ACCENT: AN ANTHOLOGY, 1940-60

ACCENT

AN ANTHOLOGY, 1940-60

Edited by
DANIEL CURLEY
GEORGE SCOUFFAS
CHARLES SHATTUCK

UNIVERSITY OF ILLINOIS PRESS   Urbana Chicago London

272795

Contents

II. POETRY

III. CRITICAL PROSE

Introduction

The story of *Accent* and the story of Kerker Quinn are so inter-related that it would be impossible to separate a history of the one from a eulogy of the other. One cannot speak of *Accent* without speaking of Kerker, nor think of Kerker without thinking of his master-work, the twenty volumes of nearly flawless editorial taste and judgment that is *Accent*.

The history of *Accent* actually began at Bradley University when Kerker was an undergraduate there in 1934. In the fall of that year, he and three associates published the first issue of "a quarterly of new literature" called *Direction*. Two more issues followed (January-March and April-June, 1935), and then *Direction* was suspended when Kerker came to the University of Illinois to begin graduate study in the De-partment of English. At that time he intended to resume publication within a few months, but five years would pass before that intention could be realized. It must be recognized, however, that in every im-portant respect—in editorial policy, in quality of contents, even in format—the true beginning of *Accent* lies in the three issues of *Direction* put together by a college senior who appears to have been born wise in the ways of the literary world.

Direction, like *Accent,* offered short fiction, poetry, critical articles, and reviews. One's first impression of the list of contributors is that it is simply a roll call of the truly best writers of the day. In the first issue we find Wallace Stevens, Ezra Pound, Robert Frost, Kay Boyle, Branch Cabell, Conrad Aiken, Vardis Fisher, William Carlos Wil-liams, and Richard Aldington; in the second Marianne Moore, R. P. Blackmur, Horace Gregory, Erskine Caldwell, Manuel Komroff, and C. Day Lewis; in the third Stephen Spender, William Saroyan, and Herbert Read, plus further work by Williams, Fisher, Blackmur, Stevens, and Lewis. This was a remarkable garnering of talent for a fledgling editor of twenty-two. But just as auspicious was another principle operating in *Direction:* together with the famous and the near-famous are the names of a few new writers. Elizabeth Bishop's "first nationally published verse" appears in the last issue; Roger Roughton, "still under twenty, is published for the first time in Amer-ica"; and Gordon Sylander, "a student at the University of Wis-consin," contributes two poems. Not only did *Direction* display an editorial knowledge of the literary scene; its success must also have convinced Kerker that writers genuinely needed such an outlet for their work.

By the time he was able to resume publication in the autumn in 1940, the title *Direction* had been taken up elsewhere, and a new title was needed. Legend has it that suggestions were tossed into a hat and the title chosen at random. Be that as it may, the choice was certainly fortunate. Not only did the name have the right ring—one charter subscriber was moved to hope that the magazine's accents would be both grave and acute—but it had the unexpected advantage of placing *Accent* in eye-catching position in library and bookstore displays and in all magazine lists.

Accent: A Quarterly of New Literature named on its first masthead seven editors: Kerker Quinn, associate professor of English at the time of his death; Kenneth Andrews, now professor at the Harvard Business School; Charles Shattuck, now professor of English at the University of Illinois; W. R. Moses, now professor of English at Kansas State University and editor of the *Kansas Quarterly;* the late Thomas Bledsoe, at one time editor of the Beacon Press and of his own publishing house, Arlington Books; Keith Huntress, now professor of English at Iowa State University; and W. McNeil Lowry, now vice-president for the humanities of the Ford Foundation. There were also three associates: John Schacht, now professor of journalism at the University of Illinois; Robert Bauer, now retired from the English department at Pennsylvania State; and Paul Proehl, now, after a career in law and university administration, president of an international business corporation.

The first issue, identical with *Direction* except in name, set the appearance and format that, with minor changes, remained constant for twenty years. It had sixty-four pages, a contributors' column, and minimal advertising on the inside covers and last page. It was priced at thirty cents (yearly subscription: one dollar). In 1949 when post-war costs began pressing, the price was raised to forty cents and was never raised again.

All of the original editors were young, and most of them were graduate students in English. Although eventually the staff would have a core of veterans, it would usually include teaching assistants and young instructors and frequently undergraduates as well. Academic mobility would, of course, regularly draw members of the staff away, but would also regularly bring new personnel. The roster included several husband-wife teams, visiting instructors, and instructor-writers whose work had already appeared in the quarterly.

Editorial meetings typically reflected openness of opinion. There were no hierarchic structures or hampering ideologies to cater to, although Kerker's taste and personality were often decisive factors in the selection of manuscripts. One editor particularly given to incautious support of bad poems remembers having his taste educated by the way Kerker would read a questionable line or shout with laughter over some unhappy image. Kerker was sometimes outvoted in meetings. If he happened to feel strongly, however, that we were dismissing a good thing or accepting a bad one, he would quietly place it back in the "Consider" drawer and hope the rest of us would come to a better way of thinking before we met again. The only absolute rules of the magazine were that no one was to eat celery at meetings and (in the late fifties) that Stanley Elkin was not to tie bundles of magazines because his bundles always came untied even before they got to the post office.

It was commonly assumed by outsiders that *Accent* was a university publication, but it was in fact private property, the owners being Kerker and, for legal purposes, one or two other editors whose names were entered in the statement of ownership filed with the post office. It is true that eventually, in recogntion of the worth of the magazine, the university made certain contributions to its welfare. During the last dozen or so years of its career, Kerker himself was relieved of a portion of his teaching load. From 1951 the Department of English provided a subsidy equivalent to about one-fourth of the annual printing bill. In the final years some of the labors of typing and mailing were taken over by the department's secretarial staff. But *ownership,* entailing legal responsibility and absolute freedom from institutional interference in editorial practice, remained strictly with Kerker and his colleagues, and was jealously guarded by them.

When *Accent* was founded it was expected to be able to pay contributors at least at a modest rate, but this was a daydream based on prewar calculations. For the most part the contributors got their greatest (sometimes their only) satisfaction out of appearing in print. When the magazine was relatively prosperous (that is to say, just this side of collapse) the pay schedule for prose was about $2.50 per page, for poetry from $2.50 to $20.00 per poem. As the national economy improved and pay schedules elsewhere rose, the *Accent* schedule declined, and, indeed, for several years was wiped out entirely. The pressure was eased during one three-year period in the 1950s when the Ford Foundation assisted the magazine by purchasing several hundred subscriptions on behalf of foreign libraries. But this relief was only temporary. Remarkably, there were few complaints from contributors, and writers of established reputation as well as newcomers ungrudgingly let their work be published *gratis*. Even so, the magazine went in the red, and its deficits were made up out of Kerker's own pocket. He would never ask for—indeed, would not accept—contributions from his fellow editors, and it can probably never be known how many thousands of dollars of his own salary went to meet the publishing bills and mailing costs.

Accent's circulation was never large. It early reached a level which it maintained more or less steadily. Kerker was not greatly disappointed, however, for he was not interested in unlimited sales. He once remarked that 5,000 would be a good ultimate figure. Actually *Accent* never came close to that. The invoice for the Spring, 1960, issue was for 1,727 copies, an average printing. Of these, perhaps 300 to 500 were over-run. Though it was pleasant to imagine the faithful expectantly awaiting their copies, there was obviously no public rush to the bookstands.

In spite of this limited circulation, there is no reason to suppose that *Accent* failed to reach the discerning readers or fell short of the ideals alluded to in its inaugural manifesto:

> The editors of *Accent* hope to build a magazine which discerning readers will welcome as a representative collection of the best creative and critical writing of our time, carefully balancing the work of established authors with that of comparative unknowns. By avoiding a biased viewpoint and rejecting the stereotyped and the trivial and the unintelligible, they will try to make the contents of each issue significant, varied, and readable.
>
> America has need and room for such a magazine. Look down the list of today's periodicals—the few that are open to the serious creative writer either allow articles on current events to dwarf the space left for him, or else specialize in poetry or short stories or criticism to the exclusion of the other fields. *Accent* has no first-rate parallel in aim and scope at this time.

The statement is a model of the declaration that has launched countless literary magazines. It aspires and it confidently assumes, with a touch of bravura. Literary quality is a given, and the existence of those who create it, those who uncover and present it, and those who gladly receive it are also givens. But literary standards are not self-evident fact. They need to demonstrate themselves—perhaps with twenty years of proving. Yet "quality" is what *Accent* and every editor who served it attempted to live by. Perhaps more immediately demonstrable in the pages of *Accent* are those parts of the manifesto which deal, first, with intent and, second, with the resolution that unknown writers should be given their chance.

Accent was to be literary in the broadest humanistic sense. It was to be committed to no particular ideology—literary, political, or social —to no specialized literary form, to no literary clique. In a very significant way it would refuse to honor mere "newness." Always inviting the experimental, it would nevertheless force the avant-garde to test itself against the established, to modify the traditional by honest means. It would post its standards by presenting the work of Stevens, Cummings, Blackmur, Burke, Welty, Porter, Moore. It would offer translations of distinguished foreign writers, some of them then practically unknown in America: Martin du Gard, LaForgue, Valéry, Apollinaire, Rilke, Lorca, Brecht, Seferis, Elytis, Svevo, Hesse. Alongside these masters it would publish writers who were still building their reputations and still wanting the assurance of recognition: writers like A. R. Ammons, Ruth Stone, Josephine Miles, Marguerite Young.

The editors' peculiar delight, however, would be to discover and give first publication to the work of the writer who was certainly on the threshold of a distinguished career—among these Flannery O'Connor, J. F. Powers, William Humphrey, Daniel Curley, Stanley Elkin, Grace Paley, William Gass.

Once in the early 1940s the editors somewhat reluctantly (and after heavy blue-penciling and "improving"—which the author surprisingly agreed to) printed a story based on the already hackneyed subject of Negro jazz musicians in a city night club. A few months later the same author submitted a second story so extraordinarily different in theme and superior in writing that the editors could hardly believe it came out of the same typewriter. It was not faultless, however: after a magnificent development it ended all too abruptly with a too easy symbolic death scene. The editors turned to outsiders for counsel, among them Katherine Anne Porter, who had already advised and befriended them in other ways. Miss Porter's response was to the effect that this piece was so superbly written that it *must* be printed, whether the ending pleased or not. Back to the author went the manuscript, with Miss Porter's opinion attached, and with such incentive the author went at it again. Within a few weeks he had developed what is now the final, climactic, and best section of one of the masterpiece short stories of our time—J. F. Powers' "Lions, Harts, Leaping Does."

No editor who was then on the staff will forget the excitement over the first submission by another complete unknown, a philosophy professor at Purdue University, William H. Gass. It fell to Charles Shattuck to be the first reader of the Gass manuscripts, a heavy package of three long stories and a critical article, and he tells the story this way. "I started through the package at home on a Saturday morning, and the first story I read was so good that I drove to the office and put it in the 'Yes' box immediately. Back home, I found the second one just as good. Before the morning was out, I'd made four separate trips." Soon thereafter one entire issue was given over to the first works of William Gass.

This kind of excitement and the hard work accompanying it are only part of the history of *Accent,* however. There is still everything important to be said: about assessment, achievement, accountability. In time others will doubtless explore the matter from a detached viewpoint. Perhaps all that is practicable now are retrospective musings. What sustains twenty years of life in a literary quarterly?·

Every editor who shared the experience can probably speak to the pleasure and excitement of his own commitment, but how do all the many editors, with their tastes and biases, speak to their joint effort scattered from 1940 to 1960? From its beginnings *Accent* was blessed with testimonials to its vitality and performance, not only from subscribers, contributors, and would-be contributors, but from professional writers and critics everywhere. Such wide and sustained acceptance encouraged at least the illusion of a singular distinction. The review of all twenty volumes, ten years after the end, in preparation for this anthology, has certainly affirmed for the present editors an astonishing wholeness. Though aware of the lapses that men and magazines are subject to, they could see that throughout its life *Accent* thrived on editorial integrity; that its first editors began with the highest ideals and quickly and firmly established standards which following editors in their turn refined and enriched; that in short it could claim its honorable place in contemporary literary history.

Risking an extravagance that Kerker himself would have deplored, one finally must see *Accent* as his creation. It is not too fanciful to say that *Accent* consists of the poetry, the stories, the criticism that he might under other circumstances have written. He was the primary source of the magazine's taste, continuity, and literary sophistication. All who knew him knew of his appetite for the arts. His life was a strenuous and continuous effort to know, to judge, and to enjoy fiction, poetry, drama, ballet, opera, music of every sort, painting, and the movies. Both catholic and wisely eclectic, he responded to the new and original as avidly as to the worthy old. To the limit that his means would permit, his possessions reflected these interests. His home overflowed with books and records. And if it can be said of anyone, it can be said of him that he had read every book and heard (many times over) every record he owned. With ritual regularity he kept up with news and reviews and the whole content of the most reputable literary journals. The cumulative enrichment of this regimen was aided by his rare memory, which, in relaxed moments, he indulgently enjoyed displaying.

More difficult to relate directly to his role as editor, but significantly germane, was an almost Jamesian sensibility, a mixture of imagination (a multi-faceted and comprehensive awareness) and scrupulosity. The manifestations of this were complex, ranging from the moral and the attractively social to the near eccentric. Kerker considered *Accent* a commitment not only to a pet project but also to the demonstration of the dynamic relation between altruism and the arts. Though he respected money as a resource and always regretted his inability to pay contributors handsomely, he was embarrassed by money and distrusted its effect on the job at hand. His commitment to *Accent* meant for him the forfeiture of personal literary distinction, and it certainly hindered his academic advancement. Yet in this he was not performing a sacrificial gesture. He was activating a belief. If he was playing a role, it was as a catalytic agent helping things happen in the creation of literature and making sure when they happened that they were displayed accurately and to best advantage.

There is a round finality in the sound of Volume 20, no. 4. Kerker surely thought so when he decided that the Autumn, 1960, issue of *Accent* would be the last. With characteristic thoroughness he wrote out for his colleagues the reasons why the magazine should fold. He believed that the magazine had served its purpose. The rapid increase in literary magazines during the fifties had spread thin the quantity of good writing available to any of them. The limited resources of *Accent* did not permit fair competition with the more richly endowed magazines. Finally, the chief editor was tired of editing. Twenty years was enough to give to anything. His fellow editors were not surprised by the announcement. They had known and understood all the reasons.

In the nine years that followed the closing of *Accent,* Kerker gave himself wholly to his students. They were the youngest and the newest writers, and whatever strength he had he would pour into them. Not only was he midwife for their artistic labors, he was their friend in trouble. He helped them up. He bailed them out. He stood best man for them and "father of the bride." It is hard to believe that any young writer on whom he lavished his great gift of serious attention could ever after that completely lose heart.

Then on Monday, October 27, 1969, Kerker met his eleven o'clock writing class in a small seminar room that had been carved out of the old *Accent* office. A few minutes later he dropped to the floor. His students spread the alarm and called for help. Shortly after noon he was pronounced dead at the hospital. Diagnosis: heart attack. In three weeks he would have been fifty-eight.

On Sunday, November 2, a roomful of his friends, colleagues, and students gathered to remember him—not to eulogize or to pray (in the conventional sense) but, as it were, to carry his life forward by listening to a few poems and a few bits of music which had been his favorites. Shakespeare and Cummings, Frost, Yeats, and Joyce were laid out like posies for remembrance. There was a tiny concerto of Domenico Cimarosa's. Bessie Smith sang. The Dorrs offered their special rendition of Kurt Weill's "Moon of Alabama." For half an hour it was as if we were all at Kerker's house for one last party.

Kerker's will was a document fit to be compared to Caesar's in that it made clear once and for all how Kerker did love his students and where his other loves were. He bequeathed the *Accent* papers, seventy-three boxes of documents, and all his books to the University of Illinois Library, all his records to the School of Music, and the financial proceeds of his entire estate to the University of Illinois Foundation to set up awards for undergraduate writers, not on the basis of need but of demonstrated talent. In keeping, therefore, with the spirit of these bequests, editors and contributors have agreed that all royalties from this anthology should be donated to the Kerker Quinn Awards.

Like Lambert Strether at the end of *The Ambassadors,* Kerker would seem finally to have been saying: "That, you see, is my only logic. Not, out of the whole affair, to have got anything for myself." And if it were pointed out to him that "with your wonderful impressions, you'll have got a great deal," he would have agreed: "A great deal."

Kerker had a way of rating parties based on the number of pipes he put down and forgot during the course of the evening. The next day he would call on his host to collect the missing pipes, and a search would begin. If he had been so excited, delighted, absorbed that he abandoned three pipes, the party was a complete success. For us who have assembled this anthology, reading through the twenty years of *Accent* has been a three-pipe party. It has been accompanied, though, by a heavy sense of the difficulty of choice. How to choose among the chosen? The many hundreds of stories, poems, and articles represent our own choices over the years, and to a remarkable extent our taste is constant. There are few items in the volumes which we would not choose again out of a stack of submissions. In fact, the riches are such that it would be possible to put together a totally different *Accent* anthology in no way inferior to the one we now present. We are convinced, however, that our selections faithfully represent what *Accent* was, and we hope that something of our pleasure will be shared by a new generation as well as by former subscribers and contributors.

I. NARRATIVE PROSE

R. V. CASSILL:

Fragments for Reference

Lust and forgetfulness have been among us . . .

Formulas of Birth

To be born is no different than they say it is, only this time it's you.

The prints your fingers make. They say nobody else has that pattern or if they had there wouldn't be that scar across the second finger (which the barbed wire tore one December day when you were hunting). There wouldn't be that lead-colored sky and the white flakes that drifted over the stubble. There wouldn't be the fence creaking and springing out from under your boot. There wouldn't be that day.

Repeatedly spring delivers you in the same harsh way it delivers buds or the first grass. Time after time you have to find out how cold the glitter of mud in March is.

The repetitive process, when you are young, keeps bearing you into a world that has centers and no edges (remember the embarrassments of childhood, your hand lifted expectantly to the center of the loaded tree, the laughter of the adults. Or watching your own fat belly. Thinking how sweet it is.) and if

you make it, to be born again old is to live with the edges. The days gone, the nights gone, the land of memory where the edge-eaters live.

The shape of a birth can be cut out of the muckiest stuff. When the months of the war of nerves are run through, the border is crossed, the pretense of decency and the scruples are cut, the loyalty forsworn, the red, loving past surely behind you. And damn them then. You're your own little man. No blood pumps into you that's not your own. After nine months waiting you need neither cord nor the shape of the sack to hold you. You can remember from that pre-world the voices of a dreaming order telling you (you not-yet child) that Lincoln freed the slaves and loved his mother, that Washington didn't lie, that boiling in oil took place in olden times, that Columbus discovered a New World (you thought the sails swelled out on big sweet winds blowing into the future), that Daniel Boone found a country that shone as green as green moss in the snow.

3

4

How, Being Born, to Get What You Want

Listen to the big boys, the boys who've been around. They'll tell you it's sure fire. Just reach out, they'll say. There, there it is. Take it.

If your eyes are as sharp as your teeth are, remember this bit of the sharpie's remark, "I'd like to sink my long yellow teeth into that and let it drag me to death."

If your heart has to be as stubborn as an iron lock, remember hearing, "I have his picture yet. It isn't a very good picture. Sometimes I go to the places we used to go. There isn't anybody I know there. But —I don't know how to tell you—I don't forget him."

Or

"It doesn't matter what she does or anything. We were happy for a while and I know she'll never be that happy again."

(In the middle of summer, this one Sunday, I felt the Dakota wind run over my body like warm water in a current. After dinner we had had a fight with corn cobs in the barnyard, and when we were all worn out, we lay on top of a shed in the sun. The little girls came walking by in a row abreast, five of them holding hands. When they saw us up there watching them, the lot of them wavered like a five-leaved vine that swings loose from a wall in a light breeze. My cousin Walter yelled at them, and they began to giggle and shiver. They muttered and mumbled then all at once gave a laughing screech and turned and ran. A little cloud of dust followed each one, a delicate cloud floating off through the pasture fence.

Once we fished a garter snake out of the cistern. Walter fastened a wire snare on the end of a pole to catch it. Four of us crouched around with our heads down in the water-smelling dark hole. We saw our faces reflected around the reflection of the clouds up behind us. The snake swam about slowly and aimlessly as though he did not mean to notice the wire slide under his belly and draw tight. A little afraid of him, we tramped and kicked him until his green hide broke and the red of him was smeared with dirt.)

(I rode one night in a coal car down across the Utah desert and when the sun came up like steel on fire, the little man with me took some bread and onions out of his shirt and we ate them. "Wunt you rather eat out like this than in some damn restrunt?" he said.)

In public parks there are shady spots where you can lie and watch the girls strutting around the pool, watch their tense bodies balancing when they go up to dive; or if you haven't anywhere else to remember

the old men with cheesy eyelids in the libraries, behind piles of books, the white-skinned hands busy on letters to the editor. The words that go on the page bitter and young, "My dear sir: The presumptions of your ignorance . . ." The minds hunting like a hawk hunting over a grassy field.

(We marched in toward the hills that afternoon, coming to the edge of them, filing in among the boulders just before dark. When we sat down for ten, I saw Martin leaning back on a rock just to my right. There was brown dust all over his face except where the sweat had run down through it. "My feet," he said, "they're throbbing like a mocking bird's ass." The taste of water washing the sand out of my mouth. I remember the flocks of sparrows sweeping over while we made our camp. In the gray light.)

Or How to Evade Reality

Reach for clouds, roads, sky, apples; imagine arms which are strong enough to hold anything that time wants. Reach your hand out of a train window into the dark, and if your hand touches a hand out there (it will seem real) get off the train and look and look and look for whom you touched.

There should be caves in reality. There should be a thicket. There should be a station along the way. Sure, Jack. But come on. Hurry.

(In the fall evenings, above the oak trees big V's of geese came over. If I pointed a stick at them, or the handlebars of a junked bicycle, they were formations of enemy aircraft. And over the mountains, when the light remained only in the top of the sky, the bombers with the orange color of the sun streaked on them were geese following an old river. The *American Boy* and *The Wonder of the War in the Air,* which had led me by the hand through imagination to the season of reality, could not lead me back.

The hills rising up sharply out of the desert at Kasserine reminded me of the river hills I'd once imagined full of battles — and seen lightning as artillery fire a long way off.)

To lie in summer looking up the trunk of a box elder tree, to watch the leaves open a soft door and to see the deep sky through it isn't

the same thing as the New Empire Hotel (walk up one flight and register as Mr. and Mrs. Jack Chance from Reno, Nevada — the clerk is an old acquaintance of the Chances) nor the cold awakening and the return down a street crackling with rain.

And finding at the edge of your own town an old house with the

roof fallen in and draped over the walls as softly as wet burlap, newspapers stacked in its cellar telling of the inauguration of Grover Cleveland, a coin and an old tin can on the damp stairway is not quite the
same

as climbing into the house in the village, the one house that looks
undamaged after the bombardment and seeing the black wall and the
chairs scorched hastily with a flame-thrower and expecting to see
the faces suddenly come back, the children reappearing at the door.
When you tell yourself the faces of the dead won't hurt you if you
don't see them. When you wonder if someone is just outside. Are
there footsteps coming up the alley?

In the movie you see certain strangers (but their caps look familiar,
their coats, too) walk through the Newsreel as though they had their
minds on the blonde in the Main Feature until the planes come up the
street behind them and they run for doorways and some of them
fall, Jesus, you're safe and indignant all at the same time, and while
the feature is on you don't have to think that if the blonde's real then
safe isn't, or if safe is

the blonde isn't and isn't anybody you knew in high school and has
never claimed to be

any particular friend of Jack's

who you aren't anyway.

(The causes of war are economic, you will learn. But what if I
said maybe that's a dollar you're giving me and maybe it isn't a dollar
and he let me bite it to see and I said maybe it's a dollar and maybe
it won't ever be a dollar. Would his surprise be real?

Or if I took the dollar without question and in good faith and held
it really there in my hand would Mrs. Chance with her best dress on,
wagging her hips in just that way that makes you cry to watch it,
come down the street and stop to say, "Hello Jack. You've been a long
time gone"?)

How to Answer a Letter Read in a Bar in 1940

Begin at once to compose a reply. Make it exact and calm but
fairly representative of your feelings. Say this is winter. The sun
looks more like a reminder than a sun. The street outside is mostly
covered with snow. In this bar there are no individual or separate
shadows.

Refer to a parenthesis of her letter (when I come in the spring).

Pause for the necessary interruptions, or, rather, those you can expect in so public a place. While the clock hand swings back and forth across five o'clock, seeking eternity, learn that the road to life leads back and forth past these epitaphs:

"I done every dirty thing you ever heard of, and I never got anything out of life either."

"I said, 'Don't tell your ma I give it to you, but here, take this money to buy the stuff for supper. Get us some nice boloney. I ain't no bum.'"

"He came home drunk and fell on the floor. His wife was pregnant and couldn't bend down to hit him. So she started kicking him."

"I wrecked his car for him and damn near killed him, and I wish it would of been me and done a good job."

"I wish to Christ they had just sewed up everything when they did that and left me open on only one end."

Resume: This place in winter is a concave monument. As for myself (what am I thinking these days?) I'll try to explain. I have imagined a mirror in which I am not yet walking. In it a figure appears burdened with talk. The talk concludes, "Maybe what I always figured, thinking I was someone special, that I could do anything I made up my mind to do, was that I'd be the American Lenin or something like that. Aaah. Boo. I've lied to myself for twenty years. Or is that true, even? Anyway, as long as I've known how to. But still, what I wanted to see you for . . .You're a writer, or you say you are, and I didn't want to do this unless everything about me, all this I've told you could be written down. I've made up my mind, but I can't get rid of the idea that my life ought to be understood. I don't think it's worth living, but maybe someday somebody will live better and it will do them good if they know about me. Just on paper it might look better than it feels. There's too many things that can be done to you while you're really alive. Your nerves are too near the skin. Think about all the clubs and whips and fire they apply to these guys in these skillful, persistent ways. And I'm as happy now as I'll ever be, so why stretch it out? Only you write it all down, everything I've told you, because just in that one way I don't want to ever die."

The imagined figure points forefinger to forehead and pretends to snap the thumb down like a gun hammer. The figure falls half out of the mirror. People I know gather before the mirror and look at the sideless head. Their voices explain that this was I. The things that persist of him, like ghosts in their minds, are the realities of my life, stripped from me and given to this one.

8

If I resist this robbery, other figures appear in the mirror — soldiers and partisans — and describing voices give them my realities. They die by millions and pass out of the mirror wearing my guises. I keep the breathing of my own life, but it too becomes caught in that mirror as in childhood we are caught in a constricting dream. You know, the dream in which tigers leap and the finger can not pull the trigger in defense.

Conclude: I have read your letter over and over. All you say is Wait. You will come in the spring. I cannot understand this, this attitude. I believe this winter is real. It will never be over just because this spring you talk about comes.

In the World You Meet the Stubborn Ones

There was the story about her, never becoming quite clear, that she had been in love once with a fellow who moved out West and never wrote back to her. Whatever it was, when she married she wasn't happy, and the children she bore did not make up for what she thought she had once seen in the world. She was always planting flowers and kept the house full of potted plants all winter. In 1927 she joined the small town's branch of the foreign missionary society. At night when she thought about it, lying awake, she told herself that the Good Lord did not intend his children in China to eat grass and mud. She could imagine then the taste of grass and mud, and it helped to believe she belonged to a society that was doing something to distribute God's Daily Bread. It helped her not to think about herself so much.

In the years when the Japanese planes flew unmolested over China and bombed unmolested, it seemed to her the bombs were destroying something very important to her, some vague imagined substance (not quite people) of her love. And it's easy to understand the devils in the planes when they blast the image you had felt secure within you. She did not ask whom she should hate.

She understood the war without the help of the columnists. It seemed very simple to her. On one side were the guns and those who owned them. On the other side she counted those whom she believed counted on her. When the war was over, she still understood those who still had guns.

And Those Who Die Young

He was nineteen when the war was over and had been knocking around the infantry camps in the States for a year. In the fall of 1945 he was sent to Japan. He arrived too late to see the Little Yellow Bastards, but he saw men and boys still walking the cold streets in the remnants of uniform, and the women with bony, expressionless faces, with children slung on their backs, kneeling gracefully before an overturned garbage can from which they took egg shells and sucked them.

He made a sight-seeing trip to Nagasaki and wrote a letter home saying, "It doesn't look any different from the other cities they bombed. It's only when you think that it all happened at once and more people were as a result of this killed that it seems different." He didn't know what to think of the Jap who told him, "It's a good thing you have bombed our cities. Now we can rebuild them with wider streets." It didn't seem quite right to say that.

He had no regular job in the outfit and one day they sent him with another GI to Sasebo to pick up a freight-car load of beer. On the way back with the load the two of them went to sleep in the freight car. The cases of beer shifted, pinned them both down, but pinning his blanket tight across his face. He could still yell for a while, but the other man couldn't get free to help him. Before the train had passed through the tunnel into Honshu, he was dead.

And another one who didn't see the end of the war. He had the name of a famous general except that his middle initial was different. He was standing in front of a plane that had just come in when one of the 50's, for no reason, not quite cold yet, blew his head into a pulp full of bone splinters.

And the Others

He was Master Sergeant in the Headquarters Company at the time they landed on Bougainville. One night after supper — they had just come back from the mess tent near the beach, he said — while they were shooting the breeze a Jap came running out of the palm trees. The little rat must of been out of his head, like, because's just running up to us screeching Kill me, kill me. And there was a Thompson slung right inside the tent where he could reach it easy. "O.K.," he said. "O.K." Damn near cut him in two.

They shoot a 45 slug, don't they — a Thompson?

10

Approach the Present

The world is always turning into now. In childhood now whips by with a whistle like a green switch in the air.

Then it slows down and as things end the ends get fuzzier and slower. The last end is a pile of the unraveled, fit for cobwebs which might as well be public property if they were property.

(When Roger came to play with my brother they hauled sand in toy dump trucks, but I wasn't old enough to play with them. I tried to kick over their trucks. They took me down, poured sand over my face, and ran away. I waited behind the front door with a club and hit them both when they came back. I made them cry and got whipped for it. When I was sent to bed, I knew I'd done wrong. Giant frogs and yellow lights from hell threatened me.)

"Never, never. Not until you're grown up."

When you're grown up some there is another voice,

"Full many a rose is born to blush . . ." the fat-rimmed eyes crinkling in amusement, "How does that go, the rest of it? Anyway, I'm sorry there's nothing we can do for you." I got what I wanted but so late I'd forgotten why

I wanted it. "No sir. I don't imagine and I didn't expect."

A parenthesis of words—the first end and the second end: "Darling, let's watch ourselves so nothing don't happen." and "Hello, I thought I recognized you when you came in, but . . ."

As a parenthesis for:

Her arms around your neck while somebody else's radio is saying (on a fine warm night) "Reichschancellor Hitler has ordered his legions to meet force with force."

We had a twelve-day passage on the troopship coming back. In our cabin nobody talked much but one Lieutenant Smith. He'd been with an outfit of niggers — "more —— trouble, but me and the old man fixed their —— wagon." "You hear the news? They want to send food to them —— —— in Europe." "One officer we had was smart in books, but he didn't know a —— thing about the army. The mens, they called themselves the mens, were asking me about him, and the old man and me snuck down to see if we could catch him at it, but it turned out there was nothing to it." "These —— —— Jews. Aren't any of you Jews, are you?" "By God, if I was commanding general there wouldn't be no mass meetings." "I'd take the —— atom bomb over there and clean them all up." In twelve days we learned he hated niggers, foreigners, politicians, enlisted men, Jews, women. Andrews said he was a radical, but nobody told him to shut up.

But Don't Worry

Stop the subscription, sell the radio, pull the blind on the window facing the street. Come and kiss and let's get acquainted. How can the world end twice when it's always ending?

Contemporary Metaphors of Birth

Toward the day and the hour, when the divisions were bulging the border and the ships lay fat with troops (while the last pretense was asking, "Do you want me? Do you need me for anything, sir?") the blood-stream thoughts split as the eyes became aware of light. The ships opened and the border broke.

When the period swelled through its last month, the only questions left were: How can we cling? How can we hide in this sweet dark?

The red expulsion into the new, new world. Through the mirrors of the rosy walls. The reflection of our frightened eyes no longer sheltering around us.

Review the Workable Formulas

In the Blood. In blood.

In concocted faith or hope that needs no object — waking on a train when the morning whistles cry out a new city, climbing ladders of a ship to see the newest harbor, sitting in a house when a new voice speaks — it may happen to you,

Or the tyranny of those who become as little children.

WALTER VAN TILBURG CLARK:

The Indian Well

In this dead land the only allegiance was to sun. Even night was not strong enough to resist; earth stretched gratefully when night came, but had no hope that day would not return. Such living things as hoarded a little juice at their cores were secret about it, and only the most ephemeral existences, the air at dawn and sunset, the amethyst shadows in the mountains, had any freedom. The Indian Well alone, of lesser creations, was in constant revolt. Sooner or later all minor breathing rebels came to its stone basin under the spring in the cliff, and from its overflow grew a tiny meadow delta and two columns of willows and aspens, holding a tiny front against the valley. The pictograph of a starving, ancient journey, cut in rock above the basin, a sun-warped shack on the south wing of the canyon, and an abandoned mine above it, were the only tokens of man's participation in the well's cycles, each of which was an epitome of centuries, and perhaps of the wars of the universe.

The day before Jim Suttler came up, in the early spring, to take his part in one cycle, was a busy day. The sun was merely lucid after four days of broken showers, and, under the separate cloud shadows sliding down the mountain and into the valley, the canyon was alive. A rattler emerged partially from a hole in the mound on which the cabin stood, and having gorged in the darkness, rested with his head on a stone. A road-runner, stepping long and always about to sprint, came down the morning side of the mound, and his eye, quick to perceive the difference between the live and the inanimate of the same color, discovered the coffin-shaped head on the stone. At once he broke into a reaching sprint, his neck and tail stretched level, his beak agape with expectation. But his shadow arrived a step before him. The rattler recoiled, his head scarred by the sharp beak but his eye intact. The road-runner said nothing, but peered warily into the hole without stretching his neck, then walked off stiffly, leaning forward again as if about to run. When he had gone twenty feet he turned, balanced for an instant, and charged back, checking abruptly just short of the hole. The snake remained withdrawn. The road-runner paraded briefly before the hole, talking to himself, and then ran angrily up to the spring, where he drank at the overflow, sipping and stretching his neck, lifting his feet one at a time, ready to go into immediate action. The road-runner lived a dangerous and exciting life.

In the upper canyon the cliff swallows, making short harp notes, dipped and shot between the new mud under the aspens and their high community on the forehead of the cliff. Electrical bluebirds appeared to dart the length of the canyon at each low flight, turned up tilting. Lizards made unexpected flights and stops on the rocks, and when they stopped did rapid push-ups, like men exercising on a floor. They were variably pugnacious and timid.

Two of them arrived simultaneously upon a rock below the road-runner. One of them immediately skittered to a rock two feet off, and they faced each other, exercising. A small hawk coming down over the mountain, but shadowless under a cloud, saw the lizards. Having overfled the difficult target, he dropped to the canyon mouth swiftly and banked back into the wind. His trajectory was cleared of swallows, but one of them, fluttering hastily up, dropped a pellet of mud between the lizards. The one who had retreated disappeared. The other flattened for an instant, then sprang and charged. The road-runner was on him as he struck the pellet, and galloped down the canyon in great, tense strides, on his toes, the lizard lashing the air from his beak. The hawk stooped at the road-runner, thought better of it, and rose against the wind to the head of the canyon, where he turned back and coasted over the desert, his shadow a little behind him and farther and farther below.

The swallows became the voice of the canyon again, but in moments when they were all silent, the lovely smaller sounds emerged, their own feathering, the liquid overflow, the snapping and clicking of insects, a touch of wind in the new aspens. Under these lay still more delicate tones, erasing, in the most silent seconds, the difference between eye and ear, a white cloud shadow passing under the water of the well, a dark cloud shadow on the cliff, the aspen patterns on the stones. Silentest of all were the rocks, the lost on the canyon floor, and the strong, thinking cliffs. The swallows began again.

At noon a red and white cow with one new calf, shining and curled, came slowly up from the desert, stopping often to let the calf rest. At each stop the calf would try vigorously to feed, but the cow would go on. When they reached the well the cow drank slowly for a long time; then she continued to wrinkle the water with her muzzle, drinking a little and blowing, as if she found it hard to leave. The calf worked under her with spasmodic nudgings. When she was done playing with the water, she nosed and licked him out from under her and up to the well. He shied from the surprising coolness and she put him back. When he stayed, she drank again. He put his nose into the water too, and bucked up as if bitten. He returned, got water up his nostrils and took three jumps away. The cow was content and moved off towards the canyon wall, tonguing grass tufts from among the rocks. Against the cliff she rubbed gently and continuously with a mild voluptuous look, occasionally lapping her nose with a serpent tongue. The loose winter shag came off in tufts on the rock. The calf lost her, became panicked and made desperate noises which stopped prematurely, and when he discovered her, complicated her toilet. Finally she led him down to the meadow where, moving slowly, they both fed until he was full and went to sleep in a ball in the sun. At sunset they returned to the well, where the cow drank again and gave him a second lesson. After this they went back into the brush and northward into the dusk. The cow's size and relative immunity to sudden death left an aftermath of peace, rendered gently humorous by the calf.

Also at sunset, there was a resurgence of life among the swallows. The thin golden air at the cliff tops, in which there were now no clouds so that the eastern mountains and the valley were flooded with unbroken light, was full of their cries and quick maneuvres among a dancing myriad of insects. The direct sun gave them, when they perched in rows upon the cliff, a dramatic significance like that of men upon an immensely higher promontory. As dusk rose out of the canyon, while the eastern peaks were still lighted, the swallows gradually became silent. At twilight, the air was full of velvet, swooping bats.

In the night jack-rabbits multiplied spontaneously out of the brush of the valley, drank in the rivulet, their noses and great ears continuously searching the dark, electrical air, and played in fits and starts on the meadow, the many young ones hopping like rubber, or made thumping love among the aspens and the willows.

A coyote came down canyon on his belly and lay in the brush with his nose between his paws. He took a young rabbit in a quiet spring and snap, and went into the brush again to eat it. At the slight rending of his meal the meadow cleared of leaping shadows and lay empty in the starlight. The rabbits, however, encouraged by new-comers, returned soon, and the coyote killed again and went off heavily, the jack's great hind legs dragging.

In the dry-wash below the meadow an old coyote, without family, profited by the second panic, which came over him. He ate what his loose teeth could tear, leaving the open remnant in the sand, drank at the basin and, carefully circling the meadow, disappeared into the dry wilderness.

Shortly before dawn, when the stars had lost lustre and there was no sound in the canyon but the rivulet and the faint, separate clickings of mice in the gravel, nine antelope in loose file, with three silently flagging fawns, came on trigger toe up the meadow and drank at the well, heads often up, muzzles dripping, broad ears turning. In the meadow they grazed and the fawns nursed. When there was as much gray as darkness in the air, and new wind in the canyon, they departed, the file weaving into the brush, merging into the desert, to nothing, and the swallows resumed the talkative day shift.

Jim Suttler and his burro came up into the meadow a little after noon, very slowly, though there was only a spring-fever warmth. Suttler walked pigeon-toed, like an old climber, but carefully and stiffly, not with the loose walk natural to such a long-legged man. He stopped in the middle of the meadow, took off his old black sombrero, and stared up at the veil of water shining over the edge of the basin.

"We're none too early, Jenny," he said to the burro.

The burro had felt water for miles, but could show no excitement. She stood with her head down and her four legs spread unnaturally, as if to postpone a collapse. Her pack reared higher than Suttler's head, and was hung with casks, pans, canteens, a pick, two shovels, a crowbar, and a rifle in a sheath. Suttler had the cautious uncertainty of his trade. His other burro had died two days before in the mountains east of Beatty, and Jenny and he bore its load.

Suttler shifted his old six-shooter from his rump to his thigh, and studied the well, the meadow, the cabin and the mouth of the mine as if he might choose not to stay. He was not a cinema prospector. If he looked like one of the probably mistaken conceptions of Christ, with his red beard and red hair to his shoulders, it was because he had been away from barbers and without spare water for shaving. He was unlike Christ in some other ways.

"It's kinda run down," he told Jenny, "but we'll take it."

He put his sombrero back on, let his pack fall slowly to the ground, showing the sweat patch in his bleached brown shirt, and began to unload Jenny carefully, like a collector handling rare vases, and put everything into one neat pile.

"Now," he said, "we'll have a drink." His tongue and lips were so swollen that the words were unclear, but he spoke casually, like a club-man sealing a minor deal. One learns to do business slowly with deserts and mountains. He picked up a bucket and started for the well. At the upper edge of the meadow he looked back. Jenny was still standing with her head down and her legs apart. He did not particularly notice her extreme thinness, for he had seen it coming on gradually. He was thinner himself, and tall, and so round-shouldered that when he stood his straightest he seemed to be peering ahead with his chin out.

"Come on, you old fool," he said. "It's off you now."

Jenny came, stumbling in the rocks above the meadow, and stopping often as if to decide why this annoyance recurred. When she became interested, Suttler would not let her get to the basin, but for ten minutes gave her water from his cupped hands, a few licks at a time. Then he drove her off and she stood in the shade of the canyon wall watching him. He began on his thirst in the same way, a gulp at a time, resting between gulps. After ten gulps he sat on a rock by the spring and looked up at the meadow and the big desert, and might have been considering the courses of the water through his body, but noticed also the antelope tracks in the mud.

After a time he drank another half dozen gulps, gave Jenny half a pail full, and drove her down to the meadow, where he spread a dirty blanket in the striped sun and shadow under the willows. He sat on the edge of the blanket, rolled a cigarette and smoked it while he watched Jenny. When she began to graze with her rump to the canyon, he flicked his cigarette onto the grass, rolled over with his back to the sun and slept until it became chilly after sunset. Then he woke, ate a can of beans, threw the can into the willows and led Jenny up to the well, where they drank together from the basin for a long time. While she resumed her grazing, he took another blanket and his rifle from the pile, removed his heel-worn boots, stood his rifle against a fork, and rolling up in both blankets, slept again.

In the night many rabbits played in the meadow in spite of the strong sweat and tobacco smell of Jim Suttler lying under the willows, but the antelope, when they came in the dead dark before dawn, were nervous, drank less, and did not graze but minced quickly back across the meadow and began to run at the head of the dry wash. Jenny slept with her head hanging, and did not hear them come or go.

Suttler woke lazy and still red-eyed, and spent the morning drinking at the well, eating and dozing on his blanket. In the afternoon, slowly, a few things at a time, he carried his pile to the cabin. He had a bachelor's obsession with order, though he did not mind dirt, and puttered until sundown, making a brush bed and arranging his gear. Much of this time, however, was spent studying the records on the cabin walls of the recent human life of the well. He had to be careful, because among the still legible names and dates, after Frank Davis, 1893, Willard Harbinger, 1893, London, England, John Mason, June 13, 1887, Bucksport, Maine, Mathew Kenling, from Glasgow, 1891, Penelope and Martin Reave, God Guide Us, 1885, was written Frank Hayward, 1492, feeling my age. There were other wits too. John Barr had written, Giv it back to the injuns, and Kenneth Thatcher, two years later, had written under that, Pity the noble redskin, while another man, whose second name was Evans, had written what was already a familiar libel, since it was not strictly true, Fifty miles from water, a hundred miles from wood, a million miles from God, three feet from hell. Someone unnamed had felt differently, saying, God is kind. We may make it now. Shot an antelope here July 10, 188— and the last number blurred. Arthur Smith, 1881, had recorded, Here berried my beloved wife Semantha, age 22, and my soul. God let me keep the child. J.M. said cryptically, Good luck, John, and Bill said, Ralph, if you come this way, am trying to get to Los Angeles. B. Westover said he had recovered from his wound there in 1884, and Galt said, enigmatically and without date, Bart and Miller burned to death in the Yellow Jacket. I don't care now. There were poets too, of both parties. What could still be read of Byron Cotter's verses, written in 1902, said,

> . . . . here alone
> Each shining dawn I greet,
> The Lord's wind on my forehead
> And where he set his feet
> One mark of heel remaining
> Each day filled up anew,
> To keep my soul from burning,
> With clear, celestial dew.
> Here in His Grace abiding
> The mortal years and few
> I shall. . .

but you can't tell what he intended, while J.A. had printed,

> My brother came out in '49

18

> I came in '51
> At first we thought we liked it fine
> But now, by God, we're done.

Suttler studied these records without smiling, like someone reading a funny paper, and finally, with a heavy blue pencil, registered, Jim and Jenny Suttler, damn dried out, March—and paused, but had no way of discovering the day—1940.

In the evening he sat on the steps watching the swallows in the golden upper canyon turn bats in the dusk, and thought about the antelope. He had seen the new tracks also, and it alarmed him a little that the antelope could have passed twice in the dark without waking him.

Before false dawn he was lying in the willows with his carbine at ready. Rabbits ran from the meadow when he came down, and after that there was no movement. He wanted to smoke. When he did see them at the lower edge of the meadow, he was startled, yet made no quick movement, but slowly pivoted to cover them. They made poor targets in that light and backed by the pale desert, appearing and disappearing before his eyes. He couldn't keep any one of them steadily visible, and decided to wait until they made contrast against the meadow. But his presence was strong. One of the antelope advanced onto the green, but then threw its head up, spun, and ran back past the flank of the herd, which swung after him. Suttler rose quickly and raised the rifle, but let it down without firing. He could hear the light rattle of their flight in the wash, but had only a belief that he could see them. He had few cartridges, and the ponderous echo under the cliffs would scare them off for weeks.

His energies, however, were awakened by the frustrated hunt. While there was still more light than heat in the canyon, he climbed to the abandoned mine tunnel at the top of the alluvial wing of the cliff. He looked at the broken rock in the dump, kicked up its pack with a boot toe, and went into the tunnel, peering closely at its sides, in places black with old smoke smudges. At the back he struck two matches and looked at the jagged dead end and the fragments on the floor, then returned to the shallow beginning of a side tunnel. At the second match here he knelt quickly, scrutinized a portion of the rock, and when the match went out at once lit another. He lit six matches, and pulled at the rock with his hand. It was firm.

"The poor chump," he said aloud.

He got a loose rock from the tunnel and hammered at the projection with it. It came finally, and he carried it into the sun on the dump.

"Yessir," he said aloud, after a minute.

He knocked his sample into three pieces and examined each minutely.

"Yessir, yessir," he said with malicious glee, and, grinning at the tunnel, "the poor chump."

Then he looked again at the dump, like the mound before a gigantic gopher hole. "Still, that's a lot of digging," he said.

He put sample chips into his shirt pocket, keeping a small black, heavy one that had fallen neatly from a hole like a borer's, to play with in his hand. After trouble he found the claim pile on the side hill south of the tunnel, its top rocks tumbled into the shale. Under the remaining rocks he found what he wanted, a ragged piece of yellowed paper between two boards. The writing was in pencil, and not diplomatic. "I hearby clame this hole damn side hill as far as I can dig in. I am a good shot. Keep off. John Barr, April 11, 1897."

Jim Suttler grinned. "Tough guy, eh?" he said.

He made a small ceremony of burning the paper upon a stone from the cairn. The black tinsel of ash blew off and broke into flakes.

"O.K., John Barr?" he asked.

"O.K., Suttler," he answered himself.

In blue pencil, on soiled paper from his pocket, he slowly printed, "Becus of the lamented desease of the late clamant, John Barr, I now clame these diggins for myself and partner Jenny. I can shoot too." And wrote, rather than printed, "James T. Suttler, March—" and paused.

"Make it an even month," he said, and wrote, "11, 1940." Underneath he wrote, "Jenny Suttler, her mark," and drew a skull with long ears.

"There," he said, and folded the paper, put it between the two boards, and rebuilt the cairn into a neat pyramid above it.

In high spirit he was driven to cleanliness. With scissors, soap, and razor he climbed to the spring. Jenny was there, drinking.

"When you're done," he said, and lifted her head, pulled her ears and scratched her.

"Maybe we've got something here, Jenny," he said.

Jenny observed him soberly and returned to the meadow.

"She doesn't believe me," he said, and began to perfect himself. He sheared off his red tresses in long hanks, then cut closer, and went over yet a third time, until there remained a brush, of varying density, of stiff red bristles, through which his scalp shone whitely. He sheared the beard likewise, then knelt to the well for mirror and shaved painfully. He also shaved his neck and about his ears. He arose younger and less impressive, with jaws as pale as his scalp, so that his sunburn was a red domino. He burned tresses and beard ceremoniously upon a sage bush, and announced, "It is spring."

He began to empty the pockets of his shirt and breeches onto a flat stone, yelling, "In the spring a young man's fancy," to a kind of tune, and paused, struck by the facts.

"Oh yeah?" he said. "Fat chance."

"Fat," he repeated with obscene consideration. "Oh, well," he said, and finished piling upon the rock notebooks, pencil stubs, cartridges, tobacco, knife, stump pipe, matches, chalk, samples, and three wrinkled photographs. One of the photographs he observed at length before weighting it down with a .45 cartridge. It showed a round, blonde girl with a big smile on a stupid face, in a patterned calico house dress in front of a blossoming rhododendron bush.

He added to this deposit his belt and holster with the big .45.

Then he stripped himself, washed and rinsed his garments in the spring, and spread them upon stones and brush, and carefully arranged four flat stones into a platform beside the trough. Standing there he scooped water over himself, gasping, made it a lather, and at last, face and copper bristles also foaming, gropingly entered the basin and submerged, flooding the water over in a thin and soapy sheet. His head emerged at once. "My God," he whispered. He remained under, however, till he was soapless, and goose pimpled as a file, he climbed out cautiously onto the rock platform and performed a dance of small, revolving patterns with a great deal of up and down.

At one point in his dance he observed the pictograph journey upon the cliff, and danced nearer to examine it.

"Ignorant," he pronounced. "Like a little kid," he said.

He was intrigued, however, by some more recent records, names smoked and cut upon the lower rock. One of these, in script, like a gigantic handwriting deeply cut, said ALVAREZ BLANCO DE TOLEDO, Anno Di 1624. A very neat, upright cross was chiselled beneath it.

Suttler grinned. "Oh yeah?" he asked, with his head upon one side. "Nuts," he said, looking at it squarely.

But it inspired him, and with his jack-knife he began scraping beneath the possibly Spanish inscription. His knife, however, made scratches, not incisions. He completed a bad Jim and Jenny and quit, saying, "I should kill myself over a phoney wap."

Thereafter, for weeks, while the canyon became increasingly like a furnace in the daytime and the rocks stayed warm at night, he drove his tunnel farther into the gully, making a heap of ore to be worked, and occasionally adding a peculiarly heavy pebble to the others in his small leather bag with a draw string. He and Jenny thrived upon this fixed and well-watered life. The hollows disappeared from his face and he became less stringy, while Jenny grew round, her battle-ship gray pelt even lustrous and its black markings distinct and ornamental. The burro found time from her grazing to come to the cabin door in the evenings and attend solemnly to Suttler playing with his samples and explaining their future.

"Then, old lady," Suttler said, "you will carry only small children, one at a time, for never more than half an hour. You will have a bed-room with French windows and a mattress, and I will paint your feet gold.

"The children," he said, "will probably be red-headed, but maybe blonde. Anyway, they will be beautiful.

"After we've had a holiday, of course," he added. "For one hundred and thirty-three nights," he said dreamily. "Also," he said, "just one hundred and thirty-three quarts. I'm no drunken bum.

"For you, though," he said, "for one hundred and thirty-three nights a quiet hotel with other old ladies. I should drag my own mother in the gutter." He pulled her head down by the ears and kissed her loudly upon the nose. They were very happy together.

Nor did they greatly alter most of the life of the canyon. The antelope did not return, it is true, the rabbits were fewer and less playful because he sometimes snared them for meat, the little, clean mice and desert rats avoided the cabin they had used, and the road-runner did not come in daylight after Suttler, for fun, narrowly missed him with a piece of ore from the tunnel mouth. Suttler's violence was dispro-portionate perhaps, when he used his .45 to blow apart a creamy rat who did invade the cabin, but the loss was insignificant to the pattern of the well, and more than compensated when he one day caught the rattler extended at the foot of the dump in a drunken stupor from rare young rabbit, and before it could recoil held it aloft by the tail and snapped its head off, leaving the heavy body to turn slowly for a long time among the rocks. The dominant voices went undisturbed, save when he sang badly at his work or said beautiful things to Jenny in a loud voice.

There were, however, two more noticeable changes, one of which, at least, was important to Suttler himself. The first was the execution of the range cow's calf in the late fall, when he began to suggest a bull. Suttler felt a little guilty about this because the calf might have belonged to somebody, because the cow remained near the meadow bawling for two nights, and because the calf had come to meet the gun with more curiosity than challenge. But when he had the flayed carcass hung in the mine tunnel in a wet canvas, the sensation of providence overcame any qualms.

The other change was more serious. It occurred at the beginning of such winter as the well had, when there was sometimes a light rime on the rocks at dawn, and the aspens held only a few yellow leaves. Suttler thought often of leaving. The nights were cold, the fresh meat was eaten, his hopes had diminished as he still found only occasional nuggets, and his dreams of women, if less violent, were more nostalgic. The canyon held him with a feeling he would have called lonesome but at home, yet he probably would have gone except for this second change.

In the higher mountains to the west, where there was already snow, and at dawn a green winter sky, hunger stirred a buried memory in a cougar. He had twice killed antelope at the well, and felt there had been time enough again. He came down from the dwarfed trees and crossed the narrow valley under the stars, sometimes stopping abruptly to stare intently about, like a house-cat in a strange room. After each stop he would at once resume a quick, noiseless trot. From the top of the mountain above the spring he came down very slowly on his belly, but there was nothing at the well. He relaxed, and leaning on the rim of the basin, drank, listening between laps. His nose was clean with fasting, and he knew of the man in the cabin and Jenny in the meadow, but they were strange, not what he remembered about the place. But neither had his past made him fearful. It was only his habitual hunting caution which made him go down into the willows carefully, and lie there head up, watching Jenny, but still waiting for antelope, which he had killed before near dawn. The strange smells were confusing and therefore irritating. After an hour he rose and went silently to the cabin, from which the strangest smell came strongly, a carnivorous smell which did not arouse appetite, but made him bristle nervously. The tobacco in it was like pins in his nostrils. He circled the cabin, stopping frequently. At the open door the scent was violent. He stood with his front paws up on the step, moving his head in serpent motions, the end of his heavy tail furling and unfurling constantly. In a dream Suttler turned over without waking, and muttered. The cougar crouched, his eyes intent, his ruff lifting. Then he swung away from the door again and lay in the willows, but where he could watch the cabin also.

When the sky was alarmingly pale and the antelope had not come, he crawled a few feet at a time, behind the willows, to a point nearer Jenny. There he crouched, working his hind legs slowly under him until he was set, and sprang, raced the three or four jumps to the drowsy burro, and struck. The beginning of her mortal scream was severed, but having made an imperfect leap, and from no height, the cat did not at once break her neck, but drove her to earth, where her small hooves churned futilely in the sod, and chewed and worried until she lay still.

Jim Suttler was nearly awakened by the fragment of scream, but heard nothing after it, and sank again.

The cat wrestled Jenny's body into the willows, fed with uncertain relish, drank long at the well, and went slowly over the crest, stopping often to look back. In spite of the light and the beginning talk of the swallows, the old coyote also fed and was gone before Suttler woke.

When Suttler found Jenny, many double columns of regimented ants were already at work, streaming in and out of the interior and mounting like bridge workers upon the ribs. Suttler stood and looked down. He desired to hold the small muzzle in the hollow of his hand, feeling that this familiar gesture would get through to Jenny, but couldn't bring himself to it because of what had happened to that side of her head. He squatted and lifted one hoof on its stiff leg and held that. Ants emerged hurriedly from the fetlock, their lines of communication broken. Two of them made disorganized excursions on the back of his hand. He rose, shook them off, and stood staring again. He didn't say anything because he spoke easily only when cheerful or excited, but a determination was beginning in him. He followed the drag to the spot torn by the small hoofs. Among the willows again, he found the tracks of both the cougar and the coyote, and the cat's tracks again at the well and by the cabin doorstep. He left Jenny in the willows with a canvas over her during the day, and did not eat.

At sunset he sat on the doorstep, cleaning his rifle and oiling it until he could spring the lever almost without sound. He filled the clip, pressed it home, and sat with the gun across his knees until dark, when he put on his sheepskin, stuffed a scarf into his pocket, and went down to Jenny. He removed the canvas from her, rolled it up and held it under his arm.

"I'm sorry, old woman," he said. "Just tonight."

There was a little cold wind in the willows. It rattled the upper branches lightly.

Suttler selected a spot thirty yards down wind, from which he could see Jenny, spread the canvas and lay down upon it, facing towards her. After an hour he was afraid of falling asleep and sat up against a willow clump. He sat there all night. A little after midnight the old coyote came into the dry-wash below him. At the top of the wash he sat down, and when the mingled scents gave him a clear picture of the strategy, let his tongue loll out, looked at the stars for a moment with his mouth silently open, rose and trotted into the desert.

At the beginning of daylight the younger coyote trotted in from the north, and turned up towards the spring, but saw Jenny. He sat down and looked at her for a long time. Then he moved to the west and sat down again. In the wind was only winter, and the water, and faintly the acrid bat dung in the cliffs. He completed the circle, but not widely enough, walking slowly through the willows, down the edge of the meadow and in again not ten yards in front of the following muzzle of the carbine. Like Jenny, he felt his danger too late. The heavy slug caught him at the base of the skull in the middle of the first jump, so that it was amazingly accelerated for a fraction of a second. The coyote began it alive, and ended it quite dead, but with a tense muscular movement conceived which resulted in a grotesque final leap and twist of the hind-quarters alone, leaving them propped high against a willow clump while the head was half buried in the sand, red welling up along the lips of the distended jaws. The cottony underpelt of the tail and rump stirred gleefully in the wind.

When Suttler kicked the body and it did not move, he suddenly dropped his gun, grasped it by the upright hind legs, and hurled it out into the sage-brush. His face appeared slightly insane with fury for that instant. Then he picked up his gun and went back to the cabin, where he ate, and drank half of one of his last three bottles of whiskey.

In the middle of the morning he came down with his pick and shovel, dragged Jenny's much-lightened body down into the dry-wash, and dug in the rock and sand for two hours. When she was covered, he erected a small cairn of stone, like the claim post, above her.

"If it takes a year," he said, and licked the salt sweat on his lips.

That day he finished the half bottle and drank all of a second one, and became very drunk, so that he fell asleep during his vigil in the willows, sprawled wide on the dry turf and snoring. He was not disturbed. There was a difference in his smell after that day which prevented even the rabbits from coming into the meadow. He waited five nights in the willows. Then he transferred his watch to a niche in the cliff, across from and just below the spring.

All winter, while the day wind blew long veils of dust across the desert, regularly repeated, like waves or the smoke of line artillery fire, and the rocks shrank under the cold glitter of night, he did not miss a watch. He learned to go to sleep at sundown, wake within a few minutes of midnight, go up to his post, and become at once clear headed and watchful. He talked to himself in the mine and the cabin, but never in the niche. His supplies ran low, and he ate less, but would not risk a startling shot. He rationed his tobacco, and when it was gone worked up to a vomiting sickness every three days for nine days, but did not miss a night in the niche. All winter he did not remove his clothes, bathe, shave, cut his hair or sing. He worked the dead mine only to be busy, and became thin again, with sunken eyes which yet were not the eyes he had come with the spring before. It was April, his food almost gone, when he got his chance.

There was a half moon that night, which made the canyon walls black, and occasionally gleamed on wrinkles of the overflow. The cat came down so quietly that Suttler did not see him until he was beside the basin. The animal was suspicious. He took the wind, and twice started to drink, and didn't, but crouched. On Suttler's face there was a set grin which exposed his teeth.

"Not even a drink, you bastard," he thought.

The cat drank a little though, and dropped again, softly, trying to get the scent from the meadow. Suttler drew slowly upon his soul in the trigger. When it gave, the report was magnified impressively in the canyon. The cougar sprang straight into the air and screamed outrageously. The back of Suttler's neck was cold and his hand trembled, but he shucked the lever and fired again. This shot ricocheted from the basin and whined away thinly. The first, however, had struck near enough. The cat began to scramble rapidly on the loose stone, at first without voice, then screaming repeatedly. It doubled upon itself, snarling and chewing in a small furious circle, fell and began to throw itself in short, leaping spasms upon the stones, struck across the rim of the tank and lay half in the water, its head and shoulders raised in one corner and resting against the cliff. Suttler could hear it breathing hoarsely and snarling very faintly. The soprano chorus of swallows gradually became silent.

Suttler had risen to fire again, but lowered the carbine and advanced, stopping at every step to peer intently and listen for the hoarse breathing, which continued. Even when he was within five feet of the tank the cougar did not move, except to gasp so that the water again splashed from the basin. Suttler was calmed by the certainty of accomplishment. He drew the heavy revolver from his holster, aimed carefully at the rattling head, and fired again. The canyon boomed, and the east responded faintly and a little behind, but Suttler did not hear them, for the cat thrashed heavily in the tank, splashing him as with a bucket, and then lay still on its side over the edge, its muzzle and forepaws hanging. The water was settling quietly in the tank, but Suttler stirred it again, shooting five more times with great deliberation into the heavy body, which did not move except at the impact of the slugs.

The rest of the night, even after the moon was gone, he worked fiercely, slitting and tearing with his knife. In the morning, under the swallows, he dragged the marbled carcass, still bleeding a little in places, onto the rocks on the side away from the spring, and dropped it. Dragging the ragged hide by the neck, he went unsteadily down the canyon to the cabin, where he slept like a drunkard, although his whiskey had been gone for two months.

In the afternoon, with dreaming eyes, he bore the pelt to Jenny's grave, took down the stones with his hands, shoveled the earth from her, covered her with the skin, and again with earth and the cairn.

He looked at this monument. "There," he said.

That night, for the first time since her death, he slept through.

In the morning, at the well, he repeated the cleansing ritual of a year before, save that they were rags he stretched to dry, even to the dance upon the rock platform while drying. Squatting naked and clean, shaven and clipped, he looked for a long time at the grinning countenance, now very dirty, of the plump girl in front of the blossoming rhododendrons, and in the resumption of his dance he made singing noises accompanied by the words, "Spring, spring, beautiful spring." He was a starved but revived and volatile spirit. An hour later he went south, his boot soles held on by canvas strips, and did not once look back.

The disturbed life of the spring resumed. In the second night the rabbits loved in the willows, and at the end of the week the rats played in the cabin again. The old coyote and a vulture cleaned the cougar, and his bones fell apart in the shale. The road-runner came up one day, tentatively, and in front of the tunnel snatched up a horned toad and ran with it around the corner, but no farther. After a month the antelope returned. The well brimmed, and in the gentle sunlight the new aspen leaves made a tiny music of shadows.

DANIEL CURLEY:

Saccovanzetti

The council of war said, Today you'll have to be Saccovanzetti by yourself. We don't have enough in it for there to be two. So, Micky, you have to be Saccovanzetti and you have to hold up the factory and you have to be dead at the end. Remember you have to be dead. You can kill the paymaster but at the end you have to be dead.

It seemed to Micky that he always had to be dead. All his life he was always being dead. Nine years old — 1927 minus 1918 gives nine — well almost nine, nine in October, and always dead. He looked down from the top of the sandpit across the glass-smooth pond where the cows stood knee deep in water and mud, up the long cool slope of the pasture and the old orchard, to the pine grove.

"OK," he said, "I'll be Saccovanzetti." He looked back at the group which had imperceptibly formed opposite him, drawing itself together and leaving him by himself. He looked away from the pond and pasture and wood and looked at the group — his brother Ed, Bobby Miller, and Don Conlin — and then he looked to his right at the level stretch of sand between him and the thicket that sloped down to the pond. He knew that after he killed the paymaster he would have to hide out in the thicket and try to outwit and outshoot those who could not be outwitted and outshot.

The loose sand near the entrance to the thicket was marked with signs of his death struggles of yesterday when he had been a German. The others liked to see him die because he died so well and so violently, because he seemed to put everything he had into dying, leaping into the the air and falling or falling in his tracks without ever putting out his hands (the sand was soft).

"OK," he said, "where will the shoe factory be?"

"In the basement of the old burned school," his brother Ed said. "Don will be the paymaster."

"Not me," Don said. "I don't want to be shot."

"Just for a minute," Ed said. "As soon as he starts his getaway you can be the one who calls the good guys, and then you can be one of the good guys who goes after him."

"OK," Don said, "but I don't see why I have to be shot all the time."

"Do you have a handkerchief to put over your face?" Ed said.

"No," Micky said.

"Give him your cowboy bandanna, Bobby," Ed said.

"Here," Bobby said, "don't lose it."

"Don't worry." Bobby, of course, should have been the bad guy: he had the bandanna. Micky began to tie the bandanna around his face. The policemen were getting into the police station — the same craterlike depression that had been the shellhole yesterday from which the doughboys had slaughtered the Germans as they came out of Belleau Wood. The paymaster was in his office counting money and glancing up every now and then apprehensively.

Saccovanzetti dropped over the edge of the sandpit and crept along the slope just below the top until he was sure he had between him and the paymaster a large bush growing inside the old foundation. Then he eased himself over the top and crawled toward the bush. The policemen watched him intently, but since no one had called them they could do nothing. As he rounded the bush the paymaster's head appeared over the old foundation. The paymaster was looking the other way. Saccovanzetti pushed his pistol forward and fired it an inch from the back of the paymaster's head. The paymaster yelled, whirled, and drew his pistol firing twice.

"I got you," Saccovanzetti said. "Drop dead. You never knew what hit you." With extremely bad grace the paymaster sat on the ground. Saccovanzetti leaped into the office and began scooping up the money. He climbed out of the office and ran toward the thicket. He could hear someone in the office frantically telephoning the police.

The police were streaming out of the police station as he ran past, but since they had first to go to the scene of the crime to investigate they had no way of knowing that he was the killer.

He sprang into the wide funnel-like opening to the thicket and took the path branching off to the right. He ran along the spine of the hill with the pond glimmering before him through the trees and the thin air of the cut-away hill on his right hand.

When he reached the place where the path dropped sharply down to the pond, he stopped and listened. He could hear nothing except the rasping of his breath and the pounding of a pulse in his throat. To get a better look back over the path he began to climb a small tree at the edge of the pit with its roots on one side reaching dryly down into sterile air. From a little way up the tree he could see Ed and Bobby and Don just running into the thicket. Without stopping they turned down the path he had taken. That was just luck — good for them, bad for him. There was no way they could tell he had come that way, for the sand everywhere was pocked with footmarks from one day to another.

Before he could get down from the tree he heard them running along the path, and before he could even think of flattening himself among the branches, they ran directly under him close together, straining forward like hounds on a scent. He held his pistol in readiness but he did not shoot although he could have shot all three of them like fish in a barrel: he was supposed to die, not they. He knew that if he started shooting they would groan and grimace and shoot him like a bird in a tree and he'd be dead. He wished that for once he could be a good guy so that when he got shot like a fish in a barrel he could get up clutching his shoulder or his side or his head, grimacing with pain, more dead than alive, but carrying on and eventually winning and, if there were girls in the game, having his head bathed and stroked in the hospital. When girls played there were always more wounded than killed outright, though sometimes the girls liked to have you die in the hospital so they could have a funeral for you.

He waited a minute. When he jumped down from the tree he dropped his gun, and as he was looking for it among the bushes he heard them coming back. He flattened on the ground not five feet from the path, his face pressed down so that it would not show white among the leaves.

"He must have gone the other way," Bobby said. They had stopped beside the tree.

"Maybe he's up this tree," Don said. He fired twice into the branches and stepped close to the trunk to look up.

Micky held his gun on Ed's head and waited, the taste of metal strong in his mouth and his sweaty body cold against the ground.

"Come on," Ed said. "We'll go back and take the other path. Let's not let him get too big of a start."

Micky rested his head on his arm and sank back against the ground, weak in the reaction. Then he got up and ran down the hill toward the pond. With one quick bound he was across the path that paralleled the pond about fifteen feet up the last precipitous slope. He sprang down to the narrow beach and huddled against the bank. He clutched his side for the pain of running and thought that he would be unable to move again and that he would have to meet them there by the pond and shoot it out hopelessly there with those who could not be killed. He waited.

Gradually the pain left his side, his pulse quieted, his breathing eased; and he knew that he could not stay there pinned against the bank. Sooner or later they would get around the corner of the pond and see him from the railroad embankment and pick him off sitting. He began to work along the edge of the pond away from the railroad. The narrow beach narrowed even further as he approached a point of land that jutted slightly into the pond.

The steep bank became steeper and dropped straight down into the water. Soon he was walking in the rapidly deepening water, and it was becoming increasingly obvious that he would never be able to reach the point. He stood in the water, his gun held high, and stared out over the pond. They passed on the path overhead while he flattened against the bank, hidden by the steep bank and the leaves. He tasted the dry metallic taste again, and his shirt clung cold to his back.

They went away. They had not yet thought of the pond. Sooner or later they would think of the pond. They would go all through the thicket and then they would think of the pond. He had to move.

The best thing to do would be to go on to the dam, climb down the dam to the river bed, and get clean away. That would be the best thing. But the pond was too deep and the bank was too steep; so there was nothing to do but go back and climb up to the path. He could follow the path to the other side of the point and then get down to the pond again.

He started back along the beach. He could hear them shouting in the thicket, and he realized that he would never get ten yards along the path.

Perhaps he could go in the other direction over the tracks. For a moment he looked at the nearby railroad embankment, but it was so high, so bare, so lonely that he knew he could never get across to the safety of the other side.

And then he found the raft. When he had gone down the beach before, he had walked right over it because it had been covered with branches. He had thought it was a tree fallen down into the water. But now when he needed it he found the raft.

He pushed the raft into the water. He found that it was level and dry only if he stood exactly in the center. If he moved or shifted his weight suddenly, the raft tipped and water sloshed across it. He worked cautiously up to the point, staying always as close as possible to the bank. Then he stopped poling and allowed the raft to drift almost imperceptibly until he could see around the point.

This he knew was the crucial moment. He had to get the raft in motion, and he had to steer its unwieldy bulk around the point. And just when he would most need his eyes to scan the bank for them, he would have to devote his entire attention to the raft. He gave a violent push with the pole. The raft jerked forward, tipping slightly. The water sloshed into his shoes.

Then he was in the wide open at the point. He felt for the bottom with his pole, but the water was too deep. He hung there like a duck on the water. He knelt down and paddled with his hands, glancing continually over his shoulder, expecting any minute to hear gunfire from the bank. Although the raft had seemed to hang motionless, he found, when he began trying to paddle, that it continued to drift farther from the shore. He paddled frantically. His arms ached with the effort, but at last the raft appeared to stand still.

If it had been difficult to check the motion of the raft, it was even more difficult to start it off in a new direction. His arms were too tired to keep up the sustained paddling needed to get under sluggish way. He sat on the edge of the raft and kicked with his feet — he was soaked to the waist anyway. When he turned to look at the bank, he saw that he was perceptibly closer. He felt with the pole for the bottom, found it, and pushed himself into the bank.

That had been luck, he thought, to get around the point without being seen. He sat for a minute in the middle of the raft holding onto a bush to keep from drifting away. When he was out there in the open, he had felt that if only he could get to the bank he would be safe, but now at the bank, he knew that he must keep moving down to the dam.

He stood up and started poling. It had been some time since he heard them. Perhaps they were up on top of the sand pit or by the railroad. He poled easily along and beached the raft beside the dam. He leaped from the raft to the bank. He sprang to the top of the narrow bank and for a moment saw the steep sliding path down to the groove of the river bed below the dam. For an instant he was poised gathering himself for the path down. From all sides deafening gunfire and close at hand. His heart stopped, his pulse exploded, and he fell to the ground.

"OK, Saccovanzetti," his brother Ed said, "get up. We filled you full of lead and now we're going to take you to Dedham for the trial."

"I'm going to be Judge Thayer," Bobby Miller said.

"No, I'm going to be Judge Thayer," Don Conlin said. "I had

to be the paymaster and be shot. I got to have something good."

"You be Judge Thayer, Don," Ed said. "Bobby, you can be District Attorney Katzman. I'm going to be Governor Fuller, and President Lowell of Harvard and Attorney General Palmer."

"Aw," Don said, "what do you say? When you're those guys you always mess everything up."

In the distance a shrill whistle like a police whistle blew two long and one short. "They want us for supper," Ed said. "You're going to catch it, Micky, for getting your clothes soaked."

"I don't care," Micky said. He was sitting on the ground trying to catch his breath.

"You better care," Ed said.

"How come you found me?" Micky said.

"We were up on top of the sand pit and we saw the ripples out in the pond," Ed said.

"We figured it was you," Don said, "so we came down and followed you along the shore."

"I never saw you," Micky said. He stood up and they all started for home.

"We didn't see you either," Ed said. "We just followed the ripples."

"How come you tried to really get away?" Bobby said.

"You must be crazy," Don said. "Don't you know Saccovanzetti never gets away?"

They went on home, Micky knowing all the way that he would really catch it. When they went into the house Micky could smell the mingled supper smells. It seemed to him that there was a chocolate cake in there somewhere.

"Oh, Micky, Micky," his mother said, "what have you done now?"

"I fell in the pond when we were playing Saccovenzetti," he said. He looked at Ed, but Ed said nothing and went on up to their room.

"George, come here and look at this boy," his mother said.

He could hear his father getting up in the other room. The paper rustled loudly. His father came to the door, the paper held in his hand.

"Speak to him, George. Tell him he mustn't play that horrid game." His mother turned back to the stove.

"What now, son?" his father said.

"I was playing Saccovanzetti and I fell in the pond," Micky said.

"There's no need to tell him not to play that game any more, Grace," his father said. "They're going to the chair tonight."

"Yeah?" Micky said. His mother crossed herself quickly and went on with her left hand taking the chocolate cake out of the oven.

"This time for sure," his father said.

"Good," Micky said, "they had it coming."

"Don't be so bloodthirsty, son," his father said.

"You said so yourself," Micky said.

"I know," his father said. "But now we have more important business to attend to. A desperate criminal who has fallen into the pond and is wet and exhausted can't very well be sent to bed without supper, but he can and should be sent to bed directly after supper and without chocolate cake. Not only without chocolate cake tonight but also without chocolate cake as long as this cake shall last."

"Run now and get washed up," his mother said.

"You might as well get into your night clothes now," his father said.

Micky ran up the stairs. It hadn't been really bad. He was tired, much too tired to go out after supper. "Ed," he called. "Saccovanzetti are getting it tonight."

"Yeah?" Ed said. He was sitting on the toilet.

"Yeah," Micky said. "You're Saccovanzetti in the electric chair. I'm the warden and I'm going to throw the switch." He reached behind Ed and flushed the toilet. A look of frustrate rage blazed on Ed's face. Micky ran laughing to their room.

HARRIS DOWNEY:

Caught

It was August. The heat pressed down the branches of the elder and the mass of coffee weeds in the fields.

The lush foliage of summer was still. Only the mimosa tree stirred; the current that moved it was so delicate that the long seed pods hung as stiff as bronze and the ragged off-season blooms sat among the leaves like balls.

The mimosa grew against the cabin but neither it nor the china-ball tree cast any shade on the roof; heat rose from the tin in waves.

Everything was silent but for the hum of bumblebees in the clematis vine of the porch and the occasional crow of a rooster that sat in the sun between the shade of the elder and the mimosa tree. It was an old black rooster with hackle and saddle of gray. He sat with his beak hanging open and his eyes closed. From time to time he would rise, stretch his neck, blast the stillness with his raucous crow, and drop again to his pool of dust.

The blinds of pine board were partially closed against the glare; yet the heat was as great inside the cabin as it was in the sun.

Two partitions divided the cabin into three rooms. In the front room an old negro lay in bed, his pillows propped against the iron rods of the bedstead that curved themselves into the shape of a harp. His head was bald but for a fringe of hair, short, kinky, and white. His chin and cheeks were as hairless as his forehead but two long mustaches, gray-white as his pillows, stretched from under his nose like

35

masquerade. His hands clutched the quilt under his chin.

The blind by the bed was partly open to the shadow of the mimosa tree and, though the room was almost dark, there was too much light for the old man's eyes. The lashless lids were heavier than the logs of his youth, or the sacks of feed, or the stray sheep that had to be lifted over the sty. He opened his eyes barely a thread, summoning all his strength to orient himself in time and place: *I yit in the bed . . . It's the daytime.*

Through the crack of the blind he saw a mimosa branch. In its mass of green foliage were three blossoms, fat pom-poms of pink, and above it was a stretch of blue sky, blinding bright. The branch was a green field slanting a hill and the blossoms were pink-ginghamed women working among indistinguishable rows.

"Lena!" Often he dreamed of being unable to run or cry out when, in the dark of night, he opened the door of the outhouse and saw a great white ghost sitting on the hole. His hand would be stuck to the rope handle of the door and his cry would well in his throat, then roll out of his mouth — as silent as thistle falling on the air. Often when he called from his bed he was uncertain whether he made any sound at all or called only as he called in the dream. "Lena!"

"Oh mighty!" The protest was like a sigh. She was sitting in the kitchen, her bare feet spread apart, her head bent towards her lap. Her gums were clamped tight on a cold cob-pipe. With one hand she held her scalp to her head and with the other she yanked the comb through her matted gray hair. She was dressed in a long white dress like a gown.

"Lena!"

"Gon' drive me crazy," she said. She stuck the comb in her hair, grasped the edge of the table, slid forward, and got up as carefully as if the chair were a rocking boat. At the door to his room, she held back the curtain and impatiently asked: "What you want, Jim Pa?"

But she didn't expect any answer. She had spoken just as she spoke to her rooster, to a rat scampering through the yard, to her wood stove, to the Lord, to all of those things that she habitually complained to and that never answered. Maybe he had fallen asleep again and she would not have to bother. She squinted against the darkness of the room as he had squinted against the light. Deep in the pillow, the old face was only a black hole with two furry tails hanging out, white and still.

"Lena!"

"Dere you go." She came to the bed and called out. "What you want?

"It's mornin'," he said. He did not open his eyes. There was no need. She was there. He was no more blind than deaf but it was easier to hear than to see. It was such an effort to open the eyes. And when he listened — when he really came awake — he felt the comfort of her being near. She existed as sound: the dropping of wood on the kitchen floor, the rattling of pans, and the voice. And when not sound, she was touch, her hands as intimate as his thoughts — feeding him, cleaning him, changing his bed. Her sounds and her touch were his wakeful-ness, his consciousness of being alive.

"It's evenin'," she said. "Pas' one o'clock. What you want?"

He wanted his syrup. "My su'up," he said. "You got my su'up yit?"

"Goin' now, like I tole you, to git it."

"The women is out in the pea field yit."

"There ain't no pea field, Jim Pa. Now you git some res'." The pea field and the women had become an argument between them.

"They *there*." He opened his eyes, saw her standing beside him. Then he closed them again. He did not like to look at her, for then she was a stranger who might turn and go away forever. "They all dressed in red. Pickin' peas."

She had looked out before and had seen only the weeds. But the women? What did he think was women? She went past his bed and looked out. Tiney, the rooster, had struggled to his feet and was flap-ping his wings. "Sho' ain't no women." She stood gazing at the rooster until he stretched his neck, blasted the droning afternoon, and dropped down again. "Gotta go feed my rooster." She pulled the blind nearly shut.

She finished combing her hair and bound it up in a cloth. She put on an old pair of canvas shoes and, about her waist, tied a long white apron.

In the yard, she put a plate of scraps — greens and corn-bread — before Tiney as if he were a dog. She touched his wing. "Eat your dinner." Tiney got up, walked off a way, spread his wings tentatively, and, stretching the hackle from his back, gave a long crow.

The mimosa tree had almost no trunk at all; it was a cluster of limbs leaning together and crossing one another like the sticks of a broken fan. In one of the low forks of the tree, Lena sat down and watched the rooster.

From out of nowhere an old hen came up to the plate. The woman got up, started to spread her arms: *Shu!* But she blinked her eyes in the glaring sun. It was her old dominecker. "Where you bin, hin?" She always was a silly old hen. "Thought the ole fool was et."

"Creola!" He was always calling her by a wrong name, lying there in the bed mixing his sleep with his waking, mixing the weeds with a pea field, mixing her with a lot of niggers she'd never heard tell of.

She pulled back the blind and looked into the window. "Don't call me by no Creola," she yelled.

"You git my su'up?"

"Ain't gone yit. Now you stop that callin'. I gotta long ways to go."

The coffee weeds were as high as her shoulders. They overhung the path. She pulled her apron and dress around her legs, holding them gently in a loose fold before her as though she were carrying a hot skillet. But the weeds brushed against her. "The drought gon' git you 'fore you make your seeds. I hope to the Lord it do."

The dust was thick in the lane. Still folding her dress in front of her, she pulled it up as high as her knees. She lifted her feet straight up in the air and put them down gingerly like a cat walking through grass. But the dust rose in little explosions, billowed directionless, then rolled suddenly forward to follow her. The weeds at the side of the road were blanketed gray. The corn stalks in the field were bent and brown. "If you drap a match, the whole world go up in a flame," she said. Then she bent forward and threw her feet out in a shuffling gait, still holding her dress before her in both hands. The dust turned back like earth from a plow, spread over the lane, and hung there.

The lane dipped down the hollow. The trees hung over like a cave. "Come all you trees and shelter this world." On one side of the lane there was an embankment as high as her head; on the other there was a marsh. "All you oaks and ash. You buckeye and pine." She was looking up at the trees on the embankment. "Now where that puckawn tree? Ole alligator, if you sittin' up in that puckawn tree waitin' to fall on me, you jes as well sidle back to your swamp. I ain't no un-suspectin' nigger." She peered ahead. "There it yonder. There the puckawn tree." She crossed to the other side of the lane, brushing against the honeysuckle.

Beyond the hollow she passed a row of cabins. She saw a woman in a red dress out in a garden picking crowder peas. She stopped and watched her. "You s'pose —?" she said, but she shook her head. "Dat cain't be what he see."

At the end of the lane she turned into a gravel road. She spread her eyes wide and prodded her toe against a pile of scrap wood by the ditch. "Gon' git me that wood," she said, "don' some nigger steal it 'fore I git back."

At Mr. Ben's store, Mr. Ben said: "The older you get the more you eat. How many men you keeping now, Lena?" He looked over at an old white man who was leaning against the ice-box drinking a bottle of pop.

Fifteen years before, she had deeded her ten acres to Mr. Ben. In return he had agreed to furnish her provisions until she died. In order to discount his advantage in the bargain he had begun almost immediately to chide her about her everlastingness and her gluttony. He hadn't expected her to live so long and even now that it seemed she would get the better of him he still made his defense — especially when others were present. It had become habit.

She didn't mind his jokes, but she didn't answer him. She sat down on a box and began flapping her handkerchief against her neck.

Mr. Ben was unpacking a carton of pepper. He ignored her. After a while she would say, "I come for some side-meat" or "I need me some coffee." It would do no good to ask her what she wanted. She would only reply, "Cain't talk tu' after I catch my bref," or, in winter, "tu' after I warm my bones," though sometimes, when Mr. Ben was alone, she would say "tu' after I recollects."

"I'm outa that su'up for Jim Pa," she said. She never turned to him but kept staring out the door to the road.

The syrup was a tonic and not strictly a provision. But their bargain had grown complex through exceptions and modifications far beyond the reach of legal definitions. Mr. Ben's protests were only formality. "Ain't that man of yours ever gonna get well?"

"Ain't no man of mine. He my papa."

He had heard this before. Yet, starting around to the other counter, he said, "Can't be your papa."

She was silent for a while, as though she had decided to pay him no mind. Then suddenly she asked, "How come?"

"Can't nobody be older than you." And when he handed her the bottle of brown liquid, he added: "We couldn'na made our agreement . . . if he was your papa."

"He my papa all right," she said. "He older un me. He in the bed."

She got up and started out the door so quickly that he had to call after her: "What else you need, Lena?"

She came back. Whenever she was doubtful, she said either corn meal or coffee. "Mite o' corn meal," she said.

On the way back, she forgot to look for the scrap wood, forgot even to skirt the pecan tree. Her mind was filled with remembering. She talked to herself — even stopped from time to time to study what she was saying — but she said nothing to the trees or the swamp, didn't look once at the cabins that, sitting in a row, their board shutters and doors closed against the sun, always reminded her of old hens asleep on a roost.

"Course he's my pa," she kept saying. But the more she said it, the more doubtful she grew.

* * *

It seemed that he had been lying in the bed with the quilt under his chin for years and years. But she could remember him sitting by the kitchen stove teasing the fire — or out under the shadetree chunking chinaballs at the mocking birds. Beyond that she lost him. He had always been an old man, no-count-no-more, sitting around and lying around, calling for his food and his tobacco and his syrup. She could remember him only when he and she were alone, long past the time that all the others had gone.

Among the kinfolks and friends that once crowded her life, she couldn't single him out at all. But then she couldn't single out anyone else. In her memory there were all sorts of people — going away, coming in, always changing somehow. But she couldn't pin them down, couldn't remember their faces. And under their feet or sitting at the table or falling out of the chinaball tree there were always a lot of children — their hair plaited in ribbons, a nail stuck in their foot, or their little black fists pushing lightning bugs into a bottle. They'd go out the back door, barefoot and half naked, a piece of bread in their hand and snot under their nose. Then they'd come in the front, grown up with a mouth full of teeth and with new city clothes, smelling of cologne, and saying *How-do*.

If she could get them together, she'd have enough to populate a whole town. Yet she was certain that, could she conjure up their faces, she would be able to call them by name. But eyes, gestures, voices were fever in her recollection, flowing sideways up and sideways down like things looked at against the sun; she could never adjust them to the vision of any definite person. Even her children were like words that you understand when you hear them, familiar and fit, but that you yourself could no more call to mind than if they didn't exist at all.

" 'Fore the Lord, he my pa," she said. She stopped in the lane. The dust moved ahead of her, hesitated, and seemed to look back, waiting. "Now when did he come to live at my house?" The wrinkles drew tight round her eyes, almost forcing them shut. And there flowed through her mind some of the pictures that had always stayed round her, like the stuff on her mantelpiece — so familiar as hardly to be noticed at all. But now she studied them just to be able to set them aside as she might set aside the bric-a-brac of her mantel while looking for some especial object misplaced: "That ain't it" and "It ain't under there."

The pictures of her memory were endless: her boy Enoch with a whirring locust flying from a string; somebody's kid walking round the yard on his heel, chicken mess on his foot; her sister Ellie's hand that somebody brought home from the sawmill in a sack. She could see the littlest details of such pictures: how the dime tied round her ankle flashed in the sun as she worked down the cotton row, now fast and now slow, to reach the end by the canebrake at the same time some man did. But the pictures were not complete: What happened to Ellie? And who was that man she wanted to meet in the canes? The pictures were no good — not for remembering; they never had faces. She brushed her hand over her forehead as if to wipe them away. She walked on, and the dust jumped up beside her like a pup excited at moving again.

She remembered her husbands. At least she remembered their names — Zeekial and Jason and Black. There had been others but they had never stayed long, couldn't rightly have been thought of as husbands. "Jim couldn'na been none o' them." Black died an old man; she was certain there had been none after him.

Bent forward towards the billow of dust, she shook her head like an old black toy. "An' if he ain't my pa, who he is? How he got in my house? . . . Now how that ole man got in my house? In my bes' bed! I sho' gon' find out. 'Fore the Lord, I sho' gon' see." She came through the coffee weeds like a gar cutting the waves.

Shadows of gum trees fell on the mimosa, brightening its flowers. She stopped. "It's them *flowers*, do Jesus. That's what he see!" She stared at the tree as though it were a miracle. "Gon' pull 'em off jes' to shet his mouf."

She shot forward, stumbling against Tiney, who, hearing her voice, had risen and was poking his neck towards a crow. She nearly fell. Tiney gawked violently and flapped himself into a cloud of dust.

She pulled the blind fully open, looked in. "Jim Pa!" she yelled. The old man lay still, not hearing. She put her packages on the sill. "Watch me git yo' women outa the field." She knew he couldn't hear, but she talked on. "Better wake up, you bug-eyed bear. You got a lot o' talkin' to do." She turned towards the tree. The flowers were beyond her reach.

She took off her shoes. "Ain't climbed a tree since Hector," she said. "Don' wanna tear my apron." She went up; but, when she reached out, she slipped. Her foot caught between two of the branches angling together. Her head struck one of the lower limbs, and her dress fell down about her.

* * *

The old man was weak. He had opened his eyes to the light and to the dark — he couldn't tell how many times. He had called. He had groaned. He wondered whether he had only dreamed that she never came.

He had heard the women out in the field singing a low sad song like a moan. Then for ever so long everything had been quiet except for the crow of the rooster.

He was thirsty. He was hungry. In his bed there was an awful smell. Something was wrong. He had to come awake: "I gotta git out o' this bed."

When he opened his eyes, the light was so bright he could hardly see. "Lena!" His voice seemed to come from outside.

He saw the women still out in the field. A big black cloud like a wobbling bird fell down from the sky and covered them. "It's a omen," he thought. "It's a cloud like a buzzard."

His mind was full of dreams and he couldn't awaken. "I'm goin' to die."

He thought he jumped up and ran down the lane, swinging his arms and whistling, the smell of fried chicken coming over the pasture, leading him on. Then he felt his fingers against his chin and the heavy quilt on his chest. "Cain't tell what's in this world and what's in the next. Maybe I'm already dead and cain't git away."

Then he thought he sat bolt up in bed and saw Lena hanging by her feet in the tree like a little old girl showing off to the boys — her old backside, big as a buzzard and nearly as black, shining in the sun that splayed through the leaves.

"Lena!" he called but he couldn't hear his voice. "Lena! Lena!" But he wasn't certain whether he had come awake at all; he was scared that he was caught in a dream.

STANLEY ELKIN:

Among the Witnesses

The hotel breakfast bell had not awakened him. The hotel Social Director had. The man had a gift. Wherever he went buzzers buzzed, bells rang, whistles blew. He was a one-man fire drill, Feldman thought.

Feldman focused his eyes on the silver whistle dangling from the neck of the man leaning over him, a gleaming, tooting symbol of authority suspended from a well-made, did-it-himself, plastic lanyard.

"Camp Cuyhoga?" Feldman asked him.

"What's that?" the man said.

"Did you go to Camp Cuyhoga? Your lanyard looks like Cuyhoga '41. Our colors too. Purple and Green against a field of white plastic."

"Come on, boy, wake up a minute," the man said.

"I'm awake. I'm awake."

"Well," he began, "you probably think it's funny, the Social Director coming into the room of a guest like this."

"To hell with caste, man. We're all Americans here," Feldman said.

"But the fact is," he went on, "I wanted to talk to you about something. Now first of all I want you to understand that Bieberman doesn't know I'm here. He didn't put me up to a thing. As a matter of fact he'd probably fire me if he knew what I was going to say,

but, well, Jesus, Steve, this is a family hotel, you know what I mean?"
Feldman heard him say, "well, Jesus, Steve," like a tee-shirted YMCA
professional conscious and sparing of his oaths. He was Arts and
Crafty, this one. "That thing yesterday, well, to be frank, a thing
like that could murder a small hotel like this. In a big place, some
place like Grossinger's, it wouldn't mean a thing. It would be
swallowed up in a minute, am I right? Now you might say this is
none of my business, but Bieberman has been good to me and I
don't want to see him get hurt. He took me off club dates in Jersey
to bring me up here. I mean I ain't knocking my trade but let's
face it, a guy could get old and never get no higher in the show
business than the Hudson Theater. He caught me once and liked
my material, said if I come up with him maybe I could work up
some of the better stuff into a musical like. He's been true to his
word. Free rein. Carte blanche. Absolutely blanche, Steve. Well,
you know yourself, you've heard some of the patter songs. It's good
stuff, am I telling a lie? You don't expect to hear that kind of stuff
in the mountains. Sure, it's dirty, but it's clever, am I right? That
crazy Estelle can't sing, she's got no class, we both know that, but
the material's there, right? It's there."

People were always recruiting him, Feldman thought. "So?" he
asked carefully.

"Well," the Social Director said, embarrassed, "I'll get out of
here and let you get dressed. But I just wanted to say, you know,
how I feel about this guy, and warn you that there might be some
talk. Mrs. Frankel and that crowd. If you hear anything squash it,
you know what I mean? Explain to them." He turned and went
toward the door.

Feldman started to ask, "Explain what?" but it was too late. The
Social Director had already gone out. He could hear him in the
hall knocking at the room next to his own. He heard a rustling
and a moment later someone padding toward the door. He listened
to the clumsy rattle of knobs and hinges, the inward sigh of wood
as the door swung open, and the introductory murmurs of the
Social Director, hesitant, explanatory, apologetic. Trying to make
out the words, he heard the Social Director's voice shift, take on a
loud assurance, and finally subdue itself into a tone of cheap conspiracy. "Between us," he would be saying now, winking slyly,
perhaps even touching with his finger his listener's chest.

Feldman leaned back against his pillow, forgetting the Social

Director. In a few minutes he heard the long loud ring of the second breakfast bell. It was Bieberman's final warning and there was in it the urgency of a fire alarm. He had once told Norma that if the hotel were to catch fire and they sounded that alarm, the guests would go by conditioned response into the dining hall to nibble sandwiches and wait for the fire engines. Well, he would not be with them at any rate. Stephen Feldman, he thought, hotel hold-out. They moved and played and ate in a ferocious togetherness, eyeing with suspicion and real fear those who stood back, who apologized and excused themselves. They even went to town to the movies in groups of a dozen. He had seen them stuff themselves into each other's station wagons, and in the theater had looked on as they passed to each other down the wide row of seats candy bars, bags of peanuts, sticks of gum. With Norma he had watched them afterwards in the ice cream parlor, like guests of honor at a wedding banquet, at the tables they had made the waiter push together. If they could have worked it out they would all have made love in the same big bed, sighing between climaxes, "Isn't this nice? Everybody, isn't this nice?"

He decided to ignore the bell's warning and forfeit breakfast, enjoying the small extravagance. But he was conscious of another feeling, vaguely familiar, and he wondered about its source. Perhaps that was really why he made no effort to get up—he was afraid of dissipating it. It was a feeling of deep, real pleasure, like waking up and not having to go to the bathroom, and he had had it for several mornings now. He had at first regarded it suspiciously, like some suddenly recurring symptom from an old illness. But then he was able to place it. It was a sensation from childhood. It was the way boys woke, instantly, completely, aware of some new fact in their lives. He was—it reduced to this—excited.

He began then his morning inventory of himself. It was a way of keeping up with his geography. He looked first for the source of his new feeling, but except for the obvious fact that he was no longer in the army and had had returned to him what others would have called his freedom, he could find nothing. But he knew that it was not simply a matter of freedom, or at any rate of that kind of freedom. It was certainly not his prospects. He had none. He was fresh out of prospects. But thinking this, he began to see a possible reason for his contentment. His plans for himself were vague, but he was young and healthy. (At the hotel old men offered, only half-jokingly, to trade places with him.) He had only to let something happen to himself, to let something turn up. Uncommitted, he could simply drift until he came upon his fate as a lucky victim of a shipwreck might come upon a vagrant spar. It was like being once again on one of those trips he used to take to strange cities. He had never admired nature. He would bear a mountain range only if there were a city on its other side, water if eventually it became a busy port. In cities he was somehow like a cautious but interested swimmer going tentatively beyond his depth. He would strike out fearfully into the older sections, into slums, factory districts, past railroad yards, into bleak neighborhoods where the poor stared forlornly out of windows. He would enter their dingy hallways and study their names on their mailboxes. Once, as he wandered at dusk through a Skid Row, meeting the eyes of bums who gazed listlessly at him from doorways, he had felt a hand grab his arm. He turned and saw an old man, a bum, who stared at him with dangerous eyes. "Give me money," the man wheezed from a broken throat. He hesitated and saw the man's fist grope slowly, threateningly, toward him. He thought he would be hit but he stood, motionless, waiting to see what the man would do. Inches from his face, the hand opened, turned, became a palm. "Money," the old man said. "God bless you, sir. Help a poor old man. Help me. Help me." He remembered looking into the palm. It was soft, incredibly flabby, the hand, weirdly, of a rich man. The bum began to sob, to tell some story of a wasted life, of chances missed, of things lost, of mistakes made. He listened, spellbound, looking steadily into the palm which remained throughout it all just inches from his body. Finally it shook, reached still closer to him, and at last, closing on itself, dropped helplessly to the old man's side. Stephen was fascinated.

The talking in the other room had momentarily stopped. Then someone summed things up and a pleased voice agreed. It sounded as though a pact had been made. A door opened and the Social Director walked out, whistling, into the corridor.

In a little while he heard others in the corridor. Those would be the guests going to breakfast. He felt again a joy in his extravagance and smiled at the idea of trying to be extravagant at Bieberman's (he thought of the shuffleboard court and the crack in the cement that snaked like a wayward "S" past the barely legible numbers where the paint had faded, of the frayed seams on the tennis nets and the rust on the chains that supported them, of the stucco main building that as soon as it had been built must have looked obsolete, out of place in those green, rich mountains); it was a little like trying to be extravagant at Coney Island. There was about Bieberman's an atmosphere of the second-rate that had little to do with shabbiness. Some places, he knew, even commanded high prices for their shabbiness. But here a thin film of compromise clung to everything about the hotel.

He had seen the expression on the guests' faces as they descended from the hotel station wagon. They came, traitors to their own causes, doubtful, suspicious of their chances, their hearts split by the hope for change, for some unlooked for shift of fortune. Later, they joked about it. What could you expect, they asked, from a mountain that had no Bronx or Brooklyn on top of it?

As for himself, he knew why he had come. And there was nothing mysterious about it. It had nothing to do with soul-searching, or with any of the other academic sports. He was fascinated by the debauch. Sin appealed to him as an art form. But he knew there must be opportunity, and that though the world existed on many levels you had to find your own. You couldn't simply run to the nearest orgy and ask to be let in. You might be a cop, a spy, a person who would throw up. Hometown boy, go home, he had told himself. Home, of course, was where you screwed around, where they knew you. Like the Catskills, a place, a kind of dark, wild closet where his race— none of that—his people—now cut that out—people like himself— that was better—could go.

In the army he had known a boy named Phil, a sort of amateur confidence man itching to turn pro, who, like a mystic, looked to the mountains. He remembered a conversation he had once had with him. They had been sitting in the PX one night during basic training solacing themselves with near-beer. Phil asked him what he was going to do when he got out. He had to tell him he didn't know, and Phil looked doubtful for a moment. He did not understand how something so important had not been prepared for. Stephen asked him the same question, expecting to hear something improbable, some pathetic little tale about night school, but Phil surprised him, reciting an elaborate plan he had worked out. All he needed was a Cadillac.

"A Cadillac?" Feldman said. "Where would you get the money?"

"Listen to him. What do you think, I was always in the army?"

"What did you do before?"

"What did I do? I was a bellboy. In the mountains. In the mountains a bellboy is good for fifteen, sixteen hundred a season. If he makes book like me, add another five."

"You made book?"

"Not my own. I was an agent sort of for a guy. I was a bellboy five seasons. I was saving for the car, you understand. Well, now I've got enough. I've got enough for a wardrobe too. When you have a white Caddy convertible with black upholstery and gold fittings, you don't drive it in blue jeans. I've got about a thousand bucks just for the wardrobe part. When I get out I'm going to pick up my car and I'll go back to the mountains, see? There must be a hundred hotels up there. All I've got to do is to drive around until I see some girl who looks like she might be good for a couple of bucks. I'll pick her up. I'll make a big thing of it, do you follow me? We'll drive around with the top down to all the nice hotels, Grossinger's and the Concord, where all the bellboys know me, and we'll eat a nice lunch in town, and we'll make a date to meet again. Then when I pick her up that night we'll go out to the different hotels—they've got all this free entertainment in the mountains— but the whole time I'm with her I'll be hanging back like, quiet, very sad. She's got to ask me what's up, right? Well, I'll brush it off, but all the time I'll be getting more miserable and she'll be all over me with questions about what's wrong, is it something she did, you know what I mean? So finally I'll say, 'Look, dear, I didn't want to ruin your evening, but I see I'll have to tell you. It's the Cadillac. I've got just one payment to make on it and it's ours. Well, I'm broke this month. I lent money to a guy and I dropped a couple of hundred on a nag last week. I missed the payment. They called me up today they're going to repossess if they don't get the payment tomorrow. Hell, I wouldn't care, honey, but I like you and I know what a kick it gives you to ride in it.' Now you know, a girl on a vacation, she's got to have a few bucks in the suitcase, am I right? Sooner or later she's got to say, 'Maybe I could lend you some money toward it. How much do you need?' I tell her that it's crazy, she doesn't even know me, and anyway that I'd need about sixty bucks. Well, don't you see, she's so relieved it's not more she knocks herself out to get the dough to me. She's thinking I'm into her for sixty bucks, we're practically engaged or something. The thing is, to close the deal, I've got to be able to make her. That's my insurance she won't try to find me later on. These girls make a big thing out of their reputation and I could ruin her. It's easy. That's the whole setup. The next day I go to a new hotel. If I'm smart I figure it's good for the whole season. And then in the winter, there's Miami."

Feldman smiled, recalling Phil's passion. It was a hell of an idea, he had to admit, and he would have to keep his eyes open for a white Cadillac convertible. But what was important was that somewhere in the outrageous plan, there was sound, conservative thinking, the thinking of a man who knew his geography, who saw his symbols in the true white lights of a Cadillac's headlamps. The plan could work. It was, in its monstrous way, feasible, and he cheered Phil on. He had not come himself for the money, of course, but to shake down a little glory from the skies; to abandon himself; in short, to make love to some nice Jewish girl or girls. Only it depended upon mutual abandon, and there was not so much of that going around. And as far as that was concerned, he was hard pressed to work up any abandon of his own. All he could be sure of was that he approved of it.

"Well anyway," he thought, playing his pleasant morning game, "I'm in a new place, and there's Norma, at least."

As he thought of Norma he felt some misgivings. It was too easy to make fun of her desperation. She was, after all, something like the last of her race, the vacationing secretary, the over-ripe vestal virgin, the only girl in the whole damned family who had not walked down some flower-strewn aisle in the Bronx amidst a glory going at four dollars a plate, toward the ultimate luck, a canopy of flowers, to plight what she would call (all the time explaining who the old uncle was who hung back and did not smile in the wedding photographs) her troth. Beauty is troth and troth beauty, that is all ye know on earth and all ye need to know. And Norma, he thought, on the edge of age, having tried all the other ways, having gone alone to the dances in the gymnasium of the Hebrew School, having read and mastered the *Journal of the American Medical Association* for the month of April so that she might hold intelligent conversation with the nephew of her mother's friend, a perspiring interne at Bellevue, and having ceased to shave her underarms because of the pain, had abandoned herself to Bieberman's and to him.

He stretched in bed. Under the sheet he moved his toes and watched the lump change shape, like a suddenly shifting mountain range. The sun lay in strips across his chest. He got out of the sun-warmed bed, and slices of light from the Venetian blinds climbed up and across his body.

He began to dress but saw that his ground level window was open. He moved up to it cautiously and started to pull the string on the Venetian blinds to slant the sunlight downward. Seeing some of the guests standing in a large group beside the empty swimming pool, he paused. He remembered the cryptic warnings of the Social Director. He shivered slightly, recalling against his will the confused and angry scene which yesterday had sickened them all. Was this the new excitement he had awakened with, he wondered.

He had even known the child slightly; she and her mother had sat at the table next to his in the dining hall. He had once commented to Norma that she was a pretty little girl. Her death and her mother's screams (the cupped hands rocking back and forth in front of her, incongruously like a gambler's shaking dice) had frightened him. He had come up from the tennis court with his racket in his hand. In front of him were the sun-blistered backs of the guests. He pushed through, using his racket to make a place for himself. He stood at the inner edge of the circle but, seeing the girl's blue face ringed by the wet yellow hair sticking to it, he backed off, thrusting his racket before his face, defending his eyes. The people pushing behind him would not let him through and helplessly he had to turn back, forced to watch as Mrs. Goldstone, the girl's mother, asked each of them why it had happened, and then begged, and then accused, and then turned silently back to the girl to bend over her again and slap her. He heard her insanely calm voice scolding the dead girl: "Wake up. Wake up. Wake up." He watched the mother, squatting on her heels over the girl, vaguely obscene, like someone defecating in the woods. She struggled hopelessly with the firemen who came to remove the girl, and after they had borne her off, her body jouncing grotesquely on the stretcher, he saw the mother try to hug the wet traces of the child's body on the cement. When the others put out their hands and arms to comfort her, crowding about her, determined to make her recognize their sympathy, he looked away.

He stood back from the window. Several of the people from yesterday were there again. "My God," he thought, "they're acting it out."

He recognized Mrs. Frankel among them. She was wearing her city clothes and looked hot and uncomfortable standing beside Bieberman's empty pool. She seemed to be arguing ferociously, in her excitement unconscious of the big purse that followed weirdly the angry arcs of her arms. The sun caught the faces of some stones on her heavy bracelet and threw glints of light into Stephen's eyes as she pointed in the direction of the pool. He did not know what she was saying but he could imagine it easily enough. He had heard her bullying before. She was like the spokesman for some political party forever in opposition.

In a moment Stephen noticed something else. Beyond the excited crowd gathering about Mrs. Frankel, he saw Bieberman who stood, hanging back, his head cocked to one side, his expression one of troubled concentration. He looked like a defendant forced to listen in a foreign court to witnesses whose language he could not understand. Beside him was the Social Director, scowling like an impatient advocate.

Stephen finished shutting the light from the room, and, turning from the window, began again to dress.

When he approached the main building the others had finished their breakfasts and were already in the positions that would carry them through until lunch. On the long shaded porch in front of Bieberman's main building people sat in heavy wicker rockers playing cards. They talked low in wet thick voices. Occasionally the quiet murmur was broken by someone bidding stridently. Stephen could feel already the syrupy thickness of the long summer day. He climbed the steps and was about to go inside to get some coffee when he saw Mrs. Frankel. She was talking to a woman who listened gravely. He tried to slip by without having to speak to her but she had seen him. She looked into his eyes and would not turn away. Stephen nodded to her. She allowed her head to sway forward once slowly as though she and Stephen were conspirators in some grand mystery. "Good morning, Mrs. Frankel," Stephen said.

She greeted him solemnly. "It won't be long now, will it, Mr. Feldman?"

"What won't?" Stephen asked.

She waved her hand about her, taking in all of Bieberman's in a vague gesture of accusation. "Didn't they tell you I was leaving?" she asked slowly.

He was amazed at the woman's egotism. He pictured her dispatching little notes via the bellboy. On each would be the cryptic message: "I'm leaving. F."

"Vacation over, Mrs. Frankel?" he asked, smiling.

"Some vacation," she said. "Do you think I'd stay with that murderer another day? I should say not! Listen, I could say plenty. You don't have to be a Philadelphia lawyer to see what's happening. Some vacation. Who needs it? Don't you think when my son heard he didn't say, 'Mama, I'll be up to get you whenever you want?' The man's a fine lawyer, he could make plenty of trouble if he wanted."

For a moment as the woman spoke he felt the shadow of a familiar panic. He recognized the gestures, the voice that would take him into the conspiracy, that insisted he was never out of it. Mrs. Frankel could go to hell, he thought. He could not tell her so, of course, for that would be a gesture of his own. He would not go through life using his hands.

Mrs. Frankel still spoke in the same tone of outrage which Feldman did not quite trust. "The nerve," she said. "Well, believe me, he shouldn't be allowed to get away with it."

Bieberman suddenly appeared at the window behind Mrs. Frankel's chair. His huge head seemed to fill the whole window. His face was angry but when he spoke his voice was soft. "Please, Mrs. Frankel. Please," he said placatingly. Stephen continued toward the dining room.

Inside, the bus boys were still clearing the tables. He went up to one of the boys and asked for some coffee. The boy nodded politely and went through the large brown swinging doors into the kitchen. He pushed the doors back forcefully and Stephen saw for a moment the interior of the bright kitchen. He looked hard at the old woman, Bieberman's cook, sitting on a high stool, a cigarette in her mouth, shelling peas. The doors came quickly together, but in a second their momentum had swung them outward again and he caught another glimpse of her. She had turned her head to watch the bus boy. Quickly the doors came together again, like stiff theatrical curtains.

He turned and saw Norma across the dining hall. She was holding a cigarette and drinking coffee, watching him. He went up to her table. "Good morning," he said, sitting down. "A lot of excitement around here this morning."

"Hello," she said.

Stephen leaned over to kiss her. She moved her head and he was only able to graze her cheek. In the instant of his fumbling movement he saw himself half out of his chair, leaning across the cluttered table, like a clumsy diver on a diving board. He sat back abruptly, surprised. He shrugged. He broke open a roll and pulled the dough from its center. "Frankel's leaving today," he said after a while.

"Yes," she said. "I know."

"In a cloud of shady circumstances. I'm going to miss her. She's a kind of Catskillian Minute Man," he said, smiling.

"What's so funny about Mrs. Frankel?"

Stephen looked at her. "Nothing," he said. "You're right. One of these days, after this Linda Goldstone affair had blown over, she would have gotten around to us."

"She couldn't say anything about us."

"No," he said. "I guess not."

"Goldstone affair," she said. "The little girl is dead."

"Yes," he said. "She was a nice kid."

"Affair," she said. "Some affair."

He looked at her carefully to see whether she was teasing him. He could not understand her coolness, her primness. Her face was without expression. What did she want from him, a *statement?*

"All right," he said, "O.K. The Goldstone affair—excuse me, the Goldstone tragedy—was just the Goldstone drowning. Norma, it was an accident. Sure, unfortunate, tragic too, in a limited, personal way, but at bottom just an accident. Everyone around here carries on as though it had implications. Even you. I suppose the thing I feel worst about, outside my common and decent sympathy for the parents, is Bieberman. He's the only one who still has anything to lose. It could hurt him in the pocketbook and to a man like him that must be a mortal wound."

He stopped. Norma looked shocked, like someone who had been slapped. It was a dodge, it was a dodge, he thought. Always, fragility makes its demands on bystanders. The dago peddler whose apples have been spilled, the rolled drunk, the beat up queer, the new widow shrieking at an open window—their helplessness strident, their despair a prop. What did they want? They were like children rushing to their toys, the trucks, the tin armies, to manipulate them, put them in situations whose consequences they could not foresee, making sounds of battle in their throats, percussing danger and emergency. He would not take back what he had said. He would not make things easier for her.

Stephen Feldman was in his bathing trunks. On his feet were the low quarters he had been discharged in. He had not had time, so anxious was he to get away, to buy other shoes, not even the sneakers appropriate for afternoon climbs like this one on the high hill behind Bieberman's.

He had lost interest in the hike. He turned his back on the sandy, rock-strewn path that continued on up the hill and into the woods he had promised himself to explore, and he looked down to see where he had come from. Below him was the resort, tricked out in artificially bright colors. He had not seen the place before from up here and its arrangement in the flat green valley struck him as comic. It looked rather like a giant Fun House in an amusement park. He had the impression that if he were to return to his room he would find, bracketed in heavy yellow frames, mirrors that gave back distorted images. In the trick rooms, constructed to defy gravity, he would have to hang onto the furniture to keep from falling. He looked at the fantastic spires that swirled like generous scoops of custard in cups too small to hold them, and he pictured Bieberman climbing at sunset to the top of these minarets to bellow like a clownish muezzin to the wayward guests. He saw the brightly colored beach umbrellas on the hotel lawn. They were like flowers grown grossly out of proportion in a garden.

He grinned, shifting his gaze from the hotel grounds and letting it fall on his own body. It rested there a moment without any real recognition and then, gradually conscious of himself, he stared, embarrassed, at his thighs which, somehow, exposure to the sun had failed to tan deeply. He traced his legs down past bony knee-caps and hairless shins and mocked in silence their abrupt disappearance into the formal shoes. Why, he was like someone come upon in the toilet. The fat thighs, the shiny pallor of the too smooth legs, like a glaucous sheen on fruit, betrayed him. He seemed to himself clumsy and a little helpless, like old, fat women in camp chairs on the beach, their feet swollen in men's shoes they had to leave untied, the loose strings like the fingers they laced protectively across their busts.

Just what was he really doing at Bieberman's, he wondered. He could dismiss his disappointment as an experience of travellers who, having left the airport in their hired cars, and spoken to clerks about reservations, and made arrangements for the delivery of bags, find themselves alone in cities strange to them, bored, vaguely depressed, sleepless in their rented beds, searching aimlessly for familiar names in the telephone directory. But what, finally, was he doing there at all? He thought of the other people who had come to the hotel. Somehow he had to remind himself that they did not live there always, had not been hired by the hotel as a kind of folksy background, a monumental shill for his benefit. Their reasons for coming were practical. They organized their pleasures, he supposed, on a quantitative basis and had chosen Bieberman's (poring over the brochure in hot apartments) for the access it would give them to the tennis court, the pool, the six-hole golf course, the floor show "nitely," the card tables, the dining room, each other. The greatest difference was that they had come to *Bieberman's,* he merely to a place in the mountains (he remembered the hot trip on the Greyhound bus, the small village where he left the bus, the suitcases he had lifted into the taxi, and his instructions to the driver to drive through the mountains until he told him to stop). He supposed that was why there were for the others no surprises, except for the death of the little girl, and for himself—except for the death of the little girl—so many.

He wondered whether to start up the path again. He turned to estimate the distance he had yet to travel and discovered, quite unexpectedly, that he was tired. He looked again below him. He could see the drained pool. A little water still remained at the bottom, like a stain on the smooth white tile. Some reflected light flashed against his eyes and he turned, instinctively shielding them with one cupped palm.

"I didn't think you'd see me," someone said.

Stephen stepped back. He hadn't seen anyone but assumed that the boy who was now coming from within the trees that bordered the path had mistaken his gesture as a friendly wave and had responded to it.

"If you're trying to hide," Stephen said, "you shouldn't wear white duck trousers. Law of the jungle." The bare-chested boy, whom he recognized as the hotel lifeguard, came cautiously onto the path where Stephen stood. Stephen thought he seemed rather shamefaced, and looked into the green recess from which the boy had come to see if perhaps one of the girls from the hotel was there.

"I wasn't hiding," the boy said defensively. "I come up here often when I'm not on duty. I've seen you at the pool."

"I've seen you too. You're the lifeguard." The boy looked down. They were standing in a circle of sunlight that seemed to ring them like contenders for a title of little note in a woodsy arena. He noticed uncomfortably that the boy was looking at his shoes. Stephen shuffled his feet self-consciously. The boy looked up and Stephen saw that his eyes were red.

"Have they been talking about me?" the boy asked.

"Who? Has who been talking about you?"

The boy nodded in the direction of the hotel.

"No," Stephen said. "Why?" he asked before he could check himself.

"Mr. Bieberman said I shouldn't hang around today. I didn't know anywhere to come until I remembered this place. I was going all the way to the top when I heard you. I thought Mr. Bieberman might have sent you up to look for me."

Stephen shook his head.

The boy seemed disappointed. "Look," he said suddenly, "I want to come down. I'm not used to this. How long do they expect me to stay up here?" For all the petulance, Stephen could hear real urgency in his voice. He added this to the boy's abjectness, to his guilt at being found, and to the terror he could not keep to himself. It wasn't fair to let the boy continue to reveal himself in the mistaken belief that everything had already been found out about him. He didn't want to hear more, but already the boy was talking again. There was no way to stop him. "I'm not used to this," he said. "I told Mr. Bieberman at the beginning of the summer about my age. He knew I was sixteen. That's why I only get two hundred. It was O.K. then."

"Two hundred?"

The boy stopped talking and looked Stephen over carefully. He might have been evaluating their relative strengths. As though he had discovered Stephen's weakness and was determined to seize upon it for his own advantage, he looked down at Stephen's knees. Stephen felt his gaze keenly.

"Does anyone else know?" Stephen asked abruptly.

"Mrs. Frankel, I think," he said, still not looking up.

Stephen shifted his position, moving slightly to one side. "She'll be going home today," he said. "I saw her this morning. She didn't say anything." He did not enjoy the cryptic turn in the conversation. It reminded him vaguely of the comical communication between gangsters in not very good films. A man leans against a building. Someone walks past. The man nods to a loitering confederate. The confederate winks slyly and moves on.

He made up his mind to continue the walk. "Look," he said to the boy, "I'm going to go on up the path." Having said this, he began to move down towards Bieberman's. He realized his mistake immediately but felt that the boy must be staring at him. He wondered whether he should make some feint with his body, perhaps appear to have come down a few steps to get a better look at some non-existent activity below them and then turn to continue back up the path. "No," he thought. "I won't give him the satisfaction." He could hear the boy following him.

Some pebbles that the boy dislodged struck Stephen's ankles. He watched them roll down the hill. The boy caught up with him. "I'm going down too," he said, as though Stephen had made a decision for both of them. The path narrowed and Stephen took advantage of the fact to move ahead of the boy. He moved down quickly, concentrating on the steep angle of the descent. Just behind him the boy continued to chatter. "He needed someone for the season. It was the Fourth of July and he didn't have anyone. I got a cousin who works in the kitchen. He told me. Mr. Bieberman knew about my age. I told him. He said, 'What's age got to do with it? Nobody drowns.' I had to practice the holds in my room." The path widened and the boy came abreast of Stephen. He timed his pace to match Stephen's and they came to the bottom of the hill together.

Stephen began to jog ahead of the boy but, soon tiring, he stopped and resumed walking. Though the boy had not run after him, Stephen knew that he was not far behind and that he was still following him. He went deliberately toward one of the tables on Bieberman's lawn, thinking that when he reached it he would turn to the boy and ask him to bring him a drink. He did not notice until it was too late that it was Mrs. Frankel's table he was heading for. The wide, high-domed beach umbrella that stood over it had hidden her from him. He saw that the only way to take himself out of her range was to veer sharply, but remembering the boy behind him and the mistake he had made on the hill, he decided that he could not risk such a sudden movement. What if the kid turned with him, he thought. They would wind up alone together on the golf course. He would never be able to get away from him. "That damned kid is chasing me toward the woman," he thought.

Mrs. Frankel, sitting in her hot, thick city clothing, looked to Stephen like a woman whose picture has just been taken for the

Sunday supplements. ("Mrs. Van Frankel, seated here beneath a two-hundred-pound mushroom she raised herself, has announced . . .") "Well," he thought, "she is always announcing anyway." When he came closer he saw that she would not do for the supplements at all. Her legs, thrown out in front of her, gave her the appearance of an incredibly weary shopper whose trip downtown has failed. Her expression was disconsolate and she seemed, brooding there, like someone who does not quite understand what has gone wrong. It was an unusual attitude for Mrs. Frankel and he stood beside her for a moment. She stared straight ahead toward the useless pool.

"It's funny," she said, turning to him. "A little girl." Stephen had never heard her talk so softly. "Did you see her? Like she was just some piece of cardboard that had been painted like a child. It's too terrible," she said. "To happen here? In the mountains? Just playing like that? All right, so a child is sick, it's awful, but a little child gets sick and sometimes there's nothing you can do and the child dies." Stephen was not sure she was talking to him. "But here, in the mountains where you come for fun, for it to happen here? It's, I don't know, it's too terrible. A thing like that." She looked directly at Stephen but he could not be certain that she saw him. "Did you see the mother? Did you see the fright in the woman's eyes? Like, 'No, it couldn't be.' I was there. The child wanted an ice cream and the mother told her that her lips were blue, she should come out. She looked around for a second, for a second, and when she turned around again . . ." Mrs. Frankel shrugged. "How long could she have been under, five seconds, ten? Is the pool an ocean, they had to search for her? No, it's more important the lifeguard should be talking to his girl-friends so when he hears the screaming he should look up and holler 'What? What? Where? Where?' Who's to blame?" she asked Stephen. "Is God to blame for such a thing? We're not savages. Let's fix the blame a little close to home."

He shifted under her direct stare. She had recovered her stentorian coloratura and for this he was grateful. She was running true to form again and her elegy or whatever it was had only been a kind of interlude as though the woman caught her breath not by ceasing to talk but by lowering her voice. However, her question still hung in the air. He didn't want to play but that didn't seem to make any difference to these people. Even saying No, he wouldn't play, was playing too in a way, and not saying no, not saying anything, but just walking away as he had done on the hill, or as he had meant to do on the hill, well, that was playing too, and if he had to get into the game, he might as well get in on the side he believed in.

"All right, Mrs. Frankel," he said. "What is it? All morning you've been hinting at some dark secret. Is it that the lifeguard wasn't old enough?" His voice sounded louder than he had intended. He heard it as though he were listening to a recording he could not remember having made. "Is that what's bothering you? Is that the little secret you're determined to let everyone in on? Well, relax, it's no secret. Everybody knows about it. It's too bad, but even if the kid had been eighteen instead of sixteen the little girl would still have drowned."

"The lifeguard was only sixteen?" the woman asked. It was impossible that she didn't know. She must have guessed, must have suspected it. That had to be the reason for her outrage.

"The lifeguard was only sixteen?" she repeated. It was too much; he couldn't be the one she learned it from. He would renege. "Only sixteen?" she insisted.

"I don't know how old he is," he said. "That's not the point. It was an accident. What difference does it make how old he is?" Only now was he conscious that the boy had not left them. He was standing about twenty feet away, listening. Stephen remembered seeing Bieberman stand in the same attitude just that morning, his head bowed low under the weight of his embarrassment, buffered from his enemies by the Social Director. No, Stephen thought, he would not be anyone's champion.

Blithely he changed the subject. Seemingly without reason he began to tell Mrs. Frankel of the walk he had just taken, of his vague plans for the future. She listened politely and even nodded in agreement once or twice to things he said. He remained with her in this way for about ten minutes, but when he started to leave he caught for a moment Mrs. Frankel's angry stare. "It's better we should all get out," she said.

Stephen lay beside Norma beyond the closed-in tennis court. He watched the moon's chalk silver disintegrate and drift icily to the lawn. They had not spoken for a quarter of an hour. He did not know whether she was asleep. The ground was very damp. He could feel, beneath the blanket, the evening's distillation like a kind of skin. He raised himself on one elbow and looked at Norma's face. Her eyes were closed and he lay back down again and watched the sky.

The lawn was deserted; the exodus of late that afternoon had ended; the last cars from the city had gone back. He thought of Bieberman, alone beside the pool, and could still see the old man's awful face as he waved at the departing guests, pretending that it was only the natural end of their vacation that took them back.

Stephen pulled a blade of grass from beside the blanket.

"The slob," he said aloud.

Norma stirred beside him, made a small sound, like a whimper.

Stephen only half heard her. "The slob. He stood in the driveway and waved at them. He shook their hands and said he'd save their rooms. He's been a host too long. He even told the bellboy where to put everything." He tore the grass in half and threw one piece away. "The slob. I was ashamed for him."

He rolled the grass between his fingers. Feeling its sticky juice, he threw it away in disgust. "Even the Social Director. Did you hear him? 'I'm sorry, Bieberman, but I've got to have people. I've got to have people, right?' And Bieberman told him, 'You're a fine actor. You give a professional performance.' It made me sick. And Mrs. Frankel didn't say a word. She didn't have to. He gave himself away."

"The poor thing," Norma said. Her voice was low and cool, not sleepy at all. He turned to her and smiled.

"Who, Bieberman?"

"I meant the little girl," she said. Her voice was flat. He studied her pale face and the skin which looked cooler and softer than he remembered ever having seen it. She seemed smaller somehow and, in a way he did not mind, older. It may only be the moon, he thought.

He touched her cheek with his fingers. "You would have gone with them, wouldn't you?" he asked softly. She didn't answer. She turned her head and his hand dropped to the blanket. "You've done that twice today," he said.

"Have I?"

He looked at her body. She lay straight back, her arms at her sides. He rolled toward her quickly and his arm fell across her breast. She tried to move away from him, but she seemed unsure of herself. He grabbed her arms and pinned them to her sides and kissed her on the mouth. In a few minutes, he thought, my vacation

begins. A nice Jewish girl in a nice deserted Jewish hotel. She shook
her head ferociously. His face fell on top of hers and he forced it
with his weight toward the blanket. He felt her body stiffen, her
arms go rigid. Then her arms shook in a rage against him and he
was helpless to hold them at her sides. She was very strong and with
a sudden convulsive movement she threw him off. She sprang up
quickly and stood looking down at him.

"Get away from me," Stephen said.

"Stephen . . ."

"Get away from me."

"Stephen, I wouldn't have gone back."

"Get away."

"All right," she said quietly. She turned and started away.

"There she goes," he called after her. "Don't touch her, she's in
mourning." His anger rose in him. "Hey come back, I've got an
idea. We'll have a lynching. We'll string the kid up to the diving
board and hang Bieberman from a beach umbrella."

She was moving from him quickly, back to the hotel. He got up
and started after her. He put out his hand to stop her but she
eluded him and Stephen saw himself stumble forward, his empty
hand reaching toward her. He recovered quickly and walked along
slightly behind her, talking to her. He felt like a pedlar haggling
but he couldn't help himself. "The drowning loused things up,
didn't it? It killed a stranger, but nobody around here knows from
strangers." She broke into a run. From the way she ran Stephen
could tell she was crying. He ran after her and heard her sobbing.
"Let's blame someone. The lifeguard. Bieberman. You want to
know what to blame? Blame cramps and the kid's lousy Australian
crawl." As they approached the hotel steps Stephen halted. Norma
continued up and Stephen called after her. "Damn you. Do you
hear? I damn you." She walked into the hotel and Stephen slumped
on the steps. He clapped his palms together nervously in a raged
applause. "That kid, that lousy kid," he thought. Gradually, he
forced himself to calm. He thought of his tantrum as he would
of a disease which recurs despite its cure.

When the world had quieted he knew that he was not alone.
He realized that he had been vaguely aware of someone on the
porch when he turned from Norma and let her go inside. He looked
around and saw in the shadows about twenty feet away the silhouette

of a man propped against the side of the porch. In the dark he could not make out his face.

"Bieberman?"

The man came toward Stephen from the dark recesses of the porch. He walked slowly, perhaps uncertainly, and when he passed in front of the hotel entrance he was caught in the light slanting down from the interior like a gangplank secured to the building.

"Ah, Feldman." The voice was deep and mocking.

"Mr. Bieberman," Stephen said softly.

The man stayed within the light. Stephen rose and joined him nervously but Bieberman still did not move. "It's about time for bed," Stephen said. "I was just going up."

"Sure," Bieberman said. "So this will be your last night with us, hah Feldman?"

Stephen looked at him, feeling himself, as they stood together within the close quarters of the light, somehow under attack. "I hadn't planned for it to be."

"Planned?" The old man laughed. "The girl will be going in the morning. What will there be to keep you? The food?" He laughed again. "You'll leave tomorrow. But I thank you for staying the extra day. It will make me a rich man, and I can go myself to a hotel." Stephen noticed the bottle in Bieberman's hand. The old man followed Stephen's glance and looked up, smiling broadly. "Schnapps," he said, holding the bottle up. "A little schnapps. I've been sitting here on my porch and I'm on a deck chair on the *Queen Mary* which in honor of my first voyage over is keeping a kosher kitchen. The only thing wrong is that once in a while someone falls overboard and it upsets me. If we weren't three days out, I would call my wife she should swim up from the city and we would go back."

Stephen smiled and Bieberman offered him the bottle. He took it and, unconsciously wiping off the neck, began to drink.

"I guess I will be going," Stephen said.

"I guess you will."

It was just what he wanted, perfect for his mood, to come after the long and trying day to the councils of the sage and talk to an old man, somewhere outdoors, but with indirect lighting. "I shouldn't be here," he said. "It was supposed to be a lark. I didn't come slumming, don't think that. But it didn't work out. I guess I just wanted to fool around. I really wanted to fool around."

"Yeah," Bieberman said. "I know you guys. You've got a suit-case filled with contraceptives. Fooey."

"I just wanted to fool around," Stephen repeated.

"Nobody fools. Ever," Bieberman said.

"You said it," Stephen said.

Bieberman went back into the dark wing of the porch. Stephen followed him. "I don't want you to think I'm leaving for the same reason as the others. I don't blame you." The old man didn't answer. "I really don't," Stephen said.

Stephen almost lost him in the shadows. "A boy who likes to fool around doesn't blame me," he heard the old man say to himself.

Stephen paused. "Well," he said lamely, "goodnight." He went toward the door.

"Feldman, tell me, you're an educated person," Bieberman said suddenly. "Do you really think they could sue me?"

Stephen turned back to him. "I don't see how," he said.

"But the lifeguard, the boy. If I knew he was a boy? If I knew he was sixteen? If they could prove that, couldn't they sue?"

"How could they find that out?" Stephen said, annoyed at the insistent tone in the old man's voice.

"Well, I wouldn't tell them. I wouldn't run an ad in the *Times,* but if they knew it could they sue me?"

"I suppose they could try, I don't know. I'm no lawyer. I don't see how they could find you responsible."

"My guests did."

"They'll forget."

"Ah," the old man said.

"Next year your place will be full again."

"Yes, I suppose so," he said sadly.

"Wait a minute, it wasn't your fault."

"It made them sick," Bieberman said so softly Stephen thought he was talking to himself. "All they could do was get away. Some of the women couldn't even look at me. Sure, that's why the Cats-kills and Miami Beach and Las Vegas and all those places are so important. That's why a man named Bieberman can have his name written across a hotel, and on towels." Stephen couldn't follow him. "I mean, what the hell," he said, suddenly talking to Stephen again. "Does Spinoza get his name written on towels?"

"Why don't you come inside?" Stephen said, offering him his arm.

"When a little girl drowns in such a place where nobody must drown, where you pay good money just to keep everybody on top of the water, it's a terrible thing. I understand that. You're not safe anywhere," Bieberman said. "Not anywhere. You go to a football game and all of a sudden the man on the loudspeaker calls for a doctor it's an emergency. Not during a holiday, you think. You think so? You think not during a holiday? You think so? In a forest even, by yourself, one day you notice how the deer are diseased or how the rivers are dried up, something."

"Come on inside, Mr. Bieberman," Stephen said.

"Feldman, listen to me. Do me a favor, yeah? Tomorrow when you get back to the city, maybe you could call up those people and tell them what the lifeguard told you. You're the only one who knew about it."

The old man lighted a cigarette. Feldman could see the glowing tip pulsating softly as Bieberman spoke. He tried to see his face but it was too dark.

"You're crazy," Stephen said finally.

"I'm responsible," he said sadly.

"Well, I'm not," Stephen said.

"You are, Feldman. You're a witness. A witness is responsible. There's always something he can do. He can call the police. He can try to take away the robber's gun. A witness is responsible."

Stephen got up quickly. He walked across the darkened wing of the porch and came abruptly into the slanting yellow light. Bieberman called him and he turned around. "Feldman," he said. "I mean it, tell them you heard me brag once how I saved a couple hundred bucks." Stephen shook his head and started carefully down the steps, afraid he would stumble in the dark. "Feldman, I mean it," Bieberman called.

He took the rest of the steps quickly, forgetting the danger. He was going toward the empty pool. He turned around. A light was on in Norma's room. He could still hear Bieberman calling his name. He stood among the beach umbrellas on the wide dark lawn and listened to the old man's desperate voice. "Feldman. Feldman." It was as though he was hiding and Bieberman had been sent out to look for him. "Feldman, I mean it."

All right, he thought, all right, damn it, all right, all right. He would wait until the morning and then he would go to Norma's room and apologize and they would go back to the city together and he would investigate some jobs and they would continue to see each other and, after a while, perhaps, he would ask her to marry him.

WILLIAM H. GASS:

Mrs. Mean

1

I call her Mrs. Mean. I see her, as I see her husband and each of her four children, from my porch, or sometimes when I look up from my puttering, or part my upstairs window curtains. I can only surmise what her life is like inside her little house; but on humid Sunday afternoons, while I try my porch for breeze, I see her hobbling on her careful lawn in the hot sun, stick in hand to beat her scattered children, and I wonder a lot about it.

I don't know her name. The one I've made to mark her and her doings in my head is far too abstract. It suggests the glassy essence, the grotesquerie of Type; yet it's honestly come by, and in a way, it's flattering to her, as if she belonged on Congreve's stage. She could be mean there without the least particularity, with the formality and grandeur of Being, while still protected from the sour and acrid community of her effect, from the full sound and common feel of life; all of which retain her, for me, on her burning lawn, as palpable and loud and bitter as her stinging switch.

I may have once said something to her—a triviality—and perhaps once more than that, while strolling, I may have nodded to her or I may have smiled. . . . though not together. I have forgotten.

When I bought my house I wished, more than anything, to be idle, idle in the supremely idle way of nature; for I felt then that nature produced without effort, in the manner of digestion and breathing. The street is quiet. My house is high and old, as most of the others are, and spreading trees shade my lawn and arch the pavement. Darkness is early here at any time of year. The old are living their old age out, shawled in shadows, cold before fires. A block away they are building stores. One feels the warmth that is the movement of decay. I see the commercial agent. He wears gold rings. His hand partitions. Lamps will grow in these unlucky windows. Wash will hang from new external stairs. No one has his home here but myself; for I have chosen to be idle, as I said, to surround myself with scenes and pictures; to conjecture, to rest my life upon a web of theory—as ready as the spider is to mend or suck dry intruders. While the street is quiet, the houses whole, their windows shaded; while the aged sit their porches and swap descriptions of their health; the Means, upon the opportunity of death, have seized the one small house the neighborhood affords. Treeless and meager, it stands in the summer in a pool of sun and in the winter in a blast of air.

My house has porches fore and aft and holds a corner. I spy with care and patience on my neighbors but I seldom speak. They watch me too, of course, and so I count our evils even, though I guard my conscience with a claim to scientific coldness they cannot possess. For them no idleness is real. They see it, certainly. I sit with my feet on the rail. My wife rocks by me. The hours pass. We talk. I dream. I sail my boats on their seas. I rest my stories on their backs. They cannot feel them. Phantoms of idleness never burden. If I were old or sick or idiotic, if I shook in my chair or withered in a southern window, they would understand my inactivity, and approve; but even the wobblers make their faithful rounds. They rake their leaves. They mow and shovel. They clip their unkempt hedges and their flowers. Their lives are filled by this. I do no more.

Mrs. Mean, for instance: what could she think? She is never idle. She crowds each moment with endeavor.

When I had my cottage I used to see, on Sabbaths, a wire-haired lady drive her family to the beach. She rented everything. Her family dressed in the car, the windows draped with blankets, while the lady in her jacket rapped on the hood for speed, then rushed them to the surf. She always gestured grandly at the sea and swung a watch by its strap. "So much money, so much time, let us amuse," she always said, and sat on a piece of driftwood and shelled peas. The children dabbled at the water with their fingers. Her husband, a shriveled, mournful soul, hung at the water's edge and slowly patted his wrists with ocean. Inertia enraged her. She thrust her pods away, pouring her lap in a jar. "Begin, begin," she would shout then, jumping up, displaying the watch. The children would squat in the sand until foam marked their bottoms, staring in their pails. Papa would drip water to his elbows and upper arm while mama receded to her log. The children fought then. It began invisibly. It continued silently, without emotion. They kicked and bit and stabbed with their shovels. When she found them fighting she would empty her lap and start up, shaking the watch and shouting, but the children fought on bitterly, each one alone, throwing sand and swinging their pails, rolling over and over on the beach and in and out of the moving ocean. She ran toward them but the sea slid up the sand and drove her off, squealing on tiptoe, scuffing and denting the smooth sand. The children plunged into the surf and broke apart. "Don't lose your shovels!" The waves washed the children in. They huddled on dark patches of beach. At last their mother would run among them, quickly, between breaths of ocean, and with her hands on her hips, her legs apart, she would throw her head back in the mimic of gargantuan guffaws, soundless and shaking. "Laugh," she would say then, "there is only an hour."

The people by me primitively guess that I am enemy and hate me: not alone for being different, or disdaining work, or worse, not doing any; but for something that would seem, if spoken for them, words of magic; for I take their souls away—I know it—and I play with them; I puppet them up to something; I march them through strange crowds and passions; I snuffle at their roots.

From the first they saw me watching. I can't disguise my interest. They expected, I suppose, that I would soon be round with stories. I would tell Miss Matthew of Mr. Wallace, and Mr. Wallace of Mrs. Turk, and Miss Matthew and Mr. Wallace and Mrs. Turk would take the opportunity to tell me all they knew of one another, all they knew about diseases, all they thought worthy of themselves and could remember of their relatives, and the complete details of their many associations with violent forms of death. But when I communicated nothing to them; when I had nothing,

in confidence, to say to anyone; then they began to treat my
eyes like marbles and to parade their lives indifferently before me,
as if I were, upon my porch, a motionless, graven idol, not of their
religion, in my niche; yet I somehow retained my mystery, my potency,
so that the indifference was finally superficial and I fancy they felt
a compulsion to be observed—*watched* in all they did. I should say
they dread me as they dread the supernatural. How Mr. Wallace dreads
it, dead as he nearly is, twisted on his cane. Every morning, when he
can, he comes down the block past my porch, his left arm hung like
a shawl from his shoulder, shuffling his numb feet, poking cracks.
"I'll have to go back." His voice is hoarse and loud. "I used to walk to
the end of the street." He mops his face and dries his running eyes.
"Hot," he shouts, propped against his cane. "Last summer I went to
the end." The cane comes out of his belly. He sways. Will he die like
this? palsy seize him? sweat break before that final clip of pain and
his surprise? The cane will gouge cement. His hat will float into my
privet hedge and the walk drive blood from his nose.

He turns at last and I relax. His eyes are anxious for a friend to
cry at, to bellow to a stop. He squints up the street, and if, by any
chance, someone appears, Mr. Wallace grins and howls hello. He inches
forward, pounds the walk, roars reports of weather for the middle
of the night. "Know what it was at one? Eighty-seven. June, not
hell we're in, but eighty-seven. I ain't even eighty-seven. There was
a cloud across the moon at two. It rained alongside five but nothing
cooled." And the dawn was gray as soapy water. Fog lay between
garages. A star, almost hidden by the morning light, fell past the Atlas
stack and died near Gemini. The friend is fixed and Mr. Wallace
closes, his face inflamed, his eyeballs rolling. He describes the contours
of his aches, the duration, strength, and quality of every twinge, the
subtle nuances of vague internal hurts. He distinguishes blunt pains
from sharp, pale ones from bright, wiry from watery, morning, night.
His brown teeth grin. Is it better, he discourses, to suffer when it's hot
or when it's cold, while standing or sitting, reading or walking, young
or old?

"I say it's better to be cold. You'll say not. I know what you'll say.
You'll say, 'the knuckle, now, if rapped when cold, will ring.' I know.
A cold shin on the sharp, hard edge of something—that's a real one. I
know. Never mind. Hurts are all fires. Keep you warm. Know those
fellows like that fellow in a book I read about? His name was Scott.
You know him? Froze. Scott. If I'd been with him, freezing, I'd of

pounded on me some great sore so when I hit it I would burn all over. Keep you warm. Say, they didn't think of that, did they? Froze. I read about it. I read a lot, except for seeing, or I would. Half an hour. I used to, all the time. My eyes burn through. Your eyes burn sometimes? Scott. Froze. Hey, you know freezing's quiet. Ha! You know— it's warm!"

Mr. Wallace wavers on his stick and spits. The whole street echoes with him. His friend dwindles.

Portents are next. They follow pain as pain the weather. Anyone is a friend of Mr. Wallace who will stay.

The starfall past the Atlas stack—a cruel sign. They are all bad, the signs are. Evil is above us. "Evil's in the air we breathe or we would live forever." Mr. Wallace draws the great word out as he's doubtless heard his preacher. The cane rises with difficulty. The tip waves above the treetops. "There," bellows Mr. Wallace, his jowls shaking. "There!" And he hurls the cane like a spear. "Smoke, sonny, comes out and hides the sky and poisons everything. I've got a cough." His hand is tender on his chest. He taps with it. He hacks, and stumbles. Spit bubbles on the walk and spreads. The friend or friendly stranger bobs and smiles and flees while Mr. Wallace waits, expecting the return of his cane. "I can't bend," he almost whispers, peering at the disappearing back. His smile stays, but the corners of his mouth twitch. Wearily his eyes cross.

"Cane cane cane," Mr. Wallace calls. His wife hurries. "Cane cane," Mr. Wallace calls. She waves her hankie. "Cane," he continues until it's handed back. "Hot." Mrs. Wallace nods and mops his brow. She settles his hat and smooths his sleeve. "You threw your cane again," she says. Mr. Wallace grows solemn. "I tried to kill a squirrel, pumpkin." Mrs. Wallace leads him home, her face in tears.

What a noise he makes! I thought I couldn't stand it when I came. His puffed face frightened me. His eyes were holes I fell in. I dodged his shadow lest it cover me, and felt a fool. He's not so old, sixty perhaps; but his eyes run, his ears ring, his teeth rot. His nose clogs. His lips pale and bleed. His knees, his hips, his neck and arms, are stiff. His feet are sore, the ankles swollen. His back, head and legs ache. His throat is raw, his chest constricted, and all his inner organs—heart, liver, kidneys, lungs, and bowels—are weak. Hands shake. His hair is falling. His flesh lies slack. His cock I vision shriveled to a string, and each breath of life he draws dies as it enters his nose and crosses his tongue. But Mr. Wallace has a strong belly. It is taut and smooth and round, like a baby's, and anything that Mr. Wallace chooses to put into it mashes up speedily, for Mr. Wallace, although he seeps and oozes and excretes, has never thrown up in his life.

I could hear him walking. That was worst. When I raked the yard I faced in his direction and went in when I saw him coming. With all my precautions his voice would sometimes boom behind me and I would jump, afraid and furious. His moist mouth gaped. His tongue curled over his bent brown teeth. I knew what Jonah felt before the whale's jaws latched. Mr. Wallace has no notion of the feelings he creates. I swear he stinks of fish on such occasions. I feel the oil. It's a tactile nightmare, an olfactory dream—as if my smell and touch divided from my hearing, taste, and vision, and while I watched his mouth and listened to its greeting, fell before whales in Galilee, brine stung and bruised while the fish smell grew as it must grow in the mouth of a whale, and the heat of an exceptionally hardy belly rose around.

It grew upon me that my budding world was ruined if he were free in it. As a specimen Mr. Wallace might be my pride. Glory to him in a jar. But free! Better to release the sweet moving tiger or the delicate snake, the monumental elephant. I was just a castaway to be devoured. It was bad luck and I rocked and I cursed it. Mr. Wallace spouted and I paced the porch with Ahab's anger and his hate. Mrs. Mean wanted my attention. She passed across my vision, brilliant with energy, like the glow of a beacon. Each time my stomach churned. Her children tumbled like balls on the street, like balls escaping gloves and bats; and on the day the boy Toll raced in front of Mr. Wallace like a bolting cat and swung around a sapling like a rock at the end of a string, deadly as little David, then I saw how. Well, that's all over now. Mr. Wallace dreads me as the others do. He inches by. He looks away. He mumbles and searches the earth with his cane. When Mr. Wallace completes his death they will wind crepe around his cane and stick it in his grave. Mrs. Wallace will stand by to screech and I shall send—what shall I send?—I shall send begonias with my card. I say good morning Mr. Wallace, how did you pass the night? and Mr. Wallace's throat puffs with silence. I cannot estimate how much this pleases me. I feel I have succeeded to the idleness of God.

Except in the case of Mrs. Mean. I am no representative of preternatural power. I am no image, on my porch—no symbol. I don't exist. However I try, I cannot, like the earth, throw out invisible lines to trap her instincts; turn her north or south; fertilize or not her busy womb; cause her to exhibit the tenderness, even, of ruthless wild things for her wild and ruthless brood. And so she burns and burns before me. She revolves her backside carefully against a tree.

2

Mrs. Mean is hearty. She works outside a good bit, as she is doing now. Her pace is furious, and the heat does not deter her. She weeds and clips her immaculate yard, waging endless war against the heels and tricycles of her children. She rolls and rakes. She plants and feeds. Does she ever fall inside her house, a sprung hulk, and lap at the dark? The supposition is absurd. Observation mocks the thought. But how I'd enjoy to dream it.

I'd dream a day both warm and humid, though not alarming. Leaves would be brisk about and the puff clouds quick. This, to disarm her. She'd be clipping the hedge; firmly bent, sturdily moving, executing stems; and then the pressure of her blood would mount, mount slowly as each twig fell; and a cramp would grow as softly as a bud in the blood of her back, in the bend of her legs, the crook-snap of her arms, tightening and winding about her back and legs and arms like a wet towel that knots when wrung.

Now the blood lies slack in her but the pressure mounts, mounts slowly. The shears snip and smack. She straightens like a wire. She strides on the house, tossing her lank hair high from her face. She will fetch a rake; perhaps a glass of water. Strange. She feels a dryness. She sniffs the air and eyes a sailing cloud. In the first shadow of the door she's stunned and staggered. There's a blaze like the blaze of God in her eyes, and the world is round. Scald air catches in her throat and her belly convulses to throw it out. There's a bend to her knees. The sky is black and comets burst ahead of her. Her hands thrust ahead, hard in the sill of the door. Cramp grasp her. Shrivel like a rubber motor in a balsa toy her veins. Does her husband waddle toward her, awag from stern to stem with consternation? Oh if the force of ancient malediction could be mine, I'd strike him too!

. . . the vainest dream, for Mrs. Mean is hearty, and Mr. Mean is unpuncturable jelly.

Mr. Wallace can bellow and Mrs. Wallace can screech, but Mrs. Mean can be an alarm of fire and war, falling on every ear like an aching wind.

Among the many periodicals to which I subscribe is the very amusing *Digest of the Soviet Press* and I remember an article there which described the unhappiness of one neighborhood in a provincial Russian city over the frightfully lewd, blasphemous, and scatological shouts a young woman named Tanya was fond of emitting. She would lean from the second story window of her apartment, the report said, and curse the countryside. Nothing moved her. No one approached without blushing to the ears. Her neighbors threatened her with the city officials. The city officials came—were roundly damned. They accused her of drunkenness, flushed, and threatened her with the party officials. The party officials came—were thoroughly execrated. They said she was a dirty woman, a disgrace to Russia—an abomination in the sight of the Lord, they would have said, I'm sure, if the name of the Lord had been available to them. Unfortunately it was only available to Tanya, who made use of it. The party officials told the city officials and the city officials put Tanya in jail. Useless. She cursed between bars and disturbed the sleep of prisoners. Nor was it well for prisoners to hear, continually, such things. They transferred her to another district. She cursed from a different window. They put her in the street, but this was recognized at once as a terrible error and her room was restored. The report breathed outrage and bafflement. What to do with this monster? In their confusion they failed to isolate her. They couldn't think to shoot her. They might have torn out her tongue. Abstractly, I'd favor that. All the vast resources of civilization lay unused, I gathered, while Tanya leaned obscenely from her sill, verbally shitting on the world.

Mrs. Mean, too, dumbfounds her opposition. There have been complaints, I understand. Mrs. Mean, herself, has been addressed. The authorities, more than once, have been notified. Nothing has come of it. Well, this is wisdom. Far better to do nothing than act ineptly. Mrs. Mean could out-Christ Pius.

Thus the trumpet sounds. The children scatter. They run to the neighbors, pursued by her stick and her tongue, so she can mow and tamp and water her crop of grass that it may achieve the quiet dignity of lawn. At the distance of oceans and continents, I admire Tanya. I picture her moving lips. I roll the words on my own tongue—the lovely words, so suitable for addressing the world—but they roll silently there, as chaste as any conjunction; whereas Mrs. Mean's voice utters them with all the sharp, yet exaggerated enunciation of an old Shakespearean. They are volumed by rage and come sudden and strident as panic. Mrs. Mean, moreover, is almost next door and not oceans and continents and languages away.

"Ames. You little snot. Nancy. Witch. Here now. Look where you are now. Look now, will you? God Almighty. Move. Get. Oh Jesus why do I trouble myself. It'll die now, little you care. Squashed. That grass ain't ants. Toll, I warn you. God, God, how did you do that? Why, why, tell me that? Toll, what's that now? Toll, I warn you now. Pike. Shit. Get. What am I going to do with you? Step on you like that? Squash. Like that? Why try to make it nice? Why? Ames. Damn. Oh damn. You little snot. Wait'll I get hold of you. Tim. You are so little, Tim. You are so snotty, so dirty snotty, so nasty dirty snotty. Where did you get that? What is that? What's it now? Drop that. Don't bring it here. Put it back. Nancy. Witch. Oh Jesus, Jesus, sweet, sweet Jesus. Get. Did you piss in the flowers? Timmy? Timmy, Timmy, Timmy, did you? By God, I'll beat your bottom flat. Come here. You're so sweet, so sweet, so nice, so dear. Yes. Come here. All of you. Nancy. Toll. Ames. Tim. Get in here. Now, now I say. Now. Get. I'll whale you all."

It is, however, an old play and Mrs. Mean is an old, old player. The recitation, loud as it is, emphatic, fearsome as it is, everyone has heard before. The children almost wholly ignore it. When her voice begins they widen away and start to circle, still at their little vicious games. Mrs. Mean threatens and cajoles but she does not break the rhythm of her weeding. Toll digs with his shovel. "Don't dig, don't dig," Mrs. Mean chants, and Toll digs. "Don't dig, Toll, don't dig," and Toll digs harder. "Didn't you hear me? didn't you? Stop now. Don't dig." Toll comes red with effort. "I'll take that shovel. Don't dig. Toll, you little creeping bastard, did you hear me? I'll take that shovel. Toll!" The earth is pierced and the turf heaved. Mrs. Mean drops her trowel, rushes upon Nancy, who is nearest, and slams her violently to the ground. Nancy begins screaming. Toll runs. Ames and Timmy widen out and watch. Mrs. Mean cries: "Ah, you little stink—eating mud!" Nancy stops crying and sticks out her muddy tongue; and perhaps this time she learns, although she isn't very bright, that Mrs. Mean always moves on her real victim silently and prefers, whenever possible, surprise.

Toll and Ames are hard to catch. They keep an eye out. If Mrs. Mean leans on her rake and yells pleasantries at Mrs. Cramm— unfortunate Mrs. Cramm—Toll and Ames push each other from their wagons; but they keep an eye out. The sudden leap of Mrs. Mean across the tulip bed deceives only tiny Tim, his finger in his nose. Mrs. Cramm pales and shrinks and endures it like a slave.

Once I went to a lavish dinner party given by a most particular and most obstinate lady. The maid forgot to serve the beans and my most particular dear friend, rapt in a recollection of her youth that lasted seven courses, overlooked them. I did not nor did the other guests. We were furtive, catching eyes, but we were careful. Was it asparagus or broccoli or brussel sprouts or beans? Was she covering up the maid's mistake like the coolest actress, as if to make the tipped table and the broken vase a part of every evening's business? She enjoyed the glory of the long hours of her beauty. The final fork of cake was in her mouth when her jaws snapped. I would have given any sum, then, performed any knavery, to know what it was that led her from gay love and light youth to French-cut green beans and the irrevocable breach of order. She had just said: "We were dancing. I was wearing my most daring gown and I was cold." She went on a word or two before turning grim and silent. By what Proustian process was the thing accomplished? I suppose it was something matter-of-fact. She shivered—and there in her mind were the missing beans. She rose at once and served them herself, cold, in silver, before the coffee. The hollandaise had doubtless separated so we were spared that. But only that. We ate those beans without a word, though some of us were, on most occasions, loquacious, outspoken, ragging types. Our hostess neglected her own portion and rushed sternly back to glory. Of her sins that evening I never forgave the last.

Mrs. Mean bounds over the tulip bed, her rake falling from her, her great breasts swinging like bells, her string hair rising and whirling, while Mrs. Cramm pretends that Mrs. Mean is calm against the end of her implement and finishes her quiet sentence in her quiet voice and looks straight ahead where her neighbor was as if she were, as good manners demanded, still respectably there. Mrs. Mean roars oaths and passes the time of day. She fails even a gesture of interruption. So Toll and Ames, the older and the wiser ones, keep a good look out and keep in motion. Mrs. Cramm, however, remains as if staked while Mrs. Mean genially hammers her deeper with rough platitudes and smooth obscenity.

Mrs. Cramm is a frail widow whose shoes are laced. Her misfortune is to live by Mrs. Mean and to be kind. She bestows upon the children, as they flee, the gentlest, tenderest glances. Compassion clothes her, and docility. She flinches for boxed ears. She grimaces at the sight of Mrs. Mean's stick, but unobtrusively, so much against her will to show the slightest sign that Mrs. Mean, who reads in the world only small words written high, misses it all—the tight hands and nervous mouth and melting eyes. Too stupid to understand, too stupid, therefore, to hate, Mrs. Mean nevertheless plays the tyrant so naturally that her ill will could hardly prove more disagreeable to Mrs. Cramm than her good.

It would almost seem that Mrs. Mean is worse for witnesses. She grows particular. What passed unnoticed before is noted and condemned. The wrestling that was merely damned is suddenly broken by violence. The shrill commands rise to shouts and change to threats. It is as if she wished to impress her company with the depth of her concern, the height of her standards. I knew a girl in college who spent her time, while visiting with you, cleaning herself or the room, if it were hers: lifting lint from her skirt or the hairs of her Persian cat from sofas and chairs; pinching invisible flecks of dirt off the floor, sleeving dust from tables, fingering it from the top edge of mirrors; and it never mattered in the least as far as I could discover whether you came unexpectedly or gave her a week of warning or met her at a play or on the street, she tidied eternally, awkwardly shining the toes of her pumps on her hose, brushing her blouse with the flicking tips of her fingers, sweeping the surrounding air with a wave of her hand.

It's early. I'm waiting for the bus when Mrs. Cramm scuttles anxiously from her house carrying a string bag. I prepare to tip my hat and to be gracious for I've had little commerce with Mrs. Cramm, and what knowledge that frail lady must possess! Mrs. Mean is then in her doorway crying: "Cramm! It's a peach of a day, Mrs. Cramm, isn't it? Come over here!" And Mrs. Cramm, most hesitantly, leaves me. "A peach. Grass is a little thin in back. It's been too hot for green things. God damn you Toll, don't you move. Don't you move a shitting inch! Here. Scrubbed the kitchen floor. You can't be too particular. Kids pick up things. Nancy. Be careful. Cut her finger on dad's razor. Nancy! Bring your finger. Show Mrs. Cramm your sore-sore. There. Like to scare us to death." Mrs. Cramm is murmuring, bending, the wounded finger thrust at her nose. "Bled too," says Mrs. Mean. "Got on her dress damn her. How's your sore-sore now, Nennie? The hell it needs more medicine. Kids, kids. Barely broke the skin. Run and play, go on." Mrs. Mean pushes the child off. I avert my eyes and turn my back. She stares at me—I feel her face—and her voice drops for an instant. When it rises again it is to curse and to command. "Keep your brother off that floor, my God!" The bus comes into view and I lose all talk in its noise. Mrs. Cramm does not board with me. She takes the next bus, I can only presume.

Thus they flee: Ames, Nancy, Toll, and Tim. They pick the flowers next door to me. They tramp the garden down the street. They run through Mr. Wallace's hedge, and while Mr. Wallace bellows like a burnt blind Polyphemus, they laugh like frightened crystal. I've had no trouble myself. Maybe she's warned them. No. She wouldn't. I don't exist. And out of her reach a warning is laughter. They are a curse to Miss Matthew, to Dumb Perkins, Wallace, Turk, yet not to me. So she may cry them out of Christendom if she likes, as she would if she were put in garden charge of all the Christian grass.

Ames, Nancy, Toll, and Tim: they go. Wires are strung on little sticks and strips of cloth are bowed upon the wires. Orders are promulgated. Threats are rung over the neighborhood, and Mrs. Mean takes her turn in the famished grass, spinning like a windturned scarecrow, stubbornly and personally plump with her ambition.

It's no use. Her children pour repeatedly, end on end, across it. They find the natural path. They scuff the grass. They chaff it. They stamp and jump and drive it. They scream it down. The wires sag. The bows drag in the mud. The sticks finally snap or pull out. Nancy wraps her foot in a loop of wire and is hauled up briskly like a hare, howling; and Mr. Mean appears, sullenly rolls the wire around the sticks, over the bows, signaling his wife's surrender. The children stand in a line while Mrs. Mean watches from between her kitchen curtains.

The surrender is far from unconditional. Mrs. Mean vents her hate upon the dandelions. She scours them out of the earth. She packs their bodies in a basket and they are dried and burned. She patrols with an anxious eye the bordering territory where the prevailing winds blow the soft heads from the plants of her negligent neighbor—not, of course, Mrs. Cramm, who has a hired boy, but the two young worshippers of flesh who live on her right and who never appear except to hang out towels or to speed in and out of the late afternoon in their car. Their hands are for each other. They allow the weeds all liberty. There the dandelions gloriously flourish. From their first growth across her line, she regards them with enmity. Their blooming fills her with fury and the instant the young couple drive off in their convertible, Mrs. Mean is among the bright flowers, snapping their heads until her fingers are yellow; flinging the remains, like an insult, to the ground where no one but the impervious pair could fail to feel the shame of their beheaded and shattered condition. With a grand and open gesture, unmistakable from where my wife and I boldly sit and enjoy it, and meant for the world, Mrs. Mean lifts her soiled hands above her head and shakes them rapidly.

There are too many dandelions of course. The young couple does not go out often; and while Mrs. Mean dares, during the time of the dandelions' cottoning, to pace the property line, glaring, her arms in scorn upon her hips, her face livid with furiously staged resignation, watching helplessly the light bolls rise and float above her peonies, hover near her roses, fall like kisses upon her grass, indecently rub seed against her earth; she would not consider—honor would not permit—stepping one foot across the borders if the young couple might observe it, or speaking to them, even most tactfully, about the civic duties of householders; and indeed, she is right this once at any rate; for if those two could not see what we saw so easily, and if they were not shamed or outraged into action by Mrs. Mean's publicly demonstrated anger against them, she might plow and salt the whole of the land their castle grows on and expect no more effect than the present indifferent silence and neglect.

So there are too many dandelions and they go speedily to seed. The seeds rise like a storm and cross in clouds against her empty threats and puny beatings of the air. Mrs. Mean, then, as with all else, sets her children to it. They chase the white chaff. It dances from their rush. Mrs. Mean screams incoherent instructions. The children run faster. They leap higher. They whirl more rapidly. They beat back the invasion. But inevitably the seeds bob beyond them and float on. Mrs. Mean is herself adept. She snatches the cotton as it passes. She crushes it; drops it in a paper bag. Her eye never misses a swatch of the white web against the grass, and after every considerable wind, she carefully rakes the ground. The children, however, soon make a game of it. They gambol brightly and my heart goes out to them, dancing there, as it goes out seldom: gay as they are within the ridiculous, happy inside the insane.

The children hesitate to destroy their favorites. Instead they begin to cheer them on, calculating distance and drift, imagining balloons on tortured courses. Who would want to bring such ships prematurely down or interfere with their naturally appointed, wind-given paths?

Mrs. Mean.

She waits, motionless. The clusters come, one drifting near. Her arm flies out. Her fingers snap. The boll disappears in the beak of her hand. The prize is stuffed in her sack. Mrs. Mean is motionless again though the sack shakes. I am reminded of lizards on rocks, my wife of meat-eating plants. Mrs. Mean's patience here is inexhaustible, her skill astonishing, her devotion absolute. The children are gone. Their shouts make no impression on her. Mrs. Mean is caught up. She waits. She fills her sack. But at last the furious fingers close on air, the arm jerks back an empty hand, and Mrs. Mean lowers her head to her failure. Alive, she whirls. Her wide skirt lifts. It is a crude, ballet, a savage pantomime; for Mrs. Mean, unlike the other mothers of my street, does not shout her most desperate and determined wishes at her children. She forewarns with a trumpet but if her warnings are not heeded, she is silent as a snake. Her head jerks, and I know, reading the signs, that Mrs. Mean is seeking a weapon. The children are now the errant chaff, the undisciplined bolls, and although they are quite small children, Mrs. Mean always augments her power with a stick or strap and dedicates to their capture and chastisement the same energy and stubborn singleness of purpose she has given to the destruction of weeds.

No jungle hunt's been quieter. She discovers a fallen branch, the leaves still green. She shakes it. The twigs whip and the leaves rustle. She catches sight of her oldest boy beside the barn, rigid with the wildest suspense. His boll is floundering in a current of air. It hurtles toward a hole in the barn where cats crawl. His mother hobbles on him, her branch high, stiff, noiseless, as if it were now part of the punishment that he be taken unaware, his joy snuffed with fright as much as by the indignity of being beaten about the ears with leaves.

I think she does not call them to their idiotic tasks because they might obey. Her anger is too great to stand obedience. The offense must be fed, fattened to fit the feeling, otherwise it might snap at nothing and be foolish. So it must seem that all her children have slunk quietly and cunningly away. It must seem that they have mocked her and have mocked her hate. They must, therefore, be quietly and cunningly pursued, beaten to their home, driven like the dogs: bunched on all fours, covering their behinds, protecting the backs of their bare legs from the sting of the switch and their ears with their hands; contorted like cripples, rolling and scrabbling away from the smart of the strap in jerks, wild with their arms as though shooing flies; all the while silent, engrossed, as dumb as the dumbest beasts; as if they knew no outcry could help them; refusing, like the captive, to give satisfaction to his enemy—though the youngest child is only two—and this silence as they flee from her is more terrible to me than had they screamed to curdle blood and chill the bone.

3

Mrs. Mean seizes Ames' arm, twists it behind him, rains blows upon his head and neck. He pulls away and runs. It's to her purpose. She permits his flight. Now the words come and I understand that the silence has been a dam. Her arm points accusingly at his eyeless back. She curses him. She pronounces judgment upon him. She cannot understand his laziness, his uselessness, his disobedience, his stupidity, his slovenliness, his dirtiness, his ugliness; and Mrs. Mean launches into her list, not only of those faults she finds in his present conduct, but all she can remember having found since he first dangled from the doctor's fist and was too slow to cry or cried too faintly or was too red or too wizened or too small or was born with eczema on his chest—a terrible mortification to his mother. He has been nothing but a shame since, a shame in all his days and all his doings. The ultimate word is hurled after him as he slams the door: shame! He is given to understand by shouts directed toward the upstairs windows that there will be more to come, that she is not done with him, the shameful, disrespectful boy, the shameful, discourteous child; and now and then, though not this time, if the boy's spirits are unusually high, if he is filled more than ordinarily with rebellion, he will thrust his head from the window of what I take to be his room, for that is where he has been sent, and make a horrible face at his mother, and a horrible bracking noise; whereupon Mrs. Mean will stop as though struck, suck in her breath, pause dreadfully to scream "what!" at the affront; and then explode derisively, contemptuously, "you! you! you!" until she sputters out. She rounds up the other children if they remain to be rounded up and some minutes later howls of pain and grief can be heard over the whole block.

It is on these occasions, I think, that the children are really hurt. The cuffs, the slaps, the switches they receive are painful, doubtless, but they are brief. They are also, in a sense, routine. The blows remind me of the repertoire of the schoolyard bully: the pinch, the shove, the hair pull, the sudden blow on the muscle of the arm, the swift kick to the shin, elbow in the groin. Evil that is everyday is lost in life, goes shrewdly into it; becomes a part of habitual blood. First it is a convenient receptacle for blame. It holds all hate. We fasten to it— the permanent and always good excuse. If it were not for it, ah then, we say, we would improve, we would succeed, we would go on. And then one day it is necessary, as if there's been a pain to breathing for so long that when the pain at last subsides, out of fright, we suffocate. So they grow up in it. At any rate, they get larger. They know the rules by heart for it's like a game, a game there is no fun in playing and no profit. Ames retreats into the house with Mrs. Mean's damnations at his back while the others, warned now, ready, circle widely out in alleys and around garages and old carriage barns, between the nearby houses, as Mrs. Mean cautiously seeks them, carefully guarding her rear, swiveling often, doubling back, peering craftily around corners until she finds one and the distance has been closed, when she makes a sudden, silent rush with her switch extended, beating before her the empty air, whipping the heels of the child as it runs for home. I don't know all the rules or I don't fully understand them but I gather that when Mr. Mean's at work the front door is always locked, for the children never try to sneak in that way; and I guess the house must be home base, must be sanctuary except in the gravest cases. If they are not let out again, they are at least not beaten. They don't have to dance after dandelion seeds in the hot yard.

My wife and I find it strange that they should all run home. It seems perverse, unnaturally sacrificial: the self leading itself, as in a great propelling crowd, blind over cliffs, stupidly to the sea. We'd run away we affirm in our adulthood to one another, knowing, as we make the affirmation, that even old as we are, adult as we claim to be, we would return to the poisonous nest as they return, children still largely on turned out feet, the girl unbreasted, the boys inadequate and bare for manhood. We would chew on our hurt and feel the pain again of our beginnings. We would languish for the glory of complaint in the old ties. The eldest Mean child may someday say, confronted by a meanness that's his own, by his own mean soul, that he was beaten as a boy; and he may take a certain solace from the fact; he may shift at least a portion of his blame to the ages. "This shit's not mine." *"Mann ist was er isst."* "Alas for the present time!"

We wish they *would* run off, certainly, as we wanted to run off, for had we run away, had we had the courage we so easily wish for them and the necessary resource, we feel we'd be as much as moral now, clear of the need to disclaim our dirt, round, holding our tail between our teeth. For that, we must exaggerate the past. We inflate it with our wrongs. Fortunately for us then, unfortunately for us now, it was really not so bad. We were not pursued and beaten. We were not beggared in our own yard. We were not flayed within the hearing of the world. Our surprise is symbolic. It is a gesture of speech. It expresses a wish of our own; and if we really felt the indignation and disappointment we put into words when we see the Mean children flying to their hive, my wife and I; if we ever borrowed to apply to them any anger from our feelings for Mrs. Mean, it would be an injustice on our part almost as great as in our power as mere observers to do them; although I am not above injustice and must confess, despite my knowledge of the dreadful circumstances of his life, a dislike of Ames, the eldest Mean child, especially upon his bike, as deep as my dislike for his cow-chested, horse-necked, sow-faced mother. "It may have been put in him, but he *is* nasty, unnaturally nasty," I'm afraid I often say. "He can't help it," my wife replies, and I glare at the children too as Mrs. Mean flushes them one by one and they run or toddle to the house because I know my wife is right. I exclaim at their stupidity, their lack of character, their lack of fight—I have my list as Mrs. Mean has hers—for I am, in these remote engagements, as fearsome, as bold and blustering as a shy and timorous man can be.

But after all there must be corners in that little house for each of them, corners that are personal and familiar where the walls come together like the crook of a soft, warm arm and some hour has been passed in quiet love with a private treasure. There must be some sight, some touch, that is a comfort and can draw them to the trap. We haven't been suckled, thank God, by Mrs. Mean, or bathed or clothed or put to bed or nursed when we've been ill. Perhaps her touch is sometimes tender and her tone is sweet. My wife is hopeful.

Really I am not. Their house is chocolate. The paint is peeling badly. It has a tin roof. The front porch is narrow. The house is narrow. The windows are low and small. The gutters need repair. There are rust stains on the side of the house. There are cracks in the foundation. The chimney tilts. I cannot think of it as sanctuary for very long. I try. I see the children orbiting. They vanish within and I try to think they could, like Quasimodo, cry their safety. But is there any reason for us to suppose that life inside is any better than the life outside we see? My wife wishes to believe it—for the children—but I cannot imagine Mrs. Mean's long dugs would not be bitter, and I cannot imagine the deep shadows of that little house full of anything warm except perhaps the rolled, damp fat of Mr. Mean, squatting like a toad in his underwear, his bright, hard eyes pinned like beads to his face, his tongue licking the corners of his mouth, his fingers rubbing softly up and down his other fingers, his legs gliding against themselves, his pale skin bluish in the bad light.

82

But then my wife is subject to failures of the imagination. I have tried to carry her but her sentiments are too readily aroused. Her eyes stay at the skin. Only her heart, only her tenderest feelings, go in. I, on the other hand, cut surgically by all outward growths, all manifestations, merely, of disease and reach the ill within. I conceive the light, for instance, as always bad, of insufficient strength and a poor color, as having had to travel through too much dust and too much muslin, as having had to dwell too long in the company of dark rugs and mohair chairs and satin shaded lamps. The air, I feel, is bad too. The windows are never open. The back door bangs but the breeze is metaphorical. All things in their little house that hang, hang motionless and straight. Nothing is dirty but nothing feels clean. Their writing paper sticks to the hand. Their toilet sweats. The halls are cool. The walls are damp.

I was playing with toy cars and digging roads around the supports of the family porch when I accidentally placed my hand upon a cold wet pipe which rose out of the ground there and saw near the end of my nose, moist on the ridge of a post, four fat white slugs. I think of that when I think of the Means' house and of pale fat Mr. Mean, and the urge to scream as I did then rises strongly in me. I bumped my head, I remember, scrambling out. I was afraid to tell my father why I'd yelled. He was very angry. Even yet I have a distaste for the odor of earth.

My wife maintains that Mrs. Mean is an immaculate housekeeper and that her home is always cool and dry and airy. She's very likely correct as far as mere appearance goes but my description is emotionally right, metaphysically appropriate. My wife would strike up friendships, too, and so, as she says, find out; but that must be blocked. It would destroy my transcendence. It would entangle me mortally in illusion.

Yes. The inside of the Mean house is clear and horrible in my mind like a nightmare no one willingly would want to enter. It may be five rooms. It can't be more. And into these five rooms, at best, the six Means are squeezed with the machinery to keep them alive, with the geegaws she buys, the bright blue china horses which trot in the windows, and some of the children's toys, for they do not lack for toys, at least the kind you ride. They have a scooter, a small tricycle, a large tricycle, one that has a wagon welded to its rear, and a sidewalk bike with which the eldest Mean child rides down flowers, people, cats and dogs. I must salute their taste this once. They haven't bought their children cycles shaped by great outriding fenders of tin and paint like rockets, airplanes, horses, swans or submarines. They have an eye for the practical, the durable, in such things. I remember with fondness my own tricycle, capable of tremendous speed or so it seemed then, and because it was not fangled up by paid imaginations, it could be Pegasus, if I liked, and it was.

There is no Pegasus—imaginary—real—in the house of the Means. There is father floating among the couches, white as animals long in caves, quiet as a weed, his round mouth working, his eyes twitching, his fat fingers twisting a button on his sleeve.

Purple bath towels hang in the bathroom. I have seen them on the line. They have some colored sheets—one lavender, one rose, one wine —and some brightly yarned doilies you can buy in the living room of a house, a block away, where articles of religion are sold among candies and cozies and pickles in mason jars. The two ladies who make them are also immensely fat and immensely pious. They furthermore sell signs which gloomily, but with a touch, I fancy, of spiteful triumph, herald the Coming of the Lord and the Eventual Destruction of the World. There is a fine one I have noticed in their dining room window which says in scarlet letters simply, Armageddon, like an historical marker. The expectation is tastefully surrounded by a dark border of crosses and small skulls. Mr. Mean bore one of their placards home and tacked it up on the door of the small barn where he keeps his car. In silver script that glitters from the black card it warns of Eternity Tomorrow, and it must have cost him a dollar and a half. At least I take it as a warning. My wife says it reminds him to drive carefully. You see how easily and dangerously she is deceived. However, perhaps for the Means it is not a warning but a hope, a promise of reward; and it no doubt speaks plainly and poorly for my destination that I regard its message so pessimistically.

The Means are Calvinists, I'm certain. They may be unsure of heaven but hell is real. They must feel its warmth at their feet and the land tremble. Their meanness must proceed from that great sense of guilt which so readily becomes a sense for the sin of others, and poisons everything. There is no pleasure. There is only the biological propriety of the penis. In another, more forthright age, they would have read to their children from *Slovenly Peter,* the picture story book of the righteous, where the reward of moral weakness, of which it was an illustrated catalogue, was a severed limb, the loss of teeth and vision, the promise of a bloody and crippling accident, a painful and malignant disease, or fits of madness—all of these disasters tailored by a wise and benevolent Providence to fit the crime. I remember very well, too, a poem of our Puritan ancestors, in rather strenuous iambics, about a child called Harry, perverse to the heart, who went fishing against his father's wishes, doubtless on the Lord's day too, and with the devil's pleasure.

> Many a little fish he caught,
> And pleased was he to look,
> To see them writhe in agony,
> And struggle on the hook.
>
> At last when having caught enough,
> And also tired himself,
> He hastened home intending there
> To put them on the shelf.
>
> But as he jumped to reach a dish,
> To put his fishes in,
> A large meat hook, that hung close by
> Did catch him by the chin.
>
> Poor Harry kicked and call'd aloud,
> And screamed and cried and roared,
> While from his wounds the crimson blood
> In dreadful torrents poured.

The pattern of punishment here is based on the principle of a comparable eye for a comparable eye but I feel sure that while the Mean children might dread their moral transmigration into ants (a steamroller mash them flat) or butterflies (their arms fall off), all ants and butterflies would dread as much their total intersection. A butterfly, I think, would prefer to die of burned off wings, with some immediacy, possessing beauty, than to be rubbed, pinched, and buffeted about, losing before the power of flight, the desire, and before the desire, the eloquence of its design.

I should like to see Providence take the side of the dandelion. A tooth for a tooth would suit me fine.

But of course all the Means have suffered metamorphosis. They are fly beleaguered bears in a poor zoo with nothing to claw but each other and a dead trunk and no one to hate but themselves, their flies, and the bare, hot, peanut spotted ground.

4

Mr. Wallace has displayed a certain strength. I had thought him shorn but he has joined the Means. They gather now on cooler evenings on the Means' front porch, the misters and the missuses, heads together. Shouts and wails of laughter, snorts and bellows as from steers rise out of the porch's shadows as out of shadowing trees by a wallow bank. It is a juncture, I must confess, that had not occurred to me although I sometimes fancy I am master of the outside chance. It was a part of *her* that I let slip. Following her gyrations in the grass, her rush and whirl and roaring curse, I forgot her geologic depth, the vein of meanness deep within her earth. Against the mechanical flutter of appearance I failed to put the glacial movement of reality.

I drove them together . . . an unpleasant end for so pleasant a beginning.

Mr. Wallace was before at large, as I have said; gigantic in the landscape, swallowing life. There was, in him, no respect for *my* mysteries, only for his own: signs, omens, portents, signatures and symbolings whose meaning he alone was privy to. Mr. Wallace was the paramour of prophecy, yet it came to me when the boy Toll catted across his path that day that it was a stone symbolic more than real that struck the light from Goliath's eyes. It was for prophecy that Jonah fled the Lord. For Jonah's flight the tempest rose, and for the tempest was Jonah flung between the whale's jaws. To be properly swallowed, then, was the secret; to cause, in going down, the oils to flow that would convulse the membranes of the stomach. What must that whale have felt, his moist cavernous maw reverberating prayers and pledges! Would Mr. Wallace be a dog and eat his vomit? I judged that I should soon be cast on dry land. Thenceforth the mystery would be mine, as it was Jonah's. To be the bait, to carry the harpoon down and in that round and previously unshaken belly stick it, then escape—that would be the trick. And prophecy would do it.

How I was enamoured of the notion! All day I lightly walked. Mr. Wallace obliged me by appearing almost at once to record his aches, to dilate upon the midnight's weather, and to wallow surely, by absolutely predictable thrashes, toward the topic. I was on a vast dry plain. Red rock rose out of its distances. Behind me and before me there were multitudes embannered—murmuring. The sun's light struck from shields and spears. I squinted at the giant. His figure wavered. I sensed the wet and dry together. Perhaps the ancient Greek philosophers were right about the wedding of these opposites. Dust clouded my shuffling feet. Spume flew to the giant's face. It is amazing how the feelings of the universal fables sometimes focus in a single burning vision. Of course that singleness of sight has always been my special genius.

I waited. The ankles were painful. I said I had a mole that itched. A bad sign, Mr. Wallace said, and I saw the thought of cancer fly in his ear. Moles are special marks, he said. I was aware, I said, of how they were, but the places of my own were fortunate and I divined from them a long life. Moles go deep, I said. They tunnel to the heart. Mr. Wallace grinned and wished me well and with great effort turned away. It was a good start. Wonder and fear began in him and twitched his face. When again he came he thought aloud of moles and I discoursed upon them: causes, underflesh connections, cosmic parallels, relations to divinity. There was a fever in him, dew on his lip, brightness in his eye. Moles. Every day. At last there was no art in how he brought the subject up. I spoke of the mark of Cain. I mentioned the deformities of the devil. I talked of toads and warts. I discussed the placing of blemishes and the ordering of stars. Stigmata. The world of air is like the skin and signs without are only symbols of the world within. I referred to the moles of beauty, to those of avarice, cunning, gluttony and lust, to those which, when touched, made the eyes water, the ears itch, or caused the prick to stand and the shyest maid to flower. My fancy soared. I related moles and maps, moles and mountains, moles and the elements of interior earth. Oh it was wondrous done! How he shook and warmed his lips like an old roué and trembled and put anxiety in every place! I was everywhere specific and detailed. *This* may correspond to *that*. The region of the spine is like unto the polar axis. But I was at all times indeterminate and vague as well. A certain hornshaped mole upon a certain place may signify a certain spiritual malignity. I informed him of everything and yet of nothing. I moved his sight from heaven to hell and drew from him the most naive response of bliss, followed first by a childlike disappointment as our viewpoint fell, then a childlike fright. His cane quivered against the pavement. He was in the grip. To be so near, continually, to dying; to feel within yourself the chemistry of death; to see in the glass, day by day, your skull emerging; to rot while walking and to fear the sun; to pick over the folds of your loosening flesh like infested clothing; to know, not merely by the logician's definition or the statistician's count that men are mortal, but through the limpsting of your own blood—to know so surely so directly so immediately this, I thought, would be a burden needing, if a man were to bear up under it, a staff of self-deceiving hope as sturdy and leveling as the truth was not: an unquenchable, blasphemous, magical hope that the last gasp when it came would last forever, death's rattle an eternity.

There were moles upon that body I was certain. And he would want to know their meaning. It wouldn't matter if he had, before me, given sense and order to their being, these things despair of guarantee. He would want to know. He would have to know. And he would fear to know. What if I said: This is the mole of death most painful? Yet what if I said: This is the mole of everlasting mortal life? What if a miracle should happen? What if?

I waited. Again and again he came, nibbling. Excitement, worry, anticipation, profoundest thought passed and repassed like winds across him. Finally I broached the deadly topic. Mr. Wallace showed his teeth and his eyes hunted in the trees. His cane chattered. He admitted his wife had a mole or two. Ah, I said, where are they? Mr. Wallace blew his nose and bade farewell. Not yet. The rogue would offer up his wife. He wanted a safe bite, a free taste of the news. Well I should freely give it. I worried only that the shriveled witch had moles upon her privates—this shame silencing speech. Such a sign, if I could pronounce upon it, I would deed the whole of fortune to.

Again and again he came until I grew so sick of the smell of oil and the sound of water that I thrust the question boldly toward him. Each time, in silence, he refused it. Again and again he came. I had no heart any more. I feared his coming. I hesitated to enter my yard. And then he said that there were moles upon her body, on her thigh. The thigh, I exclaimed, the home of beauty. The right side or the left? The left. The left! Momentous conditions are being satisfied. Are they low upon it? high? Near the hip. The hip! Glorious! Were there two? Two. Two! And the color: brown? red? black? Yellow. Yellow! What a marvel! And the hair that grew there? the color of the hair that grew there? Surely there was hair. There must be. My friend, you must look again. Look again. Again. Determine it precisely.

So he sounded with the bait. He was hooked through his throat to the tail.

Even now I dare not let my mind look upon the picture of that pair peering beneath her lifted skirts. How infernally lewd! How majestically revolting! She would ask him if he saw any. He would hesitate, realizing more than she how important it was to say yes, and yet not clearly, not surely finding grounds for an affirmation. He moistens his finger and applies it to the spot. Perhaps a brighter light. Perhaps if she removed her dress. In worry she watches him. What does it all mean? Can they say for certain that hair grows there; that it does not? She is persuaded to pronounce the negative but he holds her back. There is a doubt. There must be a doubt.

Or he has kept the substance of our conversations from her. He spies out her moles, creeps upon her dressing, at her bath, or he remembers lovelier days when he was whole and she was smooth and clean and there was flesh to glory in. Then those moles were yellow on her hip perhaps like beads inviting kisses. No. I see the moistened finger, the hiked skirt, the inquiring frown. I see it clearly, bright with color, dimensional with shadow. There is somehow a bond between them greater than comfort. She is a nurse. She is a wife. But what else really? Was there a time when that same finger touched her thigh with love? I consider it and shudder. The mind plays strange games. No. No youth for them. They were always old. Does that finger touch her now with any tenderness or is it, as I rather fancy, like the touch of a dry stick?

There was a time when my hand, too, held heat and when its touch left a burn beneath the skin and I sought beauty like the bee his queen; but it was a high flight for an old tyrant, and not worth wings. Doubtless there were sweet and brave and foolish times between them. There may be sweet times now. Such times lie beyond my conjuring. I only know that thorough evil is as bright as perfect good and seems as fair; for animals that live in caves are bleached by darkness and so shine in their surroundings as the good soul does in its, albino as the stars. But beauty or any of its brilliant semblances is foreign to Mr. Wallace and his wife and to the Means. Real wickedness is rare. Certainly it does not rest in the tawdry murder of millions, even Jews. It rests rather on the pale brow of every saviour who to save us all from death first kills. Nevertheless, it is the Jewish fleshsmoke that one smells, the burning cords of bodies, and it is hard to see the soul through that stiff irreverent wood, I suppose, just as it is hard for me to light a bright bulb in the house of the Means, or place between the boards of husband Wallace and his wife a lover's need and pleasure.

Although, as it turned out, I was unable to capture Mr. Wallace, who clung tenaciously to his secrets, my triumph was complete. I broke the weaker vessel. I heard his cane rap on the front door and I rushed from my study to prevent his entrance. However, my wife

forestalled me and Mr. Wallace was already in the living room when I
arrived, sinking on the piano bench, his face alarmingly red and his
eyes blinking at shadows. He filled the room with his hoarse hospital-
ities. I was brusque with my wife. I had hoped to hold him to the
porch. I had read of saints who kissed the suppurating sores of beggars
and I had always doubted the spiritual merit of it, but in front of Mr.
Wallace I could only marvel that the act had been performed. At last
I turned my wife away and Mr. Wallace pulled at the brim of his
straw hat and stuttered at a shout his puzzlement. He shook, poor
fellow, with anxiety. I laughed. I made light of everything. Moles are
of course, I said, the accidents of birth. There's no more to be seen in
their position than in the order of the stars. The ancient Greek
philosophers, for the most part, have spoken clearly on the subject.
Perhaps Pythagoras was not as plain as one would wish, while Socrates
had in him from his birth a warning voice and Plato was given on
occasion to behavior which was, well, scarcely consistent with his love
of mathematics; yet Aristotle remained firm and did not generally
recognize the power of premonition. The Christian Church, to be
frank, regards such things as satanic, although there have been
happenings which do appear upon their face to be . . . of a nature
nearer to . . . what shall I say? . . . the epiphany of an occult world:
nail holes on the feet and hands of even little boys, visions of the
virgin, voices, seizures, transports, ecstasies, then the miracles worked
by sainted bones, the wood of the true cross, cloth of the holy cape,
blood, excrement and so on . . . wounds in the side from which cool
water flows as pure as the purest spring. Still . . . still . . . the church
is stern. The Jews, too, are a hard-headed lot. There is of course the
Cabbala, the magical book. Nevertheless Yaweh is forthright. And so
we know the leaves of tea arrange themselves for our amusement while
the warm insides of fowl permit only the primitive to divine. Was it not
before Philippi that the ghost of Julius Caesar . . . ? however . . . all
omens are imaginings. We should laugh when we read disaster. In
medieval days the story went about of a stream of spring fresh water
so sweet and pure that on the tongue it made the spirit eloquent and
the head giddy with thanksgiving. But when men followed its turnings
to its source they found it sprang from the decaying jaws of a dead
dog. Thence the faithful spoke of how it was that from a foul, corrupt,
and wicked world the clean and whole and good would one day flow.
Mr. Wallace thanked me and tried to rise. He beckoned me and I went
close and a powerful hand gripped my upper arm and pulled. The

monster rose and his mouth broke open bitterly. Good-by.

At last. But Mr. Wallace cannot whisper. The walls rang with him. What did she think when she heard? Will she cringe again? She came with tea some minutes later and pretended surprise at finding him gone. I had to stare at her until her cup shook. Then I went upstairs to my room.

When all was well begun and seemed well ended, the Wallaces joined the Means. Perhaps the Means read moles better than I do. Better: perhaps they do not know what moles may mean.

The houses here are served by alleys. Garages face them. Trash spills over the cinders and oil flavors the earth. The Wallaces have helped themselves up the Means' porch steps and day is fading when I begin my walk through the alleys by the backsides of the houses. The house of love is first. The shades are drawn. Who knows when passion may choose to crawl from its clothes? I hear the Wallaces moving on the porch—the scrape of a chair. Eternity Tomorrow. It is tacked on the inside of the door. The letters swallow at the light. Their car is parked elsewhere but I resist the temptation to go in. Cracks in the walls net the floor. Beer cans glow. A wagon hangs precariously by its handle to the wall. I am at the entrance and frightened by it as a child is frightened by the cold air that drifts from a cave to damp the excitement of its discovery. Not since I was very young have I felt the foreignness of places used by others. I had forgotten that sensation and its power—electric to the nerve ends. The oiled ash, the cool air, the violet light, the wracked and splintered wood, the letters of the prophecy—they all urge me strangely. Mrs. Wallace hoots. I move on. The lane looks empty of all life like a road in a painting of a dream. I am a necromancer carrying a lantern. It is lit but it gives no light. My steps are unnaturally loud and I tell myself I have fallen into the circle of my own spell. Tin briefly fires. Then I hear the voice of Mrs. Cramm. Her virtuous shoes show beneath the partly opened door of her garage. She stores things there for she has no car. By her shoes are another pair—a child's. The child giggles and is shushed. I have been loud in the lane yet they have not heard me. Now stock-still, I fear to move. The door swings and I back in panic. I jump into the Means' garage. The door does not close and Mrs. Cramm remains hidden behind it with the child, conversing in low tones. Finally the feet begin to move and I duck deeply into the Means' dark. I feel a fool. Steps are coming quickly. Light steps. What a fool. They turn in. The child is in the door, a boy I think—Tim or Ames. I crouch in the dark by a tire, hiding my eyes as if he might see me with them. Fool. Why? Why have I done this? Why am I hiding here like a thief? The child's feet pass me and I hear a loud clink. Then he comes from the rear of the barn and goes out and his feet disappear onto grass. My courage returns and I follow what my ears have remembered back into the barn but I fail to find what it was he had deposited there. I bark my shin on a cycle. In the lane I put my hands in my pockets. The alley is empty. The light is nearly gone. I realize that I have breached the fortress yet in doing so I lost all feeling for the Means and sensed only myself, fearful, hiding from a child. A cat fires from a crack in Mrs. Cramm's garage and passes silently into the darkness. My stomach burns. I walk forward until I reach the turf and stand by redbud and by dogwood trees. I see her then, utterly gray and unshaped and unaccompanied, a thin gray mist by a tree trunk, and I stand dumbly too while the dusk deepens. Indeed I am not myself. This is not the world. I have gone too far. It is the way fairy tales begin—with a sudden slip over the rim of reality. The streetlights flare on Mrs. Cramm. Her arms are clenched around her. She is watching the Means' front porch from which I hear a whinny. Unaccountably I think of Hansel and Gretel. They were real and they went for a walk in a real forest but they walked too far in the forest and suddenly the forest was a forest of story with the loveliest little cottage of gingerbread in it. There is a flash in the ribboned darkness. From the corner of my eye I think I see the back door of the Means' house close. Mrs. Cramm is fixed—gray and grotesque as primitive stone. I back away. The ribbons of light entangle me. I crawl between garages. My feet slip on cans. I try to think what I'm doing. One day Jack went to town to buy a cow. Cows are real and beans are real. One day Jack went to town to buy a cow and came home with a handful of beans. I slip. There is a roar of ocean like a roaring mob. Have I gone down before the giant? Mrs. Cramm is suddenly gone and I sink home.

It was an experience from which I have not yet recovered. I go back each evening just when dusk is falling and stand by the redbud tree at the back of Mrs. Cramm's yard. I never see her, yet I know that on the evenings when the Wallaces visit with the Means, she talks to the children. I have lain like fog between the garages and only heard whispers—vague, tantalizing murmurs. Every evening I hope the streetlights will surprise her again. I know where every streak will be. I think I have seen her in the back seat of the Means' car when it is parked in the barn sometimes—a blank patch of stone gray. Is it Ames who slips out to meet her? Recently, while I've been loitering at the end of the alley, taking my last look around, I've felt I've mixed up all my starts and endings, that the future is over and the past has just begun. I await each evening with growing excitement. My stomach turns and turns. I am terribly and recklessly impelled to force an entrance to their lives, the lives of all of them; even, although this is absurd, to go into the fabric of their days, to mote their air with my eyes and move with their pulse and share their feeling; to be the clothes that lie against their skins, to shift with them, absorb their smells. Oh I know the thought is awful, yet I do not care. To have her anger bite and burn inside me, to have his brute lust rise in me at the sight of her sagging, tumbling breasts, to meet her flesh and his in mine or have the sores of Mr. Wallace break my skin or the raw hoot of his wife crawl out my throat . . . I do not care . . . I do not care. The desire is as strong as any I have ever had: to see, to feel, to know, and to possess! Shut in my room as I so often am now with my wife's eyes fastened to the other side of the door like blemishes in the wood, I try to analyze my feelings. I lay them out one by one like fortune's cards or clothes for journeying and when I see them clearly then I know the time is only days before I shall squeeze through the back screen of the Means' house and be inside.

JOHN HAWKES:

The Horse in a London Flat

It is Wednesday dawn. Margaret's day, once every fortnight, for marketing and looking in the shop windows. She is off already with mints in her pocket and a great empty crocheted bag on her arm, jacket pulled down nicely on her hips and a fresh tape on her injured finger. She smells of rose water and the dust that is always gathering in their four rooms. In one of the shops she will hold a plain dress against the length of her body, then return it to the racks; at a stand near the bridge she will buy himself—Michael Banks—a tin of fifty, and for Hencher she will buy three cigars. She will ride the double-decker, look at dolls behind a glass, have a sandwich. And come home at last with a packet of cold fish in the bag.

Most Wednesdays—let her stay, let her walk out—he does not care, does not hold his breath, never listens for the soft voice that calls goodbye. But this is no usual Wednesday dawn and he slips from room to room until she is finally gone. In front of the glass he fixes his coat and hat, and smiles. For he intends not to be home when she returns.

Now he is standing next to their bed—the bed of ordinary down and ticking and body scent, with the course of dreams mapped on the coverlet—and not beside the door and not in the hall. Ready for street, departure, for some prearranged activity, he nonetheless is immobile this moment and stares at the bed. His gold tooth is warm in the sun, his rotting tooth begins to pain. From out the window the darting of a tiny bird makes him wish for its sound. He would like to hear it or would like to hear sounds of a wireless through the open door or sounds of tugs and double-deckers and boys crying the news. Perhaps the smashing of a piece of furniture. Anything. Because he too has his day to discover and it is more than pretty dresses and gandering at a shiny steam iron and taking a quick cup of tea.

He can tell the world.

But in the silence of the flat's close and ordinary little bedroom he hears again all the soft timid sounds she made before setting off to market: the fall of the slippery soap bar into the empty tub, the limpid sound of her running bath, the slough of three fingers in the cream pot, the cry of bristles against her teeth, the fuzzy sound of straps drawing up on the skin of her shoulders; poor sounds of her counting out the change, click of the pocketbook. Then sounds of a safety pin closing beneath the lifted skirt and of the comb setting up last minute static in the single wave of her hair.

He pulls at the clothes closet door, steps inside and embraces two hanging and scratchy dresses and her winter coat pinned over with bits of tissue. Something on a hook knocks his hat awry. Behind him, in the room, the sunlight has burned past the chimes in St. George's belfry and is now more than a searching shaft in that room: it comes diffused and hot through the window glass, it lights the dry putty-colored walls and ceiling, draws a steam from the damp lath behind the plaster, warms the small unpainted tin clock which she always leaves secreted and ticking under the pillow on her side of the bed. A good early morning sun, good for the cat or for the humming housewife. But the cat is in the other room and his wife is out.

Inside the closet he is rummaging overhead to a shelf—reaching and pushing among the dresses now, invading anew and for himself this hiding place which he expects to keep from her. He stands on tiptoe, an arm is angular at the crook, his unused hand is dragging one of the dresses off the hanger by the shoulder, the other set of high fingers is pushing, working a way through the dusty folds toward what he knows is resting behind the duster and pail near the wall. His hipbone strikes the thin paneling of the door so that it squeaks and swings outward, casting a perfect black shadow across the foot of the bed. And after a moment he steps out into the room,

turns sideways, uncorks the bottle, tilts it up, and puts the hot mouth
of the bottle to his lips. He drinks—until the queer mechanism of
his throat can pass no more and his lips stop sucking and a little of
it spills down his chin. Upstairs a breakfast kettle begins to shriek.
He takes a step, holds the bottle against his breast, suddenly turns
his face straight to the sun.

*She'll wonder about me. She'll wonder where her hubby's at,
rightly enough.*

He left the flat door open. Throughout the day, whenever anyone
moved inside the building, slammed a window or shouted a few
words down the unlighted stair—"Why don't you leave off it? Why
don't you just leave off it, you with your beastly kissing round the
gas works?"—the open door swung a hand's length to and fro, drifted
its desolate and careless small arc in a house of shadow and brief
argument. But no one took notice of the door, no one entered the
four empty rooms beyond it, and only the abandoned cat followed
with its turning head each swing of the door. Until at the end of the
day Margaret came in smiling, walked the length of the hall with a
felt hat over one ear, feet hot, market sack pulling from the straps in
her hand and, stopping short, discovered the waiting animal in the
door's crack. Stopped, backed off, went for help from a second-floor
neighbor who had a heart large with comfort and all the cheer in
the world, went for help as he knew she would.

Knowing how much she feared his dreams: knowing that her
own worst dream was one day to find him gone, overdue minute
by minute some late afternoon until the inexplicable absence of him
became a certainty; knowing that his own worst dream, and best,
was of a horse which was itself the flesh of all violent dreams; knowing this dream, that the horse was in their sitting room—he had left
the flat door open as if he meant to return in a moment or meant
never to return—seeing the room empty except for moonlight bright
as day and, in the middle of the floor, the tall upright shape of the
horse draped from head to tail in an enormous sheet that falls over
the eyes and hangs down stiffly from the silver jaw; knowing the
horse on sight and listening while it raises one shadowed hoof on
the end of a silver thread of foreleg and drives down the hoof to
splinter in a single crash one plank of that empty Dreary Station
floor; knowing his own impurity and Hencher's guile; and knowing
that Margaret's hand has nothing in the palm but a short life-span

(finding one of her hair pins in his pocket that Wednesday dawn when he walked out into the sunlight with nothing cupped in the lip of his knowledge except thoughts of the night and pleasure he was about to find)—knowing all this, he heard in Hencher's first question the sound of a dirty wind, a secret thought, the sudden crashing in of the plank and the crashing shut of that door.

"How's the missus, Mr. Banks? Got off to her marketing all right?"

Then: "No offense. No offense," said Hencher after Banks' pause and answer.

The Artemis—a small excursion boat—shivered and rolled now and again ever so slightly though it was moored fast to the quay. Banks heard the cries of dock hands who were fixing a boom's hook to a cargo net, the sound of a pump, and the sound, from the top deck, of a child shouting through cupped hands in the direction of the river's distant traffic of puffing tugs and barges. And also overhead there were the quick uncontrollable running footfalls of smaller children and, on the gangway, hidden beyond the white bulkhead of the refreshment saloon, there was the steady tramp of still more boarding passengers.

A bar, a dance floor—everyone was dancing—a row of salt-sealed windows, a small skylight drawn over with the shadow of a fat gull; here was Hencher's fun, and Banks could feel the crowd mounting the sides of the ship, feel the dance rhythm tingling through the greasy wood of the table top beneath his hand. For a moment and in a clear space past the open sea doors held back by small brass hooks, he saw hatless members of the crew dragging a mountain of battered life preservers forward in a great tar-stained shroud of canvas.

"No offense, eh, Mr. Banks? Too good a day for that. And tell me now, how's this for a bit of a good trip?"

Hencher's hand was putty round the bottom of the beer glass, the black and cream-checkered cap was tight on his head, surely this fat man would sail away with the mothers and children and smart young girls when the whistle blew.

"No offense, Hencher. But you can leave off mentioning her, if you don't mind."

Perhaps he would sail away himself. That would be the laugh, he and Hencher, stowaways both, elbowing room at the ship's rail between lovers and old ladies, looking out themselves—the two of them—for a glimpse of the water or a great furnace burning far-off at the river's edge. Sail away out of the river's mouth and into the afternoons of an excursion life. Hear the laughter, feel the ship's beam wallow in the deep seas and lie down at night beneath a lifeboat's white spongy prow still hot to the hand. No luggage, no destination, helmsman tying the wheel—on any course—to have a smoke with a girl. This would be the laugh, with only the pimply barkeep who had never been to sea before drawing beer the night long. But there was better than this in wait for him, something much better than this.

In the crowd at the foot of the gangplank an officer had asked for their tickets, and Hencher had spoken to the man: "My old woman's on that boat, Captain, and me and my friend here will just see that she's got a proper deck chair and a robe round her legs."

And now the dawn was gone, the morning hours too were gone. He had found the crabbed address and come upon the doorway in which Hencher waited; had walked with him down all those streets until the squat ship, unseaworthy, just for pleasure, lay ahead of them in a berth between two tankers; had already seen the rigging, the smokestacks, the flesh-colored masts and rusty sirens and whistles in a blue sky above the rotting roof of the cargo sheds; had boarded the Artemis that smelled of coke and rank canvas and sea animals and beer and boys looking for sport.

"We'll just have some drink and a little talk on this ship before she sails, Mr. Banks. . . ."

He leaned toward Hencher. His elbows were on the table and his wet glass was touching Hencher's frothy glass in the center of the table. Someone had dropped a mustard pot and beneath his shoe he felt the fragments of smashed china, the shape of a wooden spoon, the slick of the mustard on the dirty spoon. A woman with lunch packed in a box pushed through the crowd and bumped against him, paused and rested the box upon their table. Protruding from the top of the box and sealed with a string and paper was a tall jar filled with black bottled tea. The woman carried her own folding chair.

"Bloody slow in putting to sea, mates," she said, and laughed. She wore an old sweater, a man's muffler was knotted round her throat. "I could do with a breath of that sea air right now, I could."

Hencher lifted his glass. "Go on," he said, "have a sip. Been on the Artemis before?"

"Not me."

"I'll tell you, then. Find a place for yourself in the bows. You get the breeze there, you see everything best from there."

She put her mouth to the foam, drank long, and when she took the glass away she was breathing quickly and a canker at the edge of her lip was wet. "Join me," she said. "Why don't you join me, mates?"

"We'll see you in the bows," said Hencher.

"Really?"

"Good as my word."

It was all noise of people wanting a look at the world and a smell of the sea, and the woman was midships with her basket, soon in the shadow of the bow anchor she would be trying to find a safe spot for her folding chair. Hencher was winking. A boy in a black suit danced by their table, and in his arms was a girl of about fourteen. Banks watched the way she held him and watched her hands in the white gloves shrunk small and tight below the girl's thin wrists. Music, laughter, smells of deck paint and tide and mustard, sight of the boy pulled along by the fierce white childish hands, and he himself was listening, touching his tongue to the beer, leaning close as he dared to Hencher, beginning to think of the black water widening between the sides of the holiday ship and the quay.

"What's that, Hencher? What's that you say?"

Hencher was looking him full in the face: ". . . to Rock Castle, here's to Rock Castle, Mr. Banks!"

He heard his own voice beneath the whistles and plash of bilge coming out of a pipe: "To Rock Castle, then. . . ."

The glasses touched, were empty, and the girl's leg was only the leg of a child and the woman would drink her black tea alone. He stood, moved his chair so that he was not across from Hencher but beside him.

"He's old, Mr. Banks. Rock Castle has his age, he has. And what's his age? Why, it's the evolution of his bloody name, that's what it is. Just the evolution of a name—Apprentice out of Lithograph by Cobbler, Emperor's Hand by Apprentice out of Hand Maiden by Lord of the Land, Draftsman by Emperor's Hand out of Shallow Draft by Amulet, Castle Churl by Draftsman out of Likely Castle by Cold Masonry, Rock Castle by Castle Churl out of Words on Rock by Plebeian—and what's this name if not the very evolution of his life. You want to think of the life, Mr. Banks, think of the breeding. Consider the fiver bets, the cheers, the wreaths.

Then forgotten, because he's taken off the turf and turned out into the gorse, far from the paddock, the swirl of torn ticket stubs, the soothing nights after a good win, far from the serpentine eyes and bowler hats. Do you see it, Mr. Banks? Do you see how it was for Rock Castle?"

He could only nod, but once again—the Artemis was rolling— once again he saw the silver jaw, the enormous sheet, the upright body of the horse that was crashing in the floor of the Dreary Station flat. And he could only keep his eyes down, clasp his hands.

". . . back sways a little, you see, the color of the coat hardens and the legs grow stiff. Months, years, it's only the blue sky for him, occasionally put to stud and then back he goes to his shelter under an old oak at the edge of a field. Useless, you see. Do you see it? Until tonight when he's ours—yours—until tonight when we get our hands on him and tie him up in the van and drive him to stables I know of in Highland Green. Yours, you see, and he's got no recollection of the wreaths or seconds of speed, no knowledge at all of the prime younger horses sprung from his blood. But he'll run all right, on a long track he'll run better than the young ones good for nothing except a sprint. Power, endurance, a forgotten name—do you see it, Mr. Banks? He's ancient, Rock Castle is, an ancient horse and he's bloody well run beyond memory itself."

Flimsy frocks, dancing children, a boy with the face of a man, a girl whose body was still awkward; they were all about him and taking their pleasure while the feet tramped and the whistle tooted. But Hencher was talking, holding him by the brown coat just beneath the ribs, then fumbling and cupping in front of his eyes a tiny photograph and saying: "Go on, go on, take a gander at this lovely horse."

Then the pause, the voice less friendly and the question, and the sound of his own voice answering: "I'm game, Hencher. Naturally, I'm still game."

"Ah, like me you are. Good as your word. Well, come then, let's have a turn round the deck of this little tub. We've time yet for a turn at the rail."

He stood, trying to scrape the shards of the smashed mustard pot from his shoe, followed Hencher toward the white sea doors. The back of Hencher's neck was red, the checked cap was at an angle, they made their slow way together through the excursion crowd and the smells of soap and cotton underwear and scent behind the ears.

"We're going to do a polka," somebody called, "come dance with us."

"A bit of business first," Hencher said, and grinned over the heads at the woman. "A little business first—then we'll be the boys for you, never fear."

A broken bench with the name Annie carved into it, a bucket half-filled with sand, something made of brass and swinging, a discarded man's shirt snagged on the horn of a big cleat bolted to the deck and, overhead, high in a box on the wall of the pilot house, the running light flickering through the sea gloom. He felt the desertion, the wind, the coming of darkness as soon as he stepped from the saloon.

She's home now, she's thinking about her hubby now, she's asking the cat where's Michael off to, where's my Michael gone to?

He spat sharply over the rail, turned his jacket collar up, breathed on the dry bones of his hands.

Together, heads averted, going round the deck, coming abreast of the saloon and once more sheltered by a flapping canvas: Hencher lit a cigar while he himself stood grinning in through the lighted window at the crowd. He watched them kicking, twirling, holding hands, fitting their legs and feet to the steps of the dance; he grinned at the back of the girl too young to have a girdle to pull down, grinned at the boy in the black suit. He smelled the hot tobacco smell and Hencher was with him, Hencher who was fat and blowing smoke on the glass.

"You say you have a van, Hencher, a horse van?"

"That's the ticket. Two streets over from this quay, parked in an alley by the ship-fitter's, as good a van as you'd want and with a full tank. And it's a van won't be recognized, I can tell you that. A little oil and sand over the name, you see. Like they did in the war. And we drive it wherever we please—you see—and no one's the wiser."

He nodded and for a moment, across the raven-blue and gold of the water, he saw the spires and smokestacks and tiny bridges of the city black as a row of needles burnt and tipped with red. The tide had risen to its high mark and the gangway was nearly vertical; going down he burned his palm on the tarred rope, twice lost his footing. The engines were loud now. Except for Hencher and himself, except for the officer posted at the foot of the gangway and a seaman standing by each of the hawsers fore and aft, the quay was deserted, and when the sudden blasting of the ship's whistle commenced the timbers shook, the air was filled with steam, the noise of the whistle sounded through the quay's dark cargo shed. Then it stopped, except for the echoes in the shed and out on the water, and the man gave his head a shake as if he could not rid it of the whistling. He held up an unlighted cigarette and Hencher handed him the cigar.

"Oh," said the officer, "it's you two again. Find the lady in question all right?"

"We found her, Captain. She's comfy, thanks, good and comfy."

"Well, according to schedule we tie up here tomorrow morning at twenty past eight."

"My friend and me will come fetch her on the dot, Captain, good as my word. . . ."

Again the smothering whistle, again the sound of chain, someone shouted through a megaphone and the gangway rose up on a cable; the seamen hoisted free the ropes, the bow of the Artemis began to swing, the officer stepped over the widening space between quay and ship and was gone.

"Come," said Hencher and took hold of his arm, "we can watch from the shed."

They leaned against a crate under the low roof and there were rats and piles of dried shells and long dark empty spaces in the cargo shed. There were holes in the flooring: if he moved the toe of his shoe his foot would drop off into the water; if he moved his hand there would be the soft pinch of fur or the sudden burning of dirty teeth. Only Hencher and himself and the rats. Only scum, the greasy water and a punctured and sodden dory beneath them— filth for a man to fall into.

"There . . . she's got the current now."

He stared with Hencher toward the lights, small gallery of decks and silhouetted stacks that was the Artemis a quarter mile off on the river.

"They'll have their fun on that little ship tonight and with a moon too or I miss my guess. Another half hour," Hencher was twisting, trying for a look at his watch in the dark, "and I'll bring the lorry round."

Side by side, rigid against the packing crate, listening to the rats plop down, waiting, and all the while marking the disappearance of the excursion boat. Only the quay's single boom creaking in the wind and a view of the river across the now empty berth was left to them, while ahead of the Artemis lay a peaceful sea worn smooth by night and flotillas of landing boats forever beached. With beer and music in her saloon she off there making for the short sea cliffs, for the moonlit coast and desolate windy promontories into which the batteries had once been built. At three a. m. her navigator discovering the cliffs, fixing location by sighting a flat tin helmet nailed to a stump on the tallest cliff's windy lip, and the Artemis would approach the shore and all of them—boy, girl, lonely woman—would have a glimpse of ten miles of coast with an iron fleet half-sunk in the mud, a moonlit vision of windlasses, torpedo tubes, skein of rusted masts and the stripped hull of a destroyer rising stern first from that muddied coast under the cliffs. Beside the rail the lonely woman at least, and perhaps the rest of them, would see the ten white coastal miles, the wreckage safe from tides and storms and snowy nights, the destroyer's superstructure rising respectable as a lighthouse keeper's station. All won, all lost, all over, and for half a crown they could have it now, this seawreck and abandon and breeze of the ocean surrounding them. And the boy at least would hear the moist unjoyful voice of his girl while the Artemis remained off shore, would feel the claspknife in the pocket of her skirt and, down on the excursion boat's hard deck, would know the comfort to be taken with a young girl worn to thinness and wiry and tough as the titlings above the cliffs.

He stood rigid against the packing crate, alone. He waited deep within the shed and watched, sniffed something that was not of rats or cargo at all. Then he saw it drifting along the edges of the quay, rising up through the rat holes round his shoes: fog, the inevitable white hair strands which every night looped out across the river as if once each night the river must grow old, clammy, and in its age and during these late hours only, produce the thick miles of old woman's hair within whose heaps and strands it might then hide all bodies, tankers, or fat iron shapes nodding to themselves out there.

Fog of course and he should have expected it, should have carried a torch. Yet, whatever was to come his way would come, he knew, like this—slowly and out of a thick fog. Accidents, meetings unexpected, a figure emerging to put its arms about him: where to discover everything he dreamed of except in a fog? And, thinking of slippery corners, skin suddenly bruised, grappling hooks going blindly through the water: where to lose it all if not in the same white fog?

Look sharp, look sharp . . . that's a good laugh.

Alone he waited until the great wooden shed was filled with the fog that caused the rotting along the water's edge. His shirt was flat, wet against his chest. The forked iron boom on the quay was gone, and as for the two tankers that marked the vacated berth of the excursion boat, he knew they were there only by the dead sounds they made. All about him was the visible texture and density of the expanding fog. He was listening for the lorry's engine, with the back of a hand kept trying to wipe his cheek.

An engine was nearby suddenly, and despite the fog he knew that it was not Hencher's lorry but was the river barge approaching on the lifting tide. And he was alone, shivering, helpless to give a signal. He had no torch, no packet of matches. No one trusted a man's voice in a fog.

All the bells and whistles in mid-river were going at once and, hearing the tones change, the strokes change, listening to the metallic or compressed air sounds of sloops or ocean-going vessels protesting their identities and their vague shifting locations on the whole of this treacherous and fog-bound river's surface—a horrible noise, a confused warning, a frightening celebration—he knew that only his own barge, of all this night's drifting or anchored traffic, would come without lights and making no sound except for the soft and faltering sound of the engine itself. This he heard—surely someone was tinkering with it, nursing it, trying to stop the loss of oil with a bare hand—and each moment he waited for even these illicit sounds to go dead. But in the fog the barge engine was turning over and, all at once, a man out there cleared his throat.

So he stood away from the packing crate and slowly went down to his hands and knees and discovered that he could see a little distance now and began to crawl. He feared that the rats would get his hands; he ran his fingers round the crumbling edges of the holes; his creeping knee came down on fragments of a smashed bottle. There was an entire white sea-world floating and swirling in that enormous open door, and he crawled out to it.

"You couldn't do nothing about the bleeding fog?"

He had crossed the width of the quay, had got a grip on the iron joint of the boom and was trying to rise when the voice spoke up directly beneath him and he knew that if he fell it would not be into the greasy and squid-blackened water but onto the deck of the barge itself. He was unable to look down yet, but it was clear that the man who had spoken up at him had done so with a laugh, casually, without needing to cup his hands.

Before the man had time to say it again—"You couldn't do nothing about the bleeding fog, eh, Hencher? I wouldn't ordinarily step out of the house on a night like this"—the quay had already shaken beneath the van's tires and the headlamps had flicked on, suddenly, and hurt his eyes where he hung from the boom, one hand thrown out for balance and the other stuck like a dead man's to the iron. Hencher, carrying two bright lanterns by wire loops, had come between himself and the lorry's yellow headlamps—"Lively now, Mr. Banks," he was saying without a smile—and had thrust one of the lanterns upon him in time to reach out his freed hand and catch the end of wet moving rope on the instant it came lashing up from the barge. So that the barge was docked, held safely by the rope turned twice round a piling when he himself was finally able to look straight down and see it, the long and blunt-nosed barge riding high in a smooth bowl scooped out of the fog. Someone had shut off the engine.

"Take a smoke now, Cowles—just a drag, mind you—and we'll get on with it."

She ought to see her hubby now. She ought to see me now.

He had got his arm through the fork of the boom and was holding the lantern properly, away from his body and down, and the glare from its reflector lighted the figure of the man Cowles below him and in cold wet rivulets drifted sternward down the length of the barge. Midships were three hatches, two battened permanently shut, the third covered by a sagging canvas. Beside this last hatch and on a bale of hay sat a boy naked from the waist up and wearing twill riding breeches. In the stern was a small cabin. On its roof, short booted legs dangling over the edge, a jockey in full racing dress sat with a cigarette now between his lips and hands clasped round one of his tiny knees.

"Cowles! I want off . . . I want off this bloody coop!" he shouted.

The cigarette popped into his mouth then. It was a trick he had. The lips were pursed round the hidden cigarette and the little man was staring up not at Cowles or Hencher but at himself, and even while Cowles was ordering the two of them, boy and jockey, to get a hop on and drag the tarpaulin off the hold, the jockey kept looking up at him, toe of one little boot twitching left and right but the large bright eyes remained fixed on his own—until the cigarette popped out again and the dwarfed man allowed himself to be helped from his seat on the cabin roof by the stable boy whose arms, in the lantern light, were upraised and spattered with oil to the elbows.

"Get a hop on now, we want no coppers or watchmen or dock inspectors catching us at this bit of game. . . ."

The fog was breaking, drifting away, once more sinking into the river. Long shreds of it were wrapped like rotted sails or remnants of a wet wash round the buttresses and hand-railings of the bridges, and humped outpourings of fog came rolling from within the cargo shed as if all the fuels of this cold fire were at last consumed. The wind had started up again, and now the moon was low, just overhead.

"Here, use my bleeding knife, why don't you?"

The water was slimy with moonlight, the barge itself was slimy— all black and gold, dripping—and Cowles, having flung his own cigarette behind him and over the side, held the blade extended and moved down the slippery deck toward the boy and booted figure at the hatch with the slow embarrassed step of a man who at any moment expects to walk upon eel or starfish and trip, lose his footing, sprawl heavily on a deck as unknown to him as this.

"Here it is now, Mr. Banks!" He felt one of Hencher's putty hands quick and soft and excited on his arm. "Now you'll see what there is to see."

He looked down upon the naked back, the jockey's nodding cap, the big man Cowles and the knife stabbing at the ropes, until Cowles grunted and the three of them pulled off the tarpaulin and he was staring down at all the barge carried in its hold: the black space, the echo of bilge and, without movement, snort, or pawing of hoof, the single white marble shape of the horse whose neck (from where he leaned over, trembling, on the quay) was the fluted and tapering neck of some serpent while the head was an elongated white skull with nostrils, eye sockets, uplifted gracefully in the barge's hold— *Draftsman by Engraver's Hand out of Shallow Draft by Amulet, Castle Churl by Draftsman out of Likely Castle by Cold Masonry, Rock Castle by Castle Churl out of Words on Rock by Plebeian— until tonight when he's ours, until tonight when he's ours. . . .*

"Didn't I tell you, Mr. Banks? Didn't I . . . Good as his word, that's Hencher."

The whistles died one by one on the river and it was not Wednesday at all, only a time slipped off its cycle with hours and darkness never to be accounted for. There was water viscous and warm that lapped the sides of the barge; a faint up and down motion of the barge which he could gauge against the purple rings of a piling; and below him the still crouched figures of the men and, in its moist alien pit, the silver horse with its ancient head round which there buzzed a single fly as large as his own thumb and molded of shining blue wax.

He stared down at the lantern-lit blue fly and the animal whose ears were delicate and unfeeling, as unlikely to twitch as two pointed fern leaves etched on glass, and whose silver coat gleamed with the colorless fluid of some ghostly libation and whose decorous drained head smelled of a violence that was his own.

Even when he dropped the lantern—"No harm done, no harm done," Hencher said quickly—the horse did not shy or throw itself against the ribs of the barge, but remained immobile, fixed in the same standing posture of rigorous sleep that they had found it in at the moment the tarpaulin was first torn away. Though Cowles made his awkward lunge to the rail, saw what it was—lantern with cracked glass half-sunk, still burning on the water, then abruptly turning dark and sinking from sight—and laughed through his nose, looked up at them: "Bleeding lot of help he is. . . ."

"No harm done," said Hencher again, sweating and by light of the van's dim headlamps swinging out the arm of the boom until the cable and hook were correctly positioned above the barge's hold. "Just catch the hook, Cowles, guide it down."

Without a word, hand that had gripped the lantern still trembling, he took his place with Hencher at the iron bar which, given the weight of Hencher and himself, would barely operate the cable drum. He got his fingers round the bar; he tried to think of himself straining at such a bar, but it was worse for Hencher whose heart was sunk in fat. Yet Hencher too was ready—in tight shirtsleeves, his jacket removed and hanging from the tiny silver figure of a winged man that adorned the van's radiator cap—so that he himself determined not to let go of the bar as he had dropped the lantern but, instead, to carry his share of the horse's weight, to stay at the bar and drum until the horse could suffer this last transport. There was no talking on the barge. Only sounds of their working, plash of the boy's feet in the bilge, the tinkle of buckles and strap ends as the webbed bands were slid round the animal's belly and secured.

Hencher was whispering: "Ever see them lift the bombs out of the craters? Two or three lads with a tripod, some lengths of chain, a few red flags and a rope to keep the children away . . . then cranking up the unexploded bomb that would have bits of debris and dirt sticking peacefully as you please to that filthy big cylinder . . . something to see, men at a job like that and fishing up a live bomb big enough to blow a cathedral to the ground." Then, feeling a quiver: "But here now, lay into it gently, Mr. Banks, that's the ticket."

He pushed—Hencher was pushing also—until after a moment the drum stopped and the cable that stretched from the tip of the boom's arm down to the ring swiveling above the animal's webbed harness was taut.

"O.K." It was Cowles kneeling at the hold's edge, speaking softly and clearly on the late night air. "O.K. now . . . up he goes."

The barge which could support ten tons of coal or gravel on the river's oily and slop-sullied tide was hardly lightened when the horse's hoofs swung a few inches free of that planking hidden and awash. But drum, boom, cable and arms could lift not a pound more than this, and lifted this—the weight of the horse—only with strain and heat, pressure and rusted rigidity. Though his eyes were closed he knew when the boom swayed, could feel the horse beginning to sway off plumb. He heard the drum rasping round, heard the loops of rusted cable wrapping about the hot drum one after another, slowly.

"Steady now, steady . . . he's bloody well high enough."

Then, as Hencher with burned hands grasped the wheel that would turn the boom its quarter circle and position the horse over quay, not over barge, he felt a fresh wind on his cheek and tilted his head, opened his eyes, and saw his second vision of the horse: up near the very tip of the iron arm, rigid and captive in the sling of two webbed bands, legs stiff beneath it, tail blown out straight on the wind and head lifted—they had wrapped a towel round the eyes—so that high in the air it became the moonlit spectacle of some giant weather-vane. And, seeing one of the front legs begin to move, to lift, and the hoof—that destructive hoof—rising up and dipping beneath the slick shoulder, seeing this slow gesture of the horse preparing to paw suddenly at the empty air, and feeling the tremor through his fingers still lightly on the bar: "Let him down, Hencher, let him down!" he cried and waved both hands at the blinded and hanging horse even as it began to descend.

Until the boom regained its spring and balance like a tree spared from a gale; until the drum, released, clattered and in its rusty mechanism grew still; until the four sharp hoofs touched wood of the quay. Cowles—first up the ladder and followed by Jimmy Needles the jockey and Lovely the stableboy—reached high and loosed the fluttering towel from round its eyes. The boy approached and snapped a lead-rope to the halter and the jockey, never glancing at the others or at the horse, stepped up behind him, whispering: "Got a fag for Needles, Mister? Got a fag for Needles?" Not until this moment when he shouted, "Hencher, don't leave me, Hencher. . . ." and saw the fat naked arm draw back and the second lantern sail in an arc over the water, and in a distance also saw the white hindquarters on the van's ramp and dark shapes running, not until this moment was he grateful for the little hard cleft of fingers round his arm and the touch of the bow-legged figure still begging for his fag but pulling and guiding him at last in the direction of the cab's half-open door. Cowles had turned the petcocks and behind them the barge was sinking.

These five rode crowded together on the broad seat, five white faces behind a rattling windscreen. Five men with elbows gnawing at elbows, hands and pairs of boots confused, men breathing hard and remaining silent except for Hencher who complained he hadn't room to drive. In labored first gear and with headlights off, they in the black van traveled the slow bumping distance down the length of the cargo shed, from plank to rotted plank moved slowly in the van burdened with their own weight and the weight of the horse until at the corner of the deserted building—straight ahead lay darkness that was water and all five, smelling sweat and river fumes and petrol, leaned forward together against the dim glass—they turned and drove through an old gate topped with a strand of barbed wire and felt at last hard rounded cobblestones beneath the tires.

"No one's the wiser now, lads," said Hencher, and laughed, shook the sweat from his eyes, took a hand off the wheel and slapped Cowles' knee. "We're just on a job if anyone wants to know," smiling, both fat hands once more white on the wheel. "So we've only to sit tight until we make Highland Green . . . eh, Cowles . . . eh, Needles . . . eh, Mr. Banks?"

But he himself, beneath the jockey and pressed between Cowles' thick flank and the unupholstered door, was sickening: smells of men, smells of oil, lingering smells of the river and now, faint yet

definite, seeping through the panel at his back, smells of the horse—
all these mixed odors filled his mouth, his stomach, and some hard
edge of heel or brake lever or metal that thrust down from the dash
was cutting into his ankle, hurting the bone. Under his buttocks he
felt the crooked shape of a spanner; from a shelf behind the thin
cushions straw kept falling; already the motor was overheated and
they were driving too fast in the darkness of empty market districts
and areas of cheap lodgings with doorways and windows black except
for one window, seven or eight streets ahead of them, in which a
single light would be burning. And each time this unidentified black
shabby van went round a corner he felt the horse—his horse—thump
against one metal side or the other. Each time the faint sound and feel
of the thumping made him sick.

"Hencher. I think you had better leave me off at the flat."

Then trying to breathe, trying to explain, trying to argue with
Hencher in the speeding overheated cab and twisting, seeing the
fluted dark nostril at a little hole behind the driver's head. Until
Hencher smiled his broad worried smile and in a loud voice said:
"Oh well, Mr. Banks is a married man," speaking to Cowles, the
jockey, the stable boy, nudging Cowles in the ribs. "And you must
always make allowance for a married man. . . ."

Cowles yawned, and, as best he could, rubbed at his great coat-
sleeves still wet from the spray. "Leave him off, Hencher, if he
gives us a gander at the wife."

The flat door is open and the cat sleeps. Just inside the door,
posted on a straight chair, market bag at her feet and the cat at her
feet, sitting with the coat wrapped round her shoulders and the felt
hat still on her head: there she waits, waits up for him. The neighbor
on the chair next to her is sleeping—like the cat—and the mouth is
half-open with the breath hissing through, and the eyes are buried
under curls. But her own eyes are level, the lips red, the face smooth
and white and soft as soap. Waiting up for him.

Without moving, without taking her eyes from the door: "Where's
Michael off to? Where's my Michael gone?" she asks the cat. Then
down the outer hall, in the dark of the one lamp burning, she hears
the click of the house key, the sound of the loose floor board, and
she thinks to raise a hand and dry her cheek. With the same hand
she touches her neighbor's arm.

"It's all right, Mrs. Stickley," she whispers, "he's home now."

JOSEPHINE HERBST:

Embalmer's Holiday

It happened that the three friends met for Christmas in the home of old lady Shattuck. She had lost her husband years ago and her children were scattered to the ends of the earth. It was natural that the only people available were the three friends who during the course of the year had had their homes disrupted. The two women, Mrs. Fleet and Mrs. Greer, were separated from their husbands, and Mr. Dyer had left his wife. Mr. Dyer and Mrs. Fleet had known one another for a long time; they had in fact lived in the same Connecticut valley during their first year of married life. That is, Mr. Dyer's first year of married life with his first wife. It was not known whether his second wife had left him or he her, but the two women were given to understand that she was finding happiness elsewhere.

Mrs. Fleet and Mrs. Greer had a few good crying spells before Mr. Dyer came up the day before Christmas. Old lady Shattuck was determined to have a tree and was unearthing all the old tinsel and ornaments from the attic. She meant to hang on the tip of the tree the little angel that had hung on all the trees during her life with Mr. Shattuck. Mr. Shattuck's picture was surrounded with green wreaths two days before and a tall candle stood ready to be lighted to his memory on Christmas day. Mrs. Shattuck hoped she would get a chance to recite "The Night Before Christmas" and Mr. Dyer and the two women hoped they would have a chance to get a little tight.

It was inevitable that the three friends should remember with dramatic clearness the Christmas before. At that time they had been united with their respective husbands and wife and together with six other apparently happy pairs had a big Christmas party. Mr. Dyer said that to his knowledge all but two couples were now dissolved. For some reason the news made Mrs. Fleet and Mrs. Greer very cheerful.

"They say misery loves company," said Mrs. Greer. They sat pensively trying to decide what elements had been at work for such wholesale destruction.

"It's the times," said Mr. Dyer. "The world is going to pieces. It affects everything. It's in the air."

"I don't know," said Mrs. Fleet. "Lots of people got married this year too and I don't see why it should have hit all of us so hard."

Mr. Dyer thought it was because they were peculiarly sensitive. Mrs. Greer said that she had never thought of Flossie Stone as particularly sensitive. Mr. Dyer said that Bill Stone was as sensitive a man as you'd find. Mrs. Fleet said who would have thought that last Christmas was to be the final Christmas she and Jim Fleet would ever spend together.

"Now none of that," said Mr. Dyer. "No red eyes. We're going to have a cheerful Christmas. Everybody is going to have a swell time." Mrs. Shattuck pattered in and said that someone wanted to speak to Mrs. Greer on the telephone. Mrs. Greer left and Mr. Dyer and Mrs. Fleet began talking of the early days when they had met. Mr. Dyer said that no one had been lovelier than his first wife. She was just stupid now and when he saw her as he often did in a friendly way, the past seemed an impossible dream. It was different with his second wife, they had never been happy. He didn't understand why they had come together or why they had stayed together. She was, of course, a beauty. He had to have glamour. But he had met a woman, an actress who was a real woman, not like Tillie, but a real honest to god woman with brains as well as beauty and moreover with heart. She wouldn't do the cruel things Tillie did. Tillie had never thought of anyone but herself. When he was making nine hundred a week at Hollywood they went one night to a delicatessen store to buy things for a supper and she bought everything she wanted. When he finally bought a few dill pickles for himself she had raised hell. She had made so much fuss about it you would have thought he had committed a crime. It was always like that. She had never sewed on a button for him or darned a sock and he had waited on her hand and foot. He had waited on Elsie, his first wife too, but she was at least amiable. She had even learned to bake.

"I remember her popovers," said Mrs. Fleet. "I never tasted such fluffy popovers. And the delicious coffee you made when we were in the valley and came to see you on winter afternoons, remember?"

"Remember the day we came to the valley dead broke and said you had to find us a house," said Mr. Dyer. "We didn't have a cent and had to plow through drifts up to our waists to get to your place."

"We opened the door," recited Mrs. Fleet, "and there you stood. I never saw such a lovely girl as Elsie was with her hair splattered with snow. And she was a good sport to live in that old house without complaining."

Mrs. Greer came into the room smiling. She looked around embarrassed. "Who was it?" said Mr. Dyer.

"Why you know," said Mrs. Greer, giggling a little. "It's so funny. You see in New York when I was down there I met this man. He just telephoned. He's very nice, in a friendly way of course. He's very lonely, he was married fifteen years and his wife died six months ago. He was at the hotel where I was and we talked one night and he took me to dinner. He wants to know if he can come up Christmas. Do you suppose it would be all right with Mrs. Shattuck, the poor thing is so lonely."

"Sure," said Mr. Dyer. "Has he any dough? He can buy us some scotch."

"Now don't get ideas," said Mrs. Greer. "He's just lonely, that's all. He'd like to buy something, of course. Shall I say to come?"

"Of course," said Mrs. Fleet. "Go ahead."

"That's what I thought," said Mrs. Greer. "I told him already."

"Who is he?" said Mr. Dyer.

"Well," began Mrs. Greer with some reluctance. "He's an embalmer."

"An embalmer," grinned Mr. Dyer.

"He's got a car and he's a nice person and as I say, lonely."

"Good for little Dottie Dimples," said Mr. Dyer playfully.

"Don't be silly," said Mrs. Greer. "If you do, I can't stand it."

"That's right," said Mrs. Fleet. "Don't tease her. He's just a friend."

"Only an acquaintance," said Mrs. Greer on the defensive.

Mrs. Shattuck was pleased at the new addition to their party. "The more the merrier," she said gaily. "You should have seen this house when Mr. Shattuck was alive. Teeming with people. We had everyone pouring in all day long. Mr. Shattuck made the finest rum punch you ever tasted. People didn't overdo in those days. Drank like ladies and gentlemen. Of course the times were different. People knew the earth they were standing on. They could count on one year after the next."

"Just what I was saying," agreed Mr. Dyer, balancing on his toes. "Exactly what I tried to tell the girls."

"It doesn't explain everything to me," said Mrs. Fleet. She was trying to make up her mind about Mr. Fleet. She couldn't bear not to send him something for Christmas. But she had had a talk with Mrs. Greer and both had said they didn't care a hoot what happened to their husbands on Christmas day. They didn't intend to gratify them by so much as a Christmas card. But in the morning of the day before Christmas the entire Shattuck household turned inside out. The two

young women went to town for Mrs. Shattuck and the main street of
the little suburban town with its clutter of bright Christmas trees before the hotel, its three fat Santy Clauses ringing bells before the chain
stores, and its windows full of turkeys, began to have an effect upon
the two women. Mrs. Fleet found it hard to keep the tears back. She
remembered the first Christmas she and her husband had ever spent
together in the valley. They had been broke and had promised not to
give one another presents. But Mr. Fleet had produced one of her
stockings Christmas morning stuffed with a five cent pencil, a little
sack of raisins, and some pink and white peppermints that had been
her favorite candy as a child. Every Christmas afterwards he had
bought her pink and white peppermints. She told herself it was silly
sentimentality to want peppermints or to care about Christmas anymore. In a world full of pressing events, one should not clutch at such
tiny trifles, yet she did clutch. She mourned for the peppermints and
when Mrs. Greer was busy elsewhere, she sneaked into a store and
bought her husband a carton of cigarettes with a red Christmas wrapping. She even wrote a little card. "To Jim from his old friend, Santa
Claus."

She felt better afterwards. But she hoped if she ever spent another
year so miserably she would be in her grave. She wondered what Jim
would do on Christmas and late that afternoon when she got a letter
from him she went straight with it to Mrs. Greer.

"Can you imagine such a man," she said half laughing, half indignant. "He does that to me, just walks off with that hussy and now
writes to say he wishes he could see me Christmas, it will seem strange
without me. Hopes I will have a nice time and will I write him a nice
letter and not to feel bitter about this terrible year. Imagine."

The two women just looked at one another. Then they laughed.
"Are they crazy?" said Mrs. Greer. "You'd think it was nothing more
than taking off a pair of gloves. Just a pair of gloves, like that." She
stripped her hands one over the other with an indignant yet important
gesture. "They haven't an idea what it means to us. No, they are all
right. They are happy so they can't bear to have their Christmas
spoiled. They must take a little notice of us to keep an appetite for
dinner."

But a little later in the evening when a box was delivered from the
express company for Mrs. Greer she broke down and cried in earnest.
The box was from Mr. Greer. Mr. Dyer and Mrs. Shattuck and Mrs.
Fleet stood looking on. "Jim never sent me anything," said Mrs. Fleet.

"I never got a single present and Tillie never even sent me a card," said Mr. Dyer. "All the rest of you got boxes from someone, but I don't get a thing. I'm just an orphan."

"It came from the Russian store," said Mrs. Greer excitedly, pulling out stuffing and looking at newspapers clipped fine to make a padding for something hard.

"I bet he's sending back my lamp," said Mrs. Greer. "It's nothing new."

"Don't be cynical," said Mrs. Fleet. "Open it."

"Oh I remember when Mr. Shattuck used to come home loaded down with presents. Once he bought me a velvet dressing gown and it had lovely maribou all around it," babbled Mrs. Shattuck. "We used to stay up all night getting the tree ready for the children."

"It's something hard," said Mrs. Greer tugging. Out came a samovar. She sat back looking at it, then pushed it away. She got up and began walking up and down. She couldn't help it, angry tears came.

"Don't you like it?" said Mr. Dyer.

She nodded, crying harder. "Come, come," said Mrs. Shattuck. "You mustn't carry on. He meant well. It's a lovely samovar."

Mrs. Fleet stared at it. Mr. Fleet hadn't even sent her pink and white peppermints. When she was in college her father had never forgotten to send her peppermints. So long as he was alive, he had remembered and after his death for ten years Jim Fleet had remembered. With all the responsibilities of life, Christmas had been the one time when she was certain to feel something of the old cared for security of childhood. It had warmed her to remember she was someone's little girl, that no matter how necessary it was to earn a living, to compete in the world, to constantly juggle for place, yet she had been a child with long curls, deeply loved, who on Christmas went confidently to her stocking and found peppermints, year after year. Now for the first time in her life, Santa was dead, her father was dead. Jim Fleet, though alive in the world and at that moment probably kissing the back of his new wife's neck, putting a surprise present into her hand, was dead. She looked dully at the shiny samovar and said, "It's a nice samovar."

"A samovar," sobbed Mrs. Greer. "Now—it's too late for a samovar. He knows I don't want things to do with a house anymore. I don't want possessions anymore. I don't want anything but a suitcase."

"Now, now," soothed Mrs. Shattuck. "Give yourself time, my dear. In time it will be all right. You've been treated badly but Time, as Mr. Shattuck used to say, is a Gentleman. You'll laugh a year or so from now, see if you don't."

Mrs. Greer sobbed and eyed the samovar, sitting crookedly on its bedding of snipped paper. "Why didn't he get me something to wear? All that money. He hasn't any." She sobbed again but she was thinking of how few presents he had ever given her. He had never had much money. It had taken too much to get his training. She had never given him presents either. They had gone to a show together if they had money. It had always seemed fun to spend it together but as a result she had nothing to show for her life with him now it was gone. Except the samovar. She said, "I'm going to send it back and get the money." At the moment she only thought that she could not bear to see it around reminding her of the presents they had never exchanged until it was over. That a solid samovar, a more or less useless piece of furniture, should appear now of all times, seemed too much.

Mr. Dyer stopped the flow of tears and lightened the general depression with a brisk, "Now take it the way he meant it. He meant well. Nobody thought of me. I'm just an orphan." He went on in that vein thinking to cheer Mrs. Greer but the two women friends took it somewhat seriously. They got together in a corner and although it was after nine at night decided to run into town and buy something for Mr. Dyer. It would be terrible if no one thought of him.

Mrs. Shattuck said she hadn't thought of presents. A nice dinner had been as far as her imagination had gone. The two women friends drove hastily to town and haggled over a pair of socks and muffler. Mrs. Greer said that Mr. Greer had worn a number ten sock and Mrs. Fleet said Mr. Fleet had taken a twelve. They compromised on eleven for Mr. Dyer. When it came to picking out a muffler Mrs. Fleet leaned toward a dark red with white bars but admitted Mr. Fleet would have preferred a lovely deep green one. Mrs. Greer said her husband loved green too. The two women fondled the green scarf and finally bought it for Mr. Dyer. They felt a little sad but pleased to be buying a present for some man, even if it were not for their own husbands. Mrs. Fleet said she was afraid that Mr. Dyer was making fresh trouble for himself again and his fatal weakness for glamour would involve him in the same old way. She suspected that he had hoped for a present from the actress.

By the time they returned a package had actually arrived for Mr. Dyer and the actress had remembered him with a dressing case full of ornamental and useless objects. He then admitted that he had spent an entire day packing up a little box for the actress's daughter full of tiny dogs, airplanes, and other knickknacks tied in tissue paper with ribbons. Mrs. Greer confessed that she had weakened and had sent Mr.

Greer two handkerchiefs that had been in her handkerchief box all
year and had in fact been part of her husband's present the year before. Mrs. Fleet confessed to the cigarettes. They had a good laugh
and Mr. Dyer read them the recipe for eggnog calling for twelve eggs
and a quart of cream as well as rum and scotch that he intended to
make the next day. He said it would be a little masterpiece.

It was a sunny Christmas day and the embalmer came around ten
in the morning. Mrs. Fleet was stuffing the turkey with a dressing that
had been used in her family for a hundred years and Mrs. Shattuck
was hunting for little moulds for Christmas cookies. The embalmer
was an ordinary blond fellow rather short and stocky. Mr. Dyer took
an immediate antagonism to him. He began bragging about the way
he made drinks and spaghetti.

"Not better than my wife," spoke up the embalmer, Mr. Spotwood,
with unexpected belligerency.

"Not better than your wife," screamed Mr. Dyer now the better for
several old-fashioneds. "With all respect to your lamented wife, I can
make the best spaghetti in the country."

Mr. Spotwood shrugged. "Some people would be hard up if it
weren't for their own good opinion," he said.

"My good opinion! Everybody can tell you. Mrs. Fleet can tell you.
I'm one of the best cooks in America. Mrs. Fleet is a wonderful cook.
You're sitting in this room with two unbeatable cooks and you talk
about spaghetti."

"He can make nice things," placated Mrs. Fleet. The kitchen was
somewhat crowded with everyone getting in everyone's way and the
presence of the embalmer made it seem full to overflowing. Mrs. Greer
tactfully suggested that perhaps the men might like to take a little run
into town. Mr. Dyer spitefully said in an aside that he would shame
Mr. Spotwood into buying some scotch for the day. The two men departed in Mr. Spotwood's new car and the women went ahead with
the cooking somewhat sadly. The three women were deeply thoughtful
and engaged each in her own way upon her own separate and lost
past. At that moment Christmas seemed not only wasteful but a day
of singularly cruel resurrections. Mrs. Fleet said if she ever so much as
noticed the day again they could take her for an idiot. Mrs. Shattuck
said that the day was for children and without children no one knew
what on earth it was for. Mrs. Greer said that two years before when
she and Mr. Greer had been in Chicago at her mother's home it had

been a wonderful day with old friends coming in all day long. "Just open house," said Mrs. Greer, "that's what it was."

By the time the men returned, their animosity had been drowned in Christmas spirits. Mr. Spotwood had been restrained with difficulty from buying a whole case of champagne. "I didn't have the heart to let him," confided Mr. Dyer with a benevolent air. He read his recipe for eggnog several times and began an argument concerning the amount of cream and eggs required. Mr. Spotwood said that the recipe sounded more like an omelet than an eggnog.

"What!" yelled Mr. Dyer. "That's all you know. You probably never made an eggnog in your life." The women looked pained.

"Listen feller," said Mr. Spotwood with infuriating familiarity. "I'm a lot older than you and I know eggnogs of old, before you were dry behind the ears."

"You never tasted one like this," said Mr. Dyer. But he was becoming sleepy with all the pre-dinner libations. The entire household began to nod. Mrs. Shattuck retired to her room. Mrs. Greer and Mr. Spotwood went for a little drive. Mr. Dyer fell asleep on the couch with the eggnog recipe clutched in his hand. Mrs. Fleet held out to keep guard on the turkey. It was too large for the pan and took constant basting. It was not as nice as the turkeys her mother used to make. The turkey she and Jim Fleet had when they celebrated their first Christmas had been nicer. They had made cranberry ice in a milk can set in the snow and had held hands singing "O Little Town of Bethlehem." At that moment it would have seemed the most natural thing in the world for Jim Fleet to press his face at the window in the back door and stamping off the snow come in calling out, "Hello baby, here's your boy." Half expectant she turned to face the blank glass. Something more mysterious and inexplicable than death had happened. It was as final as death and harder to be reconciled with. She tried to remember an old recipe for hot slaw but the eggs curdled.

Mr. Dyer roused himself in time and made his really tremendous eggnog. It was all they could do to restrain him from insisting they drink it before dinner. "Hey feller," called the embalmer. "I want some room for turkey." Crossly Mr. Dyer conceded, carrying the turkey with reckless vigor. It was a mammoth meal and Mr. Spotwood enlivened it with well meant comments in German. It was bad German but Mrs. Fleet attempted to respond with an understanding look. Mr. Spotwood persisted under the notion that he was giving a cosmopolitan touch to the dinner to say nothing of competing with Mr. Dyer, who had begun to sprinkle his remarks with French phrases. In spite of the efforts everyone made, the dinner had a melancholy air. Mrs. Greer struggled not to be bored with the embalmer's humor. Mr. Dyer struggled to keep awake for the eggnog. Mrs. Shattuck sank into a gentle contemplation of the past.

The eggnog was finally served and Mr. Dyer pronounced it a perfect masterpiece. "Ho, ho," cackled the embalmer, trusting to make up in sarcastic expression what he lacked in wit. Mr. Dyer was too befuddled to more than glare. With dignity he managed to leave the table and stalk to his own room. He fell down heavily on his bed and promptly went to sleep. Mrs. Shattuck excused herself. Mr. Spotwood and Mrs. Greer retired a little drearily to the parlor. Mrs. Fleet looked upon the remains of the feast.

With everyone taking themselves off Mr. Spotwood felt uncomfortable. He had the uneasy feeling he had not conducted himself properly. He longed to ingratiate himself and to buy something. When he bought something, it was his experience that popularity came to him, at least for the moment. Only his wife had been able to make him feel that it was possible for anyone to have a sustained interest in him. Now he hoped there was something he might buy. "Isn't there something you need in town?" he asked hopefully. Mrs. Greer shook her head. She was angry at Mr. Dyer for deserting the party and she wished Mr. Spotwood would let her alone. She suggested that Mrs. Fleet might like a little drive.

Mrs. Fleet did not want a little drive but she did not know how to get rid of the insistent Mr. Spotwood. His need to rehabilitate himself in someone's esteem and to divert to himself some tiny ray of interest succeeded in getting her into the car. They drove around the snow-covered streets of the little town. Everyone was indoors but the many Christmas trees made the houses unnaturally gay. Mr. Spotwood said he couldn't bear to look at them. By this time his own past Christmases with his dead wife began to be reconstructed with a peculiar halo.

"You take this country," said Mr. Spotwood impressively. "It's a country of little homes. Everyone is in his little home, like in a shell. If you have a home, it's swell, if you lose it, it's hell. There's no place to go. I often think it's very limiting, especially now I'm all alone. After fifteen years you feel pretty alone."

Mrs. Fleet had listened attentively. She tried to begin a sympathetic reply and Mr. Spotwood volunteered that he was an old man.

"Why Mr. Spotwood," said Mrs. Fleet. "That's silly. You're in your prime."

"Relatively speaking," said Mr. Spotwood, "I'm an old man. But so long as I can do anything for anyone, I'll stick around. The minute I'm useless, *schluss*. I'm never going to be a burden on anybody."

Mrs. Fleet resigned herself to cheering up Mr. Spotwood. She began to feel a little sore at Mrs. Greer for having invited the embalmer, who was not lightening the burden of the day. Mr. Spotwood began telling how a year ago he and his wife were driving to Florida and he had a little attack of appendicitis. He had instructed his wife what to do if he got worse and had taken pleasure in knowing that all his affairs were in shape. In the end, he got over it and months later it was his wife who had checked out.

Mrs. Fleet politely asked if she had been sick long. "Six weeks," said Mr. Spotwood, now speaking with a new grave voice. "I didn't know she was going to check out. She didn't know either, that's one thing I'm thankful for. Day before she checked out she cried a little. Perhaps she suspected. I said, 'Now mamma, come now, we can't have that. No tears, cheer up, we'll have you on your feet in no time.' She was game, she smiled right back at me. But that night she began to slip. My brother's a doctor but he wouldn't touch her. 'I can't do it, Ed,' he said. 'I haven't got the nerve.' I phoned another feller, doctor on Long Island, friend of mine. 'You got to come,' I said, 'you got to get right over here.' He came and they got her on the table but it was too late. She never came out of it and I never saw her again. Believe me, I wouldn't look at her after they got her fixed up. She was gone and what was left wasn't her is the way I look at it. They can talk about heaven but I can't take stock in it. It's here and now, if you ask me, and very little of that."

He had succeeded so fully in lowering his spirits and the spirits of Mrs. Fleet that he became cheerful. Mrs. Fleet's sympathetic silence soothed him for the cuts that the snobbish Mr. Dyer had handed him during the day. When he and Mrs. Fleet reentered the house, he was almost genial. Inside the party was beginning to revive. Mr. Dyer was pouring a little drink and cast a baleful glare at Mr. Spotwood, who did not flinch. We can't all write for Hollywood but he could probably buy and sell Dyer at this minute. And he had been loved devotedly for fifteen years.

Mrs. Shattuck had waked up and was ready to recite "The Night Before Christmas." Mrs. Greer was looking pensively into the fire.

Mrs. Fleet and Mr. Spotwood sat down with the other orphans and a toast was proposed to "Ye old time Christmas." Mrs. Shattuck got up and lighted the candle under the portrait of her deceased husband.

FRANK HOLWERDA:

In a Tropical Minor Key

The hotel was built for some thirty guests—ghost-guests, it turned out. Because twenty-nine of the lattice-near-the-ceiling rooms had been locked now for years, window shutters dogged down, interiors fetidly hot, dark, smelling of South American must. The ugly frame building, a cube, stood off the ground on massive brownhart uprights so that air, even searingly hot, could find means to drift. The heavy planks and outside cedar laps swelled and groaned during the rainy season and dried and shrank again and shrivelled and cracked when the equatorial rains stopped and the powdery shell-dust from the street sifted in. The rank Guiana bush, a quarter of a mile away, might, now and then, send an emissary in the form of a bat or an awari-with-young for an after-dark visit. But guests who could reach in their pockets and pay never seemed to materialize. The help tip-toed about, endlessly dusting, drowsily waiting behind potted palms, speaking in whispers.

A squad of high stools stood at attention in front of the bar on the first floor, one of them well used, bottom rungs scuffed. The tall, heat-thinned man, bony-cheeked and with eyes sunk deep in their sockets, leaned across the shiny slab of amaranth and idly watched the bartender scour the sink with fine white sand and a lime peel. He pushed his glass across the bar, then crooked an index finger and squeegeed the sweat from his forehead. "Better let me have another, Wek," he said.

"Same, Mr. Brenn?"

"One more and I'll go eat. What's for dinner tonight, Wek? Saturday night there should be . . ."

Wek poured the drink. "I'll go ask the cook," he said. He wiped his hands on his apron and his forehead on his sleeve and walked through the back door to the kitchen.

Geoffrey Brenn watched him go, drumming his fingers on the bar. He skidded his forefinger back and forth where his glass had left some moisture and swore. He stretched his long legs and pulled up the crease in his white linen pants. He was sweating behind the knees. He took a damp handkerchief from his pocket and mopped his temple with a corner. Wek came back through the door behind the bar. "There's chicken soup, red snapper, curried rice with chicken and cocoanut. Sugar pines for dessert—sliced." Wek made a simple, tired announcement of it. "Cook says it's chicken but it's really iguana—in the soup too. I saw the skin." He picked up the blackened lime peel and went back to the sink. He squeezed the lime peel into a mere button, dipped it in a saucer of sand and took long strokes with it across the drain of the sink.

"Saturday night blueplate! Hot curried rice and lizard is swell stuff in this heat, isn't it, Wek?" Jeff's voice carried sharply through the open door behind the bar. "Isn't it, Wek? Give me an answer— loud!"

"It's pretty good," Wek said without looking up. "I don't want to . . ."

"We have a bygod fire-stoker back there for a cook!" Jeff said. He had turned on his stool and spoke to the tiny polished dance floor and the empty chairs in the dining room beyond. "Wonder if that Borgian bastard ever heard of a cold salad? You know what lettuce is, Wek? Ever have it?" Wek paid no attention to him, the sweat dripping from the tip of his heavy nose as he worked.

And then in the sudden silence that followed, the heat billowed back. As though the sound of their voices had held it off, now that they were silent, it returned like a sudden hot blush.

A slight movement on the floor caught Jeff's eye. It was a mouse. He watched it dart around the potted palms and mahogany pillars, run along the base of the wall and bump into the mopboard below the bar. "Hey, Wek!" The sound of the whisper backed up the heat. "That mouse is here again! Wants a peanut! Funny thing, Wek, all I have to do is sit here a little while and he comes around. Knows me, Wek! The little grey bastard's a friend of mine. Follows me, Wek! For peanuts! Look!"

"Oh never mind the hint, Mr. Brenn," Wek said wearily, "I always serve the peanuts after your fourth drink. You won't eat them before that anyway." He slid the round basket across the bar and wiped his face on his sleeve again. "They're not my peanuts you know. And I don't really care when you eat them and how many either." He cut a fresh lime then turned and said "Sir."

"Now watch me feed my little grey friend a peanut, Wek," Jeff said. He dropped the shells on the bar and threw the kernel on the floor. The mouse nibbled it eagerly.

"That's all right, Mr. Brenn," Wek said patiently. "Throw 'em all down there. One of the boys'll sweep 'em up."

"You don't believe there's a mouse down here, do you, Wek?"

"No I don't, Mr. Brenn," Wek said politely. "I know when there's mice around. I can smell 'em."

"Take a look then."

"Can't see through the bar," Wek said. "Eyes not as good as they used to be."

"Neither's your nose! Lean over the bar then and take a look."

"Get dizzy when I lean over that far, Mr. Brenn. And I'm not supposed to leave the bar and walk out there either."

"Honestly, you just don't believe there's a mouse out here, do you, Wek?"

"No I don't think there's a mouse out there, Mr. Brenn. Sorry."

"It's not important," Jeff said. "The hell with it. And with everything else too!"

Wek said quietly, "I don't want to argue. But I still remember that time when . . ."

"OK, Wek. So you got a good memory! *Okay!*"

They stopped talking and with the silence the lid came off the giant stew-pot somewhere below, the moist heat rushing back as though filling a vacuum. It was still and quiet and as he sat thinking, Jeff wondered if either of them had spoken at all or if he'd just imagined they had, or if there really was a mouse on the floor or not. He avoided looking down.

Jeff stretched his arms and tried for a yawn that wasn't there. "Wek," he said. "Saturday night, Wek. Does she ever . . ."

"Sir?"

"Never mind. Skip it." He began flipping peanut shells at the sink, aiming and sighting carefully. "When's the next tourist boat come in, Wek?"

"About three weeks." Wek left the sink, picked up a bar rag and wiped the spotless bar vigorously. He kept his eyes down and wiped back and forth. "You could take it easy tonight, Mr. Brenn? You could have an early dinner and go upstairs to bed? Get a good night's sleep and then . . ."

"The longer I sleep, the more nightmares I have, Wek. Another one, please. Same."

"Just let me ask you one question for a simple answer, Mr. Brenn. Just one." Wek pushed the filled glass across the bar. "Do you have to get that way every night?"

"Don't have to, Wek, but it sure helps." Jeff ran a pocket comb through his damp hair. He placed a cigarette between his lips and watched the sweat-soaked match heads crumble as he struck them. Wek leaned over with a light in his cupped hand. "If I cut this out," Jeff said, "you'd be out of a job. Ever think of that, Wek? I'm just about your only customer."

"I'll find something else," Wek said.

"You'll cut cane for seventeen Dutch Guiana cents an hour and eat fish heads and iguana eggs. You'd like that, wouldn't you? You like pow-pow made of palm worms, Wek? And you can put some goddamn curry on 'em if they taste a little muddy. First you let 'em horse around in a pan of warm milk for a day or so. Keep it shallow so they won't drown and then . . ."

"I don't want to argue," Wek said.

"All right! So the next tourist boat comes in, I'll find a nice girl and wine her lopsided and marry her and live in a house and never touch another drop and you can go cut cane. And use a dull machete, Wek. More fun that way!"

"Tourists!" Wek said. "You wine 'em all right! Never even go near your office when there's a boat in. Your company back in the States is going to . . ."

"My company!" Jeff said and crossed himself. "They don't need

me in that hot little office, Wek. I trained all of them not to need me.
You should see all the money we make. I taught them to scoop it into
a big pile before we send it to New York. I'm a good teacher, Wek.
I should start a money school some place. I'd be the principal scooper!"

"You taught 'em too well, Mr. Brenn." Wek cut another lime in
two and licked the juicy ends before going to the sink with it. "Tourists!" he said. "Huh! You want to hear what they say about this
place?"

"God no! Spare me, Wek. I've heard."

"Utterly romantic," Wek said. "So *quaint!* And charming, utterly
charming!" He dropped one of the lime halves, half stooped to re-
trieve it, then straightened and kicked it through the open back door.
"You wine 'em all right, Mr. Brenn! And then they go back to the
boat all primed and you come back here alone and sit here and argue
with me."

"I won't do it anymore. Argue, I mean."

"Get yourself a nice girl from here, Mr. Brenn. From town here.
Some of them are real nice. Honest! I could . . . "

Jeff stopped him with a wave of his hand. He stared at his hand
held aloft as though it were not a part of himself. He lowered it and
examined it carefully. "Local girls, Wek," he said thickly, "they're
all sick! If they haven't got biggee-footoo, they got biggee-something-
else! Biggee-fingeree or sickee-leggee! I don't know what all they
got that's biggee. They sickee-biggee-leggee-missee!"

"Some of them got things wrong," Wek said. "Sure! A lot of them.
But you could pick one out and then have a doctor look her over. That
way you'd be sure."

Jeff leaned way over the bar. "Confidentially, Wek, the doctors
are sick too. Everybody sickee! You ever hear of the *lossfell,* Wek?"

"I've heard about it but I don't believe that kind of stuff. Nobody's
skin ever gets *that* loose! But a lot of people here got . . . "

"Sickee, sickee, that's what they got! Only you no sickee and me
no sickee too. Make you feel proud, Wek? Just think!"

"Think? Huh! Sometimes I worry," Wek said. He polished
hard at the lone faucet in the sink. "Only once in a while though—
not often. Not me! Huh! All the boys here do. And not because you
put all that money in the flower pots for them to find either. Money
isn't . . . Sometimes we all want to help. Remember the time Selfi
tried to? Remember?"

"Shuddup! Hear that, Wek?"

126

"Sorry."

"OK, Wek. All I said was 'Shuddup'. That doesn't mean a thing. Don't get sore. Tell me some more about old Gainsy, Wek."

"Mr. Gains," Wek said, "the man you replaced. And he wasn't old! He was still a young man and a fine . . . "

"He was funny," Jeff said. "He was a damn scream, old Gainsborough was. I met him in the Company office in New York before I . . . You know what he does, Wek? Wears a tight belt when he takes a hot shower. Afraid he's going to step on his own skin!"

"Nonsense," Wek said. "He was a fine young man. It was just flies. Flies bothered him and you know how that goes. All day he'd hold his hand this way and then he'd . . ."

"No flies where he is now, Wek."

"Good," Wek said. He refilled his sand saucer from a tin can stashed under the bar and placed a neat row of limes beside the saucer. "Glad to hear it, Mr. Brenn. Now let's . . ."

"Screens," Jeff said. "His room has screens now. The house furnished the small mesh ones, and the Company furnished the heavy ones behind it. They thought a lot of old Gainsy."

"Mr. Gains," Wek said. "A fine man. You should have met him when he first got here."

"Yes," Jeff said. He rubbed his hands dry on the side of his pants. "Look, Wek. I listen to you make one crack like that and I waste my last four drinks. So pour me four more." He turned to watch the porter switch on the lights. A generator throbbed faintly, the lights not yet steady. By the time the man had made his rounds, moths were beginning to flutter in. They hit the lighted bulbs with soft thuds and spiraled dustily to the floor, spinning. "Good God, Wek. Suppose I had a real, honest-to-God, live, pretty girl sitting next to me—right now. Right here! Is that too much to ask?" Wek looked up, then quickly down again. He was giving one corner of the sink minute attention. "A blonde, Wek. Just let's say a blonde. With light blue eyes. Huh, Wek? Say something! Long white arms and legs! Smooth, waxy legs—no hairs on 'em and clean and fresh and shiny! Huh, Wek? And long soft hair pulled back tight behind her ears. Clean ears, Wek! Pink! Clean face and a real red mouth. And long legs, Wek! Long and shiny! Hard ones! With a thin yellow dress on. Jesus! I'd . . ."

"A very pretty girl," Wek said quietly.

"She still comes in here once in a while? Does she, Wek? Say something! Answer me. Please, Wekker!"

"Not on Sundays."

"I didn't ask that. I just asked if she ever comes in here anymore."

"During the week only when you're in your office—when you're not here. Is that what you want me to say? You want another drink, Mr. Brenn?"

"Yes. She drinks, Wek? What does she . . ."

"Lime juice," Wek said. He dug at the corner of the sink with a rubbery fingernail. "Lime juice with a little soda in it. That's all. And a little sugar."

"Does he ever come in here with her?"

"Who?"

"Her husband."

"No."

"The dumb swine! The dumb, dirty, stupid, sick swine! He's not only a swine, he's a sick swine with a black peanut heart! He's . . ."

"Too loud," Wek said. "Please! The boys'll be peeking around the corners again and you'll start throwing . . ."

"Too loud," Jeff said. "She can play the piano as loud as she wants around here and I can't even talk. She plays so loud, I can hear it nights. She must live around here. Some time I'm going to follow her and see where. She plays Chopin, Wek. Appropriate, huh Wek? Sometimes she plays all night long when it's so Christly hot and quiet and I stand by the window and way way off across the river I can hear somebody call me and I go out there—I really do—way out there alone and . . ."

"I used to play a piano," Wek said, "back in Switzerland. And I just wish we had . . ."

"You couldn't beat a drum, Wek. Confidentially, not even in Patagonia, that is. Much less a piano in Switzerland!"

"If there was one here, I'd prove it!"

"You couldn't prove you're alive! That's what's wrong with you!"

"You want to eat dinner now, Mr. Brenn?"

"No!"

"The boys are ready to serve it and on Saturday nights they like to . . ."

Jeff walked to the dining room, stepping gingerly over the polished dance floor, careful to keep his heels from breaking the silence. His table was set and the waiter pulled back his chair, face immobile. For a moment Jeff stared at him as though he were a fixture and then at the steaming tureen of soup on an adjacent table. "No," Jeff said.

"No thanks. Maybe later," he said. "Maybe I'll have some later. Here, have some money. Take a lot and have fun! And split it with that belly-robber friend of mine in the kitchen."

He walked the length of the grass carpet to the stair and up to his room. The shutters were closed and the room was hot and sour-smelling from dead kitchen odors, trapped. He took off his white coat and threw it across the room. Then he slipped down the knot of his tie and fell diagonally across the bed. There was a mad throbbing at the base of his skull and his shirt stuck to his back.

It was a little past midnight when he awoke. The cuticle around his fingernails felt tender and sore where the roaches had nibbled it down to the live tissue. Someone had opened the shutters and a thousand stars were softly framed in the open window. He undressed and threw his damp, wrinkled clothes into a corner and stood by the washstand, soaking his fingertips in the tepid water and bathing his hot temples and aching neck. His body felt damp as he slipped into his pajamas and groped for his slippers. At the door he picked up a light walking stick and quietly let himself out.

The bar was closed and the dim night-light in the lobby threw grotesque shadows on the wall. A huge clock on a pillar, face un-glassed, slammed out the seconds. Jeff helped himself to cigarettes and matches, then pushed open the heavy door and tiptoed down the steps to the dusty ground-shell street.

The night was dark and quiet, a skyful of stars outlining the motionless palm fronds overhead, yellow sputtering lights marking the street corners. He walked slowly, not caring where he went. His slippers made only a soft scuffing sound and now and then a dead leaf scraped drily over another. He passed the shuttered frame houses and listened to the muffled coughs. Someone was always and always and forever coughing. Day and night. Dry high-pitched hawking and shell-dust coughing. The sound barked out from somewhere within the house he was passing and then from across the street and again faintly from the distance. "I walk along the Street of Sorrow!" Jeff called it out, loud, then bristled and spun around at the sound of his voice. "A Bastardly Boulevard of Broken Lungs!" he said, louder.

Listlessly, he turned a corner and found himself in front of the convent. The waist-high marl wall in front was white and chaste-looking, the tiny crystals like miniature stars. He brushed off a section of the top and struck a match, examining it closely for ants and bugs. Then he pulled himself up and dangled his feet, thumping the wall with his heels. "Quiet," he thought. "Everything's dead. Everything just died this minute!" He turned slightly as the faint tinkle of a bell reached his ears. The sound came from somewhere deep inside the darkened building behind him. "Ice in a glass?" he thought. "Could be, but isn't. Ice is habit forming stuff," he thought, "that's not it."

He kept thinking of what might be going on in there. They could be having an eyeglass-stomping party, he thought, but hardly. Slam your glasses against a stone-block wall would make a sound like that, he thought. Or how about a garter-snapping party? A little bell on a garter and then snap it on a hard white thigh would make a sound like that, he thought, if you were constituted to put up with bell-ringing preliminaries. But Naa! Think they'd wear fancy garters in there? Silk underpants? Naa! But what did they wear? Some kind of rough stuff. Sackcloth! That's what it was! Sackcloth and then ashes too, of course. Ashes on their heads and sackcloth on their be-hinds! Rattan underpants! Good, thick, substantial, woven-under-water, unbendable, sackclothable Rattan-pants!

Stop it, he thought. He jabbed his stick into the ground beside the wall. The movement startled a large rat nosing around the base of a nearby palm. It scurried to the protection of the shadows, ran whisker-to-wall along the base and disappeared between the square iron bars of the gate. "They follow me around!" Jeff said, and the high sharp sound of his voice made his body-skin suddenly crawl and pull tight. He spun around to look at the other side of the wall. Wek's right, he thought, they stink! "Rats!" he said loudly. "Where are you, Rat? Where is my wandering rat tonight? Come here, my friend. A rat is a rat is to ratify yourself!" The bell inside the building tinkled again. "Ratation!" Jeff called out. "Raterpolate! So you won't answer, huh? Well then, Ratifigoddamnation, you bell!"

It wasn't a rat at all, he thought, nor a mouse in the bar last night. But yes they were. That wasn't a bell I just heard but yes it was. It was a little silver bell, delicate, engraved with a hang-tough motto and somebody turned over in sleep and was lonely and frightened at the unearthly silence and just barely tipped the little bell over and it made a friendly sound and now . . .

He shifted his weight and leaned over on an elbow. I've got to be decent to Wekker, he thought, and quit teasing him. Because he's my friend and someday I'll tell him so too! Sometimes he worries about me, Jeff thought. Imagine! And it's not the money I hide in his eternal bar rag and the . . . And it wasn't too long ago, he thought, that I first saw her . . . He was sitting in the lobby that Sunday morning, alone, trying not to think of the insufferable heat, when she walked in. "Good morning, Wekker," she called. Even the sound of her voice was cool and light and lemon-fresh from a windswept hillside, he remembered. "All right if I play the piano?" Her eyes really were light light blue and sparkling wet.

"But of course, ma'am!" Wek said. "Anytime! Anytime at all!" Switzerland Wek who knew what it was to want to play the piano and not have the opportunity or perhaps want something as much as life itself but never get it. "An honor!" Wek said.

Jeff looked past his magazine and watched her walk to the empty corner. Her pale-yellow dress was of some wispy material that billowed out behind her as she walked. It pressed against her thighs in front and showed the outline of her knees and her firm round legs. Her blond hair was pulled back tight from her face and held in back with a simple gold clasp. Her hands were like living, tinted wax and as she struck the first experimental chord, her lips parted a splinter's width and she tossed her head to one side. She swayed gently, a soft outline undulating on the bench. Jeff looked at her round white arms, creamy and full—the shiny smoothness. And her legs! They were bare and glossy and firm. Not a scar, not a blemish, not a swollen chigger bite on the ankles. Nothing to mar the smooth white shininess.

Suddenly he felt himself rising and strolling toward the bar. As he walked past her, he averted his face, whistling drily, then suddenly aware of the vaguely-familiar, spicy perfume that beat into his veins. He sat at the bar and ordered a whiskey-soda.

"Hot today, isn't it, Wekker?"

"Yes sir," Wek said. "Make the wind come knock me today, Sahib! It's always hot here, Mr. Brenn, but feels like today's going to be a melt-me-downer!" He wiped his face in the crook of his elbow and went back to the sink.

"May I ask you a simple question, Wek, and get a simple answer? No rush. Think it over."

"But of course! Anytime! Anytime at all! An honor!"

"What the hell are you always and always and forever doing in that goddamn sink?"

"Cleaning up, Mr. Brenn."

"What makes it so dirty around here?"

"Oh, bugs and roaches mostly. Run all over everything. I got to keep washing everything. Mice too."

"You agree then?" Jeff said. "About the mice. Huh, Wek? Go ahead. Admit it now!"

"Bush mice, Mr. Brenn. You can't keep 'em out. And if you don't wash up behind 'em, Oh me Goddo! They got some kind of powder on 'em and when that gets wet . . ."

"Makes a paste, eh?"

"Smells," Wek said. "High and sort of ripe. Even a little sweet like that pink talcum when it gets wet. One time I . . . "

"OK, Wek. *Okay!* Now look at your hands," Jeff said. "Just look at them!"

Wek held his hands up and looked them over critically. They were swollen and water-wrinkled and the nails were soft and thin. "It's from always having them in water, Mr. Brenn. And the lime juice. Lime juice'll do that to your hands. Acid in the peel. And roaches. Forget to pull your net down some night and they'll fly in and . . ."

"Roaches, my foot! It's from slopping around in that sink all the time. Don't do it, Wek!"

Wek threw the lime peel into a bucket under the sink and wiped his hands on his apron.

"Give me another drink, Wek. And if you want to dissolve your hands in that sink, go ahead!"

Wek took the glass and poured the whiskey over the ice remaining in the glass and filled it with soda. He slid it deftly across the bar and turned quickly away. The heat rose in thick moist waves and through it Jeff could feel the soft, easy beat of the piano, bewitching, his whole body wanting to squirm, a huge knot in his viscera holding him rigid.

"*Wekker!* For God's sake!"

"What?"

"Who's that girl playing the piano?"

"There's a girl in here and she's playing a piano?" Wek, back turned, seemed to query the bottles he was arranging with such fine precision on the bar shelf. "Hmmmm, Mr. Brenn. I don't know who she is." He tapped one of the bottles the width of a dust mote back into line. "I never met her," he said.

"Come in here often?"

"No," Wek said. He squinted along the row of bottles and tapped another one into place. "No, I can't say she does. These shelves sure get dusty, don't they, Mr. Brenn? If I don't . . ."

"Alone?"

"Oh sure. Always. Shall I fill it up, Mr. Brenn?"

"Yes please. And thank you, Wek! That's the first time you ever asked me that." They looked at each other closely, only the width of the bar between them. "She plays a piano like an artist," Jeff said. "Just listen to it! A girl so pretty you can't breathe right and then she can . . ."

"Let me tell you about Switzerland," Wek said, "when I was young. I took piano lessons and if we only had . . ."

"Please," Jeff said, "don't! Don't repeat yourself. And don't argue. Just ask me that question again, will you?"

"Shall I fill it up, Mr. Brenn?"

"Yes please, Mr. Wekker."

"That's they way to order 'em up, Mr. Brenn! You drink a lot but not fast enough. On a day like this, drink it faster! A *piano!*" Wek said. "Good *God!*"

"I'm doing the best I can, Wek. Just don't goad me! And tell one of the boys to clean those piano keys. With alcohol!"

"Yes sir."

Jeff sat with his elbows on the edge of the bar, hearing the throbbing beat of the piano, watching Wek halve another lime. He looked into his glass, studying it intently, suddenly clenching it in his fist and draining it in one long gulp. Wek placed the bottle on the bar and turned his back.

In less than an hour she was gone. He watched her rise, her face long and narrow, ghostly pale now. She walked to the stair landing with haughty, long-limbed strides, pirouetted, her wispy dress billowing far to one side. Then she was gone.

"Couldn't you say something to her, Wek? Couldn't you even say 'Goodbye' or 'Please come back sometime'? You have to stand there like a lump of wet meat and just let her go and . . ."

"She's gone? Well, let 'em all go," Wek said. "But don't break the romantic spell by talking it over with 'em." He took a glass and started to polish it. "In these romantic places, you only say 'Goodbye' once, Mr. Brenn. You know that! Don't louse the romance! Listen!" He set down the glass, snapped the towel and swung into high falsetto. *"The romantic tropical moonlight and the motionless palms and the white sand on the beaches and the soft stars!"* He slammed the towel against the wall over the sink and dropped his voice. "Soft stars, Mr. Brenn! And soft heads! And soft bugs and hard centipedes a foot long and . . ."

"Three feet, Wek! Not . . ."

"OK. Three feet. You want to eat dinner now, Mr. Brenn?"

"What's for dinner?"

"Same thing every Sunday noon, Mr. Brenn. Chicken soup, red snapper, roast beef, string beans. Canned peaches for dessert. Libby's. Always the same Sunday noon."

"Real chicken today," Jeff said. "I can smell the wet feathers." He tore at the knot in his tie and slipped it down. The sweat ran unhindered down his neck. "Bring me a bottle of high-wine at my table, Wek. In an ice pail. And tell Selfi I want to talk to him. Right now!"

The soup was scalding hot. It tasted unsalted and smelled greasy. He could feel the hot steam of it on his face as he sat there. The steam condensed on the spoon handle and made his fingers slippery. The waiter hovered near and then, without waiting for instructions, removed the bowl of hot soup and carried it back to the kitchen, winking at the porter en route as they passed each other.

The porter stood at mock attention, eyes sparkling, grinning widely. He asked, "Something, sir?"

"Yes. Big job for you, Selfi. Makee muchee monee!"

"Yes sir."

"Know any girls?"

"Yes sir! Many!" He chuckled and bent down to laugh. "Yes sir! Fine ones! Big ones and . . ."

"Bring one up to my room."

"Just now? In the daytime?"

"Right now! Bring one up there and tell her to wait. I'll be up in a little while. After I eat. Here, take this." He placed a bill on the corner of the table.

"Thank you! Thank you, sir!" The man scooped up the bill and stepped aside as Wek brought the ice bucket to the table.

The door of his room was ajar and Jeff knew someone was inside even before entering. She sat on the edge of the bed, sagging it deeply, grinning coyly.

"Hello," she said simply. "You send for me?"

"Yes I did," Jeff said. "It was nice of you to come. Selfi told you?"

"Oh yes! I know!" She smiled.

"Would you like some wine? Or some coffee or some cigars or something? What would you . . ."

"You want I off my clothes now, Mahn?"

"Well, yeah, off 'em. Might as well." He was leaning against the door-jamb, trying to run his wet fingers through his hair.

She leaned over and took off her shoes. Her feet were wide and flat to the floor. Her ankles were thick and chigger-bitten and the backs of her heels were grayish-pink. She undid her blouse and slipped it off, not looking up. The blouse was spotlessly white, stiff with starch and wax-ironing. She hooked it stiff on the back of a chair and as she reached over, Jeff saw the backs of her heels again. They were turning brilliantly pink. Then she loosened one of the straps holding her slip. The harsh white light beat through the open window and the heat-flies buzzed madly about the room. There was a sweat-dried-in-talcum-powder smell in the air. Chalky and acridly sweet. She coughed. She struggled with the other strap and finally slipped it over her heavy shoulder.

"Let's have some wine," Jeff said. "No?"

She looked up at him. "First, Mister Mahn," she said, "I tell you wahn ting."

"Tell me wahn ting, you Percheron then! What?"

"I have wahn sickee sore."

"I don't care you have wahn hunderd! Percheron!"

"You want I put wahn piece paper over she, Mahn?"

"Wait!" Jeff said. "You wait and . . ." He whirled and struck the half-open door head on. He backed and tore through the open part, down the stairs and brought up in front of the bar.

"Wek! Wek! Here! Take this!" He shoved a roll of bills across the bar. "Take this upstairs to my room! There's somebody in there and give it to her. All of it! Tell her I'm sick or I had to go someplace and I won't be back. Quick!"

Wek took the money and melted through the door behind the bar. He was back before Jeff could light a cigarette.

"That's all right, Mr. Brenn," Wek said. "They get in the hotel sometimes. They sneak up the back stairs. I'll tell the boys to watch it better." He lighted Jeff's cigarette and then quickly averted his face. "And now, what'll it be, Mr. Brenn? So hot today!"

"Mix me some black velvet, Mahn. A lot of it!"

"The champagne's all warm. No ice either—won't get any 'til they turn on the generator tonight. How about some lime juice and soda?"

"No! Black velvet, Mahn! I like it warm!" He watched eagerly as Wek poured out the half glassful of stout and then added the fizzing, warm champagne. It bubbled and hissed as though boiling and sprayed his nostrils as he tilted his glass and poured it down. The sweat stood out in big drops on his forehead. It ran down his cheeks and dripped from his jaw. "Warm again today, isn't it, Wek?"

"It's always warm in here," Wek said. "No air gets in here. Stuffy."

"What difference does it make if air gets in here or not? It'd still be hot air, wouldn't it? Well? *Wouldn't it?*" Jeff's eyes were glassy and the sound of his voice came to him from far, far off—an old, lost, beat-up echo—returning at last. "Tell me about the hot air, Wek."

"Aw, Mr. Brenn," Wek said, "my clothes are stuck to me now. Even my shoes are wet. If we start to argue, it'll just be . . ."

"OK, then. All right. How is it with dogs then, Wek?"

"Dogs?"

"You told me to send for a dog once, didn't you? Remember?"

"Dogs are nice," Wek said. "They make good pals. Shall I keep filling it up, Mr. Brenn? Keep it full? If you drink it faster, it'll cool you off quicker."

"Yeah. Remember what you told me about how those white dogs got those black spots?"

"I wish I'd never mentioned it," Wek said. "You want me to get you a towel, Mr. Brenn? You're getting wet as . . ."

"It's raining in here, Wek. Just a romantic, tropical, tepid rainstorm. Romantic as the hell!" His elbow slipped off the edge of the bar and landed in his lap. "Or maybe this goddamn rathouse is on fire!" He teetered on his stool and tried to stand up. "Know something, Wekker?"

"What?" Wek curled his fingers over the edge of the bar as though ready to vault it. "Have another," Wek said. "A quick one!"

"You should have been on one of those trips with Columbus, Wek. The second one."

"Why?"

"Columbus'd kicked your fat butt right over the side of the Pinta Maria for saying that. About those white dogs with the black spots."

"Yes sir."

He sucked noisily at his glass and blew the foam and the sweat from his upper lip. "Dogs bark a lot, don't they, Wek?"

"Some of them do. Not all of them."

"Bark at the moon, don't they?"

"Sometimes they'll do that. They quit when you say so though. You can train them. In Switzerland I once had a . . ."

"A goddamn piano! I know! But can you train a dog to take his fur coat off?"

"No," Wek admitted. "That's all they have and . . ."

"How would you like to wear a fur coat, Wek? Come on now! Tell me! For Christ's sake tell me how you'd like to always and always and forever have to wear a fur coat! Tell me that, Wek! Give me a simple answer for once!"

"I wouldn't like it."

"Well then, quit trying to sell me a bunch of dogs!"

"Yes sir."

"And where is she?"

"Home, I guess."

"I know! But *where?*"

"Let me fill up that glass again," Wek said.

Now the heat was a solid flame that had him pinned against the bar. He struck at it, viciously, fanning with half-closed fist. His arm muscles shrivelled and shrank into hard knots as he reached for his glass again.

After a while Wek placed the empty champagne bottle and the three empty stout bottles on the sink and went around to the front of the bar. "Let's go upstairs now," Wek said. "You've had an awful lot today, Mr. Brenn. Really my fault but. . . ."

"Keep your hands off me, Wekker! Y'hear?" He brushed Wek's hand from his sleeve. "Talk but don't touch!"

"But I just thought . . ."

"Never mind what you think! Keep your fat roach fingers off me! You just want to argue! Go sit in your dirty sink!"

"Yes sir."

Jeff lurched in a long curve toward the stairs, grasped the rail loosely and stopped. The stairs extended high, high up to no ending, into the dim grayness. He took the steps one at a time, clinging to the rail, knees buckling. At the half-landing, he turned and began the second half of the climb. And then there was that rat. It was three steps above him—where it always waited for him—just obscenely quivering there, getting larger and smaller and larger and smaller. Its nose vibrated into a grayish blur and its white whisker-hairs were pulled back tightly against its long thin cheeks. Its rubbery tail dropped limply off the edge of the step, coiled itself, then lashed out like a whip. Now the rat suddenly appeared on the step above, reared up, smelling and snuffling its paws. They were pink and covered with a soft, powdery bloom. Jeff uttered an obscenity and stumbled up the stairs, kicking and lurching from rail to rail.

At the top of the stair the rat turned and humped itself down the long dark hallway, half a kick beyond reach of Jeff's feet. Just before reaching the door to his room, Jeff saw the round black hole in the baseboard. With a final snap of its tail, the rat disappeared into it while Jeff slammed into the wall, kicking at the hole below, beating the wall with his fists.

Wek was there then. Perhaps he'd followed behind or perhaps he'd taken the back stairs. Perhaps he'd been worried. His arm was around Jeff's waist and he held him in a firm grip. "What's the matter, Mr. Brenn? What happened?"

"That rat waiting for me again! Then he runs down the hall and . . ."

"A rat, Mr. Brenn?"

"In that hole down there, Wek! For God's sake! Some day I'll . . ."

The marl wall began to feel wet and clammy and through his thin pyjamas Jeff could feel the sharp little crystals numbing his skin. He slid down and let his feet touch the ground. He felt weak and old. Very old. Wearily he started back to the hotel. He stopped and listened for a possible last tinkle from the bell but two dry leaves scratched out a sound and from far off the sleepy call of a night bird. Wek was right of course, he thought, but when did you start to admit it? Infallible Wek with his sandy lime peels and his eternal bar rag was always right. Good, old anchor-man Wek. On that hot Sunday afternoon in particular, Wek was right. God, but he'd been right!

Upstairs there in that hallway, Wek released his grip around Jeff's waist and gently took his arm. "There's a hole?" he asked kindly, looking down. "Now you show me where it is and I'll have one of the boys . . . Sorry, Mr. Brenn."

ROBERTS JACKSON:

Fly Away Home

That they were alone surprised her. Something was gone and yet she couldn't think what it was. The sun was high, the air cold and exhilarating. A nice day as far as Sundays go. Stem had taken on the traffic going out to the Orange Show and steered a path through it, one so wild and serpentine that neither knew when they had reached San Bernardino and started to climb, or, for that matter, how far up the pass they had come.

It was funny, on a motorcycle, how absorbed both of them got. They paid no attention to towns. He didn't like to stop and ask directions because it wasted traveling time. Nor did the girl, because it made her think of tomorrow; more than that, because the distance to the top of a mountain was their own affair. Knowing exactly would put them in a class with tourists — flabby, self-indulged. Yet in country like this it was hard to tell where you were at. She did not like the feeling and tried to think back.

Counting local cops and gas stations and all the intersections they had snarled, putting each in its proper place as best she could — doing that might bring her up to date, although she had no idea of the actual number. They had mounted a sidewalk once, but because it was a natural thing to do in emergency, she had forgotten where it had happened. Near the state hospital at Patton, not that this mattered, but somewhere in there.

Her clearest memory was of a station wagon driven by a nun, who was dressed as she was, in black. Her riding pants were that color, and her favorite pair of boots, and, under her leather jacket, her silk blouse, which cost as much as Stem made a week. No one could say she hadn't got her money's worth, for they made a nice contrast with the white kid jacket and the jeweled belt around her kidneys. The nun would have loved such fancy material. She was sure of it. They had recognized something in each other the half-minute it took Stem to pass, something as futile as wanting to trade places if only to know what the feeling was like, and every bit as sad. Shutting her eyes, she could see the woman's expression as they went on by, the envious stares of the children in the station wagon.

Out here looked as though it didn't have much to offer in the way of excitement. She bet Sunday was the big deal, yet it was not in her to feel sympathetic, not now. Those kids had a home, and after reaching a certain age they were going to find out what she had learned at Girls' Republic: that church, though a good excuse for going into town, did not help you unwind. It never went far enough. And while she was thinking this over in relation to herself, it all slipped out of reach entirely, not because she wanted it to happen, but because of how glorious she felt.

Other things had already been dealt with: the suspicion that Stem wasn't as sick as he pretended; her hostility to Dr. Bauer. To none of it was she indifferent. She had put them off as long and successfully as this because they were men, neither one of whom listened to what she had to say. On Monday there would be a legal commitment which would make her further resistance useless — a paper bearing both signatures, so that her whole life seemed to consist of lost arguments and flattery.

The countryside was fading now as if bleached by ammonia. She was aware of it all in outline, yet there was little to cling to in the disconnected places unless it was Greyback up there ahead of them — and she couldn't do that. She wouldn't dare. For as long as possible she fought back lightheadedness, then with a grateful sigh gave up to it.

The air was delicious, so hard and pure she raised her goggles and let the knowledge of it dilate her eyes. They stung like fury, and the wet places down her cheek would chap in the wind — still, she didn't care. What trifles had concerned her never would again. She was drunk on the smell of greasewood, woozy and halfway gone, until the solitude added its finishing touch and speed brought them together as nothing else could, raw speed.

The thrust of it, the surge of noise surrounding her; noise, which couldn't be heard, burning her ankles: this was the wonderful thing about a motorbike. It seemed to lift her right out of herself, to purify any thought she had and tie it in with what was beyond and in store for them.

Already the road, just as she had dreamed it, was a strip of magnesium foil burning ahead of them through each successive foothill until it reached the mountains, there to be extinguished in a pile of boulders. Their bodies caught some of its fire as the dips grew more frequent and the pressure on the curves more exciting. Yet with Greyback no closer seemingly, the February sun cold and skeptical, with Stem unable to gauge these things for himself, she had to grasp his arm. When the pace was slow enough to suit her, she smoothed away the tiny wrinkles she had twisted into his sleeve, counterclockwise, and locked her legs tight to his body. It was imperceptible to Stem. She did it without thinking.

They were climbing now. It was colder. Sage had changed to the crooked green of manzanita. There was buckthorn in blue patches along the firebreak, like old tattooing. Both were caught unawares when the road left its course and zigzagged up a small ravine. *Broo-ahhhh* went the motor and the exhaust grew hot enough to see. They shot out of sun into shadow and back into sun; the accumulation of sound at each of these sharp turns was deafening.

She saw it hurt his vanity to have to shift into a lower gear. He was crouched forward trying to glimpse the grade in relation to some landmark that would tell him its steepness, but there was nothing to go by, which amused her. The cliffs had closed in, there were no straight stretches to speak of, no trees. Yet she knew their degree of climb without looking back at the canyon below them — at least here was something her breasts were good for, inertia pulling them up and down, back and forth, as free as a spirit level — and this advantage over him made her laugh.

However, this discovery didn't make up for the deadliness of their speed. Stretched back in the seat, just so, she let her foot drag along the hardtop. Danger made it somewhat exciting. Her toe was inches away from the orange spokes of the wheel and now and then collided with pebbles which brought it closer. He did not like her to do this, but she kept on, hoping he would sense it and turn around. She needed his attention suddenly, wanted him to tell her what a bitch she was, as if he meant it. For just sitting there didn't prove you really existed.

And how dreary it was to stare at the back of his neck while he enjoyed himself, had all the fun. Stem was at his best steering a motorcycle, but his best was not what it should be. She had felt this her first ride. What he couldn't say, what he couldn't feel, he expressed through the Harley-Davidson, and with her sure sense of timing these things came alive. At present he was somebody else, removed from all that was familiar to them, though of course he could not shut her out indefinitely. Despite talk about tomorrow being arranged "to his own best interests," she always would be on Stem's side, unlike the Doctor.

Just the same, it angered her that he failed to see this, and while she considered telling it to him for perhaps the twentieth time, they came to a rise in the hill, which brought them back into a canyon she recognized, except it was wider up here, more deeply indented. The bike again picked up speed and with it her power returned. She clung to his chest as they went singing across the Mill Creek bridge, its steel against their tires, moving brilliantly as the stream below them and as fluid.

Spruce trees floated by, and in one there was a chipmunk. She reached out her hand to it, and seemed to touch Greyback instead. The peak stood out supremely blue, and though a different shape at this angle, it dominated the range, the cleanest, most formidable of mountains. She was left a little stunned.

Looking up, she felt everything flow from her into Stem, each private thought, tiny impulses she had not been able to communicate. It was as if Greyback, seen from her bathroom window, was still fifty miles away, and they would never get there. Both worked as one vessel, leaning on the outside curves, banking on the ins. They seldom left the white line, even where the road was beginning to buckle through frost and winter rains.

The whole world lay in the swivel of her lap. Mountains seemed to respond to her slightest pressure, as did the sun, the sky, and crags towering above them, down to a blemish on Stem's neck from an old carbuncle. She was at the very center of things, and time a glint of chrome from the handlebar. Of no more importance than that.

When they got to the Forest Home and stopped at Igo's for gas, she felt shaken inside. Her legs were wobbly. And to regain composure she walked away from Stem, although it tore her to do so, up the log steps into the store where six or seven people sat by a fire, getting warm. They were quiet as she came in. A woman let her breath out, as though swallowing dry. The man in the polo shirt got up and stood behind the counter.

She bought candy, Cheese-Its, some meat spread, and a tube of camphor ice instead of Mentholatum because it didn't smell. Then she read about campfires, National Forests, and stoves in cabins, giving herself something to do while the men whispered behind her back. The woman was too timid, although she could feel the little mouse memorizing every stitch she had on. When she finally could take it no longer, she turned to stare with open hostility, her chest inflated, which had its effect on them all.

"Beer?" she asked, her voice harsh. "We'll want it in cans."

The man stopped to consider. "I don't keep it on ice, girlie. It's not worth fooling with out of season."

"That's not what I asked you."

"How much did you have in mind?"

Inside she was set against him, his whole manner, as oftentimes she was set against herself. She gave a disdainful glance around the room. "Whatever it takes for *them* to get a buzz-on, double that." She could think of things she would rather drink than warm beer. Stem wasn't crazy about it either, yet she wasn't going to let this man get the best of her, sick as he looked, nor as bothered by her now. His wasn't a weak face.

"Tell you what," he said slowly. "You folks come back — in, say, an hour." He nodded toward his living quarters. "We can crowd some into the cooler."

"No."

"All right. Give us an idea where you'll be staying and maybe one of the neighbors will haul it for you later on. That suit you?"

"We'll take it with us, thanks . . . if you can bear to part with it, Pop."

"How many?"

Everyone put off breathing in order to hear what she was going to say. If they hadn't been so nosy at first, she would have felt sorry for them. Otherwise it seemed too late for such hopeless people. They sat around here on Sundays, in a grocery store, hoping someone would stop by and give them something to think about. Well, what she had to say would last them the rest of the year, and in her mind she increased the order so they would have something good and big to hash over.

"I don't know — a case. A case and a half."

While that sank in, she walked across the room to a slot machine, her hips swinging. She jingled the change in her pocket like a man, pulled out some quarters and put in six in quick succession, then walked outside before she saw if any coins were returned. The machine was still spinning.

Stem was on his knees, fiddling with the carburetor. She knew that nothing was really wrong by the way he worked — staring hard at the ground while he made complicated finger adjustments. Let him play important if he had to, she didn't mind. She was going to kid him about the Harley-Davidson, his sore spot, except that the man brought the beer and there wasn't time. Six quarters lay on top of the carton.

Stem looked at the beer shaking his head when the man caught his eye and winked. Then wordlessly they packed it away in the saddle-bags. There was nothing she could do but sit on the steps and count them — twenty-eight cans, which was all they had room for.

"Fine-looking machine," the man said.

Stem nodded, the half-scowl making his face look ever so much darker, for he was never sure that people meant what they said.

"Much of a drain on you?"

"No more than cars," he answered. Their eyes met, but it was the man who turned away first. This seemed to please Stem for some reason. Pointing out the advantages of a motorcycle, he talked more than she had heard him in the past six months. He forgot to stand up straight, held his shoulders relaxed, so that in faded green cover-alls he didn't look so small and top-heavy and pigeon-chested.

Teeth on edge, she sat listening for fifteen minutes while it sounded like one woman urging, and the other wondering what it must be like to turn professional. She coughed at this because it annoyed her. She sighed, had an ironic conversation with herself, then caught sight of a face at the window before it disappeared, which was the last straw.

"Say, you, how's the trail up there?" she broke in, pointing toward Greyback.

"What makes you think there is one?"

The man looked at her with new interest, then back to Stem, who made a wilting gesture with his hands and pulled out a chamois to polish the metal flaps, the brightly enameled tank, the glass dials of the dash. He looked like a rebellious little ferret, poking in and out of things. His hair was too long. Some day she would make him shave off those sideburns he was so proud of, she decided.

"Why not?" Her tone was critical. "I get around." Nor was the abruptness lost on Stem.

She waited to hear more about it, but Stem remembered gasoline and the two men filled the tank, busying themselves with the saddle-bag, where they strapped on an extra can of two gallons. Half the beer came out, only part of it got packed in again. Stem took the hint when she walked over and claimed possession of the seat, climbing on, too. He knew her patience was gone, that she might make a scene, and no wonder. He'd become absolutely impossible.

"You're not going to try her on this?" said the man. "That old lady is cold and steep. You'll freeze."

Stem kicked the starter for an answer. The motor took hold, which marked the end of fooling around.

"Don't do it," the man shouted.

She touched Stem's arm to idle down. "Tell me why. Wasn't it meant for motorcycles?"

"Oh sure, sister. It's what the CCC boys used to say, but they were the ones who built it. You'd expect them to brag. That trail hasn't been kept up since then."

Stem let out the clutch, anxious to do so before she could signal, and they started up the road with the man running after them. "Your change," he shrieked. "Slot machine's broken. You didn't have a chance." She made a derisive gesture that included the people on the porch. There were no more doubts, for they were climbing in earnest. It was even a different sound, and she didn't trouble herself to look back.

On up from Igo's the road was dusty, tortuous, and unpaved. Every fifty feet they came to a deep thank-you-ma'am, which jolted the bike and set her back to aching. She tightened the belt with careful fingers, impervious to pain, and saw a dust cloud trail out in back of them for miles. Air currents scooped it from the road in a continuous piece so that it seemed to be sky-writing. To look at it made her dizzy.

They passed the Dolly Varden, a beer hall and dance pavilion, which was boarded up. She tried to imagine what it was like in the summertime, but failed.

And before long they were lost to each other. Something didn't jibe. Stem was going fast enough, yet his movements were wooden. He held himself in and headed straight for a stretch of washboard, which pounded the frame and was punishing to them both. She let that one go by until he did the same thing again, then understood that his heart had gone out of it, that he wanted to turn back.

About to lose her temper, she determined not to, to play his little game for all it was worth. She had the seat, the easiest place to ride; Stem straddled the tank up forward. His legs could take only so much pounding in that position, which was tough luck considering his insides. But since he had started this, she would see it through, and let the best man win.

They squeezed every bump out of the road until both were hurting, and it felt as though they were opposed, on different motorcycles. She had long ago lost track of time. To sit upright raised the center of gravity. Leaning out when the bike came in of its own accord, resisting Stem at every turn made it tiring for him, but her teeth ached. She tasted dirt, the goggles had grown sweaty, her thighs seemed to chafe one another while gripping the seat. Her nipples were sore and hard.

It was a nightmare swollen out of reality. She felt bruised, her nostrils were clotted with dust, each hair burned. Just holding on was all she could do, praying that something, maybe his kidneys, would give out before she did. Finally it happened. When they reached the ridge route and took the narrower fork in the road, he slowed down.

He looked in both directions for a place to stop, cheeks sucked in, his face grey. They went on a bit farther, scarcely crawling, to where the road dipped down to Barton Flats. He pulled over onto a carpet of pine needles and left the bike while it was still in motion. She fell with it, over-balanced, rolling her leg out of the way and lay there panting.

When they got back their strength and had something to eat, washed down with beer, it was obvious that neither had given in. Stem pulled off his pants to examine his leg, which was purple to the knee, the veins an angry red. He applied camphor ice to both, though the other leg wasn't as bad, wincing at his own touch. Then, while she slipped out of her jacket and blouse and bound her breasts to her body with a bandana, he turned his back on her, began polishing the bike. It was deliberate, spitefully done, and this angered her.

Suddenly he looked up and caught the expression on her face, so that she turned away — in a sense, had to back down, which was galling. She freshened her lipstick prolonging it while she wondered about his stare. He might kill her, beat her up, or leave her here marooned: they were all three possibilities, yet only the last frightened her. This was the one she would fear always, because of what it meant.

As it grew in her mind, she moved toward the motorcycle, mirror in hand to keep the thought hidden from Stem. Their eyes met, then she felt terribly let-down, disgusted with herself. He was chewing a fingernail. It was so ridiculous.

"Come here to mama, Hot Lips."

Slapping his hand away, she put lipstick on him in bold red slashes, which he suffered without being fully aware of what it was. "Hold still. This'll fix the soreness." Before he could start up again, as both were getting settled, she held the glass up to his face to let Stem have a peek at what she had done. He stiffened but said nothing. Not even to her remark: "Ahhh, isn't he sweet."

He was all business after that. His judgments were expert and sure, though they were traveling faster than seemed necessary. Stem no longer sought out bumps, just drove himself in a hard, disciplined way that was encouraging. They reached Palestine Flats and sped through yellow pine. A lone cabin flashed by. Near the turn-off at

Barton a totem pointing toward the scout camp grinned back at her. Stem behaved perfectly as scud clouds crossed a range of mountains that stood between them and the desert on the other side, and there was nothing she could find fault with.

Soon they were in sight of the control road leading up to Jenk's Lake — one lane, cut zigzag through perpendicular faults and crumbling red granite until it was lost to her at what appeared an impossible elevation. Two cars, directly ahead of them, stood waiting behind the eastbound gate, but it was closed. A big sign showed in red letters the control times for east-bound traffic — one-thirty, three, and four-thirty.

For though traffic had been meager, the attendant still observed these long intervals, and she couldn't tell whether Stem resented this or found it funny. He saw the warning, and saw the people collected outside a wooden shelter, which separated one gate from the other, but as they swung left, Stem gave no sign that he intended this maneuver seriously. It was just a chance to get even, since he was satisfied scaring her half to death; only there was no time for that: to check for cars, even to see if it were safe, before they were through the left gate and going up a steep, mountain road.

He met the first descending car at a place easy to pass. The next one came fast and so unexpectedly from around a hairpin curve, her knee was grazed as they went up the bank, over a worn retaining wall, and down ten feet. The bottom of her stomach seemed to come undone, yet somehow they regained the road and kept on climbing. When she looked back, the driver stood, both fists in the air and with a front wheel hanging in space. Seeing he was all right, they waved at the same time, which was a good omen, and Stem waggled the tail of the bike. The lipstick had sent him through, with a twenty-to-one chance of making it. It was just like him to be that embarrassed.

The third car, a pick-up truck that was olive green in the sunlight, must have been warned by telephone. It waited next to an impassable cliff, blocking the road, while a man with work gloves stood waving for them to stop, a caretaker or forest official.

Stem double-clutched down to fifteen miles an hour, until he was fifty yards away from its yellow and black-striped bumper. Then he aimed for the truck with a terrifying burst of speed. Slowing imperceptibly, he made the motorcycle backfire, his spark retarded. As they came head-on, the man jumped out of the way. The bike swung onto the outside shoulder, clearing the fender by inches, which gave them as much balance as an up-ended dime.

She sat huddled up, while poor Stem, unable to pull in his elbows, let the right one drag against the body of the truck. It made a fleshy sound until the handle grip drowned this out with a higher pitched squeal of rubber. He had to choke the handlebar farther forward and steer from there. The vibration stung his fingers — just listening to it was torture enough.

The road disappeared. The wheels, pulled by loose dirt, were opposed, floundering. She shut her eyes experimentally and everything was green. On one side lay the sensation of emptiness, nearness on the other. So immediate was their danger, she could not distinguish between them, or know which to choose, yet neither one existed while she and Stem were together as close as this, not even death.

The shoulder gave away, where the road hadn't been reinforced, it seemed to liquefy, as the bike slipped lower with her weight, then dry land came up to meet them. It was solid — and so disappointing. How foolish she had been. The momentum had led her into thinking something else. But they were coming through to each other; that's what counted most. She would slow up now and wait for Stem to feel the same way she did, and for as long as she lived this would never happen again.

Jenk's Lake was small, hemmed-in looking, and she wanted to get away from the wooded shore and its half-dozen summer camps and cabins as fast as they could. It depressed her, frozen over like this, with a little tumor of smoke coming from a chimney on the far side where there was a grey, reflected light but no sun.

Stem, also, sensed that it was tame and did not fit their mood. He skirted the lake quickly until they reached the last cabin, which must have belonged to the caretaker himself, judging by its size, the fresh woodpile, and Indian blanket washed and stiffening on the line.

He turned up the front path on impulse, drove along the porch and off the other side. Rustic bannisters whirred by, she kicked over an empty kerosene can, and the bike went down four steps without blowing a tire, through a pack of dogs, back to where the road ended in a circle and the trail up to Greyback began. Stem went around the monument a couple of times, which was a brilliant beginning and the perfect end. No one had ever shared anything as fully. She patted him for a long time to show her approval; of how unquestioning his heart could be when he didn't interfere and spoil things for them both.

Their first view of the desert came at Big Meadow; then when they left its springy peat, the field of lupin which lacked color at this altitude, water bubbling up everywhere, they were in shale, enormous pencil-like pieces of it, and the trees had changed to stunted piñons. She noticed that it was stormy. They were moving under an overcast that was part of Greyback this time of year, but every so often they stopped while Stem checked the bike to keep it from getting over-heated. This was necessary since they were dependent on the Harley-Davidson, yet she found it exasperating. The trail was furrowed out of continuous cliff now and where landslides had carried it away in places, they had to get off and walk. Neither of them could see ahead, and though Stem seemed to know which way to go, mostly by instinct, it was tiring and took longer. When they came to a small ravine, he wouldn't turn back or retrace his steps, refusing to with a look that frightened as much as it thrilled her. They tried lifting the bike across, one to the other, but it was too heavy for her and Stem could not manage alone. So she scrambled over, sending some rocks below, to sit there confident that he'd figure out a way to join her.

As Stem started the motor, her heart stopped pounding, for it was impossible for him to ride across. But he ran alongside the bike, throttling it by hand, then angled off and to his right above the trail. The rear tire shot out gravel and dust. The motor, smoking, slipped to one side and burned a scar in his boot. Yet on he came while she cheered, until he was across the gap, fifteen feet away, and almost on top of her.

The motorcycle went dead, knocking Stem off his feet, and both slid down to the lip of the trail, where she braced herself to keep the combined weight from going over the side. Pebbles flowed past her body, increasing in size, until the canyon was full of thunder. They gazed at each other without smiling. The only noise left was the pinking of the exhaust pipe as it cooled, and so immense was her pride in Stem that time stood motionless until she finally got him a beer.

He sucked it in, and drops of sweat began to ooze from his forehead and grimy face. They shared the next can, which exploded under the opener and sprayed her clothes. It seemed to exalt them, to bring release from the caution of living. They were seized by a wonderful frenzy of recklessness and started working up the trail again in perfect unison.

She pushed behind the bike till her cheek was cut by flying particles. She went ahead of him to coax. She threatened, slapped him, did everything but lie down and make a mat of her body. Stem toiled up the last forty feet with his face buried in the lamb's-wool seat, and when they got to the ridge above the timber line where lightning flickered, she saw that he had bitten it, torn a piece out of the fur —

except this didn't register. They were stupefied on beer, and how high up it was. As yet he had not noticed that her side of the bike was badly dented, not because of how dark it had grown up here, but because Stem was fascinated by the sight of his arms trembling and jerking involuntarily where they rested against one knee.

Knowing the storm would catch them, she was glad, for without it they would never make the top, and her need to get there after coming so far had increased. Her face burned where she had tripped and fallen headlong against the hot exhaust. A bolt of lightning, the purest color she had ever seen, hit close by, yet the sound barely glanced off them in the wind. Nor was there a world below, and thus undistracted, she could go on indefinitely.

"Get up," she shrieked at Stem. "Get up, get up, get up!" And it seemed one of the most natural things to be beating him with a sharp piece of slate.

He rose drunkenly. Together they set the motorcycle upright and Stem climbed on bleeding while she steadied it for him. There was nothing here but motion and cold blasts of air. The trail was smooth. It ran along the ridge unimpeded, sometimes in the open, more often buttressed by stone, and there was nothing to struggle against. They used their legs as out-riggers, which helped to counteract the wind, but it did not keep the bike from swaying.

A few minutes later Stem hit a rock. It slammed her forward, which tore something loose in her neck, and she fell off sobbing with rage while he rolled back the Harley-Davidson, unmindful of her, and smashed into the boulder again and again. The tire punctured, it began to shred, spokes stuck through. And while the steel rim flattened inexorably there was nothing she could do but watch. Her muscles were poised, there was strength in them but she could not act. Stiffening with cold, she worked her way out of the gale, still facing the summit of Greyback.

At the next flash, she saw him a quarter of a mile beyond, a small, maddened bug moving among dry ice fragments and vapor. The bike inched along like a small plow, its front wheel nearly gone. Again darkness opened and he was pulling it after him, dead weight — but not up the trail. Stem was backing into the wind, struggling to reach a place on the horizon when the summit lay elsewhere, in a quite different direction.

As she always did with Stem, she got to her feet unthinkingly, impelled to set him straight, until there came a light of much less brilliance, the flare of gasoline. He was attempting to refuel the motorcycle but spilled it over the cylinder walls instead, while wind trailed flame up the sleeve to his body turning him into a torch faster than it could explode against the heated metal.

In the end there was a blast, a final separation which offended her, then darkness and freezing. It had been her mistake. For the lives of both had been compromised when Stem chose selfishly. She felt cheated, deeply hurt, yet without crying, not even angry at this betrayal, she began to crawl in the right direction. Crawling, so she would be found farther up the slope than he.

JASCHA KESSLER:

Fat Aaron and the Night Rider

I

Fat Aaron was a bloated angel. This is what the mothers called him, winking that smile about things you weren't supposed to know. Mothers, aunts, they would have been sweetly right to put it this way —you couldn't be supposed to know yet. Then, their secret might have washed down safe with coffee and buttered rolls; then, their innocent suns would have careered unswerving and unspotted above the summer, neat and simple over the rolling haymeadows, golden with birdsong and buzzing clover, in that good morning reserved for children since the night Adam covered Eve, children who are set apart romping in an idyll, still growing quiet as appleblossoms in spring.

In such dumb warm August nights the Holstein bull over the next hill bellowed black and white through the hours of that teeming darkness; he rattled the steel chain ringed in his mist-snorting muzzle, and the clanking links of his celibate bondage rang through the roar that yearned out of the pink giant skin bags swollen between his shanks, and burst from the organ pipes of his heaving chest, thundering over the valley to rattle the boards of the sleeping barns. The fields seethed with chirruping crickets, the heavens dripped meteor milk, there! there! there! A hot wind rushed up from the panting earth; flowers, berrybushes, wheatstalks of grass burst their skins; the ground reeked with the rank musk, juice and scents from the wrestling bodies and mixed sweat of things. In such nights you squatted round the gloam of a weenyroast fire as the spuds pulsed idol eyes hot in the ruined embers of a jungle temple, looking up at those bombinating skies, humming songs, and dabbling fingers with freckled brown girls whose mouths were fruit, moss their hair, and their downy arms baskets to cradle your soft melon head. While far below on the porches of the clumped cottages the mothers miched over cards and tea, or strolled the road where their flashlights glimmered like squids' eyes beneath a hot sea.

And yet, there I was, in that August, untaught, a rough boy camping on screes in the shabby tents of childhood among the stone mountains of a no land. I had trekked out willynilly from Egypt

151

with all its wealth. I had escaped that plentiful slavery of old Nile's beastheaded wizards; my garden memory was a starveling now: palaces and towers, those cities of daisies and barley where we played with blocks, gathering straw to make the bricks to make the temples and tombs—Rameses, Luxor, Heliopolis, Pithom, Thebes—distant now, fading hieroglyphs the sands in their whorling drifts scrabbled away. And the new scrolls, inscribed with new chronicles and new behests of blood and tears, my clumsy hands could not unwind nor my shaggy eyes read. Though there was a black thunderhead beckoning in the dog days, and an arm of stuttering fire by night, there was no voice in that furious music. Until I heard Fat Aaron's. And I knew he was to be the arcane, masterful rabbin of this season.

Fat Aaron was the bakery man. He delivered to the bungalow colonies. About eight in the morning the truck would bounce, bang, hurtle up the driveway, that sassy horn tooting, and skid along to a rest as if it had no brakes and no driver. The women would collect at the back. Then he trundled out of the cab, puffing and heaving, pawing and pinching his way through them to the doors. Once at his station he dispensed breads, rye and pumpernickel and wholewheat and white, sticky jellybuns, cinnamon buns and cupcakes. They dribbled from his fat fingers into the paperbags, the endlessly fluttering doves of dough miraculous with each sweep of the arms. And like the greatest of Magi palming the eggs of milk and honey, he kept up his pudder all the while, with every bagful a daub of smut. The long rolls called saltsticks he called "pacifiers," or "Wednesday husbands"; cherries in the pie he said were gathered from the hotels clustered around Swan Lake; and the plain burntsugar drynutted coffeecake was "Ol' Sarah."

I never heard enough of the pitch to quite make sense from the outside, and I was never allowed to push through the harem of housecoats. There were the heads all pressed together, pronged with those big aluminum curling pins, from among which the gray tendrils of cigarette smoke threaded up into the clear mountain morning. I'd hear his mumbling treble mutter. They would knee each other in their blueveined thighs, wallop one another's loose rumps, and screech with laughter. He was giggling too, burbling rather; the chortle foamed out of his lungs, and coughed through the tight fat channel of his throat as if they were tickling him. And, though their ringed hands, their strong bonyknuckled, longnailed, fishchopping, meat-slapping, carrotscraping, redpainted fingers picked at and patted and poked him, could he have felt anything through that blubber massed on his breast which curved under his arms from his broad back, rolling to settle over the lead vat of his vast belly? When they had their day's bread the knot broke; each went clopping back in her slippers to her bungalow for breakfast, grinning. Sometimes one raised a word of raucous warning that Fat Aaron had had for another across the grounds: "Sadie! If you can't sleep, don't try to beat it. Go see the big specialist down at the bakery!" At which a chorus of chokes and sniggles racketed through the screendoors from half a dozen coffeemugs.

I puzzled about Fat Aaron's being a bloated angel. He weighed three hundred pounds. He had the whitest lily skin, a great round head of golden curls, moist lips, cupid lips of wet pink, and downy cheeks red as McIntoshes. His skin was so white and smooth, white as the flour on his white baker's trousers. A cherub without wings I might glimpse in him, but not a seraph. Not pure, refined from all sensuality, a mature specimen of any of the host, not one of the thrones, dominations, princedoms, virtues or powers. But even cherubic there was something terrible about him. Not the fatness, though he was like those chubby hovering infants, with their gold heads and disingenuous expression: not baby, yet not adult—and you noticed their things even if they were angelic boys. They were more naked somehow than the grand naked women sprawling on velvet, more naked than a holy fat child in its mother's lap. Maybe it was his blue eyes, chunks of lake ice they were; maybe the frizzled cigarette burning always in his mouth of sharp white teeth.

II

It was near twelve Sunday night. The town still woke. Busses and cars yapped south to the city; happy people rested in the juices of the flesh were driving to the week's sweltering work. The prison gates of the rancid theater grated shut at my back and I stood in the dusty threshold of Main Street. The ache of murder was in me: my heart lusted after payrolls and molls. Warner Brothers had marked me a snarling four-reel con; my eyes were gorged with blood, my nose pulped, cheeks and skull scarred by pistolwhippings, my feet dragged the irons of a spirit brought to book. I took desperate bearings for our cottage and cut out of town.

Then, climbing the sharp hill that led my way home, I came into the cold native air blowing from the stars. Where the last sidewalks gave out, the last houses were humped snoring shadows. I stepped onto the westering macadam road for the two miles. A young moon floated at the end of it, just above the dark world's edge. It was the sire of the Holsteins, the wonderful metalled horns of the father of bulls, who cropped whole forests in his grazing meditation. The thin arc of the young moon was a boomerang brandished by the hunter of king kangaroo, who was stalking into the long Pacific combers of the night sky, the last of the aboriginal pride. It was a Viking galley; the road unrolled towards it, wavering over a blue tundra, the track upon which the wolfpelted plunderer marched. The young crescent was the mythological brow of the silver queen: the grassroot congress of katydids fiddled her virtues night long, the cottontails mumbled praises as they munched their silver salads, the owls swooped on silver fieldmice for her sport, and in deference to her virgin nudeness most creatures dropped their eyes and slept.

I topped the rise and glanced good midnight to the town sputtering out below. A truck careened past me going downhill like the yellow ghost of a comet. It was the Manna Bakery's. I turned and walked after it. There was a crossroads a few blocks back where the bakery loomed; when I came to it the truck was parked for lading against the sliding doors. I sidled up to them and stuck my nose through to get a look at the plant.

The air inside was hot moist and delicious with the aroma of baking dough: hot poppyseed, hot sesame, nuts, nutmeg and ginger, cinnamon and cloves. At the near end were tables loaded with baking trays; on the floor the great wicker baskets were lined up, some already filled with breads and heaped rolls. In the center of the vaulted room there were grouped the mixing machines, coated with flour dust, all rumbling and churning, their pronged steel arms plunged in steel cauldrons of golden batter, revolving this way and that, backward and forward and around. Far down was the bank of roaring gas ovens, and their attendant, Fat Aaron.

He was the only one there. He was ladling loaves out of the black maws of his ovens with a twentyfoot pole. His shirtsleeves were rolled up to the bulging elbows; a linen apron stained with the stiff goo of white icing, splattered with chocolate and the blood of tarts, draped from his neck to his ankles like a white caftan. He was monumentally brisk. A dozen breads at one scoop came out on the tongue as he stepped back, balancing his staff, and tipped them into a basket. After some hundred, he clanged the last little door to and turned around. He walked deliberately to me as far as the center of the hall, holding the long heavy shovel lightly upright in his right hand, and stopped mid the cluster of his thumping dancing machines, where he planted the regal ash of his baker's sceptre. His left arm swung out to invite me in. He smiled. In his high reedy voice he laughed, "Sholom, sonny! Come into the ark of my tabernacle."

He waggled a derisive wrist at the ceiling. "There's nobody else here tonight to keep me company but the living god: Baal-Berith, the lord of cookies and cupcakes; Baal-zebub, the lord of leavened loaves; Baal-phegor, the lord of the little broken hardon. Adonai must be lonely; he needs quiff to keep him company. You should have brought a girlie with you. We'd have tickled some cunny juice from her: that makes good cake."

The batter had begun to thicken; he adjusted the mixers to a slower stroke. I was set to filling a tray with cupcake paper. After a while he switched off one of the machines; when he pressed another button the arm drew up out of the sucking yellow stuff in the vat.

"Take a taste of this," he said as he stroked the vanes of the beater. Batter dripped from them and diffused in the rest of the mixture. I ran my thumb over an edge. I said it was good, and it was better actually than after it was baked.

"Dropped from heaven," he sighed modestly, lolling a pious head to one shoulder.

"What's in it, vanilla?"

"Sure, sonny. Vanilla, and a little flour, and some scraping off the floor; ten pounds of butter, a squirt of machine oil, and a little spit." He giggled at the expression on my face. "You don't believe? The baker's spit is good: the breath of life, the smoke of ruach, like God's in the mouth of the gingerbread Adam." He hawked, and spat a nicotined glob into a pot still on the mix.

"Come here and hold this sack." He handed me a long cone-shaped linen bag which had a wooden nipple at the apex. I held it spread open; he tipped the cauldron and poured the stiff batter into the open end, shoving it over with his palm. Then he slipped a ring over the gathered ends and knotted them. The whole sack went under his arm like a suckingpig to market. As I laid out the paper molds, he squeezed the dough through the nipple with pressure from his arm against the sack as it rested on his hip, and with two fingers flipped each gobbet neatly into a cup.

We worked fast. "What about the icing?" I asked when we were done.

"It's already made for this batch. Next time, sonny, you'll help. You're young and pure. It's a boy's sweet seed I need for icing.

That makes it good!" He squealed, drumming his belly.

I helped him load the baskets of bread into the pungent truck, and we went off full gun. Fat Aaron drove with his belly, so tight did that girth press into the wheel. One arm lazed out the window, the other was dropped comfortingly on my shoulders: the roads were his, he did as he pleased. The Manna truck had been so tinkered with, the muffler magnified the blast of each cylinder's stroke, groaning and boiling on the upgrades with a monstrous catarrh, and letting off slobbish dysenteric grenades as it zoomed down slopes. The nightly passage of this dragon through fifty miles of countryside was wanton; it expressed the joyous contempt and abandon of the driver who plied the gas-pedal of the highballing thing. The slipstream dragged sparks from the cigarette in his mouth. He handed me one from his shirt-pocket and I lit it from the tip of his.

He said, "This is one of the beautiful facts of life. You don't know enough to like it. You're still a kid, cabbage is the leaf of your heart. Look at you, you're skinny with innocence. But me, I deliver the staff of life, I'm round on all sides, white bread and dark bread and nutty dough."

I laughed at him. He pulled over and stopped on the peak of the spur of Walnut Mountain. "And here's another fact." He drew a bottle of whiskey from under his seat, drank, and passed it to me. "It might burn at first, but drink it."

It seared; I swallowed bravely each time he urged me. We walked to the edge of the road. "Look at that country," he said. "Soon it's going to be all yours; but you won't like it."

"It looks all right to me," I said.

"Yes, from here that quilt looks like a bed of delights. But once you get down there for a good whiff it's all small, it crawls with scurrying sucking people. They're vampires."

I didn't say anything. From that height I made nothing of it. Yes, a bed, heaped and various, of hummocks and pastures and glacier-rolled valleys, stands of trees under starlight like patches of black broccoli, ponds and lakes where there was darkness visible, and simple scattered blocks of guileless habitation. What could he see, I wondered, in that lambent void which was to my vision mere massy landscape?

He drank and continued, "Look over there. Swan Lake. We'll drive to the hotels, The President, The Ambassador, The Swan Lake. That's a world chock full of girlies. The lights are still on in their rooms. You know what they do all night? They dance and they swizzle. They stand by the windows naked, and they comb their hair and look at the stars. Lovely. What I see in those bully buildings you couldn't imagine. Let's go, sonny."

I leaped to my saddle in the truck and he squeezed in behind the wheel once more. The road coasted around the south end of the lapping waters of Swan Lake and descended between ranks of maples and poplars. We ran down and turned into a gravel strip that led to the rear of The President. Most of the windows, line over line for five stories, were dark. We lugged several baskets into the quiet kitchen. In the vague light the long galvanized tables gleamed dimly. The stoves and sinks and dishwashing machines were empty, quite dead; the floor was a holystoned spotless deck. Only an old white tom hissed, stretched himself, and shuffled away.

While Fat Aaron scribbled the bill, I went outside to look around again. The buildings seemed asleep; there was no life of the night to be seen. I strained to see something. There, it might have been the glimmer of a languorous form; no, there, what I thought was a lifted arm and the nubile ivory of a breast, a delicate hand caressing the rondure of a young belly. No. Yet they must be there behind the bluey sheets of glass; any moment a shade would roll generously up, or a ripple of cuddled laughter would sound. But the night brought only the sough of summer through foliage, the clunk of rowboats against the little wooden wharves a hundred yards off.

We stopped at The Ambassador, The Swan Lake. We delivered orders. Fat Aaron whispered of what he'd seen just the night before; he pinched me and prophesied wonders. And, yes, there were some lights, there were momentary insignificant shadows that moved in rooms; there were some murmurous voices, the tinkle of a dropped tumbler, gushes of water in hidden plumbing; but no music, none of the promised cries of ecstasy, no noises of pleasure at all.

Each time he came from the kitchens he asked me what I'd seen, and I shrugged in disappointment. "It's there," he insisted, "you're blind, sonny. The world is too cunning for you." His eyes brimmed conviction as he flapped pictures with his obscene magical fingers. "But wait, we'll go up to Miriam's at White Lake. She keeps the gold calf. I'll show you what's what."

By that time my brains were flaring. We bowled along in the skies, plunging and rearing with the contours of the earth. Fat Aaron cursed and laughed and sang words I couldn't distinguish in queer tunes that never were, and he made the truck skitter at sixty miles an hour.

Then we were there. I stepped down in front of an old foursquare frame building sided over to simulate logs. It was a tavern backed by the lake: The Harvest Moon. About a dozen cars were parked off under the trees. Inside, the lanterns over the bar were dimmed; the front door was locked, but the lights on the second floor glowed through drawn blinds, and a jazzy hullabaloo was blaring upstairs.

He rattled the door. No one came. He kicked it, and sent me to hold down the horn of the truck. Finally, a shape appeared and moved along the bar. "Miriam," he whispered. The door was opened to us. They grappled on the sill. In a bassoon throat as deep as his was high she boomed out, "Angel cake! I thought I'd have to have a party without you. Come on in, virgin, you're on time; the joint's jumping. . . . Who's the man of the world?"

"Sonny? I was shorthanded tonight, so I snatched him from his pisspot of a mother. He's pimply, but he looks already at home with that bottle."

"Doesn't he stare!" she rumbled, and, latching hold of my ear, yanked me to her. "What a sweet present, Aaron: a ladyfinger."

Miriam, cased in green satin, bangles and bracelets of gold on her arms, loops and rods of gold freighting her ears, was as big and as fat as Fat Aaron himself. Her hair was an auburn mane: without pins or curls, it parted from the middle of her brow and cascaded to her shoulders where it fell as it wished over her bare arms, down her back, and down the freckled expanse of two breathing monadnock breasts. She crushed my head between them and I smelled the thick richness of the living body of an orchard. But when she bent her head to kiss me, it blew a west wind of gin.

The stairs climbed to a posh parlor beneath whose scarlet ceiling clouds swayed of a strange sweet smoke. In the center of the room an ivory babygrand was surrounded by clubchairs in which a trombone, a clarinet, a sax, and a trumpet slouched. They made music that no leg or heart ever beat to. I slumped in a couch.

There was a throng in the house who drifted in and out of the music joined head to knees in a kissing sigh. Like smoke they came and they went; doors banged down halls; there was singing, laughter, men growled and shouted, women shrilled in delight, in pain, in anger; there were muffled chants such as I'd never heard, though human voices made them. And the music played on and on, slow and cavernous, so slow it barely moved, or whipping, looping in the eyes so swift it dazzled like sheet lightning in the muggy glow of the room. The buzzing place was rank with the writhing and kicking of naked ruddy arms and legs.

Suddenly the trumpet flourished a clarion fanfare. I was yanked to my feet by a hand of long nails and rings twisted in my hair, and dragged to a ring where I swayed between the hips of two tall women whose arms were hot around me. The music had stopped. Then, with lonely hooched chords it began again.

Knees dipped, arms wagging loose before them, their bellies grinding and bumping, Fat Aaron and Miriam snaked to the center of the circle. Their faces shone by sweat; their eyes blank and orbed, they approached, gyred, retreated. The music stepped up its rhythm and the crowd clapped and stamped in time, shouting, "Go! Go! Go it!" The dancers thumped their backsides, bumped stomachs, swivelled, pressed and bumped, faster and faster. At the moaning climax their hands grasped each other's hair, the auburn and the gold. I joined in as the chorus yelled, "Go! Go! Go!" and I heard his whinny and her contralto laughter sounding over the music.

III

I knew in my stupor that I was back in the truck, running through mists. As we farewelled for dawn, simple years of prince and princess crowded cheering to the banks of childhood. I was aware of the wet road, the cool dripping gray trees and the dank fernery past which we rushed. He said nothing all the way. When the truck slowed on the last hill I stumbled from it with a loaf of bread under my arm. It never stopped, and as it picked up speed Fat Aaron's pinkwhite arm fumbled out and slammed the door shut. With a last sneering blat of exhaust, it disappeared over the russet crest of the hill into the jubilee of dawn.

I stood on the shoulder of the road breathing the dew-washed day. Rank upon rank of air in light, grain in the fields glinting against the first shafts of the fresh sun and rippling in the blue breeze, the grapes bunched from the green arbors, swallows barrelling over the treetops, the hawks spread in the upper skies. As I walked down to the colony across the wet lawn to the white cottage, the sun shone full hurrah for victory. .So this was Canaan! The green flesh of the world, that solemn land, was mine.

M. M. LIBERMAN:

Fineboned Shoulder and Boyish Arm

I

When you are a young boy, it is natural, I suppose, to compare other men with your father and to like them—and him—more or less, accordingly. I do not recall that I was not fond of my father, a handsome, serious man with a mustache; but I could not get very close to him in spite of his manifest love for me. Uncle Ed, his brother, was something else, altogether. He was a thinner, younger, less stolid edition of my father. He laughed a lot and treated me as an uncle is supposed to treat a nephew when he (the uncle) has two daughters; like a son, as they say, but without the uneasiness attached to the real thing. No duty, no responsibility. Uncle Ed was concerned only with making me like him and he was not disturbed, as my father often was, if I behaved in a way to suggest that I might not grow up to be a sound man.

When I spent vacations at his home, Uncle Ed seemed bent on being free and easy. The way he couldn't be with the little daughters, that's how he was with me. He would demonstrate his new camera equipment and explain the virtues of a new pipe and, when I was a little older, he would tell me vaguely off-color jokes. He even gave me, from time to time, a half glass of beer. Aunt Dorothy seemed pleased that we enjoyed ourselves.

There were other things, too, about my uncle that made visiting him better than being home. There was the atmosphere of position, of vague affluence. I could feel it especially when I was out with him. He was a dentist in a small community. Everyone knew him. They smiled and waved and called, "Hi, there, Doc." I liked sitting next to him as we drove through town. I knew everyone seemed fond of him and I could feel the good will communicated to me. At times I felt as if I might like to open the car window and shout, "He's my uncle. He's my father's brother. He likes me a lot." Then, at dinner and later there was an absence of care in the house. There was nothing there of the trials of business life brought home and displayed for everyone to be depressed over. Unlike my father's dealings with "the public" Uncle Ed's did not sour him. Finally,

160

when I went to bed (much later than at home) I fell asleep almost
before I could savor the warm feeling of being completely protected.

Sometimes I would get to Uncle Ed's place and find my grandparents Miller there and then I wouldn't have as much fun. First
of all, I wouldn't have my uncle to myself and then Grandma and
Grandpa would follow me around, directing my behavior with cross
admonitions. They, too, showed much affection for me, however. But
they gave me a pain.

Grandpa was, in a way, retired. He had come to this country with
his father. When a boy, he took to traveling around our part of the
state selling things, almost anything, house to house. Later he opened
a kind of shop and got a license to dispense glasses and was a licensed
optician. He was not really old, but looking back, it seems he was
always tired, solemn and withdrawn. I think neither he nor my
grandmother knew that there was a kind of life in which the heart-
aches, the wants and the worry, could, in ways, be watered down.
They were always poor. Grandpa finally closed his shop once and
for all, not because he could afford to but because he could ill-afford
not to. For a time they lived on what the stock brought after bills
and then he went peddling again, this time by bus, but as things
turned out, he must have done poorly.

One year, when school had let out for the Christmas vacation, I
ran all the way home to supervise the packing of my things for a
week with my uncle. It was Friday and on Sunday my parents were
to drive me in. When I got home I felt a strange atmosphere the
moment I crashed into the house, and after I yelled for attention once
and then a second time, I felt I ought to quiet down quickly for it
was more than silent in the house. Yet I knew my mother was not
out and I found this a little alarming.

I stood for a moment in my galoshes, dripping muddy water on
the hall rug in violation of strict orders about leaving them on the
porch. Moreover, in my haste, I had left the front door open. The
house was uncommonly dark, I noticed, but before I could reflect
further on the oddness of things, my mother came downstairs. Her
face was a frightful white and her eyes had a strange filmy look. At
first I was only puzzled, but when she didn't say anything about the
mud or the door and just put her finger to her lips and said, "Don't
wake Daddy," I started to cry. She cried too. Then as if on signal
we both stopped. I looked up into her face and she told me Grandpa
was dead. He had killed himself. On that cold mid-winter morning,

he had gotten off a bus and walked into a lake. He had walked until the freezing water came over his head, filling his lungs, choking the life out of his defeated body. He left a suitcase on the shore and there was a note on it. It said he didn't want to be a burden to his children. My mother sobbed as she told me this and I nearly stopped breathing to listen.

In all the unhappiness which hung in our household I forgot, momentarily, my projected visit to Uncle Ed's. But when the novelty of the death wore off, I felt disappointment.

According to custom, Grandpa Miller was to be buried the next day and I was told that while my parents went ahead to take care of Grandma, I was to stay with Mrs. Tobias. Mrs. Tobias would take me to the funeral.

A family friend of long standing, Mrs. Tobias was a fat, busy, unkempt woman, given to much talking and elaborate displaying of emotion. She had a kind of husband, a little wordless man. She took it for granted that I felt very bad about my grandfather's death. Her drab imagination would have been boggled had she known that, at most, I felt a certain mild compassion for my parents in their time of heartbreak and a great deal of annoyance at my own physical discomfort occasioned by the strangeness of the Tobias household. Moreover, I was beginning to feel that, in the way things had turned out, an injustice had been done to me, somehow. Had anyone realized that my vacation had gone out the window? Nevertheless, Mrs. Tobias persisted in looking at me pityingly and clucking and, in reference to my dead grandfather, saying again and again, "Oh, that poor man, that poor man."

That night I got to sleep with great difficulty, only to be awakened by Mrs. Tobias. She gave me a glass of warm milk, which I didn't want, and said something about catching cold. I was too tired to protest. Before I fell asleep again, I heard her talking to her husband in the next room. "Nobody took care of that old couple. I know *that*," she was saying. "*This* one's father makes a living and *Ed* does even better. It's a shame. I heard he didn't even have an overcoat. He was wearing a thin, little topcoat. They say Ed told him he was going to buy him an overcoat, but who remembers an old father? Not Ed. A happy-go-lucky, but for his father—nothing. He thought he was a burden to his children. Imagine! God in heaven it's awful. It pays to sacrifice for children. Yesterday, it pays."

All at once and for the first time, I felt a real love for Grandpa and felt sorry that he had died and I cried myself to sleep while Mrs. Tobias talked on.

At Grandma's house, after the funeral, Uncle Ed put his arm around me and tried to smile. "Come and visit us when you have your next vacation, keed," he said. I told him I would but when spring came, I convinced myself I had other things to do. My parents couldn't understand it. I told them that I would rather hang around with my father.

II

Now, more than anything else I wish I could talk to my father. During the long summer evenings when we sit on the porch and the warm sounds of my mother doing the kitchen chores and a cow lowing at the edge of town commingle with those of an anguished train whistle, he waits. I know he waits for me to say the words I would gladly say, more than gladly, if I knew them. Can anyone understand that it breaks my heart that I don't know what to say? The little, tentative, cautious, almost frightened exploratory thrusts; they mean he wants me to say something that means: father, I know, I understand, father, I can prove it, father, by telling you this or that much about my secret self, the self that I don't know and don't know for a certainty that I want to know; those little cautious thrusts like the embarrassed virgin touch of a boy-lover's hand, only the two middle fingers, say; they bring me more deep-bruising pain than a thousand exacerbated fists and still I cannot say the words and cannot be sure I could say them if I knew them. The pain is great enough to cause me in turn to strike back and the stupid circle of pain and remorse becomes ever wider, a forest fire of pain, guilt and remorse where here and there a grove gives on to an open road, which, when I get to it, closes in a sheet of red in my face as if out of sheer perversity.

He says: Oh stay up for a while, it's early, it's too warm to sleep.

I sit down again. I say: All right, I'll have a smoke and then I'll go to bed.

"Your car running OK isn't it?"

"Yes, it's all right."

"You get good mileage?"

"No, not very. I never did."

"I get good mileage."

"Good."

My mother says: Always drive carefully. Lots of crazy people on the road.

I'm tired. All day I've read. My eyes are like two pits of sand. New books have come from New York and last night I dreamt that I was locked in a room lined walls and ceiling with books and I was not worried about how I could get out, only about how I could read all the books, all the books in the world.

I have said to him: I read because it's important to me. I don't read because I have nothing better to do, because it's summer and I'm home. I read because it gives me more pleasure than anything in the world (not quite the truth but as much truth as there is for my father: do you understand that it grieves me that I don't know the truth for my father?).

"Your mother thinks you're bored."

"I read because I like to read."

"She thinks you should be out with young people."

"I like to read."

"She thinks you're worried about something."

"Oh for God's sake."

"She thinks something's bothering you you're not telling us."

"For God's sake nothing's bothering me and if there were would you expect a man my age to tell you about it?"

"It's your mother. You know I don't interfere in your affairs. I don't worry."

"I like to read."

"I understand. It's your mother."

"Ah, you're as bad as she is. Jesus Christ I'm going to bed."

She says: Gordon.

He says: OK, OK, I'll sit here alone.

I say: Mother's here.

He says, "She's tired. She'll be going to bed in a few minutes too, but g'wan, I don't care."

"You're always doing that."

"What?"

"Making me feel as if I'm deserting you. Making me feel ashamed. Here I want to go to bed and you won't let me go without making sure I feel rotten about leaving you alone."

Mother says, "Gordon, you talk like a ten-year-old. He doesn't care if you go to bed. G'wan if you want to go to bed. Nobody's stopping you. We'll all go soon."

"I've been trying to go to bed for the last half hour. Every time I get up he says what's your hurry, it's hot, it's early and he looks at me as if I were deserting him, abandoning him. He gives me that hurt look."

"Ah, what in hell are you talking about?" he says. "For God's sake go to bed. What do you want from me anyway?"

To her: "Ever hear such a thing? Just wanted to talk to him a little bit. What did I do?"

In bed I turn and fret until I see a stairway going up, up and then down into my sleep where the steps are impossibly wide and soiled and are at crazy angles to the damp, cracked walls of an old movie-house. Here my father is young and peacefully, plainly happy and handsome, the small handsome man of my earliest recollections in which he is carrying a bag of pop-corn as we go into the enormous side-street door, past gorgeously colored posters of a man in green, carrying a sword and leaping over a wall to a girl standing demurely in the middle distance. At the foot of the stairs, my father, a very young man with a black mustache, tells me we want pop-corn, don't we, and he gives the man behind the little black case something and laughs and hands me an oily paper bag and smiles, he is so happy to be with me, more loving than when he comes home at night and frowns and complains that it is impossible to make a decent living. I look at Doug Fairbanks look at the girl on the wall and push my hand into the oily bag and my father nibbles from the top of his, all the while looking at his son, not the stairs, and he stumbles and falls flat and hard on his stomach while his hands and feet are out in all directions like a crab and the pop-corn bounces like a battalion of bugs and the ticket taker at the top of the stairs and his companion laugh so hard they are nearly in tears and I hate them so fiercely I nearly cry too and inside I soon tire of Robin Hood. The evening is ruined for me in the pop-corn and sweat stink of the Happy Hour. I try to lift my head off my chest to look at Doug in the funny tight suit and then at the man next to me, my father, who is watching the screen as if he has forgotten me and I do my best to stay awake and then suddenly I am bolt upright having heard the outraged scream in the next room and my mother's voice saying you had a nightmare, Ben, and my father saying I saw my father in the water.

JACK MATTHEWS:

Sweet Song from an Old Guitar

Elsa trundled about in the kitchen, rattling her coffee cup in a saucer and pacing like a bear, her slippers flapping on the uneven floor.

"God DAMN!" Tommy yelled from the dining room. "Come in HERE to drink your coffee and stop that PACING!"

She appeared at the doorway, shoulders hunched forward, brown sweater twisted on her thick arms. Her pretty aging face was shiny with a kind of lachrymose dew which had settled upon her these past few weeks.

"Now what the HELL is the matter this morning?" Tommy demanded angrily.

"You know what's the matter, Mr. Lott."

"No I DON'T know what's the matter and I don't GIVE a damn. What's more, come in here and sit DOWN with me and drink your coffee. You know I don't like to eat my breakfast alone. That's why I took you on as my housekeeper."

Elsa followed the old man's ferocious mumbling with alarm and, when he finished, her mouth twitched and her eyes glazed with tears. She caught a warning hunch in his shoulders and decided that she had better not indulge in weeping until she was alone in her room. It was not the grouching she minded, but his nastily referring to her as a housekeeper. It brought to her mind discomforting visions of insecurity.

And when she had sat down, he asked her again what the hell was wrong . . . knowing full well, she thought, but just being mean in drawing it out.

"It's almost seven years since I came here," she said slowly, sucking on her lips after the words were out.

"Seven YEARS!" Tommy roared.

"That means, according to my brother who's a lawyer, that in the eyes of the law I'll be your wife, having lived alone and under the same roof with you for that period of time." She said this with the dignity of possessing technical information. "Seven years," she repeated, sipping her black coffee and eyeing him over the rim of her cup, while his head bobbed angrily above his scrapple and eggs.

166

"God DAMN! Don't the law know I'm already married?"

"The fact that you are already married," she said, speaking calmly and trying to straighten out the silverware at her plate, "doesn't necessarily mean that your wife inherits your estate. Since you've been apart over ten years, and she has never sued you for alimony or even divorce . . ."

"You're AWFUL God damn sure of yourself, aren't you woman? My ESTATE!" Tommy spat a piece of pork gristle out of his mouth, missing his plate and scratching it off the table cloth with his fingernail.

"No, I'm not, Mr. Lott. Who knows, I may not live to collect a thing."

"You're healthy as a damn horse, and HEALTHIER than the front end." Tommy laughed at this, stroking his eyebrows lovingly, his mouth gaping wide, a fleck of egg white on his dry lip.

His crude humour steadied and comforted Elsa. Her hand picked out the cup handle on the first try, and raising the cup six inches off the table she said calmly, "I'm not speaking of the state of my *health,* Mr. Lott."

She waited ponderously for his reaction, but seeing nothing but the top of his head, swinging in preoccupied arcs above the plate, she decided to reveal all. "I mean, Mr. Lott, that I may be DONE AWAY WITH!" She was appalled for an instant, because her voice had come out exactly like his. "That's what living with him so long has done," she told herself.

He cast a small look of interest at her. "Have you taken your nerve medicine today?" he asked.

"My nerves are all right," she said airily. "Oh, you may joke!"

He dropped her from his interest and for a full minute she sat listening to his vigorous chewing.

Then, abruptly, he raised his head enough to see her through his eyebrows and said: "Just what the hell do you MEAN?"

She sucked on her lips for an instant and fondled a teaspoon. Then she said, "I'm not so dumb. Some people may think that I don't know what's going on, but I've got plenty of time to think and my brother being a lawyer . . . don't think I haven't had some good long talks with him."

Having finished breakfast, Tommy subsided into an attitude of meditation. He fingered tobacco out of his can of Sir Walter Raleigh and rolled back in his rocker, bumping the table solidly with his knees. The old house creaked in response to the rocker, or so it seemed to

Elsa, who had never felt completely easy here.

"Just what have you and your brother found out?" Tommy said, without removing the pipe from his mouth.

"Well, what I'm talking about now isn't something I've exactly gotten straight from my brother, but it's something I've figured out with his help, you might say."

"Just what the hell IS it?" Tommy yelled, rocking violently.

"Well, it's about your wife. Mrs. Lott, that is."

"Fern? Hell, Fern wouldn't do NOTHING!" His voice, though loud and emphatic as always, seemed suddenly to lose conviction.

"I wouldn't be so sure of that," Elsa said faintly, a knowing, sad smile on her face.

"Just what would FERN do?"

"Just what wouldn't she do!" Elsa said in a hushed voice. "If you only knew some of the things she's said to me, you wouldn't put up with her ever setting foot in this house again."

Tommy puffed and hummed meditatively, his eyes rolling back in his head and his eyebrows filling with smoke.

"After all, when she left you alone it seems to me that she forfeited any rights she might have had as your wife."

"What rights?" Tommy said quickly, crossing and uncrossing his legs nervously.

"Well . . . just rights. For instance, what if something should happen to you before I go. Then what will I do? According to the law, I might get something if I've lived with you seven years, but . . . well, I've been thinking that maybe Fern means that I shouldn't live with you seven years."

Tommy took the pipe from his mouth and did not try to disguise the wonder in his voice. "You mean DO AWAY WITH YOU?" he bellowed.

Elsa nodded. "I wouldn't put it past her. That woman's not in her right mind. If you only knew some of the things she's said to me, why . . ."

"Fern knows I don't have any money," Tommy said.

Elsa pursed her lips and said nothing, but kept a stubborn look on her face to show Mr. Lott that *she* knew very well he had a sock full of fifty-dollar bills hidden away, and that she knew that *Fern* knew.

"Fern wouldn't do nothing," Tommy said. As he talked, the pipe bobbled up and down and then it sagged abruptly, where the bit was held together with a thick nub of dirty adhesive tape. "God DAMN!"

he bellowed. He righted the bowl and brushed ashes off his trousers.

"Don't forget," Elsa said, "that she's getting older, too. And she might just feel desperate enough to do something, now that she sees the seven years coming to an end. Her brother's dead now and she's all alone. She might want to come back here and get me out of the way so she . . ." Elsa's nose and eyes started burning with tears and she had just barely strength enough to sniff them back.

They sat silently for a few minutes, he puffing on the pipe and casting looks at the weather and she shivering in her sweater. To save on gas bills, he kept the thermostat on sixty-seven.

Finally she said half-aloud, "It's not just any woman who'd put up with what I've put up with, Mr. Lott. When you've been drinking and beaten me with your fists . . . oh, you don't understand what it is to be a woman and helpless and you never did understand your own strength." She said this last to mollify him, for she knew it made him feel proud.

"I've never touched you," he said mildly, still looking out the window and rocking and holding his pipe in his fist while he puffed at it mightily, making it bubble like a silex.

Elsa sucked her lips and said nothing.

Presently, Tommy went outside in his coatsweater (she warned him of both flu and pneumonia), and when he had left, Elsa climbed upstairs to the bedroom to put on a pair of shoes. She heard a car slow down and her heart beat swiftly for a moment.

But the car went on, and Elsa hurried to the window to see if she recognized the license number of Fern's car. Whoever it was had disappeared under the heavy branches of the elms up the street and Elsa calmed herself, thinking, "She'll have a fight on her hands if she tries to turn me out of this house after I've put up with him all this time."

Then she began to cry, and when she walked downstairs, she could not see clearly, feeling her way step by step, her hand on the banister. "If I fell, that would bring him running. And it would bring him to his senses, maybe. How good I've been to him!" Reaching the bottom step, she crossed the hallway and peered through the uneven glass of the door, rattling in the wind. She saw Tommy with his hedge clippers, leaning over the privet and puffing serenely on his pipe.

That evening Elsa decided that she should search for his sock in the storage shed. Tommy decided to go downtown and, when she saw him walk away down the street, she hurried to get her coat out of the closet.

It was a blustery evening, with thick, oily clouds coiling overhead. A stiff wind full of winter chilled Elsa's bare legs.

Inside the musty shed she felt even colder. She groped for the light string and when she found it and turned the light on she was— as always—startled at the clutter about her. Stacks of old newspapers and magazines, boots, old shoes, discarded suits and women's hats from fifty years ago, a neatly coiled garden hose, desiccated and cracked, a broken wheelbarrow full of jelly glasses, cigar boxes crammed with rusty nails and bolts and sticks of wood . . . so many things, indeed, that Elsa was staggered and didn't know where to look first.

But finally she started searching in the clothes, going through each pocket with numb fingers. As she was picking at an old frock coat she heard a scraping sound at the shed door.

She whirled around and there stood Fern, poised and bright-eyed.

"Mrs. Lott!" Elsa gasped.

"That's my name," Fern said, staring at her brightly and working her mouth back and forth as if she were chewing on something. She was a dumpy, erect woman with thick gray hair growing sturdily out of her head, which she kept partially covered with a felt hunter's hat sporting a long pheasant feather.

"And what are you doing in Mr. Lott's shed?" Fern asked, nodding her head up and down as if she were answering yes.

"Why, I'm just looking for a better broom than Mr. Lott keeps up there in the kitchen."

"Well, look away, my dear, for you won't find a thing in this old shed."

She turned and left Elsa standing there and looking about her at the confusion in the shed. Then she realized with horror that she was still holding the frock coat. And that despicable woman had seen her seaching it!

And what was Fern doing here?

She hurried into the kitchen, sniffing as she walked, as if she might smell disaster in the air.

But in the house all was quiet. She saw Fern in the hallway, taking off her coat, and she rushed in.

"Here, I'll take that and hang it up in the closet," she said.

But Fern drew it back sharply. "You act as if I was a stranger or something," she said, showing her expansive teeth in a hearty smile. "Goodness, I guess I know my way about my own house."

"I suppose you do at that," Elsa said numbly, fingering the newel post and gazing at the healthy roundness of Fern's body.

"Of course I do."

"You look robust," Elsa said, gathering herself together.

Fern looked above her airily and walked into the sitting room. "Same old-fashioned furniture," she said as she sat back in a rocker, kicking her feet and thumping the arms with her fists.

And then: "Where's Tommy?"

"He went out about an hour ago. Downtown, I suppose."

Fern arched an eyebrow up at Elsa. "Drinking?"

"Lord, I hope not!" Elsa said in spite of herself. And then: "May I get you a cup of coffee? Have you had dinner?"

Fern lurched out of the chair and walked to the kitchen. "My, I guess I know how to make coffee!"

When Fern had the percolator going above the gas flame (turned so high Elsa could smell the wood handle scorching), she looked directly to Elsa and said, "You know I'm still married to Tommy."

Elsa tried to say something but her throat was glued together.

Fern continued: "Now that my brother's dead, I have no place to go. And this is my home, legally speaking."

"What about my seven years!" Elsa managed to gasp.

"What's that? What's that?"

"I've been here seven years, and you've been separated over ten years! According to the law, you don't have any more rights!"

"Who's to say ten years?" Fern took off the spitting coffee pot and placed it on the frayed linoleum counter.

"The neighbors," Elsa said. "Everybody."

Fern looked thoughtful a minute. Then she sighed. "Well, let's be friends. There's no need of our quarreling . . . although I put up with him for over twenty years, and it seems a downright sin that you should just put up with him only seven, and then come in for all his money. And speaking of the money, I'm surprised you'd bother looking out there in the shed. Tommy'd never hide it out there. I guess I know him better than that.

And at that instant, they heard Tommy on the porch.

"He must be all right," Elsa said.

"Yes, at this time of night, he must be sober," Fern agreed.

Tommy walked into the kitchen, his mouth open in wonder. "God DAMN!" he said when he saw Fern.

"Hello, Tommy," she said brightly.

"You back here AGAIN?"

"That's right, Tommy."

"Well, there ain't nothing for you here, woman. You left ten years ago and that was your choice. I got nothing for you here. My house-keeper and I manage pretty well." Elsa could not help noticing a sudden meekness in him. And his glances through his eyebrows suddenly appeared guilty and abashed, instead of ferocious.

Fern was laughing confidently. "Tommy rot, Tommy Lott," she said, gurgling.

Tommy charged out of the room. "Get rid of her, Elsa," he said.

Fern looked at her and laughed whoopingly. "Isn't he a crusty old dusty?" she shrieked. And then they heard Tommy pounding the floor in his rocker.

Elsa felt she could have killed her on the spot.

Although Fern left that night, she appeared early the next morning, walking in the front door without knocking.

Tommy was smoking in his rocker at the table and Elsa was cleaning up after breakfast.

"Would you like some breakfast?" she asked Fern as she appeared in the kitchen.

"Land sakes no! I've eaten hours ago. I'm used to getting up early and getting my day organized. I couldn't get so much done if I didn't."

Elsa could see Tommy's head peering around the door at Fern every time his rocker came forward. He was puffing up a cloud of pipe smoke and his eyebrows were thick and low.

"Well, hello, Tommy!" Fern beamed, as if she hadn't seen him until this instant. "What are you doing in there all alone? Nobody to keep you company?"

"Don't need no God damn COMPANY!"

"Lord, but this house is in a mess!" Fern said, looking all around over Elsa's head. "You need a woman here, Tommy, to take care of you."

She walked with tiny, prim steps into the dining room while Tommy roared in irritation, pretending he was clearing his throat at the end.

"Just look at this house, will you? I'm going to do some cleaning and organizing for you today."

"Don't NEED any!"

"Oh, come on now, Tommy! A Tommy Lott you know about such things. Men don't even pay attention to things like that, but they appreciate it when it's done."

"I think I just ought to tell you," Elsa said at the kitchen doorway, her voice hoarse, "that I clean this house each and every day and I reckon I do a whole lot better job of taking care of my OWN affairs than some other people I could name!"

But Fern was walking into the front room, head thrown back and eyes searching the corners. "If you want to help, Elsa, you could use some wallpaper cleaner on these walls, and I'll just go upstairs and start tidying things up on the third floor. That's a regular firetrap up there. The idea of all those papers and magazines and things up there has always worried me."

Fern started up the steps. Tommy and Elsa listened in awe for a moment as the stairs creaked on up to the third floor.

"God DAMN!" Tommy whispered hoarsely. "She cleaned me out once before and now she's going to do it again!"

"What do you mean?" Elsa cried.

"Oh LORD! I've hid some money up there, some place, and I can't remember where!"

Elsa threw her hands up in the air. "Let's go up and look, too."

Tommy hurried out of his rocker and strode across the floor. "She cleaned me out once before when she left."

"She'll find the money and leave again. Just leave us alone to starve!" Elsa cried out, following him. "Are you sure it's up there? I've been through the third floor several times, just sorting things out."

"It's up there somewhere," Tommy said, panting in his pipe and stopping to rest a moment at the top of the first flight of stairs.

"Can't you remember where?"

"No. GOD DAMN if I can!"

The third floor consisted of two dingy rooms on either side of the stair entrance. The floors of both sagged away from the small hallway and the ceilings were slanted from the gabled roof. Each room had a single window with the bottom sill almost touching the floor. The rooms were filled with the accumulations of Tommy's life. He still made occasional trips to the third floor, carrying any old thing that was beginning to get in his way. Fern had frequently referred to him as a pack rat or a magpie, building his nest high up under the eaves.

Now, Fern was bending stiff-legged over a box of family photograph albums. When Elsa and Tommy reached the doorway she turned and walked swiftly toward them.

"It's no bother for me to do this. You two would just get in my way up here. Now shoo on downstairs and leave me alone while I do my work."

174

"WOMAN!" Tommy roared. "Get out of my house. You're TRES-
PASSING, GOD DAMN IT!"

"Oh, Tommy rot, Tommy Lott! Now just turn around and get
back downstairs where you belong. You go downstairs with the
housekeeper."

"Don't forget I've been here just about seven years!" Elsa shrieked.

"Seven, eleven," Fern said, frowning. "Can't you ever get that silly
number out of your silly head?"

"OUT OF MY HOUSE!"

"Just call the police, Mr. Lott!" Elsa suggested.

"Why, what an awful to-do you both are making. You certainly
don't think anybody'd put me out of my own house."

"You've been away ten years; you can't just push me out!" Elsa
said.

"Of course . . . now I know. That's it. You think you can just come
in here and take over my house, not to mention my husband, just because I happen to be living with my sick brother, and now when my
poor brother's dead, you think I don't have any right to come back.
Oh, I know your kind, but you can't pull that sort of trick on me. So
just stop trying. And you too, Tommy Lott—why, I'm ashamed of you,
siding with this woman!"

"I AIN'T SIDING WITH NO WOMAN! I JUST WANT YOU
TO GET OUT!"

"And where would you expect me to go, pray tell?"

"Go back to your brother."

"He's dead and you know it."

"Well, that's all right with me."

"Tommy, this is not time for a Tommy-joke."

"OH LORD!"

They suddenly had no more to say to one another. Tommy and
Elsa started going through things in the other room and Fern continued where she had left off.

It was not long until Elsa was attracted by a rattling semi-musical
sound. She looked up and there was Tommy with a dusty, battered
guitar in his hands, plucking a flaccid E string and frowning mightily.
Then he cast the instrument roughly aside, and when it jarred against
a cardboard box, Elsa saw a piece of faded blue cloth in the circular
hole beneath the strings. Prudently she said nothing. And by the time
they had all decided to quit for lunch, her stomach was so screwed up
with excitement that she was afraid to open her mouth lest her voice
break.

When Fern left that evening, Tommy was "in an awful state" (as Elsa expressed it to herself), fumbling about the first floor like a wounded sea lion, shagging his eyebrows at Elsa, cursing Fern with the eloquence of a blasphemous Moses, complaining of his stomach, the wind blowing leaves all over his sidewalks, aching feet, the price of lumber (God knows what he wanted to build, Elsa thought), the crime rate, deterioration of property in his neighborhood (where his house seemed to Elsa the most decrepit), sewer taxes, lawyers, over-emphasis in college athletics, and the Anti-Saloon League.

Reaching this last topic, Tommy veered steadily for the wooden cabinet beneath the sink, and Elsa thought Oh Lord several times and began to take inventory of the Tommy-inflicted bruises on her body. The old man filled a jelly glass half full of whiskey and then sloshed in some water from the faucet. He went to his rocker and sat there drinking for several minutes.

Then he made another drink and filled his pipe and turned on the radio. Elsa, sitting huddled in the living room, realized that he was suddenly as calm as a field of July wheat, and, peering around the corner of a sliding door, she saw him looking obviously contented. "He's like a little boy," she said to herself. Feeling profound, she settled down to waiting for Tommy to lurch off to bed, so she would be free to go to the guitar.

The thought made her jittery and she suddenly felt that she couldn't wait any longer. She went into the kitchen and got his whiskey bottle and brought it into the dining room, putting it on the scarred table in front of his nose.

He stared at it for a minute and then looked up at Elsa with varnished eyes.

"Well, I'll be diddledly damned!" he said in a hushed voice.

Elsa smiled at him timidly. "I like you to be happy, Mr. Lott!"

And for some reason, tears sprang to Elsa's eyes and she hustled out of the room, leaving Tommy humming into his pipe.

When the hands of the Black Forest clock pointed to ten-twenty, Tommy started fussing with the blinds. This was a sure sign that he was about to go to bed. He raised a blind, peered out into the blackness of night, hummed half-words to himself, sucked on his pipe and trotted to another blind, which he lowered all the way—for no reason that Elsa could understand. Often she had explained to herself that Tommy was just plain disorderly, and that was why he couldn't seem to go to bed with any two blinds drawn to the same height.

One of the blinds flew ripping to the top of a high window, and Tommy cursed happily, while Elsa's stomach coiled with impatience. But the old man was too far gone in liquor to find the blind now, so he rolled across the floor and potted along up the stairway.

When Elsa heard his shoes hit the floor, she called out, "Goodnight, Mr. Lott!" But he didn't answer, and in another five minutes or so Elsa heard him snoring loud enough to rattle the frame of the house.

Then Elsa climbed up to the third floor, her heart hammering and her eyes fluttering. Reaching the top landing, her hand trembled as she groped for the wall switch. The yellow light came on and Elsa went straight for the guitar. When she had picked it up, she cocked her head, listening for a moment to the snoring. Then she thrust her hand through the strings and clutched a small bundle wrapped in a faded blue bandanna. Quickly she opened it and there was the money, in a tight roll.

The bills were held together by old rubber bands which broke when she pulled on them. She laid the money out in neat stacks, counting nine fifties, twenty-seven twenties and forty-three ten dollar bills.

Downstairs, Tommy lurched on his bed and groaned. Elsa trembled all over for an instant. Then she picked up the money in both hands and started down the steps.

At the bend in the stairway she could hear the wind outside and, glancing through the narrow, ecclesiastical window there, she could see the shadows of tree limbs and of telephone wires swaying in the light from the street lamps. There seemed to be no one outside on the streets, nor even lights on in the neighboring houses.

Reaching her room, she quickly took her suitcase down from the shelf in the closet and placed two house dresses in it. Then she sat in the old oak rocker by the bed and cried a little, thinking all at once of the seven years, and terrible old Tommy, and her lost life, and the uncertainties that faced her now at the age of sixty-seven.

Then she rolled her stockings up above her knees and put on her best dress, deciding to leave the old house dress she had been wearing. She brushed her hair quickly and stuck big pins all over to hold it in place. Then she set a small, flowered hat squarely on her head and stood looking around the room.

The ticking clock by her bed said two minutes till twelve. And then another day, a new life.

She picked up her suitcase and walked into the hallway, peering into Tommy's room. A rectangle of light from the hall lay on the floor and dimly illuminated the table by Tommy's bed. On it she could see the faint sparkle of the water glass holding his teeth.

The floor of the hall creaked loudly as she picked up the suitcase and stepped forward. She realized that the old man had not drunk enough to sleep soundly. After she had descended three steps, she heard a loud, snorting noise from Tommy's room.

"Who du hell DERE?" he bellowed sleepily, his voice sounding muted with his teeth out.

"It's just me, Mr. Lott," she said in a quavering tone.

"Jut what du hell you DOING?"

She bit her lip and her face twitched and trembled all over. She was in a panic . . . she had no idea what to tell him. She opened her mouth and started to tell him the truth, then stopped with a gasp, the sound of the words in her mind terrifying her.

"Jut what du hell TIME id it?"

She heard the bed springs squeak as he leaned over reaching for his watch.

"I don't know," she answered softly.

"Well, get du hell back to BED."

For an instant she stood on the steps, her face puckered tightly, tears burning her eyes. Then, afraid he might actually get out of bed, she hurried back to her room.

Tommy called out again: "Are you going to BED?"

"Yes, Mr. Lott."

She heard him sigh and turn over.

Then she slowly undressed, and while she was hanging her dress up in the closet, the thought occurred to her for the first time that she could continue to live here and put the money in a bank. After all, it was a kind of home, even though it wasn't a very good one. "And I'll let Fern know about it," she said to herself. *"Then* she'll stay away!"

And if Tommy was ever nasty to her again—that is, really, very, *awfully* nasty—why, she could just get up and leave.

But right now, tonight, she didn't dare.

Suddenly, she felt independent, optimistic. These were strange feelings to her, and she explained to herself, as she pulled the covers up to her chin, "It just shows what money can do."

FLANNERY O'CONNOR:

The Geranium

Old Dudley folded into the chair he was gradually molding to his own shape and looked out the window fifteen feet away into another window framed by blackened red brick. He was waiting for the geranium. They put it out every morning about ten and they took it in at five-thirty. Mrs. Carson back home had a geranium in her window. There were plenty of geraniums at home, better looking geraniums. Ours are sho nuff geraniums, Old Dudley thought, not any er this pale pink business with green, paper bows. The geranium they would put in the window reminded him of the Grisby boy at home who had polio and had to be wheeled out every morning and left in the sun to blink. Lutisha could have taken that geranium and stuck it in the ground and had something worth looking at in a few weeks. Those people across the alley had no business with one. They set it out and let the hot sun bake it all day and they put it so· near the ledge the wind could almost knock it over. They had no business with it, no business with it. It shouldn't have been there. Old Dudley felt his throat knotting up. Lutish could root anything. Rabie too. His throat was drawn taut. He laid his head back and tried to clear his mind. There wasn't much he could think of to think about that didn't do his throat that way.

His daughter came in. "Don't you want to go out for a walk?" she asked. She looked provoked.

He didn't answer her.

"Well?"

"No." He wondered how long she was going to stand there. She made his eyes feel like his throat. They'd get watery and she'd see. She had seen before and had looked sorry for him. She'd looked sorry for herself too; but she could er saved herself, Old Dudley thought, if she'd just have let him alone—let him stay where he was back home and not be so taken up with her damn duty. She moved out of the room leaving an audible sigh to crawl over him and remind him again of that one minute—that wasn't her fault at all—when suddenly he had wanted to go to New York to live with her.

He could have got out of going. He could have been stubborn and told her he'd spend his life where he'd always spent it, send him or not send him the money every month, he'd get along with his pension and odd jobs. Keep her damn money—she needed it worse than he did. She would have been glad to have had her duty disposed of like that. Then she could have said if he died without his children near him, it was his own fault; if he got sick and there wasn't anybody to take care of him, well, he'd asked for it, she could have said. But there was that thing inside him that had wanted to see New York. He had been to Atlanta once when he was a boy and he had seen New York in a picture show. "Big Town Rhythm" it was. Big towns were important places. The thing inside him had sneaked up on him for just one instant. The place like he'd seen in the picture show had room for him! It was an important place and it had room for him! He'd said, yes, he'd go.

He must have been sick when he said it. He couldn't have been well and said it. He had been sick and she had been so taken up with her damn duty, she had wangled it out of him. Why did she have to come down there in the first place to pester him? He had been doing all right. There was his pension that could feed him and odd jobs that kept him his room in the boarding house.

The window in that room showed him the river—thick and red as it struggled over rocks and around curves. He tried to think how it was besides red and slow. He added green blotches for trees on either side of it and a brown spot for trash somewhere upstream. He and Rabie had fished it in a flat-bottom boat every Wednesday. Rabie knew the river up and down for twenty miles. There wasn't another nigger in Coa County that knew it like he did. He loved the river, but it hadn't meant anything to Old Dudley. The fish were what he was after. He liked to come in at night with a long string of them and slap them down in the sink. "Few fish I got," he'd say. It took a man to get those fish, the old girls at the boarding house always said. He and Rabie would start out early Wednesday morning and fish all day. Rabie would find the spots and row; Old Dudley always caught them. Rabie didn't care much about catching them—he just loved the river. "Ain't no use settin' yo' line down dere, boss," he'd say, "ain't no fish dere. Dis ol' riber ain't hidin' none nowhere 'round hyar, nawsuh," and he would giggle and shift the boat downstream. That was Rabie. He could steal cleaner than a weasel but he knew where the fish were. Old Dudley always gave him the little ones.

Old Dudley had lived upstairs in the corner room of the boarding house ever since his wife died in '22. He protected the old ladies. He was the man in the house and he did the things a man in the house was supposed to do. It was a dull occupation at night when the old girls crabbed and crocheted in the parlor and the man in the house had to listen and judge the sparrow-like wars that rasped and twittered intermittently. But in the daytime there was Rabie. Rabie and Lutisha lived down in the basement. Lutish cooked and Rabie took care of the cleaning and the vegetable garden; but he was sharp at sneaking off with half his work done and going to help Old Dudley with some current project—building a hen house or painting a door. He liked to listen, he liked to hear about Atlanta when Old Dudley had been there and about how guns were put together on the inside and all the other things the old man knew.

Sometimes at night they would go 'possum hunting. They never got a 'possum but Old Dudley liked to get away from the ladies once in a while and hunting was a good excuse. Rabie didn't like 'possum hunting. They never got a 'possum; they never even treed one; and besides, he was mostly a water nigger. "We ain't gonna go huntin' no 'possum tonight, is we, boss? I got a lil' business I want tuh tend tuh," he'd say when Old Dudley would start talking about hounds and guns. "Whose chickens you gonna steal tonight?" Dudley would grin. "I reckon I be huntin' 'possum tonight," Rabie'd sigh.

Old Dudley would get out his gun and take it apart and, as Rabie cleaned the pieces, would explain the mechanism to him. Then he'd put it together again. Rabie always marveled at the way he could put it together again. Old Dudley would have liked to have explained New York to Rabie. If he could have showed it to Rabie, it wouldn't have been so big—he wouldn't have felt pressed down every time he went out in it. "It ain't so big," he would have said. "Don't let it get you down, Rabie. It's just like any other city and cities ain't all that complicated."

But they were. New York was swishing and jamming one minute and dirty and dead the next. His daughter didn't even live in a house. She lived in a building—the middle in a row of buildings all alike, all blackened—red and gray with rasp-mouthed people hanging out their windows looking at other windows and other people just like them looking back. Inside you could go up and you could go down and there were just halls that reminded you of tape measures strung out with a door every inch. He remembered he'd been dazed by the building the first week. He'd wake up expecting the halls to have changed in the night and he'd look out the door and there they stretched like dog runs. The streets were the same way. He wondered where he'd be if he walked to the end of one of them. One night he dreamed he did and ended at the end of the building—nowhere.

The next week he had become more conscious of the daughter and son-in-law and their boy—no place to be out of their way. The son-in-law was a queer one. He drove a truck and came in only on the weekends. He said "Nah" for "No" and he'd never heard of a 'possum. Old Dudley slept in the room with the boy who was sixteen and couldn't be talked to. But sometimes when the daughter and Old Dudley were alone in the apartment, she would sit down and talk to him. First she had to think of something to say. Usually it gave out before what she considered was the proper time to get up and do something else, so he would have to say something. He always tried to think of something he hadn't said before. She never listened the second time. She was seeing that her father spent his last years with his own family and not in a decayed boarding house full of old women whose heads jiggled. She was doing her duty. She had brothers and sisters who were not.

Once she took him shopping with her but he was too slow. They went in a "subway"—a railroad underneath the ground like in a big cave. People boiled out of trains and up steps and over into the streets. They rolled off the street and down steps and into trains—black and white and yellow all mixed up like vegetables in soup. Everything was boiling. The trains swished in from tunnels, up canals, and all of a sudden stopped. The people coming out pushed through the people coming in and a noise rang and the train swooped off again. Old Dudley and the daughter had to go in three different ones before they got where they were going. He wondered why people ever went out of their houses. He felt like his tongue had slipped down in his stomach. She held him by the coat sleeve and pulled him through the people.

They went on an overhead train too. She called it an "El." They had to go up on a high platform to catch it. Old Dudley looked over the rail and could see the people rushing and the automobiles rushing under him. He felt sick. He put one hand on the rail and sank down on the wooden floor of the platform. The daughter screamed and pulled him over from the edge. "Do you want to fall off and kill yourself?" she shouted.

Through a crack in the boards he could see the cars swimming in the street. "I don't care," he murmured, "I don't care if I do or not."

"Come on," she said, "you'll feel better when we get home."

"Home?" he repeated. The cars moved in a rhythm below him.

"Come on," she said, "here it comes; we've just got time to make it." They'd just had time to make all of them.

They made that one. They came back to the building and the apartment. The apartment was too tight. There was no place to be where there wasn't somebody else. The kitchen opened into the bathroom and the bathroom opened into everything else and you were always where you started from. At home there was upstairs and the basement and the river and down town in front of Fraziers . . . damn his throat.

The geranium was late today. It was ten-thirty. They usually had it out by ten-fifteen.

Somewhere down the hall a woman shrilled something unintelligible out to the street; a radio was bleating the worn music to a soap serial; and a garbage can crashed down a fire-escape. The door to the next apartment slammed and a sharp footstep clipped down the hall. "That would be the nigger," Old Dudley muttered. "The nigger with the shiny shoes." He had been there a week when the nigger moved in. That Thursday he was looking out the door at the dog run halls when this nigger went into the next apartment. He had on a grey, pin-stripe suit and a tan tie. His collar was stiff and white and made a clear-cut line next to his neck. His shoes were shiny tan—they matched his tie and his skin. Old Dudley scratched his head. He hadn't known that the kind of people that would live thick in a building could afford servants. He chuckled. Lot of good a nigger in a Sunday suit would do them. Maybe this nigger would know the country around here—or maybe how to get to it. They might could hunt. They might could find them a stream somewhere. He shut the door and went to the daughter's room. "Hey!" he shouted, "the folks next door got 'em a nigger. Must be gonna clean for them. You reckon they gonna keep him every day?"

She looked up from making the bed. "What are you talking about?"

"I say they got 'em a servant next door—a nigger—all dressed up in a Sunday suit."

She walked to the other side of the bed. "You must be crazy," she said. "The next apartment is vacant and besides, nobody around here can afford any servant."

"I tell you I saw him," Old Dudley snickered. "Going right in there with a tie and a white collar on—and sharp-toed shoes."

"If he went in there, he's looking at it for himself," she muttered. She went to the dresser and started fidgeting with things.

Old Dudley laughed. She could be right funny when she wanted to. "Well," he said, "I think I'll go over and see what day he gets off. Maybe I can convince him he likes to fish," and he'd slapped his pocket to make the two quarters jingle. Before he got out in the hall good, she came tearing behind him and pulled him in. "Can't you hear?" she'd yelled. "I meant what I said. He's renting that himself if he went in there. Don't you go asking him any questions or saying anything to him. I don't want any trouble with niggers."

"You mean," Old Dudley murmured, "he's gonna live next door to you?"

She shrugged. "I suppose he is. And you tend to your own business," she added. "Don't have anything to do with him."

That's just the way she'd said it. Like he didn't have any sense at all. But he'd told her off then. He'd stated his say and she knew what he meant. "You ain't been raised that way!" he'd said thundery-like. "You ain't been raised to live tight with niggers that think they're just as good as you, and you think I'd go messin' around with one er that kind! If you think I want anything to do with them, you're crazy." He had had to slow down then because his throat was tightening. She'd stood stiff up and said they lived where they could afford to live and made the best of it. Preaching to him! Then she'd walked stiff off without a word more. That was her. Trying to be holy with her shoulders curved around and her neck in the air. Like he was a fool. He knew yankees let niggers in their front doors and let them set on their sofas but he didn't know his own daughter that was raised proper would stay next door to them—and then think he didn't have no more sense than to want to mix with them. Him!

He got up and took a paper off another chair. He might as well appear to be reading when she came through again. No use having her standing there staring at him, believing she had to think up something for him to do. He looked over the paper at the window across the alley. The geranium wasn't there yet. It had never been this late before. The first day he'd seen it, he had been sitting there looking out the window at the other window and he had looked at this watch to see how long it had been since breakfast. When he looked up, it was there. It startled him. He didn't like flowers, but the geranium didn't look like a flower. It looked like the sick Grisby boy at home and it was the color of the drapes the old ladies had in the parlor and the paper bow on it looked like the one behind Lutish's uniform she wore on Sundays. Lutish had a fondness for sashes. Most niggers did, Old Dudley thought.

The daughter came through again. He had meant to be looking at the paper when she came through. "Do me a favor, will you?" she asked as if she had just thought up a favor he could do.

He hoped she didn't want him to go to the grocery again. He got lost the time before. All the blooming buildings looked alike. He nodded.

"Go down to the third floor and ask Mrs. Schmitt to lend me the shirt pattern she uses for Jake."

Why couldn't she just let him sit? She didn't need the shirt pattern. "All right," he said. "What number is it?"

"Number 10—just like this. Right below us three floors down."

Old Dudley was always afraid that when he went out in the dog runs, a door would suddenly open and one of the snipe-nosed men that hung off the window ledges in his undershirt would growl, "What are you doing here?" The door to the nigger's apartment was open and he could see a woman sitting in a chair by the window. "Yankee niggers," he muttered. She had on rimless glasses and there was a book in her lap. Niggers don't think they're dressed up till they got on glasses, Old Dudley thought. He remembered Lutish's glasses. She had saved up thirteen dollars to buy them. Then she went to the doctor and asked him to look at her eyes and tell her how thick to get the glasses. He made her look at animals' pictures through a mirror and he stuck a light through her eyes and looked in her head. Then he said she didn't need any glasses. She was so mad she burned the corn bread three days in a row, but she bought her some glasses anyway at the ten cent store. They didn't cost her but $1.98 and she wore them every Saddey. "That was niggers," Old Dudley chuckled. He realized he had made a noise, and covered his mouth with his hand. Somebody might hear him in one of the apartments.

He turned down the first flight of stairs. Down the second he heard footsteps coming up. He looked over the banisters and saw it was a woman—a fat woman with an apron on. From the top, she looked kind er like Mrs. Benson at home. He wondered if she would speak to him. When they were four steps from each other, he darted a glance at her but she wasn't looking at him. When there were no steps between them, his eyes fluttered up for an instant and she was looking at him cold in the face. Then she was past him. She hadn't said a word. He felt heavy in his stomach.

He went down four flights instead of three. Then he went back up one and found number 10. Mrs. Schmitt said O. K., wait a minute and she'd get the pattern. She sent one of the children back to the door with it. The child didn't say anything.

Old Dudley started back up the stairs. He had to take it more slowly. It tired him going up. Everything tired him, looked like. Not like having Rabie to do his running for him. Rabie was a light-footed nigger. He could sneak in a hen-house 'thout even the hens knowing it and get him the fattest fryer in there and not a squawk. Fast too. Dudley had always been slow on his feet. It went that way with fat people. He remembered one time him and Rabie was hunting quail over near Molton. They had 'em a hound dog that could find a covey quickern any fancy pointer going. He wasn't no good at bringing them back but he could find them every time and then set like a dead stump while you aimed at the birds. This one time the hound stopped cold-still. "Dat gonna be a big 'un," Rabie whispered, "I feels it." Old Dudley raised the gun slowly as they walked along. He had to be careful of the pine needles. They covered the ground and made it slick. Rabie shifted his weight from side to side, lifting and setting his feet on the waxen needles with unconscious care. He looked straight ahead and moved forward swiftly. Old Dudley kept one eye ahead and one on the ground. It would slope and he would be sliding forward dangerously or in pulling himself up an incline, he would slide back down.

"Ain't I better get dem birds dis time, boss?" Rabie suggested. "You ain't never easy on yo' feets on Monday. If you falls in one dem slopes, you gonna scatter dem birds fo' you gits dat gun up."

Old Dudley wanted to get the covey. He could er knocked four out it easy. "I'll get 'em," he muttered. He lifted the gun to his eye and leaned forward. Something slipped beneath him and he slid backward on his heels. The gun went off and the covey sprayed into the air.

"Dem was some mighty fine birds we let get away from us," Rabie sighed.

"We'll find another covey," Old Dudley said, "now get me out of this damn hole."

He could er got five er those birds if he hadn't fallen. He could er shot 'em off like cans on a fence. He drew one hand back to his ear and extended the other forward. He could er knocked 'em out like clay pigeons. Bang! A squeak on the staircase made him wheel around —his arms still holding the invisible gun. The nigger was clipping up the steps toward him, an amused smile stretching his trimmed mustache. Old Dudley's mouth dropped open. The nigger's lips were pulled down like he was trying to keep from laughing. Old Dudley couldn't move. He stared at the clear-cut line the nigger's collar made against his skin.

"What are you hunting, old timer?" the negro asked in a voice that sounded like a nigger's laugh and a white man's sneer.

Old Dudley felt like a child with a pop-pistol. His mouth was open and his tongue was rigid in the middle of it. Right below his knees felt hollow. His feet slipped and he slid three steps and landed sitting down.

"You better be careful," the negro said. "You could easily hurt your-self on these steps," and he held out his hand for Old Dudley to pull up on. It was a long narrow hand and the tips of the fingernails were clean and cut squarely. They looked like they might have been filed. Old Dudley's hands hung between his knees. The nigger took him by the arm and pulled up. "Whew!" he gasped, "you're heavy. Give a little help here." Old Dudley's knees unbended and he staggered up. The nigger had him by the arm. "I'm going up anyway," he said. "I'll help you." Old Dudley looked frantically around. The steps behind him seemed to close up. He was walking with the nigger up the stairs. The nigger was waiting for him on each step. "So you hunt?" the nigger was saying. "Well, let's see. I went deer hunting once. I believe we used a Dodson 38 to get those deer. What do you use?"

Old Dudley was staring through the shiny tan shoes. "I use a gun," he mumbled.

"I like to fool with guns better than hunting," the nigger was say-ing. "Never was much at killing. Seems kind of a shame to deplete the game reserve. I'd collect guns if I had the time and the money, though." He was waiting on every step till Old Dudley got on it. He was explaining guns and makes. He had on grey socks with a black fleck in them. They finished the stairs. The nigger walked down the hall with him, holding him by the arm. It probably looked like he had his arm locked in the nigger's.

They went right up to Old Dudley's door. Then the nigger asked, "You from around here?"

Old Dudley shook his head looking at the door. He hadn't looked at the nigger yet. All the way up the stairs, he hadn't looked at the nigger. "Well," the nigger said, "it's a swell place—once you get used to it." He patted Old Dudley on the back and went into his own apart-ment. Old Dudley went into his. The pain in his throat was all over his face now, leaking out his eyes.

He shuffled to the chair by the window and sank down in it. His throat was going to pop. His throat was going to pop on account of a nigger—a damn nigger that patted him on the back and called him "old timer." Him that knew such as that couldn't be. Him that had come from a good place. A good place. A place where such as that couldn't be. His eyes felt strange in their sockets. They were swelling in them and in a minute there wouldn't be any room left for them there. He was trapped in this place where niggers could call you "old timer." He wouldn't be trapped. He wouldn't be. He rolled his head on the back of the chair to stretch his neck that was too full.

A man was looking at him. A man was in the window across the alley looking straight at him. The man was watching him cry. That was where the geranium was supposed to be and it was a man in his undershirt, watching him cry, waiting to watch his throat pop. Old Dudley looked back at the man. It was supposed to be the geranium. The geranium belonged there, not the man. "Where is the geranium?" he called out of his tight throat.

"What you cryin' for?" the man asked. "I ain't never seen a man cry like that."

"Where is the geranium?" Old Dudley quavered. "It ought to be there. Not you."

"This is my window," the man said. "I got a right to set here if I want to."

"Where is it?" Old Dudley shrilled. There was just a little room left in his throat.

"It fell off if it's any of your business," the man said.

Old Dudley got up and peered over the window ledge. Down in the alley, way six floors down, he could see a cracked flower pot scattered over a spray of dirt and something pink sticking out of a green paper bow. It was down six floors. Smashed down six floors.

Old Dudley looked at the man who was chewing gum and waiting to see the throat pop. "You shouldn't have put it so near the ledge," he murmured. "Why don't you pick it up?"

"Why don't you, pop?"

Old Dudley stared at the man who was where the geranium should have been.

He would. He'd go down and pick it up. He'd put it in his own window and look at it all day if he wanted to. He turned from the window and left the room. He walked slowly down the dog run and got to the steps. The steps dropped down like a deep wound in the floor. They opened up through a gap like a cavern and went down and down. And he had gone up them a little behind the nigger. And the nigger had pulled him up on his feet and kept his arm in his and gone up the steps with him and said he hunted deer, "old timer," and seen him holding a gun that wasn't there and sitting on the steps like a child. He had shiny tan shoes and he was trying not to laugh and the whole business was laughing. There'd probably be niggers with black flecks in their socks on every step, pulling down their mouths so as not to laugh. The steps dropped down and down. He wouldn't go on those steps. He wouldn't go on them again. He wouldn't go down and have niggers pattin' him on the back. He went back to the room and the window and looked down at the geranium.

The man was sitting over where it should have been. "I ain't seen you pickin' it up," he said.

Old Dudley stared at the man.

"I seen you before," the man said. "I seen you settin' in that old chair every day, starin' out the window, looking in my apartment. What I do in my apartment is my business, see? I don't like people looking at what I do."

It was at the bottom of the alley with its roots in the air.

"I only tell people once," the man said and left the window.

GRACE PALEY:

Goodbye and Good Luck

I was popular in certain circles, says Aunt Rose. I wasn't no thinner then, only more stationary in the flesh. In time to come, Lillie, don't be surprised—change is a fact of God. From this, no one is excused. Only a person like your mama stands on one foot, she don't notice how big her behind is getting, and sings in the canary's ear for thirty years. Who's listening? Papa's in the shop. You and Seymour, thinking about yourself. So she waits in a spotless kitchen for a kind word and thinks,—poor Rosie—.

Poor Rosie! If there was more life in my little sister, she would know my heart is a regular college of feelings and there is such information between my corset and me that her whole married life is a kindergarten.

Nowadays, you could find me anytime in a hotel, uptown or downtown. Who needs an apartment to live like a maid with a dustrag in the hand, sneezing? I'm in very good with the bellboys, it's more interesting than home, all kinds of people, everybody with a reason. . . .

And my reason, Lillie, is a long time ago I said to the forelady, "Missus, if I can't sit by the window, I can't sit." "If you can't sit, girlie," she says politely, "go stand on the street corner." And that's how I got unemployed in novelty wear.

For my next job, I answered an ad which said: "Refined young lady, medium salary, cultural organization." I went by trolley to the address, the Russian Art Theater of Second Avenue where they played only the best Yiddish plays.

They needed a ticket seller, someone like me, who likes the public but is very sharp on crooks. The man who interviewed me was the manager, a certain type.

Immediately he said: "Rosie Lieber, you surely got a build on you!"

"It takes all kinds, Mr. Krimberg."

"Don't misunderstand me, little girl," he said. "I appreciate, I appreciate. A young lady lacking fore and aft, her blood is so busy warming the toes and the fingertips, it don't have time to circulate where it's most required."

Everybody likes kindness. I said to him: "Only don't be fresh, Mr. Krimberg, and we'll make a good bargain."

We did: Nine dollars a week, a glass of tea every night, a free ticket once a week for mama, and I could go watch rehearsals any time I want.

My first nine dollars was in the grocer's hands ready to move on already, when Krimberg said to me: "Rosie, here's a great gentleman, a member of this remarkable theater, wants to meet you, impressed no doubt by your big brown eyes."

And who was it, Lillie? Listen to me, before my very eyes was Volodya Vlashkin, called by the people of those days the Valentino of Second Avenue.

I took one look and I said to myself, where did a Jewish boy grow up so big? "Just outside Kiev," he told me.

How? "My mama nursed me till I was six. I was the only boy in the village to have such health."

"My goodness, Vlashkin, six years old! She must have had shredded wheat there, not breasts, poor woman."

"My mother was beautiful," he said. "She had eyes like stars."

He had such a way of expressing himself, it brought tears.

To Krimberg, Vlashkin said after this introduction: "Who is responsible for hiding this wonderful young person in a cage?"

"That is where the ticket seller sells."

"So David, go in there and sell tickets for a half hour. I have something in mind in regards to the future of this girl and this company. Go David, be a good boy. And you, Miss Lieber, please, I suggest Feinbergs for a glass of tea. The rehearsals are long. I enjoy a quiet interlude with a friendly person."

So he took me there, Feinbergs, then around the corner, a place so full of Hungarians, it was deafening. In the back room was a table of honor for him. On the table cloth, embroidered by the lady of the house, was Here Vlashkin Eats. We finished one glass of tea in quietness out of thirst, when I finally made up my mind what to say.

"Mr. Vlashkin, I saw you a couple weeks ago even before I started working here, in *The Sea Gull*. Believe me, if I was that girl, I wouldn't look even for a minute on the young bourgeois fellow. He could fall out of the play altogether. How Chekhov could put him in the same play as you, I can't understand."

"You liked me?" he asked, taking my hand and kindly patting it. "Well, well, young people still like me,—so, and you like the theater too? Good. And you, Rose, you know you have such a nice hand, so warm to the touch, such a fine skin, tell me, why do you wear a scarf around your neck? You only hide your young, young throat. These are not olden times, my child, to live in shame."

"Who's ashamed?" I said, taking off the kerchief, but my hand right away went to the kerchief's place, because the truth is, it really was olden times, and I was still of a nature to melt with shame.

"Have some more tea, my dear."

"No thank you, I am a samovar already."

"Dorfmann!" he hollered like a king. "Bring this child a seltzer with fresh ice!"

In weeks to follow, I had the privilege to know him better and better as a person—also the opportunity to see him in his profession. The time was autumn; the theater full of coming and going. Rehearsing without end. After *The Sea Gull* flopped, *The Salesman From Istanbul* played, a great success.

Here the ladies went crazy. On the opening night, in the middle of the first scene, one missus, a widow or her husband worked too long hours, began to clap and sing out, "Oi, oi, Vlashkin." Soon there was such a tumult, the actors had to stop acting. Vlashkin stepped forward. Only not Vlashkin to the eyes . . . a younger man with pitch-black hair, lively on restless feet, his mouth clever. A half a century later at the end of the play he came out again, a grey philosopher, a student of life, from only reading books, his hands as smooth as silk. I cried to think who I was—nothing—and such a man could look at me with interest.

Then I got a small raise due to he kindly put in a good word for me and also, for fifty cents a night, I was given the privilege together with cousins, in-laws and plain stagestruck kids to be part of a crowd scene. This was for me a special pleasure, to stand behind his back and hear him breathe.

The sad day came, I kissed my mama goodbye. Vlashkin helped me to get a reasonable room near the theater to be more free. Also my outstanding friend would have a place to recline away from the noise of the dressing rooms. She cried and she cried. "This is a different way of living, Mama," I said. "Besides, I am driven by love."

"You! you! a nothing, a rotten hole in a piece of cheese, are you telling me what is life?" she screamed.

Very insulted, I went away from her. But I am good-natured, you know fat people are like that, kind, and I thought to myself, poor mama . . . it is true she got more of an idea of life than me. She married who she didn't like, a sick man, his spirit already swallowed

up by God. He never washed. He had an unhappy smell. His teeth
fell out, his hair disappeared, he got smaller, shriveled up little by
little, till goodbye and good luck he was gone and only came to
mama's mind when she went to the mailbox under the stairs to get
the electric bill. In memory of him and out of respect for mankind,
I decided to live for love.

Don't laugh, you ignorant girl.

Do you think it was easy for me? I had to give mama a little
something. Ruthie was saving up together with your papa for linens,
a couple of knives and forks. In the morning I had to do piecework
if I wanted to keep by myself. So I made flowers. Before lunchtime
every day a whole garden grew on my table.

This was my independence, Lillie dear, blooming, but it didn't
have no roots and its face was paper.

Meanwhile Krimberg went after me too. No doubt observing the
success of Vlashkin, he thought, "Aha, Open Sesame. . . ." Others in
the company similar. After me in those years were the following:
Krimberg I mentioned. Carl Zimmer, played innocent young fellows
with a wig. Charles Peel, a Christian who fell in the soup by accident,
a creator of beautiful sets. "Color is his middle name," says Vlashkin,
always to the point.

I put this in to show you your fat old aunt was not crazy out of
loneliness. In those noisy years, I had friends among interesting people
who admired me for reasons of youth and that I was a first-class
listener.

The actresses, Raisele, Marya, Esther Leopold, were only interested
in tomorrow. After them was the rich men, producers, the whole
garment center, their past is a pin cushion, future the eye of a needle.

Finally the day came I no longer could keep my tact in my mouth.
I said: "Vlashkin, I hear by carrier-pigeon you have a wife, children,
the whole combination."

"True, I don't tell stories. I make no pretence."

"That isn't the question. What is this lady like? It hurts me to
ask, but tell me, Vlashkin . . . a man's life is something I don't
clearly see."

"Little girl, I have told you a hundred times, this small room is the
convent of my troubled spirit. Here I come to your innocent shelter
to refresh myself in the midst of an agonized life."

"Ach, Vlashkin, serious, serious, who is this lady?"

"Rosie, she is a fine woman of the middle classes, a good mother to my children, three in number, girls all, a good cook, in her youth handsome, now no longer young. You see, could I be more frank? I entrust you, dear, with my soul."

It was some months later at the New Year's Ball of the Russian Artists Club, I met Mrs. Vlashkin, a woman with black hair in a low bun, straight and too proud, she sat at a small table speaking in a deep voice to whoever stopped a moment to converse. Her Yiddish was perfect, each word cut like a special jewel. I looked at her. She noticed me like she noticed everybody, cold like Christmas morning. Then she got tired. Vlashkin called a taxi and I never saw her again. Poor woman, she did not know I was on the same stage with her. The poison I was to her role, she did not know.

Later on that night in front of my door, I said to Vlashkin, "No more. This isn't for me. I am sick from it all. I am no home-breaker."

"Girlie," he said, "don't be foolish."

"No, no, goodbye, good luck," I said. "I am sincere."

So I went and stayed with mama for a week's vacation and cleaned up all the closets and scrubbed the walls till the paint came off. She was very grateful, all the same her hard life made her say, "Now we see the end. If you live like a bum, you are finally a lunatic."

After this few days, I came back to my life. When we met, me and Vlashkin, we said only hello and goodbye, and then for a few sad years with the head we nodded as if to say, "Yes, yes, I know who you are."

Meanwhile in the field was a whole new strategy. Your mama and grandmama brought around—boys.

Your own father had a brother, you never even seen him. Ruben. A serious fellow, his idealism was his hat and his coat. "Rosie, I offer you a big new free happy unusual life." How? "With me, we will raise up the sands of Palestine to make a nation. That is the land of tomorrow for us Jews." "Ha, ha, Ruben, I'll go tomorrow then." "Rosie!" says Ruben. "We need strong women like you, mothers and farmers." "You don't fool me, Ruben, what you need is dray horses. But for that you need more money." "I don't like your attitude, Rose." "In that case, go and multiply. Goodbye."

Another fellow: Yonkel Gurstein, a regular sport, dressed to kill, with such an excitable nature. In those days, it looks to me like yesterday, the youngest girls wore undergarments like Battle Creek, Michigan. To him it was a matter of seconds. Where did he practice, a Jewish boy? Nowadays, I suppose it is easier, Lillie? My goodness, I ain't asking you nothing,—touchy, touchy.

Well, by now you must know yourself, honey, whatever you do, life don't stop. It only sits a minute and dreams a dream.

While I was saying to all these silly youngsters—no, no, no, Vlashkin went to Europe and toured a few seasons—Moscow, Prague, London, even Berlin, already a pessimistic place. When he came back, he wrote a book you could get from the library even today, *The Jewish Actor Abroad*. If some day you're interested enough in my lonesome years, you could read it. You could absorb a flavor of the man from the book. No, no, I am not mentioned. After all, who am I?

When the book came out, I stopped him in the street to say congratulations. But I am not a liar, so I pointed out too the egotism of many parts,—even the critics said something along such lines.

"Talk is cheap," Vlashkin answered me. "But who are the critics, tell me do they create? Not to mention," he continues, "there is a line in Shakespeare in one of the plays from the great history of England, it says . . . 'self-loving is not so vile a sin, my liege, as self-neglecting.' This idea also appears in modern times in the moralistic followers of Freud.

"Rosie, are you listening? You asked a question. By the way, you look very well. How come no wedding ring?" I walked away from this conversation in tears. But this talking in the street opened the happy road up for more discussions. In regard to many things. For instance, the management—very narrow-minded—wouldn't give him any more certain young men's parts. Fools. What youngest man knew enough about life to be as young as him?

"Rosie, Rosie," he said to me one day. "I see by the clock on your rosy, rosy face, you must be thirty."

"The hands are slow, Vlashkin. On a week before Thursday I was thirty-four."

"Is that so? Rosie, I worry about you. It has been on my mind to talk to you. You are losing your time. Do you understand it? A woman should not lose her time."

"Oi Vlashkin, if you are my friend, what is time?"

For this, he had no answer, only looked at me surprised. We went instead, full of interest but not with our former speed, up to my new place on 94th Street. The same pictures on the wall, all of Vlashkin, only now everything painted red and black which was stylish, and new upholstery.

A few years ago there was a book by another member of that fine company, an actress, the one that learned English very good and went uptown—Marya Kavkaz, in which she says certain things regarding Vlashkin.

Such as, he was her lover for eleven years, she's not ashamed to write this down. Without respect for him, his wife and children or even others who also may have feelings in the matter.

Now, Lillie, don't be surprised. This is called a fact of life. An actor's soul must be like a diamond. The more faces it got, the more shining is his name. Honey, you will no doubt love and marry one man and have a couple kids and be happy forever till you die tired. More than that, a person like us don't have to know. But a great artist like Volodya Vlashkin . . . in order to make a job on the stage, he's got to practice. I understand it now, to him life is like a rehearsal.

Myself, when I saw him in *The Father-in-Law,* an older man in love with a darling young girl, his son's wife, played by Raisele Maisel —I cried. What he said to this girl, how he whispered such sweetness, how all his hot feelings were on his face . . . . Lillie, all this experience he had with·me. The very words were the same. You can imagine how proud I was.

So the story creeps to an end.

I noticed it first on my mother's face, the rotten handwriting of time, scribbled up and down her cheeks, across her forehead back and forth—a child could read—it said, old, old, old. But it troubled my heart most to see these realities scratched on Vlashkin's wonderful expression.

First the company fell apart. The theater ended. Esther Leopold died from being very aged. Krimberg had a heart attack. Marya went to Broadway. Also Raisele changed her name to Roslyn and was a big comical hit in the movies.

Vlashkin himself, no place to go, retired. It said in the paper: ". . . an actor without peer, he will write his memoirs and spend his last years in the bosom of his family among his thriving grandchildren, the apple of his wife's doting eye."

This is journalism.

We made for him a great dinner of honor. At this dinner, I said to him for the last time I thought, "Goodbye, dear friend, topic of my life, now we part."

And to myself I said further: Finished. This is your lonesome bed. A lady what they call fat and fifty. You made it personally. From this lonesome bed you will finally fall to a bed not so lonesome. And now comes? Lillie, guess.

Last week, washing my underwear in the basin, I get a buzz on the phone.

"Excuse me, is this the Rose Lieber formerly connected with the Russian Art Theater?"

"It is."

"Well, well, how do you do, Rose? This is Vlashkin."

"Vlashkin! Volodya Vlashkin?"

"In fact. How are you, Rose?"

"Living, Vlashkin, thank you."

"You are all right? Really, Rose? Your health is good? You are working?"

"My health, considering the weight it must carry, is first class. I am back for some years now where I started, in novelty wear."

"Very interesting."

"Listen, Vlashkin, tell me the truth, what's on your mind?"

"My mind? Rosie, I am looking up an old friend, an old warm-hearted companion of more joyful days. My circumstances by the way are changed. I am retired as you know. Also I am a free man."

"What? What do you mean?"

"Mrs. Vlashkin is divorcing me."

"What came over her? Did you start drinking or something from melancholy?"

"She is divorcing me for adultery."

"But Vlashkin, you should excuse me, don't be insulted, but you got maybe seventeen, eighteen years on me and even me, all this nonsense, this daydreams and nightmares, is mostly for the pleasure of conversation alone."

"I pointed all this out to her. My dear, I said, my time is past, my blood is as dry as my bones. The truth is, Rose, she isn't accustomed to have a man around all day, reading out loud from the papers the interesting events of our time, waiting for breakfast, waiting for lunch. So all day she gets madder and madder. By night time a furious old lady gives me my supper. She has information from the last fifty years to pepper my soup. Surely there was a Judas in that theater saying every day, 'Vlashkin, Vlashkin, Vlashkin' . . . and while my heart was circulating with his smiles he was on the wire passing the dope to my wife."

"Such a foolish end, Volodya, to such a lively story. What is your plans?"

"First, could I ask you for dinner and the theater—uptown of course? After this . . . we are old friends. I have money to burn. What your heart desires. Others are like grass, the north wind of time has cut out their heart. Of you, Rosie, I recreate only kindness. What a woman should be to a man, you were to me. Do you think, Rosie, a couple of old pals like us could have a few good times among the material things of this world?"

My answer, Lillie, in a minute was altogether yes, yes, come up, I said, ask the room by the switchboard, let us talk.

So he came that night and every night in the week. We talked of his long life. Even at the end of time, a fascinating man. And like men are too till time's end, trying to get away in one piece.

"Listen, Rosie," he explains the other day. "I was married to my wife, do you realize nearly half a century. What good was it? Look at the bitterness. The more I think of it, the more I think we would be fools to marry."

"Volodya Vlashkin," I told him straight, "when I was young, I warmed your cold back many a night no questions asked. You admit it, I didn't make no demands. I was soft-hearted. I didn't want to be called Rosie Lieber a breaker up of homes. But now, Vlashkin, you are a free man. How could you ask me to go with you on trains to stay in strange hotels, among Americans, not your wife? Be ashamed."

So now, darling Lillie, tell this story to your mama from your young mouth. She don't listen to a word from me. She only screams, "I'll faint, I'll faint." Tell her, after all I'll have a husband which, as everybody knows, a woman should have at least one before the end of the story.

My goodness, I am already late. Give me a kiss. After all, I watched you grow from a plain seed. So give me a couple wishes on my wedding day. A long and happy life. Many years of love. Hug mama, tell her from Aunt Rose, goodbye and good luck.

J. F. POWERS:

Lions, Harts, Leaping Does

"'Thirty-ninth pope. Anastasius, a Roman, appointed that while the Gospel was reading they should stand and not sit. He exempted from the ministry those that were lame, impotent, or diseased persons, and slept with his forefathers in peace, being a confessor.'"

"Anno?"

"'Anno 404.'"

They sat there in the late afternoon, the two old men grown grey in the brown robes of the Order. Angular winter daylight forsook the small room, almost a cell in the primitive sense, and passed through the window into the outside world. The distant horizon, which it sought to join, was still bright and strong against approaching night. The old Franciscans, one priest, one brother, were left among the shadows in the room.

"Can you see to read one more, Titus?" the priest Didymus asked.

"Number fourteen." He did not cease staring out the window at day becoming night on the horizon. The thirty-ninth pope said Titus might not be a priest. Did Titus, reading, understand? He could never really tell about Titus, who said nothing now. There was only silence, then a dry whispering of pages turning. "Number fourteen," Didymus said. "That's Zephyrinus. I always like the old heretic on that one, Titus."

According to one bibliographer, Bishop Bale's *Pageant of Popes Contayninge the Lyves of all the Bishops of Rome, from the Beginninge of them to the Year of Grace 1555,* was a denunciation of every pope from Peter to Paul IV. However inviting to readers that might sound, it was in sober fact a lie. The first popes, persecuted and mostly martyred, wholly escaped the author's remarkable spleen and even enjoyed his crusty approbation. Father Didymus, his aged appetite for biography jaded by the orthodox lives, found the work fascinating. He usually referred to it as "Bishop Bale's funny book" and to the Bishop as a heretic.

Titus squinted at the yellowed page. He snapped a glance at the light hovering at the window. Then he closed his eyes and with great feeling recited:

" 'O how joyous and how delectable is it to see religious men devout and fervent in the love of God, well mannered—' "

"Titus," Didymus interrupted softly.

" '—and well taught in ghostly learning.' "

"Titus, read." Didymus placed the words in their context. The First Book of *The Imitation* and Chapter, if he was not mistaken, XXV. The trick was no longer in finding the source of Titus's quotations; it was putting them in their exact context. It had become an unconfessed contest between them, and it gratified Didymus to think he had been able to place the fragment. Titus knew two books by heart, *The Imitation* and *The Little Flowers of St. Francis*. Lately, unfortunately, he had begun to learn another. He was more and more quoting from Bishop Bale. Didymus reminded himself he must not let Titus read past the point where the martyred popes left off. What Bale had to say about Peter's later successors sounded incongruous—"unmete" in the old heretic's own phrase—coming from a Franciscan brother. Two fathers had already inquired of Didymus concerning Titus. One had noted the antique style of his words and had ventured to wonder if Brother Titus, Christ preserve us, might be slightly possessed. He cited the case of the illiterate Missouri farmer who cursed the Church in a forgotten Aramaic tongue.

"Read, Titus."

Titus squinted at the page once more and read in his fine dead voice.

" 'Fourteenth pope, Zephyrinus. Zephyrinus was a Roman born, a man as writers do testify, more addicted with all endeavor to the service of God than to the cure of any worldly affairs. Whereas before his time the wine in the celebrating the communion was ministered in a cup of wood, he first did alter that, and instead thereof brought in cups or chalices of glass. And yet he did not this upon any superstition, as thinking wood to be unlawful, or glass to be more holy for that use, but because the one is more comely and seemly, as by experience it appeareth than the other. And yet some wooden dolts do dream that the wooden cups were changed by him because that part of the wine, or as they thought, the royal blood of Christ, did soak into the wood, and so it can not be in glass. Surely sooner may wine soak into any wood than any wit into those winey heads that thus both deceive themselves and slander this Godly martyr.' "

"Anno?"

Titus squinted at the page again. " 'Anno 222,' " he read.

They were quiet for a moment which ended with the clock in the tower booming once for the half-hour. Didymus got up and stood so close to the window his breath became visible. Noticing it, he inhaled deeply and then, exhaling, he sent a gust of smoke churning against the freezing pane, clouding it. Some old unmelted snow in tree crotches lay dirty and white in the gathering dark.

"It's cold out today," Didymus said.

He stepped away from the window and over to Titus, whose face was relaxed in openeyed sleep. He took Bishop Bale's funny book unnoticed from Titus's hands.

"Thank you, Titus," he said.

Titus blinked his eyes slowly once, then several times quickly. His body gave a shudder, as if coming to life.

"Yes, Father?" he was asking.

"I said thanks for reading. You are a great friend to me."

"Yes, Father."

"I know you'd rather read other authors." Didymus moved to the window, stood there gazing through the tops of trees, their limbs black and bleak against the sky. He rubbed his hands. "I'm going for a walk before Vespers. Is it too cold for you, Titus?"

" 'A good religious man that is fervent in his religion taketh all things well, and doth gladly all that he is commanded to do.' "

Didymus, walking across the room, stopped and looked at Titus just in time to see him open his eyes. He was quoting again: *The Imitation* and still in Chapter XXV. Why had he said that? To himself Didymus repeated the words and decided Titus, his mind moving intelligently but so pathetically largo, was documenting the act of reading Bishop Bale when there were other books he preferred.

"I'm going out for a walk," Didymus said.

Titus rose and pulled down the full sleeves of his brown robe in anticipation of the cold.

"I think it is too cold for you, Titus," Didymus said.

Titus faced him undaunted, arms folded and hands muffled in his sleeves, eyes twinkling incredulously. He was ready to go. Didymus got the idea Titus knew himself to be the healthier of the two. Didymus was vaguely annoyed at this manifestation of the truth. *Vanitas.*

"Won't they need you in the kitchen now?" he inquired.

Immediately he regretted having said that. And the way he had said it, with some malice, as though labour *per se* were important and the intention not so. *Vanitas* in a friar, and at his age too. Confronting Titus with a distinction his simple mind could never master and which, if it could, his great soul would never recognize. Titus only knew all that was necessary, that a friar did what he was best at in the community. And no matter the nature of his toil, the variety of the means at hand, the end was the same for all friars. Or indeed for all men, if they cared to know. Titus worked in the kitchen and garden. Was Didymus wrong in teaching geometry out of personal preference and perhaps—if this was so he was—out of pride? Had the spiritual worth of his labor been vitiated because of that? He did not think so, no. No, he taught geometry because it was useful and eternally true, like his theology, and though of a lower order of truth it escaped the common fate of theology and the humanities, perverted through the ages in the mouths of dunderheads and fools. From that point of view, his work came to the same thing as Titus's. The vineyard was everywhere, they were in it, and that was essential.

Didymus, consciously humble, held open the door for Titus. Sandals scraping familiarly, they passed through dark corridors until they came to the stairway. Lights from floors above and below spangled through the carven apertures of the winding stair and fell in confusion upon the worn oaken steps.

At the outside door they were ambushed. An old friar stepped out of the shadows to intercept them. Standing with Didymus and Titus, however, made him appear younger. Or possibly it was the tenseness of him.

"Good evening, Father," he said to Didymus. "And Titus."

Didymus nodded in salutation and Titus said deliberately, as though he were the first one ever to put words in such conjunction:

"Good evening, Father Rector."

The Rector watched Didymus expectantly. Didymus studied the man's face. It told him nothing but curiosity—a luxury which could verge on vice in the cloister. Didymus frowned his incomprehension. He was about to speak. He decided against it, turning to Titus:

"Come on, Titus, we've got a walk to take before Vespers."

The Rector was left standing.

They began to circle the monastery grounds. Away from the buildings it was brighter. With a sudden shudder, Didymus felt the freezing air bite into his body all over. Instinctively he drew up his cowl. That was a little better. Not much. It was too cold for him to relax, breathe deeply and stride freely. It had not looked this cold from his window. He fell into Titus's gait. The steps were longer, but there was an illusion of warmth about moving in unison. Bit by bit he found himself duplicating every aspect of Titus in motion. Heads down, eyes

just ahead of the next step, undeviating, they seemed peripatetic figures
in a Gothic frieze. The stones of the walk were trampled over with
frozen footsteps. Titus's feet were grey and bare in their open sandals.
Pieces of ice, the thin edges of ruts, cracked off under foot, skittering
sharply away. A crystal fragment lit between Titus's toes and did not
melt there. He did not seem to notice it. This made Didymus lift his
eyes.

A fine Franciscan! Didymus snorted, causing a flurry of vapors. He
had the despicable caution of the comfortable who move mountains, if
need be, to stay that way. Here he was, cowl up and heavy woollen
socks on, and regretting the weather because it exceeded his anticipa-
tions. Painfully he stubbed his toe on purpose and at once accused himself of exhibitionism. Then he damned the expression for its modern-
ity. He asked himself: wherein lay the renunciation of the world, the
flesh and the devil, the whole point of following after St. Francis
today? Poverty, Chastity, Obedience, the three vows. There was nothing of suffering in the poverty of the friar nowadays: he was penniless,
but materially rich compared to—what was the phrase he used to
hear?—"one third of the nation." A beggar, a homeless mendicant by
very definition, he knew nothing—except as it affected others "less
fortunate"—of the miseries of begging in the streets. Verily, it was no
heavy cross, this vow of Poverty, so construed and practiced, in the
modern world. Begging had become unfashionable. Somewhere along
the line the meaning had been lost, they had become too "fortunate."
Official agencies, to whom it was a nasty but necessary business, dispensed Charity without mercy or grace. He recalled with wry amusement Frederick Barbarossa's appeal to fellow princes when opposed by
the might of the medieval Church: "We have a clean conscience, and
it tells us that God is with us. Ever have we striven to bring back
priests and, in especial, those of the topmost rank, to the condition of
the first Christian Church. In those days the clergy raised their eyes to
the angels, shone through miracles, made whole the sick, raised the
dead, made Kings and Princes subject to them, not with arms but with
their holiness. But now they are smothered in delights. To withdraw
from them the harmful riches which burden them to their own un-
doing is a labor of love in which all Princes should eagerly participate."

And Chastity, what of that? Well, that was all over for him—a
battle he had fought and won many years ago. A sin whose temptations had prevailed undiminished through the centuries, but withal
for him, an old man, a dead issue, a young man's trial. Only Obedi-

ence remained, and that too was no longer difficult for him. There was something—much as he disliked the term—to be said for "conditioning." He had to smile at himself: why should he bristle so at using the word? It was only contemporary slang for a theory the Church had always known. "Psychiatry," so called, and all the ghastly superstition that attended its practice, the deification of its high priests in the secular schools, made him ill. But it would pass. Just look how alchemy had flourished, and where was it today?

Clearly an abecedarian observance of the vows did not promise perfection. Stemmed in divine wisdom, they were branches meant to flower forth, but requiring of the friar the water and sunlight of sacrifice. The letter led nowhere. It was the spirit of the vows which opened the way and revealed to the soul, no matter the flux of circumstance, the means of salvation.

He had picked his way through the welter of familiar factors again —again to the same conclusion. The last time when he received the letter from Seraphin asking him to come to St. Louis, saying his years prohibited unnecessary travel and endowed his request with a certain prerogative, No, he had written back, it's simply impossible—not saying why. God help him, as a natural man, he had an inordinate desire to see his brother again. One of them must die soon. But as a friar, he remembered from Titus: "Unless a man be clearly delivered from the love of all creatures, he may not fully tend to his creator." Therein, the keeping of the vows having become an easy habit for him, was his opportunity. It was plain and there was sacrifice and it was hard. And he had not gone.

The flesh just above his knees felt frozen. They were drawing near the entrance again. His face too felt the same way, like a slab of pasteboard, stiffest at the tip of his nose. When he wrinkled his brow and puffed out his cheeks to blow hot air up to his nose, his skin seemed to crackle like old parchment. His eyes watered from the wind. He pressed a hand, warm from his sleeve, to his exposed neck. Frozen, like his face. It would be chapped tomorrow.

Titus, white hair awry in the wind, looked just the same.

They entered the monastery door. The Rector stopped them. It was almost as before, except that Didymus was occupied with feeling his face and patting it back to life.

"Ah, Didymus! It must be cold indeed!" The Rector smiled at Titus and returned his gaze to Didymus. He made it appear that they were allied in being amused at Didymus's face. Didymus touched his nose tenderly. Assured it would stand the operation, he blew it lustily. He stuffed the handkerchief up his sleeve. The Rector, misinterpreting all this ceremony, obviously was afraid of being ignored.

"The telegram, Didymus. I'm sorry, I thought it might have been important."

"I received no telegram."

They faced each other, waiting, experiencing a hanging moment of uneasiness.

Then, having employed the deductive method, they both looked at Titus. Although he had not been listening, rather had been studying the naked toes in his sandals, he sensed their eyes questioning him.

"Yes, Father Rector?" he answered.

"The telegram for Father Didymus, Titus?" the Rector demanded. "Where is it?" Titus started momentarily out of willingness to be of service, but ended, his mind refusing to click, impassive before them. The Rector shook his head in faint exasperation and reached his hand down into the folds of Titus's cowl. He brought forth two envelopes. One, the telegram, he gave to Didymus. The other, a letter, he handed back to Titus.

"I gave you this letter this morning, Titus. It's for Father Anthony." Intently Titus stared unremembering at the letter. "I wish you would see that Father Anthony gets it right away, Titus. I think it's a bill."

Titus held the envelope tightly to his breast and said: "Father Anthony."

Then his eyes were attracted by the sound of Didymus tearing open the telegram. While Didymus read the telegram, Titus's expression showed he at last understood his failure to deliver it. He was perturbed, mounting inner distress moving his lips silently.

Didymus looked up from the telegram. He saw the grief in Titus's face and said, astonished, "How did you know, Titus?"

Titus's eyes were both fixed and lowered in sorrow. It seemed to Didymus that Titus knew the meaning of the telegram. Didymus was suddenly weak, as before a miracle. His eyes went to the Rector to see how he was taking it. Then it occurred to him the Rector could not know what had happened.

As though nothing much had, the Rector laid an absolving hand lightly upon Titus's shoulder.

"He can't forgive himself for not delivering the telegram now that he remembers it. That's all."

Didymus was relieved. Seeing the telegram in his hand, he folded it quickly and stuffed it back in the envelope. He handed it to the Rector. Calmly, in a voice quite drained of feeling, he said, "My brother, Father Seraphin, died last night in St. Louis."

"Father Seraphin *from Rome?*"

"Yes," Didymus said, "in St. Louis. He was my brother. Appointed a confessor in Rome, a privilege for a foreigner. He was ninety-two."

"I know that, Didymus, an honor for the Order. I had no idea he was in this country. Ninety-two! God rest his soul!"

"I had a letter from him only recently."

"You did?"

"He wanted me to come to St. Louis. I hadn't seen him for twenty-five years at least."

"Twenty-five years?"

"It was impossible for me to visit him."

"But if he was in this country, Didymus . . ."

The Rector waited for Didymus to explain.

Didymus opened his mouth to speak, heard the clock in the tower sound the quarter-hour, and said nothing, listening, lips parted, to the last of the three strokes die away.

"Why Didymus, it could easily have been arranged," the Rector persisted.

Didymus turned abruptly to Titus, who, standing in a dream, had been inattentive since the clock struck.

"Come, Titus, we'll be late."

He hastened down the corridor with Titus. "No," he said in agitation, causing Titus to look at him in surprise. "I told him No. It was simply impossible." He was conscious of Titus's attention. "To visit him, Seraphin, who is dead." That had come naturally enough for being the first time in his thoughts that Seraphin was dead. Was there not some merit in his dispassionate acceptance of the fact?

They entered the chapel for Vespers and knelt down.

II

The clock struck. One, two . . . two. Two? No, there must have been one or two strokes before. He had gone to sleep. It was three. At least three, probably four. Or five. He waited. It could not be two: he remembered the brothers filing darkly into the chapel at that hour. Disturbing the shadows for matins and lauds. If it was five—he listened for faint noises in the building—it would only be a few minutes. They would come in, the earliest birds, to say their Masses. There were

no noises. He looked toward the windows on the St. Joseph side of
the chapel. He might be able to see a light from a room across the
court. That was not certain even if it was five. It would have to come
through the stained glass. Was that possible? It was still night. Was
there a moon? He looked round the chapel. If there was, it might
shine on a window. There was no moon. Or it was overhead. Or powerless against the glass. He yawned. It could not be five. His knees
were numb from kneeling. He shifted on them. His back ached.
Straightening it, he gasped for breath. He saw the sanctuary light. The
only light, red. Then it came back to him. Seraphin was dead. He tried
to pray. No words. Why words? Meditation in the Presence. The perfect prayer. He fell asleep . . .

    . . . Spiraling brown coil on coil under the golden sun the river
slithered across the blue and flowerflecked land. On an eminence they
held identical hands over their eyes for visors and mistook it with
pleasure for an endless murmuring serpent. They considered unafraid
the prospect of its turning in its course and standing on tail to swallow
them gurgling alive. They sensed it was in them to command this also
by a wish. Their visor hands vanished before their eyes and became
instead the symbol of brotherhood clasped between them. This they
wished. Smiling the same smile back and forth they began laughing:
"Jonah!" And were walking murkily up and down the brown belly
of the river in mock distress. Above them, foolishly triumphant, rippling in contentment, mewed the waves. Below swam an occasional
large fish, absorbed in ignoring them, and the mass of crustacea,
eagerly seething, too numerous on the bottom to pretend exclusiveness.
"Jonah indeed!" the brothers said, surprised to see the bubbles they
birthed. They strolled then for hours this way. The novelty wearing
off (without regret, else they would have wished themselves elsewhere), they began to talk and say ordinary things. Their mother had
died, their father too, and how old did that make them? It was the
afternoon of the funerals, which they had managed, transcending time,
to have held jointly. She had seemed older and for some reason he
otherwise. How, they wondered, should it be with them, *memento
mori* clicking simultaneously within them, lackaday. The sound of
dirt descending six feet to clatter on the coffins was memorable but
unmentionable. Their own lives, well . . . only half curious (something to do) they halted to kick testingly a waterlogged rowboat
resting on the bottom, the crustacea complaining and olive green silt
rising to speckle the surface with dark stars . . . well, what *had* they

been doing? A crayfish pursued them, clad in sable armor, dearly de-
siring to do battle, brandishing hinged swords. Well, for one thing
working for the canonization of Fra Bartolomeo, had got two cardinals
interested, was hot after those remaining who were at all possible, a
slow business. Yes, one would judge so in the light of past canoniza-
tions, though being stationed in Rome had its advantages. Me, the
same old grind, teaching, pounding away, giving Pythagoras no rest
in his grave . . . They made an irresolute pass at the crayfish, who
had caught up with them. More about Fra Bartolomeo, what else is
there? Except, you will laugh or have me excommunicated for wanton
presumption, though it's only faith in a faithless age, making a vow
not to die until he's made a saint, recognized rather—he is one, convinced of it, Didymus (never can get used to calling you that) a saint
sure as I'm alive, having known him, no doubt of it, something wrong
with your knee? Knees then! The crayfish, he's got hold of you there,
another at your back. If you like, we'll leave, only I do like it here.
Well, go ahead then, you never did like St. Louis, isn't that what you
used to say? Alone, in pain, he rose to the surface, parting the silt
stars. The sun like molten gold squirted him in the eye. Numb now,
unable to remember and too blind to refurnish his memory by observation, he waited for this limbo to clear away . . .

Awake now, he was face to face with a flame, blinding him. He
avoided it. A dead weight bore him down, his aching back. Slowly,
like ink in a blotter, his consciousness spread. The supports beneath
him were kneeling limbs, his, the veined hands, bracing him, pressing
flat, his own. His body, it seemed, left off there; the rest was something else, floor. He raised his head to the flame again and tried to
determine what kept it suspended even with his face. He shook his
head, blinking dumbly, a fourlegged beast. He could see nothing, only
his knees and hands, which he felt rather, and the flame floating unaccountably in the darkness. That part alone was a mystery. And then
there came a pressure and pull on his shoulders, urging him up. Fingers, a hand, a rustling related to its action, then the rustling in rhythm
with the folds of a brown curtain, a robe naturally, ergo a friar,
holding a candle, trying to raise him up, Titus. The clock began
striking.

"Put out the candle," Didymus said.

Titus closed his palm slowly around the flame, unflinching, snuffing
it. The odor of burning string. Titus pinched the wick deliberately.
He waited a moment, the clock falling silent, and said, "Father Rec-

tor expects you will say a Mass for the Dead at five o'clock."

"Yes, I know." He yawned deliciously. "I told him *that*." He bit his lips at the memory of the disgusting yawn. Titus had found him asleep. Shame overwhelmed him, and he searched his mind for justification. He found none.

"It is five now," Titus said.

It was maddening. "I don't see anyone else if it's five," he snapped. Immediately he was aware of a light burning in the sacristy. He blushed and grew pale. Had someone besides Titus seen him sleeping? But, listening, he heard nothing. No one else was up yet. He was no longer pale and was only blushing now. He saw it all hopefully. He was saved. Titus had gone to the sacristy to prepare for Mass. He must have come out to light the candles on the main altar. Then he had seen the bereaved keeping vigil on all fours, asleep, snoring even. What did Titus think of that? It withered him to remember, but he was comforted some that the only witness had been Titus. Had the sleeping apostles in Gethsemane been glad it was Christ?

Wrong! Hopelessly wrong! For there had come a noise after all. Someone else was in the sacristy. He stiffened and walked palely toward it. He must go there and get ready to say his Mass. A few steps he took only, his back buckling out, humping, his knees sinking to the floor, his hands last. The floor with fingers smelling of dust and genesis reached up and held him. The fingers were really spikes and they were dusty from holding him this way all his life. For a radiant instant which had something of eternity about it, he saw the justice of his position. Then there was nothing.

III

A little snow had fallen in the night, enough to powder the dead grass and soften the impression the leafless trees etched in the sky. Greyly the sky promised more snow, but now, at the end of the day following his collapse in the chapel, it was melting. Didymus, bundled around by blankets, sat in a wheelchair at the window, unsleepy. Only the landscape wearied him. Dead and unmoving though it must be, of that he was sure, it conspired to make him see everything in it as living, moving, something to be watched, each visible tuft of grass, each cluster of snow. The influence of the snow perhaps? For the ground, ordinarily uniform in texture and drabness, had split up into individual patches. They appeared to be involved in a struggle of some kind, possibly to overlap each other, constantly shifting. But whether it was equally one against one, or one against all, he could not make out. He reminded himself he did not believe it was actually happening. It was confusing and he closed his eyes. After a time this confused and tired him in the same way. The background of darkness became a field of vari-colored factions, warring, and, worse than the landscape, things like worms and comets wriggled and exploded before his closed eyes. Finally, as though to orchestrate their motions, they carried with them a bewildering noise or music which grew louder and cacophonous. The effect was cumulative, inevitably unbearable, and Didymus would have to open his eyes again. The intervals of peace became gradually rarer on the landscape. Likewise when he shut his eyes to it the restful darkness dissolved sooner than before into riot.

The door of his room opened, mercifully dispelling his illusions, and that, because no knock, could only be Titus. Unable to move in his chair, Didymus listened to Titus moving about the room at his back. The tinkle of a glass once, the squeak of the bookcase indicating a book taken out or replaced, they were sounds Didymus could recognize. But that first tap-tap and the consequent click of metal on metal, irregular and scarcely audible, was disconcertingly unfamiliar. His curiosity, centering on it, raised it to a delicious mystery. He kept down the urge to shout at Titus. But he attempted to fish from memory the precise character of the corner from which the sound came with harrowing repetition. The sound stopped then, as though to thwart him on the brink of revelation. Titus's footsteps scraped across the room. The door opened and closed. For a few steps, Didymus heard Titus going down the corridor. He asked himself not to be moved by idle curiosity, a thing of the senses. He would not be tempted now.

A moment later the keystone of his good intention crumbled, and the whole edifice of his detachment with it. More shakily than quickly, Didymus moved his hands to the wheels of the chair. He would roll over to the corner and investigate the sound . . . He would? His hands lay limply on the wheels, ready to propel him to his mind's destination, but, weak, white, powerless to grip the wheels or anything. He regarded them with contempt. He had known they would fail him; he had been foolish to give them another chance. Disdainful of his hands, he looked out the window. He could still do that, couldn't he? It was raining some now. The landscape started to move, rearing and reeling crazily, as though drunken with the rain. In horror, Didymus damned his eyes. He realized this trouble was probably going to be chronic. He turned his gaze in despair to the trees, to the branches level with his eyes and nearer than the insane ground. Hesitating warily, fearful the gentle boughs under scrutiny would turn into hideous waving tentacles, he looked. With a thrill, he knew he was seeing clearly.

Gauzily rain descended in a fine spray, hanging in fat berries from the wet black branches where leaves had been and buds would be, cold crystal drops. They fell now and then ripely of their own weight, or shaken by the intermittent wind they spilled before their time. Promptly they appeared again, pendulous.

Watching the raindrops prove gravity, he was grateful for nature's, rather than his, return to reason. Still, though he professed faith in his faculties, he would not look away from the trees and down at the ground, nor close his eyes. Gratefully he savored the cosmic truth in the falling drops and the mildly trembling branches. There was order, he thought, which in justice and science ought to include the treacherous landscape. Risking all, he ventured a glance at the ground. All was still there. He smiled. He was going to close his eyes (to make it universal and conclusive), when the door opened again.

Didymus strained to catch the meaning of Titus's movements. Would the clicking sound begin? Titus did go to that corner of the room again. Then it came, louder than before, but only once this time.

Titus came behind his chair, turned it, and wheeled him over to the corner.

On a hook which Titus had screwed into the wall hung a bird cage covered with black cloth.

"What's all this?" Didymus said.

Titus tapped the covered cage expectantly.

A bird chirped once.

"The bird," Titus explained in excitement, "is inside."

Didymus almost laughed. He sensed in time, however, the necessity of seeming befuddled and severe. Titus expected it.

"I don't believe it," Didymus snapped.

Titus smiled wisely and tapped the cage again.

"There!" he exclaimed when the bird chirped.

Didymus shook his head in mock anger. "You made that beastly noise, Titus, you mountebank!"

Titus, profoundly amused by such scepticism, removed the black cover.

The bird, a canary, flicked its head sidewise in interest, looking them up and down. Then it turned its darting attention to the room. It chirped once in curt acceptance of the new surroundings. Didymus and Titus came under its black dot of an eye once more, this time for closer analysis. The canary chirped twice, perhaps that they were welcome, even pleasing, and stood on one leg to show them what a gay bird it was. It then returned to the business of pecking a piece of apple.

"I see you've given him something to eat," Didymus said, and felt that Titus, though he seemed content to watch the canary, waited for him to say something more. "I am very happy, Titus, to have this canary," he went on. "I suppose he will come in handy now that I must spend my days in this infernal chair."

Titus did not look at him while he said, "He is a good bird, Father. He is one of the Saint's own good birds."

Through the window Didymus watched the days and nights come and go. For the first time, though his life as a friar had been copiously annotated with significant references, he got a good idea of eternity. Monotony, of course, was one word for it, but like all the others, as well as the allegories worked up by imaginative retreat masters, it was empty beside the experience itself, untranslatable. He would doze and wonder if by some quirk he had been cast out of the world into eternity, but since it was neither heaven nor exactly purgatory or hell, as he understood them, he concluded it must be an uncharted isle subscribing to the mother forms only in the matter of time. And having thought this, he was faintly annoyed at his ponderous whimsy. Titus, like certain of the hours, came periodically. He would read or simply sit with him in silence. The canary was there always, but except as it showed signs of sleepiness at twilight and spirit at dawn, Didymus regarded it as a subtle device, like the days and nights and bells, to give the lie to the vulgar error that time flew. The cage was small and the canary would not sing. Time, hanging in the room like a jealous fog, possessed him and voided everything except it. It seemed impossible each time Titus came that he should be able to escape the room.

" 'After him,' " Titus read from Bishop Bale one day, " 'came Fabius, a Roman born, who (as Eusebius witnesseth) as he was returning home out of the field, and with his countrymen present to elect a new bishop, there was a pigeon seen standing on his head and suddenly he was created pastor of the Church, which he looked not for.' "

They smiled at having the same thought and both looked up at the canary. Since Didymus sat by the window most of the day now, he had asked Titus to put a hook there for the cage. He had to admit to himself he did this to let Titus know he appreciated the canary. Also, as a secondary motive, he reasoned, it enabled the canary to look out the window. What a little yellow bird could see to interest it in the frozen scene was a mystery, but that, Didymus sighed, was a two-edged sword. And he took to watching the canary more.

So far as he was able to detect the moods of the canary he participated in them. In the morning the canary, bright and clownish, flitted back and forth between the two perches in the cage, hanging from the sides and cocking its little tufted head at Didymus querulously. During these acrobatics Didymus would twitch his hands in quick imitation of the canary's stunts. He asked Titus to construct a tiny swing, such as he had seen, which the canary might learn to use, since it appeared to be an intelligent and daring sort. Titus got the swing, the canary did master it, but there seemed to be nothing Didymus could do with his hands that was like swinging. In fact, after watching a while it was as though the canary were fixed to a pendulum, inanimate, a piece of machinery, a yellow blur—ticking, for the swing made a little sound, and Didymus went to sleep and often when he woke the canary was still going, like a clock. Didymus had no idea how long he slept at these times, maybe a minute, maybe hours. Gradually the canary got bored with the swing and used it less and less. In the same way, Didymus suspected, he himself had wearied of looking out the window. The first meagre satisfaction had worn off. The dead trees, the sleeping snow, like the swing for the canary, were sources of diversion which soon grew stale. They were captives, he and the canary, and the only thing they craved was escape. Didymus slowly considered the problem. There was nothing, obviously, for him to do. He could pray, which he did, but he was not sure the only thing wrong with him was the fact he could not walk and that to devote his prayer to that end was justifiable. Inevitably it occurred to him his plight might well be an act of God. Why this punishment, though, he asked himself, and immediately supplied the answer. He had, for one thing, gloried too much in having it in him to turn down Seraphin's request to come to St. Louis. The intention, that was all important, and he, he feared, had done the right thing for the wrong reason. He had noticed something of the faker in himself before. But it was not clear if he had erred. There was a certain consolation, at bottom dismal, in this doubt. It was true there appeared to be a nice justice in being stricken a cripple if he had been wrong in refusing to travel to see Seraphin, if human love was all he was fitted for, if he was incapable of renunciation for the right reason, if the mystic counsels were too strong for him, if he was still too pedestrian after all these years of prayer and contemplation, if—

The canary was swinging, the first time in several days.

The reality of his position was insupportable. There were two ways of regarding it and he could not make up his mind. Humbly, he wished to get well and to be able to walk. But if this was a punishment, was not prayer to lift it declining to see the divine point? He did wish to get well; that would settle it. Otherwise his predicament could only be resolved through means more serious than he dared cope with. It would be like refusing to see Seraphin all over again. By some mistake, he protested, he had at last been placed in a position vital with meaning and precedents inescapably Christian. But was he the man for it? Unsure of himself, he was afraid to go on trial. It would be no minor trial, so construed, but one in which the greatest values were involved, a human soul and the means of its salvation or damnation. Not watered down suburban precautions and routine pious exercises, but Faith such as saints and martyrs had, and Despair such as only they had been tempted by. No, he was not the man for it. He was unworthy. He simply desired to walk and in a few years to die a normal uninspired death. He did not wish to see (what was apparent) the greatest significance in his affliction. He preferred to think in terms of physical betterment. He was so sure he was not a saint that he did not consider this easier road beneath him, though attracted by the higher one. That was the rub. Humbly, then, he wanted to be able to walk, but he wondered if there was not presumption in such humility.

Thus he decided to pray for health and count the divine hand not there. Decided. A clean decision—not distinction—no mean feat in the light of all the moral theology he had swallowed. The canary, all its rocking come to naught once more, slept motionless in the swing. Despite the manifest prudence of the course he had settled upon, Didymus dozed off ill at ease in his wheelchair by the window. Distastefully, the last thing he remembered was that "prudence" is a virtue more celebrated in the modern Church.

At his request in the days following a doctor visited him. The Rector came along too. When Didymus tried to find out the nature of his illness, the doctor looked solemn and pronounced it to be one of those things. Didymus received this with a look of mystification. So the doctor went on to say there was no telling about it. Time alone would tell. Didymus asked the doctor to recommend some books dealing with cases like his. They might have one of them in the monastery library. Titus could read to him in the meantime. For, though he disliked being troublesome, "one of those things" as a diagnosis meant very little to an unscientific beggar like him. The phrase had a philosophic ring to it, but to his knowledge neither the Early Fathers nor the Scholastics seemed to have dealt with it. The Rector smiled. The doctor, annoyed, replied drily:

"Is that a fact?"

Impatiently Didymus said, "I know how old I am, if that's it."

Nothing was lost of the communion he kept with the canary. He still watched its antics and his fingers in his lap followed them clumsily. He did not forget about himself, that he must pray for health, that it was best that way—"prudence" dictated it—but he did think more of the canary's share of their captivity. A canary in a cage, he reasoned, is like a bud which never blooms.

He asked Titus to get a book on canaries, but nothing came of it and he did not mention it again.

Some days later Titus read:

"'Twenty-ninth pope, Marcellus, a Roman, was pastor of the Church, feeding it with wisdom and doctrine. And (as I may say with the Prophet) a man according to God's heart and full of Christian works. This man admonished Maximianus the Emperor and endeavored to remove him from persecuting the saints—'"

"Stop a moment, Titus," Didymus interrupted.

Steadily since Titus began to read the canary had been jumping from the swing to the bottom of the cage. Now it was quietly standing on one foot in the swing. Suddenly it flew at the side of the cage nearest them and hung there, its ugly little claws, like bent wire, hooked to the slender bars. It observed them intently, first Titus and then Didymus, at whom it continued to stare. Didymus's hands were tense in his lap.

"Go ahead, read," Didymus said, relaxing his hands.

"'But the Emperor being more hardened, commanded Marcellus to be beaten with cudgels and to be driven out of the city, wherefore he entered into the house of one Lucina, a widow, and there kept the congregation secretly, which the tyrant hearing, made a stable for cattle of the same house and committed the keeping of it to the bishop Marcellus. After that he governed the Church by writing Epistles, without any other kind of teaching, being condemned to such a vile service. And being thus daily tormented with strife and noisomeness, at length gave up the ghost. Anno 308.'"

"Very good, Titus. I wonder how we missed that one before."

The canary, still hanging on the side of the cage, had not moved, its head turned sidewise, its eye as before fixed on Didymus.

"Would you bring me a glass of water, Titus?"

Titus got up and looked in the cage. The canary hung there, as though waiting, not a feather stirring.

"The bird has water here," Titus said, pointing to the small cup fastened to the cage.

"For me, Titus, the water's for me. Don't you think I know you look after the canary? You don't forget us, though I don't see why you don't."

Titus left the room with a glass.

Didymus's hands were tense again. Eyes on the canary's eye, he got up from his wheelchair, his face strained and white with the impossible effort, and, his fingers somehow managing it, he opened the cage. The canary darted out and circled the room chirping. Before it lit, though it seemed about to make its perch triumphantly the top of the cage, Didymus fell over on his face and lay prone on the floor.

In bed that night, unsuffering and barely alive, he saw at will everything revealed in his past. Events long forgotten happened again before his eyes. Clearly, sensitively, he saw Seraphin and himself, just as they had always been—himself, never quite sure. He heard all that he had ever said, and that anyone had said to him. He had talked too much too. The past mingled with the present. In the same moment and scene he made his first Communion, was ordained, and confessed his sins for the last time.

The canary perched in the dark atop the cage, head warm under wing, already, it seemed to Didymus, without memory of its captivity, dreaming of a former freedom, an ancestral summer day with flowers and trees. Outside it was snowing.

The Rector, followed by others, came into the room and administered the last sacrament. Didymus heard them all gathered prayerfully around his bed thinking (they thought) secretly: this sacrament often strengthens the dying, tip-of-the-tongue wisdom indigenous to the priesthood, Henry the Eighth had six wives. He saw the same hackneyed smile, designed to cheer, pass bravely among them, and marvelled at the crudity of it. They went away then, all except Titus, their individual footsteps sounding (for him) the character of each friar. He might have been Francis himself for what he knew then of the little brothers and the cure of souls. He heard them thinking their expectation to be called from bed before daybreak to return to his room and say the office of the dead over his body, become the body, and whispering hopefully to the contrary. Death was now an unwelcome guest in the cloister.

He wanted nothing in the world for himself at last. This may have been the first time he found his will amenable to the Divine. He had never been less himself and more the saint. Yet now, so close to sublimity, or perhaps only tempted to believe so (the Devil is most wily at the deathbed), he was beset by the grossest distractions. They were to be expected, he knew, as indelible in the order of things: the bingo game going on under the Cross for the seamless garments of the Son of Man: everywhere the sign of the contradiction, and always. When would he cease to be surprised by it? Incidents repeated themselves, twined, parted, faded away, came back clear, and would not be prayed out of mind. He watched himself mounting the pulpit of a metropolitan church, heralded by the pastor as the renowned Franciscan father sent by God in His goodness to preach this Novena—like to say a little prayer to test the microphone, Father?—and later reading through the petitions to Our Blessed Mother, cynically tabulating the pleas for a Catholic boy friend, drunkenness banished, the sale of real estate and coming furiously upon one: "that I'm not pregnant." And at the same church on Good Friday carrying the crucifix along the communion rail for the people to kiss, giving them the indulgence, and afterwards in the sacristy wiping the lipstick of the faithful from the image of Christ crucified.

"Take down a book, any book, Titus, and read. Begin anywhere."

Roused by his voice, the canary fluttered, looked sharply about, and buried its head once more in the warmth of its wing.

" 'By the lions,' " Titus read, " 'are understood the acrimonies and impetuosities of the irascible faculty, which faculty is as bold and daring in its acts as are the lions. By the harts and the leaping does is understood the other faculty of the soul, which is the concupiscible— that is—' "

"Skip the exegesis," Didymus broke in weakly. "I can do without that now. Read the verse."

Titus read: " 'Birds of swift wing, lions, harts, leaping does, mountains, valleys, banks, waters, breezes, heats and terrors that keep watch by night, by the pleasant lyres and by the siren's song, I conjure you, cease your wrath and touch not the wall . . .' "

"Turn off the light, Titus."

Titus went over to the switch. There was a brief period of darkness during which Didymus's eyes became accustomed to a different shade, a glow rather, which possessed the room slowly. Then he saw the full moon had let down a ladder of light through the window. He could see the snow, strangely blue, falling outside. So sensitive was his mind and eye (because his body now faint no longer blurred his vision?) he could count the snowflakes, all of them separately, before they drifted, winding, below the sill.

With the same wonderful clarity, he saw what he had made of his life. He saw himself tied down, caged, stunted in his apostolate, seeking the crumbs, the little pleasure, neglecting the source, always knowing death changes nothing, only immortalizes . . . and still ever lukewarm. In trivial attachments, in love of things, was death, no matter the appearance of life. In the highest attachment only, no matter the appearance of death, was life. He had always known this truth, but now he was feeling it. Unable to move his hand, only his lips, and hardly breathing, was it too late to act?

"Open the window, Titus," he whispered.

And suddenly he could pray. *Hail Mary . . . Holy Mary, Mother of God, pray for us sinners now and at the hour of our death . . .* finally the time to say, *pray for* me *now—the hour of* my *death, amen.* Lest he deceive himself at the very end that this was the answer to a lifetime of praying for a happy death, happy because painless, he tried to turn his thoughts from himself, to join them to God, thinking how at last he did—didn't he *now?*—prefer God above all else. But ashamedly not sure he did, perhaps only fearing hell, with an uneasy sense of justice he put himself foremost among the wise in their own generation, the perennials seeking after God when doctor, lawyer, and bank fails. If he wronged himself, he did so out of humility, a holy error. He ended, to make certain he had not fallen under the same old presumption disguised as the face of humility, by flooding his mind with maledictions. He suffered the piercing white voice of the Apocalypse to echo in his soul: *But because thou art lukewarm, and neither cold, nor hot, I will begin to vomit thee out of my mouth.* And St. Bernard, fiery-eyed in a white habit, thundered at him from the twelfth century: "Hell is paved with the bald pates of priests!"

There was a soft flutter, the canary flew to the window sill, paused, and tilted into the snow. Titus stepped too late to the window and stood gazing dumbly after it. He raised a trembling old hand, fingers bent in awe and sorrow, to his forehead, and turned stealthily to Didymus.

Didymus closed his eyes. He let a long moment pass before he opened them. Titus, seeing him awake then, fussed with the window latch and held a hand down to feel the draught, nodding anxiously as though it were the only evil abroad in the world, all the time straining his old eyes for a glimpse of the canary somewhere in the trees.

Didymus said nothing, letting Titus keep his secret. With his whole will he tried to lose himself in the sight of God, and failed. He was not in the least transported. Even now he could find no divine sign within himself. He knew he still had to look outside, to Titus. God still chose to manifest Himself most in sanctity.

Titus, nervous under his stare, and to account for staying at the window so long, felt for the draught again, frowned, and kept his eye hunting among the trees.

The thought of being the cause of such elaborate dissimulation in so simple a soul made Didymus want to smile—or cry, he did not know which . . . and could do neither. Titus persisted. How long would it be, Didymus wondered faintly, before Titus ungrievingly gave the canary up for lost in the snowy arms of God? The snowflakes whirled at the window, for a moment for all their bright blue beauty as though struck still by lightning, and Didymus closed his eyes, only to find them there also, but darkly falling.

RALPH ROBIN:

Scott Burgess and His Friends

Scott Burgess saw his parents when he was six, eleven, and sixteen. He was raised in a boarding school for the children of missionaries, and the heathen generously parted with his parents that often. They were both ordained, if that is the correct term; and they died of natural causes before he was twenty-one. When Scott finished college (a person did so then) he went to work as a cataloguer at the Library of Congress.

It was necessary to live somewhere that was not a boarding school, a college dormitory, or Uncle Doctor's. A senior at the Library introduced him to an old virgin who wanted a young man in the house to protect her from thieves and fires: one couldn't be too careful thenadays. The old lady was delighted with his respectable antecedents; she took his money regularly only to preserve his self-respect. She gave him the smallest, coldest, and worst-furnished room in the house and there he lived on. He mowed the lawn and stoked the furnace and did other chores. He didn't think this strange; he had done these things at boarding school and at college and was perhaps uneasy that he did not have to at the Library of Congress.

Nor did he find it strange that the house on First Street, Southeast, was hierarchic. Miss Lucy Pitton, the owner, ranked first; Miss Mary Klank, the companion, ranked second; and young Scott Burgess, "the boy who stays with us," was third and last. Only the head of the house preserved the house's maidenhead, though she thought all was well. Mary coupled every Saturday night with a contractor concealed as her poor old friends in Anacostia. Scott preserved his purity— except for nocturnal emissions (the heavy pajamas he wore because of the cold pretty well protected the sheets, and the Chinese laundry had an air of anonymity that left him unashamed)—only until he was twenty-seven.

Scott did not attend the war. He usually had a slight cold because of the sharp difference in temperature between his room and the Library—or because he believed that this would cause a cold on the double authority of the boarding school doctor and Uncle Doctor. The eye, ear, nose, and throat specialist (that Elizabeth, Betty, Betsy, and Bess of medicine) who examined him at the selection center had a passion for chronic sinusitis and found his chronic cold to be such and sent him back to his cold room and hot Library. A few days later a young woman struck up an acquaintance with him at a streetcar stop and took him home to her apartment with her.

They were a naive pair all right, as their acquaintance improved. He pretended to be an experienced lover and she believed him though she didn't pretend to be inexperienced. She was disappointed at his inexpertness. "He can't even find the hole," she thought, shocked but excited by her language. "He scarcely knows what to do when he is in it." But if inexpert he was not inapt. Essentially it was easier than keeping up a good fire in an old furnace with too little coal or mastering the numbering system at the Library of Congress. He soon achieved a high degree of proficiency. They soon got to like each other and finally fell in love. Her name was Eloise Darnell; she was the wife of a professor at George Washington University, but they had separated. Fifteen years passed as easily as in *The Winter's Tale* (PR 2839).

"It's white," Lucy Pitton said. She was ninety-one.

"It's good. Eat it," Mary Klank said. She was sixty-two. "See, I'm eating mine. Scott is eating his. Aren't you, Scott?"

"Yes, Miss Klank," Scott said. He lifted a spoonful of dense Cream of Wheat to his mouth. He was forty-two.

"I want Wheatena," Lucy Pitton said.

"The doctor says Wheatena is too coarse for you."

"I don't care what the doctor says. I want Wheatena. Scott, your uncle is a doctor, isn't he?"

"Yes, Miss Pitton."

"Write to him and ask him if I can't eat Wheatena. Mary, take this away and bring me Wheatena."

"Oh, all right."

"Take yours away and Scott's too. Bring us all Wheatena. I think it's nice for a whole family to eat the same thing for breakfast. It's what they call togetherness nowadays and that's something nice about these terrible times anyway. You know, I regard you both as my family. Have you given Miss Klank your check this week, Scott?"

"Yes, Miss Pitton."

"You know we only take your money to preserve your self-respect, don't you, Scott?"

"Yes, Miss Pitton."

She turned up the volume of her hearing aid. "Do I hear you getting another pot, Mary?"

"Well?"

"Don't make work for yourself. Throw away that Cream of Wheat and use the same pot."

"All right."

"Mary?"

"Yes?"

"Be sure you scour out all that Cream of Wheat before you cook the Wheatena. I won't eat if I find one speck."

Scott reconciled himself to losing an hour's leave. Now that he was head of a subsection he always charged himself an hour's annual leave when he was more than a few minutes late; he thought it set a good example. When Mary brought the Wheatena, Scott discovered steel wool in it. He didn't want to offend Miss Klank; but he didn't want to murder Miss Pitton, so he had to raise an alarm. The hullabaloo was still going on when he left. He wondered if the excitement would not be as bad for Miss Pitton's heart as the steel wool would have been for her digestion; certainly it would be worse than plain Wheatena.

Her desire to eat a food considered bad for her was a new development, and Scott somewhat admired her for it. During the twenty years he had lived in her house, she had worried so much about her digestion that he had come to consider her diagrammatically, as a long alimentary canal activated by a heart and a tangle of nerve fibers. Scott believed that she loved him and loved Miss Klank also; that Miss Klank loved Miss Pitton and loved him.

"Yoo hoo, Scott. Yoo hoo." A woman moved her arm (terminating in a flat, fat hand) at the elbow like a windshield wiper. Scott had to stand there, late as he was, because this was a friend of his, Mrs. Havelly. "The admiral would like you to stop in for a highball after work. Five-thirtyish, shall we say?"

"Of course, Mrs. Havelly. Thank you, Mrs. Havelly. How are you? And is the admiral well? I shall look forward to seeing him."

Since his retirement Admiral Havelly had helped organize five reactionary political parties. They had all sunk; but the admiral never went down. He decided he had done enough for the Republic, except for one last public-spirited task: one which he expected would be compensated for by money as well as by universal appreciation. He hired a ghost to write his memoirs. But he was only a captain in reality, retired as a rear admiral, and his ghost was an old hack writing badly enough, in a style a generation behind the times. The publishers had plenty of fake books scheduled without Admiral Havelly's. A vanity press brought it out, very attractively for the money, and Admiral and Mrs. Havelly's problems in present-giving were solved for all time. Admiral Havelly was now launching a scheme to market frozen doughnuts in the District of Columbia, Maryland, and Virginia.

Scott put his hat back on and ran up the street, aware that the policemen beside the Old House Office Building were watching him with dull interest, aware that now he was not concerned what time he got to the Library, although he was running. He was concerned about his $12,837. He had saved it by no effort, simply by not learning to want things; but he valued it highly and often thought what to do with it. Sometimes he thought he would take leave without pay for a year and travel around the world; sometimes he thought he would buy a perfect house to live in; and sometimes he thought, not actually needing the money himself, he would give it to worthy charities. He often put himself to sleep dividing his savings among the National Heart Fund, the Young Men's Christian Association, Friendship House, and the American Civil Liberties Union. (He did not share his friend the admiral's political views.)

He was plunging up First Street toward Union Station, where he often sat in the winter when he was not in his room or at the Library. There was a clenching in his chest, cold as a package of frozen doughnuts; his face would have been hot except that it was cooled by the sharp air he moved through. The hints of his friends were converging to a conclusion: tonight they would extract from him a sacred pledge of all his money. He did not suspect Admiral Havelly of intent to embezzle his money; but he knew beyond any doubt whatever that the admiral would lose it all.

The great Library was lost behind him like a disapproving but slow adult; he was not going there today. He called up from the station. Jane in his subsection answered and he told her of important personal business.

"Your friend, Mrs. Darnell, called already. She wants you to call her."

"Yes. Yes, thank you."

"You're just like the husbands here even if you are an old bachelor. That's just like my husband too; he says, 'Yes, yes, thank you,' and then doesn't call me at all. I know."

"You are very hard on me, Jane. You make me see myself as in a mirror. But you are right. Yes, right. On the bibliography for Dr. Franciosi, go right ahead."

"I'll get stuck, Scott."

"Well, do the best you can."

Then he did call Eloise, who was working now for the Teamsters' Union.

"Scott? A very good morning to you. Do you know what day this is?"

"It's not your birthday."

"Of course not. You know when my birthday is. You bought me that lovely figurine from your friend the admiral."

"No, that was from my friend the Chinese general who has a store on I Street."

"That's who I meant. I don't have a good place for it, but I do love it; I take it out of my closet and look at it ever so often. But, Scott, what day is this?"

"You ask me a very difficult question, Eloise. I'm at a loss what to say. Tuesday?"

"I'm not going to call the Library of Congress for any more information, if you can't do better than that. Today is Halfway Day. To end the mystification, it's just exactly three months—only three months —before my decree becomes final. At last."

"Congratulations. Yes, indeed. Congratulations."

"Good-bye, Scott. I have to get ready for the coffee break, as the old joke is here—but I really have a lot of work to do."

Scott wandered to a stand-up snack bar, where orange crush whirled in a glass bowl. He wanted hot chocolate. He saw on a sign, with his usual astonishment at the change, that hot chocolate was fifteen cents; it seemed abnormal to him that hot chocolate had ever risen above ten cents and did not now include two cookies. The girl there, a cheerful fat thing she looked, made him hot chocolate in an unusual manner: she put vanilla ice cream in it.

He stirred with a wooden spoon in the paper cup, and the blob of ice cream collapsed into the drink. "Oh, my God," he said. "What will I do?" He didn't really want the hot chocolate at all, but he tasted it to see if it was cool enough and drank it in several gulps. He hurried into the cold part of the station, on the way to the trains, where two 1958 automobiles turned on carpets. Everywhere on

224

Capitol Hill the home owners or their contractors were ripping and pounding to make their garages fit these cars.

He saw there was a Pennsylvania train leaving for New York in fifteen minutes. He ran back to the ticket window, and to the trains again; and he ran down the platform to the coaches. He should have wired Uncle Doctor. Uncle Doctor had always said Scott was always welcome but should always wire: by Postal Telegraph, which Uncle Doctor preferred. When the train started to move, Scott felt suddenly sick. He wanted to get off and go back to the Library to die, but it was too late. He wasn't sure what was the matter with him, but he thought it must be his heart. He had a strange feeling in his chest, and pains rippled along his arms. Miss Pitton often spoke of pains radiating into the arms. This was one of the slower trains, and he spent five hours in expectation of death.

He thought about a quotation he was trying to place (a congressman was trying to place it and all over the Library people were looking for it) and he suddenly remembered the source while his mind spun with death; it was from Herodotus. The first thing he did in Pennsylvania Station was to call up the New York Public Library and verify it; then he wired his chief. He felt that a deficit had been made good, though of necessity by Western Union.

His uncle—really the husband of his mother's older sister—had his office on the ground floor of a remodeled house on West Tenth Street. He lived two flights up, in a small apartment; Scott's aunt was dead, but she had lasted among Christians twenty years longer than her sister. When she died in 1952, he sold his old practice and new turquoise stucco mansion on Staten Island and moved with some of his oldest furniture to Manhattan. It never occurred to Scott to take a taxi anywhere, not even in Washington where they are so cheap; and finding the subway, though he had often found it before, was beyond him today. He managed to get into the air on Seventh Avenue, and walked south.

He found the building, but the door of the office was locked. Under the lettered office hours there was a typewritten card held by pieces of curling Scotch tape. It read: OTHER TIMES TRY RESIDENCE ON THIRD FLOOR IN CASE OF EMERGENCY ONLY.

Scott raced up the stairs, two flights, and pounded on his uncle's door.

"Who is it? Is it an emergency?" his uncle called through this closed door.

"It's I. Scott."

"Well." The door opened. "I'm certainly surprised to see you, Scott. You didn't telegraph. I always told you you were always welcome so long as you telegraphed, preferably by Postal Telegraph, though of course they're out of business now and it would be necessary to use Western Union. I always thought Postal Telegraph much more efficient and obliging."

"I think I'm dying, Uncle Doctor."

"What of? Lung cancer? I warned my patients to give up smoking years ago, but hardly anyone listened to me. They have to read it in the newspapers."

"I don't smoke. I think I'm dying of heart disease."

"You look flushed. How did you get here from the station?"

"I walked. I didn't feel like—"

"You walked. And I heard you run up the steps. You can't be dying very fast. Unbutton your shirt."

The doctor bent and pressed his ear to Scott's breast. Scott thought he could hear the bumps of his heart going into that medical and related brain. He felt the warm ear and cheek on his skin. He could smell his uncle's hair, the old hairy smell, a little sourer now, perhaps, but still comforting.

The doctor took his head away. He said of course—what other phrase would he have used?—"You'll do."

"What's the matter with me, Uncle Doctor?"

"I want to speak to you very seriously. Very seriously and frankly. Sit down, if you please." The doctor seated himself on an old leather couch with wooden arms. Scott looked around, and sat down on a straight chair. He had buttoned his shirt and tied his tie and straightened his jacket. Unknowingly he had picked up his overcoat and was holding it over his arm.

"A young man like you, unmarried and living in a room by himself, is apt sometimes to fall into bad habits—in fact, to be frank, one particular bad habit. To be frank with you, he is liable to the habit of masturbation."

"But I don't masturbate, Uncle Doctor. I never did."

"Well, see that you don't. That's all, Scott."

There was silence. "Look," Uncle Doctor said portentously, "it is necessary that I make a purchase uptown. I'll give you a lift to the station."

"I don't want to be a trouble" and "No trouble at all" were said.

"Before we go," said Uncle Doctor. "I'm charging you only seven and a half dollars instead of my usual ten dollars for an ordinary examination or treatment at my residence outside of office hours. But I feel that a young man like you should pay something for what he gets or the cost to him will be greater in self-respect than any monetary consideration might be."

On the train to Washington, Scott suffered bitter regret that he had forgotten to ask Uncle Doctor whether Wheatena was too coarse for the alimentary canal on First Street; he wanted to get out at every stop and take a train back to New York. It was dark outside the train windows and dark in Washington; he went through the hall past the closed door of the parlor up the stairs to his room, with the sideways walk of roomers in houses, which he thought the way to walk. His room was narrow and had a narrow window and a narrow bed and a paper wardrobe about body size and a broken chair and a broken table. There were no books of his own; books were a mess to keep clean, said Miss Klank; but there were always two or three books from the Library hidden in the wardrobe.

There was no reading lamp for table or bed. But it was possible to read, sitting up and wrapped in blankets, in the middle of the bed under the hanging bulb. Scott read mainly the books out of old curricula. Tonight it was colder than usual; the day that had begun with Miss Pitton's defying her digestion had ended with Scott's letting the furnace go out. He dressed again and walked sideways to the cellar. But when he got there he realized that to shake the ashes would wake the ladies and to start a fire so late at night would waste coal. He went back to his room and set his alarm clock an hour early.

The next morning he remembered what he had forgotten besides the furnace. He remembered his appointment for a highball with the admiral. It was necessary to apologize: he did so by telephone from his office. After accepting his apology, Mrs. Havelly renewed the invitation for that very night. His money was as good as gone, it seemed to him.

He worked most of the morning on the bibliography, in a haze; he could work with pencil and paper, but he could not coherently answer any of Jane's questions. Dr. Franciosi wandered in once from his room among the privileged researchers, but fortunately he came only to tell a long story about his wife's cat ("the little devil has got so it recognizes my existence, and yesterday evening when

I parked the car . . ."). All Scott had to do was nod in understanding and shake his head in wonderment. But Scott was tortured by a hot desire to interrupt Dr. Franciosi, an expert on debentures, to tell him about Admiral Havelly and ask his advice; to tell him of his heart attack on the train, the coldness of Uncle Doctor, his love affair with Eloise Darnell, and the stiff-stained flannelet pajamas he had taken to the Chinese laundry for so many years. Why, Scott Burgess asked himself, did he think it so fortunate that Dr. Franciosi did not suspect his agitation? Didn't his agitation have the right for once to cry out in screaming words?

How lonesome he was for Eloise; but when Eloise called around ten o'clock he talked to her as if she were a member of the public. He was reminded of something another woman had said to him, looking at him with pity (why had he not separated that woman's thighs?): "Scott, why don't you buy a house?"

Scott went out for lunch but not to lunch. He walked southeast on Pennsylvania Avenue to a real estate agency, C. T. Richard and Sons, and said to a girl behind the counter: "I want to buy a house."

It seemed to him that she said in a low, hateful voice, "What would a person like you do with a house?" but there was no reason for her to say such a thing, and people did not say things without reason. Whatever she had said in a low voice, she wriggled away and came back with a man. "Here's Mr. Richard. He'll take care of you."

"Buddy Richard," said Mr. Richard, evidently a son. Scott Burgess almost said ridiculously, "Scotty Burgess," but he said: "I want to buy a house. I am Scott Burgess, and I am employed in the Library of Congress." Each clumsily tried to let the other through the door—Buddy Richard said his topcoat was in his car—and Scott felt that the girl was watching them hatefully.

Buddy Richard turned on the radio in his 1958 automobile, but they didn't go anywhere. "I used to use the Law Library at your place when I was studying law. I'm really a lawyer, not a real estate salesman, but my father thinks this is good experience. He's C. T. Richard. I like something like this all right; what gets me is when he sits me down in a house—Open—you know—some long set time on a Sunday. Nothing to do except listen to a portable radio, if people don't come. What kind of house do you want? Some of them have been given the Georgetown treatment, you know, and that comes kind of high."

"I think I want one that hasn't been given the Georgetown treatment. I want to renovate it myself. I want to make it the perfect house to live in."

"I have a perfect house for renovation on Gwinnett Street."

"Gwinnett Street! I've always wanted to live on Gwinnett Street. But won't it be too expensive?"

"Well, this is going kind of reasonable. They're asking seventeen-five."

"Pardon me?"

"The asking price is $17,500; but I think she'll come down some. Now you know I get my commission from the seller, but my function in the real estate business is to bring buyer and seller together."

"Will you please turn off that radio? I'll give you $12,837."

"You haven't even seen it."

"I'll see it when it's mine. I'll give you the money right now. It's in the building and loan association across the street. Oh yes, and it has to include settlement charges, if that is the correct term. You're a lawyer. You figure it out, to make it come out even."

"Well, I'll certainly talk to her about it. . . ."

"Let me give you the money now. Then you can give it back to me if she won't take it."

"Yes, I can do that. But we'll ask them to make it a check, if you don't mind."

That evening the starlings went home as usual; they could not be counted. Scott watched them for a few moments (the traffic went the other way) and he ran down First Street—in quiet back yards one could hear their wings. The maid sent Scott to the rec room in the English basement, but that was no insult; for it was the admiral's favorite room and had the largest television screen. (And the admiral courteously turned off the television set, knowing Scott's prejudice.) There was also a little blond mahogany bar, the gift of a contractor when the admiral had headed up an inspection office: the admiral had done nothing dishonest to earn the bar; he had only carried on the duties of his assignment to the best of his ability. He mixed a drink for Scott as if it were a difficult thing to do but he, for one, could do it well.

"And here is a dish of the doughnuts." He did not need to tell Scott, who had eaten almost nothing for two days and was having much trouble keeping his eyes off the doughnuts he did not want to talk about but did want to eat. "Have one. Not the usual accompaniment to a highball, I admit, but these aren't your honeydip, sugar, raised, coconut, chocolate, marshmallow, God knows what, but honest-to-Christ old-fashioned solid, but not too solid, doughnuts. They're even put out by a special machine that makes 'em look hand-shaped. They're made of the finest ingredients with no artificial coloring or flavoring, and they are enriched with vitamin B. They're partially precooked by a special electronic process that insures all the old-fashioned goodness with none of the old-fashioned greasiness, and that was a fault of grandma's doughnuts, you'll have to admit, all sentimentality aside. Then thev're quick-frozen ten degrees below the usual food-freezing temperatures in a special aluminum package ready to pop into the oven without thawing, after removing the easily removable top. Well, I see you don't need much convincing." Scott was eating his third.

"Sometimes I think," said the admiral, "oh, it's just a fanciful thought, that when grandma stopped making homemade doughnuts, that was when the moral decay we see all around us set in. All these sweet-coated doughnuts, with no authority to them, are symptoms of an underlying disease. Well, frozen doughnuts is one way of restoring an old verity, humble as it is and needs to be, in a new cultural framework. Oh, I know you think I'm a reactionary, Scott, and I accept the term: but I think of a reactionary not as one who wants to turn the clock back but as one who reacts against moral decay. That's enough philosophy for any man's afternoon—I'm not inviting you to join in a crusade; I'm inviting you to come in on a business proposition that will give you an unusual return on your investment. The amount that will put us over the top is just $12,750, and if you will come in for that much—well, last one in is no cross-eyed varmint or anything like that. Last one in is the one that puts us across and will get special consideration. We'll put that in writing. What do you say? All set?"

"You paint a very attractive picture, Admiral Havelly. I would be pleased and honored to associate my capital with yours. But it is impossible; I have no money."

"Have no money! What did you do with the $12,837?"

"I bought a house."

"Where?"

"On Gwinnett Street."

"What number?"

"I don't know."

The admiral seemed surprised to find his fingers putting the cork in the bottle of bourbon. "Shall I fix you another drink?" He did not quite remove the cork again.

"No, thank you. I must go. I promised to do some work for a friend."

"Take the last doughnut." And Scott did; he wrapped it in a cocktail napkin that said "Bottoms Up" illustrated by a lady whose bottom was up.

The friend was Eloise and the work was finding some information in the stacks: he ate the doughnut while he took notes, breaking a rule of the Library. Off he went to Eloise's apartment. It was colder than ever, and he folded his black overcoat around his chin. He had walked only four blocks when he decided to buy Eloise some flowers. He turned around and hurried back. "Usual professional discount," the florist said, writing quickly on a scrap of paper.

He did not refuse the discount; this had happened before. With graying brushed hair, deep eyes, heavy-boned but lightly-fleshed chin thrusting in a manly though unaggressive fashion from the turned-up overcoat, he did look like a priest or like an actor playing the part of a priest. He often thought of himself as a monk, in his room in Miss Pitton's house.

The same man, Scott Burgess, thought Eloise's apartment too bare. Her well-waxed floor and new-painted walls, her few and open furnishings, seemed wrong to him: he wished she would hang the paper tapestries he had bought for her. If a little cracked, a little faded, that only added to their venerable symbolism, his friend, the Chinese general, who kept store on I Street, Northwest, had assured him; and had sold them to him at a reasonable price. His friend, the Chinese general, would have given them to him, except that there was a Chan Buddhist dictum against it, one word of which might be translated "respect of selfhood."

Eloise now valued a streak of white in her hair; it made her different, but not fantastically so. It had started to lighten when she was fourteen. "I talk to you with foolish jokes," she said. "Halfway Day. Getting ready for the coffee break. Oh, my God. I don't even tell you what my feelings really are for you and have been. You're dear and wonderful, if you only realized it. There is no one like you in the whole lonely world." This language means more than the other, she thought; he'll marry me when my decree becomes final. What is going on now? If he has given his money away to charity,

I don't mind—we make enough to live comfortably. Maybe he's running away to Europe—no, he wouldn't do that. Oh, my God: maybe he has turned Catholic and is joining the Trappist monks and will sell whole wheat bread from Virginia, door to door.

Scott sat in his gray suit, which was worn and dry-cleaned thin; his hands were folded and he looked at the floor. "I am not dear," he said with a silly smile. "People say my habits are cheap. I am not wonderful. I am full of horrors. May I take off my trousers?"

"Please do."

He went home at one o'clock and walked sideways to his room. The next morning, just before breakfast, he heard Miss Pitton croak and crack on the telephone. "Yes, Scott Burgess lives here. He is the boy who stays with us. No, I will not call him to the telephone. He doesn't have telephone privileges."

Scott guessed it was Buddy Richard calling, though he hadn't told him where he lived. He succeeded in escaping to the Library early; and his phone was ringing there. "I got your house for you," Buddy Richard said. ("Fine," Scott said.) ". . . on condition you assume about twelve hundred dollars still owing on a first trust."

"That's over and above the $12,837?"

"Yes, but it's still a good price. Too good—I feel almost unethical in my relation to the seller."

Jane had just come in and was settling at her desk. Scott looked sternly at his telephone: his sternness was not toward Jane, who was on time, but for her admiration. "Under the circumstances, Mr. Richard, I accept the counteroffer on condition there will not be another penny of charges. When will the closing take place?"

"Does Eloise know you've bought a house?" Jane cried.

"Allow me to finish my conversation, Jane."

It was Friday morning at ten o'clock, no later than that, when Scott walked into his house alone, protected by two hours' annual leave. The excitement of the random-length pine flooring, so desirable, moved his bowels; and he looked for the bathroom. The first thing he noticed there—there was no toilet seat. He shrugged; he crouched in the air and, content, let his wastes drop. He had a friend at the Library whose brother was a rug dealer. He would talk to them about slightly used wall-to-wall carpeting.

WILLIAM SANSOM:

How Claeys Died

In Germany, two months after the capitulation, tall green grass and corn had grown up round every remnant of battle, so that the war seemed to have happened many years ago. A tank, nosing up from the corn like a pale grey toad, would already be rusted, ancient: the underside of an overturned carrier exposed intricacies red-brown and clogged like an agricultural machine abandoned for years. Such objects were no longer the contemporary traffic, they were exceptional carcasses; one expected their armor to melt like the armor of crushed beetles, to enter the earth and help fertilize further the green growth in which they were already drowned.

Claeys and his party — two officers and a driver — drove past many of these histories, through miles of such fertile green growth stretching flatly to either side of the straight and endless grey avenues. Presently they entered the outskirts of a town. This was a cathedral town, not large, not known much — until by virtue of a battle its name now resounded in black letters the size of the capital letters on the maps of whole countries. This name would now ring huge for generations, it would take its part in the hymn of a national glory; such a name had already become sacred, stony, a symbol of valor. Claeys looked about him with interest — he had never seen the town before, only heard of the battle and suffered with the soldiers who had taken it and held it for four hopeful days with the hope dying each hour until nearly all were dead, hope and soldiers. Now as they entered the main street, where already the white tram-trains were hooting, where the pale walls were chipped and bullet-chopped, where nevertheless there had never been the broad damage of heavy bombs and where therefore the pavements and shop-fronts were already washed and civil — as they entered these streets decked with summer dresses and flecked with leaf patterns, Claeys looked in vain for the town of big letters, and smelled only perfume; a wall of perfume; they seemed to have entered a scent-burg, a sissy-burg, a town of female essences, Grasse — but it was only that this town happened to be planted with lime-trees, lime-trees everywhere, and these limes were all in flower, whose essence drifted down to the streets and filled them. The blood was gone, the effort of blood had evaporated. Only scent, flowers, sunlight, trams, white dresses.

"A nice memorial," Claeys thought. "Keep it in the geography book." Then the car stopped outside a barracks. The officers got out. Claeys said he would wait in the car. He was not in uniform, he was on a civil mission, attached temporarily to the army. It does not matter what mission. It was never fulfilled. All that need be said is that Claeys was a teacher, engaged then on relief measures, a volunteer for this work of rehabilitation of the enemy, perhaps a sort of half-brother-of-mercy as during the occupation he had been a sort of half-killer. Now he wanted to construct quickly the world of which he had dreamed during the shadow years; now he was often as impatient of inaction as he had learned to be patient before. Patience bends before promise: perhaps this curiosity for spheres of action quickened his interest as now a lorry-load of soldiers drew up and jumped down at the barrack-gate. One of the soldiers said: "They're using mortars." Another was saying: "And do you blame 'em?"

There had been trouble, they told Claeys, up at the camp for expatriates — the camp where forced laborers imported from all over Europe waited for shipment home. A group of these had heard that a released German prisoner-of-war was returning to work his farm in the vicinity of the camp. They had decided to raid the farm at nightfall, grab as much food as possible, teach the German a trick or two. But the German had somehow got hold of a grenade — from the fields, or perhaps hidden in the farmhouse. At any rate, he had thrown it and killed two of the expatriates. The others had retreated, the story had spat round, before long the expatriates were coming back on the farm in full strength. They had rifles and even mortars. The news got back to the occupational military and a piquet had been sent over. The mortars were opening fire as it arrived: but they were stopped, the expatriates respected the British. Yet to maintain this respect they had to keep a piquet out there for the night. Not all the Polskis or Czechskis or whoever they were had gone home. A few had hung about, grumbling. The air was by no means clear.

When the officers returned, Claeys told them that he had altered his plans, he wanted to go up and take a look at this expatriates' camp. He gave no reason, and it is doubtful whether he had then a special reason; he felt only that he ought to see these expatriates and talk to them. He had no idea of what to say, but something of the circumstances might suggest a line later.

So they drove out into the country again, into the green. Rich lucent corn stretched endlessly to either side of the straight and endless road. Regularly, in perfect order, precisely intervaled beeches flashed by: a rich, easy, discreet roof of leaves shaded their passage as the foliage met high above. Occasionally a notice at the roadside reminded them of mines uncleared beyond the verges, occasionally a tree bore an orderly white notice addressed to civil traffic. And occasionally a unit of civil traffic passed — a family wheeling a handcart, a cyclist and his passenger, and once a slow-trudging German soldier making his grey way back along the long road to his farm. But there was nothing about this figure in grey-green to suggest more than a farmer dressed as a soldier; he walked slowly, he seemed to be thinking slowly, secure in his destination and free of time as any countryman walking slowly home on an empty road.

All was order. Birds, of course, sang. A green land, unbelievably quiet and rich, sunned its moisture. Each square yard lay unconcerned with the next, just as each measure of the road lay back as they passed, unconcerned with their passing, contented, remaining where it had always been under its own beech, a piece of land. And when at last the beech-rows stopped, the whole of that flat country seemed to spread itself suddenly open. The sky appeared, blue and sailing small white clouds to give it air. Those who deny the flatlands forget the sky — over flat country the sky approaches closer than anywhere else, it takes shape, it becomes the blue-domed lid on a flat plate of earth. Here is a greater intimacy between the elements; and for once, for a little, the world appears finite.

The carload of four travelled like a speck over this flat space. And Claeys was thinking: "Such a summer, such still air — something like a mother presiding heavily and quietly, while down in her young the little vigors boil and breed . . . air almost solid, a sort of unseen fruit fibre . . . a husk guarding the orderly chaos of the breeding ground . . ."

Such a strict order seemed indeed to preside within the intricate anarchy — success and failure, vigorous saplings from the seeds of good fortune, a pennyworth of gas from the seeds that fall on stony ground: yet a sum total of what might appear to be complete achievement, and what on the human level appears to be peace. And on that level, the only real level, there appeared — over by the popular plumes? Or by the windmill? Or at some flat-point among the converged hedges? — there appeared one scar, a scar of purely human disorder: over somewhere lay this camp of ten thousand displaced souls, newly freed but imprisoned still by their strange environment and by their great expectations born and then as instantly barred. On the face of it, these seemed to represent disorder, or at most a residue of disorder. But was this really so? Would such disorder not have appeared elsewhere, in similar quantity and under conditions of apparent order? Were they, perhaps, not anything more than stony-grounders — the disfavored residue of an anarchic nature never governed directly, only impalpably guided by more general and less concerned governments? Was it right to rationalize, to impose order upon such seed, was it right — or at least, was it sensible? It was right, obviously — for a brain made to reason is itself a part of nature and it would be wrong to divert it from its necessitous reasoning. But right though reason may be, there was no more reason to put one's faith in the impeccable work of the reasoning brain than to imagine that any other impressive yet deluded machine — like, for instance, the parachute seed — should by its apparent ingenuity succeed. Look at the parachute seed — this amazing seed actually flies off the insensate plant-mother! It sails on to the wind! The seed itself hangs beneath such an intricate parasol, it is carried from the roots of its mother to land on fertile ground far away and set up there an emissary generation! And more — when it lands, this engine is so constructed that draughts inch-close to the soil drag, drag, drag at the little parachute, so that the seed beneath actually erodes the earth, digs for itself a little trench of shelter, buries itself! Amazing! And what if the clever little seed is borne on the wrong wind to a basin of basalt?

Claeys was thinking: "The rule of natural anarchy — a few succeed, many waste and die. No material waste: only a huge waste of

effort. The only sure survival is the survival of the greater framework that includes the seed and all other things on the earth — the
furious landcrab, the bright young eskimo, the Antiguan cornbroker
— every thing and body . . . and these thrive and decay and compensate
. . . just as we, on the threshold of some golden age of reason, just as
we are the ones to harness some little nuclear genius, pack it into neat
canisters, store it ready to blow up all those sunny new clinics when
the time comes, the time for compensation . . ."

Just then the car drove into a small town on the bank of a broad
river. Instantly, in a matter of yards, the green withered and the
party found themselves abruptly in what seemed to be some sort of a
quarry, dry, dug-about, dust-pale, slagged up on either side with ex-
cavated stones.

It was indeed an excavation; it was of course the street of a town.
This town was dead. It had been bombed by a thousand aircraft,
shelled by an entire corps of artillery, and then fought through by land
soldiers. No houses were left, no streets. The whole had been churned
up, smashed and jig-sawed down again, and some of the jig-saw pieces
left up-ended — those gaunt walls remaining — and the rest of the
pieces desiccated into mounds and hollows and flats. No grass grew.
The air hung sharp with vaporized dust. A few new alleys had been
bulldozed through; these seemed pointless, for now there was no
traffic, the armies had passed through, the town was deserted. Somewhere in the centre Claeys stopped the car. He held up his hand for
silence. The four men listened. Throughout that wasted city there
was no sound. No distant muttering, no murmur. No lost hammering, no drowned cry. No word, no footstep. No wheels. No wind
shifting a branch — for there were no trees. No flapping of torn cloth,
this avalanche had covered all the cloth. No birds — but one, a small
bird that flew straight over, without singing; above such a desert
it moved like a small vulture, a shadow, a bird without destination.
Brick, concrete, gravel-dust — with only two shaped objects as far
all round as they could see: one, an intestinal engine of fat iron pipes,
black and big as an up-ended lorry, something thrown out of a factory;
and leaning on its side a pale copper-green byzantine cupola like a
gigantic sweet-kiosk blown over by the wind, the tower fallen from
what had been the town church. This — in a town that had been
the size of Reading.

Almost reverently, as on sacred ground, they started the car and
drove off again. Through the pinkish-white mounds the sound of

the motor seemed now to intrude garishly. Claeys wanted only to be out of the place. Again, this destruction seemed to have occurred years before; but now because of the very absence of green, of any life at all, of any reason to believe that people had ever lived there. Not even a torn curtain. They wormed through and soon, as abruptly as before, the country began and as from a seasonless pause the summer embraced them once more.

Claeys stood up off his seat to look over the passing hedges. The camp was somewhere near now. The driver said, two kilometres. Surely, Claeys thought, surely with that dead town so near the men in this camp could realize the extent of the upheaval, the need for a pause before their journey could be organized? Surely they must see the disruption, this town, the one-way bridges over every stream far around, the roads pitted and impassable? Yet . . . what real meaning had these evidences? Really, they were too negative to be understood, too much again of something long finished. It was not as if something positive, like an army passing, held up one's own purpose; not even a stream of aircraft, showing that at least somewhere there was an effort and direction. No, over these fields there was nothing, not even the sense of a pause, when something might be re-started; instead a vacuity stretched abroad, a vacuum of human endeavor, with the appalling contrast of this vegetable growth continuing evenly and unconcerned. That was really the comprehensible evidence, this sense of the land and of the essence of life continuing, so that one must wish to be up and walking away, to be off to take part not in a regrowth but in a simple continuation of what had always been. For every immediate moment there was food to be sought, the pleasures of taste to be enjoyed: what was more simple than to walk out and put one's hands on a cap-full of eggs, a pig, a few fat hens? And if a grey uniform intervened, then it was above all a grey uniform, something instinctively obstructive, in no real sense connected with the dead town. The only real sympathy that ever came sometimes to soften the greyness of this grey was a discovery, felt occasionally with senses of wonder and unease, that this uniform went walking and working through its own mined cornfields and sometimes blew itself up — that therefore there must be a man inside it, a farmer more than a soldier. But the grey was mostly an obstruction to the ordinary daily desire for food, for fun, for something to be tasted. The day for these men was definitely a day. It was no twenty-four hours building up to a day in the future when something would happen. No future day had been promised. There was, therefore, no succession of days, no days for ticking off, for passing through and storing in preparation. There were, in fact, the days themselves, each one a matter for living, each a separate dawning and tasting and setting.

Suddenly Claeys heard singing, a chorus of men's voices. A second later the driver down behind the windshield heard it. He nodded, as though they had arrived. The singing grew louder, intimate — as though it came from round a corner that twisted the road immediately ahead. But it came from a lane just before, it flourished suddenly into a full-throated Slavic anthem — and there was the lane crowded with men, some sitting, others marching four abreast out into the road. The car whirred down to a dead halt. The singing wavered and stopped. Claeys saw that the driver had only his left hand on the wheel — his other hand was down gripping the black butt of a revolver at his knee. (He had never done this driving through German crowds earlier.)

"It's not the camp," the driver said. "These are some of them, though. The camp's a kilometre up the road." He kept his eyes scanning slowly up and down the line of men crowding in the lane's entry, he never looked up at Claeys. Then the men came a few paces forward, though they looked scarcely interested. Probably they were pushed forward by the crowd behind, many of whom could not have seen the car, many of whom were still singing.

Claeys stood upright and said: "I'd like to talk to these . . . you drive on, get round the corner and wait. I don't want that military feeling."

The men looked on with mild interest, as though they might have had many better things to do. They looked scarcely "displaced"; they had a self-contained air, an independence. There was no censure in their stare; equally no greeting; nor any love. Their clothes were simple, shirts and greyish trousers and boots: though these were weather-stained, they were not ragged.

Claeys jumped down. An interest seemed to quicken in some of the watching men as they saw how Claeys was dressed — beret, plus-fours, leather jacket. It was because of these clothes that the military in the car gave Claeys no salute as they drove off; also because they disapproved of this kind of nonsense, and this may have been why they neither smiled nor waved, but rather nodded impersonally and whirred off round the corner. They might, for instance, have been dropping Claeys after giving him some sort of a lift.

So that Claeys was left quite alone on the road, standing and smiling at the crowd of expatriates grouped at the entrance to the lane. The car had disappeared. It had driven off the road and round the corner. There, as often happens when a vehicle disappears from view, its noise had seemed to vanish too. Presumably it had stopped. But equally it might have been presumed far away on its journey to the next town.

The men took a pace or two forward, now beginning to form a crescent-shape round Claeys, while Claeys began to speak in English: "Good afternoon, mates. Excuse me, I'm Pieter Claeys — native of Belge." None of the men smiled. They only stared hard at him. They were too absorbed now even to mutter a word between themselves. They were searching for an explanation, a sign that would clarify this stranger. They were unsure and certainly, it seemed, unimpressed. "Good afternoon, comrades," Claeys shouted. "Gentlemen, hello!"

Without waiting, for the silence was beginning to weigh, he turned into French. "Suis Claeys de Belge. Je veux vous aider. Vous permettez — on peut causer un peu?"

He repeated: "Peut-être?" And in the pause while no one answered he looked up and above the heads of these men, feeling that his smile might be losing its first flavor, that somehow an embarrassment might be dissolved if he looked away.

The country again stretched wide and green. Claeys was startled then to see sudden huge shapes of paint-box color erecting themselves in the distance. But then immediately he saw what they were — the wings and fuselages of broken gliders. They rose like the fins of huge fish, tilted at queer angles, grounded and breathlessly still. Difficult at first to understand, for their shapes were strange and sudden, and of an artifice dangerously like something natural: brightly colored, they might have been shapes torn from an abstract canvas and stuck wilfully on this green background: or the bright broken toys left by some giant child.

Claeys tried again: "Gijmijneheeren zijt blifkbaar in moeilijkheden. Ik zou die gaarne vernemen . . ."

The Dutch words came ruggedly out with a revival of his first vigor, for Claeys was more used to Dutch and its familiarity brought some ease again to his smile. It brought also a first muttering from the men.

They began to mutter to each other in a Slav-sounding dialect — Polish, Ukrainian, Czech, Russian? — and as this muttering grew it seemed to become an argument. Claeys wanted instantly to make himself clearer, he seemed to have made some headway at last and so now again he repeated the Dutch. This time he nodded, raised his arm in a gesture, even took a pace forward in his enthusiasm. But now one of the men behind began to shout angrily, and would have pushed himself forward shaking his fist — had the others not held him.

It was not clear to Claeys — he felt that the Dutch had been understood, and yet what he had said was friendly . . . he began to repeat the words again. Then, half-way through, he thought of a clearer way. He broke into German. There was every chance that someone might understand German; they might have been working here for three years or more; or anyway it was the obvious second language. ". . . so bin ich hier hergekommen um Ihnen zu helfen. Bitte Kameraden, hören Sie mal . . ."

The muttering rose, they were plainly talking — and now not to each other but to him. The crescent had converged into a half-circle, these many men with livening faces were half round him. Claeys stood still. Overhead the summer sky made its huge dome, under which this small group seemed to make the pin-point centre. The green quiet stretched endlessly away to either side, the painted gliders stuck up brightly. No traffic.

". . . bitte einen moment . . . ich bin Freund, Freund, FREUND . . ." And as he repeated this word "friend" he realized what his tongue had been quicker to understand — that none of his listeners knew the meaning of these German words. They knew only that he was speaking German, they knew the intonation well.

He stopped. For a moment, as the men nudged each other nearer, as the Slav words grew into accusation and imprecation, Claey's mind fogged up, appalled by this muddle, helplessly overwhelmed by such absurdity, such disorder and misunderstanding.

Then, making an effort to clear himself, he shook his head and looked closely from one man to the other. But the composure had gone: they were all mouth, eyes, anger and desire — they were no longer independent. And this was accumulating, breeding itself beyond the men as men. They had become a crowd.

Knowing that words were of no further use, Claeys did the natural thing — wearily, slowly he raised his arm in a last despairing bid for silence.

An unfortunate gesture. The shouting compounded into one confused roar. One of the men on the edge of the crowd jumped out and swung something in the air — a scythe. It cut Claeys down, and then all the pack of them were on him, kicking, striking, grunting and shouting less.

Claeys must have screamed as the scythe hit him — two shots thundered like two full stops into that muddle, there was an abrupt silence and two men fell forward; and then another shot and the men scattered crying into the lane.

Those three soldiers came running up to Claeys' body. They shot again into the men crowding the lane; but then the men, bottled up in the narrow lane, suddenly turned and raised their arms above their heads. The soldiers held their fire, their particular discipline actuated more strongly than their emotions. Two of them kept their guns alert, gestured the men forward. They came, hands raised, shambling awkwardly. The other officer bent down to Claeys.

He was almost finished, messed with blood and blue-white where the flesh showed. He was breathing, trying to speak; and the officer knelt down on both his knees and raised Claeys' head up. But Claeys never opened his eyes — they were bruised shut, anyway. And no words came from his lips, though the officer lowered his head and listened very carefully.

Through the pain, through his battered head, one thought muddled out enormously. "Mistake . . . mistake . . ." And this split into two other confused, unanswered questions — weakening, dulling questions. Broadly, if they could have been straightened out, these questions would have been: "Order or Disorder? Those fellows were the victims of an attempt to rule men into an impeccable order, my killing was the result of the worst, that is, the most stupid disorder . . ."

But he couldn't get the words out, or any like them. Only — weakly, slowly he raised his right hand. He groped for the officer's hand, and the officer knew what he wanted and met the hand with his own in a handshake. Claeys just managed to point at the place where the men had been, where they still were. Then his head sank deep on to his neck. Again the officer knew what he wanted. He rose, his hand still outstretched from Claeys' grasp, like a hand held out by a splint. Then he started over towards the men.

Instinctively, for this hand of his was wet with blood, he wiped it on his tunic as he walked forward. Without knowing this, he raised his hand again into its gesture of greeting. There was a distasteful expression on his face, for he hardly liked such a duty.

So that when he shook hands with the first of the men, proffering to them, in fact, Claeys' handshake, none of these expatriates knew whether the officer was giving them Claeys' hand or whether he had wiped Claeys' gesture away in distaste and was now offering them his congratulation for killing such a common enemy as Claeys.

EUDORA WELTY:

Ida M'Toy

For one human being to point out another as "unforgettable" seems a trifle condescending, and in the ideal world we would all keep well aware of each other, but there are nevertheless a few persons one meets who are as inescapable of notice as skyrockets, it may be because like skyrockets they are radiant with their own substance and shower it about regardlessly. Ida M'Toy, an old negro woman, for a long time a midwife in my little Mississippi town and for another long time a dealer in second-hand clothes in the same place, has been a skyrocket as far back as most people remember. Or, rather, she is a kind of meteor (for she is not ephemeral, only sudden and startling). Her ways seem on a path of their own without regard to any course of ours and of a somewhat wider circuit; she will probably leave a glow behind and return in the far future on some other lap of her careening through all our duller and steadier bodies. She herself deals with the rest of us in this mighty and spacious way, calling in allegories and the elements, so it is owing to her nature that I may speak a little grandly.

The slave traders of England and New England, when they went capturing, took away the most royal of Africans along with their own slaves, and I have not much doubt that Ida has come down from a race of tall black queens. I wish I might have seen her when she was young. She has sharp clever features, light-filled black eyes, arched nostrils, and fine thin mobile lips, and her hair, gray now, springs like a wild kind of diadem from the widow's peak over her forehead. Her voice is indescribable but it is a constant part of her presence and is filled with invocation. She never speaks lightly of any person or thing, but she flings out her arm and points at something and begins, "O, precious, I'm telling you to look at that—*look* at it!" and then she invokes about it, and tolerates no interruptions. I have heard long chants and utterances on the origin and history and destination of the smallest thing, any article or object her eye lights on; a bit of candle stuck on the mantlepiece will set her off, as if its little fire had ignited her whole mind. She invokes what she wishes to invoke and she has in all ways something of the seer about her. She wields a control over great numbers of her race by this power, which has an integrity that I believe

242

nothing could break, and which sets her up, aloof and triumphant, above the rest. She is inspired and they are not. Maybe off by themselves they could be inspired, but nobody else could be inspired in the same room with Ida, it would be too crowded.

Ida is not a poor old woman, she is a rich old woman. She accepts it that she is held in envy as well as respect, but it is only another kind of tribute as far as she is concerned, and she is not at all prouder of being rich or of having been married in the home of a white lady, "in her bay window," than she is of being very wise. She expects to be gaped at, but she is not vain.

Ida's life has been divided in two (it is, in many ways, eloquent of duality); but there is a thread that runs from one part into the other, and to trace this connection between delivering the child and clothing the man is an interesting speculation. Moreover, it has some excuse, for Ida herself helps it along by a wild and curious kind of talk that sashays from one part to the other and sounds to some of her customers like "ranting and raving." It is my belief that if Ida had not been a midwife she would not be the same kind of second-hand clothes dealer she is. Midwifery set her off, it gave her a hand in the mysteries, and she will never let go that flying hold merely because she is engaged in something else. An ex-alchemist would run a second-hand clothes business with extra touches—a reminiscence of glitter would cling to the garments he sold, and it is the same with Ida. So it is well when you meet her to think what she was once.

Ida's memory goes back to her beginnings, when she was, she says, the first practical nurse in Jackson at the age of twenty-one, and she makes the past sound very dark and far back. She thanks God, she says, that today Capitol Street is not just three planks to walk on and is the prettiest place on earth, but that "people white and black is too high and don't they know Ida seen them when they carried a little tin coal-oil lamp that wasn't any bigger than their little fingers?" Ida speaks of herself in the third person and in indirect discourse often and especially when she says something good of herself or something of herself long ago. She will intone, "Ida say that she was good to the poor white people as she was to the rich, as she made a bargain to nurse a poor white lady in obstetrical case for a peck of peas. Ida said no, she couldn't see her suffer, and therefore a peck of blackeyed peas would be sufficient." She wants all she says to be listened to with the whole attention, and declares she does wish it were all written down. "Let her keep it straight, darling, if she remember Ida's true words, the angels will know it and be waiting around the throne for her." But Ida's true words are many and strange. When she talks about the old days it is almost like a story of combat against evil. "Ida fitted a duel from twenty-one to fifty-six, and then they operated on her right side and she was never able to stoop down to the floor again. She was never like those young devils, that pace around in those white shoes and those white clothes and up and down the streets of an evening while their patient is calling for a drink of water down poor parched throat —though I wore those white shoes and those white clothes. Only, my heart was in another direction."

Ida said, "I was nursing ever since there was a big road in Jackson. There was only nine doctors, and they were the best in all the world, all nine, right here in Jackson, but they were weak in finance. There wasn't nary hospital nowhere—there wasn't nary brick in Jackson, not one brick, no brick walk, no brick store, no brick nothing-else. There wasn't no Old Ladies' Home at the end of the street, there wasn't no stopping place but the country. Town was as black as tar come night, and praise God they finally put some gas in bottles on the corners. There wasn't no such thing in the world as a nice buggy. Never heard tell of a cotton mattress, but tore up shucks and see the bed, so high, and the hay pillow stand up so beautiful! Now they got all this electric light and other electricity. Can't do nothing without the clickety-click. And bless God they fly just like buzzards up in the air, but Ida don't intend to ride till she ride to Glory."

In those early days when Jackson seems to have been a Slough of Despond with pestilence sticking out its head in the nights as black as tar, Ida was not only a midwife, she nursed all diseases. "It was the yellow fever first, and the next after that was the worst pox that there ever was in this world—it would kill you then, in my girl-days, six or seven a day. They had to stretch a rope across the road to keep the poor sick ones apart and many's the day I've et at the rope and carried the food back to the ones suffering." Ida remembers epidemics as major combats in which she was a kind of giant-killer. She nursed through influenza "six at a blow, until the doctor told me if I didn't quit nursing by sixes I would drop dead in the room." She says the doctors wrote her a recommendation as long as where she will show you up her arm, saying that when they called, it never was too cold and it never was too hot for Ida to go, and that the whole town would bow and say Amen, from the Jews on. "Bless my patients," she says, "nary one ever did die under my nursing, though plenty were sick enough to die. But laugh here," she directs. "My husband stayed sick on me twenty-one years and cost me one thousand whole dollars, but you can't nurse the heart to do no good, and in the night he fallen asleep and left me a widow, and I am a widow still."

When Ida found she could no longer stoop to the floor she stopped being a midwife and began selling clothes. She was successful at once in that too, for there is a natural flowering-ground for the second-hand clothes business in the small American community where the richest people are only a little richer than the poor people and the poorest have ways to save pride and not starve or go naked. In Jackson the most respectable matron, if she would like a little extra cash to buy a new camellia bush or take the excursion to New Orleans, can run over to Ida's with her husband's other suit and Ida will sell it to a customer as a bargain at $5 and collect 25% for herself, and everybody except the husband ("Right off my back! Perfectly good suit!") will be satisfied.

It could be a grubby enough little business in actual fact, but Ida is not a grubby person, and in her handling it has become an affair of imagination and, to my notion, an expression of a whole attitude of life as integrated as an art or a philosophy.

Ida's store is her house, a white-painted little house with a porch across the front, a picket-fence around, and the dooryard planted to capacity in big flowers. Inside, it is a phantasmagoria of garments. Every room except the kitchen is hung with dresses or suits (the sexes are segregated) three and four times around the walls, for the turnover is large and unpredictable, though not always rapid—people have to save up or wait for cotton-money. She has assumed all the ceremonies of Business and employs its practices and its terms to a point within sight of madness. She puts on a show of logic and executive order before which the customer is supposed to quail; sometimes I think her customers take on worth with her merely as witnesses of the miracles of her workings, though that is unfair. Her house turns year by year into a better labyrinth, more inescapable, and she delights in its complication of aisles and curtains and its mystery of closed doors with little signs on ruled paper, "Nobody can come in here." Some day some little colored girl is going to get lost in Ida's house. The richer she gets, the more "departments" she builds and adds on to the house, and each one is named for the color of its walls, the pink department, or the blue. Even now her side yard is filled with miscellaneous doors, glass panes, planks, and little stacks of bricks that she is accumulating for a new green department she says she will build in 1943.

Her cupboards and drawers are a progressive series of hiding places, which is her interpretation of the filing system. She hides trinkets of mysterious importance or bits of paper filled with abbreviated information; she does not hide money, however, and she tells how much she has on hand ($660.60 is the latest figure), and her life insurance policy is nailed up on the wall over the mantel. Everybody knows her to be an old woman living with only a small grandchild to guard her in a house full of cash money, and yet she has not been murdered. She never will be. I have wondered what Ida would do if she saw a burglar coming after her money. I am convinced that she has no axe or gun ready for him, but a flow of words will be unstoppered that will put the fear of God in him for life; and I think the would-be burglars have the same suspicion, and will continue to keep away, not wanting so much fear of God as that.

She keeps as strict and full a ledger of transaction as the Book of Judgment, and in as enthusiastic and exalted a spirit of accuracy as an angel book-keeper should have. The only trouble is, it is almost impossible to find in it what she is looking for—but perhaps there will be confusion on Doomsday too. The book, a great black one, which she now has little William, her grandson, to hold for her while she consults it (and he will kneel under it like a little mural figure), covers a period of 26 years, concerns hundreds of people, "white and black," and innumerable transactions, all noted down in a strange code full of flourishes, for Ida properly considers all she does confidential. "You could find anything in the world in this book," she says reverently, then slamming it shut in your face, "if you turn enough pages and go in the right direction. Nothing in here is wrong," she says. Loose slips are always flying out of the ledger like notes in the Sybil's book, and she sets William flying to chase them and get them inside again.

She writes her own descriptions of the garments brought to her to sell, and a lady giving over her finest white dress of last summer must not be surprised, if she looks over Ida's shoulder, to see her pen the words, "Rally Day, $2.00" or note down her best spring straw hat as "Tom Boy, 75c." The customer might be right, but Ida does not ever ask the customer. After a moment of concentration Ida goes and hangs the object for sale on the wall in the room of her choice, and a tag is pinned to the sleeve, saying simply, "Mrs. So-and-So." Accuracy is a passion with Ida, and so is her belief in her own conscience, and I do not know what it must have cost her to pin a tag on one poor sagging dress that has hung there year in, year out, saying "Don't know who this is."

She bears respect to clothes in the same degree as she bears it to the people from whose backs they come; she treats them like these people, until indeed it seems that dignity is in them, shapeless and even ridiculous as they have seemed at first; she gives them the space on the wall and the room in the house that correspond to the honor in which she holds the human beings, and she even speaks in the proper tone of voice when she is in the room with them. They hang at human height from the hangers on the walls, the brighter and more important ones in front and on top. With the most serene impartiality she makes up her mind about client and clothes, and she has been known to say, "For God's sake take it back. Wouldn't a man white or black wear that suit out of here."

There is a magnificence in Ida's business, an extent and an influence at which she hints without ceasing, that undoubtedly inspire the poorest or idlest customer with almost an anxiety to buy. It is almost like an appeasement, and the one that goes off with nothing must feel mean, foolish, and naked indeed, naked to scorn. "I clothe them," she says, "from Jackson to Vicksburg, Meridian to Jackson, Big Black to 'Azoo. Memphis to New Orleans—Clinton! Bolton! Edwards! Bovina! Pocahontas! Flora! Bentonia! 'Azoo City! Everywhere. There ain't nobody hasn't come to Ida, or sooner or later will come."

If no one else had thought of the second-hand clothes business, Ida would have originated it, for she did originate it as far as she is concerned; and likewise I am forced to believe that if there had never been any midwives in the world Ida would have invented midwifery, so ingenious and delicate-handed and wise she is, and sure of her natural right to take charge. She loves transformation and bringing things about, she simply cannot resist it. The negro midwives of this state have a kind of organization these days and lesser powers, they do certain things in certain book-specified ways, and all memorize and sing at meetings a song about "First we put—Drops in their eyes," but in Ida's day a midwife was a lone person, invested with the whole charge of life; she had to draw upon her own resources and imagination. Ida's constant gestures today still involve a dramatic out-thrust of the right hand, and let any prominent names be mentioned (and she mentions them) and she will fling out her palm and cry into the conversation, "Born in this hand!" "Four hundred little white babies—or more," she says. "My God, I was bringing them all the time. I got 'em every-

where—doctors, lawyers, school teachers, and preachers, married ladies." She has been in the clothes business for twenty-six years, but she
was a midwife for thirty-five.

She herself has been married, twice, and by her first husband she had
one son, "the only one I ever did have and I want his name written
down: Julius Knight." Her mother (before she died) and her brothers
live out in the country, and only one little grandson has lived with her
for a long time. Her husband, Braddie M'Toy, whom she called Toy,
is remembered collecting and delivering clothes in a wagon when he
was young, and was to be seen always on some street if not another,
moving very slowly on account of his heart.

Now without Toy, Ida uses a telephone down the road and a kind
of de luxe grapevine service to rouse up her clients and customers.
Anybody who is asked to by Ida feels a duty to phone any stranger
for her and "tell them for God's sake to come get their money and
bring the change." Strange negroes call people at dawn, giving news
of a sale, white ladies call unknown white ladies, notes on small rolls
or scraps of paper folded like doctors' "powders" are conscientiously
delivered, and the whole town contrives in her own spirit of emergency
to keep Ida's messages on their way. Ida takes 25% of the sales price
and if she sells your dress for a dollar you have to take her a quarter
when you go, or come back another time, for she will not make change
for anybody. She will not violate her system of book-keeping any
more than she would violate her code of ethics or her belief in God—
down to the smallest thing all is absolute in Ida's sight.

Whether it is due to a savage ancestry or a philosophical turn of
mind, Ida finds all Ornament a wonderful and appropriate thing, the
proper materializing of the rejoicing or sorrowing soul. I believe she
holds Ornament next to birth and somehow kin to it. She despises a
drab color and welcomes bright clothes with a queenly and triumphant smile, as if she acknowledges the bold brave heart that chose
that. Inferior color means inferior spirit, and an inferior person should
not hope to get or spend more than four-bits for an outfit. She dearly
loves a dress that is at once identifiable as either rich mourning or
"rally-day"—the symbolic and celebrating kind appeal to her inevitably over the warm, or the serviceable, and she will ask and (by
oratory) get the finest prices for rather useless but splendid garments.
"Girl, you buy this spangle-dress," she says to a customer, and the girl
buys it and puts it on and shines. Ida's scale of prices would make a
graph showing precisely the rise from her condemnation of the sub-

249

dued and nondescript to her acclaim of the bright and glorious. Her customers, poverty-bound little cooks and maids and cotton-choppers, go away feeling that they have turned into queens. Ida has put second-hand clothes on their backs and, with all the abrupt bullying of a busy fairy, wrapped them in some glowing raiment of illusion, set them in a whirl of bedazzlement; and they skitter out with shining eyes and empty hands, with every hoarded penny spent. Ida has put them in inner spangles and she has taken an actual warm moist fifty-cent piece out of their palms, and in that world both items exchanged are precious above price, fifty cents being as miraculous as glory. With something second-hand, worn, yet finer than could ever be bought new, she brings to them a perfection in her own eyes and in theirs. She dresses them up and turns them with a little ceremonial jerk towards the mirror, and a magic must hang over the green cracked glass, for (I have seen it happen a hundred times) the glances that go into its surface begin to shine with a pride that could only be a kind of enchantment. It is nice on Saturdays to pass in front of Ida's house on the edge of town and see the customers emerge. With some little flash of scarf, some extra glitter of trimming for which they have paid dearly, dressed like some visions in Ida's speculations on the world, glorious or menial as befits their birth, merit, and willingness, but all rampant and somehow fulfilled by this last touch of costume as though they have been tapped by a spirit when Ida's thimble rapped them, they float dizzily down the steps and through the flowers out the gate; and you could not help thinking of the phrase "going out into the world," as if Ida had just birthed them anew.

I used to think she must be, a little, the cross between a transcendentalist and a witch, with the happiness and kind of self-wonder that this combination must enjoy. They say that all things we write could be; and sometimes in amazement I wonder if a tiny spark of the wonderful Philosopher of Clothes, Diogenes Teufelsdröckh, could be flashing for an instant, and somewhat barbarically, in the wild and enthusiastic spirit of this old black woman. Her life like his is proudly emblematic —she herself being the first to see her place in the world. It is she literally who clothes her entire world, as far and wide as she knows— a hard-worked midwife grown old, with a memory like a mill turning through it all the lives that were born in her hand or have passed through her door.

When she stalks about, alternately clapping her hand over her forehead and flinging out her palm and muttering "Born in this hand!" as she is likely to do when some lady of the old days comes bringing a dress to sell, you can not help believing that she sees them all, her children and her customers, in the double way, naked and clothed, young and then old, with love and with contempt, with open arms or with a push to bar the door. She is moody now, if she has not always been, and sees her customers as a procession of sweet supplicant spirits that she has birthed, who have returned to her side, and again sometimes as a bunch of scarecrows or even changelings, that she wishes were well gone out of sight. "They would steal from their own mother," she says, and while she is pinning up some purchase in a newspaper and the customer is still counting out the pennies, she will shout in a deep voice to the grandchild that flutters around like a little blackbird, "Hold the door, William."

I have never caught Ida doing anything except selling clothes or holding forth on her meditations, but she has a fine garden. "If you want to carry me something I really like," she will say, bringing up the subject first, "carry me dallion potatoes (dahlia bulbs) *first,* and old newspapers second." Ida has the green finger from her mother, and she says, "You're never going to see any flowers prettier than these right here." She adores giving flowers away; under your protest she will cut every one in the garden, every red and white rose on the trellis, which is a wooden sunset with painted rays, the blossoms with little two-inch stems the way a child cuts them, and distribute them among all present and those passing in the road. She is full of all the wild humors and extravagances of the godlike toward this entire town and its environs. Sometimes, owing to her superior wisdom, she is a little malign, but much oftener she will become excruciatingly tender, holding, as if in some responsibility toward all the little ones of the world, the entire population to her great black cameoed breast. Then she will begin to call people "It." "It's all hot and tired, it is, coming so far to see Ida. Ah, take these beautiful flowers Ida grew with her own hand, *that's* what it would like. Put 'em in its bedroom," and she presses forward all the flowers she has cut and then, not content, a bouquet dripping from a vase, one of a kind of everything, all into your arms.

She loves music too, and in her house she has one room, also hung with clothes, called the music room. "I got all the music in the world in here," she used to say, jabbing a finger at a silent radio and an old gramophone shut up tight, "but what's the use of letting those contrivances run when you can make your own music?" And ignoring the humble customers waiting she would fling herself down at the old pump-organ in the corner and tear into a frenzy of chords. "I make my own!" she would shout into the turmoil. She would send for little William, with a voice like a little bird's, and he knew how to sing with her, though he would give out. "Bass, William!" she would shout, and in his tiny treble he sang bass, bravely.

When Ida speaks of her mother it is in a strange kind of pity, a tender amazement. She says she knew when her mother was going to die, and with her deep feeling for events and commemorations, she gave her a fine big party. Ida would no more shrink from doing anything the grand way then she would shrink from other demands upon her greatness. "Hush now," she told me, "don't say a word while I tell you this. All that day long I was cooking dinner between niggers. I had: four turkeys, four hens, four geese, four hams, red cake, white cake, chocolate cake, caramel cake, every color cake known. The table reached from the front door to the ice box. I had all the lights burning up electricity, and all the flowers cut. I had the plates changed seven times, and three waiters from the hotel. I'd got Mama a partner. Mama was eighty years old and I got her another old lady eighty years old to march with. I had everybody come. All her children—one son, the big shot, came all the way from Detroit, riding in a train, to be at Mama's grand dinner. We had somebody play "Silent Night" and march music to follow later. And there was Mama: look at Mama! Mama loved powder. Mama had on a little old-fashioned hat, but she wouldn't take it off—had nice hair, too. Mama did all right for the march, she marched all right, and sat down on time at the right place at the head of the table, but she wouldn't take off her hat. So the waiters, they served the chicken soup first, and Mama says, 'Where my coffee? Bring on turnip and cornbread. Didn't you make a blackberry pie?' I said, 'Mama, you don't eat coffee first? But she said, 'Where my coffee? Bring on turnip and cornbread. Didn't you make a blackberry pie? What's the matter with you?' Everything was so fine, you know. It took her two big sons, one on each side, to quiet her, that's the way Mama acted!" And Ida ended the story laughing and crying. It was plain that there was one person who had no recognition of Ida's grandeur and high place in the world, and who had never yielded at all to the glamour as others did. It was a cruelty for Ida, but perhaps all vision has lived in the house with cruelty.

Nowadays, she is carried to such heights of business and power, and its paraphernalia crowds her so, that she is overcome with herself, and suddenly gives way to the magnitude of it all. A kind of chaos comes over her. Now and then she falls down in a trance and stays "dead as that chair for three days." White doctors love her and by a little struggle take care of her. Ida bears with them. "They took my appendix," she will say. "Well, they took my teeth." She says she has a paralyzed heel, though it is hard to see how she can tell—perhaps like Achilles she feels that her end is coming by entering that way. "The doctor told me I got to rest until 1945," she declares, with a lifted hand warding you off. "Rest! Rest! Rest! I must rest." If a step is heard on the front porch she instantly cries warning from within the house, "Don't set your heels down! When you speak to me, whisper!" When a lady that was a stranger came to see her, Ida appeared, but said in haste, "Don't tell me your name, for I'm resting my mind. The doctors don't want me to have any more people in my head than I got already." Now on Saturdays if a dusty battered car full of customers from across the cottonfields draws up, one by one all the shades in the house are yanked down. Ida wishes to see no one, she wishes to sell nothing.

Perhaps the truth is that she has expended herself to excess and now suffers with a corresponding emptiness that she does not want any one to see. She can show you the track of the pain it gives her: her finger crosses her two breasts. She is as hard to see as a queen.

And I think she lives today the way she would rather be living, directly in symbols. People are their vestures now. Memories, the great memories of births and marriages and deaths, are nearly the same as the pieces of jewelry ("$147.65 worth") she has bought on anniversary days and wears on her person. "That's Mama's death," she says—a silver watch on a silver chain. She holds out for your admiration the yellow hands that she asserts most of this country was born in, on which now seven signet rings flash. "Don't go to church any longer," she says—"or need to go. I just sit at home and enjoy my fingers."

REX WORTHINGTON:

Love

"OK, let's join the bird gang," he said, his voice at twelve o'clock resonant and imperious, so that at first one was fooled. And then the gesture, at complete odds with the voice, the arms lifted mechanically to form a V, and then, as though sprung from that area of tension, his arms and outspread hands smacked sharply against his body. People looked at him—the drinkers at the bar with mute childlike surprise, and Harold, the manager of the club, lighting his cigar under his hawk nose, with ill-concealed interest, looking first at the flame of his match and next at him. He always panicked under their eyes, finding release in a mad pursuit—suddenly moving to clean all the glasses and bottles off the bar. The habitual drinkers were used to this sally and jerked their bottles right back. He retreated, dervishing awkwardly behind the bar, an object of titters now, but recovered rapidly and moved toward the cash register. Calmly he rang up one cent, put a coin in the till and turned to face them, his arms folded at ease across his chest, and his face a little arrogant, supercilious, lifted above them to stare at the opposite wall. They laughed too much or too little as though they had seen more than they wanted, and they lifted their glasses and looked into them, to ease the moment, and lit cigarettes. Sometimes a newcomer asked, "What is it? What makes him do it?" Harold said, "I don't know. Willie reminds me of a woman in heat. He's got things on his mind, you know, like he was all shut up in a barrel, just waiting to be tapped. Sometimes I have half a mind to fire him." With that he emphatically blew out a puff of smoke and began to cough, a great wheezing cough that reduced him suddenly from dignity into a veritable paroxysm, that caused the snot to flow, and still coughing he said, "All right, folks, drink 'em up. You don't have to go home, but you can't stay here," and he went onto the floor to hurry the drinkers at their tables.

Many managers had come and gone in Willie's time. He was the oldest employee, in point of faithful service, of the Arnold J. Haverman Post, No. 436, Veterans of Foreign Wars. In 1934 he had joined the Post "to take my cup from friendly hands," and he was such a sober, mild, and unpretentious fellow on his side of the bargain, that hardly a year had passed before he was asked to accept a full-time bartender's position. "He'll be a good man," they said. "He'll take all the shit they throw at him, and never give any trouble. A steadying influence, that's what we need. People are talking about us, you know, they say we're a bunch of drunkards down here." Willie had been unemployed since he made his dramatic and near-fatal departure from his farm a year and a half before. That was the day he went into the stall of gentle Bessie, who had a game leg, the vital cord of which Willie touched and was so roundly kicked that he just managed to make his way back to the barnyard where he fell unconscious. There was a store a mile away to which Mrs. Fox ran and conveyed her desperation in French for several minutes, before Mr. Stump could understand that Willie was hurt, and telephoned the hospital.

Willie was in the hospital for nearly two months, through the cold, dismal part of the winter. This undoubtedly helped him decide to leave the farm for good; for had it been spring, he might have longed for the country. Still, it wasn't a hard decision to make; Willie was a farmer's son, but hardly a farmer himself. "The stupid bastard," his father used to say, "he does everything like a damn Polack." So when Bessie scrambled up his insides, Willie wondered if God were warning him—once coming from the field at night he had been set upon by three or four wild dogs, another time he was trapped digging a well, and just last year Polford's bull, brought for the cows, pinned him to the fence like an insect before they could beat it away—and in his agony Willie made a vow with God that he would never go near a farm again, if he might live. He returned once more, however, the next spring when he was lucky enough to sell the farm. Everything went, furniture, implements . . . Bessie.

"Will she pull?"

"She's a bear."

"Nice care—I can see that."

"My best, sir," Willie said, and he pulled himself straighter on his cane, full of dignity, still offended with Bessie.

"I think you've made yourself a deal," the man said. At that Willie's lip trembled and he said, "She'll treat you as handsome as handsome does."

"I mean the farm," the man said. "Everything." Willie appeared confused and reached impulsively for his wife's arm. The man picked up some dirt and let it slip through his fingers. When he saw them watching him, he threw the dirt down and rubbed his hands on his trousers.

There was enough to keep them for a while. Willie couldn't work yet, but his wife found a job in a bakery, making dainties. She was good at that. They were rather content; in the evenings they often went to the movies and Willie began to read. He bought a subscription to the *Reader's Digest;* the pithy sayings especially appealed to him. And he discovered poetry. "Who would've ever thought I had such stuff in me?" he said to his wife after reading a poem. "And I like it," he declared, and he went into the bathroom, closed the door, and studied his face in the mirror for a long time. Many poems he knew quite through, "Flanders Field" and "Trees," which he would recite for friends over a bottle of beer. There was no way to stop him, he had a superb voice. When he said, "Poems are made by fools like me," his friends snickered in spite of themselves and fooled with their beer bottles. "It ain't nothing he does that you can see. It's his damned face."

Willie liked the people he met in the city, he liked people about him, he joined the Veterans of Foreign Wars. And his wife took membership in the Auxiliary. It was natural enough that they should join such an organization, for they had both suffered from the war. When Willie reached the front lines in October, 1918, his path was crossed by a bullet that shot him through the groin. He fell in a hump, but rose instantly, the blood streaming through his crossed hands. He tried to smile, foolishly, but his eyes expressed terrible anguish. "Well, there go the family jewels," he said, and he fell unconscious to the ground.

When Willie was well enough to be about, the war was over. He and some other soldiers at the hospital received passes to go into Paris. At a little bistro in Montmartre they met the barmaid Genevieve. She was pretty and petite, quite French-looking, they thought, and therefore desirable. Actually she was Belgian; she had lost her home early in the war, then her father and mother, and had come to Paris. Her face was square and rather gaunt, with high cheek bones. Several strands of premature grey appeared in her naturally curly hair, and her eyes were light blue. They were dreamy and melancholy. Altogether she expressed woeful feminine sadness—as though her misery were too apparent to be all her own but rather a

friendly mask of sympathy for the soldiers, which made them itch
to possess her. They did for a price and came away nonplussed.
"Well, she's French all right, 'cause that's all she talked, even when
I pinched her, but boy she ain't no more limber than a board, is
she?" Willie ignored them; this was his first, even though he was
last, and his best. He came back all the nights of his pass. When he
paused for rest, after the early thrills, he became alarmed at the girl's
chronic, even sorrow. He intuitively felt a need to talk down that
abjectness, lest the light go out of his pleasure, perhaps never to
return. "Tell me," he said in the full power of his voice, "how did
a girl like you get in this awful business?" as though the expression
were being uttered for the first time. She was combing her hair—
that gesture. "Comment—comment—" he tried again, leaning toward
her. Something he did made her whimper, at the corners of her
eyes two sparkling tears. He went to her and put his arms around
her. "Ah, my little petite," he said, feeling his manhood rage through
him. Tears were running pell-mell when she lifted her face. Mandibly
they clutched and fell on the bed. Genevieve became his wife, and
he married her in that very country.

On the farms along Merrifield Pike, Genevieve seemed destined
for scandal. "No, that's what I say, 'A real French woman from
Paris.' I suppose she'll have all the boys lathering at Fox's gate like
bulls. Why, an American woman won't be able to step outside the
house."

"You mean she sure enough is Willie's wife?"

They went to see her. For a month of Sundays they stormed
Fox's place, eating his food, dirtying up the parlor, and clapping
Willie on the back, till even he could hardly smile any more. They
brought her in from the kitchen for each round of visitors. "Why,
she's sort of old, you know. And such a poor mournful-looking
creature that I could hardly keep from laughing." The men, smiling
their disappointment, withdrew as quickly as they could and went
out and sat on the fence, where they told horrendously dirty stories.
But a couple of hardy boys, who had remembered what their parents
said at home, tried to touch her, and they were cuffed out the door.
At last they went away, suddenly old and irritable, and were hard on
their horses all the way home.

Genevieve and Willie had time then, to begin to know one another,
and to enter into the life of the farm. A room had been furnished for
them up under the eaves where they went at the blind scrabbling busi-

ness of making love as man and wife. Willie was perplexed. It was a pity how simple she was, rather like a secret box into which he could stuff his lust night after night—and as unresponsive. Willie thought of lighted Paris and the things soldiers had told him; he whispered in her ear. "Ah, you want me to be *comme ces bêtes*," she said, and for two nights she slept on a chair and wouldn't come near him. The second day he turned away from wrath and pulled the warm blankets from his mouth in order to speak. "Genevieve, this just doesn't seem right." The red morning light made him seem as rosy as a baby, and seeing the child's look of anguish on his face, she went over and got in bed with him so that he might be comforted

On the farm Genevieve was a willing helpmeet. She milked the cows, she gathered kindling, she was underfoot in the kitchen. It was apparent to Mr. and Mrs. Fox that Genevieve hadn't brought their son up in the world one bit. "They're like one cripple leading another," Mr. Fox said.

"You'd think they were brother and sister," his wife said, astonishing herself. They viewed the young couple with alarm, and Mr. Fox set himself up as a stern lord to both of them.

Though Mr. Fox presently changed. Occasionally he helped Genevieve with tasks she couldn't master; he laughingly mocked her attempts at English and would pat her on the bottom when she came in from out of doors. His wife had fallen ill. She had always had respiratory trouble and a catarrh which sometimes made her breath unbearable. Now she was probably dying of tuberculosis.

One spring day she was seriously ill. Mr. Fox sat in their room by her bed, smelling the fetid air and looking at the sun outside. A robin came to build a nest on one of the crude cross-beams under the eaves. "There ain't no room there," Mr. Fox said aloud. But the crazy robin returned, bringing twigs and grass and laid them on the beam. Many of the twigs fell, and she knocked others off with her feet and wings when she tried to build. She came back again and again till finally her mate arrived, scolding and dancing about. He tried to push her off the beam, till they both fell and flew away. Mr. Fox rose. "By God, there's only one thing a French woman's good for," and he charged from the room. He found her in the kitchen and went straight about his business; she called for Willie. Willie, who had been working in the barn, arrived with a shovel still in his hand, and saw his father trying to drag Genevieve out from behind the kitchen stove. He hit him on the back. Mr. Fox lifted himself, trembling, looking at odd corners of the room; but catching hold of dignity he said, "I'm your father, do you realize that?" Which took Willie back, and Mr. Fox sidled out the door.

Mr. Fox died soon after that, of a stroke, while beating a horse on the head. The news shocked his wife into a coma, but after having withdrawn from the world for a few days, she began to recover and was soon able to come out and sit on the back porch, in the sunshine. Much to Willie's relief, his mother took over the direction of the farm and, still sitting on the porch, she guided their operations the summer long. That winter she brought her husband's easy chair out into the kitchen by the range. She had a notebook and a pencil with her, and from time to time would scribble something. "There, you see," she said.

Willie said, "I don't know what I'd do without you, Mother." Her eyes were as bright and searching as bugs. Willie wondered if he could tell his mother about Genevieve—that she didn't seem to be all he had expected. Late one afternoon in February, when Genevieve was out milking the cows, he went to his mother; but, lo, she was dead, a twisted smile on her face. The farm had fallen to Willie. "Mother," he said in utter humility.

Johnny the fat man came into the bar. He was pulling at his pants. "Boy, this heat gets me down," he said. Willie put a cocktail shaker on the bar, then two bottles of beer and a jigger of whiskey. Johnny mixed them into the shaker and finished the drink in two long draughts. "I don't seem to have any room for my balls," he said. Willie got out two more bottles of beer. Johnny watched him pour the whiskey. "Every time I walk down the street I feel like I'm wrestling with somebody." This time he took a little longer with the drink. "Did you hear about that new beer distributor?"

"That Smith fellow?" Willie said.

"Yeah, Smith—seems like his name ought to be Schultz or something, don't it?" Johnny finished the drink.

"Did he die?" Willie said.

"Die—no—he's giving a stag party. Didn't you hear about it?" Willie crossed his arms and looked angry. "Nope," he said defensively.

"OK, OK, it wasn't in the papers, you know. It's for the taverns and their employees. Men. I'd go if I were you."

Willie wiped down the bar. "Free beer and food, eh?"

"And women, they tell me. Nu-ude women. Be quiet—mum's the

word, as they say." Willie picked up Johnny's cocktail shaker and wiped under it. He washed the whiskey glass and held it up to the light. "Ain't you going?" he said belligerently.

"Me, I ain't no employee. I wouldn't risk it in the summertime anyway, I'm too fat." Johnny paid for a sack of peanuts and left.

Genevieve would worry if Willie went to the stag party. They had never been very far apart. From the first days on the farm they had huddled together, instinctively, as animals do. It was not to be supposed that they liked one another or were even curious after the first few months, but against the world, they were inseparable. One time they went to a party. Everyone was young, they had applejack and some whiskey, and they played a lot of rough-and-tumble games like kids. Post office was suggested. Willie took delight in the thought of kissing another woman. The girls were outside the door and the men in. A postman stood by the door to announce the mail. "Your turn, Willie," he said. Willie went to the door and the postman opened it. Genevieve. Everyone almost died, and Genevieve and Willie stood staring at one another for the longest time, as before a mirror. At the same moment they folded in each other's arms, and fighting back their tears they gently patted one another's backs. It grew awfully quiet in the room, and the men got out the whiskey.

After Willie's parents had died, he and Genevieve went to see a doctor. They had been married four years and didn't have a child. "There's not a thing wrong with either of you," the doctor said.

"In the war I was shot down there," Willie said. "I got a Purple Heart, and I thought—"

"Nope. Nothing to it. You'll be all right. Just keep it up."

"In the same old way?"

"Why—yes," the doctor said.

That winter Genevieve became pregnant. At the top of the landing she felt dizzy. She fell downstairs and broke her arm and miscarried. She had to lie in bed to mend. When the doctor had gone, Willie broke into the bedroom, his face contorted with anger. "I just don't know what to say," he yelled. "Sometimes I get scared, dammit." She choked crying and turned toward the wall. They had no children. Afterwards, when the comrades talked about the soldiers who died, Willie went them one better. "I didn't give my life," he said. "I gave my children's lives. My children's lives." He had to repeat it. "In the war I was shot down there. I got a

Purple Heart and it did something to me." The comrades showed their respect.

"You understand that I don't have anything to complain about. I'm not grudging life. There's still me and Genevieve."

When Willie took the bartender's job, Genevieve quit work at the bakery and took her place in the home. "I'll take care of you, Curlylocks," Willie said. "You sit at home on a cushion and sew a fine seam, like a woman should."

But she was lonely without him. The neighbor women depressed her; they were always so excited, and the way they talked about their poor husbands made her blush. Willie never did any of those things—she longed for him. Late in the evenings now, when the bar was about to close, she went down to the club to wait for Willie and to walk home with him. She felt keenly his disapproval of her presence, but pretended not to notice. Sometimes on Friday or Saturday, after a busy night, she tried to help him put fresh bottles of beer into the depleted iceboxes. "Now, stop it," he said, scolding in a low tone. "Go away."

"You're awful tired, Willie. I'll just stay and help." The rest of the employees, watching them wrestle with the beer cartons, went about their work with serious faces. "God," they laughed when the Foxes had left, "they're like one cripple helping another."

When they got home Willie said, "If you do that one more time, I'll never go to work again. We'll starve like rats. I'll show you." Genevieve had never heard him talk such violence. He seemed so independent since he took the new job. She was afraid, she began to mother him. If it rained after Willie had gone to work, she ran down to the club with rubbers and an umbrella; in the winter she lugged his galoshes and an extra sweater for him. In hot weather there were always his salt pills which he had forgotten. Willie put on weight, and lolled in bed on Sunday mornings. He thought maybe he had heart trouble, and his kidneys didn't seem the same on both sides. Once it was necessary to take two weeks off from work in order to have his hemorrhoids removed. "Aw, it was nice," he told the comrades. "Genevieve was a wife and a nurse all rolled into one. I couldn't have done better in a hospital." Then one day Genevieve slipped on the ice and broke her arm for the second time. The ladies of the Auxiliary thought it was simply amazing how concerned Willie was. "Why, I hear he turned as white as a sheet when he heard the news, and ran straight home," they told their husbands.

"I thought, gosh, I wish all men were like that." Sitting by her bed, Willie leaned back and smiled indulgently up at the ceiling. Genevieve was all right, she was sleeping. She stirred. "There, there, Genevieve, you're OK. Now don't cry. I'm not angry with you."

"Do you like me, Willie?"

"Why yes, you know. Like I read in a poem once, you and I are one."

Through the years their lives had settled down to give and take. The most they asked for was mutual kindness, and they had become zealous for each other's welfare. Genevieve waited one night for Willie to come home from work. The bar had closed, he should be along any minute now. Out in the street Genevieve heard people, boys, calling harshly and laughing. They were abusing someone. "Willie!" she thought and ran outside. At a safe distance the boys had Willie surrounded, and they were pretending to laugh as if their sides would burst. Frightened, Willie saw Genevieve and seemed to fall back against her. "Genevieve, what's the matter, what's the matter?"

"Willie, come inside."

"They're crazy, Genevieve. They're crazy."

"Oh, come away, dear," and she pulled him into the house.

"I'll get the cops," Willie said.

"Oh, darling, it's your apron." The night had been a busy one, and Willie had put his overcoat on over his apron and walked home. She took it off and threw it on the floor. Then they sought each other's arms. Their hearts grew quiet at last, the world was outside.

Willie never forgot that incident. Whenever he wanted to intensify a particular affront, he could call it up at will, sucking at it like a sore tooth. He looked around at the persons in the club—Jasper Williams abusing the slot machines and cursing, Billy Hokes the waiter and Jonesy, Connie the Sailor and Roy Hayes arguing over their beer—probably every last one of them knew about the party and hadn't told him. Willie was furious; he thought of other insults, real and fancied. Many years ago they had elected him chaplain of the Post, and then the next year and the next till finally it became automatic, and he was given the office each year without even a preliminary nomination. They told him it was because he had such a wonderful voice, and a flair for words; and sometimes when he spoke about a recently deceased comrade, their hair bristled on their necks. When they elected him each term, they rose, smiling, and gave him an ovation, but out of the corner of his eye Willie saw them belabor each other with their elbows. And those damned Auxiliary women. They had told Willie how much they liked his wife's hair, that they just loved to look at it. Genevieve's hair had turned completely grey, silver in appearance, but it still retained its natural curl. She had it done up in ringlets so that she would only have to run her comb through it in the morning; life was easier that way. Willie knew that the women lied. They were as appalled as he was and only spoke because they just had to say something. He knew what poor Genevieve looked like, she looked like ornamented death. Willie grabbed for a rag and wiped down the bar. Harold the manager came in; Willie met him in the middle of the floor. "Why didn't you tell me about that damned stag party?" he said.

"Well, Willie—"

"I'm just as responsible as you are."

"Now, listen, Willie—" Willie left him and went behind the bar. "You—Jasper Williams—get away from those slot machines," he announced like a trumpet. They turned. Willie dervished and found the cash register. He turned back, smiling, and his eyes refused to meet them out of contempt.

The party was held one Sunday evening. They hadn't wanted to profane the Sabbath, but Sunday was the only day on which the bars were closed. "Oh, comrades," Willie said. "It's good to be here with you. The air is so gentle."

They were assembled on an abandoned farm, located by a small lake. A chateau was at their disposal, perched on the bank above the water. On the second floor of the chateau a little stage had been built. Some of the fellows had been out earlier in the week to make it. They did it gratis. Outside there was food, and cooks to serve it. Ham and beef, pork, Canadian bacon, fish and venison. Barbecues, hamburgers, hot dogs, potato salad and baked beans. There was even celery. "Try some of that venison," they said; the sauce ran down their chins. And beer. All the brands that Smithy the distributor handled were iced away in a series of large beer tubs which resembled horse troughs. Each tub of beer had its trademark and an advertisement tacked on a scaffolding behind it. At their pleasure the men could select their favorite brands. "Now stick with me," Harold said.

"Horsefeathers," Willie said and drank his beer.

As the sun went down, the games of chance came out. Food was cleared off the tables and a craps board laid; the wheel of fortune went up, card parties were starting, and for Smithy the distributor and a few, roulette.

"God, look at them with their money," Harold said. "And some of them don't have a piss pot nor a lid to keep it holy."

"It's astonishing," Willie said. They found a friendly game of craps. "Come on in," Billy Hokes said. "This is for family men." Willie dug in his pockets for change.

"What's that?" Harold said. Among the coins in Willie's hands were some pills. "Salt pills," Willie said. "Genevieve thought I better bring some." They laughed. Willie smiled and put one in his mouth and drank it down with beer.

"Atta boy," they said and clapped him on the back.

Willie won over two dollars the first time he had his hands on the dice. He went for more beer. When he had the dice once more, he doubled up on snake eyes and won again. Harold offered him a cigar, and Willie blew smoke through his nose. There was a scuffle nearby. A young man, marvelously muscled and nude to the waist, jumped on a table. He waved a quart of whiskey. "I can lick any man here," he said, "and I'll drink whiskey if I want to." Then he stepped backwards and lay moaning on the ground with a broken collar bone. "Say, that's that Haines boy," Harold said. "You'd better drive him into town, Willie."

"I don't have a car, what's the matter with you?"

"I'll lend you mine."

"Nope," Willie said, wiping off the mouth of a beer bottle.

"Didn't we all fight in the wars together?" Willie drank his beer and looked at Harold askance. They laid the Haines boy in the back of a panel truck and drove off. "Damn fools," Willie said.

Willie kept winning; he counted off ten dollars, put it away in his wallet, and finished another bottle of beer. A hush fell over the players. Harold stood up. "What's that?"

"A big truck."

"I know it's a big truck," Harold said annoyed. "And what's more they're delivering a piano at the house."

"Well, don't get hostile."

"Why didn't they deliver it in the daytime, that's what I want to know," Harold said. They stood up to watch the unloading of the piano. "She shall have music wherever she goes," Willie said.

Billy Hokes picked up his money and left. "Where you going?" Harold said.

"I think I'll go on up to the house and wait," Billy said.

"Billy's a widower," Willie said. They returned to the game. Occasionally they had to shout to make themselves heard because that bartender from the Shangri-La Tavern kept walking back and forth among the tables screaming. Three fellows got him and took him down and threw him in the lake. The ensuing silence made them jittery. Harold stood up, and then the others. "Oh—it's nothing, I guess," Harold said, and they knelt down once more. But a minute later Harold was up again. "What's that?"

"A big black sedan."

"Dammit, I know it," Harold said. Some women got out of the car and ran into the house like celebrities. The men threw a few more dice, but shortly in groups of two and three they picked up their money and strolled toward the house. They talked of automobiles, hunting, and the New York Yankees, leaving at the tables only those who were winning and the men who were desperately losing.

Inside the house it was terribly hot and the smoke made the eyes burn. Willie took another salt pill. "Well, now's the time," Harold said; "I always believe in going whole hog at these things," and he pulled a bottle of whiskey from his pocket. He offered Willie some. A man climbed on the stage and began poking at the piano, and a fiddle player joined him. The men fell silent. The musicians faltered into "Sweet Georgia Brown," and the first girl came out. "Thank God she's young," Harold said. Willie was astonished. He had seen pictures of girls before but this one was real. Her flanks were so trim and white, and her breasts. The girl finished her act and the men applauded and called for more. "More!" Willie bellowed and the men looked at him. He grabbed Harold's whiskey and took a long drink. Two more girls came out and went through a routine much like the first. When they had finished, the applause was unanimous. The men were roughhousing; they loosened their ties and called for beer, and here and there some of the old fellows like Harold and Willie had wormed closer to the stage. The musicians bounced into a jazz number, and the first girl reappeared. Obviously this was different, she meant business. Billy Hokes stood up on a chair. She capered and gamboled and finished in a sweat. The next girl came out like a comet.. "Look what she's doing," Harold said. With one leap Willie sprang up on Billy's chair and knocked Billy among the crowd. That would have meant a fight except that in the melee Willie fell too, and Billy didn't know who pushed him. Picking himself up from the floor Willie realized what it was that had been bothering him for the last hour or two. He had lost the tie-clasp which Genevieve had given him for Christmas. But he wasn't sure yet; he would look in his pocket later. When the third girl finished, the men were knocking each other around, and several fights nearly started. Someone stood on a chair, waving a bottle. "God bless you, Mr. Smith. I've never had such a good time." He fainted. Mr. Smith accepted the tribute smiling, and one of his friends pushed his hat down over his eyes.

The little band rested, but the men couldn't stand it. They broke into yells and staccato clapping. At an invisible cue, the piano player beat down on his instrument, and the three women, nude, came out in a group. They danced and were bold together. Willie was right by the stage; he couldn't look at them for guilt. He put his hands over his ears, unconsciously hearing the crescendo of sound each time he released his fingers. Genevieve in France, he thought; he grabbed for Harold's bottle.

They were proposing something special on the stage. "Here's your man," Harold said. "Give an old man a chance."

"Aw, now," Willie said, but he felt himself lifted bodily onto the stage.

"Now, let's be sensible," Willie said, turning around and preparing to go down, but the girls were encouraging him. They were beside him warm and golden in the naked light. He could touch them. They were dragging him toward the center of the stage and pulling at his clothes. "Don't," he said, slapping at them. One stood directly before his eyes, and Willie felt annihilating lust flood up from somewhere in his loins. He wanted to speak something tender. "Oh, young ladies," he said. They were all around him, interring him with their foreign smell. He reached out, he wanted to hold her young body before everyone—

Blood was coming out of Willie's nose. It had covered his chin and was spreading on his shirt front.

"Oh Genevieve," Willie said. The men began to mutter. Willie dropped to his knees and lowered his head. Blood dripped onto his trousers. "Our Father, who art in Heaven," he began. One of the girls cried out. She was hitting Willie on the shoulders and head. "Make him stop. Help me. Stop the damn fool."

II. POETRY

CONRAD AIKEN:

The Footstep

The intermediate will have its uses: here will come
the half-light, blue, in the snowdrift's shadow, the down
of fledgling grass which shines like a green mist
on the waste earth, iridescent and sensitive,
slight beyond notice, a deception to the eye,
a delight to the hand—

or a sleight to the mind, subtle creative solstice,
that farthest point in time or place in space
when light falls rarest on the dreaming world:
here the fine needle of the first dream, touching
such painful thought as the world itself dreams only
when light is scarce.

And here the dream itself, magnificent angel
swift beyond flight of mind or hand, the shape
unshaped by hand or mind, wonderfully loosed
into the void of future, the void of past:
whirlwind of will, which takes all things to self
and bids them live.

This is the moment when the heart must wait,
pause, between times of beating, and be still—
hear its own waiting, and be still serene.
The moment when the tree, with no despair,
lets the last leaf fall from last season's loss,
yet without hope.

Come here and touch, the hand which has not grasped!
wake here and see, the eye which has not seen!
and the mind think here, which has never thought.
All shall be shaped which never yet was shaped,
in this or any world; and all shall find
intrepid way—

intricate as may be, but dreadful too—
into the unknown of the inward world,
which, as it inward works, will outward flower.
Come, it is spring, and we shall find our speech
giving itself a guise of branch or leaf
as we shall live.

A. R. AMMONS:

Whose Timeless Reach

I Ezra the dying
portage of these deathless thoughts
stood on a hill in
the presence of the mountain
and said wisdom is
too wise for man it
is for gods and gods have little
use for it so I do not know what
to do with it
and animals use it only when
   their teeth start to fall and it
is too late to do anything
else but be wise and stay
out of the way
The eternal will not lie
down on any temporal hill
   The frozen mountain rose and broke
its tireless lecture of
repose and said death does
not take away it
ends giving halts bounty and
   Bounty I said thinking of ships
that I might take and helm right
out through space

dwarfing these safe harbors and
their values
taking the Way in whose timeless reach
cool thought unpunishable
by bones eternally glides

The wind coming down from

summit and blue air
said I am sorry for you
and lifting past
said you
are mere dust which I
as you see control

yet nevertheless are
instrument of miracle

and rose
out of earshot but
returning in a slow loop
said while
I am always just this bunch of
compensating laws
pushed pushing
not air or motion
but the motion of air

I coughed
and the wind said
Ezra will live
to see your last
sun come up again

I turned (as I will) to weeds and
the wind went off
carving

monuments through a field of stone
    monuments whose shape
wind cannot arrest but
taking hold on
    changes

while Ezra
    listens from terraces of mind
wind cannot reach or
weedroots of my low feeding shiver

Sumerian

I have grown a marsh dweller
subject to floods and hard wind,
drinking brackish water on long hunts,
    brushing gnat smoke
from clumps of reeds, have known

the vicissitudes of silt, of
shifting channels flush
by dark upland rains, of mounds
rising no more firmly than
    monsters from the water.

On the southern salty
banks near the gulf the ducks
and flying vees of geese have
avoided me: the bouncing spider's net,
strung wet over narrows of reeds, has
broken dawn terror cold across my face.

Rising with a handful of broken shells
    from sifting underwater mud,
I have come to know how high
the platform is, beyond approach,
of serenity and blue temple tiles.

FREDERICK BOCK:

The Jays

Before the blinded flutters of our eyes
Can tell the jaybird breaks winter in two,
So quickened is the brightness
Of sun and snow about us
That we who are often lonely often use
A shimmer for repose.

We hear, above, their bluer quartz
Spoke light like a shout
Exultant in our waste of hearts—
Yet to be, bird-loose, stretched out
Beside you is enough
To make love love: we lie
Like snowbanks on our warmth.

Their cries are axis-creaks of May!
But half-turned hills of sun
Roll back to your whiteness,
In itself halcyon:
Performed before us is our quietness.

Dying, the brightest of the snows,
We feel our drifted moments vie
With local centuries passing by
That brought no jay upon the sill,
    As this hour will,
To look at you, sidewise, as we at him
    With all our power,
For still we live on where we die—
Nothing changes but the flight of birds.

MILLEN BRAND:

An Old Man Toward the End

1

Age lets go, unembarrassed,
relaxing the bellows of the thorax,
the valves of the heart,
to quiet.
If this were all,
it would be easy, but as he draws the blanket several times
to his face,
he finds
sickness
loud in his eyes.

2

All day he holds it back.
His eyes are hinged, here
and with a furtive pivot, there with the second world.
Sometimes he follows it in the air
across the end of the room.
"Do you see . . . ?"
all those dots
that swarm like a fine dust
from his eyeballs
and fill up the presence of the walls.
When he was younger, in fever
walls went away, shook in a concave shudder,
or moved near
in a terror without images.
Now there are images.
His eyebrows, darker than his hair,
keep young, making his eyes older.
His left eyeball reddens,

suffused, threatened,
blood in it visibly
burning.
"He ain't so good as he was.
Ain't doin' good.
I pity him." (softly)
Mabel goes
to him and away
down the stairs,
and so, for long hours,
he lies alone.
    Once on a train
when fatigue remade the world
(a little uremic poisoning),
he pointed out in one seat
Favario, the sculptor of the angels;
and in another, his cousin, Eddie Leacraft;
and in another, that one —
"the florist, what was his name?"
George smiles from the dresser
his invisible smile.
"I'm always fighting my father
in my dreams."
    Dreams
come with the dark.
The dark descends
over the rear building, slowly,
down over the steep-pitched roof
and the two gable windows drawn on a line
like a ledge, in a saffron struggle,
the light creaming
to a roar as it gives out.
Then the dangerous time begins:
the unwilling guard at the cellar door
lets through
the upward-riding shadows.
These shadows are desire,
desire of years,
desire of hard body,

desire of love.
He wants a mist of perfect light
around its contour, vapor
on its sides.
Sensuous angels
reach for his bed.
They are not definite,
they are edged with blue outlines
like the sky,
like water.
And they have voices.
    Between waking and sleep,
between waking and dream,
between desire and fear,
with the force of a walking bear
he gets up from bed.
He clings to the railing of the stairs
going down.
The brain's portals
open, their arachnoid knots
flashing
under the dura
their warning
of the drowned.
They find him on a chair in the kitchen,
unable to say
how he got there.
    Old, old,
he asks no pity.
His eyebrows shadow
his eyes. He knows
where he is
in his woken
sockets.

3

From the bed,
he sees the street
and does not see it, resting.
Perhaps the pillows' comfort arranges it
into hypnoid landscapes,
into railroad stations.
He can close his eyes today
to the steam roller
and to those heavy half shoes
coated with the spring's black asphalt as with mud
the workmen wear,
and journey
in his eyelids'
mirror.

4

He tells it gently:
"I had my hand under the cover —
like this — and he — or she — grasped it —
like this. I didn't make any remonstrance.
I waited for him — or her — to discover that I had discovered —
him."
To exist with the unsuspecting suspected,
the unconfronted confronted.
The cover lay solid as a mountain
over his arm. Between his arm and the wall
there was no space, but in that spacelessness
fear took his pulse.
He accustoms himself to it the way
a bird in the woods complains
at sunset.
He accustoms himself to it the way
a half-asleep child winks
the sound of the truck's airbrake
into dream.

5

He raises his hand
to get the light behind it, its fire
taking fire from the sun,
penumbral flame
softer than blood.
The loneliness is all
in waiting, the heart
letting its bell
like a tongue
fall.

6

It is the smoke
leaking out of "your picture" that does it,
beginning perhaps at the row of medals
and the blue breast leaning
away from the kamikaze rockets and the momentary
boiling of the sea. The smoke
moves up over the black border
of the mirror in which the night light
makes its milk saucer, it blots the saucer,
and continues to the ceiling.
It is when it creeps toward him
from the blue-vested heart
that he screams. Lost.

7

   He failed to get a bed that cranked,
he notices.
When the morning nurse lets the light
into the ward,
he finds himself racked up
in a crib,
his mind clear
and the seas gone that scratched
their sharp saw
on the sky.

Calm has come with light.
His faint heels with their live calluses
hit the footrail.
    In the next bed
a man sits, patient:
down over his nose
a glass tube draws a silver line
like an interplanetary
apparatus. He stares at it
in a mirror.
On the other side a man
sleeps.
    "Where's my watch?"
"We don't have your watch, Dad."
He left it home, then.
No money, either.
And from his neck the nightgown bib,
like a king's coarse linen,
falls away over his chest
and slips up above his knees.
His friends, the two men,
rise into his eyes.
They are real,
the nurse's arm
is real.
It is a mistake
inflicted by the night
in its lonely, long bazaar.
"Let me go home."

JOHN MALCOLM BRINNIN:

Marianne Moore's

not an attitude
but a climate—
   native riviera
   where light, pale but successful, spots
     a lank destroyer stopped in a gorgeous calm,
     or a shark-like sloop.

Nothing predicted
her, unless the
   sea did, tossing, like a
   diamond in Kansas, a mil-
     limeter's labyrinth of coral on the
     tides of Rockaway;

unless another
age did, when, in
   a sky-blue vestal gown
   and ice-blue jockey cap (the stripes
     were meaningless, the sporting kings were dead) she
     rode a merry race

near Paris in the
Degas steeplechase,
   figuratively, of
   course. Vision cracked with a pin, its
     voyages at a standstill, its purposes
     exposed yet honored—

polarities that
span the world, while
   Yankee-jawed camels, the
   chariest most north-of-Boston
     types, scheme through the needle's eye to find, if not
     their proper heavens,

facsimiles there-
of. It is not
    that another couldn't
    match her method of embalming
        mirrors but that, like so much which passes for
        life in Brooklyn, she

happened there first. To
an age of art-
    ifice she brings laurels
    of artifact. How special, then,
        are these few poems of a rectitude so
        insular they will

be saved as saints are
saved whose palms bleed
    annually, because
    like the glass flowers at Harvard
        (lessons in perfect lifelessness) they are what
        they're talking about.

LEONARD CASPER:

Movement Toward a Close

I. Inception

Jittered in hotbed, the pendulum of brass-seed
is set in motion. A wind a wheel within
a wind; a flare on the surface of the sun
which has no surface. Now, Porter, begin.

For the first time, a foot inside a door;
then handed a bill-of-goods and told to sell.
Tourist rooms with the almost-maniac smell
of ammonia; barroom tan; winking dogs.

"Friend, you never know what it's like until
you've tried it." Glad-hands above the slopjar;
rocker-voices on a porch. — Think
of concern, in a hotbed turnover when wind is still!

(Man of the world, we burn in your effigy.)
Scratch a man who itches, and you'll find
Porter! cup-bearer to Sangreal and Son.
(Man of a thousand trades, we are your pedigree.)

— Think what association means *(Think!*
is a plywood slogan from the office head),
with marginal men who win their daily bread
by economy of inquiry and guarantee;

met in a winecellar of winds, with badly mixed
couples, looking ambidextrous
and sinister in medicine hats and spouting
windjammer words of ads (Think!) ventuous.

II. Involvement
Night-flight through darkness seen edgewise,
driving back to trailer that's become his home
in this new territory.
Slumbering engine (late trade-in model)
coaxes; he becomes impelled by the ply of tires,
an elegy for the memory.

Like wind passing through wind, the groundswell
scoops him forward, as to deep layers of sleep . . .
Buyers don't exist anyway:
this is the meaning of meaning, this fast road,
unsunned, unmuddied, lonely before a weekend
without landmarks to gainsay . . .

Singing, "Beyond the blue phenomena",
while the concrete-strips redistribute, and
secondhand time sweeps
around and around like obsessive tires
pressing the roadway flat as a process,
and the forward curve grows steep.

Maps say: it's no farther from the center
of the forest out than in, except
that meanwhile rivers flow
the world slips east, and things have happened:
there's no rate of exchange for *that* — unless
you forget stopping and start to *go!*

III. Fulfillment

Like naked light bulbs, thoughts
arouse him from the black of bed.
Crows' feet walk across his head
in wonder. His hurried hand is caught
in the sticky field of a strange woman,
his wife, now his bed companion
only, her bedspring voice distraught.

From the edge of silence, a voice
that sets an edge on silence cries
through a luminous clock. It pries
him alert. (The wind within had a choice
to write or not a "Manifesto, Should the Day
Ever Come".) But he knows only the way
to think, "It is time: O rise and rejoice!"

E. E. CUMMINGS:

Three Poems

1.

in time of daffodils(who know
the goal of living is to grow)
forgetting why,remember how

in time of lilacs who proclaim
the aim of waking is to dream,
remember so(forgetting seem)

in time of roses(who amaze
our now and here with paradise)
forgetting if,remember yes

in time of all sweet things beyond
whatever mind may comprehend,
remember seek(forgetting find)

and in a mystery to be
(when time from time shall set us free)
forgetting me,remember me

2.

o by the by
has anybody seen
little you-i
who stood on a green
hill and threw
his wish at blue

with a swoop and a dart
out flew his wish
(it dived like a fish
but it climbed like a dream)
throbbing like a heart
singing like a flame

blue took it my
far beyond far
and high beyond high
bluer took it your
but bluest took it our
away beyond where

what a wonderful thing
is the end of a string
(murmurs little you-i
as the hill becomes nil)
and will somebody tell
me why people let go

3.

it was a goodly co
which paid to make man free
(for man is enslaved by a dread dizziz
and the sooner it's over the sooner to biz
don't ask me what it's pliz)

then up rose bishop budge from kew
a anglican was who
(with a rag and a bone and a hank of hair)'d
he picked up a thousand pounds or two
and he smote the monster merde

then up rose pride and up rose pelf
and ghibelline and guelph
and ladios and laddios
(on radios and raddios)
did save man from himself

ye duskiest despot's goldenest gal
did wring that dragon's tail
(for men must loaf and women must lay)
and she gave him a desdemonial
that took his breath away

all history oped her teeming womb
said demon for to doom
yea(fresh complexions being oke
with him)one william shakespeare broke
the silence of the tomb

then up rose mr lipshits pres
(who always nothing says)
and he kisséd the general menedjerr
and they smokéd a robert burns cigerr
to the god of things like they err

ALAN DUGAN:

Love Song: I and Thou

Nothing is plumb, level or square:
    the studs are bowed, the joists
are shaky by nature, no piece fits
    any other piece without a gap
or pinch, and bent nails
    dance all over the surfacing

like maggots. By Christ
    I am no carpenter. I built
the roof for myself, the walls
    for myself, the floors
for myself, and got
    hung up in it myself. I
danced with a purple thumb
    at this house-warming, drunk
with my prime whiskey: rage.
    Oh I spat rage's nails
into the frame-up of my work:
    it held. It settled plumb,
level, solid, square and true
    for that great moment. Then
it screamed and went on through,
    skewing as wrong the other way.
God damned it. This is hell,
    but I planned it, I sawed it,
I nailed it, and I
    will live in it until it kills me.
I can nail my left palm
    to the left hand cross-piece but
I can't do everything myself.
    I need a hand to nail the right,
a help, a love, a you, a wife.

BREWSTER GHISELIN:

On the Disappearance of God among the Mackel

For Carl Gustav Jung

A thousand shuttles of green light through the seaweb thrown
Swerve to the pepper of chum bowled about us, flash
To the bowstring leap of the line and thump the boards of the boat:
Motion without emotion, flexible metal, eyes without thought.

Except where the black shark lags rolling like a long log
They crosswhip all the waters with flashy feeding, around him
An electric field. But when he is hooked aboard, his gone
Presence widens over the ocean. And they dazzle like a mad loom.

HORACE GREGORY:

Police Sergeant Malone and the Mysterious Case of Captain John Farley

"When John Farley said, 'I need a rest;
I want to live as though I were the Duke of Windsor
In a pair of tennis shorts, sun-glasses and a cork helmet
To keep the heat out of my brain,' I knew that something
Had gone wrong. When he said, 'Even my dentist
Tells me I need a rest and that the color of my eyes
Is turning pale.' I could have broken his case
Two weeks before he passed out of sight; I could have told him
That a trip to Cuba might end in disaster,
That you don't find heaven on a Sunday in Key West.

For some people that I know
The holiday runs like poison in their veins,
Yet millions fly from the city every year, the rich, the poor:
The school teacher who raises goats and chickens on a farm
Is almost certain to fall apart too soon;
The bank vice-president on his ranch in Arizona
Who owns a rodeo and sings 'cruel Barbara Allen'
Won't live too long or keep his name out of the papers;
The pretzel-vendor who takes his stand on a windy corner
Is likely to have a heart-attack at Far Rockaway—
Whether it's drink or manslaughter or a neighbor's wife
You can be sure it is the holiday again.
Even five-star generals after a war are found next morning
Under three inches of windshield glass and snow
And are posed for their last headlines
In the *Daily News*.

288

In New Years' celebrations
You can see the beginning of the end
For those who have the holiday fever in their eyes—
When the wish is to step out of doors for a breath of air
And you feel yourself dropping down sixty-seven floors
To the earth below the street where darkness is
The inside of Jonah's whale, it is then you know
The deep body of earth and sea is around you everywhere.
To save your nerves
You might call it an accident,
But you can't break a case unless you know the cause.

When they picked up Farley at Miami Beach
They said his mind was gone, that he had bought tickets
For a place to Mexico, that he had promised
A Louisville bathing beauty to take her swimming
On his *hacienda*.
                    I had needed a rest myself, but I said at last
'It is not the innocence, it is not the crime,
It is something else—' and if it happens
All your best friends are glad to forget your name.
I had been prepared to take a trip to Maine,
But I unpacked my trunk and decided to stay at home."

EDWIN HONIG:

The Tall Toms

All told the gray world
Sponges hopelessly on swift
Tall Toms, fliers in the
Howling highways, scorchers
Of the lush long countries.

Hats on or off they
Head through glass,
Through bowls of
Winter roses, through
Women hard as diamonds.

Floods and crosses
Kiss their shoes, and
Trolleys late for work
Pray like snails till
Sirens rinse the streets.

Their failure is success
In the eye highballing
White and black, and if
They end, even grim lids in
Grass jaws ponder over them.

A Man

How old is a man when he takes his life in his own
Bare hands and crumples it into a wad? How heavy
He is and strong beyond his knowing, a Samson
Of broken causes, whitened and bleeding his brain
To fix the one cliff passing clearly his own
Dark ship. Past this wishmark he pushes, willing it out,
To the last pulsing black nerve of his sleep.

Whose hero is he when it's done and the world
Anyhow chokes on a mouthful: Was he sick?
Was he broke? Was he right in the head? Did he love
His dead wife too much? Then munching it down
With the cold cuts insists, It took guts! — meaning not
That he may have been right, but the thing was almost as great
As fear's tyrannical acts where praises are pinned.

Many men who grow old so fast they are dead
On their feet do not tumble from twelfth-storey windows
Or smother regrets roped stiff to a stone
In the creek. Those who do, trouble our sleep
For a week while we reel to our jobs in the glare
Of inscrutable chances, heaped with a criminal hunch,
Stranger than wolves at large among friendly sheep.

Somehow, though chipper as ever the minute before,
The minute nobody looked he did it, alone,
With the handiest thing — or planned it for months,
Paid his debts, left notes to his cousins, even a text
For the preacher. He was friend to a friend (surly or dull
Or quick), who now for a honey-eyed moment is young
As someone remembers, old as the wine-dark sea.

TED HUGHES:

The Little Boys and the Seasons

One came out of the wood. "What a bit of a girl,"
The small boys cried, "to drive my elder brother daft,
Tossing her petticoats under the bushes. O we know,
We know all about you: there's a story.
Well, we don't want your tinny birds with their noise,
And we don't want your soppy flowers with their smells,
And you can just take all that make-up off our garden,
And stop giving the animals ideas with your eyes."
And she cried a cloud and all the children ran in.

One came out of the garden. A great woman.
The small boys muttered: "This one's not much either.
She keeps my dad out till too late at night.
You can't get through the bushes for her great bosom

And her sweaty arms round you wherever you go.
The way she wears the sun is just gypsy.
And look how she leaves grownups lying about."
Then they all sat down to stare her out with eyes
Hot as fever from hostility.

One came over the hill, bullying the wind,
Dragging the trees out of each other's arms, swearing
At first so that the children could hardly believe it. No one
Believed the children when they clapped he had come.
The weathercock would have crowed, but was in his hand,
The sun was in his haversack with hares,
Pheasants and singing birds all silent. Whereon
Parents pointed warningly to barometers.
But the small boys said: "Wait till his friend gets here."

Who came out of the sea, overturning the horses,
The hard captain, uniform over the hedges,
Drilling the air till it was threadbare, stamping
Up and down the fields with the nails in his boots
Till the cobbles of the fields were iron as nails.
Birds stood so stiff to attention it was death.
The sun was broken up for sabres. O he was a rough one.
And the little boys cried: "Hurrah for the Jolly Roger,"
And ran out, merry as apples, to shoot each other
On landscapes of his icelocked battleships.

MASON JORDAN MASON:

Consummatum est

Jerusalem, oh Jerusalem
thou crown of creation
thou jeweled crown

And if I owned a mad dog
ugly as you are
I would name him

Shamen

And shave his ass
with a broken mirror
and paint it with turpentine

And train him to walk backwards

Whizzbone the Warbleloot

Handsome walking the platform
so mighty
       with a tail
like a slender yellow gal

Whizzbone whizzbone
warbleloot so mighty
walking that platform
like a high yellow gal

Like spats
       like cane
like a high hat and all
but them old eyelids
drooped like a debauched turtle's

Sing 'em low warbleloot
tap 'em loose
to a highboot cane

Tap 'em warbleloot
to a highbone shinny
make that platform walk around too
like he had spats
         and striped garters

walk around
like he was sporting it too
to a highboot
highboot cane

The Mother of Hamos

In the theological seminary
I read by accident
some books reserved
only for Doctors of Divinity

It shake my faith less
than some things

The cathedrals in New Orleans
filled up with crockery
which give me the creeps
with all the glass eyes hanging

And all the little signs
THANK YOU
THANK YOU SO MUCH

And the saints sitting up
in heaven with nothing to do

He could at least learn
to play a zither
but only the angels
have to work like that

Providing of course
these books
know what they make out like

W. S. MERWIN:

A Dance of Death

King

I saw from a silk pillow
All high stations and low
Smile when I spoke, and bow,
And obey and follow.
All men do as I do.
I went in gold and yellow,
Ermine and gemmed shoe,
And was human even so,
Et, ecce, nunc in pulvere dormio.

Monk

I hoped that all sinners who
Wore a saintly sorrow
Into heaven should go.
All this did I do:
Walk with the eyes low,
Keep lonely pillow,
Many days go
Fasting and hollow,
All my bounty bestow,
Et, ecce, nunc in pulvere dormio.

Scholar

I sat like a shadow,
The light sallow,
Reasoning yes and no.
One thing I came to know.
I heard the mouse go,
Heard whispers in the tallow,
Wind disputing, "Although . . ."
Night on the candle blow,
Et, ecce, nunc in pulvere dormio.

Huntsman

The wind blew
In the cold furrow;
The falcon flew;
These did I follow:
Deerhound, doe,
Fox upon snow,
And sent the arrow,
And was chased, who did follow,
And came to this burrow,
Et, ecce, nunc in pulvere dormio.

Farmer

I walked with plow
On the green fallow;
All I did harrow
Dirt does undo.
Out at elbow
I lie to mellow,
Set in a furrow,
The weeds' fellow,
Quod, ecce, nunc in pulvere dormio.

Woman

I was as green willow,
My hands white and slow,
Love and increase below.
Be reaped as you did sow.
I am bitter as rue.
Now am I also
Defaced and hollow,
Nursing no shadow
Quod, ecce, nunc in pulvere dormio.

Epitaph

Lords, I forget what I knew;
I saw false and true,
Sad and antic show,
Did profane and hallow,
Saw the worthies go
Into the still hollow
And wrote their words, even so,
Et, ecce, nunc in pulvere dormio.

JOSEPHINE MILES:

Accompaniment

Mercedes was the lady's name and she had in her voice
A batch of tunes to tell the day how it was doing.
Often about eleven she would start one after another
Very silently, and come to no conclusion.

Afternoon, though, the day could stop any time,
Break up its traffic, bid its criers peace,
Seize the miraculous instant, and hear tuned
Under Royal keys what Mercedes thought of it.

Audience

He sang to his dog who was sitting on the hearth
And sang the dog his heart
With a tremulo tremulo tremulo
And a bass baritone.

But the dog was not there to hear, he was running
Right in field, caught in sunlight
Called unfinite though he didn't know,
Along the line of sun and in the field
Racing, as he would.

Nevertheless at many hearths the listeners
Leant to the tremulo and gave heart
Back to that baritone, so he felt
Heard as he would.

Gypsy

The entire country is overrun with private property, the
    gypsy king said.
I don't know if this is true,
I believe in the gypsy kingship though.

The lost tribes of my own nation
Rove and rove.
In red and yellow rough and silent move.

I believe
The majesty pot mending, copper smith
On the hundred highways, nothing to do with.

And black eyes, black I never saw,
Searching out the pocket lines of cloth
The face lines and the furrows of belief.

It's a curious fact, Stephan, King, if you are made to doubt
Aegyptian vision on the Jersey shore,
Property's private as ever, ever.

SAMUEL FRENCH MORSE:

The House That Kept Them Warm

Her careful silence in the room below
Distracts him idly now, although her name
Falls in his mind like light across the snow.

He listens for a moment till the slow
Despair returns, but he cannot disclaim
Her careful silence in the room below,

The ghost she has become. She must not know
He loves her thus. Her image, white as flame,
Falls in his mind like light across the snow,

Unchanged by what she is, as to and fro
She keeps the darkness round her, still the same.
Her careful silence in the room below

Is all she cares for now, who long ago
Had known the truth, that more than empty blame,
Falls in his mind like light across the snow.

They keep their word, whatever else they owe
Each other now, the debt of hopeless shame.
Her careful silence in the room below
Falls in his mind like light across the snow.

HOWARD MOSS:

Animal Hospital

(For Dick Wilbur)

Uncomprehended pain,
More savage and more sad
Than ours, waits while the rain
Outside is wet with God.
Inside, the choking lights
Panic the pawned eyes
Of cats and dogs and birds
Who wait for the light to die.

Brute shadows on the wall
Are silhouettes of dogs;
And crazy birds call
Through their dwindling fogs,
And let a feather fall
And let a song begin
In a jungle in the hall
In a zoo of pain.

Luck having lost to life,
The cat, our subtle friend,
Meets murder under the knife;
If it could comprehend
The charity of the brain,
Its claws would sever rope
And clinging there, insane,
Butcher the heart of hope.

One eye on the cuckoo clock,
A love bird, once blue-green,
Now drab, with rotted beak
Suffers the chloroform,

And lets a feather fall
And lets a song begin
In a jungle in the hall
In a zoo of pain.

These in the dark, dumb,
Lie where they cannot speak;
Premonition will not come,
Heaven will not awake.
Into the black they go,
Stiff in their witless skins,
While we at the end know
The whole taking in.

All loss is human then,
Even animal pain;
It takes away the sun,
It swallows up the brain,
And lets a feather fall
And lets a song begin
In a jungle in the hall
In a zoo of pain.

HOWARD NEMEROV:

To Lu Chi*

Old sir, I think of you in this tardy spring,
Think of you for, maybe, no better reason
Than that the apple branches in the orchard
Bear snow not blossoms, and that this, somehow,
Seems oddly Chinese. I too, when I walk
Around the orchard, pretending to be a poet
Walking around the orchard, feel Chinese,

---

* Author of the Wen Fu, or Prose Poem, on The Art of Letters, A.D. 302. See
E. R. Hughes' *The Art of Letters* (Bollingen XXIX).

A silken figure on a painted screen
Who tries out with his eye the apple branches,
The last year's shriveled apples capped with snow,
The hungry birds. And then I think of you.

Through many centuries of dust, to which
We both belong, your quiet voice is clear
About the difficulties and delights
Of writing well, which are, it seems, always
The same and generally unfashionable.
In all the many times I have read your poem,
Or treatise, where the art of letters turns
To the inspection of itself—the theme
(I take your phrase) of how to hold the axe
To make its handle—your words have not failed
To move me with their justice and their strength,
Their manner gentle as their substance is
Fastidious and severe. You frighten me
When you describe the dangers of our course,
And then you bring, by precept and example,
Assurance that a reach of mastery,
Some still, reed-hidden and reflective stream
Where the heron fishes in his own image,
Always exists. I have a sight of you,
Your robes tucked in your belt, standing
Fishing that stream, where it is always dawn
With a mist beginning to be burned away
By the lonely sun. And soon you will turn back
To breakfast and the waking of the world
Where the contending war lords and the lords
Of money pay to form the public taste
For their derivative sonorities;
But yet that pure and hidden reach remains.

Lu Chi, it's said the world has changed, and that
Is doubtless something which is always said,
Though now to justify, and not in scorn,—
Yet I should think that on our common theme
That sort of change has never mattered much.
In letters as in many other trades

The active man and the contemplative
May both engage, and each in a different way
Succeed. The alphabet, the gift of god
Or of the gods (for, modern as we are,
We have no better theory yet), was not
Devised to one use only, but to all
The work that human wit could find for it,
Is honorably employed in government
And all techniques; without it, nothing. Yet
The active man, because he is active,
Expropriates as if by natural right
The common ground to his singular use,
And spits on everything he cannot use;
Not knowing, or not caring, that to use
Means also to use up. So I have read,
In works by sages of the active side,
And heard them say, that poetry is dead.
This ancient paragon and type of arts,
They claim, was magic when the world began,
And when the old magicians died in scorn
Among the ruins of unsuccessful spells,
Their childish children, living in the dawn
Of intellect and conscience, said those spells
(Which could not move a mountain or a mouse
In a real world) for courage and consolation,
Making those holy places in their hearts
Not masonry nor magic made elsewhere.
But now, in the objective, brazen light
Shed by the sciences, they say, the arts,
And poetry first, considered as their trunk,
The nearest to the root, and bearing branches
Aloft with flower and fruit, and spreading seed
To all societies, must wither away
By supersession in nature and men's hearts.
So in our day wisdom cries out in the streets
And some men regard her.
                              And in your day,
Lu Chi?
          We know these theories, which are not new,

And know the sort of man these theories
Produce, intelligent and serviceable
So long as he can see his language as
Coin of the realm, backed up by church and state,
Each word referring to a thing, each thing
Nicely denominated by a word—
A good mind at its best, a trifle dry . . .
But in bad times, when the word of command
Fails to command, and when the word for bread
Dries and grows mouldy, he is, of all men,
The likeliest to panic as he sits
In his bomb shelter and commissions war songs
From active poets with aggressive views.
Nor on the day when all civilization
Quite visibly and audibly collapses,
When Paris burns as merrily as Sodom,
When London looks like Hell or Hiroshima,
Not even then will this man of his own
Free choice consult those who consult the source—
Who by then, in any case, can do nothing.
Meanwhile, in riches, insolence and honor
Pride is twisting his tongue. What an old joke!
These things, Lu Chi, cannot have changed so much.

What then? Nothing but this, old sir: *continue.*
And to the active man, if he should ask
(If he should bother asking) Why? say nothing.
And to the thinker, if he should ask us once
Instead of telling us, again say nothing,
But look into the clear and mirroring stream
Where images remain although the water
Passes away. Neither action nor thought,
Only the concentration of our speech
In fineness and in strength (your axe again),
Till it can carry, in those other minds,
A nobler action and a purer thought.

So much I gather from your poem: *continue.*
And now the sun shines on the apple trees,
The melting snow glitters with a great wealth,
The waxwings, drunk on last year's rotten apples,
Move through the branches, uttering pretty cries;
While portly grosbeaks, because they do not drink
That applejack, chatter with indignation.
How fine the Chinese day! delicate, jeweled,
Exactly spaced, peaceably tense with life.
I shall pretend to be a poet all
This afternoon, a Chinese poet, and
My marvelous words must bring the springtime in
And the great tree of speech to flower and fruit
Between the two realms of heaven and earth. So now
Goodbye, Lu Chi, and thank you for your poem.

JOHN FREDERICK NIMS:

In Glass: City of God

I

Downstreet, the palmed rose
Of windy matchfire blows.

For hours, overhead pass
Stars like edge of glass;
In vacant lots, by sprawl
Of backfence, garage wall,
Broken bottles gash
Orions in the ash.
Eccentric, brief, rare,
Through exposed air
Where sharp cables blow
Falls one flake of snow
Whose prisms catch
Star, lamp, sulphur-match.

On streets, in the blown arclight
Wider with late night,
Like snow to a vague goal
Floats the unsure soul:
Half in street, half out,
Robbed in saloon bout,
Sailor with cut head
Rocks from beer to bed.

In brick shadows lurk
Rumpled typist, clerk;
Her hips forced to wall,
Face upturned, where small
Sulphur kisses strike.

Mirrors are most like:—

II

Rameau's day, suppose:
A seigneur, his dark-rose
Silk coat shot like sun,
At fierce cards having won
Park and chateau, finds
(When first throwing the blinds)
Its gilt elegance thin—
He fits mirrors in.
The chandelier, glass storm,
Proliferates one form
And, wherever you look,
Explodes on a gold hook.
Flame's treasure, box on box,
Glass in one room locks.

III

In and beneath sky
Nests of reflectors lie:
Moon, prominent, calm,
Round as poolball in palm;
Dew's retina in grass;
Alleys of midnight glass;
Snowflake, whose prisms catch
Red restaurant-sign and match,
In each of whose hundred eyes
The entire streetcar lies,
Clatters and bumps free;

And last, like snowflakes, we
Whose prisms in cold wire
Turn, jibe, flood with fire:
Nursery, big schoolroom pages,
Wars, planets, domains, ages,
Girl's lip in locked park,
Bach's ember, Donne's spark,
Reflections off-hue, odd
From the far light of God.
We in our tears and blood
Make that one candle flood
(Already great) world's-end;
Our pain to prisms bend
And (as flakes from night, seek night,
One moment arclamp-bright)

Between smashed bottles pass
And the sky's edge of glass.

Hey Spinoza!

Bishop, mayor, and quarter-back,
Doctor, lawyer, merchant, quack—
What are your credentials, mac?

"Never mind. The code is sin,
Virtue, love. And now begin."
Wait—whose blueprint am I in?

Eat, think, labor, love, and sleep.
Five little hitlers my soul keep.
In the bonds I cuss and weep.

Honest Abe, who swore to see
Rastus and Jemima free,
Take a thoughtful look at me.

Love is shiny clockwork. Lo!
Gin and starlight make it go.
That's what every young man should know.

Though the heroes die for Spain
(Gesture of the lovely brain)
Human bondage will remain.

Hormones in their witches' cup
Stir a Great Emotion up.
Heroes sniff it like a pup.

Gland and psyche, bright as steel,
Clang and trap us. No appeal:
We in Prison Ego reel.

HOWARD NUTT:

Weary-Water Sue

A blue-blood blonde descends the stair,
Stands liquid-like before a mirror,
Dabbles the whirlpool of her hair,
Flows to a table, somersaults
The little hearts of cork and rubber
Upon her weary-water waltz;
Then pours herself into a chair
And ripples back her wrap, like froth,
And (without splashing on the cloth)
Congeals in exquisite despair.

It's rather hard
To be so bored
And O SO tired
And SO desired.

SYLVIA PLATH:

Tinker Jack and the Tidy Wives

"Come lady, bring that pot
Gone black of polish
And whatever pan this mending master
Should trim back to shape;
I'll correct each mar
On silver dish,
And shine that kettle of copper
At your fireside
Bright as blood.

"Come lady, bring that face
Fallen from luster;
Time's soot in bleared eye
Can be made to glister
For small charge.
No form's gone so awry,
Crook-back or bandy-leg,
But Tinker Jack can forge
Beauty from hag.

"Whatever scath
Fierce fire's wrought
Jack will touch up
And fit for use.
What scar's been knocked
Into cracked heart
Jack shall repair.

"And if there be
Young wives still blithe,
Still fair,
Whose labor's not yet smoked
Their fine skin sere,
From their white heat
Before he part
Let Jack catch fire."

MAGGIE RENNERT:

Loss of the Navigator Near Kansas City

He was reading the stars when the bubble broke.
The end of a factory worker's night on the town?
Or the devil in a rivet?—Anyway, like smoke
he was drafted upward on the sucking air,
stunned, spiralled, then became his weight, and down,

a lifetime downward tumbled in silence where
four engines had fled and left him alone.
If, when the night plucked him, despair
leadened him, or all his sins upon his head
were grave—he fell no faster, that much we've known

since Pisa. A man of faith in Plexiglas is dead
of a moment's constellation. A disciple of limit,
mistaken, he rose from error when the infinite
included him. His death was never unexpected.

ANNE SEXTON:

Torn Down from Glory Daily

All day we watched the gulls
striking the top of the sky
and riding the blown roller coaster.
Up there
godding the whole blue world
and shrieking at a snip of land.

Now, like children,
we climb down humps of rock
with a bag of dinner rolls,
left over,
and spread them gently on a stone,
leaving six crusts for an early king.

A single watcher comes hawking in,
rides the current round its hunger
and hangs
carved in silk
until it throbs up suddenly,
out, and one inch over water;

to come again
smoothing over the slap tide.
To come bringing its flock, like a city
of wings that fall from the air.
They wait, each like a wooden decoy
or soft like a pigeon or

a sweet snug duck:
until one moves, moves that dart-beak
breaking over. It has the bread.
The world is full of them, a world
of beasts thrusting
for one rock, like hideous hens.

Just four, bread scooped out and fierce
go swinging over Glouscester
to the top of the sky.
O see how
they cushion their fishy bellies
with a brother's crumb.

Portrait of an Old Woman on the College Tavern Wall

O down at the tavern
the children are singing
around their round table
and around me still.
Did you hear what it said?
                    I only said
how there is a pewter urn
pinned to the tavern wall,
as old as old is able
to be and be there still.
I said, the poets are there.
I hear them singing and lying
around their round table
and around me still.

Across the room is a wreath
made of a corpse's hair,
framed in glass on the wall,
as old as old is able
to be and be remembered still.
Did you hear what it said?
I only said
how I want to be there and I
would sing my songs with the liars
and my lies wilt all the singers.
And I would, and I would but

it's my hair in the hair wreath,
my cup pinned to the tavern wall,
my dusty face they sing beneath.
Poets are sitting in my kitchen.
Why do these poets lie?
Why do children get children and
Did you hear what it said?
I only said
how I want to be there,
O, down at the tavern
where the prophets are singing
around their round table
until they are still.

RADCLIFFE SQUIRES:

Extinct Lions

Where lions are extinct you will see some afternoon—
Some lion's afternoon, that is—the golden web
Of the lion's face smiling at you from an ordinary lane.
You will watch him stretch the lazy fluting of his ribs
And soar into a wall of leaves. You may not see him again.

Is it true that the lion stood like an ember in your eyes?
Or that years ago the last lion died toothless in his lair
Beyond back valleys where his skeleton still lies
Half clasped in loam, half clasping loam in the bare·
And loveless bones? You ask this, yet would you tease

The savage body forth unless with a severed will
You were thinking of the time you will break through the wall
Of leaves and into forests where extinct lions prowl,
Even as you mark time with the somnolent guile
Of passenger pigeons, cooing of the sangreal?

WALLACE STEVENS:

Conversation with Three Women
of New England

The mode of the person becomes the mode of the world,
For that person, and, sometimes, for the world itself.
The contents of the mind become solid show
Or almost solid seem show — the way a fly bird
Fixes itself in its inevitable bush . . .
It follows that to change modes is to change the world.

Now, you, for instance, are of this mode: You say
That in that ever-dark central, wherever it is,
In the central of earth or sky or thought,
There is a drop that is life's element,
Sole, single source and minimum patriarch,
The one thing common to all life, the human
And inhuman same, the likeness of things unlike.

And you, you say that the capital things of the mind
Should be as natural as natural objects,
So that a carved king found in a jungle, huge
And weathered, should be part of a human landscape,
That a figure reclining among columns toppled down,
Stiff in eternal lethargy, should be,
Not the beginning but the end of artifice,
A nature of marble in a marble world.

And then, finally, it is you that say
That only in man's definitions of himself,
Only encompassed in humanity, is he
Himself. The author of man's canons is man,
Not some outer patron and imaginer.

In which one of these three worlds are the four of us
The most at home? Or is it enough to have seen
And felt and known the difference we have seen
And felt and known in the colors in which we live,
In the excellences of the air we breathe,
The bouquet of being — enough to realize
That the sense of being changes as we talk,
That talk shifts the cycle of the scenes of kings?

The Sick Man

Bands of black men seem to be drifting in the air,
In the South, bands of thousands of black men,
Playing mouth-organs in the night or, now, guitars.

Here in the North, late, late, there are voices of men,
Voices in chorus, singing without words, remote and deep,
Drifting choirs, long movements and turnings of sounds.

And in a bed in one room, alone, a listener
Waits for the unison of the music of the drifting bands
And the dissolving chorals, waits for it and imagines

The words of winter in which these two will come together,
In the ceiling of the distant room, in which he lies,
The listener, listening to the shadows, seeing them,

Choosing out of himself, out of everything within him,
Speech for the quiet, good hail of himself, good hail, good hail,
The peaceful, blissful words, well-tuned, well-sung, well-spoken.

Less and Less Human, O Savage Spirit

If there must be a god in the house, must be,
Saying things in the rooms and on the stair,

Let him move as the sunlight moves on the floor,
Or moonlight, silently, as Plato's ghost

Or Aristotle's skeleton. Let him hang out
His stars on the wall. He must dwell quietly.

He must be incapable of speaking, closed,
As those are: as light, for all its motion, is;

As color, even the closest to us, is;
As shapes, though they portend us, are.

It is the human that is the alien,
The human that has no cousin in the moon.

It is the human that demands his speech
From beasts or from the incommunicable mass.

If there must be a god in the house, let him be one
That will not hear us when we speak: a coolness,

A vermilioned nothingness, any stick of the mass
Of which we are too distantly a part.

316

RUTH STONE:

The Season

I know what calls the Devil from the pits;
With a thief's fingers, there he slouches and sits.
I've seen him passing on a frenzied mare,
Bitter-eyed on her haunches, out to stare;
He rides her cruel and he rides her easy.
Come along spring, come along sun, come along field daisy.

Smell the foxy babies, smell the hunting dog;
The shes have whelped, the cocks and hens have lost their wits;
And cry, "Why," cry the spring peepers, "Why," each little frog.
He rides her cruel and he rides her easy.
Come along spring, come along sun, come along field daisy.

The Splinter

I had a little silver mannikin
Who walked and talked and petted me.
I pampered him, he pampered me, we
Were convivial. On the gray streets
Of many a gray city he wept with me.
Oh then how miniature was sin,
How clear its purpose like a looking glass
To show me my young girl's skin.

But I looked and looked again
And saw a blue cadaverous vein.
I will grow old, I cried,
You are a silver groom,
I will be a brown leather bride.
You are imperishable, still by my side
You will shine in the wine
That puckers my hide.

And in these sad reflections
I took a silver hammer made of words,
And hit him and he shattered like bright birds
Flying in all directions.
All night and all eternity I cried,
And in the morning by the gray light
I found his splinter in my side,
And when I drew it out, I saw it was glass —
The finest concave mirror, silver white
And backed with brightest silver. Oh alas,
He was a mannikin of glass with all his light turned in,
And mirrored in the dark, the mannikin.

An Old Song

When I was young I knew that I would die,
The fear of an old death went out with me.
The rank green wasted; fiddle, so did I,
But I was long-lived as the hemlock tree.

Yes, I was strong as juniper. The pitch,
The amber resin, all of those strong tars,
The pungent aromatics of the bitch,
I kept in fascinating rows of jars.

All those other odors. Love's a smell.
I'll dance the diddy on a wrinkled knee;
The empty udders dangle on the shell.
Now the fat's gone, some gnaw the bone with me.

I tell you death's hard fought for, hard to kill.
On powdered mirrors these death's eyes outstare
The old bold adversary of the will.
I am the death, and who comes for his share?

NANCY SULLIVAN:

Celebration and Requiem

i—at the station

As I await the train beside this ghost-green station
Under these vacant trees that line the arbitrary spaces
With unknown sidewalks as in read-about places,
Harsh flutterings suddenly shuttle in and out my heart
In hushes, with purple, terrible, painted-on faces:
Hawks askew, perched on a dream's resurrection.

Memory, at this cormorant vigil, is all at once in action,
And awaiting new agains with the old friends soon
To usher through that knell of hellos at noon,
I recall the horizontal poles of a cagey life,
My own; and wing back, fledgling at this rune,
To chant again in a plain song of celebration

Of creed, digit, and letter in this initialed primer:
Annotations of strum and dirge from the wayward Mays
Of me, lyric in navy jumper on those Mary-blue days
At school, or on contralto scaling in Central Park
Exploring rooty pluckings of magic, crannied ways
For use here: Rhyme'ster, rime' ster (rim'ster), n. Rhymer.

ii—a matinal

Balloons, balloons are everywhere.
The spectacle of the morning rises
On the faint string of day. Everywhere
Shouts and hurrahs of what will be.
I lean on the sill of this morning window
Alive through the concessions of the night
To a vision of the paradox of death
Guileless now on sleep's hazardous pillow.

On the street, my morning milk stands sentry at the door;
A paperboy flings newsprint at my stoop.

Look! Abstractions march resplendent in the morning light!
The past convenes on the steps today
As though for a parade.
What is there, after all, but what was?
And it does march,
And it does fade.
Sounds
        Accordion
                Through the memory.
The click-clack of names, like agate marbles,
Across the hard conversations in my family:
Cracker Burns and Butts Murphy,
Timmy the Woodhooker, and the Gentle Sheean—
Muted now in the metallic music of the past.
Many are dead; the rest, repaired and raging, twitch
                      in this morning sunlight.
Sights
        Of brave flags
                And sailor suits
Stifle the memory with the sandy debris of summers
Through which, my brother, you scuffed your way
Toward bald and mealy manhood.
I kiss that daring child in you and clasp your hand.

Wait! Listen to my riddle. It is about you and all of us:
What has so much heart it cannot love,
So much sight it cannot see,
So much soul it cannot sanctify itself?
Give up. I never found the answer.
Now memory, giddy with power, walks across my mind.
And
        Down
                Down the stairs
                        To the door
(Death's hinged door.)

I go to fetch this day's nourishment, this day's news,
And to watch from there, the second it's ajar,
The past convene on the steps
As though for a parade.
For what is there, after all, but what was.
And it does march.
And it does fade.

iii—nones: ". . . and above all, Truth."

Our Lady of Succour, pray for us . . .
Amid the veils and vines in that graded garden
Of grammar school. And find, too, some pardon
For changing griefs as the years harden
And the schools after toss loss upon loss.

All my history, redundant and loosely bound,
Bracketed by this lawless alpha-and-omega myth
Of curious symbols: A.B. and M.A.; i.e., *Truth*
Worries itself into a lopsided bauble of crystal, Sooth-
Sayer, lady, to break or to blossom on the fair ground.

iv—matinee: ". . . for the tenth part of a dollar."

"Step up, step up, right up. Give ear and eye
To the whirlpools of light which speak
In multi-colored glances and round-and-round whispers
Of sawdust stars and ambrosial puffs of pink
Fragility balanced as a windowed bubble on the seal's nose.
Everything, heart's own engine, breaks eventually.
Look, ladies and gents, here at Captain Bob Tate,
Petrified Man. Does he live or die?
Does he sing in the confines of that pearly coffin?
And can he marry? Flap, flap flaps the petal
Of his tent's opening: To this Saul no David plucks
A tinny melody. Asquat nearby, his dusty nurse laps
With a lick a moat round her frozen custard's turreted castle.
The wheel spins round a-round a-round a-round . . .
You'll ring a dream with these concentric circles . . .
Step inside, sonny: it's the eighth wonder of the world."

I was there as you were with those
Fountains, fountains everywhere
Feeding on limited water,
From whose down-deep, grim machinery
Abundance spurted, showered, flirted
With those who through a turnstile
Turned the bitter outside inside out
To walk rowdy and gaudy all
Of a topaz daytime, wondering
Much later only if
Dreams too feasted on themselves.

v—a vesper song

The people assemble in their assigned places
                                  with bakery boxes,
Night's promises thick on their hearts and faces
As the evening swoops down in navy-blue birds
To curve an iridescent rainbow over them
In feathers of virtuous color.
How like a warm place come into
Is love. I entered into
Its soft, geometric mystery
Of questions and promise one evening
To find that love too points its purple and terrible moral
As parenthesis to the dream: (Nothing, nothing satisfies.)

No one in legend or in a play
Told of what it was
That urged a virgin yield her womb to God
Or made of Abelard a poet.
I find this guarded page blank as shade.
Know it: nothing, nothing satisfies.
Love's definition is by omission.

Rome and Athens shadow in the broken sun of history,
And war upon war devalues the heart to a souvenir.
The rich crumble, and everything modifies
Into statement here where the poem should shout in the throat

Of the shuddering magnificence of love
Of a thunderous evening. Nothing, nothing satisfies.
    Like a warm place come into
    Is love in the emerald evening.

vi—envoi

All at once I hear the far down, faint inflection
Of the train bearing the bodies of my friends
Somewhere on its catafalque. Am I to comprehend
Travel, like love and death, making lean baggage of identity?
But the sudden lanterns beacon their arrival and send
Me heart-high down the gravel chasing hawks in grins
                of celebration.

DYLAN THOMAS:

Ceremony After a Fire Raid

i

Myselves
The grievers
Grieve
Among the street burned to tireless death
A child of a few hours
With its kneading mouth
Charred on the black breast of the grave
The mother dug, and its arms full of fires.

Begin
With singing
Sing
Darkness kindled back into beginning
When the caught tongue nodded blind,
A star was broken
Into the centuries of the child
Myselves grieve new, and miracles cannot atone.

Forgive
Us forgive
Us your death that myselves the believers
May hold it in a great flood
Till the blood shall spurt,
And the dust shall sing like a bird
As the grains blow, as your death grows, through our heart.

Crying
Your dying
Cry,
Child beyond cockcrow, by the fire-dwarfed
Street we chant the flying sea
In the body bereft.
Love is the last light spoken. Oh
Seed of sons in the loin of the black husk left.

ii

I know not whether
Adam or Eve, the adorned holy bullock
Or the white ewe lamb
Or the chosen virgin
Laid in her snow
On the altar of London,
Was the first to die
In the cinder of the little skull,
O bride and bridegroom
O Adam and Eve together
Lying in the lull
Under the sad breast of the headstone
White as the skeleton
Of the garden of Eden.

I know the legend
Of Adam and Eve is never for a second
Silent in my service
Over the dead infants
Over the one
Child who was priest and servants,
Word, singers, and tongue
In the cinder of the little skull,
Who was the serpent's
Nightfall and the fruit like a sun,
Man and woman undone,
Beginning crumbled back to darkness
Bare as the nurseries
Of the garden of wilderness.

iii

Into the organpipes and steeples
Of the luminous cathedrals,
Into the weathercocks' molten mouths
Rippling in twelve-winded circles,
Into the dead clock burning the hour
Over the urn of sabbaths
Over the whirling ditch of daybreak
Over the sun's hovel and the slum of fire
And the golden pavements laid in requiems,
Into the bread in a wheatfield of flames,
Into the wine burning like brandy,
The masses of the sea
The masses of the sea under
The masses of the infant-bearing sea
Erupt, fountain, and enter to utter for ever
Glory glory glory
The sundering ultimate kingdom of genesis' thunder.

W. Y. TINDALL:

Felix Culpa

Banking the air into the bushy sun
Two loves in one another's plane remarked
The crocodile descending from his palm.
That was no forest for a simple man.

Hand in hand prospected underwoods
While their creature muscled on his path
Springing leaves around those innocents
Covering panther serpent and giraffe.

The serpent put his lips to hand in hand
Printing with his lips a smiling wound
And wound his length along the winding path.
Father (with retractors) said "It's sound"

And pointed to the cutting on the hill
Where flatcars carried barns along the rails
And from the roundhouse infants carried trains.
He could not tell their purpose or the scale

Or ask the two librarians if his key
Was suitable for Sunday and their door.
He pushed between them; but the lock was stiff
As twelve labors and another more.

The Section

Pigs travel in the street
Humping the concrete
Liquefying it. Their boar
Leaping through the carriage door
Seizes a finger and the underhand.
Forgiving him (O spear the horses) fretting
Roll on (with difficulties) to the cutting.

At our usual table now
High in that sterile bowl
(Our heads of hairs touching the sterile ceiling)
We order sections of sweet fowl
And all the waiters with their knives
Whisper around the central cow
Preparing her for the cutting.

See how the white meat lies
Part on breast and part on thighs
And how her rolling eyes
Follow the sections and knives.

With her knife the victim now (and then)
Removes a section from her thigh
And vertically bisects her jaw
From nostril to rolling eye. She hands
White meat to one who seems and understands.

Forgiving her (O spear the horses) fretting
Roll on (with difficulties) from the cutting.

BYRON VAZAKAS:

For Those Who Died Like Anarchists

Between the prison gate and the thoroughfare, the past
assumed its present. Sunlight waited at the curb
marking a casual cigaret, and the homely gutter
drained blue wash-water.

When they approached, time resembled death. Strangely,
the blood upon their hands was their own. Such guilt
was obsessed by no flag. Children watched them deprive
their future of its finality.

The clouds grew tall in the sun that day, and when
    they raised their eyes to them, acquired the virtue of
    the rose. Seldom happy, marking time, but like
    children who wait for summer

This was their imago, their idol laid down without
    comment or inscription: *What hurts is wrong.*
    All knew it, but somewhere, in a century,
    anaesthesia became an opiate.

The few steps forward to death or backward to recant,
    what did it matter? Bludgeoned in a car was not
    an oriental choice where law enacts the imposition
    of the many on the few.

When Rosa entered the car, the sun fell away
    from her face, and her sight diminished to an X
    on the pavement, chalked by a child
    for a memory after trouble.

After the departure, the children returned to play,
    and were tired at evening, or until their parents
    called. The corner grocery was locked, the awnings
    drawn up; a policeman

Sauntering through the twilight, and swinging his club,
    sniffed the suspicious silence and the dust,
    and rattled at the door of a vacant house.
    Empty. Empty. Empty.

NEIL WEISS:

The Knee

I believe in fright, the warehouse
where I played, ice
for nosebleed, a red carbarn,
and my mother's candy apron
where I say, good night.

The smell of the candy store
reflecting in the guilty clamber
over a roof and then jump
so that my knee struck in my mouth.

I remember, I remember
the light struck in my mind
with that blow in the face.

I carefully shielded it,
cupping my hands around
the flaring match. But I

grew up in an enlightened time
and the light went out.
I carefully nurse my face.

Until a first spat with a wife.
And how I raged and smashed
that knee, rocking back and forth
in an ecstasy, remembering

violence in the settled crouch,
the placement of the knee
against my mouth, teeth in a cloud
of sulphur — and then my laughter.
The amazing gift of laughter!

T. WEISS:

A Local Matter

I

But who does us?
Who flexes like fingers, strains
in our sinews that they sing,
one felicitous agony?
These thoughts, these thoughts
thieving through night that things —
even hope and lust everlastingly
raucous — heckling locals
trying to distract us,
fall dumb.

II

The cat all evening
lulled the mouse, licked it
and pricked it and loved it that
never a moment did it move
out of sight. O the success,
the bliss, the fittingness
of nature there; mouse
recognized its consummation, its all-
devoted, all-devouring heir,
where the future was
suddenly breathless.
Grin, claws.

III

But we, whom do we
play for and what these aches
that carried the night past itself?
The hum of mouths within me:

waters at their loom spinning out
the wild and perplexed
sea, as lilies,
in their velvet toils, break
stones, break stems to a somewhere-
rooted, roar-cored wind.

IV

But you, but you,
enchanting the maddest
din as winter pears can pipe
the speckled curves in scented air
of summer round them —
do you not, like the lady
of the wild things, discover
in your bright bending
wells, by your hand's stir
swell their waters? —
are played by what masterly hand?
Always I hear, in your least
movement, the labials
of light.

V

Always and all ways
the lights grow too strong.
Reach out: the light sweeps us
out into its shuddering darkness.
This by the crackle of leaf
we know mouse; this, cat.
But the clatter there,
the purr? Rapt upon earth
as those transparent monsters,
the winds. Let the ribs
be beaten, let them shriek
like so many women
never escaped.

VI

These the lines
I do not somehow have
to learn; they find.their parts
at the moment of burning:
the appropriate pain, the fitting
grief. Meantime I cling
to things that belong:
shag-root of a dog
not the whole world can impress,
the sparrow tucked in the sky
ticking out fall.

VII

And yet the subtle
strings twang into us all;
I think of turtles in a bowl,
their shells like painted shields,
churning upon one another,
each overwrought by private music,
rushing together to one
gleaming doom.

VIII

Now in the lute-time,
soon brute, of the year I
slouch down, the silky lounge
of one in perfect health
(hear the chestnut
gayly crying in its country fire).
I lounge as I wait the advent
of one all sinew and strain,
the lunge. Like a string tautening
to the discords of precisianist
pain, I fit: come, windy
dark, like all the kingdoms
of the North and within the gates
of my Jerusalem set your sundry
singing thrones!

IX

In the state of weeds,
high-spirited undergrowth,
there are many kinds of nests.
Themselves flashing armor and plume
before the shadow coming on
of the long summer light, locusts
clash their cymbals.
Again and again, mighty in leaves
as Nimrod, the mouse enters
that the seasons be maintained
as locally as a broken fence
beside a yawning dog,

X

till I, skinned
and glistening, one of many
hides racked in a row, as a lesser
tale in a greater, from the lean-
to of noon, sink to mouse, catgut,
fiddlings of some nameless bog.
At work religiously, maggots welcome
me passing through, good will
from one end of death to the other,
into and through that the minerals
know me, the odors use me;
how the hum becomes me,
ever and after the household
word of the air.

WILLIAM CARLOS WILLIAMS:

The Motor-Barge

The motor barge is
at the bridge the
air lead
the broken ice

unmoving. A gull,
the eternal
gull, flies as
always, eyes alert

beak pointing
to the life-giving
water. Time
falters but for

the broad river-
craft which
low in the water
moves grad-

ually, edging
between the smeared
bulkheads,
churning a mild

wake, laboring
to push past
the constriction
with its heavy load

The Resemblance

The Jewess was happy
she had no car
— though it was raining

but she had her
baby, all wrapped
up in her arms — as

she too was all
wrapped up, short as
she was, and on

her head stood a green
clown's cap that
made her look

for all the world
like a painting
by Rouault.

LEONARD WOLF:

Monsieur Chauvannes

Monsieur Chauvannes maintains a dark *ménage*
à trois, but in Des Moines; the persiflage
That from his chamber issues spoils the rest
Of safe, firm deacons in the middle west
Where two is company and three a crowd
Perhaps more glorious, but not allowed.

Back from Dubuque and to his ladies, home
The Frenchman hurries and his neighbors come
To watch his hallway and each other's eyes
For thin betrayals of the same surmise
That keeps them yearning until overhead
Sounds the weird skip-skipping of his double bed.

Those who grow corn and those who sorghum press
Are sometimes troubled by his sweet distress
Wherefore they writhe in bed or pace the floor
Who suffer with one wife and need one more;
They hear Chauvannes and his spry ladies tumbling,
The sound of peril and of deacons stumbling.

MARGUERITE YOUNG:

The White Rat

How now could body-soul's symbol be this
By love, or calculation, this white rat enraged
Caged in a theatre of emptiness,
His, a snowfall of footsteps and glittering eyes?

Nor moon, a compound of the unseen events,
Nor earth, as principle of tear or dew on flowers
Rounding, he considers now. By him are we clarified.

Who could have nurtured his body on penurious dew
Is caged, is caught like a tyrannical dragonfly
And made to actualize, O, mute actuality

In void denuded now of all but blank him
And cleaned of all but the white rat's space
And eyes like diamonds in his empty head.

Who could have walked transparent fretted on wind and waves,
Now he runs upon a branched track abstract
And is mechanical in every wintry act

And is body-soul, is the most distant hope!
Here, in this cage, Platonic double moons,
Here, in this cage, St. Augustine
Crying, O, my God, art Thou without or within?

For this rat's sensorium is his true knowledge
Nor star will shine beyond his death for him,
Nor wild rock goose be shy and wild in the dusk of foliage,
Afraid of foxes in the light of day,
Nor hoary owls like flowers skim lost in leaves.

Does God with diamond eyes look down on these
For the purposes of what intrinsic studies?

III. CRITICAL PROSE

ROBERT MARTIN ADAMS:

Now That My Ladder's Gone —
Yeats Without Myth

The need of modern poets for a myth or tradition which shall unify and order the modern experience is a commonplace of contemporary criticism. Not only modern poets, and not only poets, are said to require myth as a sort of scaffolding for their work; one is given to understand that literary artists in every genre and of every age have experienced the need. Dante is generally accepted as the happy example of a poet who possessed in Christian tradition, and specifically in the work of Thomas Aquinas, a readymade myth, tradition, or intellectual scaffold, with which his poetry could form an organic and integral connection. Modern poets, on the other hand, are said to be faced with the unhappy alternatives of reporting the infinitely varied, perpetually identical fact of chaos; or of inventing and expounding as they go along the myths by which they choose to work. In electing the latter alternative, they assume a double function, of poet and philosopher, of creator and explorer, which constitutes either a major peril or a major incitement (as one chooses) to literary achievement. Of those that have elected this double role, William Butler Yeats is given special rank as the most radical and successful innovator in the business of constructing a private mythology.*

Yeats himself, in a letter to his father dated 1917, described his religious system as a means of providing for his poetry a new framework and new patterns; and Leo Africanus, a spirit-creature who dictated a good deal of *A Vision* to Mrs. Yeats, was no less explicit. "We have come to give you metaphors for your poetry," he said. These alone are formidable authorities; and, as noted above, they have been widely echoed. But some misgivings have lately arisen. Miss Vivienne Koch, whose volume is the most recent afield, denies very largely the relevance of the system outlined in *A Vision,* as far as the

---

* The views outlined in my first paragraph have been so often expressed as to render a strict accounting of them nothing less than a bibliography of modern criticism. The basic approach to Yeats may be traced in the Hall and Steinmann anthology, *The Permanence of Yeats,* as well as in books by MacNeice, Jeffares, Ure, Ellman, Stauffer, and Koch. A full-scale discussion of myth is that of Richard Chase (*Quest for Myth,* 1949).

later poems are concerned, and seems to have proved a good many of
her points. The philosophy is not needed to read poems like "The
Wild Old Wicked Man" or "The Three Bushes." It was not particularly in Yeats' mind when he wrote these poems; and he does not use
the typical symbols, or "metaphors," which are the hallmarks of the
system — gyres, masks, anti-masks, wheels, cycles, and phases. When
he does use them in the later poetry, as for instance in "The Gyres,"
critical opinion seems to be a good deal puzzled by them. Mr.
Stauffer says, for example, that the gyres symbolize "intellect, art, and
age." Miss Koch associates them with "process"; Ellmann, following
Yeats himself, suggests so many connections with objectivity and
subjectivity, beauty and truth, fact and value, particular and universal,
quality and quantity, man and *Daimon,* the living and the dead,
sexual symbolism, Kabbalistic lore, and Solomon's Seal, as to rob the
gyres of any particular significance in any particular context. The
problem isn't lack of content; the symbol "gyre" has too many possible
contents to be anything but a lumber-room of undirected association.
Its failure to communicate is the more striking because the basic
human meaning of the particular poem is perfectly clear. If there are
any critical confusions regarding "The Gyres" (for example, as to
the identity of Old Rocky Face, whom Mr. Jeffares is seduced into
supposing the Jew from Shelley's *Hellas*), they come from the attempt
to intellectualize what is basically very simple. And in a poem like
"The Circus Animals' Desertion," of which Miss Koch makes (curiously) no use at all, Yeats specifically repudiates not only the various
mythical systems of his career, but the personages and masks which
he has had occasion to assume in fulfillment of the system.

> These masterful images because complete
> Grew in pure mind, but out of what began ?
> A mound of refuse or the sweepings of a street,
> Old kettles, old bottles, and a broken can,
> Old iron, old bones, old rags, that raving slut
> Who keeps the till. Now that my ladder's gone
> I must lie down where all the ladders start
> In the foul rag-and-bone shop of the heart.

An independent knowledge of Yeats' philosophy is not, in fact,
necessary for the appreciation of very many of Yeats' poems; of those
generally accounted great, only a handful really demand that we look
into *A Vision,* and defy our comprehension of their form till we have
done so. A poem like "Sailing to Byzantium" may surprise us with

an occasional phrase in the jargon — "perne in a gyre," for instance, shocks us with its cracked, mechanical note. But Yeats was generally craftsman enough to conceal the prosthetic devices on which his poetry supported itself, at least to the point where they did not cry their nature aloud.

But if the poems are not, in general, abjectly helpless without the philosophy, how much does the philosophy contribute to them? Additional connotations, no doubt, under all circumstances; for one who has read Yeats, a gyre is never again a simple gyre, and the phases of the moon have a permanent queerness about them. But is there anything more to the philosophy's contribution than queerness? Certainly the sort of translation which consists merely of transposing poetry into jargon, or of reading the poetry while remaining simultaneously aware of the "additional connotations" of the jargon, does not represent much more than a feat of virtuosity. Undoubtedly, one is more impressed by images, like those of tower and cavern, Byzantium, and golden birds, when he is aware of the many meanings that Yeats crowded into them. But whether this "packed" effect is significant in any way, whether the additional levels of meaning reinforce or distract the reader's attention, is a major question. One may also ask, secondarily, whether the packed effect is legitimately achieved by publication of a philosophy which aims chiefly at packing images. The poet might quite as sensibly, and rather more economically, append to each symbol a footnote, listing the connotations he wishes us to festoon about it. And if there is something to be gained by this procedure, in richness, there is also a good deal to be lost, in cumbersomeness — not to speak of the latent irritation which rises from a pronounced disparity between what a poet says he intends and the vehicle through which he offers to accomplish it.

The philosophy is, in short, a treacherous intermediary between poem and reader; it is just hazy enough to tangle the busy, hazy mind in its intricacies, but not solid enough in its referents to provide any secure resting place. Whatever reality they had for Yeats himself, the spiritual machineries of *A Vision* are intolerable as taught machines; and Yeats himself, aware of the difficulties, concluded his philosophical statement with the advice, "all these symbols can be thought of as the symbols of the relations of men and women and the birth of children . . . all the symbolism of this book applies to begetting and birth, for all things are a single form which has divided and multiplied in time and place." In other words, behind the cycles of the moon, the Platonic year, the events of history, and the twenty-six-fold personality, is a simple human pattern.

Looking at the matter with reader's eyes, I think we will feel that one not only may but must take this view of the system. If Yeats' philosophy is mere empty nonsense (something I don't for a moment believe), the poems which adumbrate it are nonsense too, though perhaps beautiful nonsense. To hail Yeats for having made explicit the modern protest against mythlessness, while reserving one's opinion of the substitute myth he created as total nonsense, is a left-handed piece of graciousness; and it doesn't lead us very far toward the poetry, which never deals directly with mythlessness as an experience. As protest, any form of behavior is justified; ancestor-worship, bombs in public squares, and nervous tics may all be protests, and as protests would all be equally valid. But unless we can believe in a poet's philosophy, if not as an actual, at least as a potential arrangement of experience, it is not much more than a hindrance to us. Yeats' philosophy may be taken as a harmless eccentricity, and it may also be made to stand like a veil between the poetry and its experience. But it may serve equally well to relate the poetry to a human experience, a human potential. To do so, it must be translated into significant, if not necessarily important human statements. One's aim in undertaking such a translation would be to salvage the poetry from the jargon, in order to relate it to something more significant. Even if the only alternative to nonsense is commonplace, commonplace at least offers a basis for dramatic contrast and construction. So that the searching out of commonplace may seem worthwhile if one bears in mind a condition and an alternative. The condition is that one isn't trying to find an equivalent for the poem, but a referent-structure to correspond with its structure as an artifact. The alternative is to accept the poem as a nonsense-jingle without referents — as a set of symbols which either symbolize nothing, or refer only to a second set of symbols which refer to nothing. Yeats, who prided himself on his "public speech," would scarcely be flattered at being taken at this level, and criticism owes him an effort at postponing the indignity.

II

Of the better-known poems, "Byzantium" certainly presents the sharpest challenge to the act of humanistic interpretation, partly because it is so largely written in the symbols of the system, partly because the system itself doesn't seem to use some of these symbols to relate to anything very clear outside of itself or the poetry, partly because the central message of the poem has generally seemed a direct repudiation of human experience. Perhaps, by looking at the things this poem says and some of the ways in which it seems to say them, we can manage to see through and around the system, with a frank eye to rendering it dispensable by making the poem's direct human meaning stronger. Though we cannot pretend that the philosophy doesn't exist, we may be able to minimize it, to explore the poetry's ability to get around or away from it. To save quotation, this tour of inspection will presume that the text of the poem is handy for comparison.

"Byzantium" opens with a strict, abrupt grammar, a violent image followed by a relatively concrete factual statement; both, however, are short phrases in which verb is tightly linked to subject, and two blunt, complete statements of recession and departure are made. A sort of relation between the "unpurged images of day" and the "Emperor's drunken soldiery" is implied by the common quality of grossness; but what exactly "images" are the poet leaves imprecise. A third short phrase ("night resonance recedes") repeats the first verb, a second subject is attached to it ("night walker's song"), and then, with deliberate casualness, an adverb phrase ("after great cathedral gong") which could refer to any or all of the preceding verbs, probably all. For the great cathedral gong, as we look backward in the poem at its receding resonance, leads thought back to the first receding of the poem. Our minds are asked to recede from day, also from night; but day and night may be taken here not as opposites but as complements. For the receding is away from earth, with its alternate day and night; from above, in the starlit or moonlit dome (again the alternative acts as a form of aggregation, as well as implying the permanent darkness of the upper atmosphere) — from the heaven's vault, we can see in perspective what is merely human. "All mere complexities" carries an implication that there is in some condition a resolution of complexities without which one's destiny is only partially fulfilled. The poem promises in this first stanza to arrogate to itself a wider vision than that of humanity, a vision which could include the perspective of either art or death or both, but which is in any case the product of astronomical distance. "Disdains" must therefore carry the force, secondarily of contempt or scorn, perhaps projected, but primarily of looking down from a height at something immeasurably below one, as the first "That" of "Sailing to Byzantium" sets everyday life at an immense distance.

Stanza 2 presents the poet's vision within the new sphere. What he sees has the form of a man; but this is the least of it, it is more like a ghost than a man and more like an image than either. The logic of the triple presentation is the logic of approach; from one error the mind leaps to a contrary error, concluding in the just middle with the word "image," which, taken in conjunction with the first line, now begins to take on meaning for us. An image is of course a figment of the imagination; but it is also a picture or figure with substance, and in fact the sort of symbol in which "Byzantium" itself is written — neither pure abstraction nor simply material. The explanation which "For" (line 3) implies is that in Hades (which is neither Hell nor Heaven but afterlife or otherlife) the experiences of physical life ("the winding path") may be unwound from man's soul as from a bobbin; and when thus unwound by death or ecstasy, man will lose the complex motion of the spindle and achieve the simplicity of rotating in a single direction on a single axis. Moreover, a purged image of this sort, half material and half spiritual, half alive and half dead, may summon other images — beget them. Whether it is art or afterlife to which the poet is making reference here doesn't really matter as yet; it is another mode of existence than the physical, within which another mode of creation or re-creation prevails; and the poet, as he pauses a moment to survey and define its character, resolves the contradiction with the words, "I call it death-in-life and life-in-death." "I call it" marks this terminology as hyperbolical, an attribution of the poet's; and that he is really thinking of the esthetic sphere as contrasted with the everyday is made clear by the next stanza.

For the breathless mouths which the image of man summons, forges, or begets in the esthetic sphere are at once described in Stanza 3 as "miracle, bird, or golden handiwork," a triple alternative which parallels in reverse order that of Stanza 2. These are the golden singing birds of the Byzantine emperors, a context which returns us to the Emperor mentioned in Stanza 1, line 2; their social character prepares us for the discovery, already suggested at the end of Stanza 2, that the withdrawal of Stanza 1 was purely a mental recession, that in fact we are still on the floor of the Emperor's palace, though in a new sphere of mental activity. The golden birds offer now an unnatural combination of sensual and spiritual appeal — hence are more a miracle than a mere mechanical or physical bird. Such birds of art have two aspects; either they summon the mind to a partaking, or they disdain and scorn it. Their summoning would be like the crowing of Hades' cocks, an act associated with the golden bough which is the passport to the underworld, and with the crowing of earthly cocks which signalize (as in *Hamlet*) the return of ghosts to their proper sphere. The summoning of the birds associates also to the dark of the moon, when even the reflected light of the sun disappears, and the way of the spirit is lit only by cold astral lights. But the presence of the moon embitters the birds; perhaps because sunlight, even reflected, provides too warm and near a perspective for works of art. But this is a hazard; and the phrase "by the moon embittered" remains a crux on any but the esoteric level. In any event, the "disdains" of Stanza 1 is here reinforced by the golden birds which openly "scorn" common birds and all human or earth-bound complexities. The last line of Stanza 3 echoes the last two of Stanza 1, in token of a general return of the poem, in its latter parts, to themes and images of the first part; as Stanza 4 will open "on the Emperor's pavement," and not within any starlit or moonlit dome — the circle of receding and returning being now complete.

The flames which flit on the Emperor's pavement are, then, at two removes from physical reality; they are the flames begotten of flames, the breathless mouths summoned by a mouth that has no moisture and no breath, the fresh images begotten by images; they are ghostly flames, yielding no heat and obedient to no physical laws. But they can also summon blood-begotten spirits (and the nature of these blood-begotten spirits is sharply contrasted with the flames begotten of flame), so that the movement of Stanza 1 is reversed in Stanza 4; after leaving mere complexities behind in the physical world (Stanza 1), man reappears in Stanza 4, summoned by images begotten of images, and bringing his complexities now to the Emperor's floor. A cycle is achieved, the mind moving from mire, blood, and complexity to image to bird or flame and back again to blood and complexity. "Dying" (line 6), though it has the additional connotation of physical death or entrancement, is merely a settling into the form of the dance; and agony, though it implies anguish, has also the overtones of struggle and conflict *(agon)*. Thus the experience of art is fitted into a recurrent cycle in the endless alternate movement of the mind from will to idea and back to will.

The last stanza opens with an image of dolphins, one new image in that series of images begotten by other images with which the stanzas of the poem begin, and which lead us forward from images to golden birds to flames to dolphins. But like the grammar of the stanza, the logic of the image itself is unstrung and loosened; the dolphin's element is mire and blood and this element the blood-begot-ten spirits are said to be astraddle. They straddle, that is, not only the dolphin but the two alternating spheres, air and sea, through which the dolphin leaps. The circle-cycle of earth-image-firebird-earth begets the dolphin-cycle of successive arcs in sea and air which com-plicates the entire cycle-concept into that of a dance. "Spirit after spirit" sets the dance in time, as "the smithies break the flood" sets the norm or surface of the artistic experience in the fury and the mire of human blood *(Nacheinander* and *Nebeneinander).* It is from this element that the dolphins leap and to it that they return. But in the dance the structure of discourse, which has been at war all along with the begetting of images, finally succumbs, and the poem dissolves into a dance or trance which is, in either aspect, an act of pure contempla-tion, a stasis. The dolphins as they leap from the mire and blood become smithies for the creation of golden birds, and the hard, smooth anvils of the smithies, where feeling is given shape, are equated to marbles of the dancing floor. The pattern "breaks" bitter furies of complexity; and the word "break," which seems to mean merely "interrupt" in line 2, adds in line 5 the connotations of "resolve" or "purify." The grammar of these statements is much relaxed; the marbles of the dancing floor may be supposed to break ("purify") not only "bitter furies of complexity" in line 5 but also "that dolphin-torn, that gong-tormented sea" in line 8; and on these terms, lines 6 and 7 are an interjection. But the "images" of line 6 may also be in apposi-tion with either "the marbles of the dancing floor" or "the bitter furies of complexity" as the object of "break." The former is the more likely on logical grounds; either reading, however, leaves the last line without grammatical connection. Lack of this connection isn't by any means fatal; return to the dolphin and the gong, with the implied equating of the two as forces which torment while purifying our complexities, fulfills the poem adequately. In any case, whether one leaves the "images" of line 6 or the "sea" of line 8 without grammatical support, there clearly isn't enough to go around; and thus the inter-jection (if such it is) of lines 6 and 7 may be justified, for the process of begetting which it describes results in the fracture of grammar and logic which it exemplifies.

The progress of the poem is from a sort of "receding" which rep-resents departure from and positive disdain of mere complexities to the vision that includes and comprehends a perpetual struggle between the esthetic forging of one's soul and the formless salt vitality of the ocean, which is womb and complexity and physical existence.

"Byzantium" is a poem about the process of writing a poem; also about a sort of poetry, perhaps about poetry in general; surely about formality and complexity, spirit and flesh, life and death, and some of the relations between them. The position it takes is that human life may include a more-than-human point of view as part of its own strenuous pattern. And to take the poem at this primary estimate, though one need not exclude the overtones which the poem still undeniably possesses, of the Platonic year and the 28 stages of history and the 26 phases of human personality, is to give it a more general human significance than can be attained through the mechanics of an abstract verbal system.

III

The fact is that the "necessity of a mythology" so much advanced in connection with modern poetry may refer either to a social necessity, felt so far as poetry is considered communication; or to a personal necessity felt by the poet alone, to give significant structure and form to his poetry. The personal necessity seems to have predominated in Yeats' own mind; "the mythology of *A Vision*," says Mr. Ure, "gave him what he desired — a sense of power, a sense of order, the revelation of a secret knowledge and metaphors for his poetry." These, it will be noted, are all personal psychological rather than public communicative values.

But the public and the private necessities, though distinct, are by no means independent of one another. Only a very special temperament can indefinitely maintain, in the teeth of the world's disbelief, and in the absence of even the simplest tools for converting that disbelief, a conviction of significant understanding. What is the proof of significance in an idea, if not its ability to control other minds? Sooner or later, failure to communicate and convince must react upon the ability of the poet to believe in his own structure. Thus the impossibility of a communicative mythology, which the poets so much desire and of which they envy Dante the possession, may have the most serious consequences, the last of which is necessarily the extinction of creative letters. But we are still a long way from last consequences. The most one can say is that a great number of myths have, visibly, broken down under the criticism of science; and Western society, if it possesses a common myth or mythology, does not yet seem (or no longer seems) to be aware of the fact. But even though we are condemned as social beings to mythlessness, and though the reaction of this fact on our private needs is inevitable, still there is a last trick to postpone the inevitability, which we may learn from Yeats. The myths will not serve as pegs to hang poetry on; but poetry may, at a price, be made to serve as a peg for supporting myth. In terms of communication, a myth which depends on a poem is doubtless absurd. But here, as in many other tight squeezes, longest way round is shortest way home; a myth may be necessary to write a poem, which is not only unnecessary but positively detrimental to reading it. This I take to be the case with Yeats; with the proviso that his myth, as elaborated in *A Vision,* had a special transparence which enables and indeed obliges the reader to look through it at the experience beyond. The reasons for which Yeats needed *A Vision* and the special freedoms of his background determined that his ideas should be solid enough to inspire him, but not so substantial as to prove opaque to a reader. When the reader is reading his best, and *A Vision* is serving its function best, one is aware of three things at once, the poetry, the philosophy, and the reality to which they both refer — like an image cast on a rough wall by a projection apparatus. The light which makes both the image and the wall visible and interesting to us is cast by the poetry; and the poetry balances on a perpetual razor's edge between the confidence which produced it and the all-but-explicit failure to communicate that confidence which its wispiness hovers on the verge of confessing. In the last poems, the failure of belief becomes explicit; and the poetry reverts to themes which are more "human" than "philosophical" and sometimes as much animal as human. The failure and revival of desire, madness, lust, pride, rage, and joy are now the poet's topics; he handles them with extraordinarily little philosophic paraphernalia, but with a splendid heroic vitalism, a tragic masculine authority, of which modern literature shows few examples. Yeats in the last poems dramatized not a particular personality but the struggle of all personalities with circumstance. The materials he uses are drawn as directly from his own experience as those of Dante and with as serene a confidence that his poetry will confer on them universal meaning; his poetic lamp burns with a pure, white, unshaded, and uncompromising light.

This particularly stripped vision, this cold capacity to accept and use some elements of experience without the usual rationalizing, ordering trim, is a quality which renders Yeats of particular interest to the modern, mythless mind. For the modern temper, so far as one can generalize on so tenuous a quality, has not been deprived of a myth or failed after enormous efforts to achieve one; it is simply mythless. There is no preliminary demolition to be accomplished, no area of freedom to establish; one may construct any myth one chooses, and none has more than an individual, personal meaning.

Yeats, when he talked (as in his later years he often did) of "his kind" had reference to the Irish Protestant gentry of whom he was descended — to the people of Swift, Berkeley, Burke, Goldsmith, and Grattan. He defined them, in several striking phrases, as "upstanding men," "bound neither to Cause nor State," as men who "all hated Whiggery," who "found in England an opposite that stung their own thought into expression and made it lucid." The negatives here are in striking preponderance; the men with whom Yeats identifies himself are notably independent of party, system, national, or parochial loyalty. Alienated from one culture and uncongenial to another, they stand apart from both, the objects of spite or admiration, far more than the participants of sympathy. The immediate past of Yeats' own family reflected this pervasive aristocratic alienation. His father, moreover, had carried out the original act of rebellion from the strict domestic and religious disciplines of Victorianism; like Henry James, Yeats never had to rebel against a paternal authority which was particularly tolerant, understanding, and therefore inescapable — like Proteus, or the Great Boyg. As a result, Yeats very early had freedom thrust upon him; he had from the beginning to construct the meaning of his life around experiences, symbols, and traditions which were not imposed from without, but of his own making. One cannot fail to notice the freedom with which, in a poem like "The Tower," he makes use of his own experience — his character Red Hanrahan, his house, his neighbors Mrs. French and Mary Hines, the old bankrupt man, the mountain of his youth, Ben Bulben. These figures are attached to no particular intellectual system or myth; the poet confronts them directly, making use of them to create or evoke what he chooses. He has in effect made them the servants, if not the components, of a "poetic personality." And, in retrospect, this seems always to have been the quality of Yeats' relation to experience, even when he was most elaborately concerned with myth; the myth was, and was intended to be, a transparent guise through which the poet and his readers might approach the creation or experience of his personality.

To say that Yeats takes his place in a tradition which makes much of personality, which finds its central integrating force in the individual temperament, may seem like a paradox. How can a tradition be built from a series of individual idiosyncrasies? A tradition of individualism scarcely seems like a tradition at all. But the paradox is only apparent. For the habit of standing alone and independent, of dispensing with supports which others feel necessary, and confronting reality with that naked personal integrity which is independent of all codes save the code of honor, may be learned from the example of others. Undeniably, a tradition of individualism will in a sense be a tradition of dispensing with traditions. But even if this is mere paradox, it is far from an empty one. Increasingly, as modern men find themselves alienated from existing myths or traditions, and the prisoners of whatever myths or traditions they can construct for themselves, they will find Yeats' position a comprehensible and necessary one. Indeed, only a personal feud with existence, such as Yeats carried on, could provide grounds for that taut, full, masculine note of tragic rejoicing which he and Dylan Thomas, alone among modern poets, have succeeded in fully sounding. Of course, the self-made mythology, however comprehensible in its functions and even in its dicta, will inevitably suffer, precisely so far as it is self-made and self-limited, from a failure to communicate. And as its formulations grow thinner and more schematic, we may perhaps look for its place to be filled, as happened with Yeats, by the last and lowest common denominator of humanity, animal desire.

Not that I would be understood to say a solitary, sober critical word against sexuality, either in itself or in poetry. But the essential progress of Yeats, unlike his terminology, does not seem idiosyncratic. He was early concerned with the expression of ideas, artistic and national; then with the development of personality, natural and adventitious; and lastly with the facts of animality, *tout court*. To say that the loss of traditions implies the loss of humanity is perhaps too abrupt. After all, the loss isn't complete, we are partly animals, and one ultimate of tragedy as well as delight is undoubtedly physical. But perhaps "The Second Coming" has voiced as forcefully as any other poem of Yeats' the protest against animality and disorder which might be widened and particularized to include as its object the whole of Yeats' "tragic phase":

> Turning and turning in the widening gyre
> The falcon cannot hear ·the falconer.
> Things' fall apart; the centre cannot hold,
> Mere anarchy is loosed upon the world.
> The blood-dimmed tide is loosed, and everywhere
> The ceremony of innocence is drowned,
> The best lack all conviction, while the worst
> Are full of passionate intensity.

Yeats as an old man did not by many means lack passionate intensity; but he drew it precisely from the "blood-dimmed tide," and amid the swirl and foam of world-anarchy is found repeating with orphic intensity that in growing old men lose their sexual powers, and that this loss is for them a frequent matter of regret. One cannot doubt it; one can only note that in "Byzantium" Yeats had for a precious moment seen out into the whole historic chaos of which even senility is but one fragment, looking into time and beyond it to one verge of human potentiality. Future ages, which will have lost not only myth but the nostalgia for myth, will no doubt feel most at home with the *Last Poems;* but if the first half of the 20th century should choose to be represented before posterity as a community of men in time, one apex of their still concentrated, complex, and strenuous selves could only be expressed by "Byzantium."

R. P. BLACKMUR:

The Loose and Baggy Monsters of Henry James:

Notes on *The Underlying Classic Form in the Novel.*

All that I have to say here springs from the conviction that in the novel, as elsewhere in the literary arts, what is called technical or executive form has as its final purpose to bring into being — to bring into performance, for the writer and for the reader — an instance of the feeling of what life is about. Technical form is our means of getting at, of finding, and then making something of, what we feel the form of life itself is: the tensions, the stresses, the deep relations and the terrible disrelations that inhabit them as they are made to come together in a particular struggle between manners and behaviour, between the ideal insight and the actual momentum in which the form of life is found. This is the form that underlies the forms we merely practice, and it is always different — like any shot in the dark — from the technical preconception of it: what you expected when you applied your technical skills in order to find it. It is also different — as anything revealed in à body of its own always is — from what your moral and intellectual preoccupations expected: for morals in action are never the same as morals prescribed; and indeed, this form, when found, refreshes and recharges your morals, remodels and revivifies your intellect. Thus there is a mutual inter-action. There is a wooing both ways; what is found is in some respect affected by the tools used, technical, moral and intellectual; and it is also true that what is found affects, for the instance, the medium in which it emerges, technical, moral, and intellectual. Out of all these in mutual relationship is created what Croce means by theoretic form for feeling, intuition, insight, what I mean by the theoretic form of life itself. This form, whatever you call it, because it persists for new emphasis, because it endures through phase after phase and through different kinds of attention after attention, I call classic: the underlying classic form in which things are held together in a living way, with the sense of life going on.

The classic, let us say, is the life that underlies the life we know: it is the source of our behaviour, it informs our behaviour, it is what we cope with when we cope with our behaviour. A little reflection tells us that the most interesting questions we can raise about the underlying classic form in the novel will be those which enquire into the relations between it and the various forms of the mind with which it is always associated in fact, and which indeed are the only handles by which we take hold of it. This is especially so in a period like our own when works tend to be composed, and are largely read, as if the only conscious labour were the labour of technical form: the labour of the game of the mind, the play of its conventions and the play of its words. That is, we have to enquire what technical mastery has been made to stand for. If we do not ask such questions we are likely to be left with the notion that all that is necessary to heroism, in art or life, is technical skill and have no notion at all what it was — in morals, in intellect, and in what underlay both — that animated into action the art we heroize.

Something like this is the situation into which a good deal of Henry James criticism has lately fallen. To say this is not to make a discovery but a commonplace in the bad sense; it has been said all along, and to little point. My point is that the technical or executive forms of Henry James, when turned into fetishes if not rules, have been largely misunderstood both with regard to themselves and with regard to their mutual relations with other forms. Both the ideal and the substantial origin of classic form has been ignored, on the one hand; and on the other hand, by critics concerned immediately with morals or what is called the liberal imagination, the poetic — the creative — aspects of James' language and the conventions of his forms have been minimised and cheapened to perception. I am not concerned to repair these damages but to meditate on them along several paths of meditation. The paths are well-known and our feet fit them, if not our thoughts; we have only to fit our thoughts to the uneven ground.

One path is the parallel path of verse. In verse, we know that the metre does something to the words, even though the metre be the most rigidly prescribed arrangement of syllables. We know also that the rhythm does something to the metre and to the words, something not the same thing but related. Beyond that we know that the metre and rhythm and words do something to both the intellectual structure and the moral perception of the poem. We understand all this because we appreciate the strains separately as well as feel them together: we know that by their joint operation something has been brought into the poem, which is vital to it, and which would otherwise not be there. What we ought to know is that something comparable to this is true of the novel and we should suspect that we need training in appreciation to recognize it: training so that we may see not only what the author consciously intended but also where he struck on something over and above, or other than, what he intended. We must understand that the poetic mind is as much at work in prose as in verse, and we must understand that nobody — not even Dante, not even James Joyce — can be conscious of, or deliberately take care of, all the skills he uses in the moment of composition. The nine muses may be conscious, but they are too many to hear at once. The poor poet — the poor novelist — must be contented to hear what he can, yet must act with the pressure and power of the others in his writing fingers — the pressure and the power he can feel conscious of only as a haunt that has just left him.

No wonder then, if such is his case, he will confuse what he does know and can hear with what he does not know and cannot hear: a confusion sometimes made with great effect. Half the English poets of the 17th century thought that if technical mastery of the heroic couplet could be had, then the English epic might be written, when the fact was that the deep form — the underlying classic form — of *Paradise Lost,* not written in couplets at all, heroic or homely, had solved the problem of the epic for Milton: had solved the problem of what new phase of being the epic of Homer, Virgil, Dante had reached in Protestant, Christian, 17th century England. Other powers, other skills of mind and sensibility had entered into the struggle than the poets knew; yet for all we know the argument over metrical form was the efficient agent for the birth of the new deep form. That there have been no Miltons since, counts nothing; there have been no Dantes since Dante; nor should we want any. It is only the path we want to follow.

If the argument about the heroic couplet helped produce Milton, and if the argument about the very language of men' helped produce Wordsworth, and if the argument about the 'heightened form of the best conversation of the time' helped produce Eliot and Yeats — all these along with a good many confusions and ignorances as to what else helped — then I think we might strike it rich for the field of the modern novel if we look at one of the most confused, most arrogant, and most fertile statements ever made — among so many — by Henry James. The statement is often quoted, and it comes in the preface he wrote to the revised version of *The Tragic Muse.* I sug-

gest that it is there precisely because at the moment of writing James
was prodded — his writing fingers were twisted — by the very muses
of deep form that he was only hauntedly aware of. Since he was
criticising, not creating, his response was irritated.

The Tragic Muse, I may say, seems to me a failure as a Henry
James novel precisely because its form is so nearly only executive form,
and not, as James partly allowed, because he did not give the executive
form warrant enough to remake the characters. I take this as the unconscious source of James' irritation in the following remarks. "A
picture without composition slights its most precious chance for beauty,
and is moreover not composed at all unless the painter knows *how*
that principle of health and safety, working as an absolutely pre-
meditated art, has prevailed. There may in its absence be life, incon-
testably, as 'The Newcomes' has life, as 'Les Trois Mousquetaires',
as Tolstoi's 'Peace and War', have it; but what do such large loose baggy
monsters, with their queer elements of the accidental and the arbitrary,
artistically *mean?* We have heard it maintained, we will remember,
that such things are 'superior to art'; but we understand least of all
what *that* may mean, and we look in vain for the artist, the divine explanatory genius, who will come to our aid and tell us. There is life
and life, and as waste is only life sacrificed and thereby prevented from
'counting', I delight in a deep-breathing economy of an organic form."

It is curious that James should have reversed the order of words in
Tolstoi's *War and Peace,* and if we had time when we got done asking
what the whole passage stands for we might ask what that reversal
stood for. In brief I think it stood for not having read the book, if
at all, with good will — for having read it with a kind of rudderless
attention. The important thing is that *War and Peace* does have every
quality James here prescribes: composition, premeditation, deep-breathing economy and organic form, but has them in a different relation
to executive form than any James would accept. Indeed, put beside
War and Peace, The Ambassadors, The Wings of the Dove, and *The
Golden Bowl* are themselves 'large loose baggy monsters' precisely
because an excess use was made of James' particular development of
executive form, and precisely because, too, of the consequent presence of
James' own brand of the accidental and the arbitrary, and because these
together make access difficult to James' own 'deep-breathing economy
and organic form.' It is these last, however, that hold us to James as
they hold us to Tolstoi, and it is in them that we must find the 'principle of health and safety' — or of deep ill and final danger — which

James found in consciously practiced executive form; just as we would have to show in Tolstoi that his practice was virtually tantamount to an admirable executive form, and must indeed have been so used by Tolstoi. In James we have to deepen the level of our interest in the creative process; in Tolstoi we have to show that the deep things of the mind and the sensibility must after all, when they become literature, be exercised as a game, in the delight of the mind's play, like waterlights, upon its experience. It is true that Tolstoi, in a worse case than Chaucer, denied any worth to his novels compared to life; and it is true that James insisted that literature stood for everything worth living in a free life: he was himself he said that obstinate finality, the artist. But we can afford the excesses of the great — though we must counter with our own smaller excesses of enquiry to which the great were not committed. The 'divine explanatory genius' will never appear to tell us why Tolstoi — let alone Dumas and Thackeray — is 'superior to art', but it seems to me possible for a talent not divine at all to suggest why both Tolstoi and James made superior forms of art. Here our business is with James; and all we have to keep in mind of Tolstoi — of Cervantes, of Dostoevsky, of Balzac and Flaubert, of Fielding, Smollett, and Scott — is that on the evidence of endurance and recurrence of interest, on the evidence of the always available and availing feeling of stature, such work must have in every significant sense at least its necessary share of 'deep-breathing economy' and 'organic form.' We must assume that if we asked we might find out indications of how that principle worked and we can be certain that we could find in such work what James meant by the principle of composition — which is what is here meant by executive form. The novel has changed, since Cervantes, and has taken on different aspects of the general burden of literature according to the phase of culture and the bent of the writer, but I doubt that since, with Cervantes, it first undertook a major expressive task, it has reached any greater degree of mastery or perfection or possible scope. It is only the criticism of the novel, not formerly needed, that has yet to reach mastery — a lack here sorely felt; and a lack you will feel for yourselves if you will think of the relatively much greater maturity of the criticism of poetry. To go on with the present job requires the assumption of a critical maturity we do not have in fact and which we do in fact need if we are to make full response to the novel.

This is not to say that James needed in fact or in any other way to ask our critical questions or any others than he chose to ask. For a man concerned with consciousness and conscience, and perhaps because of the supremacy of that concern, James had singularly little need of consciousness outside his chosen perspective of vision, and almost no need at all of conscience — in the sense of knowing things together, with or without remorse — in regard to anything but the conventional and technical aspects of his work. But even if he had been as conscious as an oyster of his pearl, or had he had the conscience of a saint over his last sin, he had as an artist only the need to ask those questions of which he needed the answers in order to look workmanlike at his work. If those answers came then the questions must have stood for everything that counted.

It is different with us; we are not at work, we are using work done; and we have a right curiosity to understand what his questions stood for in the dark as well as what they asked for in the open of daily practice. We know, in a way that no individual novelist thinking of his own work can know, that the novel is all of a piece, and that if examples have not the same end in view, they have likely the same source, analogous means, and a common fate. Thus we have to ask at once how it is that the three novels *The Ambassadors, The Wings of the Dove,* and *The Golden Bowl* should be at the same time modelled on the well-made social play, exercises in the indirect perception of human character and action, direct to the point of the intolerable expressions of the general human predicament, and, finally, symbolic patterns — themselves in their own action — of the permanent struggle between the human condition and human aspirations; how it is, in short, that the most conventional, the most abstract, approach possible should yet exemplify one of the closest scrutinies — the closest forms — ever made of life itself. We have the shudder of beauty — of the many reduced to one, as Pythagoras says; we have the shudder of beauty — the condition of more than usual emotion and more than usual order — as Coleridge says; we have the shudder of beauty — in a unity of response felt as achieved without any feeling that the substance unified has been cheated in the theoretic form in which the unity is expressed. This is the praise of the late novels of Henry James. It may be we cannot say how it happened; if we can possibly say merely *what* happened we shall have made the judgment to go with the praise.

You will remember the well-made play-like structure of these novels — one of the ways in which they differ from all other novels of similar stature. In *The Ambassadors* the hero, Lambert Strether, is sent to Paris by a widow with whom he has 'prospects,' to rescue her son from an immoral life. Once in Paris, Strether has a classic recognition: Europe is not immoral, it is life itself, and the widow's morality is blatant and empty. Then follows a reversal of roles, equally classic with the recognition: the young man insists on giving up his mistress, who is a great lady, and returning, a cad for riches and a glutton for money, to his mother's America, while, on the contrary, Strether, having discovered life at last in Paris in middle age insists on remaining at the cost of his 'prospects' with the widow, and at the worse cost of all security in life. As he has made his recognition and achieved his reversal too late in life the denouement is that he has to renounce all that has come his way in the person of Maria Gostrey, the American expatriate who picked him up at the moment of landing. Thus Strether turns out to have been less an ambassador than a pilgrim: the goods he has achieved are spiritual, to be signified best by the badge of a new face, even a new look in the shoulders seen from behind.

In *The Wings of the Dove,* an American millionairess, Milly Theale, doomed to early death, makes her pilgrimage to Europe to see and live the most she can before she dies. She falls in with an engaged couple who cannot marry for lack of money; they — particularly the girl, Kate Croy — conceive the idea of marrying the young man to Milly Theale so that after inheriting her money at her death they can marry into power and ease. Milly's pilgrimage is broken by her recognition, which is forced upon her, of the plot to get her money in the disguise of love. She dismisses the young man, dies, but leaves him her money nevertheless. The young man, recognizing what he has done in terms of Milly Theale, suffers if not a reversal a deep change of role and finds himself compelled, like Strether, to renounce the worldly goods he has gained. He is left seeing things with new eyes forever.

In *The Golden Bowl* there is a similar but more complex predicament. Adam Verver, a multi-millionaire, and his daughter Maggie make their pilgrimage to Europe innocent as lambs in their riches and their love of each other. Maggie marries Prince Amerigo who requires money and power to preserve himself. Her father marries the Prince's 'true love', the American expatriate Charlotte Stant, who requires to preserve herself with money and — not power — but further relations with the prince. In due time — in the second act — Maggie discovers that her husband and her step-mother have been improving and expanding their relations. After her recognition scene, in what might be called the third act, she too reverses her role; out of her

changed goodness and innocence — no less good and no less changed
—she draws the power to make something tragically good and ultimately innocent of the two marriages. The sacrifice that she makes is
that she renounces the old ground of her beseeching — the aspiration
of her innocence, candor, and energy, the innocence of her money —
and stands on the new and terrible ground of the conditions of life itself.

It is interesting to observe — and I think it can equally be observed
of most great European novels — that the Aristotelian terms recognition and reversal of roles apply sharply to the major motions of the
plot and that complication or intrigue applies firmly to the minor
motions. But instead of the journey of *hubris* or overweening pride,
we have the journey of the pilgrim, the searcher, the finder. And instead of katharsis — the purging in pity and terror — we follow rather
the Christian pattern of re-birth, the fresh start, the change of life
or heart — arising from the pity and terror of human conditions met
and seen — with the end not in death but in the living analogue of
death, sacrifice and renunciation. So it is in James; and so it is in
Tolstoi with the difference that sacrifice may take the form of death
as with Anna in *Anna Karenina,* subsidence into the run of things
as with Levin in that book or with Pierre in *War and Peace,* or disappearance into the heroic unknown as with Vronsky in *Anna
Karenina.* In James the end is always a heightened awareness amount-
ing to an exemplary conscience for life itself, accomplished by the
expense, the sacrifice, the renunciation of life as lived in the very
conditions on which the consciousness and the conscience are meant
to prevail. James' novels leave us with the terrible exemplars of
conscience seen coping with the worst excruciations of which their
consciousnesses are capable. The order in the three late novels is
interesting, and it is the order of composition if not of publication.
Strether, in *The Ambassadors,* is the exemplar of the life of senses.
Kate Croy, in *The Wings of the Dove,* is our lady of philosophy or
practical wisdom shown as the exemplar of all that is torn and dis-
mayed, but still persistent in that role. Maggie Verver, in *The Golden
Bowl,* is perhaps as near the exemplar as James could come to our lady
of theology or divine wisdom; she is James' creation nearest to Dante's
Beatrice, stern and full of charity, the rock itself but all compassion,
in the end knowing all but absorbing all she knows into her pre-
determined self, not exactly lovable but herself love. Not that James
would have admitted any of these conceptions except the first.

For in the first, which is Strether as the life of senses, that is exactly what James' own language shows: Strether's consciousness and his conscience are applied to render an indirect view of the beauty and the excruciation of the life of the senses: he assents to it, he knows it, but he is only an exemplar of knowledge and assent: he himself is not finally up to that life. This James clearly must have meant. But what he meant by Kate Croy in *The Wings of the Dove* must remain uncertain and I think ought to remain uncertain. Kate as construed from the notes James left behind, notes which may be read in Matthiessen and Murdock's book, was meant originally to be the villainess in a standard social melodrama, and she never entirely loses that role — which explains both her resoluteness and her strange, occasional overriding blind commitment to action. But it explains neither her beauty — she is physically the most beautiful of all James' women by a surpassing margin — nor her instructed humanity, her sense of what is what, and the necessity, in the given conditions, of her fall from that beauty and that humanity. Somehow Kate the beauty, the girl on the make who will be nothing if she makes nothing of what other people are, somehow Kate is the destructive persistent element of practical philosophy which criticises, and places, and makes intelligible, and disposes of the overweening image of moral beauty which is Milly Theale, princess in her own American right and heiress of the ages. Kate is criticism which does not destroy but modulates: under her impact we see the nominal heroine of the novel, Milly Theale, for what she is, an aspiration impossible of realization; she is that temptation seen on the high places which is the worst temptation, once seen the most corrupting, appealing with the best impossible appeal to the worst in our natures. That is not what a man wants to do with his image of moral beauty, but is it what the imaginative man, when he sees his image in terms of the actual conditions of life, sometimes must in honesty do. The wings of the dove are still clean and silvery, but the sheepfold is fouler than ever; for the dove has created its dirt.

Maggie Verver as Beatrice — the Queen or at least the Princess of all forms of knowledge walking in human flesh — is perhaps a more tremendous image than James could quite create. It is hard to turn a lamb into a sovereign even among the lions — even, that is, among those predatory creatures of necessity who are best equipped to know that the lamb of innocence exists. That is why, no doubt, James gives Maggie and her father the added strength of their limitless millions: making the godly surrogates of Caesar. The possibility is haunting, and breathless, that such a combination might be effective;

but it is not enough, for on some other level of belief — the level Dante and Shakespeare had — the conviction of unity is lacking. Maggie has the kind of imperiousness that goes with the deepest waywardness, the waywardness that is the movement of life itself; but she has no capacity for exerting the imperium itself except in aspiration. There is too much fear in her: she feels too much of her new knowledge as chill; she is too much there to be preyed on; she is too much an ideal ever to take on full power. But she does a great deal just the same; if by her goodness and innocence she cannot make other people good, she can yet by that goodness breed their wrong. By her goodness she is able to put her husband and his mistress (who is also her step-mother) between Scylla and Charybdis: between 'the danger of doing too much and the danger of not having any longer the confidence or the nerve . . . to do enough.' And that, she says, 'that's how I make them do what I like.' When her confidante Mrs. Assingham tells her, after hearing this, that she is amazing, that she is terrible, Maggie makes her great answer. No, she says; she can bear anything for love, not for love of her father, not for love of her husband, just for love. What we see is Maggie learning in the abyss of a London stage drawing-room two of the lessons Dostoevsky found in the enormous abyss of *The Brothers Karamazov:* that most men find beauty in Sodom and that love in action is a harsh and terrible thing. But Maggie can accept neither the beauty of Sodom nor the action in love. Thus Mrs. Assingham is right when she tells her husband 'we shall have to lie for her till we're black in the face.' Her goodness and her love is all of a piece; the broken golden bowl which she can barely hold together with all her force is herself; it is flawless only to those who would protect her and defraud her, who would at once plunder and deceive her, all in the name of love and admiration of her goodness.

Maggie is all of a piece in another sense as well. When early in the book Mrs. Assingham tells the Prince — that image of Old Europe, the Italy of life and crime — that he has all the senses that make a man good, he answers her, answers Maggie, answers the reader whoever he may be; answers in an image which is a major strain in the underlying moving form of the book. No, he says, the moral sense I have not got. "I mean always as you others consider it. I've of course something that our poor dear backward old Rome sufficiently passes for it. But it's no more like yours than the tortuous stone staircase — half-ruined into the bargain! — in some castle of our *quattrocento* is like the 'lightning elevator' in one of Mr. Verver's fifteen-storey buildings. Your moral sense works by steam — it sends you up like a rocket. Ours is slow and steep and unlighted, with so many of the steps missing that — well, that it's as short in almost any case to turn round and come down again." Maggie and Milly, and Strether too, work by the terrible amazing steam of their own innocence and candor and courage. They go up like rockets and somehow work great havoc on those who are led, or forced, to go up with them.

In the havoc as it moves and shapes and heaves is the underlying form of the book: the form in which is apprehended the conditions of life. The strongest shape and the sharpest motion — the deepest heaving qualm — James is able to create out of that havoc is the shaping in heaving motion of a conscience out of consciousness. The structure and the gradual emergence of that conscience seem to me the overt and visible acknowledgement of the underlying form. Conscience is the bite of things known together, in remorse and in incentive; conscience is that unification of the sense of things which is moral beauty; conscience comes at many moments but especially, in James, in those deeply arrested moments when the will is united with the imagination in withdrawal.

It is on such moments that each of our three novels ends. In *The Golden Bowl* the Prince tells Maggie "I see nothing but you." That means he is united with his conscience. "And the truth of it had with this force after a moment so strangely lifted his eyes that as for pity and dread of them she buried her own in his breast." The moment was gone. At the end of *The Wings of the Dove* our lady of philosophy Kate Croy and her lover Merton Densher feel stretch over them the dove's wings of the dead Milly Theale. "She turned to the door, and her headshake was now the end. 'We shall never again be as we were.'" Beauty and a shade had passed between.

So it was too with Strether in *The Ambassadors* and there are thoughts in his mind towards the end of that book, applied to the wonderful mistress of the caddish young man he had come to Paris to rescue, but fitting exactly the situation in other books as well. "It was actually moreover as if he didn't think of her at all, as if he could think of nothing but the passion, mature, abysmal, pitiful, she represented, and the possibilities she betrayed." These were the powers the image of moral beauty — of conscience — had attempted to transform. It is the perennial job of uprooted imagination, of conscience, choosing from beauty and knowledge, to raise such an image; but it may not transgress actuality without destruction; the images must not be mistaken for reality though the heart craves it. As Dante says (Purg. XXI-133-36):

Or puoi la quantitate comprender dell'amar ch'a te mi scalda, quando dismento nostra vanitate, trattando l'ombre come cosa salda	Now may you comprehend the measure of the love that warms me toward you, when I forget our nothingness, and treat images as solid things.

The poor shade of the poet Statius had tried to embrace Virgil, and these were Virgil's words in answer. There the shadow was the only actual. It is interesting to use an insight from Dante here, because in his construction of conscience and moral beauty, James is himself making a late gesture in the aesthetic-moral tradition of the Christian world which Dante did so much to bring into poetry. With both men, it was only a hair's breadth, a mere change of phase, between the spiritual and the sensual, the ideal and the actual; and this is because there was in them both the overwhelming presence of felt, of aesthetic, reality as it fastened like a grapple upon individual souls and bodies.

Also to think of Dante here may remind us again of the great intellectual spiritual form in which James worked: the form of conversion, re-birth, the new life. That is the experience of Strether seen against the actual world, and in that world — "in the strict human order." Not a tragedy in the old sense — that is in its end — its tragedy lies in its centre: in the conditions of life which no conversion, no rebirth, no turning, ever leaves behind — not even in saints till they have gone to heaven. The tragic tension lies partly between what is re-born and what is left over, and partly between the extremes towards which conversion always runs and the reality which contains the extremes.

The extremes with which Henry James was obsessed had largely to do with the personal human relations and almost nothing at all to do with public relations except as they conditioned, marred, or made private relations. It may be said that James wooed into being — by seeing what was there and then going on to create what might be there in consciousness and conscience — a whole territory of human relations hitherto untouched or unarticulated. I do not say not experienced, only unarticulated. So excessive is this reach into relation, there is no escape possible for the creatures caught in it except by a deepening or thickening of that relation until, since it cannot be kept up, it must be sacrificed. That is to say, its ideal force becomes so great that its mere actual shade becomes intolerable. So it was with Strether; he denied Marie de Vionnet and Maria Gostrey wholly in order to be 'right' with the ideal which the actual experience of them had elicited in his mind. But the denial was a gesture of this ideal, and it could have been otherwise, could in another soul have been the gesture of assent; for the beauty and the knowledge were still there, and the reality, which contains both the ideal and the actual, and so much more, stands, in its immensity, behind.

Behind is a good place. If we think of what is behind, and feel what we think, which is what James did, we will understand all the better the desperation out of which Strether created his image of moral beauty, the virtuous connection, and how it stood up, no matter what, as conscience. Otherwise, like Strether at his low point, we "mightn't see anyone any more at all." As it is we see with Maria Gostrey: "It isn't so much your *being* 'right' — it's your horrible sharp eye for what makes you so."

We have gotten, as we meant to, rather far away from the mere executive form — gotten into what that form merely articulates and joints and manipulates and takes into itself, itself being charged and modified thereby; but it has been there all along, that form, and we can now look at at least one facet of it with double vision: to see what it is and to see at the same time what happens to it — like what happens to a metre — in use. There are many possibilities — all those executive habits of the artist James names in his prefaces, some of them never named before; and all those other devices, rhetorical and imagistic which James uses without naming — but for my purpose, which is to show how a technical device criticises the substance it puts in motion and how the substance modifies the device, there is none so handy or so apt as James' use of the conventional figure of the confidante, a figure common to European drama, but developed to the highest degree of conventionality in the French Theatre James knew best.

Each of the three novels has examples, and in each the uses to which they are put are somewhat different. In the theatre the confidante is used to let the audience know what it otherwise would not; she blurts out secrets; carries messages; cites facts; acts like a chorus; and is otherwise generally employed for comic relief or to represent the passage of time. Generally speaking, the confidante is stupid, or has the kind of brightness that goes with gossip, cunning, and malice. In these three novels the case is different: each confidante has a kind of bottom or residual human stupidity and each is everlastingly given to gossip; but the gossip has a creative purpose — to add substance to the story — and the stupidity is there to give slowness and weight and alternative forms to the perceptions and responses which they create. This is the gossiping stupidity for which there is no name in any living language, but which the Sanscrit calls Moha, the vital, fundamental stupidity of the human race by which it represents, to the human view, the cow, or as we would say the sheep. It is what the man has been caught in when he gives you a sheepish look; he was caught a little short of the possibility he was trying to cope with. It is this role — so much more fundamental than the conventional original — that James' confidante is given to play; and saying so much it should be evident that she will qualify as well as report action, she will give it substance, and gain substance by it, as well as precipitate it.

The simplest form of confidante in our three novels is that taken by Susan Stringham in *The Wings of the Dove*. Susie is Milly Theale's paid companion; it is she who makes out of Milly a Princess and over-declares her value, volubly and credibly, until there is a general conspiracy to accept as operative truth the ideal she puts up: she gives human and fabulous names — a fairy-godmother sort of name — to the attributes in Milly which James could not at first directly present; but she is not otherwise a part of the story. In *The Golden Bowl* Fanny Assingham and her husband Colonel Bob have nothing at all of the fairy god-parent about them, but have rather just the opposite function: to make the most intolerable, grasping, greedy, predatory behaviour socially and humanly acceptable at the same time that they make out between them that the behaviour *is* predatory and *is* intolerable. They fulfill in short the old role of truth-telling, lie-making clowns at the drawing-room level. They are the comic relief, but it is a curiously ugly, unredeemable sort of penetrating, revelatory comedy that they practice. Fanny with a refinement of perception — wrong or right — past belief and with an only barely credible polish of diction, and Colonel Bob with the good-hearted cynicism appropriate to the best clubs, dig into the tenderest perfidy and the most charitable frauds they can find, and when they cannot find they create. These are the people, wonderfully rendered in voice and gesture and texture of situation, who stand for all the intrigue that passes for human motive before human motive is created. Colonel Bob assumes that any such substitute will pass muster if let alone; by such as him, the world would get by. Fanny makes a very different but congruous assumption: that no motive inspected — and inspect them she must— could ever get by unless inspected, protected, edited, rearranged, and covered up. Her great sign of the truth is that it shall be worth lying for; and her great warrant for lying is that a lie may create a truth. To her, a mistake only proves her policy right, and a real blunder only asks for redoubled effort. It is people like the Assinghams that ensure the service of the gods of this world; they are that rhetoric of manners that masquerades as decency to cover the plea of guilty or inadequate action. They create the scandal they would excuse. What they make in the world is hopelessness, futility, emptiness; but they make these tolerable by making them a game, yet without them nobody could get along, least of all the Ververs, Charlotte, and the Prince, the truly innocent and the truly wicked, for without the Assinghams they would have no meeting ground.

Maria Gostrey, in *The Ambassadors,* shares the gossip and the creativeness of the Assinghams, but with the difference that she is the go-between who has something in common with both things she goes between, and that her creativeness is not a substitute and seldom a mistake, for she is, rather, when she pushes herself, clairvoyant. That she pushes herself often makes her a part of the story and part of the emotion that holds the story together. The gift of clairvoyance, the gift of seeing so into the centre of things as to become a part of them, and of doing so merely by nature and the skill of a lifetime, gives her powers quite opposite to those of the Assinghams. Instead of hopelessness she creates hope, instead of futility possible use, instead of emptiness fullness; and she never makes tolerable that which ought to remain intolerable. That is why she becomes, in the deep sense, a part of the story, and why the story lifts her from a means to a substance. If it were not that a device ought not to be called so, I would say that this instance of the conventional device of the confidante was also an instance of classic form.

There remains the middle ground of what is nowadays called the mind or the intellect to enquire into: the conceptual, dogmatic, tendentious part of the whole mind: the part inhabited and made frantic by one's ideology. Although there has been a good deal of talk to the effect that James was defective in this quarter, I think all that talk will vaporize on the instant if the question underlying the talk is differently put. Not what ideas did James have, but with what ideas — abroad then and now — is James' imaginative response to life related? It will be these ideas that will illuminate and partake of his underlying form. In short we want to get at the ideas in James' mind that were related to his whole work; and in James these occupy a precarious but precious place. He is not a Dante or a Thomas Mann; his humanism is under cover, part of his way of seeing, part of his 'deep-breathing economy of organic form.'

But it had got twisted by his time and by the superstitions of his time; for although he was 'against' his time he had necessarily to collaborate with it — from the very honesty of his inward eye for the actual, no one more so. I do not know that the nature of this collaboration can be made plain, but a few generalizations may be risked. They have to do with the tendency towards expressionism in art and social thinking, which stem from what is meant by art for art's sake, and they have to do with the emergence of a new concept of the individual as isolated and detached from society in everything but responsiveness, which is a concept that springs, I think, from those changes in society that are related to the facts of population growth and the mass-form of society.

There is a sense in which art for art's sake as we have had it since the *Parnassiens* is itself a reflection of the shift in the bases and the growth in size of any given modern society. As the bourgeois base turns into the industrial base — as the great population engulfs the 'great society' — we get on the one hand something called pure poetry with a set of feelings in the poets who write it which has something to do with the impulse to escape (to deny, to cut away) and the conviction of isolation (the condition of the incommunicable, the purely expressive, the fatally private — the sense of operating at a self-created parallel to the new society). At the same time, on the other hand, we get a belief in that monster the pure individual, whose impulse is to take life as a game, and whose ambition is to make the individual *feeling* of life the supreme heroism; so that the tropes of one's own mind become the only real parallel to life. In both cases — in pure art and in the pure individual — we pretend that it was like this in the past just behind our past.

No doubt this is so of some past, but not where it is looked for, in the Great Europe. It is more likely so in some of the over-populated periods in Egyptian or Byzantine history, or in the Rome of the second century: each of which ended in the culture of the fellaheen, where the individual was purified to extinction, from which only Rome has so far recovered. What we overlook in our pretence to a tradition is the difference between a population-burst accompanied by the disappearance of knowledge and the shrinking of the means of subsistence, which is what the past shows us (Egypt, China, India, Rome) and a great continuing population growth accompanied by the division of culture and the specialization of knowledge, along with the tremendous multiplication of the means of subsistence and of war — all of which has been our experience. What we see is the disappearance of the old establishment of culture — culture safe from the ravages of economy — and we do not know whether another culture is emerging from the massive dark, or, if it is, whether we like it. Whatever has disappeared or is emerging is doing so without loss of vitality except in the cultural establishment (now everywhere a prey to the economy) and with otherwise what seems a gain in vitality. What has above all survived in our new mass society is the sense of the pure individual — by himself, or herself, heir to all the ages. Because of the loss of the cultural establishment we have put a tremendous burden on the pure individual consciousness. It seems to us that in order to hang on to the pure individual we must burden his consciousness beyond any previous known measure. We make him in our art, especially the art of literature, assume the weight of the whole cultural establishment — above all that part of it which has to do with behaviour, manners, human relations: with insight, with conformity and rebellion, and with the creation or ability to create absorbing human motives. For all this the artist has to find, by instinct since his culture does not sufficiently help him, what I called to begin with the underlying classic form in which things are held together in a living way, with the sense of life going on.

Sometimes this burden of consciousness seems to obscure, if not to replace, the individuals we create, whether in ourselves or in our arts. At any rate, this burden of consciousness is what has happened to our culture. There is no longer any establishment, no longer any formula, and we like to say only vestigial forms, to call on outside ourselves. There is only the succession of created consciousnesses — each of which is an attempt to incorporate, to give body to, to incarnate so much as it is possible to experience, to feel it, the life of the times, including the culture no matter what has happened to it — and including also of course all those other things which never were in any culture, but which press on us just the same.

These generalizations seem to me one of the useful backgrounds against which to look at the novels of Henry James. As background it reflects light on the extremes to which he pushed the limits of his created individual consciousnesses, so much less varied than those of Gide, Proust, Mann, Kafka, and Joyce, but no less intense, no less desperately grasping after life, and the form of life, for and in the name of the individual. In that light we can but understand what Strether, in *The Ambassadors,* is up to when he says *Live all you can!* We can understand also how Mme de Vionnet, the young man's splendid mistress, is up to the same thing under what are fundamentally the same conditions. We understand how much there is to see — to see unaided by ourselves — how much there is to intensify into form — in the simplest relation between human beings.

James at 58, when he wrote *The Ambassadors,* had experienced and therefore could dramatize the disestablishment of culture and the shift in the bases of society, and he could do so all the better because he did not, and probably could not, have understood them intellectually or historically. He was concerned with the actuality he found and with the forms under the actuality. He was himself an example of disestablishment and a forerunner of what we may expect to find a prevalent form of disinherited sensibility, the new 'intellectual proletariat', and he had therefore only to write out of himself against the society which 'intellectually' or by common assumption he thought still existed, in order to create an extreme type of transitional image of the future time. Not unnaturally his original audience — barring the young who were ahead of themselves — thought he had created sterile fantasies; the richer his subjects grew and the deeper he got into them, the more his sales fell off. His own experience of 'America' and of 'Europe', where America had apparently moved faster than Europe towards the mass society, towards the disinheritance but not the disappearance of the individual, had moved him ahead of his contemporaries; had moved him to the 1930's when he began to be read seriously, and the 40's when he got to be the rage, and now to the 50's when he seems, so to speak, an exaggerated and highly sensitised form of the commonplace of our experience: the sensitised deep form.

If Strether is our example of 1902 looking ahead, what Strether would feel now would seem like the music of Adrian Leverkühn in Mann's *Doctor Faustus:* a heightening but not a disintegration of his feelings of 1902; and it would be a heightening, as in Mann's novel, by parody and critique, because like Leverkühn he would have had so much more of the same thing behind him, and so much more of the same burden put upon him, than he had in the earlier time. Our theoretic new Strether would have found out how much more had to be re-established in a form greater than its own than he had then felt; how much more, by necessity and by choice, must be reborn into actuality out of its hidden form. But the difference between the two Strethers would be by bulk and by kind, not by quality, by scope and not by reach. The reach is into the dark places where the Muses are, and all the rest is the work we do to bring into the performance of our own language the underlying classic form in which they speak.

KENNETH BURKE:

Symbolic Action in a Poem by Keats

We are here set to analyze the "Ode on a Grecian Urn" as a viaticum that leads, by a series of transformations, into the oracle, "Beauty is truth, truth beauty." We shall analyze the Ode "dramatistically," in terms of symbolic action.

To consider language as a means of *information* or *knowledge* is to consider it epistemologically, semantically, in terms of "science." To consider it as a mode of *action* is to consider it in terms of "poetry." For a poem is an act, the symbolic act of the poet who made it—an act of such a nature that, in surviving as a structure or object, it enables us as readers to re-enact it.

"Truth" being the essential word of knowledge (science) and "beauty" being the essential word of art or poetry, we might substitute accordingly. The oracle would then assert, "Poetry is science, science poetry." It would be particularly exhilarating to proclaim them one if there were a strong suspicion that they were at odds (as the assertion that "God's in his heaven, all's right with the world" is really a *counter*-assertion to doubts about God's existence and suspicions that much is wrong). It was the dialectical opposition between the "aesthetic" and the "practical," with "poetry" on one side and utility (business and applied science) on the other that was being ecstatically denied. The *relief* in this denial was grounded in the romantic philosophy itself, a philosophy which gave strong recognition to precisely the *contrast* between "beauty" and "truth."

Perhaps we might put it this way: If the oracle were to have been uttered in the first stanza of the poem rather than the last, its phrasing proper to that place would have been: "Beauty is *not* truth, truth *not* beauty." The five stanzas of successive transformation were necessary for the romantic philosophy of a romantic poet to transcend itself (raising its romanticism to a new order, or new dimension). An abolishing of romanticism through romanticism! (To transcend romanticism through romanticism is, when all is over, to restore in one way what is removed in another.)

But to the poem, step by step through the five stanzas.

As a "way in," we begin with the sweeping periodic sentence that,

before the stanza is over, has swiftly but imperceptibly been transmuted in quality from the periodic to the breathless, a cross between
interrogation and exclamation:

> Thou still unravish'd bride of quietness,
>   Thou foster-child of silence and slow time,
> Sylvan historian, who canst thus express
>   A flowery tale more sweetly than our rhyme:
> What leaf-fring'd legend haunts about thy shape
>   Of deities or mortals, or of both,
>   In Tempe or the dales of Arcady?
> What men or gods are these? What maidens loth?
>   What mad pursuit? What struggle to escape?
>   What pipes and timbrels? What wild ecstasy?

Even the last quick outcries retain somewhat the quality of the periodic structure with which the stanza began. The final line introduces
the subject of "pipes and timbrels," which is developed and then surpassed in Stanza II:

> Heard melodies are sweet, but those unheard
>   Are sweeter; therefore, ye soft pipes, play on;
> Not to the sensual ear, but, more endear'd,
>   Pipe to the spirit ditties of no tone:
> Fair youth, beneath the trees, thou canst not leave
>   Thy song, nor ever can those trees be bare;
>   Bold Lover, never, never canst thou kiss,
> Though winning near the goal—yet, do not grieve;
>   She cannot fade, though thou hast not thy bliss,
>   Forever wilt thou love, and she be fair!

If we had only the first stanza of this Ode, and were speculating
upon it from the standpoint of motivation, we could detect there tentative indications of two motivational levels. For the lines express a
doubt whether the figures on the urn are "deities or mortals"—and
the motives of gods are of a different order from the motives of men.
This bare hint of such a possibility emerges with something of certainty in the second stanza's development of the "pipes and timbrels"
theme. For we explicitly consider a contrast between body and mind
(in the contrast between "heard melodies," addressed "to the sensual
ear," and "ditties of no tone," addressed "to the spirit").

Also, of course, the notion of inaudible sound brings us into the
region of the mystic oxymoron (the term in rhetoric for "the figure in
which an epithet of a contrary significance is added to a word: e.g.,
cruel kindness; laborious idleness"). And it clearly suggests a concern

with the level of motives-behind-motives, as with the paradox of the prime mover that is itself at rest, being the unmoved ground of all motion and action. Here the poet whose sounds are the richest in our language is meditating upon *absolute* sound, the *essence* of sound, which would be soundless as the prime mover is motionless, or as the "principle" of sweetness would not be sweet, having transcended sweetness, or as the sub-atomic particles of the sun are each, in their isolate purity, said to be devoid of temperature.

Contrast Keats's unheard melodies with those of Shelley:

> Music, when soft voices die,
> Vibrates in the memory—
> Odours, when sweet violets sicken,
> Live within the sense they quicken.
>
> Rose leaves, when the rose is dead,
> Are heaped for the beloved's bed;
> And so thy thoughts, when thou art gone,
> Love itself shall slumber on.

Here the futuristic Shelley is anticipating retrospection; he is looking forward to looking back. The form of thought is naturalistic and temporalistic in terms of *past* and *future*. But the form of thought in Keats is mystical, in terms of an *eternal present*. The Ode is striving to move beyond the region of becoming into the realm of *being*. (This is another way of saying that we are here concerned with two levels of motivation.)

In the last four lines of the second stanza, the state of immediacy is conveyed by a development peculiarly Keatsian. I refer not simply to translation into terms of the erotic, but rather to a quality of *suspension* in the erotic imagery, defining an eternal prolongation of the state just prior to fulfillment—not exactly arrested ecstasy, but rather an arrested pre-ecstasy.[1]

Suppose that we had but this one poem by Keats, and knew nothing of its author or its period, so that we could treat it only in itself, as a series of internal transformations to be studied in their development from a certain point, and without reference to any motives outside the Ode. Under such conditions, I think, we should require no further

---

1. Mr. G. Wilson Knight, in *The Starlit Dome,* refers to "that recurring tendency in Keats to image a poised form, a stillness suggesting motion, what might be called a 'tiptoe' effect."

observations to characterize (from the standpoint of symbolic action) the main argument in the second stanza. We might go on to make an infinity of observations about the details of the stanza; but as regards major deployments we should deem it enough to note that the theme of "pipes and timbrels" is developed by the use of mystic oxymoron, and then surpassed (or given a development-atop-the-development) by the stressing of erotic imagery (that had been ambiguously adumbrated in the references to "maidens loth" and "mad pursuit" of Stanza I). And we could note the quality of *incipience* in this imagery, its state of arrest not at fulfillment, but at the point just prior to fulfillment.

Add, now, our knowledge of the poem's place as an enactment in a particular cultural scene, and we likewise note in this second stanza a variant of the identification between death and sexual love that was so typical of 19th-century romanticism and was to attain its musical monument in the Wagnerian *Liebestod*. On a purely dialectical basis, to die in love would be to be born to love (the lovers dying as individual identities that they might be transformed into a common identity). Adding historical factors, one can note the part that capitalist individualism plays in sharpening this consummation (since a property structure that heightens the sense of individual identity would thus make it more imperiously a "death" for the individual to take on the new identity made by a union of two). We can thus see why the love-death equation would be particularly representative of a romanticism that was the reflex of business.

Fortunately, the relation between private property and the love-death equation is attested on unimpeachable authority, concerning the effect of consumption and consummation in a "mutual flame":

> So between them love did shine,
> That the turtle saw his right
> Flaming in the phoenix' sight;
> Either was the other's mine.
>
> Property was thus appall'd,
> That the self was not the same;
> Single nature's double name
> Neither two nor one was called.

The addition of fire to the equation, with its pun on sexual burning, moves us from purely dialectical considerations into psychological ones. In the lines of Shakespeare, fire is the third term, the ground term for the other two (the synthesis that ends the lovers' roles as thesis and antithesis). Less obviously, the same movement from the purely dialectical to the psychological is implicit in any imagery of a *dying* or a *falling* in common, which when woven with sexual imagery signalizes a "transcendent" sexual consummation. The figure appears in a lover's compliment when Keats writes to Fanny Brawne, thus:

> I never knew before, what such a love as you have made me feel, was; I did not believe in it; my Fancy was afraid of it lest it should burn me up. But if you will fully love me, though there may be some fire, 'twill not be more than we can bear when moistened and bedewed with pleasures.

Our primary concern is to follow the transformations of the poem itself. But to understand its full nature as a symbolic act, we should use whatever knowledge is available. In the case of Keats, not only do we know the place of this poem in his work and its time, but also we have material to guide our speculations as regards correlations between poem and poet. I grant that such speculations interfere with the symmetry of criticism as a game. (Criticism as a game is best to watch, I guess, when one confines himself to the single unit, and reports on its movements like a radio commentator broadcasting the blow-by-blow description of a prizefight.) But linguistic analysis has opened up new possibilities in the correlating of producer and product—and these concerns have such important bearing upon matters of culture and conduct in general that no sheer conventions or ideals of criticism should be allowed to interfere with their development.

From what we know of Keats's illness, with the peculiar inclination to erotic imaginings that accompany its fever (as with the writings of D. H. Lawrence) we can glimpse a particular bodily motive expanding and intensifying the lyric state in Keats's case. Whatever the intense *activity* of his thoughts, there was the material *pathos* of his physical condition. Whatever transformations of mind or body he experienced, his illness was there as a kind of constitutional substrate, whereby all aspects of the illness would be imbued with their derivation from a common ground (the phthisic fever thus being at one with the phthisic chill, for whatever the clear contrast between fever and chill, they are but modes of the same illness, the common underlying substance).

The correlation between the state of agitation in the poems and the physical condition of the poet is made quite clear in the poignant letters Keats wrote during his last illness. In 1819 he complains that he is "scarcely content to write the best verses for the fever they leave behind." And he continues: "I want to compose without this fever." But a few months later he confesses, "I am recommended not even to read poetry, much less write it." Or: "I must say that for 6 Months before I was taken ill I had not passed a tranquil day. Either that gloom over-spre[a]d me or I was suffering under some passionate feeling, or if I turn'd to versify that exacerbated the poison of either sensation." Keats was "like a sick eagle looking at the sky," as he wrote of his mortality in a kindred poem, "On Seeing the Elgin Marbles."

But though the poet's body was a *patient,* the poet's mind was an *agent.* Thus, as a practitioner of poetry, he could *use* his fever, even perhaps encouraging, though not deliberately, esthetic habits that, in making for the perfection of his lines, would exact payment in the ravages of his body (somewhat as Hart Crane could write poetry only by modes of living that made for the cessation of his poetry and so led to his dissolution).

Speaking of agents, patients, and action here, we might pause to glance back over the centuries thus: in the Aristotelian grammar of motives, action has its reciprocal in passion, hence *passion* is the property of a *patient.* But by the Christian paradox (which made the martyr's action identical with his passion, as the accounts of the martyrs were called both Acts and Passionals), *patience* is the property of a moral *agent.* And this Christian view, as secularized in the philosophy of romanticism, with its stress upon creativeness, leads us to the possibility of a bodily suffering redeemed by a poetic act.

In the third stanza, the central stanza of the Ode (hence properly the fulcrum of its swing) we see the two motives, the action and the passion, in the process of being separated. The possibility raised in the first stanza (which was dubious whether the level of motives was to be human or divine), and developed in the second stanza (which contrasts the "sensual" and the "spirit"), becomes definitive in Stanza III:

> Ah, happy, happy boughs! that cannot shed
> Your leaves, nor ever bid the Spring adieu;
> And, happy melodist, unwearied,
> For ever piping songs for ever new;
> More happy love! more happy, happy love!
> For ever warm and still to be enjoy'd,
> For ever panting, and for ever young;
> All breathing human passion far above,
> That leaves a heart high-sorrowful and cloy'd,
> A burning forehead, and a parching tongue.

The poem as a whole makes permanent, or fixes in a state of arrest, a peculiar agitation. But within this fixity, by the nature of poetry as a progressive medium, there must be development. Hence, the agitation that is maintained throughout (as a mood absolutized so that it fills the entire universe of discourse) will at the same time undergo internal transformations. In the third stanza, these are manifested as a clear division into two distinct and contrasted realms. There is a transcendental fever, which is felicitous, divinely above "all breathing human passion." And this "leaves" the other level, the level of earthly fever, "a burning forehead and a parching tongue." From the bodily fever, which is a passion, and malign, there has split off a spiritual activity, a wholly benign aspect of the total agitation.

Clearly, a movement has been finished. The poem must, if it is well-formed, take a new direction, growing out of and surpassing the curve that has by now been clearly established by the successive stages from "Is there the possibility of two motivational levels?" through "there are two motivational levels" to "the 'active' motivational level 'leaves' the 'passive' level."

Prophesying, with the inestimable advantage that goes with having looked ahead, what should we expect the new direction to be? First, let us survey the situation. Originally, before the two strands of the fever had been definitely drawn apart, the bodily passion could serve as the scene or ground of the spiritual action. But at the end of the third stanza, we abandon the level of bodily passion. The action is "far above" the passion, it "leaves" the fever. What then would this transcendent act require, to complete it?

It would require a scene of the same quality as itself. An act and a scene belong together. The nature of the one must be a fit with the nature of the other. (I like to call this the "act-scene ratio," or "dramatic ratio.") Hence, the act having now transcended its bodily setting, it will require, as its new setting, a transcendent scene. Hence, prophesying *post eventum,* we should ask that, in Stanza IV, the poem *embody* the transcendental act by endowing it with an appropriate scene.

There is a passage in *Hamlet* that well illustrates the "act-scene ratio." When Hamlet is about to follow the ghost, Horatio warns:

> What if it tempt you toward the flood, my lord,
> Or to the dreadful summit of the cliff
> That beetles o'er his base into the sea,
> And there assume some other horrible form,

> Which might deprive your sovereignty of reason
> And draw you into madness? think of it;
> The very place puts toys of desperation,
> Without more motive, into every brain
> That looks so many fathoms to the sea
> And hears it roar beneath.

In the last four lines of this speech, Horatio is saying that a scene itself might be enough to provide a man with a motive for an act as desperate and absolute as suicide. This idea (of natural scene as sufficient motivation for an act) was to reappear, in many transformations, during the subsequent centuries. We find a notable variant of it in the novels of Thomas Hardy. We find less obvious variants of it in the many philosophies of materialistic science according to which behavior and development are explained in terms of the "environmental." Theories of "geopolitics" would be a contemporary variant.

It involves primarily the law of dramatic consistency whereby the quality of the act shares the quality of the scene in which it is enacted (the synecdochic relation of container and thing contained). Its grandest variant was in supernatural cosmogonies wherein mankind took on the attributes of gods by acting in cosmic scenes that were themselves imbued with the presence of godhead.[2]

Or we may discern the logic of the act-scene ratio behind the old controversy as to whether "God willed the good because it is good," or "the good is good because God willed it." This strictly theological controversy had political implications. For if the pattern were carried into theories of secular government, the thesis corresponding to the second of these theological doctrines might run somewhat like this: "Acts are legal because the monarch decrees them to be." Such a formula would obviously provide a much stronger sanction for legal innovation on the part of a central monarch than would a doctrine that the monarch's decrees should merely put into legal code traditional concepts of the lawful. For this theory, analogue of the doctrine that "God willed the good because it is good," served in effect to limit the powers of monarchs by upholding traditional rights that the king's legal innovations would abrogate or modify. Psychologically, you will note, the doctrine that "the good is good because God willed it" was more "voluntaristic," more in keeping with the rising bourgeois stress upon the "sub-

---

2. In an article by Leo Spitzer, *"Milieu* and *Ambiance:* An Essay in Historical Semantics" (September and December 1942 numbers of *Philosophy and Phenomenological Research*), one will find a wealth of material that can be read as illustrative of "dramatic ratio."

jective" (the idealistic way of locating the centre of motivation in the *agent*).[3]

If even theology thus responded to the pressure for dramatic symmetry by endowing God, as the transcendent act, with a transcendent scene of like quality, we should certainly expect to find analogous tactics in this Ode. For as we have noted that the romantic passion is the secular equivalent of the Christian passion, so we may recall Coleridge's notion that poetic action itself is a "dim analogue of Creation." Keats in his way confronting the same dramatistic requirement that the theologians confronted in theirs, when he has arrived at his transcendent act at the end of Stanza III (that is, when the benign fever has split away from the malign bodily counterpart, as a divorcing of spiritual action from sensual passion), he is ready in the next stanza for the imagining of a scene that would correspond in quality to the quality of the action as so transformed. His fourth stanza will concretize, or "materialize," the act, by dwelling upon its appropriate ground.

> Who are these coming to the sacrifice?
> To what green altar, O mysterious priest,
> Lead'st thou that heifer lowing at the skies,
> And all her silken flanks with garlands drest?
> What little town, by river or sea shore,
> Or mountain-built with peaceful citadel,
> Is emptied of this folk, this pious morn?
> And, little town, thy streets for evermore
> Will silent be; and not a soul to tell
> Why thou art desolate, can e'er return.

It is a vision, as you prefer, of "death" or of "immortality." "Immortality," we might say, is the "good" word for "death," and must necessarily be conceived in terms of death (the necessity that Donne touches upon when he writes, ". . . but thinke that I / Am, by being dead, im-

---

3. This stress is usually, in practice, exemplified by what I call the "lyric" or "scene-agent" ratio, involving a likeness of quality in person and place. In typical 19th-century writing, one can find instances of the scene-agent ratio almost at random. Here is one in Carlyle's *Heroes and Hero Worship:*

> These Arabs Mohammed was born among are certainly a notable people. Their country itself is notable; the fit habitation for such a race. Savage inaccessible rock-mountains, great grim deserts, alternating with beautiful strips of verdure: wherever water is, there is greenness, beauty; odoriferous balm shrubs, date-trees, frankincense-trees. Consider that wide waste horizon of sand, empty, silent, like a sand-sea, dividing habitable place from habitable. You are all alone there, left alone with the universe; by day a fierce sun blazing down on it with intolerable radiance; by night the great deep heaven with its stars. Such country is fit for a swift-handed, deep-hearted race of men.

mortall"). This is why, when discussing the second stanza, I felt justified in speaking of the variations of the love-death equation, though
the poem spoke not of love and *death,* but of love *for ever.* We have
a deathy-deathless scene as the corresponding ground of our transcendent act. The Urn itself, as with the scene upon it, is not merely
an immortal act in our present mortal scene; it was originally an
immortal act in a mortal scene quite different. The imagery, of sacrifice, piety, silence, desolation, is that of communication with the immortal or the dead.[4]

Incidentally, we might note that the return to the use of rhetorical
questions in the fourth stanza serves well, on a purely technical level,
to keep our contact with the mood of the opening stanza, a music that
now but vibrates in the memory. Indeed, one even gets the impression
that the form of the rhetorical question had never been abandoned;
that the poet's questings had been couched as questions throughout.
This is tonal felicity at its best, and something much like unheard
tonal felicity. For the actual persistence of the rhetorical questions
through these stanzas would have been wearisome, whereas their return now gives us an inaudible variation, by making us feel that the
exclamations in the second and third stanzas had been questions, as
the questions in the first stanza had been exclamations.

But though a lyric greatly profits by so strong a sense of continu-
ousness, or perpetuity, I am trying to stress the fact that in the fourth
stanza we *come upon* something. Indeed, this fourth stanza is related
to the three foregoing stanzas quite as the sestet is related to the octave
in Keats's sonnet, "On First Looking Into Chapman's Homer":

> Much have I travell'd in the realms of gold,
> And many goodly states and kingdoms seen;

---

4. In imagery there is no negation, or disjunction. Linguistically we can say, "this *or*
that," "this, *not* that." In imagery we can but say "this *and* that," "this *with* that,"
"this-that," etc. Thus, imagistically considered, a commandment cannot be simply a
proscription, but is also latently a provocation (a state of affairs that figures in the
kind of stylistic scrupulosity and/or curiosity to which Gide's heroes have been particularly sensitive, as "thou shalt not . . ." becomes imaginatively transformed into
"what would happen if . . ."). In the light of what we have said about the deathi-
ness of immortality, and the relation between the erotic and the thought of a "dying,"
perhaps we might be justified in reading the last line of the great "Bright Star!" sonnet as naming states not simply alternative but also synonymous:
> And so live ever—or else swoon to death.
This use of the love-death equation is as startlingly paralleled in a letter to Fanny
Brawne:
> I have two luxuries to brood over in my walks, your loveliness and the
> hour of my death. O that I could take possession of them both in the
> same moment.

Round many western islands have I been
Which bards in fealty to Apollo hold.
Oft of one wide expanse had I been told
That deep-brow'd Homer ruled as his demesne;
Yet did I never breathe its pure serene
Till I heard Chapman speak out loud and bold;

Then felt I like some watcher of the skies
When a new planet swims into his ken;
Or like stout Cortez when with eagle eyes
He stared at the Pacific—and all his men
Look'd at each other with a wild surmise—
Silent, upon a peak in Darien.

I am suggesting that, just as the sestet in this sonnet, *comes upon a scene,* so it is with the fourth stanza of the Ode. In both likewise we end on the theme of silence; and is not the Ode's reference to the thing that "not a soul can tell" quite the same in quality as the sonnet's reference to a "wild surmise"?

Thus, with the Urn as viaticum (or rather, with the *poem* as viaticum, and *in the name* of the Urn), having symbolically enacted a kind of act that transcends our mortality, we round out the process by coming to dwell upon the transcendental ground of this act. The dead world of ancient Greece, as immortalized on an Urn surviving from this period, is the vessel of this deathy-deathless ambiguity. And we have gone dialectically from the "human" to the "divine" and thence to the "ground of the divine" (here tracing in poetic imagery the kind of "dramatistic" course we have considered, on the purely conceptual plane, in the theological speculations about the "grounds" for God's creative act). Necessarily, there must be certain inadequacies in the conception of this ground, precisely because of the fact that immortality can only be conceived in terms of death. Hence the reference to the "desolate" in a scene otherwise possessing the benignity of the eternal.

The imagery of pious sacrifice, besides its fitness for such thoughts of departure as when the spiritual act splits from the sensual pathos, suggests also a bond of communication between the levels (because of its immortal character in a mortal scene). And finally, the poem, in the name of the Urn, or under the aegis of the Urn, is such a bond. For we readers, by re-enacting it in the reading, use it as a viaticum to transport us into the quality of the scene which it depicts on its face (the scene containing as a fixity what the poem as act extends into a process). The scene *on* the Urn is really the scene *behind* the Urn; the

Urn is literally the ground of this scene, but transcendentally the scene is the ground of the Urn. The Urn contains the scene out of which it arose.

We turn now to the closing stanza:

> O Attic shape! Fair attitude! with brede
>   Of marble men and maidens overwrought,
> With forest branches and the trodden weed;
>   Thou, silent form, dost tease us out of thought
> As doth eternity: Cold Pastoral!
>   When old age shall this generation waste,
>   Thou shalt remain, in midst of other woe
> Than ours, a friend to man, to whom thou say'st
>   'Beauty is truth, truth beauty,'—that is all
>   Ye know on earth, and all ye need to know.

In the third stanza we were at a moment of heat, emphatically sharing an imagery of loves "panting" and "for ever warm" that was, in the transcendental order, companionate to "a burning forehead, and a parching tongue" in the order of the passions. But in the last stanza, as signalized in the marmorean utterance, "Cold Pastoral!" we have gone from transcendental fever to transcendental chill. Perhaps, were we to complete our exegesis, we should need reference to some physical step from phthisic fever to phthisic chill, that we might detect here a final correlation between bodily passion and mental action. In any event we may note that, the mental action having departed from the bodily passion, the change from fever to chill is not a sufferance. For, as only the *benign* aspects of the fever had been left after the split, so it is a wholly benign chill on which the poem ends.[5]

I wonder whether anyone can read the reference to "brede of marble men and maidens overwrought" without thinking of "breed" for "brede" and "excited" for "overwrought." (Both expressions would thus merge notions of sexuality and craftsmanship, the erotic and the poetic.) As for the designating of the Urn as an "Attitude," it fits in admirably with our stress upon symbolic action. For an attitude is an arrested, or incipient *act*—not just an *object,* or *thing.*

Yeats, in *A Vision,* speaks of "the diagrams in Law's *Boehme,* where

---

5. In a letter to Fanny Brawne, Keats touches upon the fever-chill contrast in a passage that also touches upon the love-death equation, though here the chill figures in an untransfigured state:

> I fear that I am too prudent for a dying kind of Lover. Yet, there is a great difference between going off in warm blood like Romeo; and making one's exit like a frog in a frost.

one lifts a paper to discover both the human entrails and the starry heavens." This equating of the deeply without and the deeply within (as also with Kant's famous remark) might well be remembered when we think of the sky that stout Cortez saw in Keats's sonnet. It is an internal sky, attained through meditations induced by the reading of a book. And so the oracle, whereby truth and beauty are proclaimed as one, would seem to derive from a profound inwardness.

Otherwise, without these introductory mysteries, "truth" and "beauty" were at odds. For whereas "beauty" had its fulfillment in romantic poetry, "truth" was coming to have its fulfillment in science, technological accuracy, accountancy, statistics, actuarial tables, and the like. Hence, without benefit of the rites which one enacts in a sympathetic reading of the Ode (rites that remove the discussion to a different level), the enjoyment of "beauty" would involve an esthetic kind of awareness radically in conflict with the kind of awareness deriving from the practical "truth." And as regards the tactics of the poem, this conflict would seem to be solved by "estheticizing" the true rather than by "verifying" the beautiful.

Earlier in our essay, we suggested reading "poetry" for "beauty" and "science" for "truth," with the oracle deriving its *liberating* quality from the fact that it is uttered at a time when the poem has taken us to a level where earthly contradictions do not operate. But we might also, in purely conceptual terms, attain a level where "poetry" and "science" cease to be at odds; namely: by translating the two terms into the "grammar" that lies behind them. That is: we could generalize the term "poetry" by widening it to the point where we could substitute for it the term "act." And we could widen "science" to the point where we could substitute "scene." Thus we have:

| "beauty" | equals | "poetry" | equals | "act" |
| "truth" | equals | "science" | equals | "scene" |

We would equate "beauty" with "act," because it is not merely a decorative thing, but an assertion, an affirmative, a creation, hence in the fullest sense an act. And we would equate "truth" or "science" with the "scenic" because science is a knowledge of *what is*—and *all that is* comprises the over-all universal *scene.* Our corresponding transcendence, then, got by "translation" into purely grammatical terms, would be: "Act is scene, scene act." We have got to this point by a kind of purely conceptual transformation that would correspond, I think, to the transformations of imagery leading to the oracle in the Ode.

"Act is scene, scene act." Unfortunately, I must break the symmetry a little. For poetry, as conceived in idealism (romanticism) could not quite be equated with *act*, but rather with *attitude*. For idealistic philosophies, with their stress upon the subjective, place primary stress upon the *agent* (the individual, the ego, the will, etc.). It was medieval scholasticism that placed primary stress upon the *act*. And in the Ode the Urn (which is the vessel or representative of poetry) is called an "attitude," which is not outright an act, but an incipient or arrested act, a *state of mind*, the property of an *agent*. Keats, in calling the Urn an attitude, is *personifying* it. Or we might use the italicizing resources of dialectic by saying that for Keats, beauty (poetry) was not so much "the *act* of an agent" as it was "the act of an *agent*."

Perhaps we can re-enforce this interpretation by examining kindred strategies in Yeats, whose poetry similarly derives from idealistic, romantic sources. Indeed, as we have noted elsewhere,[6] Yeats's vision of immortality in his Byzantium poems but carries one step further the Keatsian identification with the Grecian Urn:

> Once out of nature I shall never take
> My bodily form from any natural thing,
> But such a form as Grecian goldsmiths make
> Of hammered gold and gold enamelling . . .

Here certainly the poet envisions immortality as "esthetically" as Keats. For he will have mortality as a golden bird, a fabricated thing, a work of Grecian goldsmiths. Here we go in the same direction as the "overwrought" Urn, but farther along in that direction.

The ending of Yeats's poem, "Among School Children," helps us to make still clearer the idealistic stress upon agent:

> Labour is blossoming or dancing where
> The body is not bruised to pleasure soul,
> Nor beauty torn out of its own despair,
> Nor blear-eyed wisdom out of midnight oil.
> O chestnut tree, great rooted blossomer,
> Are you the leaf, the blossom or the bole?
> O body swayed to music, O brightening glance,
> How can we know the dancer from the dance?

Here the chestnut tree (as personified agent) is the ground of unity or continuity for all its scenic manifestations; and with the agent (dancer) is merged the act (dance). True, we seem to have here a commingling

---

6. "On Motivation in Yeats" (*The Southern Review*, Winter 1942).

of act, scene, and agent, all three. Yet it is the *agent* that is "foremost among the equals." Both Yeats and Keats, of course, were much more "dramatistic" in their thinking than romantic poets generally, who usually center their efforts upon the translation of *scene* into terms of *agent* (as the materialistic science that was the dialectical counterpart of romantic idealism preferred conversely to translate *agent* into terms of *scene,* or in other words, to treat "consciousness" in terms of "matter," the "mental" in terms of the "physical," "people" in terms of "environment").

To review briefly: The poem begins with an ambiguous fever which in the course of the further development is "separated out," splitting into a bodily fever and a spiritual counterpart. The bodily passion is the malign aspect of the fever, the mental action its benign aspect. In the course of the development, the malign passion is transcended and the benign active partner, the intellectual exhilaration, takes over. At the beginning, where the two aspects were ambiguously one, the bodily passion would be the "scene" of the mental action (the "objective symptoms" of the body would be paralleled by the "subjective symptoms" of the mind, the bodily state thus being the other or ground of the mental state). But as the two become separated out, the mental action transcends the bodily passion. It becomes an act in its own right, making discoveries and assertions not grounded in the bodily passion. And this quality of action, in transcending the merely physical symptoms of the fever, would thus require a different ground or scene, one more suited in quality to the quality of the transcendent act.

The transcendent act is concretized, or "materialized," in the vision of the "immortal" scene, the reference in Stanza IV to the original scene of the Urn, the "heavenly" scene of a dead, or immortal, Greece (the scene in which the Urn was originally enacted and which is also fixed on its face). To indicate the internality of this vision, we referred to a passage in Yeats relating the "depths" of the sky without to the depths of the mind within; and we showed a similar pattern in Keats's account of the vision that followed his reading of Chapman's Homer. We suggested that the poet is here coming upon a new internal sky, through identification with the Urn as act, the same sky that he came upon through identification with the enactments of Chapman's translation.

This transcendent scene is the level at which the earthly laws of contradiction no longer prevail. Hence, in the terms of this scene, he can proclaim the unity of truth and beauty (of science and art), a proclamation which he needs to make precisely because here was the basic split responsible for the romantic agitation (in both poetic and philosophic idealism). That is, it was gratifying to have the oracle proclaim the unity of poetry and science because the values of technology and business were causing them to be at odds. And from the perspective of a "higher level" (the perspective of a deed or immortal scene transcending the world of temporal contradictions) the split could be proclaimed once more a unity.

At this point, at this stage of exaltation, the fever has been replaced by chill. But the bodily passion has completely dropped out of account. All is now mental action. Hence, the chill (as in the ecstatic exclamation, "Cold Pastoral!") is proclaimed only in its benign aspect.

We may contrast this discussion with explanations such as a materialist of the Kretschmer school might offer. I refer to accounts of motivation that might treat disease as cause and poem as effect. In such accounts, the disease would not be "passive," but wholly active; and what we have called the mental action would be wholly passive, hardly more than an epiphenomenon, a mere symptom of the disease quite as are the fever and the chill themselves. Such accounts would give us no conception of the essential matter here, the intense linguistic activity.

WALLACE FOWLIE:

The French Literary Mind

I

In the literary tradition of France, eloquence, both oral and written, is a ceremony. It is true that in every literary tradition, eloquence, by its very nature, must become to some degree the stylization of language, but in the French the instinct to make of language a highly formalized expression is deeper and more permanent than in other traditions. Each of the great masterpieces in French literature seems extraordinarily aware of the public to which it is addressing itself, of the presence of a public, of a public mind which must be subjugated and enchanted according to well-established rules of subjugation and enchantment.

And that is why the first trait of the French literary mind always seems to be its sociability or even what we might call its worldliness. The French writer is always addressing some one, even when he is speaking on that subject which has become one of his favorites since the days of the Renaissance when Montaigne wrote his *Essays:* the subject of solitude. Because of this attitude of the French writer, which is more an instinct than an attitude, born of a need to communicate and to establish a relationship between his thought and the minds of other men, his works are characterized by a tone of bareness, of separateness. They often give the effect of arias sung in the midst of great silence, sung at some distance from the world, even if they are directed toward the world. This is sometimes described as the classical spirit in French art, and works composed in this spirit have the inflexions of a pleader and a lawyer whose skill is used to combat and convince and seduce.

Such works, and they have occurred at all periods in French history, illustrate the solitude of literary speech. But such speech-solitude, because of its ceremonial aspect, is floodlighted. Its contrived effect, so carefully planned to provoke, hold, subjugate and enchant, may often appear a pure theatricality. The writer in the French tradition resembles a performing artist. In French schools the primary literary exercise is that of textual explication, by which a single page of a writer serves to reveal his particular art and thought, and even the art and thought of his period. Only a very highly self-conscious and even histrionic art would permit such examination and such treatment, whereby a novelist would be studied not in his novel, but in a single paragraph from his novel, and where a poet would be studied in a single sonnet. This habit of study has helped to convert French literature into a series of celebrated set-pieces. Renan is known for his prayer on the Acropolis and Proust for the passage on the madeleine cooky dipped in a cup of linden tea.

A single page can be separated from its book and exist autonomously in its own brilliance, in much the same way as a speech in a French conversation may be struck off from its context and found to be a distinct and singular creation. At dinner parties, where the guests are French, the general effect may be that of conversation or at times of hubbub, but when listened to more attentively, the conversation of the ten dinner guests, if there be ten, will turn out to be ten monologues, each recited simultaneously and independently. French eloquence, both that in print and that produced orally under the stimulus of a physically present public, is expression ritualistically conceived.

The reason for this solitariness of the French literary voice, what we might name the primary secret of the French literary mind, is the fervent identification it establishes with the past. If the finished product of French writing often gives us the impression of an aria sung in the center of a vast space, of a form stripped of non-essentials and bare in an almost heroic vulnerability, we know that its strength comes from its alliance with and allegiance to the tradition of its past. The dependence of a French writer on other writers who preceded him is acknowledged and emphasized. French art is knowingly the renewal of tradition and not the discovery of the new. The writer in France learns his particular rôle and vocation in terms of those past writers with whom he is in sympathy as well as those with whom he is in disagreement. Many French masterpieces have been born from a quarrel. The loneliness of the French writer, which now might be termed his uniqueness, comes from this will to determine himself by his affiliations and disagreements. The French writer knows that originality is an unimportant and even an illusory goal in art. The seeming new really draws upon the old.

I have taken courses in French literature both in America and Paris where the professor actually never got to the author announced as the subject of the course, where all the time was spent in discussing the forerunners of the author. We learned all about the readings which the author had accomplished during his lifetime and to what degree he had been influenced by them, but when we finally arrived at the work itself, the final lecture had been given, and all we had learned was what the literary work had come from and nothing about what it was.

Such an approach, which treats literature as a renovation of the past, as a prolongation rather than as an original creation, explains to some degree the attitude of the French people toward their writers. The pride which the French feel in their writers, and their awareness of them even if they don't always read them, are traits found more in France than in other countries. The recent death in Paris of Paul Valéry, in July 1945, became an event of national significance. I refer to the example of Valéry in this connection because he is as far removed as it is possible to be from the type of popular writer. As a poet he is one of the most difficult France has ever produced, and one who will rank among the greatest; and as a prose writer, he is even more difficult. The stylistic and philosophical difficulty of Valéry's art would seem to relegate him to a very small circle of initiates, but it is a fact that, even long before his death, he was a universal figure in Paris, a symbol and justification of French pride in literary tradition.

In the homage which France has paid to Paul Valéry, the dignity of the literary mind has been extolled once again. The case of Valéry signifies that once more in France acknowledgment has been made to the belief that the literary artist, no matter how esoteric or difficult, represents a significant fusion between the present and the past. Valéry has not always been kind or approving in his treatment of the past. He has derided, for example, and in a tone of considerable malice, some of the most hallowed sentences of Pascal, sentences which have been explicated for generations in the *lycées* and universities, and precisely those belonging to passages which we have been calling arias. But the French, as well as possessing a sense of tradition, have an iconoclastic sense which rather enjoys a scene of destruction when it is carried out with deftness and critical sharpness. Valéry's very attack on the sentences of Pascal has thrown them into greater relief than ever, and one day there will be books written for and against Valéry's attack on Pascal.

If Valéry is anti-Pascal and anti-philosophers in general, he is on the other hand a disciple of Mallarmé, who directed him closely in his vocation as poet. This discipleship has helped to define Valéry's particular position in French poetry and to re-define the art of his master. Valéry's debt to Mallarmé is so significant that professors in future courses on Valéry will perhaps not feel compelled to go beyond a discussion of Mallarmé's poetry.

The French, more insistently than other national groups, use the names of their writers as symbols which stand for much more than the actual literary work. They represent attitudes of mind, and efforts, which have been successful in varying degrees, to study the mystery of man. The French use the names of Racine, Descartes, Villon as others say Orpheus, Venus, Socrates. And the writers also use these names, almost as talismans or as saints and sinners who are invoked during the writers' self-examinations. The literary past in France is constantly testifying and representing. Thus Valéry orientates his own thought by declaring himself a critic of Pascal and a disciple of Mallarmé.

The art of speech in France is almost identical, as we have said, with the art of persuasion. One of the surest means to persuade is to speak intimately and personally, to take the reader into confidence, to speak confidences. When the French writer employs this device, he speaks, not about his mother or wife or child as the writer of another tradition might do, but about the author whom he reads passionately and with whom he has formed a spiritual liaison. Baudelaire is most personal when he writes of Edgar Allen Poe; Claudel when he tells the effect of Rimbaud on his life; Valéry when he describes his conversations with Mallarmé.

At moments of national crisis, the French turn to their writers, because the writer is by definition in France the man who writes about the world of his heart but who also looks at the world itself and seeks to integrate in his writing some considerations concerning the affairs of the world. On the one hand, Valéry can compose such a pure poem as *Narcisse,* which contains the description of a forest scene and the exploration of a psychological dilemma. And on the other hand, he can write such an article as *La Crise de l'Esprit* which, although it was written soon after the end of the first World War, stands today as one of the most penetrating statements on the political and sociological dilemmas of modern man. The first sentence of the essay has become a celebrated exordium in France: *Nous autres, civilisations, nous savons maintenant que nous sommes mortelles.* It is this kind of sentence we have been trying to describe as the beginning of an aria. It is both resonant and arresting: "We civilizations know now that we are mortal." It has the solitariness of a single voice speaking to a vast public, which in this case is France and the modern world. It is the voice of a pleader who is going to speak, through deep sensitivity to the past, to his own world on the subject of the abyss of history.

So the literary mind in France, nourished as it is on the past, may analyze whatever subject persists in tormenting man: politics, morals, theology, philosophy. Literature, the most complex of the arts, involves all these subjects and many others, and in France, more than in other countries, the people turn to the particular form given to these problems by the literary artist. The ideas of the 16th century are perhaps best expounded in the *Essays* of Montaigne; the moral and religious problems of the 17th century may be studied in the sermons of Bossuet; modern man's psychological barriers are for the French more significantly analyzed by a Baudelaire or by a Proust than by a Freud. When we read such a passage as that of Valéry which begins with the words, *Nous autres, civilisations, nous savons maintenant que nous sommes mortelles,* we realize that the writer in France has replaced the prophet. The writer has learned, through the exercise of his form, which is the practice of lucidity, of stripping and condensing, how to see everything in its absolute meaning. Valéry in his passage on the mortality of civilization, and Péguy, another writer-prophet of France, when he speaks of the modern tendency of changing a mystical state into a political state, both attain in their writing to the absolute meaning of an event.

II

But this rôle of tradition in the make-up of the French literary mind is only one aspect. It gives to the writer a feeling of solidarity with the past and an urgency to continue a movement rather than to found a new one. This dependence of the French writer on earlier writers, which grows in many cases to something akin to religious fervor, is not however an enslavement of mind, but, paradoxically, a liberation. Montaigne is better able to formulate his own thoughts when he reads Seneca and Sextus Empiricus. Pascal, in denouncing Montaigne, found his own voice in the 17th century; and Gide, today, in his approval of Montaigne and the pleasure he derives from reading the *Essays,* has received confirmation in many of his own attitudes as writer.

The French genius, however, cannot be defined solely by this habit of integration with the past. French genius is not just one thing. It is characterized by infinite variety and richness, by the most opposing traits. After establishing a relationship with the past, it then establishes another kind of relationship with the present. The second secret of the French literary mind is the dialogue it creates with another mind of its time. No major view on man, and no particular kind of sensitivity is allowed to exist alone in France for very long. The French genius asserts itself by creating some miracle of equilibrium. It discovers in its own age an opposing voice, usually of power equal to its own, and therefore is able to grow more vibrantly according to its own distinctive qualities. French art seems to develop in the form of a dialogue. But this dialogue is conciliation, or rather balance and counterpoint. Each of the two voices remains independent and clear, but much of its clarity and independence is derived from the existence of the other voice.

The provinces of France, each one so different from all the others, prefigure and control to some degree the multiple varieties or variations of French art. Long before the classical opposition of Corneille and Racine, so minutely studied in the *lycées,* there existed at the very beginnings of France, in the 12th century, one of the most dramatic dialogues between French minds. Throughout the history of France, Brittany has produced literary minds which seem to be characterized by agility and suppleness on the one hand, and by a tendency toward mysticism and poetry on the other. Pierre Abélard, the 12th century philosopher, who was also poet and lover at one time in his life, had this kind of mind: both critical and mystical, both lyric and independent. He is usually considered one of the forerunners of the French analytical and rationalist spirit, adept in argumentation and subtlety. But Abélard's philosophy and theology were attacked by a contemporary, a man equally powerful but in a different way. Saint Bernard was Abélard's adversary. He was a Burgundian, of a race vastly unlike the Breton. The genius of the Burgundians is that of organizing, constructing, synthesizing. The Roman legionnaires had settled in Burgundy and had perhaps bequeathed some of their respect for authority and their sense of order and even their physical prowess. I understand that it is still believed that the best soldiers in France come from Burgundy.

A clash was inevitable between these two men. Abélard's spirit was critical, analytical and even destructive; whereas Bernard's spirit was bent upon protecting authority and tradition, eager to preserve and synthesize, and determined to use his full power in accomplishing those ends. So Bernard, the man of action, opposed Abélard, the reflective thinker. The passion of order and synthesis opposed the passion of thought and analysis. The same warning which Saint Bernard gave to Abélard in the 12th century has been spoken in our day by Valéry in the essay already quoted, *La Crise de l'Esprit*. Man's investigation and knowledge may grow to such an extent that they become dangerous for himself and for the world. That was why Saint Bernard intervened in the career of Abélard, and that is the reason today for Valéry's question about knowledge. A vast amount of knowledge was necessary to permit the Americans to kill in the space of a few seconds 40,000 Japanese. We can easily realize the threat which such knowledge represents for civilization. It is not exaggerated to say that today a civilization appears to us as fragile as a human life.

The 12th century dialogue of Abélard and Bernard, which was a pattern of counterpoint established between a spirit of analysis and a spirit of synthesis, continues in varying ways in each great period of French history. In the Renaissance, the humanism of a Rabelais who believed in the natural goodness of man, was offset by the humanism of a Calvin, who preached the corruption of human nature. In the 17th century, one of the most significant dialogues for the subsequent development of French writing, was that between Descartes and Pascal. Descartes furthered his so-called method of doubt so that human reason might attain to truth. It would not be fantastic to consider Descartes' philosophical treatise, *Discourse on Method,* the first of the psychological novels in French literature wherein reason in its purest state is the protagonist. But Pascal, in the same years, and in no uncertain terms, was asking reason to humble itself: *Raison, humiliez-vous!,* and telling mankind that "the heart has its reasons which reason doesn't understand." Thus the intellectual enterprise or adventure of Descartes cannot be separated from the more deeply tormented and spiritual adventure of Pascal. One was necessary for the other in this persistent pattern of French thought where each age seeks to conciliate opposing tendencies, where analysis is opposed to synthesis, realism to idealism, action to contemplation, thought to sentiment.

More than other countries, France favors and supports and values the existence of opposing minds at any given moment of its history. In that country which has developed to such a high degree the art of argument and discussion and conversation, no single voice is ever allowed to be heard for any length of time. I suppose that no teacher ever had such abundant and even hysterical success as Abélard did, and yet his revolutionary spirit, brilliant as it was, negative and demolishing according to that form which holds and stimulates young students, was not unchallenged and was finally subjugated by the sterner, more dogmatic, although far less subtle and scintillating, spirit of Saint Bernard.

III

There exists throughout the history of French literature, from the earliest writings in the French language, the courtly romances, for example, of Chretien de Troyes in the 12th century, up to the plays and novels of the existentialists in Paris today, a profound and persistent unity of inspiration. What unites all the major works of French literature is the psychological inquest of man, an inquest to which each one seems dedicated.

The effort to study man, to explore the secrets of his mind and his desires, to define his position with respect to life and death, to the cosmos and to truth, is the motivation and the activity of the French literary mind. Many answers have been given to these questions in the various periods of French history, but all the questions might be summarized by the one question: what is man? And this question provides the stimulation and subject matter of French writing, whether it be the *ballades* of the gangster-poet Villon in the 15th century or the involved psychological novel of Proust in the 20th century. The French writer turns instinctively not to the collective problems of mankind, but to the personal, more secretive and individual problem of a man. He believes that only through the laborious exploration of self can he attain to any aspect of universal truth.

In the so-called central period of French culture, in the classical age of the 17th century, there occurred an exceptional harmonization between this permanent interest of the French writer in psychological study and the philosophically Christian view of man which lies at the basis of everything we call French. The study of man became, at that time, more uniquely than it had previously, the study of man's corruption. Classicism and Christianity were united by the doctrine that man is not born good. The mystery which man brings to the world is not his innocency, but his knowledge of evil, his corruptibility. This experience of evil is the subject matter of the tragedies of Racine, the maxims of La Rochefoucauld, the fables of La Fontaine and of every other literary work of the classical age.

The very method itself of Descartes, which was expounded in France as well as in Holland and elsewhere in Europe just prior to the reign of Louis XIV, consists in a descent into one's own mind and a removal from one's mind of all those notions falsely acquired which cannot be arrived at by rational intuition. We have already mentioned Descartes' *Discourse on Method* as a kind of introduction to the impressive list of psychological novels, the type of writing which, since the tragedies of Racine, has dominated French literature. Descartes' celebrated *Cogito, ergo sum* is the axiom on which he built his metaphysical system. It is the point of departure in a revolution not so much of ideas as of a method which has had a long history and which is not yet terminated.

Pascal, contemporary with Descartes, initiated a further revolution, which has had an equally fertile history. Descartes' analysis of the basic simple truths which man discovers in himself by means of his rational intuition is paralleled in time by Pascal's revolution of the human heart and of sentiment. The logic of Descartes, which is always however that of a single hero, is offset by the turbulent dark poetry of Pascal's torment. The "abyss," which he bears within himself, is Pascal's symbol of the barrier which separates him from truth and helps to objectify the personal anguish generated by his self-inquisition.

The psychological inquiry which has been carried on uninterruptedly by the French literary mind since Descartes and Pascal, continues in varying proportions the influence or the example of these two men. On the one hand, the spirit of a method may be primary. This becomes equivalent almost to a cult of ordering and organization, of evidence, analysis and synthesis where structure and compositional form are uppermost in the mind of the creative artist. Flaubert would be a leading example of this type of writer. And then, on the other hand, a spirit of disquietude and even of anguish, manifesting itself in the lineage of Pascal, where the study of man is carried on in an austere trembling and fearfulness, where the complexities of the heart overbalance the logical reasonableness of the mind. Some of the greatest artists belong to this lineage: Racine, Baudelaire, Rimbaud, Mauriac, Malraux. To them I would attach the contemporary group of French writers known as the existentialists.

Since 1944, the existentialist movement has occupied a central position in French literary life. I refer to it in this general discussion of the French literary mind because of its own significance and value and because, as the most recent expression of French thought, it recapitulates and illustrates much of what we have already said.

Like everything new, existentialism has become a vogue. It has been examined by philosophers and by journalists, and it has been distorted by both. Even here in America, existentialism has had a kind of vogue. The leading existentialist, M. Jean-Paul Sartre, has visited America two or three times. His picture has appeared in *Life Magazine*. Existentialism has been discussed journalistically by *Time Magazine* and *The New Yorker*. More serious critical articles have appeared in *Horizon* of London, *Partisan Review* and *Kenyon Review*. Translations of the novels and plays have begun to appear. *No Exit* and *The Flies* by Sartre have been produced in several American theatres.

In Paris, the vogue has been infinitely more pronounced. In fact, at times it has been hysterical. It has obsessed every type of French mind. Especially the mind of women, perhaps. But it is always women who assure the success of any book and any literary movement. But also, professors of the Sorbonne are becoming interested in existentialism, and I am confident that the nimble-witted waiters in the Paris cafés and bistros have contributed to the popularization of the new writing.

One of the latest reports to reach me says that a young Dominican father has been lecturing on Sartre's 722-page book on existentialist philosophy, called *L'Etre et le Néant* (1943), as seriously and thoroughly as if he were analyzing the *Summa Theologica* of St. Thomas Aquinas. The report continues to say that the Dominican's public is composed of respectable ladies and innocent young girls who take voluminous notes. I keep wondering what the priest will do with the final sentence of this long work of Sartre when he comes to it. It is a very brief sentence which seemingly summarizes the book and in which Sartre gives his existentialist definition of man. The sentence is simply this: "Man is a useless passion." *(L'homme est une passion inutile.)*

The most constant criticism levelled at existentialists is the obscenity used in many of their books and the tendency to deal with the dissolute or degrading aspects of human nature. Sartre was recently told about a woman who, in a polite conversation, by mistake uttered a coarse word and excused herself by saying, "I believe I am becoming an existentialist."

For the particular purpose of our subject, existentialism illustrates all the permanent traits of the French literary mind, such as they appear to us. But especially in the close fervent exploration of psychological man. In Sartre's play, *No Exit,* he forces each of the three characters to turn inwardly upon himself and to reveal to the other two his most personal secrets and motives. The first part of the play is a reduction to zero of pretence and deceit and even imagination on the part of the three characters. It is an effort to begin all over again from the most basic and simple truths concerning the three case histories. This is in a way an application of what is usually called the Cartesian method, which is the most lucidly rational approach to any given problem. But this is only the beginning of the play. The three characters find themselves in hell, which appears to them in the form of a Second-Empire living-room, and here we come upon the Pascalian aspect of the play. The room is hell for the three characters because they are not free to escape from it. It is what Pascal called the "abyss," or the obstacle in one's nature which prevents happiness.

This play of Sartre's contains therefore two subjects which we associate especially with French literature. First, the logic of an analysis or an inquisition which may be called the Cartesian influence; and secondly, the problem of man's happiness or salvation, which may be called the Pascalian influence. Cartesian and Pascalian are two adjectives which designate method and problem, and their commingling in the writings of Descartes and Pascal themselves, as well as in subsequent writers like Baudelaire, Rimbaud and Sartre is the specifically French quality and paradox in literary art.

We use the word "paradox," or we might have used "irony," be-

cause of the extreme logicality and sense of order with which the
French artist approaches the problems of the most dizzying illogicality.
The towering disproportion between man's desire (idealism or thirst
or aspiration) and man's capacity (realism or limitation or existence)
is the subject matter of literature, and the French consider it with a
disarming clarity of vision and a mathematical preciseness, whether
the work be the 17th century *Méditations* of Descartes or the 20th century treatise on *L'Etre et le Néant* of Sartre.

Existentialism, as the newest expression of the French paradox,
takes its point of departure from a fundamental axiom, "Existence
precedes essence," as fundamental as Descartes' *Cogito, ergo sum.* Sartre has often repeated that man exists first and then defines himself
later. Man is only what he makes himself into. He projects himself
into his future. Immediately with such statements, Sartre defines
doctrines on human liberty and responsibility which are strongly rem-
iniscent of Pascal's. If the key words used by the existentialists in describing man's state, despair, abandonment, anguish, nausea, have
their counterpart in Pascal's vocabulary, Descartes' sentence about man
conquering himself rather than the world *(se vaincre plutôt soi-même
que le monde)* is likewise applicable to Sartre's belief that man is the
ensemble of his actions and that every human project has a universal
value.

Existentialism has its roots in the past. Its writers have established
a debate or a dialogue with other contemporary writers. And it has
revised all the basic metaphysical and psychological problems of man:
action, liberty, responsibility.

IV

The outstanding trait of the French genius, that on which all other
traits depend, is its spirituality. I believe that the equilibrium which
the French writer establishes between himself and the historical past,
between himself and his contemporary world, and between himself
and the problems of man, is due to an exceptional power of spiritual
discernment. It is a willingness to avow and unmask the spiritual
turmoil and aspiration of man. More than a willingness, it is a habit,
centuries old, of considering virtue common sense, of considering
intuition that faculty by which one attains truth. Literature in France
has had an incomparable tradition in its awareness of a spiritual mission. No matter what the subject matter be, and no matter what the
philosophical stand of the individual writer be, the most apparent

word in his vocabulary, and I dare say the most frequently used word in French literature, is *esprit* and its derivatives: *spirituel* and *spiritualité*. No matter what kind of writer is speaking on human destiny, a Villon or a Pascal or an existentialist, the mystery of the subject is best articulated by the word itself of spirituality.

Everything that can be designated by the world as essentially French seems to come from their understanding of the individual, of their prized concept, *la personne*. For the French, to comprehend the destiny of their country is to comprehend the destiny of man. France is the vocation and the study of the individual.

Throughout their history, the French have never ceased believing in what we might call the "absolute of man." I mean the absolute which exists in each man and which can be attained only through perpetual analysis of himself and struggle with himself. This belief in the absolute of man is what might be designated as French pride, vastly different from the humanistic pride of the Renaissance, when man was glorified sensuously by painters and poets, and vastly different from the racial pride of a culture myth. French pride has its roots in a profoundly pessimistic view of man: he has lost through greed and perversity a great heritage of peace which has to be won back by relentless struggle and purification.

This is the key to French writing in every century: in the poetry of Villon, in the story of Rabelais' giants, in the thoughts of Pascal, in the novels of André Malraux. French pride comes from this extraordinary awareness of man's imperfection and a courageous measuring of his dilemma. André Gide has summarized this in one of his sentences: *Je n'aime pas l'homme; j'aime ce qui le dévore.* ("I don't like man; I like what devours him.") But to this very special form of pessimism is added a particular kind of optimism: a belief in the dignity of this struggle, in the ultimate capacity for reform in man and society. Behind every limpid portrait of man which French civilization has produced, behind every Gothic representation of Judas, behind every character of Balzac, behind every clown of Rouault, rises the archetype of human greatness. France has given to the meaning of freedom the will to bind oneself to the ideal through a fierce embracing of what is actual and real and even debased in man.

I suppose that no nation in the world is so diverse as France, so divided, so made up of contradictory individuals. France to the outside world often resembles a multiplicity of political parties, of social classes, of beliefs and ideas. But especially, at those very moments in its history when France appears to us the most divided, it appears to each Frenchman as one and unified. At the moments of greatest fever when France seems split asunder, it is then that she is magically composing past and future, fusing them, unifying, uniting and resolving. Its literary mind never allows France to lose its conscience.

Literature is the deepest memory of the world. In France, in particular, literature is the most powerful reassembling force of conscience. It is true that dogmas, philosophies and ideals will appear contradictory in France, and in any other country, for that matter. But if these contradictions, which are the product of the mind, become also the product of the literary mind and are cast into a formalized product, the artistic work, they have the chance of becoming a stabilizing factor in periods of turmoil and crisis. Literature is a vast register of everything: myths, psychology, philosophy, theology; but it is a reality, because of its form, which helps us to bear and understand that nightmare, infinitely more chaotic and contradictory, which is life.

France has recently passed through a military crisis and is now engaged in an economic crisis. But there is a third kind, which implacably follows the other two, and which is the most subtle and significant of all: the intellectual or spiritual crisis. Here, on the third crisis, the focus and strength of literature are felt. At the beginning of this essay, I referred to the example of Paul Valéry and his lecture, *La Crise de l'Esprit,* written at the close of the first World War. At that moment of depletion, France was able to turn to one of her literary minds in order to see more clearly into the problems facing her. Valéry belongs to no recognizable group of writers, such as Communists or Catholics or Existentialists. He is therefore, as Gide is, a more purely literary figure, disinterested and supremely independent.

His death coincided with the end of the war, and again, as in 1919, France turned toward him as clarifier of contradictions. The long creative effort of Valéry's life was directed toward a study of the activity of man's spirit or of man's mind. The word *esprit* in French means both spirit and mind, and surely it is one of the most frequently used words in Valéry's texts. In one of his earliest writings, published before the end of the 19th century, Valéry asked the question, "What are the powers of a man?" *(Que peut un homme?)* and on the pages he was writing at the time of his death in 1945, he was asking the same question.

He never deviated from the most central problem of man, from a consideration of the deepest part of man's being, of what he called *le moi pur* ("the pure self"). Valéry's enterprise of fifty years, twenty of which were spent in total literary silence — an admirable lesson of rigor and severity toward oneself — was an enterprise of denuding the intellect, of stripping off false notions and percepts and prejudices from the mind. The activity of the mind consists for Valéry of two parts: transformation and conservation. By these two activities the present and the past are harmonized.

This enterprise of a literary mind, which is spiritual in its deepest sense, stimulates the demon of knowledge who always represents a grave danger for spiritual man, but Valéry pursued his adventure with an admirable French balance of wit and seriousness, of science and maliciousness, of incredulity and naiveté. There was always in him a trace of the young student's mind: brilliant and supple, affectionate and destructive. He liked to demolish traditions and then walk about joyfully in the débris. He used to call the devil "a very attractive literary character." But levity was always offset by seriousness. Valéry composed out of the problem of knowledge a work in prose and a work in poetry where light is juxtaposed with nocturnal shadows. The experience of being human for Valéry is, in its spiritual sense, equivalent to feeling that "there is something from all men in each one of us and something from each one of us in all men." *(Il y a de tous dans chacun et de chacun dans tous.)*

The most constant theme in the writings of Valéry he learned from the example and the method of Leonardo. It is a theme which, more than other literary themes, defines and limits the work of the artist and emphasizes the primacy of the spirit in the activity of the artist. An artistic work, according to this doctrine, is never terminated. It is abandoned. A poem or a painting, therefore, represents a fragment of some greater exercise or adventure carried on not within the realm of matter but within the realm of the spirit.

RALPH J. MILLS, JR.:

Wallace Stevens: The Image of the Rock

I

Poets in old age, feeling the steady approach of death, often tend to organize their attitudes, to seek out some representative symbols in which these may be embodied and preserved against the dissolution that awaits their own persons. In such efforts, they retrace the patterns of all their previous work, hoping to mount a worthy crown upon it, one which will suffuse each poem with a new light—an illumination wrenched from a struggle on the very threshold of annihilation. This action is, of course, restricted by the nature of individual cases and also by the disposition of the writer's mind toward the question of last things.

The concluding section of poems which Wallace Stevens appended to the collected edition of his work* contains, as Randall Jarrell has pointed out, some of his finest pieces. Almost without exception,

---

*All quotations of poetry, except for "The Sail of Ulysses," are from the *Collected Poems*, London, Faber, 1955. Quotations from *The Necessary Angel*, New York, Knopf, 1951, are indicated in the text by *N.A.* plus the page number; those from *Opus Posthumous*, New York, 1957, are also indicated in the text.

they are meditations on death or display premonitions of that event. The title given to the group, *The Rock,* figures in a number of the more important poems, and it becomes evident that this symbol is appointed a heavy burden. It is to give a final character to the whole body of Stevens' poetry, issuing and receiving meaning in a ceaseless flow of reciprocal relations with that body. Again, it is a place of spiritual entombment:

> There it was, word for word,
> The poem that took the place of a mountain.
>
> He breathed its oxygen,
> Even when the book lay turned in the dust of his table.

The work itself resists the treachery of time. Death is time's instrument and draws things into its apparently endless round; from this enclosure there is no real departure. But in order to understand the total significance of the rock as it appears in these late poems, we must look at some of its previous manifestations and see how they contribute to that prominence.

The first notable appearance of the rock is in "How to Live. What to Do." from *Ideas of Order* (1936). In this poem, a "man and his companion" stop before "the heroic height'" of the rock as it stands "impure" in a landscape under the pale light of the moon. The human pair, who may in part suggest Adam and Eve cast from the Garden, are explorers of the kind we often encounter among Stevens' array of *dramatis personae,* searching for a tenable view of the world:

> Coldly the wind fell upon them
> In many majesties of sound:
> They that had left the flame-freaked sun
> To seek a sun of fuller fire.

The wind's incessant and derelict motion, always a harbinger of flux and change for the poet, is the climate they have found between an old order sacrificed and a new order as yet unknown. But the rock remains the irreducible focus of the scene, cast in the remote glare of the imagination (the moon), and we are forced to accept it as *the* essential and imperfect fact:

> Instead there was this tufted rock
> Massively rising high and bare
> Beyond all trees, the ridges thrown
> Like giant arms among the clouds.

> There was neither voice nor crested image,
> No chorister, nor priest. There was
> Only the great height of the rock
> And the two of them standing still to rest.

The tone is one of religious awe, almost of veneration, before the austere and secret promise held by the rock. There is a mixture here also of the primitive man's pantheism and of the empiricist's recognition of the definite and physical, both circumscribed by the poet's mind. The first intimation we have of Stevens' idea of a *personal church* is contained in the imagery of these stanzas, along with the attendant god of the imagination and the absence of ritual or clergy.

Yet the rock cannot be bound to one meaning, and Stevens likes to clothe it in the garbs of the richest season as he does in "Credences of Summer." In this context, it turns to "the rock of summer," associated with the peak of earthly, physical existence, but once more, and from another angle, it is established as a form of objective certainty in the changing universe of Stevens' poetry:

> The rock cannot be broken. It is the truth.
> It rises from land and sea and covers them.
> It is a mountain half way green and then,
> The other immeasurable half, such rock
> As placid air becomes. But it is not
>
> A hermit's truth nor symbol in hermitage.
> It is the visible rock, the audible,
> The brilliant mercy of a sure repose,
> On this present ground, the vividest repose,
> Things certain sustaining us in certainty.

Distinguishing his symbol as real or factual in opposition to the philosopher's (the hermit's) occult conceptualization, the poet sees the rock as encompassing within itself the natural ("green") world grasped through the senses in an intuition of sheer physical being. The "immeasurable half" of "placid air" contrasts with the shifting winds that destroy or alter things in so many of Stevens' poems and corresponds to the transparence in which perception and what is perceived are brought to fruitful completion. Without this transparent medium, of which the images of the "major," "glass," or "central" man are other and more concentrated instances, man falls short of his stature and fails to realize what is given to him—the possibilities of the created world. Outside of consciousness, the rock is his only *tangible* form of assurance; it is the layer of the actual in which he has existence. Its materiality gives it a grounding in the midst of life, and Stevens insists that we, like his two travelers, start from there: "Reality is the beginning not the end," he says in "An Ordinary Evening in New Haven."

II

Since we are involved with questions of death and eschatology in Stevens' poetry, it is necessary to examine his theology. To say that this poet is a naturalist, rejecting the accepted forms of Christianity or any other belief, is not to say that a certain type of theology is irrelevant here. It is true that from *Harmonium* on Stevens frequently treats supernatural religions with irony or otherwise indicates his distrust of them, sometimes setting as his frame of reference a world not unlike Nietzsche's one of eternal recurrence, as we discover in poems like "Description without Place," where that philosopher is considered. Often, as C. Roland Wagner has said, the influence of Bergson is discernible. At any rate, though Stevens satirizes self-righteous and stiff-necked piety or militant puritanism (see, for example, his treatment of Cotton Mather), he further reveals his own misconceptions of traditional Christianity. If I read him correctly, he views it as purely spiritual, as inimical to the creation. This notion seems to lie behind satires like "Cortege for Rosenbloom," too. However, orthodox Christian thought generally stresses the unity of the person rather than an unconditional division between body and soul which diminishes the worth of the former.

Whether we accept it or not, the announcement made in Nietzsche's *Gay Science* of the destruction of God has become a commonplace of our modern experience; it is the air we breathe. While Stevens is certainly aligned with this attitude, and has set the human as his boundary, he is, at the same time, unwilling to discard wholly the idea of God. There is no struggle in his verse with an older kind of orthodoxy which is cast off; what he accepts, he takes as simply the case. Christianity is observed in retrospect. In "The Men That Are Falling" from *The Man with the Blue Guitar,* he employs the character of a sleeper awakening to a vision in the darkness of his "catastrophic room," a metaphor for the mind. Dominated by the fierce moonlight of the imagination, he finds the pillow on which he gazes "More than sudarium" and there confronts the tortured visage of a man who at once represents Christ and all other martyrs to an ideal cause. Though the intentions here are partially political, the value of the human redemption Stevens attaches to this sacrifice is not entirely clear. However, we do see that it belongs to this world, not to another. The agony and triumph are man's rather than God's, while the ideal that prompts these selfless actions is the noble vision of projected human "desire." We may be struck by the similarity in this to the *immanent transcendence* in the writings of Joyce or Yeats, a transfiguration achieved within the natural world yet raising the participants above the range of time and space. Stevens concludes: "This death was his belief though death is a stone./This man loved earth, not heaven, enough to die." Death in the shape of the stone fixes a lasting silence within the physical order; beyond this is the "blank," as we learn in "The Blue Buildings in the Summer Air." Taken as a confrontation of Christ, the poet concludes in a refusal to accept His divinity. None the less, he places important value on all such sacrificial acts, recognizing in them a pinnacle of heroic tragedy that yet belongs to the ordonnance of human imagination.

At the same time, the extent to which the significance of mortal gestures reaches is symbolic and adheres to what Stevens calls "supreme fictions." These ideas, by which we guide ourselves, lead him into the borders of mysticism. Furthermore, the attitude toward the universe implied above does not preclude the question of deity for him. Not only the poetry but the recently published "Adagia" in *Opus Posthumous* (1957) reveals a preoccupation with "God." But, in keeping with the limitations he has set, Stevens maintains his deity as indwelling; the universe, therefore, receives its structure from within itself. In one of the adages from the collection, he writes, "God is in me or else is not at all (does not exist)" (p. 172). It is evident that the existence of Stevens' "God" depends completely on the existence of man and is, further, a creative force within him, or, as he says, "God and the imagination are one" (p. 178). The transfer of the generative power from the divine Logos of St. John's Prologue to the human faculties is accomplished in "Description without Place" and parallels the attitudes of "The Men That Are Falling." The world is created not out of nothing but, we might say, *in* depth or perspective, through the description of it:

Description is revelation. It is not
The thing described, nor false facsimile.

It is an artificial thing that exists
In its own seeming, plainly visible,

Yet not too closely the double of our lives,
Intenser than any actual life could be,

A text we should be born that we might read,
More explicit than the experience of the sun

And moon, the book of reconciliation,
Book of a concept only possible

In description, canon central in itself,
The thesis of the plentifullest John.

In that space, to use a convenient metaphor, between reality and the imagination, the flatly objective and the actively subjective, is created the "book" in which we should, Stevens tells us, seek our fullest being. For "the word is the making of the world," constructing out of the bare rudiments of our situation among objects a richer climate of habitation. The lonely pair of "How to Live. What to Do." must write upon the naked rock the meanings of which they are capable. With that act, they and the rock are drawn together and figured forth in a new identity.

In a certain respect, then, poetry is for Stevens something more than the written literature alone. It is a cast of mind, a way of looking that demands the "interdependence of reality and the imagination as equals" (*N.A.*, 27). This activity is not restricted, though craft may be; it is the exercise of what is humanly possible in our experience: "the true work of art, whatever it may be, is not the work of the individual artist. It is time and it is place as these perfect themselves" (*N.A.*, 139-140). Poetry, therefore, is involved in the very instant of our contact with the real and assumes the role of a new reality born of the fusion of the imagination and raw physical things: "The poem is the cry of its occasion,/Part of the res itself and not about it." God has become man's innate ability to renew the world and to live by the abundance arising from his intercourse with the blunt facts of material being. What Stevens calls "bare fact" is transmuted into the limitless prospects offered the mind by "analogy." The scope of life's potentiality is the pursuit of our ideal images, fixed in these distances and glittering in the sunlit air. Of his thesis, the poems are "Pages of illustrations," attributing a human meaning to an otherwise indifferent, often hostile, world. Following this in detail, Stevens develops the persistent terms of his "revelation" from the elemental parts of the universe: moon, sun, stars, sea, stones, rivers, trees, and vegetation, wind and rain, the cycle of the seasons—all come through frequent use to operate as heavily weighted symbols. From such disciplined repetition, there arises a gospel of the natural man, as we gather in "Esthétique du Mal":

> And out of what one sees and hears and out
> Of what one feels, who could have thought to make
> So many selves, so many sensuous worlds,
> As if the air, the mid-day air, was swarming
> With the metaphysical changes that occur,
> Merely in living as and where we live.

This kind of man charts his horizon from the roots of his participation in the physical, and what the expansive movements of the mind can make of that.

III

The two primary components of Stevens' poetic cosmos, the brute material fact and the imagination which fills it with meaning and value, are joined in the image of the rock. These interdependent parts are plainly visible in "Credences of Summer," where the physical and vegetative level is surmounted by the transparent glaze of imagination, bringing our focus to bear on a central point of things in a curious vision of celestial majesty. Here the eye, the chief organ of the imaginative faculty, projects its ideal representation and thus provides the harmonious conditions under which things become their utmost selves:

> It is the rock of summer, the extreme,
> A mountain luminous half way in bloom
> And then half way in the extremest light
> Of sapphires flashing from the central sky,
> As if twelve princes sat before a king.

The image of the gods is the unattainable center or idea from which everything radiates outward. This is the necessary element in what R. P. Blackmur calls Stevens' "platonism," for the remote and "inhuman" unify man's creation of the believable objects of his desires. But it is the rock, not the imagined gods, that receives the illumination and seizes the religious sense with its brilliance and splendor—and that is what the poet intends. We find the same image recurring in very late pieces such as "The Poem That Took the Place of a Mountain" and "The Rock."

Before we examine the last uses of the rock, we should grasp the relationship to death which Stevens has assigned his symbol. In order to do this, we shall have to introduce another passage from an earlier poem; this is from "Esthétique du Mal," VII:

> How red the rose that is the soldier's wound,
> The wounds of many soldiers, the wounds of all
> The soldiers that have fallen, red in blood,
> The soldier of time grown deathless in great size.
>
> A mountain in which no ease is ever found,
> Unless indifference to deeper death
> Is ease, stands in the dark, a shadow's hill,
> And there the soldier of time has deathless rest.

The soldier, whose full title indicates the temporal order to which he belongs, becomes symbolic of all human life and the unavoidable *dénouement* that awaits it. Since it is really the dark or shadow side of the rock, the "mountain" serves as an image of the burial mound, of earthly solidity, and as the poet's version of the underworld. Though Stevens defines here a kind of survival, it is one which depends on life rather than any belief in God other than that already discussed. As a result, the levels of death intimated by the poem seem to identify "deeper death" with the doctrine of immortality held by Christians and unacceptable to the poet. The "concentric circles of shadows," derived from the traditional imagery of circles and rings associated with the idea of self-containment and eternity, take on a greater clarity as we proceed:

> The shadows of his fellows ring him round
> In the high night, the summer breathes for them
> Its fragrance, a heavy somnolence, and for him,
> For the soldier of time, it breathes a summer sleep . . .

This ceremony, so close to that of the funeral rituals of the seasonal gods, brings us back to "Sunday Morning" with its "ring of men" dancing and singing "on a summer morn" the glory of the sun, the joys of earthly existence. Stevens says of these celebrants that "They shall know well the heavenly fellowship/Of men that perish and of summer morn." Evidently, then, the living and the dead are connected in some final and unbroken relation which escapes close definition, but which is deeply involved with their mystical bondage to the earth— the fecund and voluptuous queen of so many of the poems. The two circling groups of men in "Esthétique du Mal" and "Sunday Morning" are one and the same; we merely observe them from a different point of view in each poem. Life and death, as both Richard Ellmann and Northrop Frye have said of Stevens' personal eschatology, belong to one another and flow into one another. It is not surprising, therefore, to find him writing, "What a ghastly situation it would be if the world of the dead was actually different from the world of the living . . ." (*N.A.*, 76). In the reconstruction of the world, there can be no difference because the imagination is "the will of things."

The interpenetration of life and death takes place through the only agent possible for such metamorphoses in Stevens' scheme—the mind itself. In a poem called "The Owl in the Sarcophagus," we are offered a somewhat heavy prophecy of "the mythology of modern death" composed of a trio of figures. There are "two brothers" in this pantheon, one is "high sleep," the other, "high peace." They share the company of that woman, the queen of many disguises, who is here "the mother of us all,/The earthly mother and the mother of/The dead." The apparitions, like the gods before them, receive their actuality as projections, through the imagination, of human wishes. Under their aegis, death brings no radical alteration to the essential nature of man's condition; instead, there is just endless repose. If Yeats sometimes thought that man created all he knew and experienced, Stevens can play him a consistently close second:

> Compounded and compounded, life by life,
> These are death's own supremest images,
> The pure perfections of parental space,
>
> The children of a desire that is the will,
> Even of death, the beings of the mind
> In the light-bound space of the mind, the floreate flare . . .
>
> It is a child that sings itself to sleep,
> The mind, among the creatures that it makes,
> The people, those by which it lives and dies.

The multiple voices of the "Interior Paramour" return us to the problems attendant on the poet's division between reality and the imagination, but these, we may add, are best visualized, as life and death are, in terms of circles.

Reality, or the physical, factual world, is a closed system in Stevens' cosmology, conditioned by "Generations of the imagination" and bounded by the seasonal periods whose importance in the poetry we have already mentioned. In "The Auroras of Autumn," I, the serpent, we gather, marks a scale of meaning for this world along his length from head to tail, "the master of the maze/Of body and air and forms and images." And his performance is a repetition of that archetypal pursuit of himself that fixes polarities of the real and the unreal: "This is form gulping after formlessness." We have the circle again. Imposed on brute reality, the imagination, though limited in the individual by the span of human existence, perpetually extends its range of meaning, as we have said previously, upon what is otherwise a "basic slate." To account for the origins and goals of being, the imagination produces figurations of its own. Through these, the reality which is man's foundation suffers a change that leaves him in control by the domination of his images. In time, these images will topple and new ones will then be forthcoming. The mind's labors swell, drawn out by what they must encompass when there is no other support. It is little wonder that Stevens deified this faculty. We discover something of the fullness and stature expected of such work in a late poem, "The Sail of Ulysses," published in *Opus Posthumous* (p. 102):

> His mind presents the world
> And in his mind the world revolves.
> The revolutions through day and night,
> Through wild spaces of other suns and moons,
> Round summer and angular winter and winds,
> Are matched by other revolutions
> In which the world goes round and round
> In the crystal atmospheres of the mind,
> Light's comedies, dark's tragedies,
> Like things produced by a climate, the world
> Goes round in the climates of the mind
> And bears its floraisons of imagery.

The mind, then, is also a circle, for it fits itself to the conditions of this cyclical whole, which is, in effect, *its* territory. Thus Stevens says elsewhere, "We live in the center of a physical poetry, a geography that would be intolerable except for the non-geography that exists there . . ." (*N.A.,* 65).

The attainment of true centrality, both necessary and desirable in this arrangement of things, is connected with death and the rock in "The Owl in the Sarcophagus," III, and in "Things of August," IX, we learn that it is the place from which meanings are perceived, and in the perceiving made:

> A text of intelligent men
> At the centre of the unintelligible,
> As in a hermitage, for us to think,
> Writing and reading the rigid inscription.

Earth itself affords the "text" of secular revelation, preserving tight order against chaos. Drawing in more closely, "The Hermitage at the Center" and "The World as Meditation" from *The Rock* show the end and the beginning as one, caught up in the figure of "the desired," the earth queen, whose youthful sensuousness promises to vanquish the apparent disorder of age. Likewise, the "Irish Cliffs of Moher" stand as the mythical ground of existence rather than mere landscape. The elements of which they are composed and the values associated with them put these cliffs in the line of the rock's appearances:

> This is my father or, maybe
> It is as he was,
> A likeness, one of the race of fathers: earth
> And sea and air.

This is the farthest backward reach of Stevens' form of genesis, the stony base permeated by the psyche's images. To the genealogy of the fathers everything will be returned, for, as he says in another poem, "The spirit comes from the body of the world." The "center" towards which life always moves and whence it reappears is at the heart of all these circles and is an integral part of them. Their unity is that imagined embrace of Penelope and the voyager Ulysses, a "form of fire," never fully achieved, yet forever coming nearer and nearer in "The World as Meditation." The closing of the ring brings about a wholeness that embodies life and death, imagination and reality, the animate and the inanimate. Stevens' belief "beyond belief," his vision of the eternal, is the persistence of this totality.

IV

The space around which the serpent coils and which the closed circle knits is the periphery of the rock, and in the poem of that title Stevens makes an effort to give a final explanation to his attitudes. There are three sections: the first begins the course of meditations from an autobiographical foundation; the second discloses the rock itself and the meanings that it brings together; the concluding portion once again places the rock in relation to death (and here we should perhaps think of Stevens' own, so closely following) which leads the poem back to the point where it began, only on a new level.

The opening section, "Seventy Years Later," has that peculiar flavor, almost a bitterness, of old age as it examines a past that no longer appears to have any ties with the present person and his condition. Indeed, the poet gazes at this earlier self in some astonishment and disbelief; they hardly seem to belong to one another, or want to:

> It is an illusion that we were ever alive,
> Lived in the houses of mothers, arranged ourselves
> By our own motions in a freedom of air.

With lines of a defiant beauty, Stevens claims that love and human relationships, at this remove in time, are grotesque: "an embrace between one desperate clod / And another . . ." But this "queer assertion of humanity," he realizes, is a necessary block against "nothingness," and it becomes at least "an impermanence / In its permanent cold." The *barren* rock itself is the substance of this negation, though human assertions come to bear the "green leaves" upon it. It stands alone, as we first saw it in "How to Live. What to Do.," an inhuman universe, and it remains meaningless, a raw fact, without the invasion of the mind and senses. The responsibility for bringing about that change lies with the lonely pair of the early poem. The gates of Eden have opened and, for Stevens, God is gone; divinity is man's burden now and the world his task. In this coming forth, there is a spring birth that is at once both purge and blossom: "the lilacs came and bloomed, like a blindness cleaned, / Exclaiming bright sight . . ." Within the orbit of the eye, the rock is made over, a rock upon a rock, looming now as the essential ground on which the "incessant being alive" flourishes.

Whether Stevens intended it or not, the appropriation of the image of the rock is in keeping with his general adoption of Biblical vocabulary for secular purposes. The rock is, of course, for the Christian associated with the origins of the Church in Christ's delegation of spiritual authority to Peter; from this there has developed an identification of the symbol of the rock with the Church. We have already pointed to several other uses Stevens has made of orthodox religious terminology and concepts. Inseparable from this practice, the ideas of redemption and reconstruction—the creation of unified being—are then allied with the harmonious function of the rock in man's attachment to it. The blossoms of green are insufficient by themselves, we are told in part II, "The Poem as Icon," and man must be "cured" or transformed, that is, identified with the "fiction of the leaves" he has made. Stevens' narcissism is revealed here, not as egoism or vanity but as the contemplation of the projected images in which we live. We might think of a set of mirrors (imagination and reality) facing each other, which in-between make a habitable world out of their compounded reflections—everything is part of everything else. The rock is the space of this world, and the wholeness which it symbolizes contains sacramental qualities for the poet. These are bodied forth in the images of the leaves to suggest a peculiar form of sanctification: "the figuration of blessedness, / And the icon is the man." In the lines that follow, three successive seasons become the property of the rock, and the complete unity is seen against the backdrop of nothingness, involving winter, which is omitted from this ideal seasonal pattern:

> The pearled chaplet of spring,
> The magnum wreath of summer, time's autumn snood,
>
> Its copy of the sun, these cover the rock.
> These leaves are the poem, the icon and the man.
> These are a cure of the ground and of ourselves,
>
> In the predicate that there is nothing else.

Stevens means, I think, that we should take "cure" in its sense of spiritual charge or curacy, as well as a remedy. Despite his naturalism, he is attempting to represent through the image of the rock a religious formulation to replace the Christian view of life, which, he feels, belongs to the past. The frequent conversion of the language of the Gospels we have previously remarked can only be understood in the light of some such end. But the formulation brought about must be of a kind that disavows doctrine or creed and, in the poet's scheme of historical relativism, can be fitted to any change—in fact, partakes of it.

At this point, I think we may, borrowing from Richard Ellmann, speak of Stevens' personal "church of the imagination," mentioned in passing at the outset of the essay. By "church" I mean a composite of sacred attributes harbored by the rock and held within the compass of the mind. These include, most broadly, the life of the natural man and the operation of the imagination therein. As such, it is, as we said before, a closed system, though an extensive one. Stevens discovers religiousness there in the desired fruition of existence:

> In this plenty, the poem makes meanings of the rock,
> Of such mixed motion and such imagery
> That its barrenness becomes a thousand things
>
> And so exists no more.

In one of the "Adagia" from *Opus Posthumous,* he writes, "After one has abandoned a belief in god, poetry is that essence which takes its place as life's redemption" (p. 158). Thus the distinctive lines of aesthetics and theology merge into this church of the solitary imagination, a bulwark thrown up at the edge of an abyss. In one respect or another, the same tendency is visible in writers like Yeats and Rilke, in the Joyce of *Finnegans Wake.* The modern poet, frequently divorced from a stable religious faith or communal vision, is not only faced with the job of creating the reality of his art but finds himself inclined by the temptations of uncertainty to make of his art the *only* reality—an imagined one. If this is his choice, the artist becomes, sooner or later, the inhabitant of his work. Because life and the "poem" are interchangeable within the boundaries of the rock, the poet endows the latter with the compressed, incipient significance of a permanent memorial—the perpetually uttered song that renews itself in time. In "The Poem That Took the Place of a Mountain," the rock appears as the final resting place, where the poet merges into his work and discovers there a substitute for the immortality of the soul and the resurrection of the person. Art is the vessel of the purified, transfigured essential self. Since the rock belongs to time, death merely replaces one relationship with the earth for another, more inexplicable one.

Parallel with this, Stevens locates Heaven and Hell, in "Esthétique du Mal," as integral areas of the mind developed from man's experience of the world rather than anything exterior to it. The rock is, at last, "the gray particular of man's life" and "The stone from which he rises up—and—ho, / The step to the bleaker depths of his descents . . ." These are first and final things, and in "The Rock" the encroachment of death stirs the memory to recount the catalogue, the book of earth well-loved:

> The starting point of the human and the end,
> That in which space itself is contained, the gate
> To the enclosure, day, the things illumined

By day, night and that which night illumines,
Night and its midnight-minting fragrances,
Night's hymn of the rock, as in a vivid sleep.

These stanzas draw round the complete ring of existence as Stevens
envisages its certainty, fortified by the prevailing substance of the physical and by the poem played upon it through a lifetime and remaining
after death. Out of this durable identification, the imagination prof-
fers its concluding gesture in the form of a chapel rising out of the
decay of an aged cathedral, as we find in "St. Armorer's Church from
the Outside":

Its chapel rises from Terre Ensevelie,
An ember yes among its cindery noes,
His own: a chapel of breath, an appearance made
For a sign of meaning in the meaningless . . .

This breath is the warmth of life and the action of the spirit. Stevens'
affirmation is built into the structure of the chapel where he is both
priest and worshipper. Set in the very teeth of ruinous time, it is
shelter from it knows not what.

While Stevens admits that "The imagination is able to manipulate
nature . . . but it is not able to create a wholly new nature" (N.A., 74),
we have seen what that manipulation entails. W. H. Auden, in a recent professorial address at Oxford on Robert Frost, prefaced his discussion by adapting two figures from *The Tempest* as metaphors
for leading types of poetry, or perhaps we should say poetic minds.
These were, he said, "Ariel-dominated" and "Prospero-dominated."
The latter category, in which he placed Frost, is representative of the
search for wisdom; the former, including Rimbaud and Mallarmé,
seeks the earthly paradise. There is little doubt, I think, that Stevens
moves with Ariel. Poets in his path hunger after that transformation
which will bring a lost history full circle and restore to man the image
and nature from which he once defected. Rilke's angels and Stevens'
imagination are burdened with these crosses, however they try to
twist away. In an age like ours, such visions are doomed to heroic
isolation, and poets must pursue them into the dark. Rejecting belief,
they have still retained an image of man's destiny from wreckage and
abandonment. Stevens never withdrew his confidence from the idea
of human regeneration, from the Just City, and from the earth in all
its flower: each thing rooted in every other and opened deeply to the
sky—ripeness as it was meant to be.

W. R. MOSES:

Where History Crosses Myth: Another Reading of "The Bear"

This reading is made in terms of the following simple propositions: Myth does not rationally "explain" anything and perhaps does not even justify anything, but it does dramatize the human situation, appealing to and flattering the various non-rational interests that principally make us men. People live by it, or may do so. History — the brute sequence of events — lacks dramatic structure; study of it may permit explanation or justification, but appeals principally if not entirely only to the predilections of rationality, and is likely to be irrelevant to the making of a useable pattern of individual life. Automatically people live in it, but little good it does them.

"The Bear" is an account of a person who as a child was able to participate in life under the conditions of myth, but early saw those conditions smashed; who then examined the historical reality around him and found it bad; who consequently refused to go with the historical drift of things and remained a myth-man all his life. From one point of view he refused to grow up: would not accept the worldly-honorable position in his community to which he was entitled, and with it his fair share of the painful social and economic problems of that community. He remained as a little child; but not from the necessity of personal weakness or limitation. Rather, he did so through exercise of the unchildish choice that would have to be exercised, one would think, by anybody deciding to become as a little child in order to enter the kingdom of heaven. The value of childishness, at least of the possible phase of childishness which involves desperate defiance of the main chance in order to serve God instead of Mammon, is heavily stressed in the later work, *Intruder in the Dust*. (Incidentally, that kind of childishness, if it is childishness — conscience-directed defiance of the probable, practical, and respectable in the service of what is believed right — did not come freshly into Faulkner's work with "The Bear." Clear back in *As I Lay Dying*, the Bundren family sealed their respect for higher principle by deliberately setting out on

416

a rationally ridiculous journey that took them about as nearly literally as possible through hell and high water. But of course the Bundrens' outline of greatness was filled in with grotesque human flesh; Isaac McCaslin's flesh is better stuff, and so is Charles Mallison's.) Though I do not remember his anywhere saying so, I have an impression Faulkner hopes that a little child shall lead them.

There has been a good deal of justified comment about the intricacy of structure found in "The Bear." Lest awareness of the outline of the forest be lost in contemplation of the variety and splendor of the trees, it is worth remarking also the simplicity of structure found in "The Bear": three sections that present, in generally chronological order, the myth-life Isaac knew as a boy and the end of it; then a section, about as long as the first three put together, that presents his examination and condemnation of historical reality and his repudiation of practicality and worldly responsibility and worldly honor; and finally a shorter section that catches up and gives final treatment to both themes. No doubt one can point to an analogy with musical composition if he wants to.

One final preliminary remark: though "The Bear" is self-contained, other stories in the volume *Go Down, Moses* further develop and illuminate its theme. Two are especially closely related: "The Old People," dealing with an episode in Isaac's boyhood, the same period covered by the first sections of "The Bear"; and "Delta Autumn," which includes Isaac, still the unfaltering myth-man, fifty years after the time of his act of repudiation. I believe it is legitimate to use bits from these two, if they come handy, to substantiate the argument.

It is doubtful whether, without a Procrustean fitting process, the events of the first three sections of "The Bear" could be made exactly conformable to any recorded mythic pattern. So much the better, so long as the spirit and suggestiveness of myth are available. Anyhow, like the opposing forces of life and death, gods of the waxing and waning year, the little group of devoted hunters and the big-game animals of the wilderness, particularly Old Ben, engaged each November in their annual contest. On the merely practical level, almost anything went in those contests: hunting with dogs, the use of shot-guns and buckshot, still-hunting, ambushing bucks at their bedding places, shooting does (we learn reminiscently from "Delta Autumn"); nothing apparently was ignored except traps and poison, which wouldn't have been very exciting anyway. To Isaac and at least some

of the other hunters, though, it seemed that the slapdash contests
were pure and sanctioned expressions of the meaningful core of life.
The participants were "ordered and compelled by and within the
wilderness in the ancient and unremitting contest according to the
ancient and immitigable rules which voided all regrets and brooked
no quarter." There was more to it than merely living in the woods
for two weeks and shooting animals, because their hearts said there
was. It was not cruel, wasteful, inhumane because such adjectives
were irrelevant to the process, beneath the dignity of men and animals
alike, where the buck circling warily back to the stand was "perhaps
conscious also of the eye of the ancient immortal Umpire" ("The Old
People.") When a colt was killed one spring, supposedly by Old Ben,
Major de Spain complained of the bear:

> 'I'm disappointed in him. He has broken the rules. I didn't think
> he would have done that. He has killed mine and McCaslin's dogs,
> but that was all right. We gambled the dogs against him; we gave
> each other warning. But now he has come into my house and
> destroyed my property, out of season too. He broke the rules.'

(But really it was Lion that broke the rules, or never admitted the
existence of any rules to be broken. We shall come to that later.)

The pattern of myth includes, besides the opposing gods, the
goddess for whom they fight, the mother-bride-destroyer who is greater
than they. The goddess here is the wilderness. This passage from the
last section of "The Bear," a kind of summary of the physical and
spiritual life of Isaac, is worth quoting entire:

> . . . summer, and fall, and snow, and wet and saprife spring in
> their ordered immortal sequence, the deathless and immemorial
> phases of the mother who had shaped him if any had toward the
> man he almost was, mother and father both to the old man born of
> a Negro slave and a Chickasaw chief who had been his spirit's
> father if any had, whom he had revered and harkened to and loved
> and lost and grieved: and he would marry someday and they too
> would own for their brief while that brief unsubstanced glory which
> inherently of itself cannot last and hence why glory: and they
> would, might, carry even the remembrance of it into the time when
> flesh no longer talks to flesh because memory at least does that:
> but still the woods would be his mistress and his wife.

Before Isaac the child consciously knew why, he felt that the
splendid mythic pattern was coming to an end. The sequence of
history, of course, had doomed his little pocket of the frontier as

frontier, and also Isaac was coming closer and closer to being chrono-
logically grown-up, and so having the contentions of rationality to
deal with and settle. Accordingly, Old Ben sometimes seemed to him
"not even a mortal beast but an anachronism indomitable and invincible out of an old dead time." When Sam Fathers said that someday
someone would get "the" dog (that could hold Ben until the hunters
arrived to shoot him), " 'I know it,' the boy said. 'That's why it must
be one of us. So it wont be until the last day. When even he dont
want it to last any longer.' " Looking back from manhood, Isaac
believed that Sam also hadn't wanted it to last any longer. The hunters
got "the" dog, Lion,

> *And he was glad,* he told himself. *He was old. He had no children,*
> *no people, none of his blood anywhere above earth that he would*
> *ever meet again. And even if he were to, he could not have touched*
> *it, spoken to it, because for seventy years now he had had to be a*
> *negro. It was almost over now and he was glad.*

Isaac spent no time, apparently, wishing the doom away. A sense of
inevitability prevented that, or merely being so caught up in circumstances that there was no time for analysis and evaluation. Because
Lion was the symbol of the implement of doom, Isaac should have
hated and feared him,

> Yet he did not. It seemed to him that there was a fatality in it.
> It seemed to him that something, he didn't know what, was begin-
> ning; had already begun. It was like the last act on a set stage.
> It was the beginning of the end of something, he didn't know what
> except that he would not grieve. He would be humble and proud
> that he had been found worthy to be a part of it too or even just
> to see it too.

The attitude of most of the community toward the wilderness was
symptomatic and explanatory of its approaching destruction, but to
Isaac the child that attitude lacked force or significance. Small back-
woods farmers were hacking clearings from the edge of the virgin
forest; to Isaac they were only "little puny humans" who "swarmed
and hacked at" ["the old wild life"] "in a fury of abhorrence and fear
like pygmies about the ankles of a drowsing elephant." There was
logging, too, in the days before Old Ben's death, but

> It had been harmless then. They would hear the passing log-train
> sometimes from the camp; sometimes, because nobody bothered to

listen for it or not. They would hear it going in, running light and fast, the light clatter of the trucks, the exhaust of the diminutive locomotive and its shrill peanut-parcher whistle flung for one petty moment and absorbed by the brooding and inattentive wilderness without even an echo. They would hear it going out, loaded, not quite so fast now yet giving its frantic and toylike illusion of crawling speed, not whistling now to conserve steam, flinging its bitten laboring miniature puffing into the immemorial woodsface with frantic and bootless vainglory, empty and noisy and puerile, carrying to no destination or purpose sticks which left nowhere any scar or stump as the child's toy loads and transports and unloads its dead sand and rushes back for more, tireless and unceasing and rapid yet never quite so fast as the Hand which plays with it moves the toy burden back to load the toy again.

But if what was or wanted to grow into the civilized community loathed the wilderness as an alien thing, there was an inexpressibly strong sympathy between the opponents in the myth-play, those who participated in the same game according to the same rules. More narrowly and accurately, there was such sympathy between the leading actors in the play: Isaac and Sam Fathers on one side and Old Ben on the other (but apparently not Lion, though only he, Sam, and Ben were "taintless and incorruptible," and he was as fatherless, childless, and solitary as they). In part the sympathy (not that this "explains" anything) was similar to the feeling attested to by many hunters at various times and places: that of loving the game one kills. In part it relates to the regular mythic pattern, in which the opposing gods may be brothers, or father and son, and the winner takes over from the loser in more than a material sense. It would be troublesome and I believe irrelevant to make the story fit the pattern exactly. Sam, who is parallel to Ben, and about as much product of the wilderness as the bear, engineers Ben's destruction by securing and training Lion, but reacts to the destruction not by taking over but by collapsing and dying when the destruction is complete. Lion outlived Ben only by a a few hours (though his spirit went marching on). Isaac on the other hand, though only a junior assistant in the actual struggle, became like Sam and Ben in solitariness and in the pride of a secret he could not share; he was the recipient of the kingship, though not of the conditions under which he could properly have exercised it.

Now all the white hunters were tainted, Isaac said when he was twenty-one and repudiating his material heritage,

by what Grandfather and his kind, his fathers, had brought into
the new land which He had vouchsafed them out of pity and
sufferance, on condition of pity and humiliation and sufferance and
endurance, from that old world's corrupt and worthless twilight as
though in the sailfuls of the old world's tainted wind which drove
the ships.

Because they were so tainted (by the spoiled civilization of Europe),
they wrecked their myth, or assisted in the wrecking, and left themselves stranded in the meaningless light of history. Or their behavior
can be described in terms that appeal less directly to the Romantic
ideal. Major de Spain, who owned the land in the Tallahatchie bottoms
and sold the logging rights and never visited his hunting camp again,
evidently held the common, often hopeless human view that change
is change and progress is progress, and to oppose either is at worst
fatal and at best artificial. (Grandparents of mine, I am told, who
homesteaded in a pocket of the frontier far from Mississippi, said long
afterward that their first years in the new land were the best of their
lives. But they worked as hard as their neighbors, apparently, to
change the conditions that made those years good.) The gross absurdity of man's, especially civilized man's, considering artificiality objectionable does not matter. When even Isaac had no impulse to own
land for the sake of keeping it wilderness, de Spain could not be
expected to keep the logging companies off his holdings forever.

Sam Fathers, as said, was taintless, and he had no reason to feel as
the white men felt; but he was old, and death calls to everyone finally.

The account of the pursuit of Old Ben with Lion is a splendid
hunting story, and a vivid account of the mythic death struggle. I
suggest that it should be read also in a simple symbolic sense in which
Lion stands for the mechanization, the applied science, which finally
caught the wilderness fatally by the throat. Lion's mechanical attributes
are not very heavily underscored, but of course they should not be.
For one thing, he was metallic in color — "almost the color of a gun
or pistol barrel." He was of super-canine size and strength, and without
ordinary canine feelings or for that matter ordinary canine individu-
ality; his eyes, when he collapsed from hunger in Sam's trap, "were
not fierce and there was nothing of petty malevolence in them, but a
cold and almost impersonal malignance like some natural force."
Similarly, when the dog was first trapped and smashing against the
door of the trap to get out, "It never made any sound and there was
nothing frenzied in the act but only a cold and grim indomitable

determination." Lion was an unnatural and unheard-of thing to turn up in the woods, just as mechanization was, and like that mechanization he possessed a complicated and hard-to-trace ancestry: "part mastiff, something of Airedale and something of a dozen other strains probably."

These quotations are not too compelling in themselves, and what Lion was — what he symbolized, rather; he *was* a big dog that got himself gutted while trying to kill a bear — is more strongly suggested by what happened after the campaign against Ben had been successful through his instrumentality. Within two years, the logging machines and their operations had become no joke. When Isaac, on his way to visit de Spain's camp for the last time, stopped at the formerly insignificant log-line junction, he

> looked about in shocked and grieved amazement even though he had had forewarning and had believed himself prepared: a new planing-mill already half completed which would cover two or three acres and what looked like miles and miles of stacked steel rails red with the light bright rust of newness and of piled crossties sharp with creosote, and wire corrals and feeding-troughs for two hundred mules at least and the tents for the men who drove them; so that he arranged for the care and stabling of his mare as rapidly as he could and did not look any more, mounted into the log-train caboose with his gun and climbed into the cupola and looked no more save toward the wall of wilderness ahead within which he would be able to hide himself from it once more anyway.

The doom of the wilderness was written plain; it would be killed by the tireless destructiveness of the machines as surely as Ben was by the tireless destructiveness of Lion, the failure of any particular machine stopping the process no more than the incidental death of the dog saved the bear.

(Two supporting illustrations of the basic inimicality between machines and living things might be mentioned in passing. The first is arbitrary and symbolic: when still very young, at the hunting camp during one of the summer trips that alternated with the real hunting trips, Isaac went far into the woods alone to find and look at Old Ben. At Sam Fathers' edict, he had left his gun behind; Sam said that the bear would not let himself be seen by a person carrying a gun. Finally he had to realize that, even gunless, he was still tainted by mechanisms. He hung his watch and compass on a bush and pushed on without them; and then he saw the bear. The second is a minor episode of the hunting trip narrated in "Delta Autumn," when a couple of

nervous horses had to be coaxed out of a truck and it fell to Isaac to
do the coaxing:

> It was himself, though no horseman, no farmer, not even a country-
> man save by his distant birth and boyhood, who coaxed and
> soothed the two horses, drawing them by his own single frail hand
> until, backing, filling, trembling a little, they surged, halted, then
> sprang scrambling down from the truck, possessing no affinity for
> them as creatures, beasts, but being merely insulated by his years
> and time from the corruption of steel and oiled moving parts which
> tainted the others.)

What it all amounted to was that, whether moved by old-world
corruption or helpless sense of the historical drift or death-wish or
what you will, in the last combat the hunters won too devastating a
victory. To kill Ben was proper enough; but the wilderness was
goddess and in terms of the myth immortal. Yet the machines
employed against it were too strong, and when it was destroyed, or
when it became apparent that it was vulnerable and faced extinction,
the old drama collapsed into recognized make-believe, incapable any
longer of making life significant. Naturally people still could and did
go hunting, but any sense of participating in equal and sanctioned
contest would have grown harder and harder to maintain. A discernible minority of hunters and fishermen today abide by the most
meticulous (and highly artificial) rules, far exceeding anything the
law requires; but I cannot help believing they do so out of a stubborn
and elevated sense of what ought to be rather than out of any sense
of congruence with the "reality" around them.

Besides Lion and the run-of-the-mill hounds, one other dog participated in the saga of Old Ben: Isaac's fyce, which, brought into the
woods on one of the summer trips and showed the bear, launched such
a fantastic attack that Isaac had to rescue him almost out of the bear's
jaws. Except in the items of mixed ancestry and courage beyond dis-
cretion, the fyce was about as opposite as possible from Lion, and he
has an opposite function in the story. He (and Isaac at the time of the
fyce-Ben incident) are described thus in the fourth section:

> a boy who wished to learn humility and pride in order to become
> skilful and worthy in the woods but found himself becoming so
> skilful so fast that he feared he would never become worthy because
> he had not learned humility and pride though he had tried, until
> one day an old man [Sam Fathers] who could not have defined

either led him as though by the hand to where an old bear and a
little mongrel dog showed him that, by possessing one thing other,
he would possess them both; and a little dog, nameless and mongrel
and many-fathered, grown yet weighing less than six pounds, who
couldn't be dangerous because there was nothing anywhere much
smaller, not fierce because that would have been called just noise,
not humble because it was already too near the ground to genuflect,
and not proud because it would not have been close enough for
anyone to discern what was casting that shadow and which didn't
even know it was not going to heaven since they had already
decided it had no immortal soul, so that all it could be was brave
even though they would probably call that too just noise.

Lion too was of indomitable courage but he represented too much
power and led to too overwhelming a victory; the lesson of the fyce
seems to be that it is necessary for a proper man (or dog) to be brave
and faithful to principle without regard for consequence even when
he has not power enough to save his behavior from seeming ridiculous;
it is the bravery and fidelity themselves which erase the ridiculousness.
Many of Faulkner's characters of all periods of his work, incidentally,
are moved by this principle without benefit of a fyce to teach it to them.

The episode at the end of section five, which shows an hysterical
Boon Hogganbeck pounding his dismantled gun under an isolated
gum tree full of equally hysterical squirrels, is comparatively obscure.
Boon was a moron, who had exercised a kind of merryman's function
toward the other hunters. From the time of the acquisition of Lion,
he devoted himself to the dog, taking more thought to Lion's welfare
than to his own; ". . . he had the mind of a child, the heart of a horse,
and little hard shoe-button eyes without depth or meanness or generosity or viciousness or gentleness or anything else . . ." The affinity
between man and dog is suggested by one description of Lion's eyes
in terms of Boon's: ". . . the yellow eyes as depthless as Boon's, as
free as Boon's of meanness or generosity or gentleness or viciousness."
After the fight in which Old Ben was killed, Boon took more immediate thought of Lion's injuries than of either Sam Fathers' collapse
or his own wounds. The suggestion of the final episode, I believe, is
something like this: the simple-minded follower, personally ineffective
(Boon could hit nothing even with a shotgun), can be given direction
and effectiveness only by devotion to an adequate principle or pattern
outside himself (with Lion, Boon pursued Old Ben more furiously
than any of the other hunters, and knifed the bear to death in the last
fight). Let the pattern, the self-perpetuating dramatic situation, fail

(the hunting myth failed with the death of Ben, and the principle Lion represented provided no substitute), throwing the simple-minded follower on his own resources, and he becomes pitiful or objectionable or both — a poor thing that gives no satisfaction. Boon, an acceptable and finally magnificent hanger-on of the party that hunted big game according to what they felt to be eternally sanctioned rules, was reduced when he had to travel under his own power to a squirrel hunter, and a marvellously inept one. It was he, the least intelligent of the party, who had given the most extreme allegiance to the very power that was to end by degrading him. Isaac was about eighteen when he witnessed the squirrel-tree episode; for a couple of years now he had been working on an adverse judgment of the historical reality of his world. Seeing Boon should have strengthened his condemnation of life not governed by, or not admitting, external moral sanctions.

It is not necessary for present purposes to write at any length about the material of the long fourth section of "The Bear," which presents Isaac's declination to go with his times and his reasons for it. It was basically in moral terms that he had understood and approved of the ruined myth-life, and it was in moral terms that he reacted to the results of Negro slavery in general and his own grandfather's part in it in particular. (He was the better prepared to do so, of course, by his devotion to Sam Fathers, part Chickasaw and part Negro.) What he said when, having gone to Arkansas to take a "legacy" to his young partly black cousin 'Fonsiba, he encountered the amazing fatuity of the partly black man who had married 'Fonsiba, illustrates his conclusions well enough:

> Dont you see? This whole land, the whole South, is cursed, and all of us who derive from it, whom it ever suckled, white and black both, lie under the curse? Granted that my people brought the curse onto the land: maybe for that reason their descendants alone can — not resist it, not combat it — maybe just endure and outlast it until the curse is lifted. Then your peoples' turn will come because we have forfeited ours. But not now. Not yet.

Isaac had little to say about the ordinary economic details and occupations of the historical world in which he found himself. An outburst from General Compson, though, delivered (toward the end of the third section) in the boy's behalf, is at least suggestive of how Isaac himself reacted to those details and occupation. After Ben's death, when the hunting party was preparing to go out, Isaac wanted to stay in the woods with Sam, whom he alone among the whites believed to be dying. McCaslin objected, on the practical grounds that Isaac had already missed enough school. Compson rebuked him:

> You've got one foot straddled into a farm and the other foot straddled into a bank; you aint even got a good hand-hold where this boy was already an old man long before you damned Sartorises and Edmondses invented farms and banks to keep youselves from having to find out what this boy was born knowing and fearing too maybe but without being afraid, that could go ten miles on a compass because he wanted to look at a bear none of us had ever got near enough to put a bullet in and looked at the bear and came the ten miles back on the compass in the dark; maybe by God that's the why and the wherefore of farms and banks.

Whatever the why and wherefore of farms and banks, to Isaac they were intrinsically foolish and based on a meretricious predicate. The earth, he thought, should be used by all and "owned" by none. When a man realized he owned it in the sense that he could sell it, then he ceased ever to have owned it in the sense of understanding and participating in its life. Having come to understanding of this as spiritual heir to Sam Fathers ("Sam Fathers set me free"), Isaac could only repudiate "ownership" of the farm McCaslin had held in trust for him — refuse to accept the terms of the historical life around him, hold true to the terms of the myth-life that had passed. To give up the farm was no shock, incidentally, to his natural inclinations, did not mean taking a radically new course. Witness the terms of a request Boon made to him once when the two were sent to Memphis for whiskey: " 'Lend me a dollar. Come on. You've got it. If you ever had one, you've still got it. I dont mean you are tight with your money because you aint. You just dont never seem to ever think of nothing you want.' " For a person whose character could be so analyzed when he was sixteen to turn in adulthood to earning a living as a carpenter need not be actively painful, even if it isn't actively pleasant either.

So far as anyone could tell, Isaac had a comparatively thin life of it from twenty-one on. He was not and did not try to be "understood," and apparently did not and did not try to exert any influence on his townsmen. When he appears last, an old man in "Delta Autumn," he is likeable and tolerable enough to his companions, but something of an odd old anachronism too. What had sustained him for fifty-odd years, a myth-king whom no one recognized, in a culture that he believed vain? Apart from the stimulus of periodic trips into the diminishing woods, apparently he lived on a belief in immortality — the immortality of his particular myth — supported, insofar as it was supported, by a version of the teleological argument. McCaslin states the argument most clearly, but other passages indicate that Isaac adopted McCaslin's belief or formed a similar one for himself. McCaslin's statement is made in "The Old People." Isaac is twelve. He has killed his first deer, and Sam Fathers has taken him to a certain place in the woods and showed him a great ghost-buck; the boy is over-wrought about it. The cousins sleep in the same bed that night and

> . . . suddenly he was telling McCaslin about it while McCaslin listened, quietly until he had finished. 'You dont believe it,' the boy said, 'I know you dont—'
> 'Why not?' McCaslin said. 'Think of all that has happened here, on this earth. All the blood hot and strong for living, pleasuring, that has soaked back into it. For grieving and suffering too, of course, but still getting something out of it for all that, getting a lot out of it, because after all you dont have to continue to bear what you believe is suffering; you can always choose to stop that, put an end to that. And even suffering and grieving is better than nothing; there is only one thing worse than not being alive, and that's shame. But you cant be alive forever, and you always wear out life long before you have exhausted the possibilities of living. And all that must be somewhere; all that could not have been in-vented and created just to be thrown away. And the earth is shallow; there is not a great deal of it before you come to the rock. And the earth dont want to just keep things, hoard them; it wants to use them again. Look at the seeds, the acorns, at what happens even to carrion when you try to bury it: it refuses too, seethes and struggles too until it reaches light and air again, hunting the sun still. And they —' the boy saw his hand in silhouette for a moment against the window beyond which, accustomed to the darkness now, he could see sky where the scoured and icy stars glistened '—they dont want it, need it. Besides, what would it want, itself, knocking around out there, when it never had enough time about the earth as it was, when there is plenty of room about the earth, plenty of places still unchanged from what they were when the blood used and pleasured in them while it was still blood?'
> 'But we want them,' the boy said. 'We want them too. There is plenty of room for us and them too.'
> 'That's right,' McCaslin said. 'Suppose they dont have substance, cant cast a shadow—'
> 'But I saw it!' the boy cried. 'I saw him!'
> 'Steady,' McCaslin said. For an instant his hand touched the boy's flank beneath the covers. 'Steady. I know you did. So did I. Sam took me in there once after I killed my first deer.'

And that, apparently, was enough. I find it hard to think of Isaac as one reborn, for rebirth implies taking up a new line of action different from one's old line. Isaac, on the other hand, held to his old line, refusing to assume the worldly responsibilities he had never had and never wanted. Having grown up with myth, and seen life take its meaning from myth, he succeeded if only by default to mythic kingship, in a world where his authority was not recognized, and his wilderness goddess-bride was fast pining into ghostliness. Nevertheless he did not abdicate, but waited — either in stoic satisfaction of his own categorical imperative or in some actual security of resuming his proper operations after bodily death. We are told little about the latter two-thirds of his life, but "Delta Autumn" shows him actually comfortable enough in his seventies:

> Because it was his land, although he had never owned a foot of it. He had never wanted to, not even after he saw plain its ultimate doom, watching it retreat year by year before the onslaught of axe and saw and log-lines and then dynamite and tractor plows, because it belonged to no man. It belonged to all; they had only to use it well, humbly and with pride. Then suddenly he knew why he had never wanted to own any of it, arrest at least that much of what people called progress, measure his longevity at least against that much of its ultimate fate. It was because there was just exactly enough of it. He seemed to see the two of them — himself and the wilderness — as coevals, his own span as a hunter, a woodsman, not contemporary with his first breath but transmitted to him, assumed by him gladly, humbly, with joy and pride, from that old Major de Spain and that old Sam Fathers who had taught him to hunt, the two spans running out together, not toward oblivion, nothing-ness, but into a dimension free of both time and space where once more the untreed land warped and wrung to mathematical squares of rank cotton for the frantic old-world people to turn into shells to shoot at one another, would find ample room for both — the names, the faces of the old men he had known and loved and for a little while outlived, moving again among the shades of tall unaxed trees and sightless brakes where the wild strong immortal game ran forever before the tireless belling immortal hounds, falling and rising phoenix-like to the soundless guns.

SHERMAN PAUL:

Resolution at Walden

I

Walden was published in 1854, eight years before Thoreau died, some seven years after his life in the woods. His journal shows that he had proposed such a "poem" for himself as early as 1841, that its argument would be "the River, the Woods, the Ponds, the Hills, the Fields, the Swamps and Meadows, the Streets and Buildings, and the Villagers. Then Morning, Noon, and Evening, Spring, Summer, Autumn, and Winter, Night, Indian Summer, and the Mountains in the Horizon." Like *A Week on the Concord and Merrimack Rivers* (1849) — "If one would reflect," Thoreau had written in 1837, "let him embark on some placid stream, and float with the current" — *Walden* took a long time maturing, a longer time, because it was more than the stream of his reflections. The *Week* had been written out of joyousness and to memorialize his most perfect excursion in nature. *Walden,* however, was Thoreau's recollected experience, recollected not in tranquillity, but in the years of what he himself called his "decay." Although one need only search the journals to find many of the events of *Walden* freshly put down, *Walden* itself reveals that Thoreau was now looking at these events with more experienced eyes: his long quarrel with society has intervened, his youthful inspiration had become more difficult to summon, the harvest of the *Week* he had hoped to bestow on the public lay in his attic, and, growing older, he was still without a vocation that others would recognize. In *Walden,* at once his victorious hymn to Nature, to her perpetual forces of life, inspiration and renewal, Thoreau defended his vocation by creating its eternal symbol.

The common moral of *Walden* is that of the virtue of simplicity; and simplicity is usually taken on the prudential level of economy with which Thoreau seemingly began the book. In terms of Thoreau's spiritual economy, however, simplicity was more than freedom from the burdens of a mortgaged life: it was an ascetic, a severe dicipline, like solitude for Emerson, by which Thoreau concentrated his forces and was able to confront the facts of life without the intervening barriers of society or possessions. For simplicity, Thoreau often sub-

429

stituted poverty, a word which both set him apart from his materialistic neighbors and hallowed his vocation with its religious associations of renunciation and higher dedication. It was the suitable condition for the spiritual crusader: the sign in a land of traders of his profession. But it also signified his inner condition. "By poverty," he said, "*i.e.* simplicity of life and fewness of incidents, I am solidified and crystallized, as a vapor or liquid by cold. It is a singular concentration of strength and energy and flavor. Chastity is perpetual acquaintance with the All. My diffuse and vaporous life becomes as frost leaves and spiculae radiant as gems on the weeds and stubble in a winter morning." Such poverty or purity was a necessity of *his* economy. "You think," he continued, "that I am impoverishing myself by withdrawing from men, but in my solitude I have woven for myself a silken web or *chrysalis,* and, nymph-like, shall ere long burst forth a more perfect creature, fitted for a higher society. By simplicity, commonly called poverty, my life is concentrated and so becomes organized, or a κόσμος, which before was inorganic and lumpish."

This was also the hope of his paean to spring in *Walden,* to "pass from the lumpish grub in the earth to the airy and fluttering butterfly." The purpose of his experiment at Walden Pond, begun near the end of his years of undisciplined rapture — Emerson said that the vital heat of the poet begins to ebb at thirty — was to build an organic life as consciously as he built his hut (and his book), and so retain his vital heat. "May I never," he had recorded in his journal, "let the vestal fire go out in my recesses." But there was desperation in his attempt to keep his vital heat, because it was only *vital* (or rather he felt it so) when he was maturing beyond the lumpish, grub-like existence. As well as the advocacy of the organic life which promised renewal and growth, *Walden* for Thoreau filled the immediate need of self-therapy. In the serenity and joy of his art this is often overlooked, but it is there in the journals behind the book. And the greatness of *Walden,* from this perspective at least, is the resolution Thoreau was able to fulfill through art. By creating an organic form he effected his own resolution for rebirth: by conscious endeavor he recaptured, if not the youthful ecstasy of his golden age, a mature serenity.

This serenity, however, is still alert, wakeful, tense. It was a victory of discipline. "That aim in life is highest," Thoreau noted during the composition of *Walden,* "which requires the highest and finest discipline." That aim was highest, that discipline the highest vocation, be-

cause the goal and fulfillment of all transcendental callings was purity
— a oneness with Nature in which the untarnished mirror of the soul
reflected the fullness of being. The cost of doing without conventional life was not too great for Thoreau, considering his desire to
"perceive things truly and simply." He believed that "a fatal coarseness
is the result of mixing in the trivial affairs of men." And to justify his
devotion to purity he wrote *Walden,* a promise of the higher society
a man can make when he finds his *natural* center, a record of things
and events so simple and fundamental that all lives less courageous
and principled are shamed by the *realometer* it provides. Like other
masterworks of its time, it has the unique strain of American romanticism: behind its insistent individualism and desire for experience,
there is still more earnest conviction of the necessity of virtue.

II

In the concluding pages of *Walden,* Thoreau remarked that "in
this part of the world it is considered a ground for complaint if a man's
writings admit of more than one interpretation." With his contemporaries, Emerson, Hawthorne, Melville, he wanted the "volatile
truth" of his words to "betray the inadequacy of the residual statement." He would have considered *Walden* a failure if it served only
to communicate an eccentric's refusal to go along with society, if,
taken literally, its spiritual courage was thinned to pap for tired
businessmen long since beyond the point of no return. For *Walden*
was *his* myth: "A fact truly and absolutely stated," he said, "is taken
out of the region of common sense and acquires a mythologic or universal significance." This was the extravagance he sought — this
going beyond the bounds. For him, only the fact stated without
reference to convention or institution, with only reference to the self
which has tasted the world and digested it, which has been "drenched"
and "saturated" with truth, is properly humanized — is properly
myth. Primarily to immerse himself in truth, to merge himself with
the law of Nature, and to humanize this experience by the alchemy
of language, Thoreau went to Walden. There, free from external
references, he could purify himself and live a sympathetic existence,
alive to the currents of being. What he reported, then, would be the
experience of the self in its unfolding and exploration of the "not-me."
The literal record would merely remain the residual statement — no
one knew better the need for concrete fact; but it would also yield a
translated meaning.

The whole of *Walden* is an experience of the microcosmic and cosmic travels of the self. At Walden Pond, Thoreau wrote, "I have, as it were, my own sun and moon and stars, and a little world all to myself." Thoreau, of course, was a great traveller, if only a saunterer. The profession of traveller appealed to his imagination; it was, he said, the "best symbol of our life." And "Walking" was the best short statement of his way of life, of his journey to the holy land. He yearned, he wrote in 1851, "for one of those old, meandering, dry, uninhabited roads, which lead away from towns. . . ." He wanted to find a place "where you can walk and think with least obstruction, there being nothing to measure progress by; where you can pace when your breast is full, and cherish your moodiness; where you are not in false relations with men. . . ." He wanted "a road where I can travel," where "I can walk, and recover the lost child that I am without any ringing of a bell." The road he wanted led to Walden. There he regained the primal world, and lived the pristine initiation into consciousness over again. "Both place and time were changed," he said in *Walden,* "and I dwelt nearer to those parts of the universe and to those eras in history which had most attracted me."

In this effort to live out of time and space or to live in all times and places, *Walden* immediately suggests Melville's *Moby-Dick.* Melville had written another voyage of the self on which he explored reality, charted the constituents of a chaos, and raised his discovery to the universal level of archetypal experience. He had elaborated the myth of the hunter which Thoreau also employed in the chapter on "Higher Laws." "There is a period in the history of the individual, as of the race," he wrote, "when hunters are the 'best men'. . . ." Hunting, he added, "is oftenest the young man's introduction to the forest [Melville's sea], and the most original part of himself. He goes thither at first as a hunter and fisher, until at last, if he has the seeds of a better life in him, he distinguishes his proper objects. . . ." It was in these "wild" employments of his youth that Thoreau acknowledged his "closest acquaintance with Nature." For Nature revealed herself to the hunter more readily than to "philosophers or poets even, who approach her with expectation" — or, as Melville knew, to the participant and not the observer of life. If Thoreau had long since given up hunting, he still found a sustaining link with the wild in his bean field.

There are obvious differences, of course, in the quality of these travels — each author had his spiritual torment, Melville the need for belief, Thoreau the need for recommunion. But both were projecting the drama of their selves, a drama that in both instances ended in rebirth; and the methods both employed were remarkably similar. Each abstracted himself from the conventional world, established a microcosm by which to test the conventions, and worked at a basic and heroic occupation. For example, the village stands in the same symbolic relation to Thoreau at Walden that the land does to Melville's sea; and it is the occupation in both that supplies the residual statement. In Thoreau's case, it is also a primitive concern with essentials: building his hut, planting, hoeing and harvesting his beans, fishing and naturalizing. And the nature of the occupation gives each its spiritual quality, because whaling (butchery) and colonizing (building from scratch) are projections of different visions of the universe of which only the central similarity remains — the exploration of self.

But this similarity is a sufficient signature for both; one recognizes the existential kinship. At the conclusion of *Walden* Thoreau declared: "Explore thyself . . . Be . . . the Mungo Park, the Lewis and Clark and Frobisher, of your own streams and oceans. . . ." —

> ". . . . . be
> Expert in home-cosmography "

For "there are continents and seas in the moral world to which every man is an isthmus or an inlet, yet unexplored by him, . . . [and] it is easier to sail many thousand miles through cold and storm and cannibals, in a government ship, with five hundred men and boys to assist one, than it is to explore the private sea, the Atlantic and Pacific Ocean of one's being alone." Melville at Pittsfield would have agreed that "herein are demanded the eye and the nerve." But if Melville needed the watery two-thirds of the world and the great whale for this quest, Thoreau, who had the gift of enlarging the small, needed only the pond and its pickerel. And where Melville needed the destructive forces of the sea to mirror himself, Thoreau, who had seen the place of violence in the total economy of nature, needed only the recurrence of the seasons.

III

Walden was Thoreau's quest for a reality he had lost, and for this reason it was a quest for purity. Purity meant a return to the spring (and springtime) of life, to the golden age of his youth and active senses, when the mirror of his self was not clouded by self-consciousness. *Walden,* accordingly, follows the cycle of developing consciousness, a cycle that parallels the change of the seasons. It is a recapitulation of Thoreau's development (and the artistic reason he put the experience of two years into one) — a development from the sensuous, active, external (unconscious *and* out-of-doors) summer of life, through the stages of autumnal consciousness and the withdrawal inward to the self-reflection of winter, to the promise of ecstatic rebirth in the spring. It was a matter of purification because Thoreau had reached the winter of decay at the time *Walden* was being revised for the press. With consciousness had come the knowledge of the "reptile" and "sensual" which he knew could not "be wholly expelled." "I fear," he wrote, "that it [the sensual] may enjoy a certain health of its own; that we may be well, yet not pure." For the mind's approach to God, he knew that the severest discipline was necessary: his chapter on "Higher Laws" is concerned almost entirely with the regimen of the appetites because "man flows at once to God when the channel of purity is open." The undeniable sensual energy — the "generative energy" — he had unconsciously enjoyed in the ecstasy of youth, now needed control. "The generative energy," he wrote, "which, when we are loose, dissipates and makes us unclean, when we are continent invigorates and inspires us." He was consciously using instinct for higher ends, seeking chastity by control.

In Walden Pond he saw the image of his purified self — that pristine, eternal self he hoped to possess. In 1853, while he was working on his book, he noted in his journal: "How watchful we must be to keep the crystal well that we were made, clear! — that it be not made turbid by our contact with the world, so that it will not reflect objects." The pond, he recalled, was one of the "oldest scenes stamped on my memory." He had been taken to see it when he was four years old. Now, playing his flute beside its waters, his beans, corn and potatoes replacing the damage of the years, he felt that another aspect was being prepared "for new infant eyes," that "even I have at length helped to clothe that fabulous landscape of my infant dreams. . . ." Later, he recalled his youthful reveries on its waters: "I have spent many an hour, when I was younger, floating over its surface as the zephyr willed . . . dreaming awake. . . ." But time (and woodchoppers) had ravished its shores: "My Muse may be excused," he explained, "if she is silent henceforth. How can you expect the birds to sing when their groves are cut down?" It was the confession of the Apollo who had had to serve Admetus, a confession he made again in "Walking." Visited by fewer thoughts each year, he said that "the grove in our minds is laid waste — sold to feed unnecessary fires of ambition. . . ."

But Thoreau discovered at Walden that even though the groves were cut down, the pond itself remained the same — it "best preserves its purity." "It is itself unchanged," he learns, "the same water my youthful eyes fell on; all the change is in me. . . . It is perennially young. . . ." Catching sight of his eternal self and realizing that the waste of years had only touched his shore, his empirical self, he exclaimed, "Why, here is Walden, the same woodland lake that I discovered so many years ago . . . it is the same liquid joy and happiness to itself and its Maker, ay, and it *may* be to me." The pond, so constant, clear and pure, was truly the *Walled in* pond, the undefiled soul of which the Thoreau-in-decay said, "I am its stony shore. . . ."

If Thoreau spent his youth drifting with the inspiring zephyrs on Walden's surface, he now plumbed its depths, angled for its pickerel and its bottom. For it was the purpose of *Walden* to find bottom, to affirm reality; and the reality Thoreau discovered in the soul and in the whole economy of Nature he found at the bottom of the pond. What renewed his faith was the sign of the never-dying, all-promising generative force which he symbolized when he wrote: ". . . a bright green weed is brought up on anchors even in midwinter." The hope of a renewed life, rhapsodized in the concluding chapters of *Walden* and there symbolized in the hardy blade of grass — the green flame of life —, was the assurance he now had that "there is nothing inorganic."

And by sounding the bottom Thoreau also discovered the law of the universe and of the intellect that made possible his organic participation in the process of renewal and provided him the guarantee of its expression in natural objects. "The regularity of the bottom and its conformity to the shores and the range of the neighboring hills were so perfect," he wrote, "that a distant promontory betrayed itself in the soundings quite across the pond, and its direction could be determined by observing the opposite shore." He found, too, that the intersection of the lines of greatest length and breadth coincided with the point of greatest depth; and he suggested that this physical law might be applied to ethics. "Draw lines through the length and breadth of the aggregate of a man's particular daily behaviors and waves of life into his coves and inlets, and where they intersect will be the height or depth of his character. Perhaps we need only to know how his shores tend and his adjacent country or circumstances, to infer his depth and concealed bottom." *Walden* was just such an account of

Thoreau's moral topography, and if the lines were drawn, the pond itself would be his center. For wasn't the eternal self, like the pond, " 'God's Drop' "?

The search for the bottom was conscious exploration. Here, and in the passages on fishing for pickerel and chasing the loon, Thoreau was not a naturalist but a natural historian of the intellect, using the natural facts as symbols for his quest for inspiration and thought. In "Brute Neighbors" he had asked, "Why do precisely these objects which we behold make a world?" And he had answered that "they are all beasts of burden . . . made to carry some portion of our thoughts." The natural world merely reflects ourselves. Having overcome his doubts of this central article of transcendental faith by assuring himself of the regularity of Walden's depth — that the hidden reality corresponded to its visible shores, that "Heaven is under our feet as well as over our heads" — he could trust once more his own projection of mood and thought to be reflected in its proper and corresponding object. He had noted in his journal that the poet "sees a flower or other object, and it is beautiful or affecting to him because it is a symbol of his thought, and what he indistinctly feels or perceives is matured in some other organization. The objects I behold correspond to my mood." His concern with the pond and the seasons, then, was symbolic of his soul's preoccupation. "Our moulting season . . . must be the crisis in our lives," he said; and like the loon he retired to a solitary pond to spend it. There, like the caterpillar — to use another symbol —, "by an internal industry and expansion" he cast off his "wormy coat."

IV

Thoreau went to Walden to become an unaccommodated man, to shed his lendings and to find his naked and sufficient self. Of this, the pond was the symbol. He also went to clothe himself in response to his inner needs. Building an organic life was again a conscious endeavor which was chastened by the necessity of maintaining his vital heat — the heat of body and spirit; for his purpose was not to return to nature, but to combine "the hardiness of . . . savages with the intellectualness of the civilized man." "The civilized man," he said, "is a more experienced and wiser savage," meaning, of course, that the instinctive life was most rewarding when channeled by intellectual principles. "What was *enthusiasm* in the young man," he wrote during the crisis of his life, "must become *temperament* in the mature man." The woodchopper, the animal man, must be educated to consciousness, and still retain his innocence. Properly seen in the total economy of Nature the once freely taken gift of inspiration must be earned by perceiving the law of Nature, by the tragic awareness that inspiration, like its source, has its seasons. The villagers, Thoreau wrote indignantly, "instead of going to the pond to bathe or drink, are thinking to bring its waters, which should be as sacred as the Ganges at least, to the village in a pipe, to wash their dishes with! — to earn their Walden by the turning of a cock or drawing of a plug!" The spiritual soldier had learned that after laying siege to Nature, only passivity would bring victory.

Thoreau earned his Walden by awaiting the return of spring, by sharing the organic process. Of this his hut and his bean-field became the symbols. The latter, as we have seen, helped to renew the aspect of the pond; as the work of the active self, it was rightly an alteration of the shore. And the pond, as the pure, eternal self — the "perfect forest mirror" —, was the calm surface on which these purifying activities were reflected. Thoreau labored in his bean-field because he took seriously Emerson's injunction to action in *The American Scholar*. He knew that the higher ends of the activity of the empirical self were self-consciousness, that the eternal self, the passive center, only acquired consciousness by observing the empirical self at work on the circumference. He recognized "a certain doubleness by which I can stand as remote from myself as from another." "However intense my experience," he wrote, "I am conscious of the presence of and criticism of a part of me, which, as it were, is not part of me, but spectator, sharing no experience, but taking note of it. . . ." The reward of activity, the result of this drama of selves, was self-reflection, insight. "All perception of truth is the detection of an analogy," Thoreau noted in the journal; "we reason from our hands to our head." And so through the labor of the hands, even to the point of drudgery, he was "determined to know beans." He did not need the beans for food but for sympathy with Nature; he needed to work them because, as he said, "They attached me to the earth, and so I got strength like Antaeus." His fields were also symbolic of his attempt to link the wild and the cultivated. And the "immeasurable crop" his devoted hoeing yielded came from the penetration of the earth's crust — a knowledge of the depths similar in significance to Melville's descent to the unwarped primal world. "I disturbed," Thoreau wrote, "the ashes of unchronicled nations who in primeval times lived under these heavens. . . ." In his bean-field beside Walden he was not serving Admetus, for he had found a way to delve beneath the "established order on the surface."

The prudential value of this labor came to $16.94, but the spiritual value was the realization that the Massachusetts soil could sustain the seeds of virtue — that in Thoreau's case at least, the seed had not lost its vitality and that the harvest of his example might be "a new generation of men." Later on, in the chapter on "Former Inhabitants," he again disturbed the surface by delving into the past, comparing his life at Walden to the defeated lives of its previous occupants. Here, Thoreau expressed his desire for the higher society, the ideal community in which he could wholly participate and which he hoped he was beginning. "Again, perhaps, Nature will try," he wrote, "with me for the first settler. . . . I am not aware that any man has ever built on the spot which I occupy." Like Joyce's Finnegan, he was to be the father of cities, not those reared on ancient sites, but cities growing out of the union with the earth. Looking back to Concord from the distances of past and future, Thoreau felt that *Walden* was not so much his quarrel with society, but an expiation. "Through our recovered innocence," he confessed, "we discern the innocence of our neighbors." He was willing to share his regeneration, for above the constant interplay of Walden and village, there hovered a vision of an ideal village that transcended both. In the radical sense of the word, Thoreau, who had given up the wilder pursuit of hunting for farming, was a civilizer.

When he came to build his hut — the container of his vital heat — Thoreau used second-hand materials and borrowed tools and showed his dependence on civilization. He did not abandon collective wisdom: his intention was to practice philosophy, to come directly at a conduct of life, that is, to simplify, or experience the solid satisfaction of knowing immediately the materials that made his life. He scrupulously accounts for these materials, he tells their history — where he got the boards, who used them and under what conditions. And James Collins' life in the shanty is implicitly contrasted with Thoreau's, especially in Thoreau's remark that he purified the boards by bleaching and warping them in the sun. He also acknowledged his debt for tools. He did not push his economy too far, to the verge of self-sufficiency that some believe necessary to a defense of *Walden* as social gospel. He said — and this is the only way of repaying one's social indebtedness — that he sharpened the tools by use. In a similar way, he applied the funded wisdom of man to his experiment on life. Individualist that he was, he often confirmed his experience by the experience of others: he made his use of the classics and scriptures, Indian lore and colonial history, pay their way. He was starting from scratch, but he knew that the materials were old.

The building of the hut is so thoroughly described because on the symbolic level it is the description of the building of the body for his soul. A generation that was read in Swedenborg might have been expected to see this correspondence. "It would be worth the while," Thoreau suggested, "to build still more deliberately than I did, considering, for instance, what foundation a door, a window, a cellar, a garret, have in the nature of man, and perchance never raising any superstructure until we found a better reason for it than our temporal necessities even." He was speaking the language of functionalism that Swedenborgianism had popularized; and after listing his previous shelters, he remarked that "this frame, so slightly clad, was a sort of crystallization around me, and reacted on the builder."

Thoreau built his hut as he needed it, to meet the progressing seasons of developing consciousness, a development which was as organic as the seasons. He subscribed to Emerson's use of the cycle of day and night as the symbol of the ebb and flow of inspiration and extended it to the seasons: "The day is an epitome of the year. The night is the winter, the morning and evenings are spring and fall, and the noon is the summer." In this way be also followed Emerson's "history" of consciousness. "The Greek," Emerson wrote, "was the age of observation; the Middle Age, that of fact and thought; ours, that of reflection and ideas." In *Walden,* Thoreau's development began in the summer, the season of the senses and of delicious out-of-door life. This was the period when he was in sympathetic communion with Nature, refreshed by the tonic of wildness. The chapters on "Sounds" and "Solitude" belong to this period, during which he enjoyed the atmospheric presence of Nature so essential to his inspiration. And the hut, which he began in the spring and first occupied at this time, was merely a frame through which Nature readily passed.

When the "north wind had already begun to cool the pond," Thoreau said that he first began to "inhabit my house." During the autumn season of harvest and preparation for winter, he lathed and plastered; and finally as winter approached he built his fireplace and chimney, "the most vital part of the house. . . ." By the fireside, in the period of reflection and inner life, he lingered most, communing with his self.* It was the time of soul-searching, when he cut through the pond's ice and saw that "its bright sanded floor [was] the same as in the summer"; and before the ice broke up he surveyed its bottom. Even in this desolate season Thoreau looked for all the signs of

---

* Hawthorne in "Peter Goldthwaite's Treasure" and Melville in "I and My Chimney" also made imaginative use of the house and the chimney.

spring's organic promise, and in the representative anecdote of his despair, he told of Nature's sustaining power: "After a still winter night I awoke with the impression that some question had been put to me, which I had been endeavoring in vain to answer in my sleep, as what — how — when— where? But there was dawning Nature, in whom all creatures live, looking in at my broad windows with serene and satisfied face, and no questions on *her* lips. I awoke to an answered question, to Nature and daylight." Even in the winter of his discontent, Nature seemed to him to say " 'Forward' " and he could calmly await the inevitable golden age of spring.

V

Rebirth came with spring. In one of the best sustained analogies in transcendental writing, the chapter "Spring," Thoreau reported ecstatically the translation of the frozen sand and clay of the railroad cut into the thawing streams of life. Looking at the sand foliage — the work of an hour — he said that "I am affected as if . . . I stood in the laboratory of the Artist who made the world and me. . . ." The Artist of the world, like Thoreau and like Goethe whom he had in mind, labored "with the idea inwardly" and its correspondence, its flowering, was the leaf. Everywhere Thoreau perceived this symbol of creation, and in ascending forms from the sand, the animal body, the feathers and wings of birds, to the "airy" butterfly. "Thus it seemed," he wrote, "that this one hillside illustrated the principle of all the operations of Nature. The Maker of this earth but patented a leaf." And the moral Thoreau drew from this illustration was the central law of his life, for it was the law of renewal: "This earth is not a mere fragment of dead history, stratum upon stratum like the leaves of a book, to be studied by geologists and antiquarians chiefly, but living poetry like the leaves of a tree, which precede flowers and fruit, — not a fossil earth, but a living earth; compared with whose great central life all animal and vegetable life is merely parasitic. Its throes will heave our exuviae from their graves." And furthermore the law applied to man and the higher society: ". . . the institutions upon it [the earth] are plastic like clay in the hands of the potter."

For Thoreau, who had found that the law of his life was the law of Life, these perceptions were the stuff of ecstasy. Reveling in the sound of the first sparrow, Thoreau wrote, "What at such a time are histories, chronologies, traditions, and all written revelations?" The spring had brought forth "the symbol of perpetual youth," the grass-blade; human life, having died down to its root, now put forth "its green blade to eternity." Walden Pond had begun to melt — "Walden was dead and is alive again." The change in the flowing sand, from excremental to spiritual, had also been accomplished in him by the discipline of purity: "The change from storm and winter to serene and mild weather, from dark and sluggish hours to bright and elastic ones." Like the dawning of inspiration this "memorable crisis" was "seemingly instantaneous at last." "Suddenly," Thoreau recorded that change, "an influx of light filled my house, though evening was at hand, and the clouds of winter still overhung it, and the eaves were dripping with sleety rain. I looked out of the window, and lo! where yesterday was cold grey ice there lay the transparent pond already calm and full of hope as in a summer evening, reflecting a summer evening sky in its bosom, though none was visible overhead, as if it had intelligence with some remote horizon. I heard a robin in the distance, the first I had heard for many a thousand years, methought, whose note I shall not forget for many a thousand more, — the same sweet and powerful song as of yore. . . . So I came in, and shut the door, and passed my first spring night in the woods."

With the coming of spring had come "the creation of Cosmos out of Chaos and the realization of the Golden Age." And with his renewal had come the vindication of his life of purity. He had recorded what he felt was nowhere recorded, "a simple and irrepressible satisfaction with the gift of life. . . ." He had suggested what the eye of the partridge symbolized to him, not merely "the purity of infancy, but a wisdom clarified by experience." He had recounted the experience of his purification so well that even the reader who accepts only the residual statement feels purified. "I do not say," he wisely wrote at the end of *Walden,* "that John or Jonathan will realize all this [the perfect summer life]; but such is the character of that morrow which mere lapse of time can never make to dawn." To affirm this eternal present, to restore, as he said in "The Service," the original of which Nature is the reflection, he fashioned *Walden* as he himself lived, after the example of the artist of the city of Kouroo. This parable unlocks the largest meaning of the book. The artist of Kouroo "was disposed to strive after perfection," Thoreau wrote; and striving, he lived in the eternity of inspiration which made the passing of dynasties, even eras, an illusion. In fashioning his staff, merely by minding his destiny and his art, he had made a new world "with full and fair proportions." The result, Thoreau knew, could not be "other than wonderful," because "the material was pure, and his art was pure. . . ."

JOHN CROWE RANSOM:

Eliot and the Metaphysicals

The most famous and valuable of T. S. Eliot's essays, and probably at the same time the most difficult of them all, is "The Metaphysical Poets," written in 1921 in review of Grierson's new anthology of metaphysical verse. This school of poetry is either very brilliant or else very pretentious; a critical talent is heavily tried to say which, and then to say why. The critical observations which Eliot makes in this essay are quoted more than any others of his, or so at least in my own critical circles. Its public effect has been to have just about upset the old comparative valuations of the great cycles of English poetic history: reducing the nineteenth century greatly and the Restoration and eighteenth century a little less, elevating the sixteenth and early seventeenth centuries to supreme importance as the locus of the poetic tradition operating at its full. Yet there is difficulty in following Eliot's argument precisely; and it does not contain much real analysis of metaphysical poetry proper.

Eliot considers the usual way of defining metaphysical poetry in terms of its conceits, or metaphors, but rejects it; the historical body of this poetry is too various to admit so simple an explanation. Page 241 (of the *Selected Essays*):

> Not only is it difficult to define metaphysical poetry, but difficult to decide what poets practice it, and in which of their verses. The poetry of Donne (to whom Marvell and Bishop King are sometimes nearer than any of the other authors) is late Elizabethan, its feeling often very close to that of Chapman. The "courtly" poetry is derivative from Jonson, who borrowed liberally from the Latin; it expires in the next century with the sentiment and witticism of Prior. There is finally the devotional verse of Herbert, Vaughan, and Crashaw (echoed long after by Christina Rossetti and Francis Thompson); Crashaw, sometimes more profound and less sectarian than the others, has a quality which returns through the Elizabethan period to the early Italians. It is difficult to find any precise use of metaphor, simile, or other conceit, which is common to all the poets and at the same time important enough as an element of style to isolate these poets as a group. Donne, and often Cowley, employ a device which is sometimes considered characteristically "metaphysical"; the elaboration (contrasted with the condensation) of a figure of speech to the farthest stage to which ingenuity can

carry it. Thus Cowley develops the commonplace comparison of the world to a chessboard through long stanzas (*To Destiny*), and Donne, with more grace, in *A Valediction,* the comparison of two lovers to a pair of compasses.

But generally there are complications. He cites an example from Donne of the "telescoping" of images, or the passing from one metaphor into a second which depends on it, a procedure that cannot possibly be the same as the farthest possible elaboration of the one metaphor. He quotes Johnson's unfavorable saying (based chiefly on Cleveland and Cowley) that in metaphysical poetry "the most heterogeneous ideas are yoked by violence together." But a degree of heterogeneity of material is always present in poetry (though uncommonly in prose), and Eliot can cite Johnson's own verse to this effect. And if the "violence" that Johnson objected to refers to some outrageous forcing of the sense, Eliot can say that

> in one of the finest poems of the age (a poem which could not have been written in any other age), the *Exequy* of Bishop King, the extended comparison is used with perfect success: the idea and the simile become one, in the passage in which the Bishop illustrates his impatience to see his dead wife, under the figure of a journey:
>
>> Stay for me there; I will not faile
>> To meet thee in that hollow Vale.
>> And think not much of my delay;
>> I am already on my way,
>> And follow thee with all the speed
>> Desire can make, or sorrows breed.
>> Each minute is a short degree,
>> And ev'ry houre a step towards thee.
>> At night when I betake to rest,
>> Next morn I rise nearer my West
>> Of life, almost by eight hours sail,
>> Than when sleep breath'd his drowsy gale . . .
>> But heark! My Pulse, like a soft Drum
>> Beats my approach, tells Thee I come;
>> And slow howere my marches be,
>> I shall at last sit down by Thee.

That is the only full-bodied and extended passage of metaphysical poetry that Eliot quotes. And presently he is saying that the language of the metaphysical poets is usually "simple and pure"; but that the grammatical *structure* (his italics) may be "far from simple."

Eliot then proceeds to his own thesis. Metaphysical poetry cannot be defined as some tricky habit of metaphor. It should be defined as a very various poetry of the seventeenth century which was "the direct and normal development of the precedent age." That would make it a highly inclusive poetry. But Eliot spends almost the rest of the essay on a very wide speculation as to how this class of poetry differs from later poetry, with regret that its virtue was allowed to lapse. The virtue which lapsed was not something peculiar to Donne and other metaphysical poets, but something entirely common in poets of Donne's time and even before him:

> It is certain that the dramatic verse of the later Elizabethan and early Jacobean poets expresses a degree of development of sensibility which is not found in any of the prose, good as it often is. If we except Marlowe, a man of prodigious intelligence, these dramatists were directly or indirectly (it is at least a tenable theory) affected by Montaigne. Even if we except also Jonson and Chapman, these two were notably erudite, and were notably men who incorporated their erudition into their sensibility: their mode of feeling was directly and freshly altered by their reading and thought. In Chapman especially there is a direct sensuous apprehension of thought, or a recreation of thought into feeling, which is exactly what we find in Donne:

> > in this one thing, all the discipline
> > Of manners and of manhood is contained;
> > A man to join himself with th' Universe
> > In his main sway, and make in all things fit
> > One with that All, and go on, round as it;
> > Not plucking from the whole his wretched part,
> > And into straits, or into nought revert,
> > Wishing the complete Universe might be
> > Subject to such a rag of it as he;
> > But to consider great Necessity.

> We compare this with some modern passage:

> > No, when the fight begins within himself,
> > A man's worth something. God stoops o'er his head,
> > Satan looks up between his feet—both tug—
> > He's left, himself, i' the middle; the soul wakes
> > And grows. Prolong that battle through his life!

I skip a passage in which the antithesis between the old and the modern is illustrated by another pairing, Lord Herbert and Tennyson, and resume:

> The difference is not a simple difference of degree between poets. It is something which had happened to the mind of England be-

tween the time of Donne or Lord Herbert of Cherbury and the time of Tennyson and Browning; it is the difference between the intellectual poet and the reflective poet. Tennyson and Browning are poets, and they think; but they do not feel their thought as immediately as the odour of a rose. A thought to Donne was an experience; it modified his sensibility. When a poet's mind is perfectly equipped for its work, it is constantly amalgamating disparate experience; the ordinary man's experience is chaotic, irregular, fragmentary. The latter falls in love, or reads Spinoza, and these two experiences have nothing to do with each other, or with the noise of the typewriter or the smell of cooking; in the mind of the poet these experiences are always forming new wholes.

We may express the difference by the following theory: The poets of the seventeenth century, the successors of the dramatists of the sixteenth, possessed a mechanism of sensibility which could devour any kind of experience. They are simple, artificial, difficult, or fantastic, as their predecessors were; no less nor more than Dante, Guido Cavalcanti, Guinizelli, or Cino. In the seventeenth century a dissociation set in, from which we have never recovered; and this dissociation, as is natural, was aggravated by the influence of the two most powerful poets of the century, Milton and Dryden. Each of these men performed certain poetic functions so magnificently well that the magnitude of the effect concealed the absence of others. The language went on and in some respects improved; the best verse of Collins, Gray, Johnson, and even Goldsmith satisfies some of our fastidious demands better than that of Donne or Marvell or King. But while the language became more refined, the feeling became more crude. The feeling, the sensibility, expressed in the *Country Churchyard* (to say nothing of Tennyson and Browning) is cruder than that in the *Coy Mistress*.

The second effect of the influence of Milton and Dryden followed from the first, and was therefore slow in manifestation. The sentimental age began early in the eighteenth century, and continued. The poets revolted against the ratiocinative, the descriptive; they thought and felt by fits, unbalanced; they reflected. In one or two passages of Shelley's *Triumph of Life*, in the second *Hyperion*, there are traces of a struggle towards unification of sensibility. But Keats and Shelley died, and Tennyson and Browning ruminated.

It is a brief exposition, worth far more attention than we shall have time for. With the fall of the metaphysical poets the direct line of tradition was broken; it happened rather suddenly. The metaphysical poets were the last in the old line, but the first we meet as we go back; therefore they tend to look more odd to us. Eliot argues that if the tradition had been carried on, they would not have come to look odd, and would not even have been specially designated as "metaphysical" poets. For they were, at best, engaged in the task of trying to find the verbal equivalent for states of mind and feeling. And this means both that they are more mature, and that they wear better, than later poets of certainly not less literary ability.

This is about the sum of Eliot's remarks. Now feeling is distinguished by the critic from thought; but Eliot seems to say that the older poets did not make this distinction, and were superior to the modern poets in being able to do without it. Modern poets think awhile, and then decide to work in some feelings; but they should be able to assimilate thinking into feeling, as once the poets did. Lamenting the modern dualism of thought and feeling, Eliot thinks he finds it bridged in the older order of English poetry, though the technique by which it was accomplished was let go and has never been rediscovered.

I confess that I know very little about that; and I must add that, having worked to the best of my ability to find the thing Eliot refers to in the seventeenth century poets, and failed, I incline to think there was nothing of the kind there. I have often tried—as what critic has not—to find some description of poetry which would regard it as a single unified experience, and exempt it from the dilemma of logic; but we must not like some philosophers become the fools of some shining but impractical ideal of "unity" or of "fusion." The aspiration here is for some sort of fusion of two experiences which ordinarily repel one another: the abstracted exercise in hard fact and calculation; and the inclusive experience of literally everything at once. But we cannot have our theory magical and intelligible at the same time. For it would seem that from that precise moment when the race discovers that what has seemed to be an undifferentiated unity is really a complex of specialized functions, there can be no undifferentiated unity again; no return. We do not quite know how to feel a thought. The best we can do is to conduct a thought without denying all the innocent or irrelevant feelings in the process. The dualism remains. But a poem is an experience in time; and after we have had it once we can have it again, and better, by reading the poem a second time. We think through the poem at more leisure this time, and leisurely or even sprawling thinking, thinking that is in something less than entire bondage to the animal or scientific will, is the only poetic formula that I, at any rate, can find.

Such a formula indicates that we can realize the *structure,* which is the logical thought, without sacrificing the *texture,* which is the free detail—or, if anybody insists, which is the feelings that engage with the free detail. For, again, Eliot's talk is psychologistic, or affective, but we may easily translate it into objective or cognitive terms. We recall his big emotion as attaching to the main thought, and translate that simply as the logical structure of the poem; then we recall the little feelings attaching to the play of the words, and translate them as its local texture. "Sensibility," the term which Eliot has presented to the new critics, is the organ which excretes the feelings, as he would say, or the detailed perceptions, as we would say. But I think we must waive the psychological magic involved in the act of feeling our thought in honor of something much tamer and more credible: the procedure of suspending the course of the main thought while we explore the private character of the detail-items. We stop following the main thought, and take off in a different direction, as we follow the private history of an item; then we come back to the main thought.

That may be only a formula which will do for most poems. And what is different and new about a metaphysical poem? Most of the new critics still prefer to take metaphysical as describing a poetical effect which is not in Chapman and the Elizabethan dramatists unless very slightly; nor in the French Symbolists, of whom Eliot in his essay takes a notice I have not mentioned; and consists apparently in the structural device of making the whole poem, or some whole passage of it, out of the single unit metaphor. There are many such poems in Donne and other poets, and they seem distinct enough structurally from other poems. Henry King's poem is the example Eliot cites.

I should not regard Chapman's passage about the Universe as "metaphysical"; nor deny on the other hand that it is very fine poetry and does not have to be metaphysical. It has an explicit thought-structure, even attended by an explicit moral valuation; it would not be entirely ineligible for the discourse of a modern Hegelian, like Josiah Royce. It is what we should call "reflective" or philosophical verse. But it is not without a local texture, which gets in very cunningly though without recourse to magic; it is slight and unobtrusive but positive and sharp; it is perhaps most visible in the phonetic quality contributed to the object everywhere by the excellent metric. But beyond that, it is in a few local items such as a man's *main sway*, the idea of his going on with the Universe in the *round*, the witty aside which corrects *into straits* to *into nought*, and the calling of the man a *rag* of the Universe. This is not what we think of as metaphysical poetry, and it is not for being metaphysical that we prefer it to Browning's passage, which is entirely comparable. Browning's structure consists in saying: "When a man's fight begins within himself, his soul wakes and grows." It too is explicitly stated. The principal piece of texture is in the parenthetic remark—a violent interpolation—which stops to give a sort of rough-neck picture of the man's fight within himself: it is a tugging match between God and Satan. Eliot may very well talk about the modern crudeness of Browning's "feeling," though he could talk as easily about the crudeness of Browning's imagination or perception.

And now for Bishop King's poem. The passage here is one long unitary metaphor. Its fact-structure or thought-structure is not given away (it is almost given away once, inadvertently); we have to infer it from the metaphor. The language is simple and logical enough; if we could remove sleep's drowsy gale and the military-voyage business about the drum, the language might be said not to have a texture. (In some of Herbert's metaphysical poems, Eliot says, the language is perfectly plain; it has no texture.) In that case we seem to have a metaphysical poem without either a visible structure or a local texture. But the structure which we require for an understanding of the poem is not hard to supply. His wife has died, and what he says to her in the poem is in lieu of something like this: "You are in Heaven, and I am eager to join you. I think of each passing minute and hour as bringing me that much nearer, and I wake each morning thinking I have traveled by eight hours nearer. Can you not hear my pulse, ticking away the moments which separate us?" (The pulse initiates a showy local metaphor within the grand metaphor, so that I feel that a corresponding metaphor might be read back into the factual original; the pulse might become the Bishop's watch, if it is not an anachronism.) But all that, however accurately we imagine we render it, has disappeared—if it ever existed—or has been "assimilated" into the image of an impatient seventeenth century explorer-traveler, following across land and sea a lady who has made an incomprehensible journey to an ocean paradise in the West; a very secular transformation.

We think normally of metaphor as developing from a detail of the poem and making an item of local texture, centrifugal or tangential with respect to the central structure; "importing" something foreign into it, as Richards has it. But King's poem without its metaphor would have no structure, and no being. Mr. Cleanth Brooks has written about the importance of such "functional" metaphors: they are all "vehicle," to quote Richards again, with no specified tenor. (Thus, in

"O, my luve is like a red, red rose," the poet's lady-love is tenor, the rose is the vehicle; but in "O, I will ask my red, red rose," no lady, no tenor, is apparent—only the vehicle, which we must translate into a tenor.) Little functional metaphors are common, I believe, as when Hamlet speaks of his "sea" of troubles. The metaphysical conceit is a variety of the functional metaphor when its central structure, and not merely a casual detail, has no explicit tenor or fact-structure but only a "vehicle" covering it. Is this sort of metaphor to be considered structure or texture? The answer would be that, to whatever degree, it must serve both purposes. It must be transparent enough to reveal its unstated tenor, and that tenor will have to be an experience rather generalized and of little distinctness, such as love, death, valediction, or conventional religious experience. But in addition to having this structural purpose, the metaphor commonly, though not necessarily, includes details which claim an energetic character of their own, which are foreign to the tenor and must therefore be called texture.

The consequence is that the tenor of a metaphysical poem is conventional and generalized and that its texture is thick and odd. The texture can easily be grotesque and raise considerations of propriety. The tenor is forced into a tight-fitting, barely feasible form; in being particularized, it is distorted. In Bishop King's poem the drum image comes out of the exuberance with which he plays the game of the traveler, but it may seem jaunty for the actual occasion, or even wrenched. Where in the old Bishop is the actual pulse-aspect which is like this Admiral Drake's drum?

The example of metaphysical poetry most commonly mentioned (by Johnson, by Eliot, by everybody) is the passage from Donne's "Valediction" about the compasses. The poet is leaving his mistress but their souls are still joined:

> If they be two, they are two so
> As stiff twin compasses are two;
> Thy soul, the fixed foot, makes no show
> To move, but doth if the other do.

> And though it in the center sit,
> Yet when the other far doth roam,
> It leans, and hearkens after it,
> And grows erect as that comes home.

> Such wilt thou be to me, who must,
> Like the other foot, obliquely run;
> Thy firmness makes my circle just
> And makes me end where I begun.

The compasses as a mathematical instrument may be for Donne's age a symbol of great Necessity, and the activities they throw back upon the lovers' souls identified with them may be dignified, but they are awkward. He must run obliquely, in a circle, instead of going straight to his errand and dispatching it; she must lean towards him most when he is most distant, and grow erect instead of running to meet him as he returns. And after his return, what activity remains for this pair? These are strange little patterns of behavior for lovers, but the all-vehicle metaphor insists upon them, allows no others; it particularizes the lovers, and tries to endear them to us by making them slightly—in spite of the compasses—eccentric. The Restoration and the eighteenth century felt that such poetic representations were irresponsible though interesting. We today are grown again more susceptible to their brilliance as sharply-textured representations. They offer us an art which has a very formal code of composition, but in it the texture dominates the structure and all but threatens its life.

The formula of the metaphysical conceit is evidently close to that of satire: where the general behavior of the victim is so particularized, or identified with some well-known analogous behavior so exclusively, as to become ridiculous. And that fact is fair index to the peril that metaphysical poetry is in.

We must concede the sharp texture. And it gives confidence in this manner of reasoning to reflect that Donne, and such poets as use the metaphysical conceit, are gifted with a passion for the sharp texture—always, and in common figures as well as in metaphysical ones. Donne has many poems ordinary enough in their principle of structure, not in the metaphysical method, which still in the vigor of their detail differentiate him from the nineteenth century, and from Chapman too. There is, for example, "On His Mistress," the one in which he forbids his secret bride to attend him abroad in the disguise of a page. For men will spy out her womanhood:

> Men of France, changeable Camelions,
> Spittles of diseases, shops of fashions,
> Loves fuellers, and the rightest company
> Of Players, which upon the worlds stage be,
> Will quickly know thee, and no lesse, alas,
>
> Th' indifferent Italian, as we passe
> His warme land, well content to thinke thee Page,
> Will hunt thee with such lust, and hideous rage,
> As *Lots* fair guests were vext. But none of these

> Nor spungy hydroptique Dutch shall thee displease,
> If thou stay here.

Spittles, of course, are hospitals; as we might say, walking hospitals. The passage has rhetorical generalizations in it; it is almost Miltonic, but inserts the spungy hydroptique Dutch carefully as an afterthought, not as a member of the co-ordinate series as Milton would have had it. And altogether it has sharper details than Milton fancies. The poem concludes:

> Nor let thy lookes our long hid love confesse,
> Nor praise, nor dispraise me, nor blesse nor curse
> Openly loves force, nor in bed fright thy Nurse
> With midnights startings, cry out, oh, oh
> Nurse, o my love is slaine, I saw him goe
> Oer the white Alpes alone; I saw him I,
> Assail'd, fight, taken, stabb'd, bleed, fall, and die.
> Augure me better chance, except dread *Jove*
> Thinke it enough for me to have had thy love.

The detail in the dream is not metaphorical at all; but at least it is imaginative. We say such detail is fresh, sharp, energetic, and lively or vivid; but surely one term is better than another for the critic. In ontological language we might say that Donne enforces the particularity of his object. In our present terms we say that his texture is unusually distinct; that is, it distinguishes itself more than usually from the train of the prose structure.

Eliot might contend that Donne in this last poem "feels" the thought of leaving his mistress at home, to be safe, to be discreet. That way of language is Eliot's most extravagant piece of philosophizing. But in his more usual terms he would be content to say that there is naturally a leading "emotion" attaching to the given thought, and that in developing it the poet uses language which causes the play of a great many little "feelings" also.

And now if Eliot cared to go back and analyze what happens in the King passage about the journey and the Donne passage about compasses, he would doubtless say that the poet does not openly have the emotion of his actual situation, since he does not explicitly think it, but only has it somewhere in the back of his head—since he has instead a more luxuriant emotion, which attaches to another and co-ordinate thought. But that would be an unhappy locution, and worse than mine.

MARK SPILKA:

Was D. H. Lawrence a Symbolist?

In recent studies on D. H. Lawrence, two veteran critics have tried to align him with the *correspondance* tradition established by Baudelaire.[1] They have called him a symbolist out of the reasonable belief that *symbolisme* means the use of private images to suggest or evoke the ineffable. But the question soon arises—which ineffable? There happen to be two, at least in philosophical and religious circles, and Lawrence himself was always conscious of the fact. Thus, in *Twilight in Italy* he speaks of the twofold Infinite: "the Father and the Son, the Dark and the Light, the Senses and the Mind, the Soul and the Spirit, the self and the not-self. . . . The consummation of man is twofold, in the Self and in Selflessness. . . . And man must know both." Now *symbolisme* implies a wholly different metaphysic than this, since most or perhaps all of its adherents are searching for the spiritual infinite. It seems wrong, therefore, to speak too readily about Lawrence, the symbolist, or even to be led astray by the suggestive nature of his language, or by the use in his novels of dominant symbols like the *symbole littéraire*. As Mark Schorer has pointed out, Lawrence is essentially a ritualist; his symbols function through the larger pattern of the ritual, and, as I hope to show in this essay, they also function at a different level of language, and for different ends, than the *symbole littéraire*.

To grasp the problem clearly, we must turn, for a moment, to an extremely pertinent theory of language, myth, and religion put forth by Ernst Cassirer. As the German philosopher explains it:

> Language moves in the middle kingdom between the 'indefinite' and the 'infinite'; it transforms the indeterminate into a determinate idea, and then holds it within the sphere of finite determinations. So there are, in the realm of mythic and religious conception, 'ineffables' of different order, one of which represents the lower limit of verbal expression, the other the upper limit; but between these bounds, which are drawn by the very nature of verbal expression, language can move with perfect freedom, and exhibit all the wealth and concrete exemplification of its creative power.

For Cassirer, then, the religious symbol operates at the upper level of language; in metaphorical terms, it reaches out, encircles some aery corner of the spiritual infinite, then pulls it down within the middle kingdom and holds it there within its determinate form. And the *symbole littéraire* (or the pure poem itself, as conceived by Mallarmé) performs essentially the same function. But at the lower level of language the problem is altogether different. Speaking again in metaphorical terms, when the mythic symbol reaches out, it encounters *mana*,[2] that vague, mysterious, holy power which pops up out of a mythical field of force and appears now here, now there, in any guise, in front of primitive man. Unlike the spiritual infinite, which is static, absolute and eternal, *mana* is a highly relative and kinetic force which occurs in time. Hence the mythic symbol can only focus our attention, at best, upon the ebb and flow of this relative force, while the religious symbol, or the *symbole littéraire,* can theoretically hold or fix the spiritual infinite within a timeless moment. And neither symbol can perform the other's function.

In the light of these arguments, the distance between Lawrence and the symbolists becomes enormous: for Baudelaire and his followers, Nature was a mere "forest of symbols," an outward front for the spiritual infinite; but Lawrence found the force of life itself in Nature, and he made a close connection between that force and the *mana* concept. He utilized that concept, for example, in novels like *The Rainbow* and *Women in Love,* where the moon sometimes becomes a sudden "presence" to his protagonists; and he wrote about it directly in *Apocalypse,* where he deals specifically with the old Greek version of *mana,* the *theos* concept:

> To the ancient consciousness . . . the universe was a great complex activity of things existing and moving and having effect. . . . Everything was *theos;* but even so, not at the same moment. At the moment, whatever struck you was god. If it was a pool of water, the very watery pool might strike you: then that was god; or a faint vapour at evening rising might catch the imagination: then that was *theos;* or thirst might overcome you at the sight of the water: then the thirst itself was god; or you drank, and the delicious and indescribable slaking of thirst was the god; or you felt the sudden chill of the water as you touched it: and then another god came into being, "the cold": and this was not a quality, it was an existing entity, almost a creature, certainly a *theos.*

The difficulty which Lawrence has in describing *theos* is not his own: for primitive man, *theos* (or *mana*) was too vague and impermanent for precise description; hence he used the term as noun, verb, adjective, or adverb with equal readiness. This helps to account, incidentally, for much of the well-known "carelessness" in Lawrence's writing. The symbolists can afford to be precise in their poems: their version of the infinite is fixed and static, waiting for the proper language to encase it. But *mana* demands a much more volatile medium, not to encase it, but simply to keep pace with it and to keep it in focus. So it seems unfair to isolate a nebulous passage by Lawrence, as some critics have done, and to compare it unfavorably with a more precise example of symbolist art. For the truth is that Lawrence actually fused the *mana* concept with this own particular view of "quickness" in both life and language. We see this, unmistakably, in a passage from an essay called "The Novel":

> We have to choose between the quick and the dead. The quick is God-flame, in everything. And the dead is dead. In this room where I write, there is a little table that is dead: it doesn't even weakly exist. And there is a ridiculous little iron stove, which for some unknown reason is quick. And there is an iron wardrobe trunk, which for some still more mysterious reason is quick. And there are several books, whose mere corpus is dead, utterly dead and non-existent. And there is a sleeping cat, very quick. And a glass lamp, that, alas, is dead.
>
> What makes the difference? *Quién sabe?* But difference there is. And I *know* it.
>
> And the sum and source of all quickness, we will call God. And the sum and total of all deadness we may call human.
>
> And if one tries to find out wherein the quickness of the quick lies, it is in a certain weird relationship between that which is quick and—I don't know; perhaps all the rest of things. It seems to consist in an odd sort of fluid, changing, grotesque, or beautiful relatedness. That silly iron stove somehow *belongs*. Whereas this thin-shanked table doesn't belong. It is a mere disconnected lump, like a cut-off finger.
>
> And now we see the great, great merits of the novel. It can't exist without being "quick." . . . For the relatedness and interrelatedness of all things flows and changes and trembles like a stream, and like fish in the stream the characters in the novel swim and drift and float and turn belly-up when they're dead.

All this is close, in a modified and intelligent way, to the *mana* concept; and we might even note, in passing, the equally close connection Lawrence makes between life and the novel, in terms of organic flow. But for the moment the important points to stress are these: (1) that Lawrence had found corroboration for his independent sense of the quickness, the interrelatedness of all things, by reading the anthropologists—not Baudelaire; and (2) that he seems to have borrowed the holiness and perhaps the volatility of *mana* and merged this with his own concept of the life-flame, to arrive—not at synaesthesia—but at the God-stuff, or the life-force, which flows through all "live" objects and binds man to the living universe. We can see this force at work, very clearly, in a lengthy excerpt from the opening pages of *The Rainbow:*

> So the Brangwens came and went without fear of necessity, working hard because of the life that was in them, not for want of the money. . . . They felt the rush of the sap in spring, they knew the wave which cannot halt, but every year throws forward the seed to begetting, and, falling back, leaves the young-born on the earth. They knew the intercourse between heaven and earth, sunshine drawn into the breast and bowels, the rain sucked up in the daytime, nakedness that comes under the wind in autumn, showing the birds' nests no longer worth hiding. Their life and interrelations were such; feeling the pulse and body of the soil, that opened to their furrow for the grain, and became smooth and supple after their ploughing, and clung to their feet with a weight that pulled like desire, lying hard and unresponsive when the crops were to be shorn away. The young corn waved and was silken, and the lustre slid along the limbs of the men who saw it. They took the udder of the cows, the cows yielded milk and pulse against the hands of the men, the pulse of the blood of the teats of the cows beat into the pulse of the hands of the men. They mounted their horses, and held life between the grip of their knees, they harnessed their horses at the wagon, and, with hand on the bridle-rings, drew the heaving of the horses after their will. . . .
> It was enough for the men, that the earth heaved and opened its furrow to them, that the wind blew to dry the wet wheat, and set the young ears of corn wheeling freshly round about; it was enough that they helped the cow in labour, or ferreted the rats from under the barn, or broke the back of a rabbit with a sharp knock of the hand. So much warmth and generation and pain and death did they know in their blood, earth and sky and beast and green plants, so much exchange and interchange they had with these, that they lived full and surcharged, their senses full fed, their faces always turned to the heat of the blood, staring into the sun, dazed with looking towards the source of generation, unable to turn round.

Lawrence is decidedly moving about, in this passage, at the lower level of language; he is dealing with a vague but nourishing force or flow which occurs *in time,*[3] and which plays an important and distinctly religious role in the novel: the Brangwen men enjoy "blood-intimacy" with the life around them; they must learn to utilize this contact for creative ends; and in order to achieve organic being, they must also learn to transcend it. But opposed to the "rainbow," or the round arch of full organic life, is the pointed arch of the cathedral, the symbol of Christianity. And to treat Christianity properly, Lawrence had to shift over to the upper level of language and deal in terms of "soul-intimacy" with the Christian infinite, during the *timeless* moment of prayer: which is precisely what happens, midway through the novel, when Will Brangwen enters Lincoln Cathedral.

> Then he pushed open the door, and the great, pillared gloom was before him, in which his soul shuddered and rose from her nest. . . . His soul leapt up into the gloom, into possession, it reeled, it swooned with a great escape, it quivered in the womb, in the hush and the gloom of fecundity, like seed of procreation in ecstasy. . . .
>
> Away from time, always outside of time! Between east and west, between dawn and sunset, the church lay like a seed in silence, dark before germination, silenced after death. Containing birth and death, potential with all the noise and transitation of life, the cathedral remained hushed, a great involved seed, whereof the flower would be radiant life inconceivable, but whose beginning and whose end were the circle of silence. Spanned round with the rainbow, the jewelled gloom folded music upon silence, light upon darkness, fecundity upon death, as a seed folds leaf upon leaf and silence upon the root and the flower, hushing up the secret of all between its parts, the death out of which it fell, the life into which it has dropped, the immortality it involves, and the death it will embrace again.
>
> Here in the church, "before" and "after" were folded together, all was contained in oneness. . . .

If we compare this with the previous passage in aim, texture, and execution, we can see at once that Lawrence worked at opposite levels of language, and with two distinct concepts of the ineffable. That he could do so successfully is not simply an indication of versatility, but a confirmation of the actual religious dimension of his writings. We find this same striking contrast in still other works: in *Sons and Lovers* there is the close, heavy, timeless spiritual communion over flowers between Paul Morel and Miriam Leivers, and there is the bright, open, sensual engagement with the natural world which Paul and his mother enjoy; in "The Man Who Died" there is the dramatic contrast between the cold, timeless nullity of the tomb and the bloom of life in the peasant's yard:

> The man who had died looked nakedly on life, and saw a vast resoluteness everywhere flinging itself up in stormy or subtle wave-crests, foam-tips emerging out of the blue invisible, a black and orange cock or the green flame-tongues out of the extremes of the fig-tree. They came forth, these things and creatures of the spring,

glowing with desire and with assertion. They came like crests of foam, out of the blue flood of the invisible desire, out of the vast invisible sea of strength, and they came coloured and tangible, evanescent, yet deathless in their coming.

Even the young gamecock is a crest on "the swaying ocean of life," and we see, perhaps for the first time, that the quickness and spontaneity of Lawrence's prose—its transcendent quality—is almost always "supplied" by the primitive indefinite, the life-force, and not, as some writers have suggested, by either the Christian or the symbolist version of the infinite.[4]

II

But the distance between Lawrence and the symbolists is more than a matter of language and metaphysics. There is also the problem of "the self and the not-self" to contend with. In their search for the spiritual absolute, for example, the symbolists lead us away from life toward realms of non-being. One thinks of Mallarmé, who sat before a mirror while writing his poems—not out of vanity, but to prevent his disappearance into nothingness; or of Valéry's preoccupation with suicide, and of the positive value which he placed upon non-being. What is at stake here, then, is the whole symbolist effort to "transcend man." Their version of the infinite occurs outside of *life* as well as time, since life is merely finite. So by definition, the symbolist poem is an organization of sensory material for static, timeless, and essentially non-human (or non-finite) ends. Of course, the final product may "transfigure life," but the structure of the poem remains unaltered.

On the other hand, Lawrence saw the life-force as the source of all vitality, and accordingly he found a central and significant role for "his" ineffable in daily life, in time, in basic human experience. Thus the chief emphasis, throughout his work, is on greater fullness of being, through love, friendship, and creative labor—through situations, in other words, which involve some vital form of communion between man and man, or even between man and the living universe. In the short story "Sun," for instance, a woman moves from the sterile touch of her husband to life-giving contact with the sun. This contact is organic and dramatic, but only in a focal sense, symbolic. Through daily rites with the sun, new powers of consciousness are aroused within the woman's body. She becomes a fuller person through these rites: and this is the pattern—resurrection through ritual—which Lawrence follows in most of his works.

Or destruction through ritual, the other side of the coin. And for

this, take the chapter called "Rabbit" in *Women in Love,* where Gerald
Crich and Gudrun Brangwen attempt to subdue the stubborn rabbit,
Bismarck, the squirming bundle of life which young Winifred Crich
values as *un mystère, ein Wunder.* But each of them is badly scratched
in the process, and as the rabbit bursts wildly around a small enclosed
yard, they mock it, they show each other the deep scars on their arms,
and smile obscenely, as initiates to the "abhorrent mysteries" which
will surely follow. This is their bond or pledge, then, their ritual
initiation to the violent ripping at each other's souls which will end
in Gerald's death. Only the child Winifred sees the rabbit as magnificently alive: "Let its mother stroke its fur then, darling, because
it is so mysterious," she says as the chapter ends.

Now the whole interplay between Gerald, Gudrun, and the rabbit
is direct and vivid, and relative to a particular stage in the novel. As
a symbol, the rabbit simply holds that stage in focus, but as a living
animal he participates in the rite between Gudrun and Gerald. This
is not, in other words, a vague, suggestive, static moment—a *symbole
littéraire*—but a definite and spontaneous pledge between two future
lovers to destroy the life within themselves, to deny or exploit the
life-flame itself, the mystery and wonder embodied by the rabbit.

> "Isn't it a *fool!* [cried Gudrun]. Isn't it a sickening *fool?"* The
> vindictive mockery in her voice made [Gerald's] brain quiver.
> Glancing up at him, into his eyes, she revealed again the mocking,
> white-cruel recognition. There was a league between them, abhor-
> rent to them both. They were implicated with each other in
> abhorrent mysteries.
> "How many scratches have you?" he asked, showing his hard
> forearm, white and hard and torn in red gashes.
> "How really vile!" she cried, flushing with a sinister vision.
> "Mine is nothing."
> She lifted her arm and showed a deep red score down the silken
> white flesh.
> "What a devil!" he exclaimed. But it was as if he had had
> knowledge of her in the long red rent of her forearm, so silken and
> soft. He did not want to touch her. He would have to make
> himself touch her, deliberately. The long, shallow red rip seemed
> torn across his own brain, tearing the surface of his ultimate con-
> sciousness, letting through the forever unconscious, unthinkable
> red ether of the beyond, the obscene beyond.

Such ritual scenes occur as early, in Lawrence's work, as *Sons and
Lovers,* where the living relationship between men, women, and
flowers is used to push the story along: take Mrs. Morel's garden-
swoon, for example, before Paul's birth; or the whole attempt by

Paul and Miriam to commune over flowers, *à la* Wordsworth; or the extraordinary flower-picking scene between Paul, Miriam, and Clara; the floral benediction as Paul and Clara make love; and finally, the spontaneous gift of flowers to Miriam at the novel's end. But there is no space here to explicate such complicated patterns. For the moment I simply want to emphasize that most of Lawrence's works move forward through ritual scenes, toward ritualistic ends. For just as the essence of religious ritual is communion, so Lawrence saw all deeply significant contacts—between human beings, or even between man and the living universe—as spontaneous forms of communion, either sacred or debased, either nourishing or reductive; and just as the old primitive "rites of passage" always centered upon such basic events as birth, rebirth into manhood, death, and resurrection to the greater life beyond, so Lawrence's stories always center upon "rebirth" and "death"—the emergence into greater or lesser forms of being. But therefore the sexual scenes in *Lady Chatterley's Lover* can only be understood as "dramatic" rites of communion. And even the famous moon scenes, in both *Women in Love* and *The Rainbow,* can only be understood in terms of actual rapport, pro and con, between the protagonists and the moon-as-living-force: these men and women participate, that is to say, in ritualistic situations which fall within the larger flow of the novels. And so, as the novels move along, these figures rise up toward organic being, as certain statues of Rodin rise up out of a raw rough marble base—still rooted in the vague unknown, but nonetheless organic in themselves.

III

If this line of argument proves correct, then Lawrence scarcely qualifies as a symbolist; if anything, he stands opposed to this tradition on metaphysical and ontological grounds. But there is still another category to consider: the realm of "pure aesthetics." It is true, for example, that some of the later poets did not pursue the infinite; they concerned themselves with formal or aesthetic matters, to the point where symbolism became a mere question of technique. Yet even these disciples aimed at static and gratuitous beauty, if only to give order to their poems. In the meantime, Lawrence saw the novel in terms of organic *flow,* as a delicate balance of wholly fluid relationships, and he evolved his own kinetic brand of art to handle them.[5]

A typical short story, "The Blind Man," may help to clarify the problem. For the central and pervading symbol of the story—Maurice Pervin's blindness—is only a point of focus for a special condition of being in Pervin himself, and for the special conditions of his marriage; and though these various conditions might be vague and obscure in texture, they are never static, and their nature and direction are known to both Lawrence and the reader. Here, for example, is a revealing description of Pervin's blindness:

> Pervin moved about almost unconsciously in his familiar surroundings, dark though everything was. He seemed to know the presence of objects before he touched them. It was a pleasure to him to rock thus through a world of things, carried on the flood in a sort of blood-prescience. He did not think much or trouble much. So long as he kept this sheer immediacy of blood-contact with the substantial world he was happy, he wanted no intervention of visual consciousness. In this state there was a certain rich positivity, bordering sometimes on rapture. Life seemed to move in him like a tide lapping, lapping and advancing, enveloping all things darkly. It was a pleasure to stretch forth the hand and meet the unseen object, clasp it, and possess it in pure contact. He did not try to remember, to visualize. He did not want to. The new way of consciousness substituted itself in him.

This new way of consciousness is the famous "phallic" or bodily form of consciousness, and Pervin's sense of the life-flow can easily be traced to its awakening. His blindness has resulted, in other words, in a change of being, and this change has led in turn to closer contact with the primitive indefinite. This is the nature of his emotional state, and a moment later Lawrence reveals its direction:

> The rich suffusion of this state generally kept him happy, reaching its culmination in the consuming passion for his wife. But at times the flow would seem to be checked and thrown back. Then it would beat inside him like a tangled sea, and he was tortured in the shattered chaos of his own blood. He grew to dread this arrest, this throw-back, this chaos inside himself, when he seemed merely at the mercy of his own powerful and conflicting elements. How to get some measure of control or surety, this was the question. And when the question rose maddening in him, he would clench his fists as if he would *compel* the whole universe to submit to him. But it was in vain. He could not even compel himself.

Thus Pervin, like the Brangwen men in *The Rainbow,* is caught and held within a state of blood-prescience. And the potential danger of that state is kept in focus by a series of kinetic, if symbolic, scenes. The blind man moves forward toward his wife, Isabel, for instance, out of the fecund darkness of the barn. His wife can actually *feel* him coming toward her, and the darkness itself seems like "a strange swirl of violent life . . . upon her." She feels giddy, and afraid even of her husband as she meets him in his own rich world of unresolved blood-intimacy—so that the scene can only be described, in ritualistic terms, as a communion of fear.

A similar scene occurs when husband and wife sit down to dinner with their special guest, the intellectual "neuter," Bertie Reid. But here, in the safety of the house, the scar on Pervin's face suggests to Isabel that her husband, "so strong-blooded and healthy," is also cancelled out. The scar strikes Bertie this way too. He looks away from it with difficulty, and, "without knowing what he did," he picks up "a little crystal bowl of violets" and sniffs at them. The flowers, of course, are alive and organic, while Pervin remains fixed within a single form of consciousness. Thus an awkward moment occurs when Reid places them in Maurice's hands, so he may smell them too. Both Isabel and Reid are afraid and deeply disturbed at this point, and again we have, in ritualistic terms, a mounting communion of fear.

This fear is dissolved, however, with the final ritual scene. Later that evening, Bertie looks for Maurice and finds him in the barn, pulping turnips. The two begin to chat about Isabel's happiness, Maurice's scar, and the casual nature of their own acquaintanceship. Then Maurice suddenly asks if he may touch him. Bertie complies, reluctantly, and Maurice gathers his head in his sensitive fingers, shifts and adjusts his grasp until he has covered the whole face, then grasps the shoulder, arm, and hand before him. The bachelor lawyer feels annihilated by all this; he quivers with revulsion as Maurice asks him now to touch his own blind eyes. But again he complies:

> He lifted his hand, and laid the fingers on the scar, on the scarred eyes. Maurice suddenly covered them with his own hand, pressed the fingers of the other man upon his disfigured eye-sockets, trembling in every fibre, and rocking slightly, slowly, from side to side. He remained thus for a minute or more, whilst Bertie stood as if in a swoon, unconscious, imprisoned.
>
> Then suddenly Maurice removed the hand of the other man from his brow, and stood holding it in his own.
>
> "Oh, my God," he said, "we shall know each other now, shan't we? We shall know each other now."

Where Joyce might see an epiphany in such an experience (a static, timeless manifestation of some spiritual essence), Lawrence sees instead a kinetic transformation of being, in both Pervin and Reid. Thus Maurice stands "with his feet apart, like a strange colossus," when the two return to Isabel; while Bertie is now "like a mollusc whose shell is broken." Through the friendship rite, one man moves toward greater fullness of being; his blindness is transcended, his unresolved blood-intimacy released, and the limited circle of marriage itself is broken by "the new delicate fulfillment of mortal friendship"; but the other man is destroyed by the experience—his outer bulwark against life is smashed, his inner vacuum thoroughly exposed. Thus the ritual pattern of the story is complete.

By setting off Lawrence against the symbolists in this manner, by giving as much credence to his metaphysics as we normally give to theirs, we are able to see what sort of artist Lawrence actually is. And seeing this much, becoming more familiar, as it were, with the ritual pattern of his work, we can at last answer some of the more popular charges against him: namely, that he had no operative sense of form; that his work was merely impressionistic; or that he kept remarkable faith with the living moment, yet never produced a complete work of art. As Frederic Hoffman states it:

> Form for Lawrence was unimportant—though he was capable of writing aptly finished short tales and novelettes, his longer novels are held together by a succession of moments of crucial experience; its continuity is fitful, the *modus vivendi* a series of revitalized crises of bodily relationships.

This criticism is sound, in part, but Hoffman falsely assumes that emotional life is formless in itself. Apparently, Lawrence felt otherwise. His faith in the living moment was uniquely counterbalanced by his faith in the human soul, whose death and resurrection, within the living body, was his chief concern. And so, to accommodate his concept of the soul, as a stable but ever-changing element, a kind of second ego which moves along within the flux of life, waxing and waning in accord with man's emotional experience, he discovered and employed emotional form; he learned to deal, directly or obliquely, with specific states of being; he learned, quite literally, to chronicle the movements of the soul. Thus, in the better part of his writing, the "crucial moments" always mount or flow toward definite ends, and Hoffman, among others, fails to account for this fact. Granted, the emotional form breaks down or backs against itself, like Pervin's sensual flow, whenever Lawrence wrestles with those problems which he cannot solve. But significantly enough, this breakdown coincides with the troubled middle period of his life—the period stretching from *The Lost Girl* through *Aaron's Rod, Kangaroo, The*

Boy in the Bush, and *The Plumed Serpent.* But the four major novels
—those which express his finest psychological and moral insights—
are all well-organized along ritualistic lines. It seems scarcely accidental, then, that a man is born at the end of *Sons and Lovers;* a
woman, as *The Rainbow* ends; while in *Women in Love* a man and
a woman meet and marry—and conceive a child some eight years
later, in *Lady Chatterley's Lover.* For these four novels represent an
impressive and decidedly artistic attempt, on Lawrence's part, to set
forth the conditions of manhood, womanhood, and marriage, as he
felt or understood them in his own life. These novels coincide, that
is, with his own "rites of passage."

NOTES

1. In *The Later D. H. Lawrence,* William York Tindall makes extravagant
and extensive claims for Lawrence-as-symbolist. In *The Life and Works of
D. H. Lawrence* and more recently in *The Achievement of D. H. Lawrence,*
Harry T. Moore takes a much more qualified approach; he simply holds that
Lawrence used symbolist techniques during a particular phase of his career.
Such notions are not, of course, without cause or precedent. In the early 1930's
both Anaïs Nin and Francis Fergusson had written on the suggestive and subjective nature of Lawrence's symbols, though without comparing him specifically
with the *symbolistes.* This paper owes its genesis, incidentally, to conversations
with Mr. Fergusson, who might not agree with all its contents, but who at
least made them possible.

2. Presumably, it might also encounter Wordsworth's religious flux,
Nietzsche's Dionysian force, or Bergson's *élan vital.* At any rate, we can safely
lump these various beliefs together under the general heading of the primitive
indefinite, since each of them involves some vague, indefinite force or flow of a
religious nature.

3. At the end of the novel, for example, Ursula Brangwen wants "to create
a new knowledge of Eternity in the flux of Time."

4. In *D. H. Lawrence and Human Existence,* Father William Tiverton
speaks of the sense in Lawrence's work "that what is shown as alive owes its
aliveness to something behind or above—to the transcendent." But he fails to
connect this observation with "dramatic" structure, and he also fails to separate
Laurentian transcendence from the usual Christian sense of the term, and
thereby robs us of the full import of Lawrence's accomplishment.

5. Mr. Tindall tries to avoid this conclusion in *The Later D. H. Lawrence;*
he cites Loerke's notions, in *Women in Love,* on art as non-representational form,
to show "that Lawrence had an artist's conception of significant form." And
undoubtedly Lawrence did, but he also rejected it: as Ursula Brangwen tells
Loerke in the same novel, "The world of art is only the truth about the real
world." In other words, Lawrence saw art as a representation of reality, and
a kinetic one, and not as "an arrangement of material for an aesthetic [and
static] end," as Tindall would have us believe. Unfortunately, Tindall seems
to equate Lawrence with other novelists, like Joyce and Mann, who *do* write in
the symbolist tradition.

JARVIS THURSTON:

Anderson and 'Winesburg': Mysticism and Craft

The Sherwood Anderson letters[1] and manuscripts in the Newberry Library collection support Lionel Trilling's suggestion that criticism has paid too little attention to Anderson's "mysticism," or religiosity, for it does underlie, with an amazing persistency, so much of what he did and thought. It is a central determinant not only of his view of the nature and function of art but, in consequence, of his working habits, his characteristic theme and tone, and his approach to such problems of craft as characterization, action, setting, point of view, style, and structure. An examination of *Winesburg*—in which, for the first time in his literary career, Anderson found the way of closing the gap between his mystical impulses and the formal demands of art— will reveal the essential Anderson; *Winesburg* is particularly central to a critical definition of Anderson's art, for it is a volume of stories and, though not a *novel* in any ordinary sense of the term, it is, significantly, his only success in a longer form. But before turning to a scrutiny of *Winesburg* let us look at the linkage between his mysticism and art more generally.

I

Unlike that mysticism which seeks its expression within traditionally organized religious beliefs and rituals, or that which has a force and imaginativeness capable of creating a new myth complex enough to offer a satisfactory metaphysics, Anderson's mysticism is bare, inchoate and diffused. As idea, expressible outside art, it goes little beyond a rejection of materialism and a yearning for the selflessness of permanent "brotherhood." That this mysticism was unattached before he became a writer is seen in his account of the marching experience, at the age of twenty-two, described in *A Story-Teller's Story:*

---

[1] Quotations from unpublished letters are used with the permission of Eleanor Anderson and the Newberry Library; quotations from Howard M. Jones and Walter B. Rideout's *Letters of Sherwood Anderson* with the permission of Little, Brown & Company and the Atlantic Monthly Press, copyright 1953, by Eleanor Anderson.

> The constant marching and manouevering was a kind of music in the legs and bodies of the men. No man is a single thing, physical or mental . . . There was a kind of physical drunkenness produced . . . One was afloat on a vast sea of men . . . One's body was tired but happy with an odd new kind of happiness. The mind did not torture the body, asking questions. The body was moved by a power outside itself.

And there is the evidence of numerous worshipful acts recorded in the various memoirs: "I had suddenly an odd, and to my own seeming a ridiculous desire to abase myself before something not human and so stepping into the moonlit road I knelt in the dust."

Some time when he was around the age of thirty-five the mysticism became attached to art inseparably, since it was through the medium of words that Anderson experienced his basic conversion from businessman to artist. That he saw this as a kind of Saul-Paul conversion is clear in the account he made public in *A Story-Teller's Story*—the trance-like walking out of the factory in the midst of dictating a letter and the catching of a train toward Chicago and Art. Biography's disclosure of the facts—the "nervous breakdown" and the amnesia—does not alter the symbolic truth of an experience that fixed for Anderson his view of art and artist. Since he himself had come out of the wilderness he saw himself as a voice crying out. "In the *Testament*," he said, "I want to send the voices of my own mind out to the hidden voices in others, to do what can't be done perhaps." About these prose poems he wrote to Paul Rosenfeld:

> In this book I am trying to get at something that I think was very beautifully done in some parts of the old testament by the Hebrew poets. That is to say, I want to achieve in it rhythm of words with rhythm of thought . . . The thing if achieved will be felt rather than seen or heard, perhaps. You see, as the things are, many of them violate my own conception of what I am after. In making this book I have felt no call to responsibility to anything but my own inner sense of what is beautiful in the arrangement of words and ideas. It is in a way my own Bible.

If in the role of the artist Anderson saw himself as the prophetic man, the practice of art itself was both wafer and confessional. In encouraging his son, John Anderson, to become a painter, he said:

> . . . You may come to get out of canvases what I get out of sheets of paper.
> I presume it is the power of losing self. Self is the grand disease. It is what we all are trying to lose. . . .

How people ever lose themselves who are not artists I do not know. Perhaps they, some of them, do it in love.

To love a woman and possess her is a good deal. It isn't enough for an eager man . . .

In art there is the possibility of an impersonal love. For modern men it is, I think, the only road to God.

And in "Song of Theodore" in *Mid-American Chants* Anderson wrote:

. . . . I caress all men and women. I make myself naked. I am unafraid. I am a pure thing. I bind and heal. By the running of the pencil over the white paper I have made myself pure. I have made myself whole. I am unafraid. The song of the pencil has done it.

What cunning fingers I have. They make intricate designs on the white paper. My cunning fingers are flesh. They are like me and I would make love always—to all people—men and women—here— in Chicago—in America—everywhere—always—forever—while my life lasts.

Though Anderson saw the primary function of art as the personal salvation of the artist, he thought art served a religious function for the audience as well. By an extension of his own experience he saw human beings as potential creators that only the artist-priest could awaken by art-love. The primacy of art as a means toward salvation in the modern world is a frequent topic in his letters. Typical is his letter to his psychoanalyst friend, Trigant Burrow, rebuking him for having sent a book on social reform in England: "You see, I believe that the artist must come before all the others, the remakers of the social state; and always when such men as yourself who have at bottom the artist's point of view are carried aside from it by any movement of any kind for the present betterment of society, I am a bit sore and ugly."

Seeing life and art from a mystical frame of reference, Anderson rarely thought of the human character as something in process, as shaper and shaped, or as a complex product of both internal and external realities. His vision was focused on the "soul," on an essential *innerness* (whether of an individual or a society) that the artist can disclose by imaginative, *loving identification,* by "entering into lives" and going "beneath the surface." It was the staying outside, the concern with outer reality, that Anderson disliked in Sinclair Lewis; in Edgar Lee Masters it was the hate. Hemingway, he complained, always saw life "as rather ugly." Sophisticated writers like Hawthorne and James, he felt, revealed in their concern with form an unwillingness to "enter in." His first impression, which he inevitably revised, of *Women in Love* was that "so sophisticated a manner is in some way indicative of spiritual weariness . . . When one has become sufficiently weary the next best thing is to invent a manner—a point of view. One is not relaxed, does not receive freely impressions of life."

Form, for Anderson, was essentially opposed to the function of art, and as we might expect, the creative process for him contained a stronger element of daydream than it does for most artists. One has a clear impression of this in reading *A Story-Teller's Story,* in which Anderson creates several "tales" before our eyes. The genesis is invariably some everyday tableau, or little anecdote, in which an individual unknowingly reveals—through a gesture, a small act, or an unguarded speech—a hidden aspect of personality. This is interpreted by the writer, through the lens of his own spiritual preoccupations, as being a revelation of the *inner* person. Though a few exterior details are provided—vocation, setting, a brief history—the chief process is an elaboration by "fancy" of other corroboratory moments of self-revelation. Daydreaming is, of course, essential to the artistic process, but in getting stories down most writers thoughtfully test daydream against outward reality and transform by selection, by invention of new detail, and by ordering all the materials for the dramatic exploration of meaning. In his worst and most mystical writings—*Marching Men* and *Many Marriages*—Anderson seems little more than an amanuensis for a daydreaming, secondary self; in *Winesburg* and in the other volumes of stories, though there is still a very strong element of the free association and spontaneity of the daydream, he generally manages enough control to make the daydream become a part of his odd strength. Though all his inclinations were opposed to control and form (he firmly opposed any attempts of his writer-friends to "correct" him), he had his occasional insights into the problem: "From the beginning there has been, as opposed to my actual life, these grotesque fancies. Later, to be sure, I did acquire more or less skill in bringing them more and more closely into the world of the actual."

If the materials of art, as Anderson once said, have to take the place of God, it follows that writing should be approached rapturously. Anderson wrote ecstatically at break-neck speed with an absorption that could leave him sitting on a milk-can while his train pulled away. While working on *Dark Laughter* he wrote to Alfred Stieglitz:

> I have been on a grand bat, am still on it. Put aside the Lincoln thing [never finished] and made several starts at a novel. Suddenly, a week ago, Sunday, I really got into it. Since then I've been dead and blind to everything else. I am calling it a "fantasy" rather than a novel. No realism in it. An attempt to catch the spirit of things now. The War, after the War, the puzzle of things, weariness of people, laughter, Europe.
>
> It has danced so far. Often 3 or 4,000 words a day, writing until I could not sit at the desk any more and all my body trembling.

Most of his stories were written at a single sitting, and as he attempted the novel in the same headlong rush, his letters are full of pathetic accounts of novels that could never be completed because the inspiration was lost after opening rushes of 10,000 to 40,000 words: *Thanksgiving* (about advertising), *Brother Earl* (about his derelict brother), *A Late Spring* (about Thomas Wolfe), and many others.

Anderson's asking of art more than it can give, or carry, and his consequent wasteful manner of working were costly for him in both his human relations and his art. And costly as far as his critical reputation is concerned. A reading of the memoirs and letters—and all the novels except, only in part, *Poor White* and *Dark Laughter*—leave us with such a strong sense of irritation at his haphazard invention, his prophetic tone, and an over-all mindlessness that we tend to approach even his best work with too little sympathy. We are also irritated at the eddying of his thinking about American life; he was never able to get much beyond the thesis sentence: industrialism, the acquisitive, material life of contemporary America is depersonalizing mankind and destroying the spiritual entity that is the source of all beauty in human relations and art. But that was certainly an important idea—it served, among others, both Eliot and Pound well; Anderson, however, lacked the education to pursue conceptually what for him was less an idea than a personal experience and a vision.

In recognizing Anderson's lack of thematic range and his inability to analyze we must not fall into the error that he himself saw in Van Wyck Brooks' critique of Mark Twain: looking for the writer that might have been we fail to see the one we have. If the religiosity and the mindlessness, the approaching of both art and life through feeling are contributory to his failures, they are also central to his strength. In fact, it was Anderson's partial surrender to intellectuality and sophistication that contributed to the failure of the later career, as remarked by Irving Howe:

> It was his tragedy that after the early 1920's he was trapped be-
> tween two worlds: he could find sustenance neither in the deep
> kinships of the folk bard nor in the demanding traditions of the
> sophisticated artist.

In his letters, early and late, Anderson compensated for his intellectual insecurity—which grew as his circle of literary acquaintances
widened—by attacking reason, with a crafty insistence on feeling:

> Please don't always apply your reason to these things. They are to
> my mind fragments that will be more keenly realized in the minds
> of the reader than you fellows think.
> There is a danger that always besets a group of keen fellows like
> yourself. It is the sort of thing that has happened to the crowd
> over at the *New Republic*. You become too keen; a madness for
> analysis takes hold of you.

For himself, Anderson was right. For him there was only the way of
vision. What is remarkable, then, is not his many failures, but the
successes in not a few of the stories of *The Triumph of the Egg,
Horses and Men, Death in the Woods,* and *Winesburg, Ohio.*

Let us turn now to our examination of *Winesburg,* first to what is
essentially Andersonian in theme, tone, characterization, action, and
setting.

II

Probably no other sentence of Anderson's is more central to *Winesburg* (and to Anderson's own life) than Elizabeth Willard's statement
about herself: "I wanted to run away from everything but I wanted
to run toward something too." There is, on the one hand, the desire
to escape from the walls of the self, from the repressions and frustrations that warp the personality; on the other, there is the desire to fly
toward some kind of unnameable spiritual union with God, man, or
nature. It is this kind of homespun Platonism that drew Anderson
toward Whitman, colored his view of Mark Twain and the Mississippi,
and determined (but after the writing of *Winesburg*) his strong
admiration for D. H. Lawrence.

All of the Winesburgers are frustrated spiritual questers. Most of
them are unable to articulate their "vague and intangible hunger"
(in varied forms, a motif phrase in *Winesburg*); a few, like the
stranger in "Tandy," can say: "I am a lover and have not found my

thing to love . . . It makes my destruction inevitable, you see." The thing to love, though, seems never to be of this world. At times Anderson would seem to suggest that the frustration is sexual—notably with Alice Hindeman and Kate Swift—but there is always the implication that something deeper than unsatisfied sexual desire lies beyond. Even though Louise Bentley has a lover, she still has her "intangible hunger." Elizabeth Willard has had many lovers, but "like all women in the world she wanted a real lover. Always there was something she sought blindly, passionately, some hidden wonder of life."

Although he uses Freudian concepts, chiefly learned secondhand, Anderson's remarks about Freud in the memoirs and letters are always patronizing or tinged with mockery, for, like Lawrence, he tended to see the sexual relation mystically. Through sex, Anderson seems to say, we approach union, tantalizingly sense the greater union beyond the reciprocal love of man and woman, but are unable to make the last leap to the goal so poignantly and momentarily realized.

The not-finding-the-thing-to-love makes all the characters in *Winesburg* grotesque, a few like Joe Welling, Dr. Parcival, and Enoch Robinson so markedly so that they seem to have come out of a psychiatrist's case records. By juxtaposing these patently psychotic or psychoneurotic characters against the surface placidity of other characters who are revealed to be seething inside—Dr. Reefy, Rev. Hartman, Elizabeth Willard—Anderson indicates a common bond of spiritual frustration that links all humanity.

And it is the compulsive symptomatic act, frequently explosive and irrational, that Anderson typically uses to symbolize the blockage of the spiritual quest: Wing Biddlebaum's picking up of the crumbs; Dr. Reefy's rolling of his paper pills; Jesse Bentley's attempted sacrifice of the lamb; Alice Hindeman's running naked into the rain; Elmer Cowley's beating George Willard with his fists; Ray Pearson's running to warn Hal Winters.

Anderson's inchoate mysticism is evident in more than the central theme of *Winesburg*. It is also in his frequent use of religious symbolism: for instance, in the conclusion of "Hands," throughout the four-story sequence of "Godliness," and in the stained-glass Christ and child in "The Strength of God." It is also pervasively present as a kind of quaintness in the use of Biblical (King James) phrases and cadences: "the sadness of a growing boy in a village at the year's end opened the lips of the old man, the sadness was in the heart of George Willard and was without meaning," and "something new and bold came into the voice that talked"; and in the frequent use of the language of religion in word, phrase, and act: "pray," "prayer," "virgin," "god," "to see a light," "true word," "miracle," "she thought that the rain would have some creative and wonderful effect on her body," "the voices outside of himself whisper a message," "I wanted to suffer, you see, because everyone suffers and does wrong."

In one of the few perceptive essays on Anderson, Lionel Trilling has said:

> He spoke in visions and mysteries and raptures, but what he was speaking about after all was only a quiet place in the sun and moments of leisurely peace, of not being nagged and shrew-ridden, nor deprived of one's due share of affection. What he wanted for himself and others was perhaps no more than what he got in his last years: a home, neighbors, a small daily work to do, and the right to say his say carelessly and loosely and without the sense of being judged. But between this small, good life and the language which he used about it there is a discrepancy which may be thought of as a willful failure of taste, an intended lapse of the sense of how things fit.

Even though Anderson had his Ripshin Farm and a successful marriage with Eleanor Copenhaver, the last years, as revealed by the letters, show him, even if somewhat tamed by age, desperately seeking for not only a continuance of his life as an artist (and art, as we have said, he always saw in a religious sense as a way toward "otherness") but for something "beyond desire" that drew him successively toward the labor movement, Communism, and the New Deal. In much of Anderson's writing there is, in effect, a failure of taste, particularly in the novels, but the failure is the consequence of faulty craftsmanship and of not finding the proper vehicle for a religious view of the world. Also, Anderson tended to drift spiritually, to not avail himself of what organized religion could offer; and certainly he came too late and lacked a mind sufficiently disciplined to construct, like Yeats, an artistically adequate metaphysics. It is significant that it is in adolescence as a symbol that Anderson found his best vehicle.

Interwoven among the portraits of adult grotesques in *Winesburg* are the adolescents. We cannot know how clearly Anderson saw their relationship, but the charged atmosphere of adolescence with its diffused emotion, uncertain yearning, idealization, and emotional explosiveness—and with its alternating cruelty and tenderness—*is* the atmosphere of *Winesburg*. The asexual love of George Willard for Helen

472

White in "Sophistication" is Anderson's closest definition of *love*. It stands in contrast to the George Willard–Louise Trunion sexual relation and as a suggestion of the love sought by the grotesques. "He had reverence for Helen. He wanted to love and be loved by her, but he did not want at the moment to be confused by her womanhood . . . In that high place in the darkness two oddly sensitive human atoms held each other tightly and waited." At the end of the story: "Man or boy, woman or girl, they had for a moment taken hold of the thing that makes the mature life of men and women in the modern world possible." *For a moment*. But as Anderson saw the contemporary world—a world in which the Virgin and Venus have yielded to the imperatives of "Keep Smiling" and "Safety First"—he might as appropriately have ended his sentence with *impossible*.

The unwillingness of Anderson's characters to accept the less rapturous life of everyday human relations may be considered, psychologically, as a fixation of the emotional life at the level of adolescence. Floyd Dell, among the first of Anderson's literary friends in the Chicago days, said so in his review of the posthumous *Memoirs:*

> In his memoirs Sherwood Anderson does not say much of anything about his various marriages; and I shall follow his example. He had tried being grown up and responsible—a husband, a father, a provider—and he had failed at it dismally because his heart was never in it. He wanted to be in life what he managed to be in writing—a child, more than ordinarily self-centered. He wanted to be loved and believed in and encouraged, and allowed to love only his own dreams and the words he put on paper . . . He gave us his childhood; it was the best he had to give American literature—perhaps all he ever had to give to any one on earth.

There is considerable truth in Dell's statement, but he confuses too closely creator and creation. Anderson was not unaware of what he was doing, in *Winesburg* particularly; in a touching letter to Van Wyck Brooks he once said:

> When in speaking of *Winesburg* you used the word "adolescence," you struck more nearly than you know on the whole note of me. I am immature, will live and die immature. A quite terrible confession that would be *if I did not represent so much*.

What he thought of himself as representing was a voice crying out in the wilderness; he may have been immature but at least he knew it. If the emotional life of the Winesburg people is adolescent, Anderson rose above it in using it as a part of the controlled meaning of his book: maturity is impossible in a world without spiritual values. Mature people have no place in this generic portrait of contemporary life.

Those characters that are most adjusted to the modern world are the minor characters that flit in and out the stories—the Tom Willards, Banker Whites, and Will Hendersons—and they are the only ones treated unsympathetically. While George Willard is talking to Dr. Parcival, Will Henderson is "slipping in at the back door of the saloon . . . Will Henderson was a sensualist and had reached the age of forty-five. He imagined the gin renewed the youth in him. Like most sensualists he enjoyed talking of women, and for an hour he lingered about gossiping with Tom Willy."

It is the sensitive and the imaginative who become "queers" in a world that values more the Tom Willards. Anderson affectionately saw his grotesques and adolescents as both victims and "signs." George Willard, about to leave Winesburg, "sees himself as merely a leaf blown by the wind through the streets of his village," but he also carries with him the communion he has experienced with Helen White. The grotesques and the adolescents are closer to some kind of salvation, for the former have rejected the secular world and the latter have had some vague dream of what might be.

As a story-teller Anderson had a Christ-like forbearance of passing judgment; he sympathized with both the kind-and-loving (the Dr. Reefys) and the cruel-and-hating (the Wash Williamses). In "Surrender" he said:

> Before such women as Louise can be understood and their lives made livable, much will have to be done. Thoughtful books will have to be written and thoughtful lives lived by people about them.

It is clear that Anderson saw *Winesburg* itself as one of these books. By "peering beneath the surface of lives" he hoped to widen the reader's sympathy for the grotesqueries and weaknesses of his fellow creatures. Only by understanding the illness in ourselves and others, through sympathy, can we break through the sterilizing interrelationship of the sick individual and the sick society. Although he did not read Van Wyck Brooks' *America's Coming-of-Age* (1915) until 1918, after the *Winesburg* stories were written, Anderson excitedly found in it what he thought himself to have been saying in story:

> You cannot have personality, you cannot have the expression of
> personality so long as the end of society is an impersonal end like
> the accumulation of money. For the individual whose personal end
> varies too greatly from the end of the mass of men about him not
> only suffers acutely and becomes abnormal, he cannot accomplish
> anything healthily fine at all. The best and most disinterested indi-
> vidual can only express the better intuitions and desires of his age
> and place;—there must be some sympathetic touch between him
> and some visible or invisible host about him, since the mind is a
> flower that has an organic connection with the soil it springs from.

Though there are, perhaps, some notable exceptions, there is a
basic incompatibility between the mystically oriented mind and the
writing of fiction, especially the longer forms, for fiction by definition
involves characters who change in time. It is no wonder that Anderson was never able to write a novel and was successful only in those
short forms that tend toward the prose poem. For Anderson, character
is—something to be "revealed," not something that devolves. Outer
reality is of no real importance. To his painter brother Karl he wrote:
"What we have got to do is to feel into things. To do that we only
need to learn from people that what they say and think isn't of very
much importance."

The Winesburg characters are not the "rounded" portraits of so
many novels and stories: the doctors do not practise medicine, the
farmers farm, or the teachers teach. There is little analysis or dissection
of motive, and the histories of the characters—what little is offered—
do not adequately explain the genesis and development of their individual responses to life. There is in Anderson's characterization much
of the simplicity of the "folk" character sketch and of the kind of
"folk" psychology that nicknames Biddlebaum "Wing" and Williams
"Wash" and sees the village grotesque as the product of a single
experience or environmental fact: "he was forced to shoot a man
when he was the village sheriff," "his father beat him all the time," or
"Doc took to drink when his wife ran out on him."

The Winesburg people rarely see, smell, or taste their world; if
they go for walks, it is because they are driven by spiritual turmoil. If
they observe the beauty of the country about them, as does Ray Pearson in "The Untold Lie," it only serves to awaken in them their inner
tragedies:

> Every time he raised his eyes and saw the beauty of the country in
> the failing light he wanted to do something he had never done
> before, shout or scream or hit his wife with his fists or something
> equally unexpected and terrifying.

How little *Winesburg* is a portrait of village life is made obvious by reading, say, any of the stories of Ruth Suckow. What realism there is in *Winesburg* serves symbolic and structural purposes. The constant reference to places and their spatial relationships (the Fair Ground to Wine Creek, Moyer's livery barn to Voight's wagon shop) creates a background of sorts, but more importantly it serves as one of the means of linking the stories together. By setting his twenty protagonists, and numerous minor characters, with their varied occupations (farmer, reporter, minister, teacher, telegrapher, store clerk, doctor, etc.) in a village Anderson makes of Winesburg a microcosm. The use of the village setting, the symbol in the American mind of normality and healthful living, also gives emphasis to the revealed frustrations of the characters. This is life, he suggests, as it will be found anywhere if one probes beneath the surface. As Anderson's philosophizing Dr. Parcival says: ". . . everyone in the world is Christ and they are all crucified." It is a universal illness. That Anderson himself (though it may be a post-view) saw his village in terms of larger meanings is apparent in his remark in *The Intent of the Artist:*

> I myself remember with what a shock I heard people say that one of my books, *Winesburg, Ohio,* was an exact picture of Ohio village life. The book was written in a crowded tenement district in Chicago. The hint for almost every character was taken from my fellow lodgers in a large rooming house, many of whom had never lived in a village. The confusion arises out of the fact that others besides practising artists have imaginations.

III

Of the numerous relationships that can exist between author and audience it is significant that Anderson rarely chose the relationship involved in the dramatic method for which Henry James was such a persistent spokesman. The authorial self-effacement of the frequently anthologized "I'm a Fool" and "I Want to Know Why" is distinctly uncharacteristic. Anderson's lack of interest in "what men think and say," his view of the function of art, the kind of meanings he was usually working with, would almost preclude the use of objective narrative methods. In *Winesburg* he found the relationship between author and audience appropriately suited to an uneducated, intuitive man, who had come out of the wilderness of the business world and had something to tell: it is essentially the role of the wise epic poet as it has come down into modern times in a long line of English and American oral story-tellers. The role permitted Anderson the close relationship of teller to audience, permitted the authorial "wisdom," the apparent artlessness of episodic structure, the moving back and forth in time, and the moving in and out of the story as narrator and commentator. In the adaptation of the oral story to the written Anderson found for the first time in his literary career *(Windy McPherson's Son* and *Marching Men* had fumbled toward the "literary") a way of closing the gap between spiritual content and technique.

Though certain features of oral telling can be seen in more exaggerated form in some of the other *Winesburg* stories, "The Untold Lie" has most of the basic characteristics: the laying in at the beginning of blocks of background before the story proper is taken up; the apparent wandering away from the story because of some associational interest provoked by the mention of a name, object, or place; the frequent authorial intrusions in the form of "insights" and self-dramatizations; the shifts in time, and the occasional stopping of the story to lay in apparently overlooked materials necessary to the "point" of the tale.

In the opening page of "The Untold Lie" we are summarily told the names of the two characters—Ray Pearson and Hal Winters—where they live, their occupations, ages, marital status. Ray is characterized swiftly as "an altogether serious man . . . quiet, rather nervous . . . with a brown beard and shoulders rounded by too much and too hard labor." So much for Ray Pearson. Anderson then turns to Hal Winters. With the oral teller's fondness for the associational, he asks us—as if we might know him—not to confuse him with Ned Winters' family, a respectable family, for Hal is "one of the three sons of the old man called Windpeter Winters who had a sawmill near Unionville, six miles away, and who was looked upon by everyone in Winesburg as a confirmed reprobate." In oral telling the mention of any person, even though he may have little relation to the story, commonly results in a digression. And so it is here. One of the ten pages of the story is an account of Windpeter's death (as with most of Anderson's apparent digressions in these stories, this serves a purpose: Hal Winters comes from a spirited family that does not easily succumb to the traps of life that have defeated the weaker and more respectable Ray Pearson). To get back from the digression the teller has to address his listeners:

But this is not the story of Windpeter Winters nor yet of his son Hal who worked on the Wills farm with Ray Pearson. It is Ray's story. It will, however, be necessary to talk a little of young Hal so that you will get into the spirit of it.

It is not until page four that the tale promised us begins with "And so these two men, Ray and Hal, were at work . . . ," but the story is immediately interrupted by the teller's addressing us again to insist upon the reasons for Ray Pearson's "distracted mood":

If you knew the Winesburg country in the fall and how the low hills are all splashed with yellows and reds you would understand his feeling.

From this point on the story is presented dramatically with only two more brief interruptions; the latter of these—"Ray Pearson lost his nerve and this is really the end of the story of what happened to him" —is disarming, for the one page that follows is really not the after-thought it appears to be; the teller is enjoying his craftiness.

The *Winesburg* stories are "oral," but are not, of course, merely oral stories written down. Since the meanings with which he was working needed a subtlety of handling that had little to do with the oral story as he knew it, Anderson solved the problem of telling stories in which nothing much happens externally by using a narrator-bard whose sympathetic vision is never far away. His bard is like the writer in the prefatory "Book of the Grotesque" (and not unlike Anderson's conception of himself as a "story-teller"):

. . . he had known people, many people, known them in a pecu-liarly intimate way that was different from the way in which you and I know people. At least that is what the writer thought and the thought pleased him.

He is a wise old man who has "entered into lives" and who has kept alive the "young thing" (imagination, fancy) within him that in that state between sleeping and waking (the daydreaming, creative state) brings a vision of truth (out of which the artist makes his art). For the old writer it is the truth that all the people he has known are gro-tesques: "Some were amusing [Joe Welling], some almost beautiful [Dr. Reefy], and one, a woman all drawn out of shape [Elizabeth Willard?], hurt the old man by her grotesqueness." Like Anderson he has written a book called "The Book of the Grotesque" (Anderson's title for *Winesburg* until his publisher persuaded him to change it) and has been saved from becoming a grotesque himself by the creative "young thing inside him."

Far from being the intrusive character that criticism has complained about, the narrator of *Winesburg* is central to the stories he tells. It is no accident that he occasionally appears as an "I" (for instance, in "Respectability": "I go too fast") or frequently appears as a commentator (in "Hands": "The story of Wing Biddlebaum's hands is worth a book in itself. Sympathetically set forth it would tap many strange, beautiful qualities in obscure men. It is a job for a poet."), for it is his presence, never very far away, that unites the stories through a consistent tone and perspective, and justifies the characterization, structure, and style. It is his oblique vision and pervasive sympathy which persuades the reader to tolerate what on the surface seems to be little more than character sketch or anecdote.

If Anderson's narrator seems to share his creator's traits, he is, nevertheless, a *persona* that makes possible Anderson's use in story of a frame of reference that might more appropriately have been used in poetry. That Anderson's poetry (his letters show a continuing fondness for *Mid-American Chants* and *New Testament* in spite of unanimous critical rejection) is a formless mélange of Whitman, Sandburg, and the Old Testament does not disprove the rightness of Rebecca West's view that Anderson was a poet who was trying to write prose. Writers of the private life, as she observes, used to write verse.

In *Winesburg* Anderson used his narrator's mixture of inarticulate wisdom and naiveté in a controlled way that constantly suggests more than is said. Even risky passages like those in "Hands" ("it needs the poet there") carry, in the context of the book, an air of rightness. The inarticulateness seems appropriate to his spiritually confused characters and to a narrator whose wisdom is more of the heart than the head. But by the time Anderson had got to *Tar* he had begun to overwork exaggeratedly and too self-consciously the approach he had discovered. In *A Story-Teller's Story* and in *Tar* the narrator's naiveté frequently seems sham and the wisdom an unconvincing sly smile, but the successful portions—and this is true of not a few of Anderson's casual pieces in such books as *Hello Towns!* and *Puzzled America*—depend upon that principle discovered for *Winesburg:* the exploitation for art of his own quaint and quirkily religious personality. How much of the narrator's personality is Anderson's and how much a *persona* we cannot determine, but as Howard Mumford Jones and Walter Rideout have observed in their introduction to the selected *Letters,* there are few writers whose letters so completely reaffirm what we have sensed about the personality through acquaintance with the art.

IV

It is also the pervasive presence of the quirkily religious author-narrator that determines the essential characteristics of Anderson's prose style, which, much criticism to the contrary, is not adequately defined by Edmund Wilson as "a series of simple declarative sentences of almost primer-like baldness" or by Oscar Cargill as a "conscious simplicity of style." Such a language would be obviously inadequate for a writer who has a prophet's insight into modern spiritual desolation and who feels that art is salvational. The role demanded a heightened language that is expressive of "wisdom," sympathy, and humility; and this language Anderson created out of a mixture of elements that he had natively at hand:

(1) the "literary" (a kind of belated village Johnsonese learned in the advertising experience and through his attempts to reproduce the educated language of the 19th and early 20th century novelists he read —Cooper, Borrow, Austen, Wells):

> Hidden, shadowy doubts that had been in men's minds concerning Adolph Myers were galvanized into beliefs.
>
> ("Hands")

> The fruition of the year had come . . .
>
> ("Loneliness")

(2) the Biblical poetic (in the use of incremental repetition; expanded, rounded cadences; and diction—Anderson carried about with him pages torn from the Gideon Bibles that he found in the hotels in which he spent so much of his time both before and after he became a professional writer):

> Youthful sadness, young man's sadness, the sadness of a growing boy in a village at the year's end opened the lips of the old man. The sadness was in the heart of George Willard and was without meaning, but it appealed to Enoch Robinson.
>
> ("Loneliness")

> Wing Biddlebaum became wholly inspired. For once he forgot the hands. Slowly they stole forth and lay upon George Willard's shoulders. Something new and bold came into the voice that talked . . .
>
> ("Hands")

(3) the American colloquial (the kind of language commonly used by the American oral story-teller—Anderson was a great admirer of *Huckleberry Finn;* before his *Winesburg* was written he had a considerable reputation among his Chicago acquaintances as a story-teller, and by the testimony of both Anderson and the people in Clyde, Ohio, who knew him, Anderson's father was a memorable story-teller; interestingly Anderson, who hated his father and loved his mother, came to remember his father with affection in *A Story-Teller's Story,* for he recognized in him one of the sources of his own craft):

> Hal was a bad one. Everyone said that. There were three of the Winters boys in that family, John, Hal, and Edward, all broad shouldered big fellows like old Windpeter himself and all fighters and woman-chasers and generally all-around bad ones.
> Hal was the worst of the lot and always up to some devilment . . .
>
> ("The Untold Lie")

(4) the English and American informal (the "middle" world of diction and syntax that is used wherever the English language is spoken):

> Hop Higgins sat down by the stove and took off his shoes. When the boy had gone to sleep he began to think of his own affairs. He intended to paint his house in the spring and sat by the stove calculating the cost of paint and labor.
>
> ("The Teacher")

Though it is the fourth of these ingredients that provides the basic stock of Anderson's narrative style, it is given an air of quaintness by being constantly flavored with the other ingredients, and particularly by the Biblical poetic when Anderson is seeking to express the inarticulate intensity of feeling that seizes his characters. No one of the ingredients is used unmixed for more than a few sentences. Shifts from the language of the oral teller to a more formal diction and sentence structure, or to a mixture of the two, occur frequently in *Winesburg.* "A Man of Ideas" opens with the baldness of "He lived with his mother . . . His name was Joe Welling" and continues:

> He was like a tiny little volcano that lies silent for days and then suddenly spouts fire. No, he wasn't like that—he was like a man who is subject to fits, one who walks among his fellow men inspiring fear because a fit may come upon him suddenly and blow him away into a strange uncanny physical state in which his eyes roll and his legs and arms jerk. He was like that, only that the visita-

tion that descended upon Joe Welling was a mental and not a physical thing.

The colloquial element in *Winesburg* has been overstressed by critics, chiefly because of their looking backward from such stories as "I'm a Fool" and "I Want to Know Why," in which Anderson temporarily abandoned his author-narrator role for the objectivity of the uneducated main character telling his own story; these are the pieces that most closely link Anderson to Mark Twain and Gertrude Stein. Anderson commonly uses the colloquial in *Winesburg* as an indirect means of characterization, speaking about Hal, for instance, in the language that Winters himself might have used. We can observe, also, that the colloquial appears less frequently in the story about the philosophic Dr. Reefy (one of Anderson's self-portraits).

That the mixed language of *Winesburg* does not represent merely a stage toward a more colloquial language—even though there is a decrease of the "literary" that so mars the early novels—is indicated by the revisions of the stories for magazine publication (curiously, as William L. Phillips has proved, the magazine versions, though published before *Winesburg,* are revisions of the *Winesburg* manuscript). At the same time that he is increasing the role of the narrator by changing some of the commentary into the first person, he is also changing *that's* to *that is, couldn't* to *could not,* and seeking the economies of written language by eliding, for instance, the italicized clause in such a passage as this: "the puzzled look he had already noticed in the eyes of others *when he looked at them."*

V

As I have already said, practically everything about Anderson—the mystical cast of his mind, his working habits, his views of the human personality and the function of art, to mention only a few items—precluded success as a novelist. All the novels, from *Windy McPherson's Son* to *Kit Brandon,* leave one with the impression that they are, in spite of occasional good scenes, planless mixtures of narrative summary, hortatory exposition, and weakly rendered drama. Clearly Anderson had no interest in how a character moves from A to D in time. He had the lyric poet's interest in D. If A is mentioned at all it is as a contrast to D; there is no concern for intermediate points or process. But the very cast of mind that made the novel an uncongenial genre for Anderson permitted him his kind of story, the "feel into things" (and the kind of sensitive, Lawrencean reportage in *Hello Towns!* and *Home Town*). Only in *Winesburg* did Anderson manage with some success a structure larger than the single story. The nature of that success needs to be defined and explained.

Anderson's earliest comment about *Winesburg* is in a November 14, 1916, letter to Waldo Frank:

> I made last year a series of intensive studies of people of my home town, Clyde, Ohio . . . Some of the studies you may think pretty raw, and there is a sad note running through them. One or two of them get pretty closely down to ugly things of life . . .
>
> This thought occurs to me. There are or will be seventeen of these studies [there were finally twenty-four]. Fifteen are, I believe, completed. If you have the time and the inclination, I might send the lot to you to be looked over.
>
> It is my own idea that when these studies are published in book form, they will suggest the real environment out of which present-day American youth is coming.

Though the passage hints at George Willard's role, we cannot know at what time, before or rather late during the composition, Anderson saw *Winesburg* as both a collection of tales and a novel about Willard. Since Anderson had not formed any close literary acquaintants outside Chicago before the fall of 1916, most of the literary comments in the letters are post-*Winesburg*. (The majority of the stories seem to have been written in late 1915 and early 1916—the earliest of the pieces, "The Book of the Grotesque," was in the February, 1916, *Masses,* and was followed in March by "Hands." A few of the pieces—certainly parts of the "Godliness" sequence and, possibly, the three closing stories —were written in 1917, or later.)

After the publication of *Winesburg* (1919) Anderson wrote to Van Wyck Brooks that "the novel form does not fit an American writer . . . it is a form which has been brought in. What is wanted is a new looseness; and in *Winesburg* I made my own form." And in December, 1919, he wrote to Waldo Frank:

> Out of necessity I am throwing the Mary Cochran book [another of the unfinished novels] into the *Winesburg form, half individual tales, half long novel form*. It enables me to go at each tale separately, perhaps when I am ready to do it *at one long sitting*. My life now is too broken up for the long sustained thing. Every few days I must go wade in mud, in the filth of money making. [One of the most tortured periods of Anderson's life followed upon his being given by Horace Liveright a five-year guarantee of $100 a week for writing a novel a year.]

These statements and the interlockings of characters and places in the opening stories of *Winesburg* would seem to be evidence for Anderson's having begun with George Willard's dual role as confidant and protagonist in mind, but this does not necessarily indicate a unifying conception much more complicated than that he had observed in his reading in 1915 of Masters' *Spoon River Anthology*. Whatever the original conception may have been, a reading of *Winesburg* suggests that the novel was superimposed upon the tales at a rather late date and that the earlier pieces were not reworked to fit as well as they might into a new structure. (Anderson's revisions were usually minor; as we might expect, he rewrote rather than revised, since he depended upon a mood to carry him through to form.)

In sixteen of the twenty-four stories George appears as either protagonist or secondary character; in three other stories he is mentioned in some such passing remark as that in "The Untold Lie": "Boys like George Willard and Seth Richmond will remember the incident . . ." Of the five stories in which George is not mentioned, one, "Paper Pills," is placed so early in the volume and is so definitely linked by its manner to the other tales that George's absence is not noticeable. The other four are the parts of the "Godliness" series, a self-contained unit which rests uneasily among the other stories. The heavy-handed preaching about industrialism there, the overt spiritual seeking, and the almost burlesque use of Biblical symbols and allusions in the Jesse Bentley parts are the more mystical Anderson of *Many Marriages* and *Marching Men*. Some years ago I wrote that "Godliness" was probably the matrix of a novel which Anderson intended to write about several generations of the Bentley family but recast, probably because he could not finish it, to form part of *Winesburg*. This supposition is now supported by an August 27, 1917, letter to Waldo Frank, written during the summer Anderson spent in the Chateaugay Lake country in New York:

> . . . My mind has run back and back to the time when men tended sheep and lived a nomadic life on hillsides and by little talking streams. I have become less and less the thinker and more the thing of earth and the winds. When I awake at night and the wind is howling, my first thought is that the gods are at play in the hills here. My new book, starting with life on a big farm in Ohio, will have something of that flavor in its earlier chapters. There is a delightful old man, Joseph Bentley by name, who is full of old Bible thoughts and impulses.

The Jesse (as he was renamed) Bentley stories are the only ones not set in Winesburg, and even though the story of George Willard is being told, as Anderson said in 1931, "by telling the stories of other people whose lives touched his life," the story of Jesse Bentley seems to be no part of Willard's environment.

In casting George Willard in the role of village reporter Anderson generally makes credible his being the recipient of so many intimate stories, but the esthetic effect of the individual stories is occasionally weakened by Willard's unnecessary appearance as listener or secondary participant. He interferes, for instance, with the role of the "wise" author-narrator in "Loneliness" in being introduced near the end of the story in explanation of how "we know about him [Enoch Robinson]." In stories like "Queer" and "Departure" the author-narrator makes no explanations as to the source of his knowledge of his characters' private acts and thoughts.

The writing of both a book of stories and a novel in the same volume results in some inconsistencies, but it also explains certain matters. It explains the unnecessary endings, if one thinks of them as independent stories, of "Teacher" and "Death." It also explains why some of the stories like "Nobody Knows" and "Death" have a limited or ambiguous meaning if looked upon independently. "Nobody Knows" takes on an added significance when seen from the perspective of the George Willard-Helen White story in "Sophistication." "Death," broken into four sections, begins with Dr. Reefy, turns to his relationship with Elizabeth Willard (which involves much retrospective material about her early life and her marriage with Tom Willard), shifts to George's reactions upon the death of his mother, and ends on a footnote about the $800 that Elizabeth had hidden away. As part of the George Willard novel "Death" is not confusing; in it and the closing two pieces—"Sophistication" and "Departure"—Anderson is preparing for a conclusion that the George Willard story makes possible. The three final pieces pull together the fragments of George's experience. The sense of the past which has hung over the stories is brought into the present, and George leaves Winesburg carrying with him the sadness of a world that makes us lovers but does not give us our thing to love.

Though less successful as a novel than as a collection of tales, *Winesburg* is a kind of portrait of the Midwestern artist as a young man. Between the opening story in which Willard is fascinated by the love and fear expressed in Biddlebaum's hands and the closing story in which he leaves a Winesburg which is to "become but a background on which to paint the dreams of his manhood," much has happened to him: he has had his first sexual relation in an atmosphere of secrecy and guilt, been humiliatingly used as bait by a woman in securing a husband, experienced the communion of adolescent love, suffered at the death of his mother, and observed, as reporter for the village newspaper and as confidant of Winesburg's grotesques, the sadness and ugliness of life—and a little of its happiness and beauty.

In spite of Willard's unifying function, it is not, really, as a novel that *Winesburg* has its success as a totality. Structurally, like all of Anderson's longer work, it has serious flaws. The book's unity rests ultimately in its being, in effect, a series of mutually supporting prose poems on a theme, held together by the consistency of the author-narrator's attitude—a blend of the oracular and the sympathetic—toward subject and audience. This Anderson seems to have never clearly understood. Ironically it was *Winesburg,* his only long success, that confirmed for Anderson notions dangerous for a novelist. In 1930, in the wake of numerous novels rapturously begun and never finished, and after the bitterly unproductive years following *Dark Laughter* (1925), Anderson could still write to friends:

> I have put away the machine thing for the time and am at work on a long story. The machine thing must, it seems to me, be let to come as it will. It must have poetic content. It can't be reasoned out or buttressed with facts. [As if he had ever reasoned his works out or buttressed them with fact.] It is all in a field where there are no facts.
>
> As you know, poetry—the carrying of conviction to others through feeling through the medium of words—is a complex, difficult thing.
>
> The very color of the words themselves, the feeling in the artist trying to release itself is a part of what must get over to the reader.

He never fully realized that it was his "vision" of life, the consequent views of art and artist, and his working habits that blocked his doing "the long sustained thing"—and gave to his short stories their quaint strength.

VERNON YOUNG:

"Hardly a Man Is Now Alive": Monologue on a Nazi Film

You hear that the Museum of Modern Art is to show a film of the Olympic Games, made at Berlin in 1936: in two parts, for God's sake!—two afternoon sessions of an hour and forty minutes each! You ask yourself, "What's in this for me, besides the occupational compulsion of the critic to see everything? Three hours and twenty minutes of the Extrovert Ideal? Strictly for mesomorphs!"

Supervising director, Leni Riefensthal. The name rings a cracked bell: a German actress who became a Hitler favorite. Memory prods: called by some a genius, by others an upstart given credit for the achievements of her production staff. She received especially high praise from Robert Flaherty, did she not, in a footnote to an article on film-making? You're not in agreement with the Orthodox who believe in Flaherty as the Holy Ghost of that Trinity which allegedly comprises D. W. Griffith and Eisenstein as well. Still, you look up the reference. (Penguin-Pelican: *The Cinema,* 1950)—"Robert Flaherty Talking":

> Hitler was a very clever fellow. . . . He spared no effort to make films and use them . . . wonderful films made by Leni Riefensthal, but terrifying like her *Triumph of the Will.* Here was a film made in 1934 in which you saw even then that the Nazis were a psychopathic case with whom to reason was impossible. But that film, which because of its revelation could have had a vital influence on subsequent events, was suppressed. . . .

486

Instantly you're intrigued, if not intimidated. Whatever you think of Flaherty's place in the hierarchy of film-makers, you believe him to have been a decent, humane personality who would scarcely have extended compliments lightly to a Naziess. You can argue privately and some other day as to whether the cinematic "revelation" of Nazi psychosis would have had any influence on anything whatever. For the present you are going to see an Important Film—unquote. But two-days'-worth of the Olympic Games! The knees boggle. How documentary can you get?

Sunday afternoon and it's raining on 53rd St. Everywhere else, too. Not without misgivings, you enter the wet crush in the Museum's own bargain basement and wait among the aquatints and the lithographs with All Those Others: the Look-At-Me contingent from The Village, the earnest (heavily or mildly) boys and girls from Columbia (or N.Y.U., or C.C.N.Y., or The New School), the neutrals who pardonably just want the most from their sixty-cents'-worth of admission—and perhaps even an aging hero or heroine who competed in the Games of 1936 . . . You take a seat within reasonable distance of the door, just in case. The girl next to you opens a pocket-book edition of *The Life of the Bee*. Maybe she's smart. The houselights go down; small subtle ones come on in the ceiling. Just enough light for taking notes—*if* it's necessary.

Olympia, 1936! Part One. Martial music. The introductory credit informs you that this colossal reportage was undertaken by a horde of photographers who employed everything from pocket Leicas to telescopic lenses and took their vantage points in towers, in undergrounds pits, on wheels, in underwater compartments and in balloons (also, as you will later infer, hanging by their thumbs). Four language versions of the film were made, and two years were occupied in the cutting process . . . All right, so it's thorough. You can just bet it's going to be thorough!

The opening image is a mass of clouds or murk which the camera slowly penetrates. Boulders. Slabs of stone. A fractured landscape, wuthering . . . Broken columns. Weed-riven steps. A collapsed cornice.

You get the point. Greece: ruins of the Olympiad site.

Flames. A naked youth apotheosized to carry the torch in relay. Leisurely cutting, as a succession of beach-boys trots the Grecian landscape, down to the verge of the sea and then, by way of "dissolves," up through the ages. The four elements—air, earth, fire and water.

Inevitable? All the same it's pretty damned impressive. Within five minutes you're more enthralled than patient; within twenty minutes it dawns on you that if this keeps up you're seeing one of the very great cooperatively made fact films on record . . . And it keeps up.

Much of it is Siegfriedian; all of it is imposing . . . At the top of a spectacular flight of steps, a Nordic male animal lights a cauldron which is to burn throughout the Olympiad. They've placed the cauldron where the sun will set directly behind it (like Reinhardt, who timed the striking of all the clocks in town for a scene in his open-air production of *The Miracle*); and there is one stunning shot of the flames licking and consuming the molten star as it sinks: a terrifying conceit when you recall the date—1936. *Morgen die Welt!*

After the fanfares, the shots of Hitler, the panorama of flags and the release of about a million doves (what a touch!), *Olympia* gets under way; from now on you're in the hands of an excellent (if, at times, unconsciously comic) British announcer, of you don't know how many hundred cameramen as ubiquitous as Mercutio's Queen Mab, and of a film editor (or staff of them) brilliant as they come. The announcer gets his first laugh from the audience (let's agree: there's nothing sharper than a New York audience): naming the entrants for the first event, he declares cheerfully, "Another American! They keep popping up!"

Now the strategy, generally speaking, is established. Wide-angle shots of the event, the particular stage, so to speak: the stretch, the pit, the circle; move in, oversee, participate. From the total action to the detail. Whole to part; part to whole. Medium-distance shot, close-up face on, profile, low-level, overhead.

Jesse Owens' jaw-muscle tightens; a vein throbs in his temple; he swallows.

The man in the white coat (he looks like a village butcher) warns, with an upward inflection, *"Fertig!"* Runners up on their toes and fingertips. Two seconds of dry-mouthed tension. The gun goes off and the sprinters leave with a velocity suggesting they've been shot from its barrel.

The cameras do their jobs, methodically, and with unflagging variety of witness point, reporting their subject—Competition. The track event, the shot put, the discus, the hurdles, high jump, broad jump. You're overhead, underneath, running parallel, out in front, or standing by politely. Cameras pan, swivel, tilt, track or just wait. You confront the polevaulter as he begins his run, or you concentrate on the pole's point, merely, as it goes into the ground. Or you wait and crane your neck as the vaulter comes over on top of you. Or you go up with him on a pole of your own and just grunt. And in one shot you remain focused on the pole pit, and see the action in shadow only.

Slow motion. The weight throwers bounce in an unearthly levitation, sponge-like, straining to keep their momentum from carrying them over the chalk line.

The girls take the high jump; legs almost horizontal scissor suggestively before your eyes.

Faces: Nordic, Celtic, Mediterranean, Oceanic, Asiatic. Monkey faces; dog faces; horse faces; pig faces. And bull necks.

Heads: Dolicho-, brachy- and mesocephalic.

The look of strain.

The set of determination.

The expression of surprise.

The controlled elation.

Chewed lips, knit brows; the shrug, and the faint smirk that says "Take *that!*"

The British announcer again: "It's a serious business, this putting the shot."

Tensions of the Olympics audience, intercut. Italians jump into the air, gesticulate and yell. Germans look stolid or allow themselves a quiet, triumphant tic, one side of the face at a time. Hitler grins (Germany has just won something). The German rooting section intones *"Sieg Heil,"* the Japanese chant "Nish-i-da, Nish-i-da"; the French project crisply something resonant you don't quite catch; an American claque gives its rah-rah-rah, though not as intensely organized as on native ground. And somewhere in the middle of it all, a tidy group of English youngsters enunciates: *"We want you to win! We want you to win!"*

Fertig!

Most of the music (by Herbert Windt) sounds like Richard Strauss (even when it's good) and the rest like the Mars movement of "The Planets" suite, by Holst, most effective where it accompanies the flight of the javelins, a trembling roar and a high-pitched chord as they plunge, quivering, into the ground. The Japanese and the Filipinos look atavistic as they grasp their javelins weapon-wise—suddenly centuries (or at least oceans) removed, spearing a boar in the jungle or a seal from a hide boat.

Sieg Heil! We are the great companions! What do you see, Doktor Freud? *I see men and women everywhere*—mutually exclusive. The primary sexual inhibition of our time here gets conditional sanction. Never has there been so much public intrasexual hugging and kissing, as the vicarious embrace the victorious, and not all of it unconscious. A German girl, the favorite in the high jump, leaps to success, the focus of hungry female eyes, caught by the cameras with their usual impartial pertinence (or shall you say impertinent partiality?). She throws herself to the ground and is covered by a blanket; a minute later the camera pivots back as she watches her competitor. In the corner of the frame you glimpse another girl's arm moving to encircle her . . . Behind you in the theater a woman's startled voice asks, "Who's *that?!*" and her male companion answers knowingly, "Her *coach,* I suppose!" . . . You hear a low rumble, apparently from the sound track, which you can't quite identify in the context: premonitory, subterranean. Later you realize it was merely subterranean: the 8th Avenue subway train on its way to Jamaica, reverberating beneath the Museum's auditorium.

Night comes down over the Berlin field. The cauldron burns brightly, illuminating the hopes of thousands, heating the sinister ambition of millions . . . The pole-vaulters carry on. A record must be broken. Up and over! Hands leave the pole only at the last inch of moment, as if the pole were being gently planted, while its planter rises reluctantly to the dark sky. A weary Japanese boy shakes his head in the flickering light, resigning himself visibly to the fates before he starts his brief run; you can feel him calling up all his reserve of adrenalin. Up!—and over. Not quite! He dislodges the bar and the film audience, well in it now, expresses disappointment with a kindred groan. The British announcer says, extenuatingly, "Oh well—he must be tahd!"

Shot of empty stadium, ringed by searchlights, like a mountainous shower-curtain. Dissolve to a tolling bell, from the bell to the cauldron, from the cauldron to the flags of all nations, revolving, ascending and descending in double exposure. The Olympics flag with its linked circles. The cauldron again and smoke rising. Berlin, 1936. Trumpets. Lights . . .

Indubitably you are still at 11 E. 53rd St. You rise, disoriented but surcharged with vicarious energy. The girl in the next seat is finishing another paragraph in *The Life of the Bee.* You wonder if she comes here to read. Why not? Probably it's more comfortable and no more distracting than where she lives . . . Swaggering from the auditorium, you take the stairs to the street floor, three at a time, potentially invincible. You consider inspecting the authentic Japanese house which has been reassembled in the Museum's garden, but the consideration is short-lived; your Sagittarian impulses resent being Librafied. Corrupted by kinesis, you want nothing so much as to broad-jump the pond or to polevault over the garden railings into the middle of 54th St. You telephone a friend with whom you're to have dinner. You ask him if he has any liniment.

Second day. No rain but the streets are damp. The quiescence of the Japanese house seems more appealing—the uncluttered life . . . The Museum theater is not as full and the Monday audience has a more distinct air of professional curiosity. The Bee-girl is not in attendance. Perhaps she has resumed her studies in the more cavernous privacy of the Radio City Music Hall.

Olympia, Part II, is clearly the object of more artifice than Part I. Reportage is giving way further to poetry. . . . The opening is pastoral: a Siegfried idyll or an ode to matutinal joy. Dawn; beetle on a dewy leaf and birds caroling. No Disneyizing. No editorial comment. The camera speaks, unaided . . . The houses sleep. Only the lawn sprinklers are active. Contracted sun-rays splinter, making crosses and stars in the interstices of the trees, and a lone youth lopes through the woods. The community stirs itself—not yet to compete but to limber. Men shadow-box, relax their necks, kick soccer-balls, walk with ludicrous short steps, raising their knees high, like herons. Others merely have their calves massaged while they lie smiling at the sun. Even the Germans look happy. The girls enact similar prologues but since on the whole they are less attractive, clouds and sunbeams are wisely superimposed on the montage.

The stadium fills again; the preliminary exhibition is an unstinting display of *Kultur.* This is gymkhana with a vengeance. Battalions of German man- and womanhood (but you can barely tell women from men without a program) perform a joyless if intrepid ceremony of calisthenics. They leapfrog leather-bound horses and indulge in tendon-pulling feats of skill on horizontal bars, evoking every moment an intent if unintentional political myth: tempting the precarious balance, straddling the pit, suspended cruciform in mid-air with horizontal arms clutching iron rings. The women distend their thigh muscles, clench their jaws, knot their biceps, split themselves through the pelvis, as if to see how far they can submit their femininity to the test of rupture . . . Hitler smiles. (He's got doves in his gloves).

International rivalry is resumed, and the swimming matches are as fleet, as breathtaking, as anxiously observed by the omnipresent and nimble cameras as everything else . . . With the high-diving event, objectivity falters; the provocation for a sortie of expressionism was too strong. At this point, Fraulein Riefensthal or whoever must have decided, with sweeping disregard for the nominal subject, "To hell with the Olympics! Let's just make a glorious movie!" . . . Shots, low-level and diagonal, of a diver impelled from the springboard, hinging in air against a sun-edged cloud. Cross-cut to another. Increase of pace by cutting the duration of each shot. The sequence becomes a fantasia of springing divers, outlined against the chiaroscuro sky, "not to eat, not for love" but only diving. You no longer know or care who is diving for what team or with what score. Surely these flexed and soaring figures are meant to poise themselves, step tiptoe, bounce, jack-knife, twist in half gainers, spiral, swallow-flight and swan eternally, with trumpets to herald their abrupt ascent and their plummeting fall. The camera as Wagner? Yet more to the point of analogy you are reminded, by way of Malraux, of the clay models of divers Tintoretto used from which to paint his cloud-borne angels.

After hours (or should you say miles of footage) at a nervously dynamic *presto,* modified only by intermitted snatches of slow-motion, an *allegro moderato,* nautical, sets in with the yacht races on the Kiel canal. In order to preserve the necessary ratio of tension, since to the eye a racing sail-boat has a totally different rhythm of suspense from a running man, a zooming javelin or a bounding diver, the camera's witness point and the tempo of the cutting are artfully manipulated. As the boats veer into the wind around the buoys with gunwales almost under, you move in suddenly to get the vertigo sensation of a slumping list to port and glimpse the quick action of hand-over-hand hauling or a scramble for the tiller; and in one magnificent head-on shot, with a convoluting wave in the foreground, the victor's bow rights on a swell to perpendicular and the spinnaker sail bellies out like a triumphal banner, beautiful and strange as a sea-born flower.

There is no breaking of stride in this cinematic ingenuity. Still Aquarius-bound, you are next parallel with and abreast of the shell-racers, whose brief, synchronous, exacting efforts compose one of the most rhythmically exciting effects in the world of organized sport.

Here you can only guess, wildly, how some of the shots were obtained, for during one explosive sequence you are in a half-dozen boats within fewer seconds, each time squarely confronted by a faceless coxswain with a megaphone strapped over his mouth like a gas-mask, yelling "Stroke!" in six different languages! . . . Surely this is the climax, you hope, since you are by now solicitous of the film editor's ability to keep this material going with sustained interest. You need not be. After this, the cross-country bicycle grind, the appalling steeple-chases and that punishing trial of versatility, the Decathlon, captured in a walkaway by a prodigy from California, Glen Morris—now a name in a sports almanac (after an inglorious interlude as one of Hollywood's Tarzans).

Not the least remarkable job of photography (again challenging your credulity and your inferences) is the exhausting marathon, cross-country, where, in one instance, you conclude that the cameraman is either sitting on the contestant's shoulders, like Sinbad's Old Man of the Sea, or is spying from a low-flying balloon that casts no shadow. (Nothing would surprise you; Abel Gance, a French film director, once tied his camera to the tail of a "runaway" horse!). But in this case the plausible (and more prosaic) explanation is that the runner (the plodder) was followed by a car from which a camera was suspended from a boom over his head. (This is your guess and you're stuck with it). Anyway it's uncomfortably astonishing to look down and see those feet as close as if they were your own, lifted up and set down in a grueling battle against fatigue and spots before the eyes. You wonder if he felt like a donkey, with the carrot above instead of beyond his reach. Or was he past feeling anything but the unyielding ground and the cruelly receding finish line?

The Finale involves more swirling flags, the stadium in a long shot and again the tolling bell . . . . *Never send to know—*

Well, what *have* you seen? A documentary record of the Olympic Games—it says here. You can do better than that. The organization of a life-force made into art by the collaboration of sensitive instruments . . . But as you leave the auditorium you overhear a skeptic saying, "With all those cameras, you couldn't miss!" The hell you couldn't and the hell they don't! Try to find an equal five minutes in the billion feet you've seen of Fox Movietone, Pathé and Paramount: The Eyes, Ears, Nose and Throat of the World. You saw nothing like this. *Olympia, 1936* is not a newsreel; it is history, aestheticized. And what else? For the hindsight implications are rampant while you smoke your cigarette among the lithographs once more. Berlin, 1936—made possible by Berlin, 1934—the Reichstag. The flames rise as they'd risen before and would again: 1939, 1941, 1945 . . .

The participants. What happened to *them?* Where are they now —the ones who didn't play Tarzan or who didn't survive to cherish the fallen arch, the fatted calf, the varicose vein? *By brooks too broad for leaping?* . . . All that prowess and mindless agility. The gratuitous beauty of keeping fit. Two thousand sets of coordinated muscles dedicated to an exhibitionism where victory (apart from the scoreboard) is so often a collapse, a speechless gasp or an ugly convulsion, like a parody of sexual ecstasy; where the reward is a wreath of myrtle placed on the brows, in this case by the Reichsführer's Rhinemaidens, in khaki with overseas caps. *Sieg Heil! Allons enfants! Of Thee I Sing!* Images of humanism disporting not only for national aggrandizement but also for the edification of a piece of human filth who will subsequently break their limbs on the beaches of Normandy, bury their torsos under the leaves of the Ardennes, splinter their javelins on the coasts of Italy, shatter their swan-dives over the fires of Kiel. *Pro patria mori.*

The massive folly of the physical. Organized athletics, a perennial structure for collectivizing the beautiful, the belligerent and the hollow; valid symphony of and for Hydra, and pandemic rationale of the third sex for whom, like Whitman, life can be verified only by the smell of sweat from a million armpits . . .

All the same, you've seen a great movie, and you wonder whatever happened to Loki Riefensthal. *(The Thane of Fife had a wife. Where is she now?)* Did Adolf the Hammer ever realize that *Olympia, 1936* was an act of treason? The redemption of the adrenal cortex by the creative eye? The vindication of mass by perspective?

The aim was to win. The Americans won—that is, the contest. But Germany won, too. You've just seen the winner: a lyric wrested from the enemies of the lyrical.

The bust outlasts the citadel . . . . Sometimes.

Outside the Museum it's raining again.

Editors of Accent

Kenneth Andrews
Peggy Bachman
James Ballowe
Mary Bath
Robert Bauer
Jerry Beaty
Kenneth Bennett
Jerome Birdman
Claire Blaufarb
Thomas Bledsoe
Herbert Bogart
Janet Bragg
Charlotte Bruner
Glenn Carey
Arthur Carr
Marion Carr
Edith Clark
Gordon Clarke
Frances Conlin
Daniel Curley
Joseph H. Dugas
Stanley Elkin
Walter Edens
Donald Finkel
Rocco Fumento
Robert Gard

W. H. Gass
Leon Gottfried
Irwin Gold
Lloyd Goldman
Carl F. Hartman
Penny Hartman
Allen Hayman
Lester Heller
Ward Hellstrom
Frederick Highland
Donald Hill
Helen Hill
Allan Holaday
Keith Huntress
Adelaide Jauch
Sally Jauch
David Joel
Leo Knopf
Edith Lambert
Nina Logan
W. McNeil Lowry
Ruby Mason
W. R. Moses
Morton Moskov
Earl Oliver
Gayle Neubauer
Frank Pacelli

Glen Park
Jeannette Parquette
Mary Kay Peer
Paul Proehl
Verne Purcell
Kerker Quinn
Wanda Revell
Oliver Rice
Edgar Rosenberg
Martha Louise Royce
David Rudolph
John Schacht
George Scouffas
Roberta Scouffas
Betty Sereno
Herbert Shaner
Charles Shattuck
Gertrude Shumway
Benjamin Sokoloff
Ruth Stone
Walter Stone
Sidney Warschausky
Virginia Welsh
Lura Williams
George Wiswell
Bruce Youle

Contributors

ROBERT MARTIN ADAMS (1915———), professor of English at UCLA, is a critic and interpreter of a broad range of literary subjects. His books include *Ikon: John Milton and the Modern Critics* (1955), *Strain of Discord* (1958), *Nil: Episodes in the Literary Conquest of Void during the Nineteenth Century* (1966), *James Joyce* (1966). His work in progress includes an examination of literary translation and a study of how artists of the Renaissance sought to re-create themselves in images of ancient Rome.

CONRAD AIKEN (1889–1973) was editor of *The Dial,* 1917–19. Generous to new magazines, he contributed to Kerker Quinn's short-lived *Direction* (1935) as well as to the first volume of *Accent* (1940). By then he was already the author of seventeen volumes of poetry, five novels, a book of stories, and a critical volume. After 1940 he added another fourteen volumes of poetry, two volumes of criticism, a play, and an autobiography.

A. R. AMMONS (1926———). When "Sumerian" appeared in the Spring, 1956, issue, A. R. Ammons had just published his first book of poems, *Ommateum* (1955). He has since published *Expressions of Sea Level* (1964), *Corsons Inlet* (1965), *Tape for the Turn of the Year* (1965), *Northfield Poems* (1966), *Selected Poems* (1968), *Uplands* (1970), *Briefings* (1971), and *Collected Poems,* 1972. He held a Guggenheim fellowship in 1966 and a traveling fellowship from the American Academy of Arts and Letters in 1967. He is now professor of English at Cornell.

R. P. BLACKMUR (1904–65) was for many years a free-lance poet and critic, but from 1940 he was identified with Princeton, New Jersey—first as a fellow of the university, then as a member of the Institute for Advanced Study, and finally as professor of English. In 1935 he contributed two articles to Kerker Quinn's magazine *Direction* and in the same year published his first major critical work, *The Double Agent.* His further works include *The Expense of Greatness* (1940), *Lectures in Criticism* (1949), *Language as Gesture* (1952), *The Lion and the Honeycomb* (1955), and *Eleven Essays in the European Novel* (1964). He was a Guggenheim fellow and held honorary degrees from Rutgers and Cambridge.

FREDERICK BOCK (1916———) appeared in *Accent* with some regularity from 1942 through 1959, practically the entire life of the magazine. He is the author of a collection of poems, *The Fountains of Regardlessness* (1961). From 1955 to 1960 he was on the staff of *Poetry.* He is now living in Brooklyn and is working on a new book of poems.

MILLEN BRAND (1906——) is the author of five novels, among them *The Outward Room* (1937) and *Savage Sleep* (1968), and a collection of poems, *Dry Summer in Provence* (1966). He is co-author of the prize-winning screenplay *The Snakepit*. For twenty-five years he has been at work on a volume of poetry, *Local Lives,* which he expects to finish in 1972. He is now senior editor at Crown Publishers.

JOHN MALCOLM BRINNIN (1916——) is the author of six volumes of poetry including *Selected Poems* (1963) and *Skin Diving in the Virgins* (1970). He has written two books about Dylan Thomas, who was a close friend: *Dylan Thomas in America* (1955) and *Dylan* (1964), and has edited the poems of Emily Dickinson. He is now professor of English at Boston University.

KENNETH BURKE (1897——) is perhaps best known for his critical volumes, among them *The Philosophy of Literary Form* (1941), *A Grammar of Motives* (1945), and *A Rhetoric of Motives* (1950). He is also the author of a collection of stories, *The White Oxen* (1924), and *Collected Poems* (1967). He lives at Andover, New Jersey, which he says is fifty miles due west of the New York Public Library and fifty miles due north of the Princeton Library.

LEONARD CASPER (1923——) is the author of a study of Robert Penn Warren, *The Dark and Bloody Ground* (1960), and of a collection of stories, *A Lion Unannounced* (1970), a National Council on the Arts selection. He has also published poetry widely in the quarterlies and is author/editor of five critical volumes on Philippine literature. He is now a professor of contemporary American literature and of creative writing at Boston College.

R. V. CASSILL (1919——) is the author of two books of stories, *The Father* and *The Happy Marriage,* and of several novels including *Clem Anderson, The President, Pretty Leslie, La Vie Passionée of Rodney Buckthorn,* and *Dr. Cobb's Game.* He is working on a novel tentatively entitled *The Judgment of Paris.* He is professor of English at Brown University.

WALTER VAN TILBURG CLARK (1909–71). When "The Indian Well" appeared (Spring, 1943) Walter Van Tilburg Clark was living in Cazenovia, New York, where he taught English, dramatics, and sports. He later taught at Montana State, San Francisco State, and the University of Nevada. His books are *The Ox Bow Incident* (1940), *The City of Trembling Leaves* (1945), *The Track of the Cat* (1949), and *The Watchful Gods* (1950).

E. E. CUMMINGS (1894–1962) is an outstanding example of the generosity of established writers to *Accent*. His contributions span nearly the entire history of the magazine, from Volume 3 to Volume 18. He was a painter as well as a poet—as the intensely visual quality of his poems might suggest—and was the author of the classic war-prison novel *The Enormous Room* (1922).

DANIEL CURLEY (1918———). Daniel Curley's first published story was "The Ship" (Spring, 1947). He was then teaching at Syracuse University. In 1955 he moved to the University of Illinois and was one of the editors of *Accent* until it ceased publication. He is now professor of English at Illinois. He has published two collections of stories, *That Marriage Bed of Procrustes* (1957) and *In the Hands of Our Enemies* (1971), and two novels, *How Many Angels?* (1958) and *A Stone Man, Yes* (1964).

HARRIS DOWNEY (1917———), a free-lance writer of Baton Rouge, Louisiana, has published fiction, poetry, and criticism in the *Virginia Quarterly Review, Epoch, Poetry,* and many other magazines. His three novels are *Thunder in the Room* (1956), *The Key to My Prison* (1964), and *Carrie Dumain* (1966).

ALAN DUGAN (1923———) is the author of *Poems* (1961), *Poems 2* (1963), and *Poems 3* (1967). He won the National Book Award in 1961, the Pulitzer Prize in 1962, and the Levinson Prize in 1967. He has also received grants from the Guggenheim and Rockefeller foundations. He lives in New York and in Truro, Massachusetts, and is a member of the Fine Arts Work Center in Provincetown.

STANLEY ELKIN (1930———) was a graduate student at the University of Illinois and a member of the staff of *Accent* when "Among the Witnesses" appeared in 1960. He has since published *Boswell* (1964), *Criers and Kibitzers, Kibitzers and Criers* (1966), *A Bad Man* (1967), *The Dick Gibson Show* (1971), and *The Making of Ashenden* (1972). He is now at work on a collection of novellas. He has held a Guggenheim fellowship (1966–67) and a Rockefeller grant (1968–69). He is professor of English at Washington University in St. Louis.

WALLACE FOWLIE (1908———), critic, translator, and interpreter of French literature, is presently the James B. Duke Professor of French at Duke University. He has published book-length studies of Stendhal, Mallarmé, Rimbaud, Proust, Gide, Claudel, and Cocteau, and of French criticism, surrealism, and the modern French theater. He has edited works of Valéry, Mauriac, and numerous post-war French poets, and is the author of a novel, *Sleep of the Pigeon.* He is now working on a study of Lautréamont.

WILLIAM H. GASS (1924———) is the only contributor who ever had an issue of *Accent* devoted to his work. His stories and his article in the "Gass issue" (Winter, 1958) were his first published fiction and criticism. Since then he has published a novel, *Omensetter's Luck* (1966), a collection of stories, *In the Heart of the Heart of the Country* (1968), an experimental novella, *Willie Master's Lonesome Wife* (1971), and a collection of essays, *Fiction and the Figures of Life* (1971). He is now professor of philosophy at Washington University in St. Louis and is at work on a novel to be called *The Tunnel*.

BREWSTER GHISELIN (1903———) is the author of three volumes of poetry: *Against the Circle* (1946), *The Nets* (1955), and *Country of the Minotaur* (1970). His poems, stories, and essays have appeared in magazines here and in England and Italy. He was founder of the Writers' Conference at the University of Utah and directed it from 1947 to 1966. In 1970 he received an award from the National Institute of Arts and Letters. He is now professor emeritus at the University of Utah and continues to write criticism and poetry.

HORACE GREGORY (1898———) contributed to Kerker Quinn's magazine *Direction* in 1935. At that time he was about to publish his third volume of poetry. He has now published nine volumes of poetry (*Collected Poems,* 1964), a number of critical and biographical studies, Latin translations, and anthologies, these last often in collaboration with his wife, Marya Zaturenska. In 1969 he published an edition of the poems of Byron. He now lives in Rockland County, New York.

JOHN HAWKES (1925———). "The Horse in a London Flat" (Winter, 1960) is also an episode in John Hawkes's novel *The Lime Twig* (1961). His other novels are *The Cannibal* (1949), *The Beetle Leg* (1951), *The Goose on the Grave* (1954), *Second Skin* (1964), and *Blood Oranges* (1971). He has also published a collection of short plays, *The Innocent Party* (1967), and a collection of stories, *Lunar Landscapes* (1969). He has received grants from the National Institute of Arts and Letters, the Guggenheim Foundation, the Ford Foundation, and the Rockefeller Foundation. He is professor of English at Brown University.

JOSEPHINE HERBST (1897–1969) was the author of seven novels, from *Nothing Sacred* (1928) to *Somewhere the Tempest Fell* (1948), and a biography of John Bartram, *New Green World* (1956). Her literary and personal history of the 1920s and 1930s, left unfinished at her death, is being prepared for publication.

FRANK HOLWERDA (1908–71) worked in Wall Street in the late 1920s, turned common seaman about 1930, became a South American representative for Standard Oil in 1932, served in the army from 1940 to 1943, and afterward ranged from the tropics to the Arctic doing such things as importing, truck driving, drilling, horse racing, cat skinning, turkey farming, and gold mining. In the early 1950s he began to write adventure stories, but soon thereafter *Accent* and other "quality" magazines began to publish him and (he once complained to us) ruined his career as a writer for the "pulps."

EDWIN HONIG (1919——) is the author of five volumes of poetry: *The Moral Circus* (1957), *The Gazebos* (1959), *Survivals* (1965), *Spring Journal* (1968), and *Four Springs* (1972). Also the critical volume *Dark Conceit: The Making of Allegory* (1959) and *Selected Essays* (1972). He has also translated widely from Spanish literature. He is now professor of English at Brown University.

TED HUGHES (1930——) is the author of several volumes of poetry starting with *Hawk in the Rain* (1957), several volumes of poetry for children and stories for children, and a collection of plays, *The Coming of the Kings* (1970). He has received numerous awards, among them the Guinness Poetry Award, a Guggenheim fellowship, the Somerset Maugham Award, and the Hawthornden Prize. He was married to Sylvia Plath. "The Little Boys and the Seasons," an early work, was published in the Spring issue of 1957.

ROBERTS JACKSON. When "Fly Away Home" was published (Spring, 1952) Roberts Jackson was living in New York City.

JASCHA KESSLER (1929——) had his first published story in *Accent* in the summer of 1952. He is the author of two volumes of poems, *Whatever Love Declares* (1969) and *After the Armies Have Passed* (1970), and a collection of stories, *An Egyptian Bondage* (1967). He has also had a play and an opera produced in New York. He is at present professor of English at UCLA and is at work on a novel, a long play, a new book of poems, and a new collection of stories.

M. M. LIBERMAN (1921——) is the author of a collection of stories, *Maggot and Worm* (1969), and a critical volume, *Katherine Anne Porter's Fiction* (1971). He holds the Oakes Ames Chair of English Literature at Grinnell College, where he has been head of the department and dean of humanities. He is at work on a new book of stories.

MASON JORDAN MASON. The only thing we could ever ascertain about Mason Jordan Mason was that he lived in a lock box in Taos along with Judson Crews and others. We don't even know that any more.

JACK MATTHEWS (1925——). When "Sweet Song from an Old Guitar" appeared, Jack Matthews was working for the Columbus *Dispatch*. He has since become professor of English at Ohio University. He has published a volume of short stories, *Bitter Knowledge* (1964), a volume of poems, *An Almanac for Twilight* (1966), and four novels, *Hanger Stout, Awake*

(1967), *Beyond the Bridge* (1970), *The Tale of Asa Bean* (1971), *The Charisma Campaigns* (1972). He is now at work on another novel.

W. S. MERWIN (1927——). "A Dance of Death" (Spring, 1952) appeared in W. S. Merwin's first volume of poetry, *A Mask for Janus* (1952). His seventh volume, *The Carrier of Ladders,* won the Pulitzer Prize in 1971. He has held grants from the *Kenyon Review,* the Rockefeller Foundation, the National Institute of Arts and Letters, the Arts Council of Great Britain, the Rabinowitz Foundation, the Ford Foundation, and the Chapelbrook Foundation.

JOSEPHINE MILES (1911——), whose "Accompaniment" appeared in the first issue of *Accent,* lists as her major publications *Poems 1930–60* (1960), *Eros and Modes in English Poetry* (1964), *Kinds of Affection* (1967), *Style and Proportion* (1967). She does not mention, however, twelve other volumes of poetry and criticism. She has held fellowships from the American Association of Arts and Sciences and the Guggenheim Foundation and has won the Shelley Award and awards from the Institute of Arts and Letters and the National Endowment for the Arts. She is professor of English at Berkeley and is at work on a book on language in literature and on what she says is to all appearances a book of poems.

RALPH J. MILLS, JR. (1931——) is the author of *Theodore Roethke* (1963), *Contemporary American Poetry* (1965), *Richard Eberhart* (1966), *Edith Sitwell* (1966), *Kathleen Raine* (1967), and *Creation's Very Self* (1969). A collection of essays on contemporary American poetry will appear in 1973 and an edition of the notebooks of David Ignatow in 1974. A later version of the *Accent* essay appears in Marie Borroff's *Wallace Stevens: A Collection of Critical Essays.* He is now professor of English at the University of Illinois, Chicago Circle.

SAMUEL FRENCH MORSE (1916——) is the author of three collections of poetry, *Time of Year* (1944), *The Scattered Causes* (1955), and *The Changes* (1964), and two books for children, *All in a Suitcase* (1966) and *Sea Sums* (1970). He has also written a critical biography of Wallace Stevens—*Wallace Stevens: Poetry as Life*—and has edited two volumes of Stevens' poetry—*Opus Posthumous* (1957) and *Poems, a Selection* (1959). He is now professor of English at Northeastern University and is at work on a collection of essays on modern poetry.

W. R. MOSES (1911——) was one of the editors of *Accent* in its earliest years and is now professor of English at Kansas State University. His poems, published widely, have been collected in *Five Young American Poets* (1953) and *Identities* (1965). He has published other essays on Faulkner in *Modern Fiction Studies,* the *Georgia Review,* and the *Mississippi Quarterly.*

HOWARD MOSS (1922——) was about to publish his second book of poems when "Animal Hospital" appeared in 1954. The complete record is: *The Wound and the Weather* (1946), *The Toy Fair* (1954), *A Swimmer in the Air* (1957), *A Winter Come, a Summer Gone* (1960), *Finding Them Lost* (1965), *Second Nature* (1968), and *Selected Poems* (1971). He has also published criticism, *The Magic Lantern of Marcel Proust* (1962) and *Writing Against Time* (1969), and has edited the work of Keats (1959) and of Edward Lear (1964). He is now at work on a play, a critical book on Chekhov, and a new book of poems. Since 1948 he has been poetry editor of the *New Yorker*.

HOWARD NEMEROV (1920——) is the author of seven volumes of poetry, from *The Image and the Law* (1947) to *The Blue Swallows* (1967), and of three novels and two collections of short stories. He held a *Kenyon Review* fellowship in fiction (1955), a grant from the National Institute of Arts and Letters (1961), a Guggenheim fellowship (1969), and a fellowship from the Academy of American Poets (1971). Among other honors he won the first Theodore Roethke Memorial Award (1968) for his volume *The Blue Swallows*. He is now professor of English at Washington University in St. Louis.

JOHN FREDERICK NIMS (1913——), poet and translator, has collected his work in the following volumes: *The Iron Pastoral* (1947), *A Fountain in Kentucky* (1950), *The Poems of St. John of the Cross* (1959, 1968), *Knowledge of the Evening* (1960), *Of Flesh and Bone* (1967), and *Sappho to Valéry: Poems in Translation* (1971). Formerly of the English department at Notre Dame, he came to the University of Illinois at Urbana in the early 1960s and is now professor of English at the University of Illinois, Chicago Circle. He has also taught at the universities of Toronto, Milan, Florence, Madrid, at Harvard, and at the Bread Loaf School of English.

HOWARD NUTT was one of Kerker Quinn's collaborators on *Direction,* the magazine which Quinn started in Peoria in 1934 and which was the prototype of *Accent.* In 1940 he published a volume of poetry, *Special Laughter.*

FLANNERY O'CONNOR (1925–64). "The Geranium" (Summer, 1946) was Flannery O'Connor's first published story. A thorough rewriting of this story was her last completed work, published under the title "Judgement Day." "The Geranium" in its original form was not reprinted until the posthumous *Complete Stories* (1971), which includes the stories of her Iowa thesis (1947), *A Good Man Is Hard to Find* (1955), and *Everything That Rises Must Converge* (1965). She also published two novels, *Wise Blood* (1952) and *The Violent Bear It Away* (1960). A collection of essays, *Mystery and Manners* (1969), was published posthumously.

GRACE PALEY is the author of *The Little Disturbances of Man* (1959).
She lives in great seclusion in Greenwich Village, where she is active in
PTA and other local politics and where she maintains her anonymity by
the subtle device of having her phone listed under her own name. "Goodbye and Good Luck" was her first published story (Summer, 1956).

SHERMAN PAUL (1920——) is the author of *Emerson's Angle of Vision* (1952), *The Shores of America* (1958), *Louis Sullivan* (1962), *Edmund Wilson* (1965), *Randolph Bourne* (1966), *The Music of Survival*
(1968), and *Hart's Bridge* (1972). He held a Ford fellowship in 1952 and
a Guggenheim fellowship in 1963. In 1957 he was a visiting professor at
the University of Vienna. When "Resolution at Walden" appeared in 1953
he was in the English department at the University of Illinois. He is now
M. F. Carpenter Professor of English at the University of Iowa.

SYLVIA PLATH (1932–63) was the author of three volumes of poetry,
The Colossus (1960), *Ariel* (1965), *Uncollected Poems* (1966), and a
novel, *The Bell Jar* (1963), which she published under the name Victoria
Lucas. She was married to Ted Hughes.

J. F. POWERS (1917——). "Lions, Harts, Leaping Does" is one of the
earliest of the many short stories J. F. Powers contributed to *Accent*. His
work has appeared widely—in *Commonweal*, the *Partisan Review*, the
Kenyon Review, Horizon, Tomorrow, and especially the *New Yorker*—and
has been translated into the principal European languages. He has collected
his stories twice—*Prince of Darkness* (1947) and *The Presence of Grace*
(1956). His novel, *Morte d'Urban* (1962), won the National Book Award.
His wife is Betty Wahl, whose novel *Rafferty & Co.* appeared in 1969. He
lives near Dublin and is working on a novel, two sections of which have
appeared in the *New Yorker*.

JOHN CROWE RANSOM (1888——) is the author of several volumes
of poetry, culminating in *Collected Poems* (1963), and several volumes of
criticism, among them *The World's Body* (1938) and *The New Criticism*
(1941). He was editor of *The Fugitive* and of the *Kenyon Review* (1939–
59). Among many other honors he has received a Bollingen Award and a
grant from the National Council on the Arts. He lives in Gambier, Ohio.

MAGGIE RENNERT. "Loss of the Navigator Near Kansas City" (Summer, 1956) was only the third of Maggie Rennert's published poems. She
has since published a novel, *A Moment in Camelot* (1968), several dozen
poems, and many reviews. She says that she is currently planning a work
in verse and along with it a mystery novel "to help pay for that excursion
into art." She now lives near Boston.

RALPH ROBIN (1914——) is the author of a book of poems, *Cities of Speech* (1971). Trained as a chemist, he has taught creative writing as an adjunct professor of English at the American University in Washington. Since 1949, when *Accent* published his first work, his stories and poems have appeared in some two dozen magazines in America and abroad.

WILLIAM SANSOM (1912——) was in the advertising business in London until World War II. Then he served as a fireman and discovered a new and serious texture of life. The title story of his first collection, *Fireman Flower* (1944), reflects this new orientation, and he has gone on to add twenty-four volumes of fiction and travel, most recently *Christmas* (1968). According to *Who's Who*, his hobby is "watching."

ANNE SEXTON (1928——). The poems of Anne Sexton have been collected in the following volumes: *To Bedlam and Part Way Back* (1960), *All My Pretty Ones* (1962), *Selected Poems* (1964), *Live or Die* (1966), *Love Poems* (1969), and *Transformations* (1971). She won the 1967 Pulitzer Prize for Poetry for *Live or Die*. Other awards have come to her from the American Academy of Arts and Letters, the Ford Foundation, the Congress for Cultural Freedom, and the Guggenheim Foundation. She has taught at Harvard, Oberlin, and Boston University and has recently been appointed Crashaw Professor of Literature at Colgate University.

MARK SPILKA (1925——) is the author of *The Love Ethic of D. H. Lawrence* (1955) and *Dickens and Kafka* (1963). He edited the D. H. Lawrence volume in the Twentieth Century Views series (1963) and is now working on a collection of his own essays and a critical book on modern theories of fiction. He is chairman of the English department at Brown University and managing editor of *Novel: A Forum on Fiction*.

RADCLIFFE SQUIRES (1917——) has published three volumes of poetry—*Where the Compass Spins* (1952), *Fingers of Hermes* (1965), and *The Light under Islands* (1967)—and critical studies of several modern writers, including Robinson Jeffers, Robert Frost, Frederic Prokosch, and Allen Tate. He is professor of English at the University of Michigan and editor of the *Michigan Quarterly Review* and is working on a new collection of poetry.

WALLACE STEVENS (1879–1955) was a generous contributor to *Accent*, where a round dozen of his late poems first appeared. He began to write before World War I and brought out his first volume, *Harmonium*, in 1923. A reissue of *Harmonium* in 1931 was followed by a steady flow of volumes, including *Ideas of Order* (1935), *The Man with the Blue Guitar* (1937), *Notes toward a Supreme Fiction* (1942), *Transport to Summer* (1947), *Collected Poems* (1954), and *Opus Posthumous* (1957).

RUTH STONE was one of the editors of *Accent* in the early 1950s. She has published two collections of her poetry: *In an Iridescent Time* (1959) and *Topography* (1971). She has received grants from the *Kenyon Review,* the Radcliffe Institute for Independent Study, the Guggenheim Foundation, the National Endowment for the Arts, and the National Institute of Arts and Letters, and has won a number of prizes, including the Bess Hokin Poetry Prize, Borestone Mountain Poetry Awards, and the Shelley Memorial Award. She lives in Vermont but has taught as a visitor at Wisconsin, Brandeis, Wellesley, Radcliffe, and Irvine. She has most recently returned to the University of Illinois for the academic years 1971–72 and 1972–73.

NANCY SULLIVAN (1934——) is the author of *The History of the World as Pictures* (1965), for which she won the first annual Devins Memorial Award, and of a critical volume, *Perspective and the Poetic Process* (1968). Her poetry has been widely published in the quarterlies, and she has just finished work on a new collection. She is professor of English at Rhode Island College.

DYLAN THOMAS (1914–53), whose "Ceremony After a Fire Raid" appeared in the Winter, 1945, issue, published the following volumes of poems: *Eighteen Poems* (1934), *The Map of Love* (1939), *Deaths and Entrances* (1946), and *Collected Poems* (1953). His prose was collected in *Portrait of the Artist as a Young Dog* (1940) and *Adventures in the Skin Trade* (1955). Perhaps his best-known single work is the radio play *Under Milk Wood* (1954).

JARVIS THURSTON (1914——) is co-founder and co-editor (with his wife, Mona Van Duyn) of *Perspective* (1947——). He is editor of several collections of short stories and compiler of a checklist of short fiction criticism. He has contributed articles and stories to the quarterlies and is now working on a collection of his own short stories and on a commentary on the poetry of Wallace Stevens. He is professor of English at Washington University in St. Louis.

W. Y. TINDALL (1903——), who is now professor emeritus at Columbia University, claims to be "doing nothing much, but liking it." Of his more than a dozen major critical works, including studies of Bunyan, D. H. Lawrence, Yeats, Wallace Stevens, and Beckett, those which he now regards as the principal ones are *Forces on Modern British Literature* (1947), *The Literary Symbol* (1954), *A Reader's Guide to James Joyce* (1959), and *A Reader's Guide to Finnegans Wake* (1970). He has been a Guggenheim fellow, and in 1968 he was awarded an honorary doctorate from Iona College for his work in Irish literature.

BYRON VAZAKAS (1905——). The poems of Byron Vazakas have appeared in over forty magazines and many anthologies of modern verse. He has collected his poetry in four volumes: *Transfigured Night* (1946), *The Equal Tribunals* (1962), *The Marble Manifesto* (1966), and *Nostalgia for a House of Cards* (1970). He lives in Reading, Pennsylvania.

NEIL WEISS (1914——) published his first poem, "Song for Blackbirds," in the Spring, 1948, issue. He was listed then as having been a shipyard worker and merchant seaman and reader for a film company. By summer, 1949, when his next poems appeared, he had had work accepted by *Poetry* and *Quarterly Review of Literature*. By spring, 1953, he was preparing a volume of poems to be called *Song for Blackbirds*. In autumn, 1954, he was "one of the *Five Poets*" published by the Golden Goose Press. In summer, 1955, he had become "a frequent contributor" to *Accent* and was about to have his first book published by Indiana University Press, *Changes of Garments* (1956). In 1960 he published another collection, *Origins of a Design*.

T. WEISS (1916——), formerly of Bard College, is now professor of creative writing and English at Princeton University. He is editor and publisher of the *Quarterly Review of Literature*. His poetry, widely published, has been collected in the following volumes: *The Catch* (1951), *Outlanders* (1960), *Gunsight* (1962), *The Medium* (1965), *The Last Day and the First* (1968), and *The World before Us* (1970). He has recorded selected poems for the Library of Congress, Harvard University, and the Yale Series of Recorded Poets. His most recent work, *The Breath of Clowns and Kings* (1971), is a study of Shakespeare's early comedies and histories, and he is currently preparing a study of Shakespeare's tragedies. He has received awards from the Ford Foundation, the Wallace Stevens Awards, and the National Institute of Arts and Letters.

EUDORA WELTY (1909——) has published three collections of stories—*A Curtain of Green* (1941), *The Wide Net* (1943), and *The Bride of the Innisfallen* (1955)—and six novels—*The Robber Bridegroom* (1942), *Delta Wedding* (1946), *The Golden Apples* (1949), *The Ponder Heart* (1954), *Losing Battles* (1970), and *The Optimist's Daughter* (1972). Two camera studies of Ida M'Toy ("Ida M'Toy," Summer, 1942) may be found in Miss Welty's volume of photographs of life in Mississippi in Depression days, *One Time, One Place* (1971). She has been honored by degrees from several colleges and universities and has received grants from the Rockefeller Foundation, the Merrill Foundation, the Guggenheim Foundation, and the National Institute of Arts and Letters. In 1973 she was awarded the Pulitzer Prize for Fiction.

WILLIAM CARLOS WILLIAMS (1883-1963). His first book, *Poems,* appeared in 1909, and his poetic masterwork, *Paterson,* appeared in five volumes between 1946 and 1958. He also wrote five novels, a study of the American cultural past called *In the American Grain,* an autobiography, several plays including *A Dream of Love,* and numerous essays. The Pulitzer Prize for Poetry was awarded him in 1963, but posthumously.

LEONARD WOLF (1923———) has published poems and stories in the *Atlantic Monthly,* the *New Yorker,* the *Sewanee Review,* the *Kenyon Review,* and elsewhere. His books include *Voices from the Love Generation* (1968), *The Passion of Israel* (1970), and *A Dream af Dracula* (1972). He is currently doing research on vampires for a forthcoming study called *The Annotated Dracula.* He is professor of English at San Francisco State College.

REX WORTHINGTON. Rex Worthington's first published story was "A Kind of Scandal" (Winter, 1953). He was then working in the library at the University of Indiana. When "Love" appeared (Winter, 1955), he was on the staff of the Writers' Workshop in Iowa City.

MARGUERITE YOUNG (1909———) lives in Greenwich Village. Her books include *Prismatic Ground* (1937), *Moderate Fable* (1944), *Angel in the Forest* (1945, 1966), and the novel *Miss MacIntosh, My Darling* (1965). She is currently preparing a study of James Whitcomb Riley.

VERNON YOUNG (1912———). At the time of writing "Hardly a Man Is Now Alive," (Spring, 1955) Vernon Young was film critic for *Arts Digest.* He later became an art critic for the same magazine (by then known as *Arts*), first in New York and then in such European cities as Copenhagen, Stockholm, London, Rome, and Munich. He is now film editor for the *Hudson Review* and lives in Stockholm as a free-lance writer. He has published two books on film, *Cinema Borealis* (1970) on Ingmar Bergman, and *Vernon Young on Film* (1972), a collection of his essays from the past sixteen years. He is working on a critical volume on contemporary poetry.